Ashes
of Roses
and War

Sibyl Jarvis Pischke

"ASHES OF ROSES AND WAR"
A Civil War Saga
Copyright ©1994 by Sibyl Jarvis Pischke

Library of Congress Card Number—81-82894-2

Reprinted with permission by Mountain Memories Books.
Printed in the United States of America.

10   9   8   7   6   5   4   3   2   1

ISBN-13: 978-0-938985-20-4
ISBN-10: 0-938985-20-5

Distributed by:

West Virginia Book Company
1125 Central Avenue
Charleston, WV 25302
www.wvbookco.com

❦ About the Author ❦

Sibyl Jarvis Pischke born in West Virginia, is a talented novelist with several books, and other writings to her credit. She began her writing career later in life.

Attending Marshall College in Charleston, W. Va. she graduated as a Cosmetologist, with thirty years in this field. She and her husband Harry went into the Florist business and Sibyl has a wall full of ribbons for her talent in floral design.

Writing, and especially about her beloved West Virginia hills is her first love.

"The Legend of Mammy Jane," based on her grandmother's life in the 1800's, is now into its second printing.

"Matches at Midnight," a popular supernatural Mystery, is a page turner.

Sibyl's latest book, "Ashes of Roses and War," A Civil War saga, will keep you on the edge of your seat, waiting to see what will happen next.

Letters cram Sibyl's mailbox from all over the country, asking questions about her characters and when a next book will be out. Saying— "I couldn't put it down. Hurry with another one!"

Writing has become one of her first loves, but must be "squeezed" into her busy schedule of R/V'ing, book signings, and taking care of her poodle Angel and of course Harry.

❦ In Appreciation ❧

The Author would like to thank all those who had a part in this Novel. Richmond's Historical and Genealogy records. Also Williamsburg, Spotsvania, and other local record departments. William and Mary College for their help on military records.

Linda Kelly for her editing, and comments which helped more than she will ever know.

Those who read the manuscript, Mr. Ashley who said he couldn't put it down until he had finished it to the end.

My sister Irene Jarvis Gunn 'the school marm,' and my strictest critic, for her, "It's wonderful."

Jannette, for her "don't ever let anyone say you can't write," comment.

My husband Harry, for his endless hours of laser scanning the manuscript, and his tireless work on the 'Book Jacket.'

Thanks to each and every one of you.

I want to dedicate this Novel to:

My husband Harry and my son William.

Sibyl

❦ Prologue ❦

The winds of war roared across the mountains, sending echoes across every valley. Virginia was marched across so many times that the footprints would last a hundred years. Only the strong would survive the ravages of war.

Jane, a gusty eight year old, who followed her country-doctor grandfather on his rounds, learning to mix the herbs, and elixirs to treat the sick as well as the doctor, declared that she would become a doctor. Told many times, that females could never be doctors, Jane never lost her enthusiasm for medicine. Becoming a lovely woman, she watched as her sisters, and friends married, becoming mothers and wives.

Doctor Connolly, enlisted in the Union Army shortly after the conflict started. He ask to be sent to a field hospital where he thought he could be of more use to the soldiers. After many tears, and threats to marry the village idiot, Jane was given permission to accompany her grandfather to the tent hospital that followed the war into the wilderness. Jane was a strong beautiful young woman, who endured the hardships of the primitive hospital, helping with amputations, when all the anesthesia to be had was 'corn licker.' After four years of blood and gore, Jane has a break-down, and is sent to Barrlette Plantation in Carolina, who are friends of Dr. Connolly's. There she meets the Barrlette's grand-son, who is a dashing, Major in the Confederate Army. He falls madly in love with Jane and asks her to be his wife.

The war finally ends, with reconstruction taking over those who are left. Jane has become a strong, intelligent woman, who is now a plantation owner. The running of the Barrlette Plantation falls on her shoulders as circumstances beyond her control takes a hand. Never having dealt with slavery, she is left with the Bar-rette 'People' to care for and ease into their new life as free people. Deeding each a small parcel of the Barrlette land, and disman-tling the slave quarters, using the lumber, to build each of the couples who are left, a small cottage for their own.

An advertisement the Railroad has in the newspaper for homesteaders in the Oklahoma Territory, interests Jane. Going to hear the talks she is impressed with the hearty souls who are considering the venture. Knowing she didn't want to remain in Carolina where the memories are so painful, and not being sure she wants to return to her home in Virginia which is now a new state, West Virginia, she decides to join the Wagon Train that headed for the Oklahoma Territory.

During the harrying trip West, Jane's dream become a reality, when the wagon doctor, becomes ill and she has to take over the care of the many on the wagon train. They encounter renegade army deserters, Indians, and many more hardships.

This is a story of hardship, romance, and determination to make a home in the new territory. There is laughter, tears, and many surprises along the way, making this a rollicking page turner to be remembered long after the written pages are finished. The story of a strong woman!!!

❧ Chapter One ❧

Late summer had come to the hills of Virginia. A slight tinge of color touched the tips of the tallest windblown trees that stood high on the distant mountaintops. The year—1861.

Virginia with its wide rivers, fertile valleys, and rugged mountains to the West were being torn asunder, by those who owned slaves in the flatlands against the hearty mountaineers who scratched out a living, without the dependency of slavery. Rich plantation owners, against the lowly hill-farmer—each firmly entrenched in their own beliefs and ready to fight to uphold those beliefs.

Thomas Jarvis was proud to be a Virginian. He and his young bride, Ailsey, had come into the mountains as a newly married couple, and had patented fifteen hundred acres of virgin land from The Commonwealth of Virginia. Toil, sweat, and more than a few tears had made it into a prosperous farm. Thomas was looked to for advice and council by neighbors and acquaintances. His well organized holdings were proof of a sharp mind and good management. The big family that had been born and reared there were part of the land; it was their birthright.

Ominous dark clouds of war roared across the mountains, sending vibrations up each hollow, with trembling echoes racing across the valleys. Fear and distrust seeped into every household as neighbor turned against neighbor, and many a father against son. The least unguarded, casual word would wrench families apart with bloodshed—and even death.

Danger lurked at every bend in the road, and hid behind every haystack, as mothers warned sons and husbands; "Be careful of what you say, and don't go out alone" as they stood, dressed in homespun, a worried look on their faces, watching their menfolk about their chores.

Every crossroad, country store and mill, found men and grown boys' bunched in groups deciding their fate. The Connollys, Keatons, Deweeses, Ellison, Cottrells, McClains, Parsons, Hunts, Jarvis, and many, many more. All close knit families, with young

1

men ready and willing to defend their mountain way of life, and the flag they respected and loved.

The Jarvis' big majestic two-story white house standing tall and proud by the rolling West Fork, became a favorite mustering place for some of the groups that gathered to discuss the coming conflict.

There were thirteen sons and daughters in this big pioneer family—all proud of their ancestors who had fought in many bloody wars; John Jarvis, their great-great-great-grandfather, in England who had fought with Lord Nelson, and knighted after the English and Spanish War. And Solomon Jarvis, their great-great-grandfather, with his son John their great-grandfather who had fought in the Revolutionary War, as had many cousins and uncles and other relatives. All had been proud to fight for their country and set an example for those to come; their heads held high with pride and determination.

Thomas, with his hat brim turned up in back, and tilted jauntily over his piercing blue eyes, his slight frame weaving its way among the milling men gathered in the spacious barnyard, listened to the talk. His keen eye and alert mind took in everything that was being said. He shook his head at the many who were expounding on their views, ready to split families and friends apart. Most of those gathered were either related by blood or by marriage.

Tom saw the four Cottrell brothers, William and Thomas tall and dark, with high cheekbones, confirming their claim to Indian blood on their father's side. Euan and Jackson, favored their mother who was related to the Jarvis'. As he watched, a fist-fight broke out between the brothers. Euan and Jackson had announced they would join the Rebels, against Thomas and William, who took a firm stand for the Union. The fight didn't amount to much, resulting in a lot of yelling and a couple of bloody noses. Fights had became an every day occurrence between families and friends, with bloody noses and raging tempers in the best of families—a dark hint of what was to come.

Euan and Jackson, with a murderous look and a shake of their fists toward their brothers, took off toward home. They had walked the ten miles or so from Cottrell Town, which was over on the head of Beach. Tom remembered the first land he had sold to their father, William, who had added more and more acres to it over the years as the log cabins and Jenny-Lynn houses began to dot the landscape. One enterprising Cottrell named Ben, had even built a fieldstone house that stood out among the other less pretentious ones. With more and more Cottrells that came into the area, a village had sprung up in the hollow called Cottrell Town. Old Bill Cottrell was a highly respected member of the community that he oversaw, and had a large family of his own, and a big sprawling home to house them. Tom's heart went out to him, for the sorrow he knew would follow his son's decision, and the rift that was bound to come in the family.

Thomas ruled his family with a firm hand, and was proud of his tall, strong, handsome sons, who towered above his slight frame. He listened to the talk around the supper table that evening where the family met together and where the events of the day were being discussed. The last few days had brought to his attention a cross-current of descent among his sons and sons-in-laws. Josiah, strong, close mouthed and stubborn, their second son, gave cause for a shiver to run up his father's spine, as he sat listening and observing him. "Surely my sons all believe in the Union and an undivided Virginia," he said to himself as he glanced out the window at the red, white, and blue flag, its stars a symbol of this new nation, as it waved in the breeze from the tall flagpole that had been planted when the house was built. When supper was over Tom saw Josiah and one of his son-in-law, John H. H. Keaton, huddled out by the fence in deep conversation, out of hearing of the rest of the family. A worried frown creased Tom's forehead, as he wondered how to handle the situation that was developing under his roof. His mind went to the Cottrell family who were facing the same problem, and in his heart he knew more and more families would join them in sorrow and shame.

The explosion that was building up and facing him now had no easy solution. He and Ailsey had faced many, what seemed insurmountable obstacles, but nothing so devastating concerning their family as this. He knew the sorrow that Ailsey would go through, knowing her sons would be fighting against each other, and who knew how soon?

The dark descended over the valley, and the household settled down for the night. Tom knew that the night wouldn't solve anything and that the problem would still be there with the break of day. There was very little sleep for Tom that night, as he tossed and turned, trying to think of a way to unite his family again. As the big clock in the downstairs hall struck four, he swung his feet over the side of the bed and lighted the lamp on the bedside table.

Ailsey raised herself up in bed; "What is it Tom? What has been troubling you all through the night? You weren't yourself all during supper—was it the Cottrell boys fighting? What is it? What's worrying you so?" She looked intently at her husband, noticing the strained look on his face.

Tom sat on the bed his elbows on his knees, shaking his head from side to side. "Oh Ailsey I don't know what we're going to do, it's the boys, and this talk of war. I don't like to alarm you, but it's coming, and you will be part of it as will all our family. To think that Virginia will be divided; but how can it stay united when it looks as though our own family won't be? I'm not sure yet, but it looks as though Josiah, and John may not think as the others do, or as you and I do. Virginia must not secede from the Union but remain as a whole! I quake in my boots to see the families and friends that we know being divided, even our own. The Union must stand no matter what it takes! What's to become of our families? We have kin throughout Virginia. They'll be fighting against each other in what will be the bloodiest war ever fought, mark my words!"

"Oh, My God Tom what are we to do? What are our boys thinking of? Surely you must be mistaken! They'll stick together, as they always have. I know that they will, they couldn't do anything different. Oh, Dear God! Tom, you must be mistaken. It would be bad enough having them fighting, without fighting each other." Ailsey started to weep, as she leaned against her husband. "Do something Tom! Stop them! You've always had influence over them," she sobbed as she looked imploringly into her husband's face.

Tom's arm went around her as he said, "it's coming like a whirlwind that will gather every mother's son, and destroy many households! I just hope that the fighting doesn't reach the wilderness area where we live, and destroy all we have spent our life working for." They sat with their arms around each other, rocking back and forth. Tom gave a long sigh as he started to dress. Another day had to be faced, and what it would bring was anyone's guess.

* * *

4

As the day progressed, with the men and boys all busy. Tom decided to take time to ride into the village of Minnora. He wanted to know what was being said at the store concerning the war, and if any news had come in from the South. Saddling his riding mare, he started at a canter down the West Fork road, toward Chenowith's store. As he dismounted and tied his mare to the hitching rail in front of the big sprawling, gray, weather-beaten store, he saw the three McGlowthrin boys, tall and lanky, with their black hats pushed well back on their head, their black hair escaping in a mass of curls onto their forehead. They all resembled each other—Hurshel, Earl, and the youngest, Dowel, standing lax and loose, each one holding a well-oiled gun. The sun sent out sparkles from the shine on the barrel and the stock of the rifles they held. They always traveled together, usually dressed all in black, and riding plump, well-fed horses. The boys at a casual glance, looked relaxed as they stood together on the store porch; but Tom could see their shining, black eyes darting this way and that taking in everything that moved. On each of their faces was a perpetual smile, their snow-white teeth glistening against their dark skin, as they stood watching Tom at the hitching rail.

"Morning boys! Going bear hunting this mornin'? Looks like a fine day for it," Tom said, looking at the guns they held in their slender, tanned hands. Tom, going into the store thought to himself, "I never saw such white teeth and glittering black eyes in my life." The boys had a name of being wild, but Tom had never seen anything wrong, and they were always together, quiet and polite when he had been around them.

As Tom entered the cool dark store, those sitting around inside looked up, "Howdy Tom, nice day." Their looks told Tom that they knew of the ruckus at his house, concerning the Cottrell boys, and were waiting to hear the details. He didn't intend to fill them in with facts until he had asked some questions of his own.

Worth Cheniworth leaned his large boned frame on the counter, his head resting in his propped up hands, as he listened to the gossip in the store. He lazily, pulled his lanky frame to an upright position as Tom walked toward the counter.

"Howdy Tom, something I can do for you?" He scratched his shaggy head as he looked at Tom, waiting for him to make his needs known.

"Howdy, Worth, when does the mail come in?" Not waiting for

an answer, Tom asked another question, "Is there any news from the south?"

"As to mail, there's no telling' when its likely to be here.

We han't had any for some time now. The news—it's not good Tom. From what I can gather there's been a lot of fightin' off and on, and things not rightly organized yet. There have been some folks coming from that direction mostly menfolk who were working over the mountains and trying to get back to their families. They tell that those who sympathies are with the Union are being driven from their homes. Zeke Arnold, came through going to his family over on Crummies Creek; he's been working on a timbering job down somewhere close to Richmond, said he passed a Reip family. I think he said their name was Peter and Ellen, with a passel of youngens, and their household plunder piled on a wagon. Said they got out just in time, they could see the smoke from their house burning when they were five miles away. They told him they were going to try to go as far as Ohio, guess they have ken thereabout. They declared for the Union it seems.

Tom's face blanched, "It's going to be bad. What do you think about calling a meeting of all the able-bodied men and boys, and decide what we should do in this area?"

"I don't know, Tom." Worth shook his scraggley head.

"People seem upset enough without calling their attention to the fightin' down South. I don't think the womenfolk would take kindly to calling their men out to talk about war. Maybe if we leave it be, things will settle down."

Tom knew Worth wasn't one to get excited about things, being easygoing, and as Tom sometimes thought a little lazy from hanging around the store all the time. "I don't think things will settle down Worth. It's my opinion that we should be prepared, make any preparations that we can for any future emergencies that may come." Tom heard the men stirring behind him and knew they were moving closer to hear what was being said.

"I'm all for calling a meetin'! Me too!" several of the men in the room spoke up. "How about posting a notice on the storehouse door announcing a meeting? Let everyone decide, by coming or staying away" one of the men asked, as they all nodded in agreement. It was decided that Worth would make up an announcement naming the time and place and post it on the door where everyone could see it, and decide for themselves.

Tom nodded, "I'll miss my guess if the whole countryside doesn't turn out. This is a serious situation, with all of us concerned, or should be. It's going to affect every family in the Colonies, and those who are closest to the South will be in the greatest peril. You all have sons, sons-in-law, and family that will be involved. Think seriously! Make your decisions carefully! You will all be affected." He touched his hatbrim and bid them goodday as he went toward the door, mounted his mare and rode away toward his home. His troubled mind going to Ailsey, and the year 1822-23, and the memory of their journey through the mountains, to this fresh green virgin valley, where they had made their home, and raised their large family.

❧ Chapter Two ❧

Doctor Connolly opened the door from his office, which connected with the hall to the dining room to see if there was any sign of dinner. There didn't seem to be anyone about but he heard doors slamming upstairs, and he could hear voices. The house was in an uproar, the girls were like ghosts flitting from room to room calling out to each other. A Play-Party was planned for the evening, and the preparation and excitement among the girls could be heard through out the house. He heard Ailsey's voice echoing from above, "do you have the list of games done yet, Ellen"? Her footsteps sounded on the attic stairs as she called to her younger sister. "Hurry with it I have to finish your dress for the party, or we will have to lock you in the attic, you won't have anything to wear." He could hear them both giggling and knew that was a far fetched possibility. "Sirena, don't forget the—" her voice came to a stop as she came into sight on the winding staircase, and seeing her father she called, "Poppa, do you want something? Are you looking for Mamma? I think she's out in the kitchen-shed with Amelia, looking for the big copper kettle, to make the taffy in. We have to have it for the party you know.." She smiled at her father.

Shaking his head at all the excitement, he asked, "will dinner be served in this household today I wonder? Tell your mother I have a half hour now, and then won't be finished until five." He silently closed the door and returned to his office.

Ailsey hurried to find her mother, calling as she went, "Mamma, Mamma hurry, Poppa wants his dinner he doesn't have much time.

Mrs. Connolly rushed into the kitchen where she had a mutton stew simmering for her husband. Quickly pouring hot water from the teakettle she made an herb tea. "Get your father Ailsey, I'll have it on the table by the time he washes up." Setting the big blue bowl of stew on to a plate, she added the cornbread warming in the warming closet and poured a cup of tea for them both. She made a practice of setting with Dr. Connolly while he ate. He hated eating alone and liked to talk to her while he enjoyed his meal.

Seating himself he unfolded the big snowy napkin by his plate, tasted the stew, "mumm, this tastes good my dear, as I've said

8

many times before, I'm a lucky man to have such a beautiful wife and a good cook into the bargain." He patted her hand and smiled at her as he ate. "I'm worried about the little Parson girl—she's into the seventh month, big as an elephant, and still has morning sickness. She has swelling in the feet and legs, and I don't like her color. She said that she doesn't have an appetite. It's hard to believe looking at her. She lost one child since she and Okey have been married. She shouldn't have gotten with child so soon but it does happen." Dr. Connolly looked toward the window, with sadness in his eyes.

Margaret smiled at her husband, knowing she was the luckiest of women to have such a devoted husband and so many wonderful children. The people who he doctored were very fortunate to have him looking after their ills. "Don't worry dear, women are much stronger than you think. I'm sure you will think of something to help her keep this baby," she smiled encouragingly at her husband.

Their children were leaving the homestead at an alarming rate, Patrick, and Polly his wife had gone to the wilderness with her grandchildren that she had only seen a few times. Sirena was married to Caleb Hayse, and Amelia to Bee Hopkins. Only the Lord knows where they might decide to move to.

Smiling to herself she thought about the plans her daughters were making for the 'Play Party' tonight. She knew Ailsey had her eye on Thomas Jarvis, who seemed somewhat shy, the girls planned to bring it to a head this night. She would be surprised if he got away this time without making his intentions known to the whole county. Ailsey was past seventeen and as old as most girls who married. She was such a help, being able to turn her hand to anything and she dreaded losing her, but knew it was time for her to have a home of her own. Thomas was a fine young man, from a wonderful family and was a suitable match for Ailsey. She was as anxious to have the two wedded as the girls were.

The boys had made up bonfires out by the meadow, where the games were to be, they would be lighted at dusk. The flickering light would help the faint hearted and encourage the young men to boldness and more than one lass would be pledged before the night was over or she would miss her guess. She smiled at all the plans and enticements the girls were thinking up. All of the games planned would be ones where there would be touching, hugging and shy kissing, which was permissible at a 'Play Party'. They

9

had even planned a "Cake-Walk" which let the young people hold hands without raised eyebrows. The 'taffy pull' would also pair off couples and some were known to steal shy kisses during the giggling and laughter that would ensue. Mrs. Connolly smiled remembering when she was a girl, and envied her daughters the fun they were going to have with all the other young people. Boards had been placed upon blocks of cut trees for seats; these had been set back somewhat from the fires to be in the shadows, and would encourage the shy young men in the romance department.

Mrs. Connolly looked around her big dining room, seeing that everything was sparkling clean and in place, her home was always ready for unexpected company. Thank heavens the young people would be outside for the festivities; they did tend to get a little on the rambunctious side, and some of the young men seemed to become clumsy when around so many pretty girls. She wouldn't have to worry about any disasters to her house. She smiled at her husband as he folded the big napkin, "Delicious my dear, thank you," pushing back his chair he kissed her cheek, and then went back to his office.

Margaret picked up the dishes and carried them into the kitchen as she returned to the shed to help Sirena to bring the big kettle. The molasses would be boiled in the kitchen then taken outside for the 'taffy pull' where everyone could get into the fun without the mess that usually occurred.

Supper was hurried a half an hour earlier than usual due to the party. The girls didn't have to be coaxed to finish tidying the kitchen. Hurrying through the dishwashing, they flew up the long staircase to dress for the big event.

Dr. Connolly could hear the girls calling to each other, their laughter a joy to hear, as he sat looking over a medical book. He was looking for something to ease the woes of the small petite Parson girl. He was worried that she nor the baby would survive this pregnancy. She was such a sweet girl only 17 years old and already into her second trial of becoming a mother. He shook his head as he read page after page. It seemed to him that someone could come up with a different treatment, so many births where both mothers and babies were lost. It wasn't as if it was a new phenomenon. The death rate was much too much—too many young deaths. The tears that were shed when a young mother was lost— his beloved Margaret cried as though her heart couldn't stand the sadness. He dreaded to bring home the news at losing another young girl to motherhood. He let out a sigh as he put the book aside and wiped his eyes.

Dusk was falling and the sound of horses, and vehicles were heard outside, as the guests began to arrive.

Dr. Connolly walked toward the barn where buggies, and wagons as well as riding horses were arriving. Some of the families brought their girls, and visited together in a quiet area while the young people enjoyed themselves. Most of the wagons were full of laughing young people who had been picked up along the way. A lot of the available bachelors rode in on their sleek saddle horses, their bridles and gear shining with ornamentation. Showing off their mounts, with side-stepping and occasionally a dancing horse would rear and cause the girls to catch their breath, in fear for the rider. The young men got a kick out of astonishing their audience of charming female admirers, causing them to shriek and scream in fear.

The bonfires were beginning to be lighted. Every other one until it became darker when all would be lighted. Cheers went up as two of the boys did the honors using a long torch. It was time for the party to begin. The milling crowd was greeting each other with hugs and laughter, "Where have you been? I haven't seen you in a Coon's age," "What have you done to yourself? You've grown like a tree." "When are you going to jump the broomstick?" Laughter and questions from this direction and that, till it all blended into a mixture of exited voices.

Several older men arrived with an assortment of musical instruments; they went to an area where some chairs had been arranged for them. Beginning to tune up, the crowd surged this way and that, calling out "How about Barbara Allen?" "How about Floyd Went a Courtin'?" someone called out changing it from Froggy to one of the boys names. Everyone howled with laughter, and poor Floyd hid behind his friends. The musicians soon had the tuning to suit them and began to play a soft sentimental song that the girls began to sway to holding hands with each other.

The stars had began to light the sky and darkness descended. The other bonfires were lit and the crowd began to clear a place for the games—the parents and older members filling in at the edge of the cleared space to watch.

"Choose your partner, choose your partner, we're ready to start. Come on everybody." Some of the girls had to go fetch their choice of partner, pulling them into the area saved for the games. Other boys were first to choose the girl of their choice before she went to someone else. "Old Dusty Miller" was the first game to be played. The couples lined up two abreast—the girls on the right the boys on the left, their arms were crossed behind with them holding each other's hands. The march began, "Old Dusty Miller, lived by the mill, every time the wheel turned—with that the couples turned without dropping hands the girls now on the left and boys on the right. At this point everyone got mixed up and couldn't seem to make the cross-over and laughter rang out from all the young people. Some of the boys didn't want to go on with the game—the confusion embarrassed them. The more experienced players helped the others in the turning and soon the game progressed again. In the mean-time most of the participants had had a good laugh and hugging which was the main purpose of the game.

An oil-cloth cover had been put on a table of boards laid across saw horses. The big three-layered nut cake made especially for the cake walk sat in its splendor of nutty frosting on the table. One of the musicians stood with a broom handle, which would be dropped between the couples to see which one would be the winner of the cake. The cake walk slowed down as each couple came close to the person with the broomhandle, hoping to be the winner. The musicians were to sound a note when they thought the walk had continued long enough. The broom handle would fall and the couple it fell in front of would be the winner. The banjo let out a loud twang, the handle fell in front of Ailsey and Thomas. Ailsey let out a scream and then began to giggle, as the rest of the group whistled and cat called.

"Is this a wedding cake, Tom?" someone called out.

Thomas answered with a grin, "This is a walking cake, and old Tom's walking."

Ailsey took Thomas' hand and went to the table. They were to cut the cake and serve it to the group. The line formed and the cake was cut and laid in the hands that were presented for a slice. Everyone ate from their hand, licking fingers and laughing—no forks or dishes were used for the cake. There was not quite enough to go around and seeing that they were short Mrs. Connolly brought another cake from the house for the rest. Everyone enjoying the cake, expressing oh's and ah's. The games began again; 'Skipp to my Lou', was played next. All the young people crowded around for a place in the game.

While the games were played an eye was kept on the molasses that was simmering in the kitchen; it took time to cook down into taffy. Ailsey went to check on the big kettle dragging Thomas along. "Are you having fun, Tommy?" she asked as she smiled into his eyes. "Isn't this fun? I just love a 'Play Party.' Everyone is having such a good time."

"Ailsey, please don't call me Tommy; it sounds like a babe in arms." He dropped his head embarrassed about asking her, but he couldn't abide being called such a babyish name.

Taken by surprise Ailsey said, "I'm sorry Thomas, I'll remember. Did you hear about Susan Criss? She and Wade are going to be married, she just told me—in a month it's to be. Isn't that exciting?" She cast a glance at Thomas. "Oh I do hope he asks me tonight," she thought as she looked at him out of the corner of her eye.

Picking up the big wooden spoon she began to stir the bubbling molasses. "I hope they don't scorch, I think someone will have to stay and keep stirring, they are cooking down and may burn. Do you want to stay and keep me company, Thomas?"

Thomas walked to the window and looked out. "I'll stay if you want. I wanted to talk to you anyway." He took a few steps toward her and then turned and walked back to the window.

Ailsey smiled to herself. "You want to talk to me? What about Thomas?" She smiled as he turned again to her.

"You sure do look pretty tonight, and you smell good too." Thomas looked at the floor color staining his face.

"Is that what you wanted to talk to me about Thomas? I thank you for the nice compliment; you look nice too. I like the way you ride your horse, you sit so straight and tall, almost like a soldier." She continued stirring the pot, casting glances at Thomas.

"That's not exactly what I had in mind to talk about. You know I've been working in the timbering, and have just finished a job. I have my team paid for, and a little money put aside. I don't know any girl I like as well as you." He headed for the window again, his hands deep in his pockets. "I'm old enough to head out on my own; I was wondering how you would feel about maybe coming along, I mean we could get married maybe."

Ailsey dropped the spoon, letting out a squeal, ran to Tom and throwing her arms around his neck said, "Oh, Thomas I thought you would never ask me. I've waited and waited for you to say you wanted me. I love you and want to be your wife more than

13

anything. You can kiss me now."

Thomas grabbed Ailsey and gave her a hug that almost cracked her ribs, and holding her more gently gave her a kiss on her laughing pink lips. "Oh, Ailsey I was so afraid you would say no. So many of the fellows have had their eye on you. I'll try to take good care of you and be good to you. When Ailsey? Don't make me wait too long, I don't think I can stand waiting for you to be mine.

"How would Christmas do? That's only a couple of months. I don't want to wait either. We will have to make plans and talk to Mamma and Poppa. I'm so happy Thomas. Just think in a short time I will be Mrs. Thomas Jarvis. I can't wait," she twirled around the room, laughing and smiling at Thomas.

Thomas felt like his head was swimming, and his feet wanted to leave the floor. He had never been so happy in his life. Ailsey was the prettiest girl around. And she would make a good wife. He had lots of plans to talk over with her, but first would come the talk he must have with Dr. Connolly. He wasn't looking forward to that. He felt that the Dr. and Mrs. Connolly both liked him; he looked up to them both, and would feel so lucky to belong to their family.

Ailsey hurried back to the big kettle, stirring like mad to keep the molasses from being scorched. "I sure hope someone comes to help stir, I want to go outside and tell everyone that we are to be wed."

Thomas made the trip to the window again; turning to look back at Ailsey he said, "Do you have to tell right away', I kinda' wanted to keep it to ourselves for a while," he smiled a shy smile.

"Oh, Thomas, you're just shy; everyone is expecting it tonight. They will know just by looking at me, I'm that happy.

Thomas stood looking at Ailsey; she is so beautiful, he thought to himself. "I'll have to talk to the Doctor right away then. I'll go find him and see if I can get someone to help you with the taffy." With that he left the house going toward the area where the party was. He spotted Dr. Connolly talking to some men over by the fence. He went over and leaned on the top rail waiting to see if the Doctor would leave or if there would be a break in the conversation. He finally caught the eye of the Doctor.

"Excuse me, I want to talk to Thomas a minute," the Doctor said as he walked the short distance to where Thomas leaned against the fence. "Did Ailsey desert you? I thought I saw you two together."

"She's in the kitchen stirring the taffy. I would like to talk to you if you have time Doctor," Thomas said as he shuffled from one foot to the other.

Doctor Connolly knowing what was on the young man's mind, smiled to himself. He couldn't help teasing him a little. "What's wrong Thomas? Don't you feel well? You look kind of peaked come to think of it."

"I'm fine. As you know I'm eighteen now, and Ailsey and I have been seeing each other a while. I don't know of any girl I like as well as I do her. We've talked it over, and we want to marry; I hope you will want me in your family. I'll try to give Ailsey a home and treat her right." Thomas seemed out of breath, as he looked at Dr. Connolly.

Dr. Connolly cleared his throat, and looked at Thomas under his drawn eyebrows. "Well now, this comes as a surprise. What does Ailsey have to say about this?"

"She's willing and we want to marry at Christmas time." I have some money saved, not a lot—but my team is paid for, I think we can get along." Thomas looked doubtful at the Doctor, knowing he couldn't possibly offer what Ailsey had at home.

Dr. Connolly could tell that Thomas was becoming more nervous by the minute and just might take off into the night. Ailsey would never forgive him, and he would get the wrath of God from Margaret if he discouraged him any further. He remained looking straight at Thomas, "Well now! He then stuck out his hand toward Thomas—I want to welcome you to this family. I think you and Ailsey are suited and will have a fine marriage. Do you want me to announce it tonight?"

Thomas dropped his head, "Ailsey is set on it; I'll appreciate it if you will, and thank you. You'll tell Mrs. Connolly?" Thomas didn't want to go through this again.

"Leave everything to me," Dr. Connolly said as he left the fence and went toward the crowd.

"Whew!" Thomas said under his breath, "I sure wouldn't want to go through that every day. I'd better find some help to stir the taffy for Ailsey, or I'll be in even more hot water."

Amelia and Sirena were standing together on the edge of the circle where the games were being played; Thomas walked over to them. "Ailsey needs some help in the kitchen; can you find someone to stir the taffy—she's tired and needs some time off."

"We'll get help, don't you worry Thomas." They took off into the crowd and he soon saw them heading toward the house with several other women.

Mrs. Connolly went into the kitchen to check on the taffy knowing it was about time it should be worked. She found several of the young women each taking turns with the big wooden spoon. I've come to test the taffy. Going to the big kettle she lifted the spoon on high, seeing the molasses begin to thread—the amber threads flying around the kettle. Give me a glass of cold water please. It was handed to her and she dropped a dollop into the water, watching it instantly become a ball. It's ready for the working; bring some smaller pans. Someone fill the dishpan with water for hand washing and get a couple of towels. Bring the pan of butter I have ready." She dished up the taffy into bowls so the girls could carry a portion out to the table, where they would find partners to join in the pulling.

When they reached the table the musicians were told to announce the taffy-pull. The girls chose their partners, guiding them toward the pan of water to wash. Soon the couples had handfuls of the sticky mess. "Put butter on your hands so it doesn't stick. How much butter?" someone asked. "Just a little but put it on often, that way it doesn't stick and the butter makes it tasty and turns it a light yellow. Come on work it—;" the taffy was pulled out until it started to sag between the couple then quickly lapped over to the other person and pulled out again as far as they dared. This continued until the taffy became stiff and pale yellow. It was then placed on a greased bread pan or platters and left to completely harden and cool which took very little time. It was then cut into squares or pieces to be passed around and eaten. Needless to say, little conversation went on while the gooey taffy was being eaten.

It was nearing ten o'clock when Dr. Connolly approached the musicians, "I want to make an announcement, he said. He looked around noting that the party was beginning to tire the older folk. When things quieted down, he said, "It's come to my attention that there will soon be a wedding in this family; young Thomas Jarvis has asked for my daughter Ailsey's hand in marriage. The wedding will be on Christmas Day at one o'clock—you are all invited." A big smile lit the Doctor's face as he reached out an arm and embraced his wife. There was an uproar of voices and laughter at the announcement, the young people milled around the happy couple, as the party began to break up. Goodnights were heard as the rattle of wagons and horses gear jingled as they mounted and road away.

* * *

Ailsey was so happy; she thought at times that she just couldn't wait for her wedding. Christmas finally rolled around and the day arrived. The girls had trimmed the house with Hemlock and greens; big pots of wild fern scrounged from the deep ravines by the creek were placed around the parlor where the ceremony would take place. Ailsey and Sirena had made new dresses for all the women folk. Ailsey's was a lovely white gown, with pale blue flowers, a sash of blue tied in a big bow behind and hung to her dress hem. A big blue satin bow adorned the braids of her hair, making her look like a little girl playing dress-up. Thomas looked stiff and uncomfortable in a dress suit and starched white collar. Amelia sat at the Pianoforte and began to play softly, as the bride came down the winding stair case and entered the parlor. The ceremony was short and over quickly. Everyone hugged the bride and wished the groom good luck with hearty handshakes.

The guests were asked to adjourn to the dining room for refreshments.

Ailsey's eyes were sparkling as she held Thomas' arm and approached the big wedding cake. She cut slices and presented them to her parents as she kissed their cheeks. Then beaming she cut a piece for her new husband, kissing him on his cheek. Thomas lit up like a light with his red face, so embarrassed that he couldn't have told you his own name at that moment. Ailsey looked at Thomas and knew she had better get him away; taking a slice of cake for herself, she handed the knife to her sister Sirena who would serve the guests. Ailsey linked her arm through Thomas' and guided him back to the parlor to a chair.

"Oh, Thomas, finally I'm your wife. I know we will be so happy, I can't keep the tears from flowing," she turned to him with tears in her eyes.

Thomas looked frightened as he extracted a snowy handkerchief from a pocket and gently wiped Ailsey's tears away. "Don't cry Ailsey, I don't know what to do when you cry." He causally slipped an arm around her and pulled her head to his shoulder, as he looked around to see if anyone was watching.

Just as suddenly Ailsey started to laugh. It's all right Thomas;

17

we are an old married couple now." She could see that Thomas was uncomfortable nevertheless, "Don't worry, we will soon be in our own little home." They had moved their belongings into a small cottage belonging to one of their distant cousins. It was small but was enough for now. It had been scrubbed and tidied by Ailsey and her sisters. The presents she had received would be opened as soon as everyone finished their cake and coffee, and would be taken to the cabin that would be their home. Thomas' horses waited to take them there. A milk cow that Ailseys father had given her was at the cabin; as were some chicks and a pig. Ailsey felt like their home was becoming a real home for them—only lacking the happy couple.

The gifts were all opened and handed around to be admired, and Thomas began to think that the guests would never leave—it was late afternoon.

"What do they want to stay for?" he asked Ailsey. "It's all over, I want to go home and take off this stiff collar before it cuts my throat.

Ailsey looked at him and let out a giggle, "If you start bleeding they may want to stay longer," she giggled even more.

"You don't care if I suffer," sighed Thomas looking at her, his mouth drawn down, a woebegone look on his face.

Ailsey couldn't help the giggles that assailed her as she looked at her husband. "You're so funny Thomas. I have began to think that Tommy is the perfect name for you—you are a baby; can't even stand a little throat cutting without complaining," more giggles filled the air, and everyone had began to take notice.

Ellen walked over to them. "What's so funny?" she asked.

Ailsey, looked at her sister; Thomas is getting his throat cut by his stiff collar—watch out for the blood." The girl's doubled over in laughter; they would look at each other and start in again.

Thomas got up from beside Ailsey, "I'll get a cup of coffee if you don't mind," he said as he removed himself from the giggling girls.

Thomas remained in the other room and noticed that people were starting to leave; several shook his hand and wished him happiness and good luck. He was so relieved to know that soon everyone would be gone—all but the family. They were a crowd themselves; he just hoped there would be no more fits of giggles and teasing from his new relatives. This had been the longest day of his life—he wanted to go home now.

❧ Chapter Three ❧

Patrick Connolly, Ailsey's brother had come from over the mountains with news for Tom about a parcel of land that was available next to his acreage. He stayed several days, telling Tom and Ailsey of the beauty of the area which had rich soil, good water and timber, and abounded with wildlife for food and hunting. The area he told them about was a small parcel on the banks of a nice stream, well wooded and in an area that was sure to be settled quickly. Thomas and Ailsey had married on Christmas Day, 1822. To have a place in the virgin wilderness of Virginia for a home of their own was their dream.

Tom and Ailsey talked it over and had decided on Patrick's recommendation that they were interested enough for Tom to go and look at the acreage and buy the land—if it was all Patrick said it was, which they both felt sure that it would be.

Tom and Patrick left riding their saddle horses just at dawn, on a mild, sunny March morning. Their saddle bags stuffed with food to last them several days, and ears of corn for their horses. Tied behind their saddles were their rifles wrapped in their bedrolls, tarp and rain gear needed for the trail. Cooking pots, and a small ax included in their gear clanged and rattled as they started off down the Trace. Ailsey, with tears in her eyes, bid her husband and brother farewell with many warnings to be careful along the way, and to come back soon. She stood watching until they were out of sight, tears streaming down her face. There was always danger on the trail, especially with the men traveling so far, although the two being together lessened the danger and Ailsey soon dried her tears.

The preparations had been going on for several days as Ailsey went over all her belongings, carefully repairing and washing all her clothes as well as her new husband Tom's. She was getting ready for the journey over the mountains to their new home. Knowing Tom, Ailsey was quite sure he would buy the land her brother had selected for them. From the description Patrick had given, it was just what she and Tom had set their hearts on. They were both young, with good health and ambition to own their own farm and build a home for the family that was sure to come.

Ailsey smiled to herself as she worked, her family was already on its way. She hadn't told Tom, but she knew that they would have a child in several months. He had enough on his mind now without the worry of her. If they were lucky they would have their own cabin, before the birth of their first child.

The sparsely furnished cabin they now occupied belonged to relatives. Tom had made them a lovely bed from birdseye-maple, and he had taken great pains in making it; and Ailsey was very proud of both her husband and her new bed. They didn't have much in the way of household plunder, just the bare necessities. "It's just as well," Ailsey said to herself with a smile. "We couldn't take much over the mountains anyway." Patrick had told them that a small wagon could make it over the Trace, if the weather permitted. The bed—she wouldn't think of leaving it behind, cedar chest, kitchen plunder, the few tools Tom had, and their animals would be as much as they could take.

Ailsey took everything from the cedar chest that set at the foot of their bed. The chest had been a wedding gift from her mother. Her father had made it many years ago, and had recently made her mother a new one. She was so thankful to have it and wanted to air all the linens and quilts that were packed in it. There would be room to include all their clothes in the chest for the journey, where they would be protected from the weather. Everything would be ready when Tom returned. Ailsey knew that time was of the essence if they were to clear the land and put in a garden. No doubt they would stay in her brother's home until they could build their own cabin.

Ailsey had collected several packets of seeds from relatives and friends; among them roots of rhubarb, horseradish, sage and other spices for starts in her new garden. She had the roots buried in dirt in an old kettle that had holes in it; they might even have roots started by the time they reached their destination, and should start much faster when planted in her garden. She knew that it would be hard to get plants and herbs in a new sparsely settled area. Even her sister-in-law, Polly, might not have enough to share; she knew she shouldn't take anything that wasn't needed, but couldn't resist a small root from her mother's lilacs bush, she must include some roots of Ground Ivy and Skull Cap, for teas which were good for small infants. Most of the things were necessary for medicines and seasoning for cooking; salt was dear and sometimes hard to come by in the wilderness, and herb-seasoned food was palatable.

Ailsey had gotten over her crying spell and sang as she hung the things outside in the sweet-smelling spring air. Everything would be in readiness on Tom's return, to be loaded into the wagon for the journey. It was quiet in the clearing where the cabin stood, she could hear the pee-wee's as they looked for mates, and were noisily building their nests. "Just like Tom and I. Soon we will be building our nest, one that will last a long time, I hope." Her laughter rang out in the stillness. Ailsey hurried around the clearing gathering the things that would be taken with them—anything to keep busy until her younger sister came to spend the night with her. Tom had made sure she wouldn't be alone while he was gone, especially, at night.

Ailsey had milked their one cow, and gone back to the cabin and made a pan of cornbread, when she heard her sister's voice as she entered the clearing calling out to her.

"Sister, come see what I've brought you! Come see!" She called as she came across the clearing toward the cabin.

"What is it? What have you brought me?" Ailsey asked as she hurried to the cabin door to meet her younger sister Ellen.

Ellen held a snow-white, furry, little kitten, which she immediately placed in Aisley's arms.

"Oh! You beauty! It's so soft and sweet, Ellen; but what am do with it? I can never take it over the mountains; it's too far and Tom would never allow it."

"You'll want to keep it. You won't have a chance to get one where you are going. Besides, isn't Tom going to take his dog? You have as much right to a kitten, don't you?"

"Since you put it that way, I suppose I do." Ailsey laughed. "I would love to keep her; it is a her, isn't it?" She laughingly asked as she held the bundle of fur to her face. She could hear the little thing purring, as she petted it. "You're as sweet as taffy," she cooed.

"I especially picked a female; they are more loving and you won't run out of cats with her around." Ellen's laughter rang out in the stillness as the two girls laughed together.

"Thank you for the gift—I just love her. Come in while I give her some warm milk from old Bossie; I just this minute brought in a pailful." She fed the kitten, which lapped up the warm milk hungrily; Aisley then placed it on the rug by the fireplace where it immediately fell asleep. "Have you had supper? I made a pone of cornbread and I'm going to have a big bowl of cornbread and milk for my supper."

"I'd love some. You make the best cornbread ever." Ellen said with a giggle.

"I'll have to lead the team to the run for water, and feed the chickens. Come you can help me before it gets any colder!" Ailsey told her sister as she wrapped a shawl around her head, picked up a pan of food for Tom's dog that was also in the shed.

The girls quickly led the big team out to the creek where they drank thirstily, then took them back to the shed where they gave them a meager feeding of hay and a handful of grain. Ailsey taking a handful to scatter for the chickens that were penned in a corner of the shed said, "That'll do it," she said patting Tom's dog, Rowdy, and quickly closed and latched the shed door and the two girls hurried back to the cabin.

Ailsey lifted the compone from the Dutch-oven where she had left it to steam and keep warm. The kitten still slept rolled into a ball of fur on the hearth. Ailsey took two pewter bowls from the kitchen shelf and poured a pitcher of milk from the big bucket, setting it and the cornbread on the slab table. The two girls sat on the bench and gossiped while they ate. After clearing the table and putting the vittles away, they sat by the fire talking and giggling about the trip that Ailsey was soon to take. As the cabin became dark, Ailsey banked the fire and they both went to bed.

The girls had been in bed some time when Ailsey awoke; she had been dreaming of a big white house beside a wide stream where she lived happy and contented. The sound of rain on the roof and wind blowing with the cold seeping through every crack and crevice—she decided was what had awakened her. "I do hope the men have found a warm place to camp, out of the wind and cold," she thought to herself. The little kitten mewed beside her bed. "Are you cold little one?" she whispered, as she leaned over and picked it up, cuddling it close to her side among the quilts.

* * *

Tom and Patrick, keeping up a steady pace, covered mile after mile. They were soon into an uninhabited area where the woods were thick with just a slight cut through the trees to mark the Trace. Stopping late in the afternoon beside a fast-moving stream, they dismounted and watered their horses letting them rest while the men ate some of the cold meat and bread that Ailsey had packed for them.

"We've made good time so far," Tom remarked. "I'd say about fifteen miles. What do you think?"

"I'd allow about that far. We can make another ten before we camp, if the weather holds. I don't like the looks of those clouds rolling up over that far mountain." Patrick looked worried as they both observed the cloud formation.

"We had better be on our way. The wind seems to be picking up; now that we are out of the sun, it seems to be much colder. I sure hope we don't have a snowstorm building up." Tom said as he packed the saddlebags and threw them across his mare.

"We had better hurry along; there's a cabin over that next hill—we'll see if we can stay the night out of this wind. I have a feeling we're in for a storm," Patrick said as he mounted and started on ahead.

The two men kicked their mounts into a fast pace for the next several miles. A few windblown raindrops encouraged them along, they put all their energy into guiding their horses over the safest route. Their conversation came to a halt as they hurried along their eyes watching the storm clouds and the road ahead for any dangerous down trees, or potholes that a horse might stumble into.

They were approaching the upgrade that led over the hills ahead when the rumble of thunder sounded behind them. Patrick pulled his mount to a halt, seeing that Tom was a little way behind him. "Let's let the horses blow before tackling the hill; we can break out our rain gear while they rest a minute. I think we'll need it very shortly," Patrick called to Tom.

"I think that's a fine idea; we've been making tracks for the last few hours." With that; Tom dismounted and untied the slicker from behind his saddle; after putting it on, he carefully wrapped his gun and bedroll in the tarp and tied them behind the saddle. Looking toward Patrick, he saw that he was ready to tackle the steep hill before them.

"Ready?" Patrick called. "I'd like to get over this hill before it starts to rain harder. The other side could be treacherous if it

23

becomes soggy." They started up the hill, each man concentrating on keeping his animal to the best route.

They had almost reached the top when the wind picked up, blowing a gale as they neared the crest of the hill. A loud clap of thunder sounded behind them as a gust of wind snapped a dead limb from a tree close by. Tom's horse shied, side stepping, sending a clatter of stones cascading over the hill almost unseating Tom and slamming him into a large tree by the trail, bruising his leg. With a firm hand on the reins Tom brought the shaking animal under control. Patrick, turning in the saddle, looked back, seeing Tom having trouble called, "You all right?"

Tom nodded; his leg had been scraped from hip to knee against the tree. He couldn't tell if it was bleeding, but it sure hurt like the devil. They finally reached the crest where the wind was blowing so hard that the men and horses were in danger of being blown into the ravine below. Starting their descent, their horses slid on the wet leaf-covered trail; but gaining their footing, they carefully descended the hill. Slipping and sliding they took a zigzag path to where it leveled out at the bottom.

The men were tiring as were their horses; the storm was increasing in its fury. Traveling slowly and cautiously for another half hour they could make out the cabin in the distance. It didn't look very big to Tom, but maybe they could at least take shelter in a shed till morning, if the folks didn't have room for them in the cabin. He surely didn't like the idea of camping out with a storm such as was building up minute by minute roaring down on them.

"There's the cabin ahead," Patrick called out; they could hear a hound dog barking somewhere near the cabin.

The cabin door opened and a tall rangy man emerged holding a rifle at the ready, his big shaggy dog by his side.

"Ho, the cabin.'" Patrick called out, as the two men advanced slowly. "Howdy John, it's Patrick Connolly, and my brother-in-law Tom Jarvis, on our way back to the West Fork." Patrick had stopped and talked to John as he came through several days ago; dusk had fallen and he wasn't sure that John could recognize him.

"Evenin' Patrick, come in by the fire till I get a coat and we can care for your animals. We've got a humdinger of a storm coming over the mountains; it's no time for man or beast to be out."

Dismounting, Patrick answered, "We don't want to put you to

any bother John; we would appreciate a dry place to bed the night though."

"I see you have bedrolls—there's plenty of space by the hearth to spread them; you'll need warmth before this night is over or I will miss my guess. Come on in, warm yourselves; I'll be ready in a minute."

The two men walked into the cabin; it was surprisingly larger than they had at first believed, with a lean-to built on the back for extra space. A large fireplace covered one wall and sent out a cheerful welcome. Tom and Patrick wasted no time going to the fire and turning their backs to the heat as they watched John don his warm coat, and a heavy pair of boots.

"Let's get your animals settled before the weather worsens," John said as he headed toward the door. The two men followed close behind in a hurry to get back to the welcome warmth of the cabin.

"Looks as though you've lived here for some time and have the makings of a nice homestead started," Tom remarked as they walked through the rain, leading their horses toward the shed.

"We've been here goin' on to ten years. Had to clear the land to plant; of course, we used the logs for the house and barn, killing two birds with one stone as the saying goes. Had a little trouble with wild animals at first—they've thinned out considerably now. Some made good eating till we had our own hogs to butcher. We've got four boys, and one girl commin' up which will be a big help." They had reached the barn and John showed them where they could house their horses for the night.

"We've brought corn for our horses, and some food for ourselves; we don't want to impose on you folks. We appreciate a place to sleep out of the cold and wet," Tom hurried to inform their host.

"Don't you worry none; Etta has a big pot of boiled pork ribs and 'taters cooking, and cornpone in the Dutch oven. We just butchered a big fat hog—there's aplenty for us all. You'll need some hot vittles to thaw you out," ha, ha. John acted as though they were honored guests, as he helped them unsaddle and feed their horses. "That will do it," he said as he hung the last bridle on a peg on the wall. "Let's head back to the fire out of this weather; you two go ahead I'll close the door this old latch is a little tricky."

When the three men came into the cabin a trestle table had been brought in from the lean-to and set up in front of the fire;

two split-log benches lined each side. Etta had been out of sight in the lean-to when the men had first entered. Now she and her daughter, who looked about eight years old, were carrying bowls and plates to the table from the other room. Three boys came down a 'peg in the wall' ladder from the loft to join them.

There's warm water and a towel for the men in the lean-to John—would you show them where to go?" Etta asked as she continued work at the table.

"This certainly is a nice surprise, John; we appreciate your hospitality more than you know. I hope you aren't putting Etta to too much trouble," Tom said as they began to wash up.

"No trouble 'tall; Etta likes to cook She's a tolerable cook, if I do say so myself. And we both like company, don't see much of it around here though." They had finished drying their hands, and going back into the other room. Tom had noticed a mound on one of the beds in the corner, the fourth boy must be a babe, he decided.

Steam was coming off a big mound of cornbread, and several pots sent up vapor almost to the rafters. Good smells brought rumbles from the men's stomachs as they sat around the table. It seemed that Etta had outdone herself.

The men talked as they ate the hearty meal—the children and Etta listening to every word. When they had finished they moved the benches to each side of the big fireplace and continued their talk. Etta and her daughter cleared the table taking the leftover food and dishes to the lean-to to wash. By the time they were finished the men were ready to say goodnight. They spread their bedrolls by the fire.

Tom's leg hurt him terribly; turning to Patrick he asked, "you got any liniment in your saddlebags, Patrick? I sure could do with some." Tom knew they would get an early start as soon as it was light and that he would be too stiff to ride if something wasn't done for his leg.

"What's the trouble, saddle sore?" John asked his guest. Tom proceeded to tell of his mishap.

"We'd better take a look at that leg; come into the lean-to and shuck your clothes, I'll bring something to put on it. John brought a pan of warm water and a cloth to wash Tom's leg. When he removed his clothes there was a raw burn from the scrape; he washed it with soap and water and applied the salve that John handed him and wrapped some clean cloths around the area.

"Looks bad Tom; but that salve of Etta's will do the trick. Should feel better by 'mornin," John told him.

"Feels better already; I'll sleep good tonight. Thanks a lot" Tom said.

Their first night out had turned into a welcome surprise. Tom doubted there would be many such comfortable nights ahead on their journey through the wilderness.

🎋 Chapter Four 🎋

The old barnyard rooster crowing before daybreak, awoke Tom. He looked around in the dark trying to remember where he was. As he listened he could hear Patrick begin to stir; it was then Tom realized, they were bedded down beside the fireplace in John Murphy's cabin. The fire was almost out. Tom rolled out of his bed and began to build it up from the bucket of chips that was at hand. Soon the blaze sent a welcoming glow into the dark cabin.

"Mornin' Tom, how do you feel this mornin'? How's your leg?" Patrick asked as he began to roll up his bedding.

"I'll live; don't feel too bad." Tom said as he rolled and tied his bedroll ready for departure.

"You boys are parful' early risers," John called, from the corner bed, as he let out a low chuckle. "I'll be right with you; by the time we get your horses fed and saddled, Etta will have the biscuits ready." They could hear John putting on his clothes grunting and mumbling to himself.

"Don't wake Etta, we'll eat on the trail; she's done enough for us already," Tom answered.

"Shucks! If Etta couldn't feed you boys a good breakfast, she'd think you didn't like her vittles," John answered with another chuckle.

"Nothing like that!" Tom hurried to tell him. "It's just we hate putting you folk out."

"There, I'm ready to go and help with the saddling up. Don't you worry none about Etta she's enjoying having you two here," John said as he started toward the door.

By the time they had led the horses out to water, fed and saddled them, the aroma of country ham was wafting its way to the barnyard. "Boy!" Patrick said. "I didn't think I would ever be hungry again after that feed of hog-ribs we had last night, but that smell would drive an old hound-dog up a tree. Ha, Ha."

"My Etta makes fine biscuits, fried ham, and red-eye gravy; you can hardly set still when you eat it, it's that good," John laughingly told the men.

"I'll be glad if my new wife and I can live so well in ten years, John. You give a man heart; makes him want to get out there and dig," Tom told him.

"Well now, it does take a heap of digging, lugging, and pulling, and maybe a little cussin' when the wimmin-folk hain't around. Looks like you're the kind of man that'll waste no time," John answered, looking Tom up and down as they entered the cabin.

"Etta's really been rattling the cook-pots. Looks as though it's ready when you get washed up." John said with a smile as he steered them toward the lean-to and the big washpan of warm water. The men wasted no time getting to the table, and the savory meal they knew they were about to enjoy.

"I think Etta should open up an Inn; everyone would soon be going out of their way to come by here," Patrick said with a laugh. "I thought my old lady was a good cook till I ate Etta's cooking; now I'll have to tell her to take a back seat." They could see the blush of pleasure on Etta's face at Patrick's words.

The men finished their last cup of coffee, and quickly pushed back from the table. "We had better be on our way, Patrick; I'm sure our next stop won't be this pleasant," Tom said as he turned to shake hands with John. "Etta, we sure are beholdin' to you; you've made a cold night very pleasant for two weary travelers. I'll see you folks again soon. I would like you to meet my wife Ailsey. Thanks again. Tom, went out the cabin door as Patrick turned to shake hands with the Murphy's.

"Wait, Etta called, as she hurried to hand Tom a small homemade wooden container. This is some of my salve; you may need more of it for your leg—I hope it has helped," she smiled at Tom.

"It certainly did. I had a good night's sleep, thanks to you. You'll have to give my Ailsey the recipe for your salve. She's pretty good at doctoring; her father has been a doctor for sometime—guess she picked up some of it from him," Tom told her with a smile.

Bringing their horses from the shed they mounted up, waving a farewell to the household as light began to show in the East. They could see the rough trail that lay ahead through the trees.

The men put their minds to making as many miles as possible—watching the trail ahead and guiding their mounts over rough places and around down trees. The storm of the night before seemed to be over. Fleecy white clouds floated above the treetops. A weak sun sent a few shadows on the Trace through the leafless trees. The bitter wind had quieted, and Tom thought to himself it's going to be a much more pleasant ride today. He didn't get his hopes up too much, knowing that this time of year the weather could change in a matter of minutes, especially in the mountains.

Patrick kept a steady pace; having been over the trail only a few days before, he was sure of the way. The storm had downed some trees and broken limbs that had to be avoided. They were entering the foothills of the Alleghenys and would have some big mountains to cross. The men had to favor their horses, keeping them at a steady pace not riding too hard or too long without a rest watching that they didn't stumble into an animal hole, where they could be injured.

Tom knew that it was getting on to noon by the shadow of the trees. He saw a small meadow opening up just ahead and noticed that Patrick had started to slow, waiting for Tom to catch up. As Tom came abreast, Patrick said, "We'll stop here for an hour and let the horses graze on the dead grass and rest before we tackle the mountains. I sure hate camping in the high mountains, but there is no way we can avoid it," he looked beyond the meadow at the mountains in the distance.

"Is there danger there Patrick?" Tom asked looking at his brother-in-law.

Patrick took a minute to answer as he continued to gaze at the mountains before them. "There's danger—several kinds, to be sure. If we were caught in a snowstorm, we could freeze to death. It's a little early for bear, but there are some big ones in there. One of us could get injured, or our horses; it's a long walk from there to anywhere," Patrick turned to Tom with a wide grin on his face. "There are wolves and other animals, and occasionally an Indian or two. It's not a place where I want to spend a lot of time. We'll camp about two thirds of the way to the top of that big peak just ahead there where the clouds are hanging. I don't want to arrive at dark. I want to find us a safe place to camp before nightfall. I sure wish we had some of Etta's cooking—that would perk us up," Patrick said with a grin. They rode on till the meadow was almost behind them before stopping by a small stream. Patrick dismounted and announced, "We'll turn the horses out for a while. Take the bit out of their mouths—leave the bridles on though. We will have some grub and rest for a while," he lifted the saddlebags off laying them on a large downed tree.

"This is a pretty place," Tom observed. "Someone coming across the mountains will like it enough to stay one of these days."

"When more people settle, things will be safer." Patrick commented as he gathered dead branches for a fire. Soon he had a small fire going; taking out a blackened pot from his gear, he filled it with water adding coffee and set it on the coals. It wasn't long till the aroma of boiling coffee filled the little valley. Tom brought out the bread and meat that Ailsey had packed for them and they ate as they watched their horses nibbling at the dried grass. It was too damp to lay down for a nap on the ground and Tom sat on the dead tree and leaned back on one of the big branches and dozed until Patrick called, "Let's hit the saddles; we have a long way to go before nightfall."

The two men walked over to their horses and bridled them, leading them to the stream to drink, mounted, and were on their way.

The trail zigzagged around the mountain in switch backs, going first one way and then the other, up, up, and up. They circled around big boulders, dipped down into gullies and up again. Tom began to wonder how they would ever get a wagon over such terrain to bring their household plunder to the other side of the mountain.

Patrick stopped on a flat where the ground leveled off for some distance. Tom coming alongside asked, "Who ever blazed a trail through here, and is this the best way there is to go?"

Patrick looked at Tom, knowing he was as awed as he had been when he first traveled the Trace. "It's an old hunting trail of the Indians, and at one time, the buffalo came from the low lands across the mountains and down into the valleys on the other side. People and animals have been following this Trace for 50 years or more; they have brought wagons across these mountains moving their families to the other side. It's not easy, but it can be done," Patrick told him.

"I can see it sure won't be easy. Ailsey will be scared to death. I'm not looking forward to bringing a wagon across myself," Tom told him.

"Who knows, you may not like the area where we're going Tom and you won't have to move over the mountain." Patrick looked at Tom and laughed. "Well, I guess we had better move on. Dark will come early in the mountains and we have a way to go yet. I'm glad the wind hasn't picked up." He moved on up the mountain with Tom close behind watching each turn in the Trace, marveling at the large trees that towered over them.

It wasn't long until Tom noticed snow caught in among down trees, and filling gullies. Icicles hung from the stone ledges above them. The horse's nostrils sent steam swirling around their heads. Tom pulled his coat collar up around his neck as a chill sent shivers down his back. The further they climbed up the mountain the colder it became. The trail through the towering trees were free of underbrush cleared by nature. What a wonderful forest for hunting Tom thought, as he looked around him. "Preferably in warmer weather," he muttered to his horse. Looking ahead he saw that Patrick had stopped on a level spot and he went on to join him and let the horses blow. The cold air of the mountain seemed to tire the horses considerably. "I think we will walk a while Tom. It's not too wet here on the downed leaves, give the horses a chance to rest a mite," Patrick dismounted, leading his horse as Tom followed his actions. The two men trudged up the mountain leading their horses, what Tom thought, was a grueling long time.

Looking up the mountain Tom saw that Patrick had found another flat and had stopped to wait for him. When Tom came along side Patrick said, "if you are coming over the Trace by wagon, you should camp in the meadow for the night and start out at first light. You could make the other side of the mountain in a day, and not have to camp in the mountains."

Tom nodded, looking off down the Trace to where they had traveled that morning. He could see for some distance through the stark, bare-branched trees. Just a hint of the meadow where they had stopped at noontime could be seen.

"That sounds like a sensible way of crossing the mountains; I'm not sure I would want to camp here in warm weather when the leaves are out. You wouldn't be able to see anything until it was on you," Tom, said as he continued looking around him.

Patrick didn't say anything but there had been men who came up missing, when they had traveled through this same area—not for some time, however, but they were never heard of afterwards. Anything could have happened to them; no one ever knew what.

"Break out your gun Tom. We'll keep them handy from here on

up the mountain. There's no telling what we might run on to." This demand sent a shiver up Tom's back. His hair seemed to lift his woolen cap on his head. He had been keeping a look out but would make it even sharper than before from now on.

The shadows were deepening as they climbed. Tom could see the skyline above them. Patrick had slowed, and Tom knew he was looking for a camp for the night. He finally stopped walking his horse from the trail about a hundred yards to a solid wall of stone with an overhanging cliff above; there was no hint of a cave underneath. Caves were likely to have bears holed up for the winter and they didn't want to be close to caves for that reason. Patrick carefully looked at the terrain, noting plenty of dead firewood close by. They could camp against the cliff with their backs protected.

After careful scrutiny, Patrick said, "I think this will be reasonably safe. We can build a lean-to with pine branches close to the cliff, and there's water coming down that gully there more than enough for us and the horses; we'll feed, water and tie them beside the cliff close to us. We don't want to take a chance of losing them in the night." Patrick undid his saddle laying it near where the lean-to would be built. Tom followed with his saddle.

"Tom, you start gathering firewood—lay a big pile along about there," he pointed where he wanted it. "Then another pile close by. We have to have enough to burn through the night. We'll tether the horses between us and the second wood pile. I'll cut branches for our lean-to and build it between those two trees close in to the cliff. With that he started off to a big pine tree with branches hanging to the ground. As Tom gathered wood he could hear the thump of the ax strokes as Patrick hacked branches for their shelter.

Tom had to forge farther and farther from the area to drag in the big limbs of dead trees. He had one pile taller than his head piled against the cliff. "That should be enough for one pile," he said to himself; he could see why Patrick wanted it there—it would be a protection on the other side of the horses. He went in the opposite direction gathering for the second pile. He didn't want to skimp and wanted to have more than enough to last the night. He knew it would be dark directly, and would be as black as the inside ·of a cave in a short time. When the wood pile was tall enough to suit Tom, he saw that Patrick had a sizable, sturdy looking lean-to built for the night.

"That looks like home Patrick; you sure you don't plan to take up homesteading here?" Tom laughed.

"Not me; I don't hanker to live on no mountain myself.

You can start your fire down there close to the open side of the lean-to. We don't want it too far away from the opening."

Tom squatted down laying rocks in a circle building them up to about a foot on the far side, leaving the front toward the lean-to open. He brought dry twigs and leaves from under the overhanging cliff and soon had a warm blaze going. "That sure feels good Patrick," Tom called as Patrick finished the lean-to and brought pine branches for the floor to put their bedrolls on, off the damp ground. Tom took their coffee pot to the gurgling mountain stream and filled it with water, adding a measure of coffee and placed it on the coals. Soon, the smell of boiling coffee penetrated the surrounding woods.

The men led their horses the short distance to the small stream and watered them, feeding them the meager feed of ears of corn they had brought in their saddlebags. They took rope from their saddles and tethered the horses to trees between their camp and the woodpile Tom had built.

"I think that is as good as we can make it," Patrick, said as they finished and went back to the fire.

"You don't think we will have any trouble do you?" Tom asked looking nervously around at the darkness creeping in.

"I hope not; I've camped very little in the wilderness myself. I think it best to be prepared, and keep a keen eye out—You never know." An owl hooted close by in a tree, sending Tom's heart racing. He didn't consider himself a coward or afraid of much, but there was an uneasy feeling to this place. There's something out there he decided as he checked his rifle moving it close to his side. He noticed that Patrick was doing the same. They warmed themselves waiting for the coffee. Taking the meat from their saddle-bags Tom stuck it on a stick and held it over the fire to thaw it out. They talked of the day as they ate their supper of bread and meat.

Tom was dozing by the fire when he heard a hair-raising howl coming from the opposite hillside. Jerking awake, he looked around, and asked, "what's that ungodly sound, Patrick?"

"I would guess it's wolves—They aren't close. Sounds like they may be five miles away." He had barely made that observation when an answering howl came from the opposite hill. The horses began to stomp and move about. They didn't like the howling of the wild animals and were letting the men know it.

Tom had heard tales of wolf-packs stalking people and sometimes attacking. He looked at Patrick who seemed to be listening to the howling but didn't seem nervous. "Do you think they are dangerous Patrick?" Tom asked. Patrick turned to look at Tom, "They're out there, that's enough for me. You go lay down and try to sleep, I'll take the first watch. I think we should take turns and keep the fire going just in case."

Tom took the two bedrolls into the lean-to and spread his out on the pine branches. He could see Patrick sitting by the fire with his rifle across his knees. The warmth from the fire could be felt inside the lean-to and with the springy pine-branches on the ground, made for a comfortable bed. Tom was soon asleep, the warmth and the quiet seeping into ever fiber of his bones.

Suddenly Tom awoke out of a deep sleep. His mind instantly alert. He held his breath as he listened to a stealthy sound outside the lean-to where the pine branches were laced to form the back and sides. His eyes adjusted to the darkness as he looked to see if Patrick was still by the fire. He could hear the horses restless stomping and snorting, and could see that Patrick stood at their heads, his hand resting on their noses. Tom quietly unrolled from the blankets, grabbed his rifle, and moved outside into the shadow of the lean-to watching Patrick. He didn't want to move farther until he knew what Patrick intended to do. He seemed to be listening and watching the woods. Tom, stood quietly, listening. He could hear the scrunch of dead twigs and leaves. Whatever it was moving around in the darkness he decided was more than one. Tom picked up a pine branch with a knot of resin on the end and carefully edged over to the fire and lit it, holding it away from him so he would be in the shadow as much as possible. Glancing toward Patrick he saw him motion that whatever it was lurked behind the lean-to. Tom drew back his arm and threw the pine torch several feet in the air, judging it would come down about twenty feet from the lean-to. The torch lit up the area, and by the time it hit the ground Tom was ready; with his rifle cocked, he carefully edged around the lean-to. Fiery red eyes and growls met him as he quickly let off a shot toward the middle of the pack of wolves that had gathered. He quickly counted and made out ten as one let out a howl, and headed back into the dense woods dragging a broken leg from Tom's shot. He got off another shot in the direction they had gone, knowing it wouldn't reach a target but hoping to scare them far enough away to discourage them from coming back. "Got one, Patrick," he called. Patrick came over to where Tom stood looking after the departing wolves. Tom walked over and retrieved his pine knotted limb that was still smoldering. "I'll keep this handy—may need it again," Tom said. "I doubt they will come that close again," Patrick said. They waited and watched for a while. "You go have a sleep Patrick, I'll keep watch—I'm wide awake," Tom told him. "I feel rested, and had a good sleep; those branches sure make a good bed, and smell good too." Patrick went into the shelter and Tom could hear him readying his bedroll for sleep.

Tom watched and waited, fearful that the wolves would sneak around from another direction. He knew that the horses would sense them before he did and he kept a sharp ear tuned to their every move. Tom could hear Patrick's soft snoring, as he sat by the fire feeding branches into it when needed to keep it going. The horses had settled down and Tom knew no animals were lurking about. After a while the sky to the East began to turn a pale pink and Tom knew daylight couldn't be far behind. Patrick would be waking soon. Tom went to the stream and filled the pot for coffee, setting it on the fire and waited for Patrick to rise; he knew the aroma of the fresh brewed coffee would bring Partick from his bed.

Tom stood up and stretched glad that the dark of night was over and that he and Patrick and their horses were safe.

❧ Chapter Five ❧

Patrick, came yawning and stretching from the shelter. "That coffee smells good Tom; I'm sure ready for a cup"

Tom sat by the fire toasting their bread and meat on sticks. "I'll have you a warm breakfast in a minute; looks like it's gonna' be a nice day. It didn't get too cold here last night; the cliff knocked the wind off and with a fire going it's not bad," Tom said as he stuck the stick with Patrick's portion into the ground next to him, and poured them each a tin-cup of coffee.

They sat in silence, eating their meager breakfast. Tom looked toward the horses noticing that they had eaten the corn from the cobs, and were now chewing on the cobs, which he had fed them while the coffee boiled.

The two men finished eating and Patrick took the horses to the stream and watered them, while Tom stored the food and coffee pot. Their beds were rolled, and ready to be tied behind, as soon as the horses were saddled. It took only minutes until they were ready to head up the trail. Day was just breaking with mist hanging over the lowlands obscuring the view of the little valley below. They walked their horses to the top of the mountain. The early morning walk would take the kinks out of their legs and start their circulation going.

As they reached the top they stopped, looking around. A majestic view spread out before them—with the tops of the mountains tipped in snow, and the valleys filled with foamy white mist that swirled and moved. "My God!" Tom remarked. "To look at something this beautiful Patrick, you know there is a God" Patrick nodded, speechless, as he feasted his eyes on all the beauty that lay before him.

In silence the two men mounted their horses. The west side of the mountain wasn't as steep as the other side had been, leveling out to a valley that followed a good size stream flowing through a cut between the tall mountains. The horses kept a steady pace, knocking off mile after mile. Tom's eyes took in all the strange, awesome things that they passed. He caught sight of deer in the edge of a laurel thicket, and he noted that jack rabbits were plentiful throughout the valley. Tom had never seen so many different birds. There were flocks of yellow birds with black wings, and beautiful blue birds by the dozens. What a beautiful place he thought to himself. If the land that Patrick was leading him to was half as bountiful he would be more than satisfied. He couldn't wait for Ailsey to see this beautiful valley.

The sun was overhead before Patrick called a halt, pulling up beside the rushing mountain stream in a small grove of trees.

"Guess it's time to let the horses rest, Tom. If we had us some fish-hooks, I'll bet we could catch some good eating fish. That stream looks as though there might be mountain-trout in it."

"Sure is a pretty stream; and this is beautiful country and so full of game. This wouldn't be a bad place to live, if the weather didn't get too bad," Tom said, as he looked around him.

"That's just it—being situated between these tall mountains I doubt crops would get the sun they needed. If you wanted to just raise cattle or sheep, it would probably be a good place for that. Do we have any more food left? " Patrick asked.

"Just about enough for our dinner. We will have to shoot us a jack-rabbit for supper; I saw some sleek deer back about a mile— they would be good eating." Tom was getting what was left of the food from his saddlebags as he talked. Patrick was busy starting a fire for coffee. They needed hot coffee to take some of the chill off. As soon as they ate and watered their horses they were off again—following the stream through the valley over the smooth hard-packed Trace. There wouldn't be much trouble taking a wagon through this area Tom thought, as he watched the landscape pass before him.

The pale sun had gone behind the mountains, warning the travelers that night would soon be on them. They had traveled to the end of the beautiful valley and were coming to more hills. The mountains they were approaching were not as tall, and seemed to roll into level valleys that spread out between them. Patrick had kept a brisk pace all afternoon which added miles to their travels. Tom knew he must have in mind a place to camp for the night, and was trying to make it before dark.

As dusk began to fall, they left the trail and went a short distance to the base of a small hill, where large rocks and pine trees would offer them some shelter. Patrick dismounted, and waited for Tom to join him.

"I think this will do for a camp tonight Tom. You take care of the horses and build a fire; I'll take my rifle and scout around and see if I can find us some supper." Patrick started out around the foot of the hill, and as he entered the woods he was soon out of sight.

Tom unsaddled and tied the horses with long ropes that would allow them to nibble at the dry grasses that grew around the rocks. He busied himself with finding dead branches for the fire and soon had enough wood stacked for the night. Branches weren't as easy to find here as they had been on the mountain where there were more dead trees.

Tom shouldered his rifle checking the firing chamber and started toward the stream to look around; as he moved causally out from the grove of pines, he spotted movement along the stream-bed. "I wonder what that can be?" he asked himself, as he moved slowly toward the rushing stream, keeping behind small trees and rocks. He checked his gun as he hunkered down studying the movement before him. Dusk was slowly covering the valley, and as his eyes adjusted to the shadows, he saw a small flock of wild turkeys that had been to the stream to drink, and were now scratching among the debris washed up by the stream. Tom knew he was too far away to get a good shot and crept slowly toward them, bending over to make himself as small as possible. When he thought he was in range, he stood up and sighted his rifle on a big gobbler. The sound of the shot was hardly heard when he chose a turkey hen and shot again. Both of the turkeys tumbled over onto the ground as the others with a swooshing roar, took to wing, and soon disappeared into the brush. "Boy we'll eat good tonight!" Tom yelled, as he did a little dance, slapped himself on the leg and hurried toward his kill. The two turkeys were all Tom could handle; their heads were dragging the ground as he took them back to camp. Piling more wood on the fire, he began butchering the game. Cutting the head and feet from the birds, he decided to skin out the best parts instead of trying to pick the feathers from them. He soon had the legs and breasts cut apart; the liver, gizzards and hearts were saved, on a tin plate; he would fry these in some of the fat for their breakfast. Taking the ax he cut two forked sticks and several straight hickory limbs; removing the bark from them he skewered the pieces of meat and placed them across the forked sticks that he had driven into the ground on each side of the fire. The turkeys were fat and plump, and soon the dripping fat from the skewered meat was sizzling into the fire, sending smoke and good smells through the grove. Tom knew that Patrick would have heard the shots and soon be investigating. When he looked up he saw Patrick trotting toward him from the woods.

"What's going on? I heard two shots," Patrick said, as he came rushing up to Tom all out of breath. He saw the turkey cooking on the splits, "I should have sent you hunting and me stay with the fire. That sure smells good, how many did you get? as if I need to ask. Two shots, two kills."

"I was lucky; about twenty wild turkeys meandered almost into camp—they were very accommodating I'd say. I got me off two good shots before they took off like a whirl-wind. I never heard such a racket. We'll have a good feed tonight with enough for our nooning tomorrow. I'm cooking all the good parts saving the giblets for our breakfast." Tom talked as he worked cutting up the turkey.

"I spotted a herd of deer, about ten I guess; but when you shot they took off for the deep woods—I might have gotten one otherwise." Patrick said, with a hint of irritation in his voice.

"I'm sorry about that; if I had known I could have passed the turkeys by. Of course I didn't know if you would find game or not. I figured I had better take what was at hand." Tom told Patrick, a crooked smile on his face.

"You did right; two birds in the hand is worth one deer in the bushes," Patrick said with a laugh.

The two sat talking of other hunting episodes waiting for the turkey to cook. Then Tom announced that it was done, and he piled a big tin plate full between them, they sat on their saddle-blankets leaning their backs against a rock, savoring the crisp roasted turkey until Patrick declared, "I can't eat another bite. You're almost as good a cook as Etta," Patrick laughed so loud that even the horses lifted their heads looking toward them.

Deciding not to build a lean-to for the night noting that the wind had died down, Patrick went to the nearest pine tree and cut an armload of branches and piled them close to the fire where they would spread their beds for the night.

There were no wolf-packs to keep the men awake; however they kept their rifles close to hand in case they were needed.

When morning came, they both awoke at about the same time. The birds in the valley had begun chirping before dawn, waking them. Patrick poked up the fire, and Tom grabbed the pot and went to the stream to fill it with water for coffee. He could just see enough in the pre-dawn to find his way there and back. They gave their horses a small feed of the corn, while the coffee boiled. Tom brought out the roasted turkey that he had stored, tied in the cloth Ailsey had wrapped their food in. "You want to warm yours?" Tom asked as he handed Patrick a stick. They both sat with a couple of pieces of turkey on sticks over the fire. Tom stirred the liver and hearts in a small pan; it didn't take long for them to fry and each speared a browned morsel, smacking their lips as they savored the tasty treat.

Saddling and storing their gear, they were off before the sun came up behind the mountain. They made good time up the small hills and across the numerous valleys, they finally came to a well-traveled road beside a wide stream that Patrick said was a branch of the Little Kanawah River, called The West Fork.

"I like the lay of the land through here Patrick," Tom said as their horses moved along. Patrick nodded, "We'll soon be coming in sight of the place I've been telling you about." He began pointing out landmarks that was familiar to him. "We'll be home in about an hour or so; I don't know if you are aware of it, but we've traveled about a hundred and twenty-five miles. We've made real good time—something like thirty miles a day. That's what I call good time through the mountains."

"My God! I never realized it was that far. We have been making good time; I've enjoyed every minute, even the fight with the wolves," Tom told him.

They traveled along for another half hour, when Patrick turned off the main road down another trail that was well-traveled but not as wide as the one they had been on for the past two hours. Fording the wide creek that Patrick said was The West Fork, Tom saw a log house in the distance nestled back against a tall tree-covered hill. This was not a cabin, but a house of hewed logs, with chimneys on both ends, and a veranda across the front.

"There she is," Patrick announced proudly, pointing toward the big, long, sturdy-looking, log house.

"That's your house? I thought it must be a judge's at least. That's a mansion in this wilderness, Patrick." Tom was impressed; he knew that Patrick was one of the first to build in the area, but never dreamed that he would be so well-fixed.

"I own a hundred thirty-eight and a half acres, and plan to buy another tract which has another hundred. See that land that lays on the other side of the Fork?" Patrick pointed in the direction; that's the thirty-eight acres that I picked for you and Ailsey. There are more acres surrounding that parcel that will be open soon. The man that had this parcel, as I told you, gave it up when his wife died with their first child. He didn't have much done on it yet—some clearing and fence. They lived down the creek with another family for awhile. He left the area, going to fight Indians out in the West somewhere. We'll get up early in the morning after we've slept in a bed for a change, and walk over the land and you can decide what you want to do."

"I can tell you now, I like it! You have a fine homestead, your house is outstanding for the area. Just wait till Ailsey sees it— she'll want one just like it, I'm sure of that. I can see that the land is rich and the timber is prime." Tom couldn't take his eyes from the surrounding area.

Suddenly, there was a yell as the door onto the veranda flew open, and Patrick's wife Polly came rushing to meet them. "You're home! I've been so worried. I was so afraid something happened to you." She flung her arms around Patrick as he dismounted hugging and kissing him.

"Nothing happened to me I'm fine; you remember Ailsey's husband, Thomas?" "How are the youngins? Is everything all right?" Patrick asked one question after another. Tom knew he had been anxious about his family, even though he had John and Matilda Barber looking in on them from time to time. They were a young couple who lived up on Owl's Fork, and were their nearest neighbors.

Two small children stood waiting on the porch for their father's attention. With his arm around Polly, Patrick hurried to the veranda grabbed up both of his children in a bear hug, and carried them inside calling, "Come on in, Thomas."

When the horses were fed and stabled the evening meal was ready for them. They sat at a big long table with Patrick's family, in a warm comfortable house for a change. The talk was lively with Polly wanting to know all about the trip. The children's eyes popped out hearing about the attacking wolves. They were put to bed and the grown-ups soon followed. As weary as Tom was he still was thinking of the land, and what was to be his and Ailsey's new home.

Patrick and Polly were up at first light—She cooking their morning meal and Patrick outside seeing to the animals. Tom, usually an early riser, slept on until the smell of coffee awoke him. He was embarrassed to have slept so long, and not be out helping Patrick with the chores.

"Why didn't you call me, Patrick?" He asked as he entered the kitchen where Patrick now sat at the table talking to Polly.

"It's just now getting daylight, I knew you could stand a few extra winks, Tom. When we eat and the sun gets up a little we will take our rifles and go for a walk over your land." He laughed as he looked at Tom. "I think it will be yours when you see it."

Thomas smiled his crooked smile. "So far I'm taken with it; I think it is all you've said it would be and I'm anxious to see every inch of it."

The men started out carrying their rifles and a small ax. They followed the road for a short time then cut off into the tall trees following the banks of the West Fork, as Patrick called the muddy stream. The topsoil was so rich that they sank into the loam as they walked, leaving deep tracks in the soil.

"When this is cleared it'll grow just about anything," Tom remarked.

They had gone a short distance when Tom spied two animals, romping beside the stream. "Patrick, look, are those mink?" Patrick turned to look as two sleek animals slid into the water, and disappeared, "Yep, that's what they are and prime ones too. They will fetch a pretty price come cold weather next winter—it's too late to harvest them this year," Patrick explained.

The two men spent most of the morning covering the area, spotting several kinds of game which added to Tom's excitement about the land, knowing some cash money could be gotten from trapping.

Patrick shot a small doe that was grazing in a savanna close by; and they decided it was time to return to the homestead. He cut a slender sapling, peeled the bark from it and slitting the hamstrings he slid the pole through so they could both carry it through the woods. It didn't weigh much, about sixty pounds all told, but was too much for one man and cumbersome to manage through the woods.

When they came in sight of the house, Polly and the children waited at the open door. Seeing the deer Polly called out, "Take it to the back to clean up, Patrick, I'll bring a pan for the meat.

The two men went around the house with their burden where there was a flagstone work area. It extended out from the kitchen door and around a spring tail, which ran through a stone, water-storage box that was made from field stone. They lowered the deer to a worktable at one side of the terrace.

"This is a fine work area Patrick; don't think I ever saw one so handy before."

Patrick looked around as Tom was doing, "This is Polly's doing; she said she couldn't stand to be in mud every time she stepped out to get water. She and the youngins hauled the flat, creek rock, and built it themselves—it is handy at that."

Tom shook his head in amazement, "She's done a fine job. I wouldn't have thought of building something like it myself."

The tasty dinner and another night's sleep in a comfortable bed made Tom and Patrick feel like new men. Tom noticed that Polly and Patrick were having some long talks together, finding excuses to go to the barn or out-buildings alone.

Patrick suddenly suggested, "Tom, I think you should stay one more night; and we'll look around some more. I want to take you to meet the Barber's; they haven't been married long, and are a fine couple. There's a small trading post on down the West Fork where mail comes in occasionally, and where you can get the necessities; I want to show you that too."

"That sounds fine to me. Give my horse a chance to feed up some, and of course me too," he smiled his one-sided smile. "I'll have to get an early start the next mornin' though."

The two men as always carrying their rifles, started off down the valley. Turning off the main Trace they headed up what looked like to Tom an animal trail winding up a hollow—tall trees and brush almost obscuring the faint trail at times. They walked about three miles up the hollow when it widened out into a valley containing Tom estimated, around thirty acres with hills sloping back from the valley becoming level enough for tilling.

"I wouldn't have thought there would be this much level land after coming up such a narrow hollow," Tom remarked. "There's a nice farm here with plenty of space fitter' for cattle, or crops. It looks good land, but sure was a surprise."

"A lot of the land is like that around here. You can't tell how it lays till you are right on top of it. Some of these hills have wide flat land on top of them that goes for miles. You wouldn't think to find it like that after climbing for an hour to get to the top and there she is!" Patrick, looking at Tom, took off his hat and waving it around to demonstrate what he meant.

There was a small, neat-looking log cabin just ahead of them. As they approached, a big brindled hound came bounding to meet them, bellowing in a deep voice that could rouse the whole valley. A pretty young woman came out onto the small porch; she was dressed neatly in a dark homespun that covered her completely from the high neck to her shoe tops.

"Howdy Patrick, nice to see you this lovely day." Her voice was sweet and friendly, Tom decided. "Won't you come in"? she invited.

"This is Thomas Jarvis my brother-in-law; he married my sister, Ailsey, a few months ago. They're living over in Lewis County now. I've persuaded him to look at the Jess Moss farm and buy it. I think he might make a nice neighbor," Patrick looked at Tom and smiled.

"Tom, this is Matilda Barber; where's John, by the way?" Patrick asked, as Tom stepped forward to shake Matilda's small hand.

"He's around somewhere—Old Boomer will bring him," she smiled.

"That dog's named right," Tom thought to himself as he listened to Boomer's booming voice.

The introductions to Matilda were hardly over when a tall dark-haired young man came somewhere from the back around the side of the cabin toward them.

"Howdy, there Patrick!" He said, a big smile of welcome on his craggy face as Patrick made Tom known to him.

"Why don't you and Matilda get acquainted, Tom; I have a little business to take care of with John," Patrick said as he and John walked around the house out of sight.

"Won't you come on the porch and sit a while? No tellin' how long those two will be." Matilda motioned to a bench along one end of the small porch. Tom came up the two steps and sat down— Matilda sat beside him.

"Did Ailsey, come with you, Tom?" she asked with a smile as she looked at him.

"No." "She stayed at the cabin, caring for the stock and reading things for the trip here, if I decide to buy the acreage. Her sister, Ellen, is to stay with her at night," Tom explained.

"You are going to buy, aren't you? John says that it's prime land. We would have taken it if we didn't already have more than we can manage now." Matilda told him.

"You have a nice piece of farmland here; It takes you by surprise. Patrick has explained that it's common here about," Tom answered, noticing that Matilda gave a proud smile.

Patrick and John soon appeared; Patrick called out to Matilda, "See you soon." Tom said good-by and joined him, and they started back down the trail.

Patrick had a big smile on his face; Tom was at odds to know what was going on, that was so secret from him. He looked at Patrick, knowing whatever it was he wouldn't keep it to himself very long.

"I guess you've been wondering what's going on? I have a surprise for you!" Patrick was smiling from ear to ear. Tom waited, wondering what now? "I've asked the Barbers to stay with the youngins. Polly wants to make the trip back over the mountains with us. We will take our wagon and can bring all your things in the two wagons without loading them too heavy. Our corn crop can't go in for awhile yet; and the Barbers will come and stay at our house and take care of everything for the few days we will be gone. Polly is dying to go—she hasn't been away from the Forks for over two years. Says she is getting till she won't know how to talk to grown-ups she spends so much time with the two little ones."

🐚 Chapter Six 🐚

Patrick was pleased and excited about the trip, and taking Polly along. Tom wasn't too sure that they weren't asking for trouble. However, it would be nice having another man along to help when coming back over the trace; bringing a wagon over wasn't going to be something that he was looking forward to. He knew that Ailsey would be 'tickled to death' to see Polly, and have her along for company on the trip back.

It wasn't yet daylight when Patrick and Polly were out of bed. Polly hurried to make breakfast, and as they all sat down to pancakes, sausage and applesauce, the Barbers came, carrying a lantern to light their way. Their old dog Boomer tagged along at their heels, his tongue hanging out as he plunked down onto the porch, hard enough to shake the cabin.

"Mornin' Matilda, John—sit down; I have plenty of pancakes; I'll get you each a plate," Polly called, all smiles. The two took their outwear off and Matilda hung them on pegs in the mud room. They sat down at the big table, as Polly brought plates heaped with pancakes and poured coffee.

"We didn't expect breakfast. I thought I could feed the boys, and make us something instead of starting a fire at home and have to go off and leave it," Matilda said. "Not that I object to having my breakfast made for me," she said with a laugh. "I don't remember when I've had someone else cook my breakfast. Your pancakes are light as a cloud, Polly, and they sure are good, and just hit the spot. John loves pancakes; just look at him eat." Everyone's eyes turned toward John, as they all laughed.

John looked in her direction, "Don't bother me woman, don't you see I'm busy?" Their laughter rang out as they looked around the table at the others.

The men hurried out to the barn, rushing to have the wagon ready to roll as soon as they could see well enough.

Patrick lifted down the four curved, wooden, braces that hung on the wall and John helped him attach them to the wagon, sliding them down into iron brackets that were attached to the wagc body. They would then stretch the tarp over the top tying it at both ends. This trick had been learned from the pioneers that had moved from place to place in their search for a home. The wagon became a home of sorts, and provided a covering for whatever they wished to take along including bedding for sleeping out of the weather. The men filled the wagon bed with a thick layer of hay. This could be used for feed for the horses, as well as a soft bed for them through the nights ahead. Corn that had been shelled and tied in a sack went under the seat where the driver of the team would sit. Polly had been busy the day before while the men hunted and looked over the acreage, baking bread for the trail, and cooking things that she could take for them to eat. She had cooked a big bucket of dried beans; These could be set on a campfire and warmed for a meal. She cooked potatoes in their jackets, they could be sliced and fried or put in the coals to heat. If they weren't cooked they might freeze and be wasted. She knew the men would kill fresh game along the way so there would be no shortage of meat. A bundle of clothes were wrapped in a small clean piece of tarp to keep them dry in case of wet weather. She had blankets ready, as was her warm coat, and high boots, and woolen stockings. She took along clean linen strips, in case they would be needed for any injury—with liniment, turpentine, and a few herbs. She wanted to be ready for any unforeseen emergency.

The men had the horses harnessed and hooked to the wagon. Tom's horse was saddled and ready to mount.

"John, I'll leave my saddle mare for you to use, to go back and forth to your house or to the store. I don't know how many days we will be gone. I trust you to look after things. There's plenty of flour and meal, and potatoes in the hill cellar. Use whatever you need. I'll leave extra shells for your gun—it's the same gauge as mine. You can find plenty of meat close by. I have a 'tab' at the store in case there is anything else I haven't thought of." He shook John's hand.

"Don't you worry none. Matilda's good with youngins, and I know we won't starve. We can eat what we would have if we were home. Old Boomer'll find us some fresh meat. He wouldn't do without his share of that." John laughed.

"Did you think to look for fish-hooks, Patrick? I'm hankerin' for me of those big fish from that stream we camped by." Tom remarked.

Patrick went to the back of the shed that was attached to the barn, and brought out two long fishing poles with line and fish-hooks attached. He slid them in under the hay in the wagon. "There you are I'll get a couple of extra hooks I have in the house, just in case one of the big ones runs off with yours." He laughed long and hard. The men were in a rare mood with anticipation of the trip before them.

Bringing the wagon to the front of the house, Polly was waiting on the veranda, with all the things she had ready to be loaded. While Tom and John loaded them, Patrick went to look for the extra fish-hooks.

"Here they are, I'm ready to go." Patrick called out as he held the fish-hooks out to Tom, who carefully placed them in a pocket. Patrick helped Polly climb over the wheel onto the high seat. She place her pillow on the seat to sit on. Her face was flushed and her eyes sparkled with excitement as she waved to her friends and her two little boys, who stood yawning and waving.

Tom went riding ahead of the wagon looking for anything in the trail that needed to be moved; he would see it before the team and wagon came onto it. He looked back several times, seeing Patrick and Polly laughing and talking. They were a nice couple, and Tom knew that Ailsey would be over joyed at seeing her brother and sister-in-law before she had expected to. The trip would be even more exciting having them along. Tom set a fast pace while they had a good road to follow. They hoped to be at the stream below the hill where they would camp for their first night, then they could make it over the mountain as Patrick had said in one day.

They reached the place where they would turn toward the mountains, and where the trail narrowed. Tom waited till he saw the wagon come around a bend in the trail. Patrick waved him on. Tom wanted to make sure he hadn't made a mistake in the turn off. Going on ahead, he dismounted several times to lift large rocks from the trail, or tree limbs that would catch in the wheels. It would mean just that many more they wouldn't have to remove on their return with loaded wagons. The time passed fast, with Tom getting on and off his horse to clear the trail. The pale March sun was overhead when Tom began to feel that the big plate of pancakes he had eaten before daybreak had hit bottom. Finding a wide place that had water close by where they could rest, he stood waiting for Partick and Polly.

Soon they pulled into the area Tom had chosen. Polly laughed as she climbed down from the wagon-seat. "I feel like I have black and blue spots in the strangest places," she continued to laugh as she walked around the cleared space stretching and moaning trying to get the kinks out, as she brought out biscuits with fried deer-steak between for their noon meal.

"You'll have to drink water. We don't have time to build a fire for coffee," she informed them.

"You're right. We'll make and extra big pot tonight," Tom answered.

After bringing each horse a bucket of water—not wanting to unhook them for such a hurried stop, they were on their way again, Tom still riding ahead, looking for anything that would be a danger to the wagon. Tom was riding back down the trail to warn Patrick of a deep hole that he might not see at a turn in the trail when he saw that he had waited too long; Patrick had cut too close and a rear wheel went down into it. Thomas hurried to help as the wagon became stuck, one side of the wagon higher than the other, the wheel lodged in the hole. The men went to the wheel to see what should be done to extract it from the hole without damage.

"Shall I get down, Patrick?" Polly called from the high seat, where she sat holding the reins.

"No. Stay where you are, we can manage," Patrick said as he and Thomas wedged a long pole under the rim of the wheel lifting it and piling rocks under the wheel, elevating it enough so that it could roll out of the hole. Patrick went to the horse's heads and holding the bridles gently eased them forward as Thomas put pressure on the wheel. "That will do it," Thomas called as the wagon rolled onto safe ground. "We don't want to forget this hole on the way back Patrick," Thomas said as he stood the pole upright in the hole to warn them on their return.

It was late afternoon when they came to the beginning of the hills they would have to cross, and where they planned to camp for the first night. They had been lucky to get this far with the wagon, and slight accident that had befallen them.

Camp was soon set up. Polly set the big pot of beans onto the fire and put on a pot of coffee to boil. The cornbread was put into the Dutch-Oven and set close to the fire to warm. After they ate, Polly spread out the blankets on the hay in the wagonbed and they were soon asleep.

They were up early, ate a hurried breakfast and were on their way by the time the sun looked like it would peek over the mountains in the distance.

Polly kept up a continuous chatter as she looked at the landscape around her—always finding something to catch her interest. After stopping for a hurried dinner they continued their journey, the men wanting to reach the beautiful little valley where Tom had his heart set on fishing; and Patrick planned to join him; like Tom he was itching just to throw out a line.

By late afternoon they topped a small hill and the valley was in sight.

"Oh, what a pretty place," Polly exclaimed looking around as they entered the valley. Patrick halted the wagon beside the small grove of trees where their fire-hole and pine branch bed were still intact. The men soon had the team on long ropes grazing on the dried grasses of the valley.

"Do you want me to build you a fire, Polly?" Tom asked.

"No you two get to your fishing—I want a good catch for supper," she said, knowing they were like kids when it came to fishing, and couldn't wait to get started. There was plenty of wood left from where the two had camped before, she soon had a fire going and was organizing her cooking things to be ready when they came with their fish and it wouldn't take long for her to cook them a meal. They had backed the wagon in close, and everything was handy. She let the end-board of the wagon bed down to form a table for working and keeping things off the ground. It was still too cold for ants and most bugs, but it was also handier to work from. Their first night had been such a hurried affair, she wanted to enjoy tonight in this beautiful place.

Suddenly, there were whoops and yells, "Got One.'" "Me too!" Polly knew they would soon have enough at that rate for them all a feast. It didn't seem more than half an hour when they came with a bucket full of beautiful trout, cleaned and in fresh water ready for the fry-pan. Polly dipped them in cornmeal and soon the smell of frying fish sent their appetites soaring. Polly quickly made little balls of cornmeal dough and dripped those into the pan beside the fish to fry, and heaped three tin-plates full of crisp brown fish and fried bread. She had more ready in the big fry-pan as she handed each a plate. The coffee was boiling; setting it from the fire, she brought tin-cups and poured each a helping. For the first few minutes there were only sounds of pleasure as they ate the tasty meal.

"They're even better than I expected," Tom remarked finally, as the edge of his appetite diminished. " They sure are choice, I've never ate better; course, I have to give the cook some credit," Patrick said, As he gave Polly a squeeze, and kissed her cheek.

"She's a good cook, no doubt about it," Tom answered, as he took a last piece from the pan. Polly smiled at all the compliments she was receiving, as she watched the two men enjoying their supper.

"Do you reckon' we could take a bucket of fish to Etta and John? I think it's cold enough that they wouldn't spoil. I'll add some snow and ice to them when we get on the mountain tomorrow," Tom asked as he looked toward Patrick.

Patrick laughed "You sure do like fishing; we still have some daylight—why don't we try it?" The two men grabbed their poles and the bucket and headed for the stream. Polly cleaned up the supper things, and added more wood to the fire; she then went to the wagon to spread their bed for the night. The two men would sleep feet to feet, as they had the night before with Polly on the side, and they would all be comfortable under cover and out of the wind. Polly finished and sat by the cheerful fire, waiting for the men to return. Soon she heard them. Dark had fallen and they were almost on her before she could see them. They had a bucket full of fish, all cleaned and in icy water from the stream. "You two bank the fire; I'm going to bed. I ache all over from the jouncing of the wagon," she told them. The men did her bidding and soon followed.

Tom was out of bed first and had the fire going and the coffee pot on. Patrick and Polly soon following, stretching and yawning.

"How do you feel this morning, Polly," Tom asked as he smiled at all the faces she was making.

"Better, I'll get used to it by tonight; I'm enjoying every minute," Polly answered with a laugh. She was a very happy woman and showed it in her attitude toward things. After a quick breakfast of bread and meat, they hooked up the horses to the wagon and headed out toward the mountain.

"I'm gonna' get me a wooden barrel and some salt and on the way back to the West Fork, I'll catch me a bate of fish to put down in brine to take back." Tom said to himself, the memory of all the crisp fried fish Polly had made still on his mind.

🌺 Chapter Seven 🌺

Tom started out ahead, looking for anything that would interfere with the wagons progress over the Trace. He could hear Polly and Patrick in the distance talking and laughing, as his horse jogged along lengthening the distance between himself and the wagon. He rested his loaded rifle on the saddle horn in front of him. If he was lucky he might sight a deer or possibly a wild boar; and if so, he intended to get enough fresh meat to last them for a while. Reaching the hills where the switchbacks started, he rounded a large cluster of rocks with trees growing among them; his horse, Babe, suddenly threw up her ears, attracting Tom's attention. He knew something was ahead, just out of sight beyond the outcropping that he was approaching. Bringing his rifle up he checked the firing chamber; and glancing behind he saw that he was out of sight of the wagon, but he knew that if there were shooting that Patrick would be there in minutes to back him up. Pulling Babe to a slow walk he started easing himself around the obstruction. When about halfway around he stopped to listen; he could hear a soft, swishing movement in the leaves and dead grasses. He knew there were animals of some sort just ahead, but couldn't tell what kind. Slowly he nudged his horse ahead to make it seem as though she were leisurely grazing. He didn't want to frighten whatever it was. Tom was bending from the saddle, this way and that, peeking through the evergreens which were mixed in among the leafless trees, trying to see toward where the sound was coming from. Walking Babe slowly, stopping every few steps, he finally saw a slight movement through the trees ahead. Nudging Babe onward, he carefully raised his rifle ready to sight. A few steps more and he rounded a dense pine tree with branches hanging to the ground, and saw before him a small Savanna which seemed to Tom's eyes was covered with deer. There were at least twenty-five or thirty of the prettiest deer that Tom had ever had the good luck to see in one herd. Raising his rifle he leveled his sights on a young buck who proudly waved two velvet covered spikes. He was slick and rounded from feasting on the dried Savanna grasses—and at what looked to be two years of age, was in his prime to make good meat. Tom gently pulled the trigger. The report sent echoes from the hills which surrounded the pretty little meadow. Before the rifle shot began to echo the crash of the fleeing deer racing through the trees, shook the surrounding ground. Tom let out his victory yell, "Yee—e—ah!" He knew that Patrick and Polly would hear and know that all was well. Going over to his kill he began to butcher the deer, carefully preserving the skin for tanning. He could tell the meat was tender and juicy by the way the knife slid through. Tom had half the meat cut from the carcass, carefully stacking it onto the deer hide as he worked, when he heard the wagon coming toward him. He worked as quickly as he could so they wouldn't be held up on the trail.

The wagon rolled to a halt beside where Tom hunkered over his work. Patrick handed the reins to Polly and jumped to the ground hurrying over to Tom. "what've you got there Tom? Look's like you made a lucky shot, ha, ha," Patrick joshed Tom.

"Seems I can never wait on you to get in a shot, Patrick. That was the prettiest bunch of deer I have ever seen; I could have gotten two but decided to settle for one—I figured that would be enough to haul across the mountain. This is a prime young buck, and should make good eating.

"Sure looks that way. I'll bring a pot to put the small pieces in; do you want a tarp to wrap around the meat?"

"I'm going to tie it in the hide. It will be fine till we get over the mountains. We can divide with John and Etta when we reach their place. You can help tote it to the wagon though," Tom told him.

Patrick hurried to the wagon for the big cooking pot. Polly sat holding the reins and could hear the men talking and she already knew about the kill.

Soon the men came carrying the load of meat, which they had wrapped and tied with a rope. Watching them she said, "Push back the hay so no blood gets on it. We may have to use it for a bed again. And don't get my quilts dirty you two," she laughed as she bossed the men around.

The wagon wasn't held up long for Tom to finish the butchering, and they were soon traveling the switchbacks that climbed up the mountain. There weren't many limbs and stones to move from the trail as they made their way up through the thick woods, the giant trees towering above them. It was early yet; turning to look at the sun, Tom decided about ten o'clock, and they should be over the mountain by nightfall. Keeping in sight of the wagon as they climbed up the mountain, Tom didn't want to be too far ahead in case Patrick needed help over a bad place. There was little conversation as they all concentrated on the uphill climb. So far the wagon had followed the Trace without much difficulty. The sun climbed high up the mountain with the travelers. Reaching the top was an exhilarating experience, as they stopped to look over the valley below, and to look on the snow capped mountains in the distance that surrounded them.

Polly raised her arms high above her head stretching, "I wouldn't have missed this for the world. I don't think I've ever had such a good time, and the beauty of this place just can't be described." She gave a sigh when the wagon moved forward over the top, her eyes still lingering on the snow-capped mountains.

"It's all downhill from here Patrick," Tom called from up ahead, as the wagon lumbered and creaked over the crest.

When they came abreast of their old camp, (Wolf Camp Tom had named it thinking of the wolves that had attacked them in the night) he pulled his horse to a stop and dismounted, remembering the snow in the crevices that he wanted to pack around their meat, and the bucket of fish he was taking to Etta. It would be much warmer in the valley they had to cross after leaving the mountains, and the snow would keep the meat fresh. When the wagon came abreast, they all dismounted to fetch the snow and walk around to stretch their legs. Polly brought the large square of tarp as the men went ahead to find the best snow. They soon had a big mound of packed snow piled up on the tarp. Patrick and Tom took two corners each and carried it back to the wagon, where they turned the packing of the snow around the food over to Polly. As she finished she said, "Why didn't you two hearty woodsmen do this? My hands are numb," she laughed as she held her hands under her armpits to warm them.

They made good time going down the mountain, soon reaching the meadow in the valley where they would camp for the night.

Thomas built a fire for Polly as she quickly cut the meat and skewered it on sticks to roast. Patrick had the horses unharnessed and on long ropes to feed on the dried savanna grass.

When they had eaten their meal they talked for a short time around the cheerful fire and were soon ready for bed. They still had about twenty miles to go before reaching John Murphy's homestead, and should make it the next day if they kept their schedule and had no trouble on the trail.

Leaving the valley in the early dawn Thomas watched Polly who never seemed to tire as she craned her neck this way and that as they traveled, picking out birds that were building nests, and watching for wild flowers blooming in sheltered spots, chattering about all she saw. Soon conversation lagged as they hurried along, the wagon bouncing and clattering over rocks.

Their stop at noontime was very brief, and in the late afternoon the sound of a dog barking was heard several minutes before they came in sight of the cabin.

As the cabin came into view Polly exclaimed, "What a pretty homestead. Just look at the size of the garden they are planting." When the children started appearing from behind several buildings, and gathering in front of the log cabin, she could see why. Etta emerged from the front door onto the porch, and waved to the wagon, having recognized Tom who was riding ahead.

By the time Patrick brought the wagon to a halt in front of the cabin, John was coming from the direction of the barn, a big smile of welcome on his rugged face.

"Howdy' Tom, Patrick; help the little woman down and then drive on over to the barn with your team.

"This is my wife, Polly," Patrick said as they shook hands with the Murpheys. Tom had already shook hands and was unloading the bucket of fish, and opening up the deer to take out a quarter of it, repacking the snow around the rest.

"What have we here?" John asked, as he came around the wagon, watching Tom as he opened the large bundle.

"We brought you a mess of the prettiest trout you ever saw, and a quarter of a fine buck," Tom said, as he lifted it out of the wagon.

"My, my," Etta said as she looked into the bucket of fish. "I've been hankerin for some fried fish, and this looks enough to feed an army, I'm thinking I'll have my fill of these" she said as she gave Tom a shy smile.

"Would you like some of the deer heart and liver for supper?" Polly asked.

"Bring it in, we'll have both; I can't wait to sink a tooth in some fried fish though." She laughed as she started toward the cabin, almost dragging the heavy bucket of fish.

"Here Etta, let me carry that for you," Tom said as he grabbed the bucket and carried it into the kitchen where he lifted it to the work table.

"We've been looking every day for you to come back over the mountain. Etta couldn't wait to have you visit again. It'll be even better since you brought your wife along" John told the men as they took care of the team. They lingered in the barn talking, knowing it would take some time for the women to have supper ready.

"You have a nice farm, Etta; and everything seems to be handy for your work. And what a pretty little girl you have—did you say her name was Charity?" Polly asked with a smile.

"Thank you, Polly; yes, her name's Charity, after my mother. She's a heap of help to me; She can cook most as good as I can. I have four boys too. One is a babe, eight months now. How many youngins do you and Patrick have?"

"We only have two boys, as of now. I m sure we will have a large family though. Patrick and I both come from large families, and I guess we want the same," Polly let out her cheerful laugh which brought a smile to Etta's face, and caused Charity to giggle behind her hand.

The trestle table was brought in from the lean-to and placed in front of the fireplace, and it was soon loaded with food—big platters of the fried fish, heart, and liver, and cornbread with a big bowl of cooked turnips and Etta's dried fruit dumplings, and the two-gallon, granite, enameled coffee pot was set on the corner of the table, handy to Etta for filling the coffee cups. It was a lively group that sat around the table talking and laughing, as they stuffed themselves on the good food.

When supper was over logs were thrown on the fire, and a cheerful glow lit the cabin; the men sat talking, while the women were in the kitchen at their chores. Polly's laughter could be heard as the women talked. The men knew that Etta was enjoying Polly's cheerful nature. It was a treat for Charity as well, not often having anyone to visit with.

Charity was sent with the boys to the loft to sleep; her bed was readied for Polly and Patrick. Tom had brought in his bed roll and would sleep by the fire again. As he settled for the night he thought of Ailsey, and knew that tomorrow night he would be holding her in his arms. A happy smile lit his face with the thought.

They made an early start from the Murphy farm with a dinner of biscuits and meat packed for them. The weather held and the sun peeked through the trees; a chorus of birds were heard from the roadside. The men remembering the storm they had ridden through on their way over the mountains before, were thankful that their trip would be more pleasant this time. Polly added cheer to the dreariest days, making things bright for them all as they struggled through mud holes and across swollen streams.

Tom became impatient the nearer they came to his home, finding himself urging his horse to a faster pace, leaving the slower-moving wagon behind. He would then pull back on the reins and ride alongside the wagon for a short distance. "Won't be long now Polly," he told her.

"I can't wait to see Ailsey! Will she ever be surprised! This has been such fun but will be twice as much fun with her along on the way back," her eyes sparkled as she smiled at Tom.

The cabin finally came into sight; this had seemed the longest mile that Tom had had to endure. Watching, Tom wondered how long it would be before Ailsey heard them. Suddenly, old Rowdy came tearing down the trail, Ailsey a very short distance behind— her hair flying out behind, her arms reaching toward him. Tom jumped from the saddle trailing the rains of Babe, as he swung Ailsey around and around, kissing her soundly.

"I was never so glad to see anyone in my life" Ailsey said, hanging on to Tom. Suddenly looking toward the wagon and seeing Polly smiling at her she rushed forward, "Polly, Polly, it's you! It's you! oh, what a surprise! Get down, do get down, let me give you a big hug. Am I ever glad to see all of you." She was laughing and crying at the same time. The men stood with a silly grin on their faces seeing the joy the girls felt on seeing each other.

Polly and Ailsey walked toward the cabin their arms around each other, talking and laughing forgetting the men who were following meekly behind.

When they entered the cabin, Polly looked around her. She could see that Ailsey and Thomas were living very sparsely. "You don't have much room, do you Ailsey?"

"Oh, we have enough I guess. I'm glad we don't have much now that I have been packing things to move," Ailsey laughed as she looked around the room, as though for the first time.

Ailsey went to the fireplace and threw some logs on the fire. I had better start some supper," she said as she got a Dutch-Oven from the shelf for cornbread.

"The men can bring in the deer Tom butchered; I'll make us some steak while you make bread and whatever else you plan to cook" Polly said. "It won't take so long with both of us working."

Ailsey went to the shelf and took down a bigger Dutch Oven for the steak. Thomas brought in the deer wrapped in the hide, and deposited it on the table, untied the rope and spread out the meat, you'll have to bring in the meat-box from under the porch and take it to the run and scrub it good. I'll have to salt down the meat or it will spoil."

"I'll do that while Patrick takes care of the team" Tom started outside, he was soon back with the box, he had taken ashes from the hopper in back of the cabin and scrubbed the box till it was almost white.

"That looks good, Tom. Set it over by the fire to dry out some. I'll salt the meat down after supper." Ailsey had a smudge of flour on her pert little nose, and Tom smiled as he looked at her. He sure had missed her the few days he had been gone, and hoped that he never had to leave her again. He couldn't wait to tell her about the beautiful acreage that was now theirs. No more living in a house that belonged to someone else; they would soon have their own cabin.

Ailsey was dying to know about the farm, but knew that she would find out everything as soon as they sat down at the table for supper; there were chores to do now. She looked over at Polly as she pounded the steak and floured it and arranged it in the big Dutch-Oven to set on the fire. She could see that she was well-acquainted with cooking and was neat and fast.

The girls had worked the better part of an hour on the supper which was sending stomach-growling smells throughout the small cabin. Even "Taffy's" nose was twitching from the good smells. That's what Ailsey and Ellen had decided to call the little kitten since Ailsey had said she was sweet as taffy.

Polly made brown gravy in the pot after lifting out the beauti-fully-browned steak onto a platter, and supper was finally ready. They all sat around the table, ready for the treat that was piled up on the slab table before them.

Polly laughed as she sat down, "I still feel like I'm in motion. Riding that wagon so far just keeps me bouncing around now that I'm sitting still." They all laughed at Polly and her descriptive comments.

Their mouths watered as they piled their plates full of the good smelling food. "This sure is good steak, I can't sit still while I eat it," Tom remarked with a laugh remembering John's words.

"You said it," Patrick added grinning from ear to ear.

"Ailsey, you wouldn't believe how well Patrick and Polly live— they have a mansion. True, it's a log house but so big and well thought-out, and comfortable; there's a great room, with a fireplace you could throw a whole tree in. A kitchen, with a mudroom off that, and three sleeping rooms, and a veranda all across the front. The land is rich and lays well for farming, with lots of trees, and game. It's the perfect place for us, I know you will like it. You are now the owner of a farm." Tom looked at his pretty wife and smiled, a proud look in his blue eyes as he seemed to sit up a little straighter.

"Oh, Tom, I m so happy! However did you build such a home so soon? Do we have neighbors? How many people live in the area? Is there a store? Tell me more." Ailsey was looking from one to the other, her eyes sparkling as she looked around the table.

"Well, there's Patrick and Polly and their two boys, and the Barbers—they are a nice young couple, with a real nice lay-out. A small trading post that carries staples. I didn't have time for visiting, but Patrick says there are a few more not too far away. I doubt we will have time for much socializing with neighbors anyway for a while." Tom felt good being able to tell Ailsey that they were on the verge of having their own home. He knew that they would have to work hard but felt sure that they could do as well as Patrick and Polly had in time.

After the supper things had been put away, and the girls had washed the dishes, Tom brought a strawtick which was stuffed with fresh straw, from the loft, and laid it in a corner, where Ailsey made it up into an extra bed.

"I want to be up early, I'm going over to visit Dad and Mother, while I'm here," Patrick said, as they all got ready for the night.

"We're always up early, Polly you can ride old Babe if you want. It's not far but you may want to bring back something. If I know your mother she will be sending everything under the sun for

Polly to take back with her." Tom smiled at Polly.

The cabin was located just on the outskirts of the village, and the Connolly's lived on the other side of the village on a large farm. Ellen had walked the mile or more each night to stay with Ailsey. Most people thought nothing of walking that distance to have a cup of coffee with a relative or friend.

Ailsey and Tom insisted that Patrick and Polly sleep in their bed and they slept on the made-up one on the floor. Fortunately, a neighbor was passing by and Ailsey had sent word to Ellen that she need'nt come that night.

Before it started to get daylight Tom had a fire going and Ailsey had coffee boiling and biscuits in the Dutch-Oven. She cut up the leftover steak and made more gravy in it to put over the biscuits for breakfast. When she was ready to set the table Polly had it already done.

"Thanks for the offer of Babe, but we have decided to go in the wagon. It's not that far and won't tire the horses that much," Patrick told Tom. "Why don't you and Ailsey come along? You'll want to see the folks before you leave. When we come back I'll help you get things ready and loaded." Patrick and Polly looked from Tom to Ailsey.

"That's a wonderful idea Tom, I want to see everyone; Lord knows when we'll see them again," Ailsey looked at Tom.

Tom nodded, "I guess that is a good idea. Ailsey, why don't you take them a leg of that deer? We'll probably be there for dinner; we can get more when we need it, and I don't want to carry it back over the mountains."

They all arrived at the Connolly homestead, among laughter and tears. They were all glad to see each other, and it was an unexpected pleasant surprise.

The Connollys also had some surprises of their own. Dr. George, Patrick's and Ailsey's father, had decided to sell out and head for the Oklahoma Territory, where he could patent five thousand acres of good land with just a few improvements. They had been selling some of the livestock and had already sold the farm to someone who wanted to take possession immediately. They were having a sale of household plunder that afternoon. Seems that Dr. George had heard from a long-time friend who had settled in the territory and who urged the Connollys to join them. They planned to leave in a very few days.

"Ellen, why didn't you tell me," Ailsey asked.

"I didn't know—, that is for sure. Mom and Dad mentioned it but I didn't pay any attention. They are always talking of moving somewhere in the wilderness." Ellen had tears in her eyes as she answered her sister.

Patrick and Polly were so shocked that they didn't say much, just stood listening to the talk around them.

"Mom, what are you going to do with all your lovely things?" Ailsey asked.

"Well, some of them your Dad is having shipped—they have to be taken by wagon train, and we will sell what we can. The rest, who knows? I've followed your father to quite a few new homes you know. I should be getting used to it, don't you think?" She smiled her sweet smile at her family.

Ailsey and Tom walked among the things that were being brought from the big over-crowded house and strewn over the lawn for the sale. "I don't believe this," Ailsey said to Tom.

Tom shook his head. "At their age what would possess them to move to a new territory and have to start all over again, when we have a homestead to equal this, we are staying put!"

Ailsey looked at her husband, and smiled. "You are just as bad. It always gets too crowded for you and then you're looking for a new wilderness to conquer."

Thomas smiled his crooked smile, "You're right I have to admit, but when we settle on the West Fork we're going to stay put for awhile. It's going to take awhile to conquer that area. And just wait until you see Patrick's and Polly's home—you'll want one just like it."

Ailsey smiled, "I sure hate to see mother sell her lovely things. If I had a way to get it to where we are going I would love to buy the Pianoforte. I play a little, and have always loved it. I feel sorry for Ellen, she won't have much of a chance to marry, she's a little young yet, but I worry about her."

"She could come and live with us; I doubt she would have any better chance there though." Tom looked at his wife, knowing how much being in love meant to them, and being together as newly-weds.

The women-folk had dinner ready and they all sat down together; Patrick and his sister Ailsey were still in shock, knowing that their parents were going on such an adventure, and so fa away. They were even going to drive a herd of their cattle West; and no telling how many wagons would go. They would be joining a wagon train that was headed out.

The meal was scarcely over when the wagons began to gather for the sale, with men and women walking among the many things out on the lawn to be sold.

"Mother, you aren't going to sell the Pianoforte, are you?" Ailsey held her breath waiting for her mother's answer.

"I doubt it. You girls all liked it so well. However, I don't see how I can drag it all the way to the Oklahoma Territory. I haven't decided yet," her mother smiled at her. "Maybe I can have someone keep it until I do decide."

Ailsey felt as though she had received a reprieve, and smiled appreciatively at her mother.

The sale on the lawn became lively, with things being loaded onto wagons and hauled away. The women stood in groups gossiping, and listening to the talk of the men, who were more interested in tools and farm animals than the household goods that were offered for sale.

Almost all the things offered were sold by late afternoon. Mrs. Connolly and her daughters, Ailsey, and Ellen and her daughter-in-law Polly, had retired to the house; Ailsey had made a big pot of coffee and brought out a tray of sliced chocolate cake for refreshments. Ellen was sent to see if the men wanted to join them.

The last wagon was just pulling out, leaving Dr. Connolly, Patrick and Thomas looking over the few things that were left on the lawn. Most that was left were odds and ends, which didn't amount to much.

"Dr. Connolly looked at his son and son-in-law. What do you boys think of coming along to the Oklahoma Territory with us? You could both patent two thousand acres each. That makes for a nice ranch for horses, cattle or sheep. You're both young and could make a nice home there," he looked from one to the other.

"I'm not sure I would like living out West so far; besides I've just bought land close to Patrick's. I'm taken with that area, and I think Ailsey will be too when she sees it." Tom shook his head.

"If I tell Polly, she's going to want to go. I never saw such a woman. She would travel from one end of the country to the other 'f I gave her a chance, and enjoying every moment of it." Patrick ▪ughed as he talked, his mind going this way and that, he had to admit it sounded like a wonderful opportunity—two thousand acres in comparison to two hundred acres.

As they sat down to eat Patrick turned to his father, "Is there that much land to be had? And how long do you have to make improvements? And how much do you have to improve on it? What costs if any are involved?"

"You have at least a year, and all you have to do is start using it and have a dwelling to live in. If you turn out cattle, or any animals and they graze, that is enough to prove it I'm told. You do have to own it at least a year before you can sell. And it must be sold to someone who is going to live on it and work it. The government is encouraging the move West. As far as costs, there may be a small filing fee. Then it's up to you to spend whatever you can or want to on your dwelling or fencing or whatever you feel that you want to invest. You don't have to spend anything if you do all the work yourself. The Government is anxious to have reliable people settling the area. The more they have the less trouble they have with Indians," Dr. George looked around the table at the wide eyes of everyone.

"Indians!" Everyone at the table exclaimed at the same time. The word seemed to echo around the long table, everyone looking at each other, then at Dr. Connolly.

"There's no need for alarm; the Army is close by to keep an eye on the savages. If there is an outcry they are there to control the situation. They are being driven back toward the mountains in the West. I don't anticipate any problems where we are going. I intend to take some strong fellows with me who will be working the herd, driving wagons, and able to shoot and hold their own in any situation. There will be a considerable wagon train going along with experienced men heading it up. From what I can gather more than fifty wagons are all ready signed up to go."

"That's quite a train; how many wagons do you expect to have? And how many cattle will be in your herd?" Patrick asked.

"Well, I'll have about eight or ten wagons, and around sixty of my best breeding stock. I understand there will be eight hundred cattle and horses in the herd. I will take a few beef cattle too, in case we need meat and can't find it on the land. I don't intend to go hungry." Dr. Connolly laughed at the stricken look on the faces around him.

Ailsey was listening very closely, wondering what this was all about, turning to look at first one and then the other.

"I took a trip into Richmond when I heard about the land being up for grabs. They referred me back to Charleston; I talked to an attorney by the name of Lilly. He gave me the papers to fill out and he also told me that there was acreage in the West Fork area for patening also," Dr. Connolly looked around the table at his family.

"Why didn't you want the West Fork area if that was the case Dad?" Patrick asked.

"In the first place, it's too hilly for a cattle ranch. And after mother and I talked it over we decided we wanted the five thousand acres and settled for it," he answered.

Thomas was listening carefully, his ears glued to every word. "What about you, Patrick? Are you interested in patening on the West Fork?" Tom asked as he turned to look at Patrick.

"I doubt I would be. I would have to start all over and maybe not as good as I already have. I have an option on another hundred acres as I told you before. Unless I would make a drastic move I don't think I would want to go into another place." He looked toward Polly.

Tom felt sure that Patrick and Polly had been talking about going with his mother and father to the Oklahoma Territory, and wondered what they had decided. If he had a home like theirs he couldn't be hired to leave it.

"I brought two other sets of papers for the Oklahoma Territory, with maps and descriptions, and also the map and description of the West Fork area. If either of you boys are interested we will look at them and talk it over. All you will have to do is fill them out and get them back to Charleston and you're in business." Dr. Connolly left the table to get the papers he was talking about.

Ailsey hadn't had time to tell Tom about their expected baby. She was worried; what if Tom decided to go to the Oklahoma Territory? She had some morning sickness, so far nothing too drastic, but could she make a trip that far without problems, or injuring her unborn child?

The women hurried to clear the big dining table for the men to spread the maps on. Everyone gathered around to look as Dr. George started to explain them, and point out the area that he had chosen.

Patrick and Thomas were both wide-eyed at the possibilities, as they leaned over the large maps. They could see from the location of the acreage Dr. George had chosen that he had taken in every eventuality and chosen well.

"It's beautiful country but I don't think I would be interested in going so far. It will take you two or three months to get to the area. Then another two to build a cabin; by then the winter will be on you. It's a rugged life, and I have to admit with great possibilities." Thomas had declared himself. Ailsey heaved a sigh of relief. She knew it would be exciting but she would rather not go so far either; seemed Thomas knew her pretty well.

"Remember I told you that Polly would want the adventure?" Patrick looked toward Polly whose laughter rang out filling the room with joy. "We've talked some about it and are undecided at this point; we would be leaving so much we have worked for. We have to talk some more. Now if we could get Tom and Ailsey to take our house, it might make it more inviting." He looked toward Tom and Ailsey.

Tom's eyes widened. Things were moving too fast for him. He looked at Ailsey, her mouth was open in surprise, her eyes sparkling, "Let's do it, Thomas." she said so softly only he could hear her.

❧ Chapter Eight ❧

The talk went on into the night, with Ailsey and Tom casting doubtful looks at first one and then the other. They wondered just what was going to happen, and who would go and who would stay; they knew that they weren't interested in leaving Virginia and going so far away.

Ailsey kept thinking of the house that belonged to Patrick and Polly that Thomas had described to her. She already loved it just from his description, but never dreamed that they could ever have anything half so grand for themselves.

When leaving the family to retire for the night, Ailsey turned to Thomas, "What do you think? Will Polly and Patrick leave everything to go with Mom and Dad? I was surprised that they would even consider it, and was shocked when they wanted us to take over their house. What do you think, Thomas?" She looked long at her husband, knowing that he had had nothing else on his mind all evening as the talk went this way and that between the group.

"Well, we won't have to prove the thirty-eight acres that I bought, and we could just add it to Patrick's one hundred thirty eight acres. I'm not sure that we could afford to buy Patrick's place. I have some money that I planned to build with and stock our farm. We will soon need to get cattle, sheep, and hogs; it won't be much of a farm without stock; if we took his place we wouldn't have to build and could use that money toward the payment. It would all depend on how much he would want for it; it would sure save a lot of time. We could get right to farming and not have to take time to build. I'm interested in it, and also in patening the acreage on the West Fork Dr. George talked about. In fact, it joins what I already bought, but how could we manage? That's a lot of land! That would be almost as much as your dad and Patrick are going so far away for." Tom shook his head, his mind going round and round. "I wouldn't want to get in so deep that I couldn't see my way clear," Tom looked at Ailsey, not having a ready answer to the problem.

"Let's get a good night's sleep, we can talk to everyone in the morning; maybe there will be some answers by then," Ailsey told him as they went to the third floor of the big house to the room that not so long ago had been Ailsey's.

It was a long night for Tom as he tossed and turned his body in the big feather bed. He was going over in his mind every detail as he thought of all the talk of the evening past and the way it had been presented to them. He could hear Ailsey moan and mumble in her sleep as she lay beside him in the big comfortable bed, and knew that her sleep was disturbed as was his. He was overwhelmed with the possibility of so much land when his plans had been on a much smaller scale. He could remember his old grandfather saying, "Think big, you can always come down one way or another," and his roaring laugh that always followed which always brought a smile to Tom's face. He lay with his hands behind his head watching the dawn as it began to peek through the lace curtains.

One old rooster that was still left in the barnyard let out his morning call as Thomas swung his feet toward the floor and started to dress. "Nothing ventured, nothing gained," he murmured as he prepared himself for the day and what it would bring.

Ailsey turned toward him, "Is it time to get up already? Seems I just this minute got to sleep; and I dreamed all night about the house as you described it," she yawned and raising herself up in bed, she reached her arms toward her young husband. "Oh, Thomas let's do it. Let's take over Patrick's house and farm. We'll never get a chance like this again."

Thomas sat down on the bed beside Ailsey and put his arms around her, kissing her on the sweet mouth that was turned up to his. "You are so beautiful in the early morning with sleep still in your eyes—and they are sparkling now like a mountain stream with the sun shining on it," he told her as he held her close and stroked her mass of curly hair that cascaded down her back.

"Oh Tom, I think you are a poet when you say such beautiful things to me and I love you so," she said as she snuggled against him.

"You had better restrain yourself; if you keep cuddling against me I may come back to bed," he said as he smiled into her upturned face.

"We had better not linger—there are big things to be decided today, and everyone who plans to go will be busy with the preparations for the trip." Ailsey laughed her tantalizing laugh and almost fell over the edge of the tumbled feather-bed onto the floor, as she grabbed for her clothes on a chair close by.

Thomas was still pulling on his shoes as he cast sly glances toward his young bride of only a few months, watching as she dressed for the day.

When Thomas and Ailsey had made their way from the third floor to the kitchen, smells of fresh-ground coffee and the clatter of cooking pots greeted them from the bright cheerful kitchen. Sounds of laughter were coming from somewhere in the house as Polly and Patrick made their way toward the kitchen area their arms entwined, laughing as they tried to maneuver through the doors holding onto each other.

"You two seem in a good humor this morning; you must have slept better than I did last night," Tom said with a grin as he looked at the laughing couple.

"I love thinking of a trip and all the exciting things happening on the way," laughed Polly.

"You may not feel that way when some Indian takes that mass of hair you have and hangs it on his lodge pole," Dr. George said, his eyes sparkling with humor as he looked toward the laughing couple.

Polly looked at her father-in-law with alarm. "Are there really likely to be Indians along the way? Savage Indians? I think you are just joshing to scare me," she said with a toss of her head and another laugh.

"Oh, there'll be Indians, no doubt. But with the size wagon train we will be with and all the men with guns, I doubt there will be any trouble. I'm told that the Indians will follow wagon trains for miles hoping on a wagon dropping out or stragglers who fall behind that they can pounce on. This won't concern us—we will have good equipment and plenty of able-bodied hired help to take care of our interests.

The two young women became busy helping with the breakfast. Polly still looked doubtfully at her father-in-law, wondering if there was really danger to be expected on the trip. Finally putting it from her mind—he wouldn't expose his wife to danger, or his herd of beloved full-bred Herefords.

Breakfast was hurried through and the big table cleared for

the maps and papers to be spread to be gone over by the men. The two young women were as interested as the rest and leaned over the table pouring over the maps as the men pointed out the different areas, roads, and rivers—reading the names of the mountains and rivers that were depicted on them and noticing that the area that they would be settling would be between two forts, Fort Smith on the south and Fort Gibson on the North. That made Polly feel better about the Indians.

"There are several mountain ranges that have to be crossed looks like," Patrick ventured as he studied the maps.

"I believe some of the mountains are circumvented by rafting some of the rivers; and the tallest peaks won't have to be scaled. We have competent scouts and wagon-masters who have the route planned. I understand they have been over it several times and will know every problem," Dr. Connolly told the interested listeners, as they all stood studying the maps of the area in question.

Dr. Connolly took a chair and stretched his long legs out in front of him as he looked at the young couples. "Well, have any of you made a decision yet? We don't have a lot of time. If you and Polly decide to go, Patrick, we have to arrange for you a new sturdy wagon or two and decide what belongings you will take over the trail. I have some neighbors who are good wagon-builders, and may already have a new one built. They haven't been in this country long but are good hard-working men. There are three brothers and one sister by the name of Brown. Came over from, I believe Germany; one of them is the best stone mason I have ever come in contact with and one a carpenter and builder of wagons, and buggies—farm workers and honest. Between them they have several trades, one was a miller at one time, I believe. They build the big stone mill-wheels for grinding; good at shop and mill work. I've been thinking Thomas, if you were to patent the fifteen hundred acres, they could be a heap of help in proving it for you. Once you have the land, they could build grist-mills, shop-houses, wagon-building and etc. It would be done in no time, and your land proved for you."

Patrick looked at Polly, "We spent almost all the night talking about this; needless to say, Polly is ready to start this minute, Indians or not," Patrick told his father with a laugh. "Thomas and I haven't had a chance to talk about my farm, have you made any decisions Tom?"

"Like you two, Ailsey and I talked some; and like Polly, she is all for the venture. A shy smile flitted across his face as his glance went to Ailsey. "I don't have a lot of ready cash to go into something so grand, even though I would be proud to have your place, Patrick." Thomas looked at the family, all their eyes were turned on him.

"Seems to me then, all that is to be decided is the price and how the moneys are to be paid to Patrick," Thomas' father-in-law remarked as he turned to Thomas.

The girls seemed to be holding their breath as they listened to the talk, looking first at one and then the other of the men.

Patrick turned to Dr. Connolly," You know my place, Dad; what do you think it should be worth? I'll need some cash for the journey and for wagons and equipment; I have some that I had planned to buy the other 100 acres of land with, but not nearly enough for an adventure such as we are thinking of."

"Well now, if someone would come by and was urging you to sell it would go up in price. But since you want to sell, that's another matter." He turned a smiling face on the two young men.

"I think things can be worked out between you two. Patrick, you will need between five hundred and a thousand dollars to make this trip and do what needs to be done when you get there. I have a suggestion to make—the Brown brothers that I mentioned have been hinting that they want to move out of this area and get into a less-settled location. If Thomas and Ailsey wanted to patent the fifteen hundred acres and made a deal for them to have say twenty-five acres, let them put in a grist-mill and work at their other trades; maybe that could be the improvements that would qualify Thomas for the land, helping the Browns in the bargain. They are the kind of neighbors you want by to help in an emergency. You two decide on a price that you can both live with, with the stipulation that if Patrick wants to return he can have his place back at the same price, plus improvements. That way neither one will be left high and dry. Thomas will have all the land he will need and not lose out on the available land. What I think is we should get all the papers filled out for Thomas and Ailsey, then go see the Brown's, tell them that you have papers being filed on the land, Thomas, and see what they say

Thomas looked pleased, "That sounds fair and if I have enough money it suits me." He looked toward Ailsey and she nodded, a big smile on her face.

Patrick nodded, as he spoke "Suits me; can you give me three hundred dollars for the kit and kaboodle? I don't know how much will be left behind, but most of the furnishings and etc. Polly may want some of it in the future—that can be worked out between us," Patrick looked toward Thomas.

Thomas looked a little worried as he scratched his head, thinking hard as he counted in his mind the money he would give and what he would have left. Finally coming to a decision he said, "Let's go talk to the Brown brothers, see what they say; I sure want that fifteen hundred acres, and if Patrick comes back and wants his back I wouldn't be left out in the cold. If they will come in with me, I'll go and get the papers taken care of. The price is fair Patrick; I just have to do a little studying on it. If the Brown's say "yes", then you can order your wagons. "Thomas smiled at everyone after the—long speech he had just made. Laughter broke out from the girls as they jumped up and hugged each other.

The three men sat down to fill out the many pages of legal papers; Dr. George meticulously went over each page neatly filling in the information that was called for. "You will have to sign them when we file them in Charleston, Thomas; we can let Ailsey sign them now—she won't have to make such a long trip. It will all be perfectly legal; I can sign as witness to her signature." As the papers were finished he called, "Ailsey come and sign your name, here." As she came, he pointed out the line where she was to sign, dated it and signed his own name as witness. "There, that's done."

They wasted no time in saddling their riding horses and heading the several miles down the trail to talk to the Brown's.

The two girls talked and laughed, comparing what would stay and what would go on the long journey that each would soon be taking.

Ailsey's mother suddenly said, "If you want the Pianoforte Ailsey, now that Patrick will have a larger, newer wagon, I think it could be taken over to your new home. I have lots of things I can't take and don't want to sell that you can have—things I would like to keep in the family. We will have to do a lot of sorting and packing; do you want to start?"

Ailsey ran to her mother throwing her arms around her and kissing her, tears stood in her eyes as she said, "Oh, Mamma, you have made me so happy. I love you," she said as she kissed her again.

The women went to search from the attic to the first floor for treasures that weren't sold or packed for transport to the Oklahoma Territory. Finding, to Ailsey's satisfaction, lots of things that would grace her new home, and also adding memories of the home she and her family were leaving. The girls carried all the salvaged things to the big living area and stacked them close to the pianoforte. The bedding that Ailsey's mother said she could take would be packed around the instrument to keep it safe on the journey.

Ellen made a big pot of stew and put it to simmer for when the men returned for their supper, it wouldn't matter what time they came it could simmer until then. Ailsey decided to make a big pan of baked apple-dumplings. She had in mind to soften the menfolk so they wouldn't mind all the things she had gathered to be taken over the mountains.

The women had washed themselves and changed clothes after the scrounging in all the dusty corners of the big house. They now sat waiting, talking among themselves. "Mamma, I know there's a dozen things I need to ask you, but I can't think of a thing. You know so much about medicines, cooking and preserving; I just know as soon as you are out of sight I will forget everything you ever taught me." Ailsey looked at her mother with tears brimming in her eyes.

Her mother smiled her sweet smile at her daughter. "I know dear, I felt the same way when I went so far away from my mother. You will be surprised just how much you know when you have to cope on your own. I know you will need your mother in a few months, but there will be someone around who will know just what to do, and be a mother in my place—just take care of yourself in the meantime."

Polly looked toward Ailsey, seeing the blush that crept over her face at her mother's words. "Don't tell me". I missed the whole thing; I should have known—you look so radiant and so full of the Dickens. You." Why didn't you tell me?" She jumped up and gave Ailsey a big hug.

"I don't know how you could tell. I haven't been quite sure myself until the last few days. I haven't told Tom yet, so you two keep quite and give me a chance." Ailsey was blushing and smiling happily.

They heard the horses as they came into the barnyard and the men laughing and talking as they were unsaddling and leading them to water.

"Let's get the supper on the table. They will be washed up by the time we get everything ready," Mrs. Connolly told the girls.

It was dark enough that lamps had to be lit by the time they sat down at the big dining table. Tom and Patrick had given their wives a peck on the cheek as they sat down to eat.

"Everything seems to be falling into place," Dr. George said. The Brown's are more than willing to go; and they all seemed excited, even though Tom may have given them a bit more of the fifteen hundred acres than anticipated. He generously gave them each twenty-five acres—even the girl, with the stipulation in writing that they will receive a clear deed and title after the year of proving the land. They will each build their business and work their portion as though they owned it outright during that year. I think it will well be worth it to Tom and to them too. Now all that is lacking is getting the papers on file in Charleston, and the contract with the Brown's written and signed. I can spare a couple of days to go with you, Tom; I need to see Banister Lilly again before leaving the area—and Patrick will need to file his patent too. What do you say that we leave early tomorrow? There's one other thing, Patrick—now that you are going along, I think you should take a herd of cattle of your own. I know of a small herd close to Charleston that is for sale. Perhaps if you want to look at it, we three could drive them back when we return," he looked toward his son, and son-in-law.

"I would appreciate that. I don't know my way around the city and not too sure where to go and how to go about this," Tom said.

"Then that's settled. What about you, Patrick? Are you interested? We can take the time to look the herd over on the way down, and after your papers are processed you can buy them on the way back. Patrick, decide how you want your contract with Thomas and Ailsey written up and I will do that too, and you can file them when we reach Charleston. Then all we have to do is load the wagons," Dr. George said with a smile.

The men talked on and worked on the wording of the bill-of-sale while the women tidied the kitchen for the night.

The men had finished as the women came back to the dining

table. "I think we had better get to bed early; we will have to leave about four in the morning, Tom; even then I don't know how soon we can be back. It may take several days—if we are driving a herd it will take longer—depends on how much waiting around we will have to do in the city." With that Dr. George rose from his chair and started toward his bedroom. "Goodnight," he said.

Goodnights were said all around and everyone went to their beds—hopefully to sleep better than most had the previous night.

Ailsey hugged Tom to her. "I'm so excited Thomas, just think we haven't been married even six months and look what we already have. I think you are a wonderful husband, and you will appreciate the fine son who will soon be able to help you." Her eyes twinkled up at him as she saw the shocked expression on his beloved face.

"Oh, my God The world is moving too fast, I won't make it to age twenty-five at this rate. I've aged fifty-years in the past two days." He put his arms around her and gave her a soft sweet kiss. "I love you, Ailsey. I may not tell you often enough, but rest assured that I do. Are you all right? You haven't been doing too much have you?" He looked anxiously at her.

"I'm just fine. I had a little morning sickness but it's nothing to be alarmed about. I'm healthy and besides it will be some time before there is danger. She laughed into his face as she gave him a peck on the cheek. "Papa," she said as she ran on ahead.

"I'll Papa you," he said as he caught her to him in a hug. "Let's get to bed, Mama." He kissed her again, as he thought to himself, how I love that girl; if anything ever happened to her, I wouldn't want to live.

🎗 Chapter Nine 🎗

Members of the household were up moving about well before daylight—the kitchen a beehive of activity; breakfast was in progress with Lottie making donuts, pancakes, and fried country ham while Mrs. Connolly made sandwiches and was packing food to be taken with the men on their journey to Charleston. The womenfolk busied themselves in the kitchen while the men were in the barnyard readying their horses—making sure all their equipment was in good shape, and things they would need on the trail was packed into saddlebags and tied behind each saddle.

Doctor Connolly, his son and son-in-law, with one of the hired men, started out well before daylight; well-wishes and advice still ringing in their ears from the wives that were left behind.

Ailsey had tears in her eyes as she watched her husband leaving her again so soon after his return from the West Fork. She knew it was for them that he had to go; he was carving out their homestead from the wilderness—a place for their home and the family which would follow. She felt lonely as she watched her young husband ride off with the other men. She knew she was being silly and she dried her tears quickly, realizing that being in the family way was part of the strange feelings which seemed to overwhelm her now.

The women, after their tearful good-bye to their menfolk, soon finished with the kitchen chores. There were jobs aplenty to keep them occupied; big barrels waited, with sacks of meal standing ready for the packing. The meal was spread into large bread pans and put into a hot oven for several minutes; this would ensure that it was well-dried and wouldn't mildew or get musty, and also keep the weevils from it. The meal was layered in big waterproof barrels, and bric-a-brack and cherished dishes were packed between the layers. This would serve two purposes—the meal could be used later for bread and ensure the breakables arriving all in one piece. There were six barrels lining the parlor walls to be filled. The girls, making trip after trip, gathering all the beautiful things from the big house, worked all morning making sure all

77

were free of dust as the meal would later be used to eat. They had most of the precious things packed by the time the sun was up.

Ailsey and Ellen had to return to the cabin to tend the stock, old Bossie had to be milked and the chores done. They hurried down the road soon reaching the little cabin where Ailsey and Tom lived—finishing the chores, they then quickly returned to the farm to finish the packing.

Mrs. Connolly's hired-girl, Lottie had come early, and while the girl's were gone was busy moving all the things from the top floor of the big house and was systematically cleaning each room as it was emptied.

After several hours of work, Polly, called out, "I can't bend over another time. My back is broken into little pieces and my fingers are numb; I for one have to stop and have a cup of coffee." She had the coffee heating on the big kitchen stove and a big platter of the fresh made donuts on the table as they all came to sit for a time, gossiping and talking of all that needed to be done yet.

"I don't know how I could have managed without you girls. Ellen and I couldn't have done one third what you have accomplished, even with Lottie's help. You have really made things fall into order. And with Lottie cleaning as the rooms are emptied, things will soon be organized. I'll have Lottie's husband come in and nail the barrel tops on, and you can label them so I will know which I will need first when we settle. There are several trunks in the barn that he can bring in, and all the quilts, blankets and extra clothing can be packed into those; by the end of the day we should be in good shape.

I'll have to go home tonight. I can't keep running back and forth, and leave our animals to fend for themselves," Ailsey said as she looked toward her mother. "We'll have most of the things packed by then. You'll need to keep things to cook with and bedding while you're here. Will you cook on the trail, Mother?"

"I'm not sure. I think there will be a communal kitchen for each group. Your dad usually has those things organized. It is too much for the women to have to cook for so many; usually there will be a wagon equipped and a man to do the cooking".

"That will be a blessing. I had visioned cooking, cleaning, washing clothes on rocks, and taking care of my boys—and getting scalped by the Indians in the process, that was the one thing I wasn't looking forward to," Polly said with a laugh. They all looked at her and smiled. She certainly could lighten their day.

In the late afternoon, Ailsey and Polly started out to the cabin — the big Connolly house was in a semblance of order from the days work. All the packed barrels and trunks were labeled and set in the big parlor off the front entrance where they could easily be loaded on wagons, when the time came. Mrs. Connolly heaved a sigh of relief, knowing so much had been accomplished. Her girls had surprised her with the efficient way they had gone about the work and had accomplished so much. She could rest easy now until her husband returned to take-over the wagon loading.

* * *

The four men rode hard for the first few hours, wanting to make as many miles as they could. Finally stopping for half an hour at noontime to rest the horses and eat some of the food the women had packed. By late afternoon they reached the cattle farm where they intended to buy their stock. Approaching the big plantation house, they could see workers at the barns and they headed in that direction. There they saw a herd of cattle milling in a corral that joined the big sprawling barn. The men sat their horses watching the workers moving and culling the cattle, and sending the culls down a fenced-off chute toward another smaller lot. They were fat and slick, proof of good health and of good feed through the past winter.

"That's a fine herd, Dad; I don't know when I've seen cattle come through the winter so fat and slick as they are," Patrick said as he turned to Dr. Connolly.

"As I told you, they are prime. Now if we can get a good price on them, so much the better. I would suggest you take about twenty-five yearling steers and another twenty-five heifers that are already bred, if possible. That will give you a good start on a fine herd. The army buys beef cattle for their own use and to give to the Indians to keep them pacified. There will be a big market for beef and getting bigger all the time; the wagon trains going further west are also a good market; our ranch will be right on the trail west. The buffalo are still hunted but most people prefer beef if they can get it," Dr. Connolly told them.

They sat watching the work until the owner, Clent McCullahan noticed them, waving his hat as he made his way through the cattle in their direction.

"Howdy, Dr. George; didn't expect to see you down this way so soon again. Get down, we'll go to the house and see if we can rustle up some coffee or something stronger if you want. Hey Joc, come take the gentlemen's horses and see to them." A young Negro boy came; and gathering the reins of the four horses led them toward a shed and water box close by.

"Come on up to the house. It's about time for dinner; we'll just have time for a little snort first. Come to the back and you can wash up before dinner if you care to." He led them to a small washroom at the back of the house where pitchers of water and large porcelain bowls waited; snowy-white linen towels for their use were folded nearby.

They entered a big pleasant room with a well-scarred round table, where they were all invited to sit. A tray with a bottle and glasses and a big pitcher of cool water were brought in by a coffee-colored woman, who deposited them beside their host. The men looking around could see that this was a man's room and not the plantation regular dining room. A big cluttered desk with a sturdy chair sat in one corner by a window.

"Do you's want your dinner served in here, Mr. McCullen? It's most ready now," the servant asked.

"This will do fine, Winnie. We'll be ready in a few minutes. You can set up any time, whenever you're ready".

The men savored their drinks and talked business as the plates of vittles began to arrive. The contract for the cattle was made while they ate. They were all satisfied with the deal, and made arrangements to pick the herd up on the homeward journey.

Walking back toward the barn they saw that Joc was leading their horses out. "Thanks Joc," Dr. George said. Joc grinned and nodded his head.

Mounting up, Dr. Connolly turned to Clint, "We'll see you in a few days. I'm not sure just how long our business will take but I would think not more than a couple of days. We will pick up the herd then. Thanks Clint, so long." They were on their way with Clint's, "Good luck, hurry back," following them.

"I have one more stop to make. We will have to go about two miles from the Trace for this stop," Dr. George said as they started off at a brisk pace. "We need to buy some teams to haul our wagons; there's a man down here that breeds mules. I think it would

80

behoove us to buy two or three teams while we are here. Patrick, you'll need at least one more team. There will be no problem disposing of them once we reach the Territory; plenty of pilgrims going west will need new horseflesh by the time they reach our place. We'll be able to use them for our trip and even make a profit when we sell them."

"Dad, I wish I had your knack for making money; I don't know how you do it. Seems you turn everything you touch to a profit," Patrick laughed as he looked at his father.

"That's a knack I would like to learn too," Tom said. "If you have a ready recipe, I'll take it," he laughingly told his father-in-law.

When they reached the mule-breeder they were invited to sleep in the bunkhouse overnight, and thankfully took up the invitation. They would have another day's travel to Charleston after leaving there, and would be more comfortable staying the night than camping on the trail.

When they arrived in the city, they went directly to the office of Attorney Lilly. He looked over the papers that they presented to him and escorted the men to the courthouse to file, and perform all the legalities associated with the patening of the land and the contracts of sales. The business was conducted quickly and the travelers were on their way. They arrived back at the mule-farm where they spent another night—collected their ten mules, tied them loosely on ropes and started toward the McCullen plantation to collect the cattle they had bought.

When they reached the McCullen's, he insisted on sending two of his farmhands to help get the cattle started on the trail. They would help drive them the first twenty-five miles to trailbreak the animals—they would then be easier to handle on the drive. One of the boys that Clint sent along suggested that a man go ahead of the herd leading the mules—that way the cattle would follow. Strangely enough, they were much more docile with this arrangement; few of them tried to leave the herd, and followed closely together behind the mules.

Finally the Connolly farm came into view. It was a welcome sight to the travelers, even though the drive had been easier than they had expected it to be. They soon had the cattle turned into a meadow where they began to graze contentedly. "That's a big worry completed; I think we can relax for a time now boys," Dr. Connolly told them.

"I'll go on home," Tom announced; "I'll bring my team and wagon back tomorrow to collect the things I'm sure Ailsey has waiting for me," he laughed as he started out.

"See you tomorrow," Patrick answered as he and his dad went into the house.

Ailsey had walked a dozen miles to the window and back, looking down the Trace every little while for her husband. "Why don't you sit down? You'll have a hole worn in the floor, not counting in your shoes," Polly laughingly told Ailsey.

"I have a funny feeling that Tom will be here soon. I'll leave him some supper to warm on the hearth; I know he won't take time to eat at Dad's."

"You lovebirds." It won't be long till you won't even miss him when he's gone," Polly joshed her.

"I'll just bet! I've watched you and Patrick, always holding on to each other and look how long you have been married Ailsey answered.

Suddenly Ailsey jumped up from where she sat and hurried to the small window. "I knew it; here he comes." She hurried out to the porch where she waited for Tom. He slid from the saddle and gathered her in his arms. "Are you all right? You look peaked; are you sure you are all right.?"

"I'm fine; well a little tired; we've been helping Mamma with her packing. We really accomplished a lot—got all her dishes and nice things packed for her."

"I don't think you should do so much; you have to take care of yourself. That's my son you're carrying, you know." He kissed her cheek as they entered the cabin.

"Ho, Polly, you have a lot of cattle now to worry about besides worrying about that red hair of yours," Tom looked at Polly and laughed. "Oh, and I forgot the mules, Indians like mules, I'm told." He smiled his crooked smile at the two girls.

"Mules! Cattle! Tell us about this," Polly demanded.

"Wash up first; I'll get your supper; your horse can wait until you have eaten, and I want to hear everything," Ailsey said as she hurried to dish up the vittles that were warming by the fire.

As Tom ate, he told of the trip and all that Attorney Lilly had told them, and that they now had fifteen hundred acres on file at the courthouse. "I'll be notified when I can move onto the land, it may take a month or more for it to be processed. This scares me half to death. Although Mr. Lilly said not to worry it was just a formality and didn't mean too much as long as the papers are in order." Tom looked proudly at his wife and sister-in-law.

Ailsey sat stunned. When the papers were being filled out it hadn't hit her—the enormity of such an adventure. Now all at once she realized that they would be wealthy, or at least thought so by everyone who knew they had so much land. "Oh Thomas, do you think we can handle this? It seems so much responsibility; I'm scared I think," she looked at them both, her eyes big as saucers.

"Dr. George seems to think everything will fall into place. He says not to worry, that with the Brown's to help that we won't have any problems. I intend to believe every word he says; he is a much wiser man than I am and has had a lot more experience. You should have seen him dealing today for fifty head of cattle and ten mules. I learned a lot by just being with him and standing off and listening. He sure bought some nice animals. Patrick will have a wonderful start on his ranch when he gets to the territory with the herd he starts out with," Tom said with a new confidence about him.

"Oh, Polly, I'm so happy for you. Maybe you have made the right choice. I wouldn't have had the nerve to do it myself," Ailsey said to her sister-in-law.

Polly stayed the night even though Tom had returned. They would all return to the Connolly farm the next day together and get loaded to go over to the West Fork and their home that they would be turning over to Ailsey and Thomas.

The morning came all too soon it seemed to Ailsey; she was still tired from the packing and had no desire to get out of bed. Thomas was up when she awoke and had the fire going in the fireplace. She knew that he would want breakfast when he came back from tending to the chores, and quickly dressed and started their meal. The smell of coffee brought a giggle from Polly as she tried to get up from the bed that had been made on the floor for her. As she stood up she said, "I felt like I was in a hole, but I sure had a good night's sleep; I was more tired than I thought. I'll bet you were tired, too; she looked at Ailsey as her laughter rang out.

"I didn't want to get up either. I could have slept on for hours; but we have a lot to do today at Mamma's, and need to get started.

We will probably leave this area tomorrow if the weather holds and everything is ready. I know Thomas is anxious to get started on all the work we will have to do. Thank heavens, we won't have to build but will have a house to move into, thanks to you and Patrick," Ailsey told her her smile lighting her pretty face.

"What can I do?" Polly asked, after washing her face and combing her hair.

"Have it all ready when Thomas comes from the barn. I made biscuits and scrambled some eggs, and I have apple butter for the biscuits, that should fill us up. I can't take eggs on the trail, so decided to use them up. Whatever is left we can boil and take along to eat," she told Polly as she finished her work.

Thomas entered the back door and washed up for the meal that waited. "I'm all ready to go. The team's hitched up to the wagon. We can load whatever you have at your mother's and then come back here and load the stuff here," he told them as he sat down at the slab table. "We should be ready to leave tomorrow if Patrick's ready. I don't think they will have much time—the wagon train leaves in a few days. He has to allow time to come back here unless he decides to meet them somewhere on the trail."

"I don't think he will do that. He will want to go along with the cattle even though dad has help to drive them," Polly answered.

"I expect you're right. I know if I had a beautiful bunch of cattle like that I would want to sleep with them to make sure they were all right," Tom said with his crooked smile.

"You would too! I can just see you curled up to a big fat cow, and her reaching around and licking your face every now and then," Ailsey said with a grin. They all broke out in laughter that filled the little cabin with echoes.

After the house was put in order they piled into the wagon and soon arrived at the Connolly's farmhouse.

Lottie opened the door to them as she went outside to empty a bucket of scrubwater. She was still cleaning the upstairs, having finished the third floor the day before; she would soon have the second floor finished. Mrs. Connolly had Lottie's husband dismantle all the beds, and had set one up in the living room for them to sleep the last few nights. All the furniture had been moved from the top floors to the bottom one, except some bureaus and a couple armories that were too heavy for him to handle by himself. The big house was taking on a deserted look. All the curtains had been taken down, washed and stored; the blank windows looked sad from the outside.

Thomas looked around at all the barrels and trunks. "Don't tell me I have to cart all this over the mountains, Ailsey?"

Ailsey giggled, "Oh you! I don't have that much. That's Mamma's things. I don't know how she will ever get it so far. But she doesn't seem to be worried. Says dad will take care of everything."

Patrick and Dr. George had gone to the Brown's to see if the wagons were ready. Patrick was going to take a team of the mules and one of the new wagons to fetch his and Polly's belongings from their farm. He had decided that the new wagon he had ordered and the one he already owned would be enough to take what they would want. The smaller one would do for their clothing and a place for the four of them to sleep. His father had said if they needed more space that another wagon could be provided. He had loaned Partick the extra cash he needed.

There was the sound of wagons in the distance. They all rushed on to the veranda to look; Patrick and his father with the new wagon were coming down the road—another wagon was behind them. Ortho, one of the Brown brothers was driving it. The two wagons were equipped with the curved braces and had new canvas stretched over the top. They looked big and clumsy as they came to a halt in front of the veranda. Proud smiles lit the faces of the men, as they called, "Well, how do we look?"

"I don't know," Tom said with a shake of his head. "That's a big wagon to haul so far, even when it's not loaded. Are you sure it can be done?"

Ortho, climbed down from the seat, wrapped the lines around the brake and came toward the veranda, "It will go," he announced. "Been building wagons long time. Go anywhere fully loaded, take hills, take rivers, take mud, much good, strong, wide rims on wheel, make good." He looked proudly toward his work as he spoke.

Dr. George came up on the veranda, Ortho has decided to go with you over to the West Fork. He wants to look around at the land and decide on where he will want to build the mill and ect. He can help Patrick and Polly on the way back here—they won't have to travel alone. I think it is a good idea; if there is any trouble with the wagons we will know about it in time."

Thomas shook hands with Ortho, "good to see you again. I think it's a wonderful idea. I had worried about them coming back alone, although I had intended to see them over the mountain before leaving them on their own. This way he will have a reliable man with him and Ortho can see the lay of the land for their trip when they come over."

The wagons were ready to be loaded; Thomas had just found out that Ailsey intended to take the pianoforte. With a shocked look he turned to the men, "Do any of you know how to load something like this?"

Ortho came into the room, took a look at the instrument, "I know, take apart, wrap pieces, then put together again," he stood nodding his head.

"I guess it should be loaded first," Tom remarked.

"I get tools, I take apart, take on my wagon," Ortho went to fetch his tool-box that he had brought along. Soon he had each delicate filigreed piece of ornamentation dismantled and wrapped in the blankets Ailsey had ready. The top of the piece was removed; the base didn't look so overpowering after that was done. The men took the base to the wagon where it was wrapped and placed against the front seat of the wagon, and tied down; the other pieces laid together and tied so they didn't bounce around and become broken. Ailsey watched as Ortho carefully stored everything and was so grateful that he was taking such good care of the precious instrument.

All the bundles and bedding and things that were piled beside the pianoforte for Ailsey was loaded. Since there would be three wagons going Ailsey hurriedly gathered more—jugs, stone churns and things that she had had to pass by before. Hay was brought from the barn and they were packed in layers of hay in the wagon-bed. She kept running to her mother, "Are you going to take this? How about this?" Until Thomas said, "Enough, Ailsey. We still have to take the things from the cabin."

The three wagons were ready to go; a tearful good by was said, with Ailsey running back to hug her mother one more time. "Write to me Mamma, Poppa, I'll miss you." She sobbed as she climbed aboard the wagon that Patrick was driving, with Polly beside her. Polly put her arm around Ailsey holding her tightly. Thomas climbed up to his wagon-seat. Ortho, in his wagon, followed behind.

Reaching the cabin, they decided to get everything organized and load all they could that evening and wait until the next morning to leave. Ortho had left an area with hay for him to sleep. He could still take more things, even if they would have to be lifted down for the night so he could have a place to sleep.

The men went to the barn and began to load tools and etc. into Patrick's wagon. The chickens were put into coops, and stacked to one side. The hay that Tom had in the barn was put into the wagon too, he and Polly could sleep on it. That left the cabin furniture to be loaded into Tom's wagon. Ortho had brought his own blankets and insisted on sleeping in his wagon that night. Patrick and Polly slept on the straw-tick on the floor.

As soon as daylight came, everyone had been fed and the bed taken apart—it and the cedar chest were loaded onto the wagon. All the cookery was packed into Ailsey's washtub, and put into Patrick's wagon. The straw-tick was put in for a bed for Thomas and Ailsey. The chicken coops were set in Ortho's wagon and could be lifted out at night. All was ready as the sun began to peek over the mountains in the east. The wagons creaked as they started out. Old Bossie tied to the tailgate gave a bellow of displeasure as the rope tightened on her neck when the wagon began to roll. Thomas's riding mare, Babe, was tied to Patrick's tailgate. Ailsey turned to take a last look at the cabin. "I hate to leave our first home somehow," she said as a tear rolled down her face. Thomas put an arm around her for a brief minute, giving her a sympathetic squeeze.

The three wagons soon paced themselves a comfortable distance apart as they began to move along. There was little conversation as everyone seemed lost in their own thoughts, and the men with their minds on driving. Old Rowdy seemed happy as he bounded along beside the wagon, going off into the woods now and then looking for new trails. Ailsey held her beloved Taffy, in a lidded-basket on her lap.

The wagons covered the trail without problems, and they arrived at the Murpheys homestead around five o'clock. The Murphey's met them in the yard urging them to stay the night. Patrick and Thomas had decided that they wouldn't stay as there were too many to impose on the Murpheys. They could make another few miles and camp on the trail. The wagons moved along for another hour; they couldn't make the area where they had camped before but found a suitable camp and stopped for the night. The girls were tired, and a hurried meal was made with cooked food they had brought along. A big tin of Lottie's donuts and coffee would be enough, as they were all ready for a night's rest.

They were now into the wilderness, moving along at a steady pace, stopping for rest every few hours. They ate a dinner of biscuits and meat and moved along again, planning to reach the mountain and camp in the meadow at its base and get an early start over the next morning. Thomas milked old Bossie; the men tended the animals and bedded them down for the night. No one had to be coaxed to go to bed as goodnights were said.

The wagons were ready to make the move up the mountain, just as the sun tipped the tallest crest. Patrick took the lead, slowly climbing the grade, watching every inch of the trail for danger. The mules were sure-footed and climbed effortless up the mountain, maneuvering through the gullies, and around the large rock formations and back and forth along the switchbacks—the other two wagons following at a slower pace. Thomas looking back down the Trace could see Ortho following without any problems. "Looks like we will make it over without mishap," he told Ailsey.

Reaching the level flat where the Wolf Camp was located Patrick swung wide, off the Trace waiting for Thomas to come alongside. "Let's take a breather here, Thomas; Ortho can pull alongside on the other side of the Trace, and we can rest the horses a bit. This is the only level place where we can pull out before reaching the valley." Thomas pulled up on the Trace leaving room for Ortho. "That's a good idea; We have the steepest part right ahead. The horses need a breather." Ortho came up and pulled out on the right side of the Trace and stopped his wagon. "Good, good, horses need breather. Air thin on mountains, we rest," Ortho said as he got out of the wagon and began checking his horses' gear and the wagon for anything that might have come loose or had a problem, the other men were doing the same.

Polly couldn't sit still any longer and climbed from the wagon; Ailsey followed suit. They walked around the area, Polly pointed out where they had stopped for the snow, curious to see it again. Taking food from the wagon, they handed sandwiches to the men. There wouldn't be a place to stop further up the mountain.

After half an hour's rest, they mounted up and started the climb to the top of the mountain. Soon they were on their way down the west side. No problems had developed so far and they all considered themselves lucky. They reached the valley and the beautiful stream just at twilight and pulled the wagons in a half circle for the night.

"Thomas, I guess you want to fish?" Patrick called with a laugh, as they unhitched the wagons.

"You bet your life. I have me a barrel that I intend to fill with fish. Got me some extra salt and I'll salt them down so they keep for a while," Tom called back. "You want to help me catch a barrel-ful?" he asked.

"I've nothing better to do; might as well help, or you won't be finished till mornin'" Patrick answered. "Maybe I can persuade Ortho, to help." He laughed so hard the mules he was working with shied.

They showed Ortho how they put the horses out on long ropes to graze on the dried grass for the night.

Polly and Ailsey were organizing things to make a meal. "You want fish for supper, you had better get busy," they called as they gathered dry grass and wood to build a fire.

Thomas grabbed up the fishing poles and a big bucket, "Come on you two. Ortho I have one for you, too, if you want to fish," he called as he started toward the stream.

"I fish, I like. Never fish much in this country, no time," Otho explained as he hurried off to join the others.

It wasn't long before the yells started and the girls knew that the fish were landing in the bucket. Everything was ready when Tom came with several cleaned and ready for the pan. "Time your-self, we will have supper in an hour. You should have your barrel full by then," Polly laughingly told Thomas.

When the hour was up a big bread-pan was filled with fried fish and fried bread; another pan turned over it to keep them warm until the men decided to come for their supper. "The smell of boiling coffee should bring them any minute," Polly remarked. Soon the girls smiled at each other; the men were coming in to eat. "How many do you have so far, Thomas?" Polly asked.

"Well, not enough to fill my barrel, but won't be long. As soon as we eat we will try again; should have enough by bedtime," Tho-mas answered as he filled a tin plate with fish.

The girls had gone to bed before the men returned to join them— Tom's barrel full to the brim with fish, cleaned and salted down, the lid hammered tight on top.

Another two nights and they would reach the West Fork. When

Ailsey saw the house in the distance, her eyes rounded as she looked; "Is that it? I don't believe it. That's almost as big a house as Poppa and Mamma has, and in the wilderness—it's too much to hope for. Polly, thank you, I'll never forget this day," tears rained down Ailsey's face as they drove toward the house that was to be her home.

Polly's two boys came racing to meet them, all laughter, kisses and hugs for their mother and father—a shy hello to the rest.

The girls were busy packing, sorting and storing the things that Polly wanted to move, while the men looked over the patented acres. Taking Ortho down the West Fork to where another stream joined it, Patrick was of the opinion that it would suit for the location of a mill. Ortho had a solemn look on his face as he gazed at the land. "I pick twenty-five acres for each?" he looked at Thomas unbelievably. "For each?" "One hundred acres of this beautiful land?" Thomas nodded, "That's right" Ortho had tears in his eyes, as he looked lovingly this way and that. "We work hard; you never be sorry; we be your friend always." He grabbed Thomas's hand almost shaking it off in his enthusiasm. "Right here mill for corn and wheat, over there shop-house, on hill for sister, India, we build house," he looked toward Thomas doubtfully.

"Suits me, as soon as the papers are processed we will have a surveyor mark this area, and we will be in business. If you want to come and live at the house till you build I think we can manage. Whatever you work out will be fine with me," he smiled at Ortho's bewildered look.

The two wagons were loaded and ready to go by first light. Polly and Ailsey had been cooking for hours, getting things ready for the trail. They both shed tears at the thought of their parting and maybe never to see each other again. "What am I going to do?" Ailsey wailed. "Everyone I love will be leaving me. What will I do when my time comes?" her sobbing could be heard all over the house.

"Stop it, Ailsey; you may hurt your baby. You'll have Ortho's sister, and Martha Barber, and who knows, by your time there may be more women around. It will be all right—just wait and see," Polly held her tight, patting her on the shoulder.

The wagons were ready to roll. Patrick helped Polly up to the wagon-seat, then handed the two excited little boys up to sit between them. He mounted to the driver's side and looked around at the buildings before waving a last good-bye and starting the wagons to roll. Ortho moved out behind him. Ailsey and Thomas stood watching as long as they were in sight. "Oh Thomas, we're alone in the wilderness." "Not for long." He answered. "Not for long."

🦢 Chapter Ten 🦢

Worth Chenowith had made up the notice and posted it on his store-house door. WARNING—meeting called to discuss WAR. Here on Saturday next, 2:00 P.M.

The hollows began to spew out scare-crow looking men and boys, each holding a squirrel rifle in their dirty callused hands. Their patched clothes hung on skinny frames; long, lank, greasy hair framed uneducated faces; their sharp eyes darting this way and that—an uneasy look about them as they joined the milling crowd.

Thomas and Worth stood on the store-porch watching them gather. "Those will be our best solders," Tom said as he nodded toward the rugged, poorly dressed hill people. "They may not know formations and drills, but they will know how to survive in the wilderness and live off the land—Good hunters every one; when they aim and pull the trigger, their bullets will find a mark."

As Thomas had predicted, everyone in the area for miles around was gathering. It looked as though they expected Tom to take the lead. There were others there that could do a better job than he could, he thought; but at least he could start the ball rolling; seemed everyone was interested. He saw the Cottrell boys, separated this time by the crowd; the McGlotherin boys stood well in the back together. He had heard they were scouring the country buying up every riding horse that they could find. From what he heard they had a considerable herd now; they had always been good horse-traders, and would have a ready market for horses when the army started recruiting. He saw Absalom Knotts, standing over by himself, an eye on the people around him. There was Nathan Ellison, from over on Beech. The Bailey brothers, Shadrach Badget, the Deweese brothers; the Jarvis's and their in-laws made up about half of those gathered. Thomas knew that the beliefs were divided; it wouldn't take much to set off a powder keg right here and now.

The gathering had been called for two o'clock and the time was growing near. There hadn't been any new arrivals for several minutes. Thomas could see that the crowd was dividing itself—those who were strongly Union, and those who favored the confederacy. The crowd was becoming restless.

Worth nudged Thomas, "Let's get started before we have trouble. I don't know what you're going to say that won't start it anyway. They're a little edgy now to my notion."

Thomas wasn't looking forward to this; what could he say that would please everyone? Clearing his throat, he raised his hand for quiet; the crowd quieted, waiting, "I want to thank you all for coming out today. I find it hard to talk to so many whose interests are so divided. I know there are families, like my own, who are divided. These are trying times, with heartbreak, disappointment, and anger in every household. The fighting further south has intensified. There are people who are being driven from their homes. There are people being killed every day. There are those here today who are sympathetic to the cause of the Confederacy. And many who want the Union to survive. I can't read your hearts and minds. I only know I want the Union to stand! I have friends and relations throughout the South. I don't want to be separated from them or to fight against them. However, there is no alternative, except to make a choice. I don't think there is anyone here today who relishes the thought of going to war! If they do, they don't know what war is all about! For those of you who still have not made a choice—think carefully; weigh every advantage; we will all have to take one side or the other. Every able-bodied man and boy old enough will have to choose. Recruiters will soon be combing these hills, and will take you regardless of your wants. I would suggest that you do choose before you are forced to fight for a cause you don't believe in; choose while there is still time. Are there any questions?"

Someone in the back yelled, "We don't have slaves! Why do we have to fight for them?"

"I've never been over the mountains; I don't know any slaves or anyone who has any. I'm not mad at anyone—why do I have to fight if I don't want to?" a grown boy asked.

Thomas held up his hand, "This is not entirely a matter of slavery; however, I myself don't believe in slavery. To my knowledge the Jarvis' have never kept slaves; We have had Africans working for us when we lived down south, but they were paid like everyone else—they were not slaves. The whole issue as I see it, is that the southern states want to secede from the Union. Not only the southern states but some of the eastern states as well; at this time I believe eleven states have declared for the South. They want to have their own government—make their own laws. They will rule the sea-board, making the states to the West isolated from the oceans where foreign goods come for marketing. We wouldn't be able to ship without high tariffs. I know some of you don't think this affects you—you are wrong! You use many things here that are shipped in—Coffee, sugar, medicines, to name a few. I am not an educated man; I may not be explaining this so you understand. I am here for one simple reason—WAR! That doesn't have to be explained. It's here regardless of the reason It's already been decided.' There's a War—and you—you—and you will have to go," Tom pointed at those on all sides. I am here only to ask you, and to warn you—think carefully; think seriously; this has come like a whirlwind, and you will have to decide or those who come for you will decide for you." Thomas stepped back waiting to see if anyone else would take the porch to speak.

Abaslom Knotts stepped up onto the porch, and in a quiet voice began, "Neighbors, I think most of you know me; I want to say here and now that Thomas Jarvis is a good neighbor and an honest man. Like he says, you have to decide. I want our way of life to continue as it always has. I think the South deserves to make its own laws and control its destiny; I will be starting to recruit and train men toward that cause; those who want to join it may contact me anytime at my home." He left the porch to mingle with the crowd. Several gathered around him—the Deweeses, Baileys, the two Cottrell boys, and several others that Tom lost count of.

Tom spoke again, "After the meeting there will be a place for you to sign-up, here in the store; we need Home Guards which will be those who are too old to march, and who will guard our homes and families while you go off to fight. We need doctors, blacksmiths, cooks, timbermen, ditch-diggers, men who are good with horses, and teamsters; we need to know what you like doing and where you will best fit into the organization of an army. You will have to go, so it's best you go where you will be the most help. God bless you all and be with you through the trying times ahead." Tom tipped his hat and made his way toward his horse.

Several mounted up and followed Tom from the gathering. "Where will we muster?" they wanted to know. "We want to join the Union." They all nodded, as they followed Thomas.

Thomas looked them over, "Follow me home, we might as well get started." He had a large following by the time he reached his farm. He dismounted by the barn, and they all followed suit. "Wait here, I'll get a ledger to register you." He soon returned with a book and pen and ink. Going to a work-bench inside the shed to the barn, he had them line up; took their names name of wife, if married. Parents' names if not married; post office address and what they did best; if they owned a gun, and horse. "Come back here next Saturday; I'll see if I can find someone to give you some training; I'm not knowledgeable in army training, he told them." Tom watched as the scraggly bunch left, shaking his head. "How many will be alive by next year? The youth of this land—including his own sons." With a heavy heart Tom walked toward the house.

After the meeting things seemed to speed up. The feelings of the surrounding area were changing. First one and then another's property was being destroyed, barns were burnt, fences torn down. Thomas spent much of his time riding here and there on his holdings, keeping track of all who rode across his land and making sure that the damage was kept under control.

Thomas had found an old German soldier by the name of Colonel Gurshner, who had come over to fight in the Revolutionary War, and never returned to his home in Germany. He was an old man, it was true, but knew how to organize the groups into a fighting force. Maybe his tactics were outdated, but it was the best Thomas could come up with, and was thankful that the young men could have some training before going off to war. Gurshner stayed at the farm and trained all who came in the evenings and on Saturday. Thomas watched from the sidelines. The lean-looking boys from the hills and hollows were soon marching in a straight line, their weapons over their shoulders—holding themselves straight and tall. The old German seemed to know what he was doing; he trained them how to follow orders—to mount up and dismount on command—how to keep themselves free of injuries—what they could eat to be healthy—from forging on the land—and how to boil water that wasn't safe to drink—how to stay reasonably dry when it rained—how to keep warm—what to take with them from home and what to leave behind. There were so many things to learn that some wondered how they would have time to fight a war?

Colonel Gurshner watched his men closely; Shadrach Badget caught onto the drills and became expert in the maneuvers Colonel Gurshner conducted for his men. The Colonel then assigned Badgett to a smaller group of men, thus cutting down on such a big group to command. As he found men he thought fit to command, he kept dividing the bigger groups and placing some of them with new recruits as they came in from the hills. This seemed to cut down on the training time, as the older recruits could herd the newcomers through the training.

There were battles being fought that left many dead and wounded; they were coming closer and closer to the West Fork.

Nathanial Ellison was appointed in command of the Home Guards, and was training them.

Captain Absalom Knotts, commanding a well-organized, well-equipped cavalry unit had gone South; word was that he was in the midst of battle for the Confederate Army—making a name for himself.

Thomas Jarvis's sons began to enlist—Caleb in June, John H. in Oct. Solomon, Thomas P. and Wesley Jan. 7, Ailsey's heart broke when her three sons left together going somewhere into the South where Caleb and John already were. Thomas, when his second son Josiah, and his sons-in-law John H.H. Keaton joined the Confederacy, hung his head in shame and disappointment, seeming to age years in just a few minutes.

There were enough tears shed in the household that if they had been diverted to the mighty West Fork, it would have flooded its banks.

The country was in an uproar; many who had grudges against neighbors found it convenient to get back at them—burning houses, barns, shooting them from ambush, stealing cattle and live stock.

Perry Conoly, a young, foolhardy man of twenty-some years, married, and not much of a husband or farmer, gathered a bunch of renegades and formed a bush-whacking group he called the Moccasin Rangers. They rode the countryside taking what they wanted and causing mischief wherever they roamed. They were a wild unruly bunch as they went roaring through the county drinking, singing, and raising hell. They rode the best horses with new army saddles and gear, and carried the finest rifles; it was no guess where or how these fine adornments had been attained.

The word was out to beware of the Moccasin Rangers, no atrocities were too bad for them to commit.

The wife of Perry Conoly was left alone in a small log cabin in an outlying area where she tended a garden and took care of their one cow and a scraggly bunch of chickens—trying to keep her two small children fed, this wasn't unusual as she had been doing this since marrying Perry.

Word came that Perry had taken up with Nancy Heart—a wild young red-haired woman who could ride and shoot as well as any man. Perry's wife Lucenda, upon hearing this went into a decline— her family had to fetch her to their home, and look after the children and what animals there were; She lingered and languished upon her sick-bed upon hearing the tales of murder, robbing, and burnings that followed her husband and his beautiful, red-headed mistress.

Perry wasn't bothered one bit with the word he received about his wife's illness and of his family, going on his merry way—now with a woman who was becoming as notorious as himself. She had become a brilliant spy, by cozying up to the Confederate soldiers, getting information from them that she would pass on to the Union Army—for a price. The information she gathered in this way was used to advantage by Captain Perry and his Moccasins.

Perry was a striking man; his well built towering six-foot one-inch frame, black piercing eyes and shock of black curly hair would turn any woman's head. Nancy, on the other hand, was just as handsome. She entertained the Moccasins with her singing and her vivacious personality. There was always a smile on her rosebud mouth, even when she sighted down the barrel of her rifle and pulled the trigger.

Late one afternoon Perry and Nancy were coming from a dense pine grove, from no doubt a lover's tryst, with Nancy leading, when the Home Guards appeared suddenly on the road. Perry, being the gentleman that he was silently slid back among the trees, leaving Nancy to face the Guards. They took her prisoner back to their headquarters, questioning her about the Rangers and about Perry. They soon came to the conclusion that she was an innocent young girl in love with a scoundrel, caught up in something she didn't know anything about, and let her go. Pretty Nancy had charmed her way out of a bad situation. She knew where Captain

Conley was likely to be camped and soon joined him with information on the movements of the Federal troops as well as with information for their coming movements to raid supply trains and collect army payrolls for their own use. Captain Conley roamed far and wide throughout the State of Virginia, violating every form of decency as his men killed, robbed, raped, and ravaged the countryside. Captain Conely's fate was long overdue as rewards for his capture and for the capture of his lover, Nancy Heart, was advertised. They were as elusive as quicksilver, it seemed to those who were trying to track them down and capture them for the reward. Some of those who trailed them would have killed them just to have the country free of the evil they did, and not for the reward.

The beautiful Nancy continued her spying; when the Rangers became short of money and supplies, she would scout out the location of what they needed. On one such occasion pretty Nancy was picked up by Union scouts. She was taken back to a big two story farmhouse where the Union Army had their headquarters. Nancy was led to an upstairs bedroom, with a solder posted to guard her.

It wasn't long until Nancy was bored and opened the door; seeing her guard sitting on the staircase she watched him; soon realizing he was a mere boy she called to him. "Will it be all right to leave the door open to let some air in? It's hot up here.

"I guess it will be all right," he answered her, his face turning red.

Nancy pulled a chair close to the open door and started to talk to the young man. She soon had his undivided attention. "I like your hat; do you mind if I try it on?—I always wondered how I would look in a Union cap." The young man, so proud of his Union uniform, handed her his cap. Cunning Nancy took it to the mirror and pulling her beautiful red hair this way and that tried the cap. She turned, twirling in front of the mirror giving the young soldier a first-hand look at her luscious figure. Convinced she had him mesmerized, she smilingly handed the cap back. Looking at the rifle he held she asked, "Are you a good shot?"

"Good enough I reckon—I got guard duty." He smiled a shy smile at the beautiful Nancy.

The cagey Nancy walked to the window and looked out. "Whose big bay is that out there?" she asked.

Now trusting his prisoner, the boy came into the room to look down at the hitching rail, "That's the Captain's, Miss."

Nancy moved closer to the young man. "My you're tall," she said smiling up at him. "Show me how you aim your rifle at a 'Reb'." The young man raised his rifle and aimed it out the window, "I wish I had one out there now." He turned to the smiling Nancy.

"Let me try it," she said taking the rifle and pointing it out the window. Suddenly she turned toward the young soldier, fired two shots into his chest, grabbed the box of shells that protruded from his pocket, and before he hit the floor she was down the stairs and out to the hitching rail. She flung herself into the saddle of the big bay and racing toward the nearest woods, disappeared, pretty Nancy had made good another escape.

Captain Conely finally met with disaster; he was holed up alone waiting for Nancy in a mountainous hide-a-way where he felt safe for the time being, when one of his men gave away his hide-out for the reward—or some above-average hunter had hunted him down. A battle of wits and gunfire began; Perry fought long and hard, he was wounded badly at the beginning of the fight, and blood drenched his clothing and the battle area around him. He gallantly fought on until his ammunition gave out; he was in a very weakened condition from pain and loss of blood when the Federal troops, after waiting for sometime, went in to get him, clubbing him unconscious, tied him across his saddle taking him back for hanging. When they arrived back at their headquarters the notorious Captain Perry Conely, organizer of the Moccasin Rangers, was dead.

Nancy Heart resumed her lifestyle for a while after losing her famous lover; she was friend to whichever side suited her purpose at the time. The flamboyant Nancy finally faded from the limelight. It was never known if she had been killed, captured, or had just gotten tired of the rough, hazardous life she was leading and faded into the countryside.

* * *

Dr. George Connolly had spent several years in the Oklahoma Territory making a name for himself breeding fine Hereford cattle, and practicing his calling. His son, Patrick, who had taken up land in the territory when he did had returned to the West Fork several years before Dr. Connolly selling his two thousand acre ranch to his father. Dr. George remained in the Territory for some seven years. When more and more people moved into Oklahoma he sold his vast holdings to a neighbor rancher for, at that time, an unheard of amount of money. He returned to the West Fork, teaching one of the first schools in the area and returning to his doctoring.

Ailsey was now the mother of thirteen grown children; her daughter, Jane, adored her grandfather Dr. George, and wanted to be a doctor just like him. He let her help around his office from the time she was eight or so. She could sterilize his equipment, keep his medicines arranged on the shelves in order of their importance by the time she reached her teens. Still wanting to become a doctor, her grandfather had to set down with her and explain that women didn't become doctors—maybe midwives, or nurses, but never doctors. "I'll be a doctor some day, you just wait and see ," she would tell him with a toss of her head.

When the rumblings of war began, Dr. George began to settle his affairs, and was one of the first to offer his services to the Federal Army. Jane was brokenhearted to think that her beloved grandfather would be going off to war and she could no longer help with his doctoring.

As the time approached when Doctor Connolly would be going to man a field hospital, Jane begged, "Gramp, take me with you. I'm eighteen now; you need me. Please Gramp; I can't do without you, and you need me. Please Gramps." Her big blue eyes turned up to her grandfather was innocent and pleading.

Dr. George looked at his beautiful granddaughter; what would life hold for one so determined, now that war covered the land. Thinking there was no harm, and that she would let him be for a time he told her, "If your mother will let you go, then I'll take you along," never for a minute thinking that her parents would allow such a thing.

Jane hurried to her mother. "Mamma, Gramps wants me to go along to his new hospital to help him; you'll let me go, won't you? You have to Mamma; I just can't live if I can't help with medicine. Please Mamma, please! Don't say I'm not old enough! Lots of boys younger than I am are going to fight. Please, Mamma. I'll just die if I can't go." Tears stood in her big, blue eyes as she ran to her mother and threw her arms around her, laying her head on her shoulder she sobbed as though her heart would break.

"Jane, foolish child, control yourself. Men are supposed to fight a war—women remain at home to keep the home fires burning and furnish a semblance of order for them to come back to. I've let you follow your grandfather around since you were big enough to walk. I should have put a stop to it long ago. It has been explained to you, by me, as well as your grandfather that girls aren't supposed to be doctors. Why can't you understand that? Girls aren't doctors, can't ever be doctors. That is a fact of life, Jane. Look at your sisters, they want to get married and have a family—that's the way of things; that's their place in life. Why can't you be more like them? Why do you have to worry yourself and me over something that can never be?" Ailsey patted her daughter on the back and kissed her tear stained cheek. "There now, go help the girls in the kitchen."

"Mamma, please! I'm not like the other girls; I have to do this, I thought you understood. Mamma, if I can't go with Gramps, I'll do something terrible, I'll,— I'll— run off and join the Moccasin Rangers, like Nancy Heart. I will Mamma, I swear I will.

I'm old enough to have some say in what I want to do," she was hiccuping and sobbing—her eyes red and her nose running, as she looked imploringly at her mother.

"Jane, I've lost five sons to the war and two sons-in-law; what more can a mother bear? Why do you have to act this way? Why can't you be normal like other girls? If you don't behave, I'll have to speak to your father." Ailsey turned to leave the room as Jane slumped down onto the floor sobbing.

Ailsey could understand the determination of her daughter. She was strong-willed herself, and was determined to move to the wilderness when she was her age. She couldn't let a pretty, young girl like Jane go among so many men—and most of them rough, uneducated mountain fighters. What would become of her? Her grandfather was an old man; he couldn't always protect her.

She continued to think of the problem all afternoon. "She'll settle down; she knows in her heart that we would never allow her to follow her grandfather into the battle zone to a field hospital. If he were going to a regular hospital in a city maybe then she could go. But not this, never this!

Jane went back to helping her grandfather, packing all the

medicines in his office. She cleaned and packed all his instruments, leaving out the ones he would carry in his black satchel. She equipped it with bandages, sterilized instruments, and what she thought he would need for an emergency or for quick use. A big, new wagon had been equipped for the Doctor. It had two bunks that let down from the wall of an enclosed house that had been built on the wagon. Thick mattresses were laid on these for sleeping at night, and could be removed during the day for an operation, if necessary, until the hospital tent was erected. Jane made sure that plenty of sheets, blankets, and clothing for the Doctor was packed into a large wooden box that fit under the seat. There were weather-proof boxes mounted outside between the wheels of the wagon, against the side; the doors let down on strong strips of rawhide to form a worktable. There were shelves for the large containers of herbs and medicines that would be needed. She was familiar with all of them and could mix and match herbs for any treatment as well as her grandfather could. She worked quickly and without effort doing something that she was expert at and loved dearly.

Doctor George watched Jane at her job. The girl was a wonder at knowing just how to place the things that would be needed in order of their importance. She knew almost as much medicine as he did; what a shame she wasn't a male—she would have done her family proud as a doctor. "How did you make out with your mother?" he asked, curiosity getting the best of him, although he knew Ailsey wouldn't part with her daughter, especially to go to a war area.

Jane smiled a sad smile at her grandfather, "She won't even listen; she doesn't know how important this is to me and to you. Who will look after you? You know you have to have an assistant. Who is going to know just how you like things? I've worked with you so long, I know the way you think. Who can do that, I ask you?" she stood with her hands on her hips, waiting for an answer from him.

Dr. George shook his head. "I was afraid of that. If you were only a man, there would be no problem. I'm sorry, I will miss you more than you will know. This is something I have to do, and I can understand how you must feel," he looked sadly at his granddaughter, as tears forming in her eyes she ran from him.

Jane ran all the way home; she went to the back of the house where a hammock swing sat under the big cedar tree that stood by the back door. The branches hung down forming a private place where she had worked out her problems many times. She felt that the cedar tree was her friend, and she told it many things she would never tell to a living soul. She sat twisting her hands together, thinking of what she could do to convince her mother. "She will never let me go; never!" She sat swinging back and forth. The movement calmed her, and she wiped the last tear from her face. "Gramps always says that tears don't solve anything—that the energy you use crying you could be doing something about the problem. He's right, I'll not cry again. I have to use my energy thinking; Gramps says I have a good mind; then surely I can think of a solution." Jane sat for more than an hour—she was calm now, her thinking powers intensified. Suddenly she clapped her hands, jumping to her feet. "That's it, that's it. I'll get married, and then I can do as I want. First I have to find someone who won't want to boss me around, or I'll be in the same situation. And someone who will not want to set-up housekeeping. I sure don't want any babies—for that matter, I don't want a husband. Who can I turn to? Who? Who? I know—Timmy Miller, he's a little off his noggin, can't even learn how to march; he's always casting 'sheep-eyes' at me. Just the other day he told me he would do anything for me; I can manage him—I know I can. He will let me do as I please. This will do it," she smiled to herself, and went to look for her mother.

Finding Ailsey in the kitchen overseeing the preparation for the coming meal, Jane said, "Mamma, can I see you for a minute in the Parlor?"

Her mother turned to her, "I thought we finished our discussion this morning, Jane."

"This is something else, Mamma. I need to get your advice on something." Jane left the room and headed for the parlor, knowing that her mother would be too curious not to follow.

"Jane, I thought you understood how your father and I feel about this doctoring thing, and that it was settled," Ailsey said in an annoyed voice. "I don't have any more time for your foolishness; now what have you got cooked up?"

"Mother, I understand. You aren't going to let me go to help Gramps. If that is the way you feel, I know I can't change your mind even though Gramps needs me. You're certain you won't let me go with him?" Jane asked, with a half smile on her pretty mouth.

Ailsey feeling that she had finally gotten the upper hand, nodded, "I'm most certain! You are much too young and a girl besides. So get that foolishness out of your mind once and for all. There are always things on the home front that girls can do to help in the war effort." Seeing the smile on her daughter's face she couldn't help feeling that she had missed something.

"Mamma, since I can't go with Gramps, I've decided to get married. I would like to have the wedding here, say tomorrow at around two o'clock? I've been asked several times, and have finally decided. You won't have any more problems with me. My new husband will be responsible for me after the wedding. I do hope this meets with your approval?" she smiled a radiant smile at her mother.

"Married!.' Why you have never even had a serious beau! Who would you be marrying, I'd like to know? Not one of these fly-by-night soldiers, I hope;" she cast an outraged look toward her daughter. "Your father will hear about this, young lady."

"Timmy will be here this evening to talk to Pappa, and ask for my hand. I know Pappa will be pleased that I'm marrying a neighborhood boy. I hope you will be too, Mamma. I love you and Pappa, and don't want to make you unhappy; but I think the sooner we are married the better it will be for all of us.

"The sooner you're married—My God! What do you mean? You surely don't mean that idiot Timmy Miller who casts 'sheepeyes' at you every time he's around? Ailsey put a hand over her mouth as she looked at her daughter who stood with downcast eyes, her head hanging down. "Oh, My God!" Ailsey exclaimed again as she hurried from the room.

As soon as Thomas came from the fields, he and his wife were closeted in the parlor for some time; when they emerged Thomas roared, "Jane! I want to see you in the parlor immediately! Now!" he stomped ahead of her toward the parlor. The minute the door closed he roared again, "What is this hurried-up wedding you have asked your mother to have for you? Answer me! And Timmy Miller—you' re out of your mind! Answer me I say!"

Jane turned slightly away from her father to hide the grin that flitted around her mouth. She knew he was in a rage and at this moment wanted to kill her. Knowing her father, she knew he wouldn't lift a hand to her though—he might bellow but he would never hit her.

"Pappa, I'm sorry you're upset; Mamma seemed to be, too. After all I'm past eighteen; most girls are married by this time. Timmy will be here this evening to ask for my hand, all proper and all; he's asked me several times. He wants to go to the war and all," she was twisting a hankie she held in her hand for effect, as she stumbled over her words. "He and I have decided to be married and both of us go with Gramps, to help. Timmy says he will be proud to help Gramps; and proud to be my husband. He said he will treat me good and let me do whatever I want to help in the war." Jane raised woe-be-gone eyes to her father's face. "I know you wouldn't want anything shameful to happen; we want it all proper and all." She still twisted the handkerchief as slow tears rolled down her face.

"No daughter of mine is going to marry an idiot, just to get her way. If you're so set on getting yourself talked about, and maybe killed or maimed, go with your grandfather. I'll trust he can look after you. But there will be no marriage; you can't fool me with your hinting that it's a necessary hurry-up wedding. You have never in your life looked seriously at a man. You are old enough to know your own mind; if you get into trouble it will be of your own doing. Go! If you are that determined!"

Jane ran to her father threw her arms around his neck, "oh Pappa, thank you! Thank you!" She was smothering him with her wet kisses. "I love you Pappa, you won't be sorry." She kissed him again. She looked at him with eyes filled with mischief, "Thanks, for saving me from a fate worse than death. I couldn't have stood to have Timmy Miller touch me. Will you do me a favor and announce my going tonight at supper?"

"I'll do that daughter; you do us proud, do you hear?" Her father gave her a hug as they went toward the dining room where the supper bell had just rung.

Poor Timmy would have been surprised to know he was so near to marrying the prettiest girl around. Naturally Jane hadn't bothered to inform him.

❦ Chapter Eleven ❦

Jane and her father arm in arm went into the dining-room for their supper. Jane had a big smile from ear to ear; she was bursting with excitement, just thinking of the wonderful adventure ahead of her. This was something she had wanted all her life; she knew that it would be a hard life she was heading into, but helping her Gramps would counteract any of the hardships that she would have to endure.

When they entered the big dining-room everyone looked toward them, noticing the big smile on Jane's face and the frown on her father's, wondering what was making them have two such opposite expressions.

Thomas pulled out Jane's chair for her. As they both became seated the tablefull of people still stared toward them with a questioning look on their faces.

Ailsey looking toward her radiant daughter knew that she had won out over her father. His frown was witness to that fact; she wondered what Jane had come up with to win him over.

Thomas cleared his throat to make the announcement before filling his plate. "As you all know, Jane has been interested in medicine since she could walk, and has helped her grandfather with operations and many emergencies. She has convinced me that her Gramps can't do without her, and she wants to go with him to war, she has offered me two choices, war or marriage."

"Marriage?" everyone at the table exploded together.

"Marriage to who?" they asked.

"Timmy Miller" Thomas answered, a half smile flitting around his mouth.

"Timmy Miller?" Again a chorus of voices resounded around the table—all eyes on Jane, who had the decency to drop her head shamefully. Beyond her control, a smile flitted around her pretty rose-bud mouth.

"Thomas couldn't keep from smiling his lopsided smile himself at the reaction of the family.

"I've decided that she is to go to war with her grandfather to help in his doctoring. I think she will be reasonably safe with him. As I'm sure you know, I wouldn't welcome just anyone into this family as her husband, and I think I've made the best decision." He looked around the table at the nodding heads. "If there are no questions, let's eat our supper."

The conversation was limited that night as everyone ate, some casting quick questioning glances toward Jane.

Jane kept her head down as she pushed the food around her plate. She was too excited to eat much of what was placed before her. Her mind was busy with all the things she needed to do before she was to leave. Her Gramps would be surprised, as was she, in a way; she didn't think she could convince her father to let her go off to war. She had accomplished the impossible. "Oh, I'm so happy," she silently said to herself.

Jane excused herself just as she saw her father getting ready to raise from the table. She hurried off to the upstairs going all the way to the attic where she selected a small trunk for her belongings. It was small enough that she could handle it herself; who knew where or when she would have to manage it all alone. Taking it to the room she shared with her two sisters, she set it out of the way, and threw open the lid to let it air out; she was surprised that her mother had put a potpourri of wildflowers tied in a handkerchief in the bottom before storing it, and it smelled nice as she lifted the lid. Jane smiled to herself. "I'm glad it doesn't smell musty, it would have been nice for my wedding trip, with all the lovely flower fragrance; Timmy, would have loved it," she laughed out loud, as the door opened and her sister Catherine entered.

"What's so funny? Are you still thinking of your betrothed? Shame on you! telling Papa that you would marry Timmy Miller." You wouldn't marry him if he was the last person around, you can't fool me!" Catherine sat down on the bed and they both broke out into hilarious laughter, until tears stood in their eyes.

"You know me well, sis; I had to do something! You should have heard what I told Mamma!" She bent over in a fit of laughter.

"Tell me." I know it must have been earth-shaking."

"I told her I would join the Moccasin Raiders—I can't say that she believed me though; she did seem to believe that I would marry Timmy. Wouldn't he drool if he knew?" They both fell onto the bed giggling.

The days were busy with Jane sorting and putting aside things that she knew she wouldn't have use for where she was going; she decided to take one good dress just in case she would ever need to dress up. After talking to her mother she went to the store and bought two pairs of boys pants and shirts, also a pair of high-top shoes for a boy, with several pairs of woolen stockings—her mother was busy making her some warm bloomers to wear beneath her clothes knowing that she and her grandfather would be working in all kinds of weather. She made her two flannel night dresses and a warm robe to wear over them. Jane also selected rain gear to take along. She only selected dark calico dresses and having seen her grandfather wear a big rubber apron while operating to catch splattering blood, she bought herself one of those. She wanted to be prepared for all emergencies. She took a small sewing box, cramming it into a corner of the trunk, a clock, tablet, pencil, and stamps also were stored. She had packed, sorted, and re-packed several times until she was at last satisfied that she had everything she would need and all that she could take; her trunk was full. She took a small carpet-bag of things—her comb and brush, smelling salts, (she just might get faint,) some scented soap, and a couple of soft towels.

Jane's grandfather was surprised when she told him that the family was allowing her to accompany him, but was pleased that she would be there to help him. He was sure that she could be of great use to him in the coming conflict, but wondered if she could stand up to the hardships. If not, she could always be sent home or to a city hospital where she would be safer and could be of use to the Union, and still be doing what she liked most.

Almost a week had gone by since Jane knew for sure she would go with her Gramps; of course she had been sure all along—it just took some doing. The wagon was finally being loaded; the trunk was put aboard and stored under one of the bunks. A big basket of food had been prepared by her mother and sisters—enough to last a week. Her mother had put a bushel of apples in and some dried fruit to be used in an emergency when food would be scarce. Jane was so excited that she couldn't eat her breakfast, afraid she would lose it when the wagon hit the first bump.

Finally her grandfather came with the driver he had decided on; a saddled mare was tied to the tail-gate of the wagon. "I know I can't sit in that confounded wagon for long; Jane and I can take turns riding—it will give us a rest from bumping along in a rough wagon." They were ready to mount to the tall seat and be off, when Ailsey came with another armload of quilts. "I want to be sure you have enough warm things so you won't get sick," she told her father and her daughter. Tears were streaming down her face as the wagon began to roll; Jane turned and waved "Goodby all—I'll write—take care." The clatter and clank of the wagon could be heard for several minutes after they were lost to sight.

When the last of the familiar landmarks were gone, Jane turned to her grandfather, "Thanks Gramps, you won't be sorry you took me along; I'll be a lot of help to you; I'll take care of you, too." She smiled her dimpled smile at her grandfather.

"Well! I'm glad it's me and not Timmy going off with you; I think maybe the rest of the family are too," he smiled at his pretty grand-daughter.

Jane's laugh rang out making the ears of the team of mules perk up. "To tell you the truth, Gramps, I couldn't have stood going off with Timmy. He really isn't my type. Like I told Papa, he saved me from a fate worse than death by letting me go with you," she giggled as she looked affectionately at her Grandfather.

Dr. Connolly smiled at his granddaughter, "I certainly am proud that you chose me over Timmy; I know we have some trying times ahead, but there will be fun days too, I'm sure." He patted Jane's hand.

Zolly Figgins the driver, who had worked for Dr. Connolly for many years and was too old to fight in the war paid little attention to the two, keeping his mind on the wagon as it creaked and rattled along. The mules were strong, and the wagon was as nothing to them to pull as they lumbered along the rutted, dirt road.

Jane and Dr. George had started out just at daybreak; they moved along at considerable speed for a wagon and team. Dr. George didn't know exactly where they would meet up with the Army. He was to check in at Charleston, which should take them about three days to reach—since they had enough food and bedding along it should be no problem; hardships would have to be gotten used to, and now was the time they were to start practicing. Zoll had a bedroll along, also a small tent that he could erect if the weather was bad. He could sleep under the wagon if they were in dry weather; he wasn't worried—he had slept out many times on cattle drives and on the way to and from the Oklahoma

Territory with the doctor. If worse came to worse he could sleep on the floor of the wagon between the let-down beds.

They stopped around ten o'clock for a short break; letting the mules rest a bit. Jane and Dr. George alighted from the wagon and walked around; Jane had folded a thick quilt for them to sit on, but they neither were used to sitting for long periods of time and needed to exercise their legs which were becoming numb. "Would you like an apple, Gramps? Zoll?" Jane asked.

"Say that sounds nice, get one for Zoll too. We could stand a pick-me-up, ha, Zoll?" Dr. George said.

"Sounds right by me," Zoll replied as Jane opened the back door of the house built onto the wagon bed, and pulled the basket of apples over where she could take three out; then pushing the basket back under the beds where it had been stored. "Here you are, nice and crisp, that will keep the doctor away," she laughed as she handed one to Zoll and one to her grandfather. "Ummm," she said as she bit into the crunchy apple and the juice splattered her face. "They sure are juicy," she commented with a giggle as she wiped her face.

"That hit the spot; now I believe I can survive until dinner," Dr. George said, and Zolly nodded in agreement.

"Let's saddle up," Zoll called to Jane and Dr. George, who walked along the road. They climbed into the wagon and soon hit their stride again, the mules pulling as though they were as fresh as in the early morning.

Everyone sat quietly, Jane looking around as the wagon progressed. There wasn't much to see—the weeds were beginning to brown, and the leaves were falling—everything in the process of dying sent a gloomy feeling over her. She was dressed in a dark somber calico dress that came to her shoe tops, a dark woolen shawl covered her shoulders. She removed it and folded it over her lap, as the sun warmed the day. Her mind wondered as she pictured what they were going toward. Not only the trees would be dying—some mother's son was no doubt dying at this very moment. A tear rolled down her cheek, thinking that it could be her own brothers, or sister's husbands. She soon dried her tears as they entered an area where there were houses along the way. She watched as she saw people digging and holing potatoes, and some making apple-butter. She could smell the spicy aroma of the apples cooking, and the wood smoke curling toward the blue sky as they passed.

"There's nothing like fall, with the smell of apple picking, and the earth being turned for the winter to cure—and new hay in the barns, thing's settling in for a long, cold winter—a big fire on the hearth," Dr. Connolly reminisced.

"I look at it differently; everything is dying; I feel so lonely and sad to see all the birds leave and the trees bare and the grasses dying. I think it is very depressing," Jane remarked looking at her grandfather.

They discussed the pros and cons of the fall and winter months as they drove along, looking at the surrounding fields and hills through different eyes.

It was noontime before they were aware of it with all the conversation that was going on between them.

Zoll found a church beside the road that had a well in the yard. He began the pull-off into the yard and positioned the wagon beside the church. The well curb was laid up with ledge-rock, and stood thirty six inches high, a shingled board roof covered it. The wooden arm and handle went across the well, and through a hole in the curbing; a rope was attached to the arm, which would lower and raise the big wooden bucket which was attached to one end of the rope; a wooden cover was mounted to leather hinges. The well was kept covered when not in use, to keep bugs and dirt from falling into the water. Zoll unhooked the mules, and tied them to the church hitching rail. Going to the well he loosened the handle and threw the bucket over the well curb letting it down with the rope. He soon had a bucket of cold clear water which he poured into the bucket he brought from the wagon. Taking it to the mules he held it for them to drink their fill. It took two buckets each before they were satisfied; he fastened feed-bags with shelled corn over their heads.

While Zoll tended the team, Jane brought out the basket of food. She let one of the side work tables of the wagon down and sorted out what they would have for dinner. She gave each of the men a piece of bread and fried chicken. They all walked around while they were eating—enjoying being on solid ground instead of in a swaying wagon. The men ate three pieces each of chicken and bread, Jane stopped at two. She handed each a handful of molasses cookies. "Do you want anything else?" she asked as she looked at the two men.

"That will do it for me," they both said in unison. "Except for a drink of that cold water," Dr. George said as Jane handed him a tin cup.

As they rode along, the afternoon began to get cooler. Jane soon had her shawl around her shoulders again; and the men had put their sweaters back on.

Dusk was fast falling when they came in sight of a prosperous looking farm. "Why don't we ask if we can shelter here for the night?" Dr. George said.

Pulling into the large area in front of the big white farmhouse, the owner and his wife came out onto the front portico to greet the travelers.

Dr. George alighted from the wagon and went toward them.

"Good evening, I'm Dr. George Connolly, from over in the West Fork area, on my way to Charleston to help the cause. My granddaughter and driver are accompanying me.

"Good evening, I'm Danial Cook, and this is my wife Madie. Won't you come in. We were just about to sit down to supper. Bring your granddaughter in, I'll send one of my men to help your driver stable your animals. You'll spend the night? We have plenty of room. We would welcome you heartily, Doctor."

Dr. Connolly called to Jane, "Come on in darlin'" Zoll, you drive over to the barn with Mr. Cook's man. Throw a cover over that basket of apples so they don't freeze."

The evening was spent talking about the war, and becoming acquainted with their hosts. A warm bed and plenty of food was a welcome surprise for the first night on the road. Dr. Connolly knew most people welcomed travelers; however, some had become skittish since the conflict started.

Arriving in Charleston, Dr. Connolly was directed to the Union Compound where things seemed in a confused state. He soon made contact with the Medical Corp, and found that they would be needed as quickly as they could reach the battlezone further South. They were to go by troop train, with their mules and wagon on the train with them. As for Dr. George, he welcomed the faster rate of travel; it would not only be quicker, but warmer and easier.

They spent the night in a tent at the compound. There were guarded glances at Jane, but she tried to keep out of sight as much as possible—remaining in the tent while her grandfather arranged things for their train trip. Due to the weather becoming colder he also wanted to install a small stove in the wagon, and he and Zoll went to find one suitable. They had taken a small buggy that was put at their disposal and were soon back with a perfect little stove with a flat top where water could be heated, or as Dr. George thought to make coffee, which he was very fond of.

Zoll had soon found the tools he needed and had a hole cut in the roof of the covered wagon, and a stove-pipe protruded from the wagon. They couldn't have a fire until they stopped—it would be too dangerous, and might set a fire to the woodcovered wagon. However, it would come in mighty handy at night to keep them warm.

"We'll be going down to the Carolina border and will be pulling out about three in the morning. It's best if we can get some sleep before then. The orderly will bring us some food as soon as it's ready; you won't have to go to the mess tent to eat—at least not tonight; then we will sleep. It will be a long day. We should be there by late evening, I'm told," he looked toward his granddaughter, "How do you feel?"

"I'm fine, just a little scared I guess. I'm glad you are with me; maybe I wouldn't make a good doctor after all," she said with a smile at her grandfather. "I think I will be ready for bed when we eat. I should have been practicing traveling, then I wouldn't be so tired," she sat on the edge of the cot, with a droop to her usually straight shoulders.

"You'll be just fine. Takes a day or two to acclimate yourself; after about three days, you don't even notice. I've been all over this country, and that is how it has been with me," he smiled at Jane.

"There's water over in the bucket; I've already freshened up. I left some for you Gramps," she pointed toward an upturned wooden box that held a bucket and tin wash basin.

"Thanks. I need a wash-up; I'll do it now. Our chow will soon be here—that's what it's called in the Army," he remarked as he went to the basin and washed.

Dr. Connolly had just finished when an orderly brought in two trays and set them on the cots.

"You know this isn't bad," Jane remarked as she ate the stew that was served over rice. "I don't have to wash dishes do I?" she asked her grandfather with a smile.

"I doubt they would want you in the mess tent, you're far too pretty; nothing would get done with you around, so I would say you are safe from washing dishes," her grandfather answered with a smile.

"I think I may like being waited on." Jane answered.

As they finished eating Zoll came by the tent. "Dr. George, I have word that the train will be leaving around three o'clock in the morning, I'll come by and wake you in time. Is everything all right?"

"Everything's fine Zoll. Did you get something to eat?" Dr. George asked.

"I ate. I'll go now, and be here early for you in the morning." Zoll's footsteps faded in the distance; he would sleep in the wagon and guard it through the night.

"We had better get some sleep; three o'clock will come awful early Jane." Dr. George set the trays outside the tent and closed the flap.

Jane brushed out her hair, braided it, and removed her dress for the night. She lay for a while thinking of the coming days ahead. She heard her grandfather's soft snoring, and knew he was sound asleep. She became drowsy and the next thing she knew Gramps was shaking her gently.

"Zoll just came by with coffee, time to get up," Dr. George told her.

"Seems I just this minute went to bed; I'm so tired, Gramps," she said as she stretched and yawned.

He handed her a cup of the hot black coffee, "This'll perk you up; hurry, we have to drive about a mile or more to the depot, and that train won't wait for us."

Jane pulled her dress over her head and went to the washpan and splashed cold water over her face. "Oh," she said as the cold water hit her. She hurried and brushed and braided her hair, crossing it in the back and pulling a small bonnet on. When she laced her high top shoes, she was ready. Finishing her coffee she rinsed the two cups and packed them in her small bag, the ones they had brought were in the wagon and she didn't know if she could get them to take on the train. Just maybe there would be hot coffee at least. She would take the basket of food on the train with them— they would have something to eat if nothing was served. She doubted that the Army would furnish food along the way. It was best to be prepared she planned as she finished dressing.

"I'm ready Gramps." She gathered the bag she carried and headed for the tent opening.

"Good, here comes Zoll, let's get aboard."

The town was lighted by street lamps, as they drove through it. They were soon on the edge of Charleston, coming into the depot, where the lighting was very scarce. The train waited on the tracks by a low dingy building that showed some dim light from the interior as they left the wagon.

"Zoll, fetch the food basket; we'll take it aboard with us. When you get hungry come and eat." Jane told him, and he proceeded to lift the basket from the wagon and hand it to Dr. George.

The conductor motioned them to hurry toward the last car. The steps were at the door, and Jane went into the dark interior. The conductor led them to a seat on the back wall that had been reserved for them. Jane went in first. The plush covering was worn, and the windows were grimy. Dr. George placed the basket at their feet, and seated himself beside Jane.

Jane's eyes adjusted to the dimness of the car and she saw that it was filled with young men and boys. Some were in assorted uniforms, some still wore the over-all's of the mountains—all carried weaponry of some sort. She saw one overgrown boy, with a knife stuck in his belt; another had a loop on his belt from which a tomahawk swung; they all had bundles of clothing and blankets. Some toted what looked like dinner buckets. Knowing mothers, Jane knew that fried chicken, cakes, and pies were packed solid in them for the beloved son, sweetheart or father, who carried the buckets.

Some of the men were asleep—sprawled down in the seats; some leaning against the wall or against their buddies.

As Jane looked at her surroundings she thought, "How many will be alive in a week?" Her heart went out to the young men who had to leave family and friends to fight a war.

With a screech of wheels on steel tracks, the train began to move. The steam from the powerful engine swirled around the windows, blocking out what view there was. Jane strained to see the last of the lights of Charleston as they picked up speed, and the town was gone. Jane, tired of leaning forward to see the passing countryside whizzing by in darkness, leaned back into the corner where they sat. The train's clickety clack, clickety clack, soon lulled her to sleep. Dr. George had also succumbed to the lulling sound of the train and snored softly.

Jane slept for some time—it was daylight when she awoke; the train was into the mountains and they were traveling at considerable speed. The silver tracks spanned deep gorges, where mountain streams plunged and roared over large rocks below sending spray and foam high into the air. Jane was fascinated with the view before her. A couple of times she was sure she had seen deer peeking from dense pine thickets. "They won't last long with soldiers forging for food," she decided with a sigh.

The train finally arrived at a small hamlet on the edge of the Carolina border. A low building served as a depot, where the train pulled to a stop. There were several men at the building, some on horseback, apparently waiting for the train to arrive. The recruits left the train and were met by the waiting soldiers, they were counted off into groups, with one of the soldiers over each group. Jane watched the rag-tag bunch as they were marched off down the railroad tracks and out of sight.

When Dr. George and Jane left the train, they saw Zoll down the track where the horses were being unloaded. He soon had the mules hitched to the wagon, and came toward them.

As they waited, an orderly came from the depot, "Chad Tanner, sir, are you Dr. Connolly? sir," he asked.

"At your service private," Dr. Connolly answered with a smile. "This is my nurse, Jane."

The Private nodded, "Mam. Come with me sir; I'll show you to your unit; is this your wagon sir?" he looked with surprise and amazement at the wagon, made into a house.

Zoll standing at the wagon, smiled at the young soldier's expression.

"That's right soldier. I have my equipment along; I'm ready for whatever is required of me," Dr. George replied.

Jane was looking right and left taking in all the action that was going on with the unloading of the train. She was amazed at all the men who had been on it—there must be at least a thousand, and a large bunch of horses were being brought down a ramp at the back end of the train. Excitement was in the air as the men called to one another over the noise of the braying mules and neighing horses. Several head of cattle were taken away by two men on horses; their mooing added to the noise and confusion.

"Let's get aboard Jane," Dr. George said.

In minutes the wagon was on its way. The private, on horse-back, took them down the railroad tracks a short way, then turned East down a dirt road. It seemed an unused rural road leading through trees and over creeks that had no bridges, and had to be forded. Fortunately, they were not deep and could be crossed without problems. They traveled through this wooded area for quite some time. Suddenly, Jane could hear what she took for thunder in the distance. "Is that thunder, Gramps?" she asked looking at her grandfather with a note of fear on her pretty face.

I'm afraid not darlin'; what you are hearing are cannon—, I'd say about ten miles away. Looks as though we will be working sooner than we thought; I was hoping we could have a good night's sleep before we saw action. Are you ready?" he looked at Jane and smiled, giving her a quick squeeze, as she nodded yes.

Topping a hill they saw the camp in a small clearing close to a stand of trees—a large tent set to one side. Jane had never seen a hospital in the field before; she knew that was what she was looking at. She could hear yelling and moaning as they neared; her heart raced and the blood drained from her face. "This is it.'" she said to herself. "Can I do it?" She was nodding to herself when her grandfather looked toward her.

Zoll brought the wagon to a halt, "You'll do; don't think about it; I'll be right beside you." He knew Jane was scared—he was himself, and he had an idea what it would be.

The private dismounted and hurried into the smaller tent which he had said was the operating tent; it was separate from the large one, where the patients were. He soon came back with a tall thin man, who had a bloody apron over his clothes. "This is Dr.. William Fugate, Dr. Connolly, and his nurse. He shook hands with Dr. George. "I'll be leaving now. Good luck sir; mam," he said as he rode away.

"Welcome Doctor I'm glad to have you aboard; when you get settled, I can use some help, if you're up to it after your trip here; you too, miss, excuse me I'll have to get back—they are piling up on me," he said as he hurried back to his work.

Zoll had looked around the compound and had decided to park the wagon on the east side of the tents—any smells would blow the other way—and the noise wouldn't be so noticeable. He pulled in close to a big low-branched pine tree, it would afford some privacy for the doctor and Jane. The spring was close too; there had been a privy built from small logs over the branch from the spring—it was situated about three hundred feet from the spring itself. When Zoll got the wagon level to his satisfaction, he unhooked the mules, and would be taking them to the corral where the other horses were.

Jane pulled her trunk from under the seat and took out her rubber apron; her grand father was sorting his instruments to take into the operating tent. He had his big white rubber apron on too. "Ready, darlin'? let's see if we can be of any help."

When they entered the operating tent, the smell of blood, urine, and turpentine, was overpowering. A rough table had been set up for Dr. Connolly. Dr. Fugate looked up and nodded toward the other table. A flat-top stove stood to one side with pans of boiling water; Jane hurriedly placed the tools of doctoring into one of the pans. By the time she lifted them from the scalding water, Dr. George had a young boy on the table, slitting his pants leg to the thigh, where there was a bullet wound; seeing the bullet was lodged close to the bone, "probe," he said to Jane, as he handed a small swatch of cotton saturated with ether to her. She held it under the nose of the moaning, thrashing boy. He was soon fast asleep, as Dr. George probed for the bullet; Jane had forceps handy for Dr. George; when it was extracted, he threw it into a tub at the end of the table. Jane hurried cleaning the wound and applied a clean dressing; she hardly finished when two orderlies grabbed the boy by the legs and the shoulders and took him toward the large tent. Two more orderlies had another patient ready for the table before she could clean the blood from it.

Dr. George took time to wash the blood from his hands and dip them into a pan of water laced with turpentine before tackling the new case.

Jane cleaned the instruments—sterilizing them as quickly as possible. This wound was more serious than the one before—the arm had been shattered below the elbow. She looked at her grandfather as he quickly examined it. "It'll have to come off," he said, as he raised his eyes to Jane. "Saw, clamps," he ordered. Jane hurried to the stove and extracted the bone saw, where it boiled in the pan. Laying it on a clean towel she brought it to the table, quickly applying the ether-soaked pad to the patient's nose and mouth—his whimpering and moving stopped, the saw had cooled enough for the amputation. Dr. George poured a weakened solution of water and turpentine over the area, marking where the cut would be. He looked at Jane. "Ready?" he asked, as he motioned the two orderlies to hold the man steady.

Jane had never helped with an amputation before; she fought against faintness and the urge to close her eyes. The young man still moaned, even though she knew he had enough ether that he wouldn't feel the saw. She pressed the swatch of cotton to his face again to make sure. She looked at her grandfather as he took a scalpel and made an incision where the arm would end. He motioned for Jane to help staunch the flow of blood as he clamped the arteries. She quickly mopped the blood from the incision, as the doctor inserted the saw. The men holding the patient looked away as the saw grated into the bone and suddenly the hand and lower portion of the arm dropped into the tub with a thud; the flap of skin that was left on the underside was brought up and folded neatly around the stub. Jane wet a small swatch in turpentine and wiped around the folded skin, as Dr. George sewed it together. Jane applied a bandage, and she had hardly finished when he was whisked from the table. Hour after hour the men appeared on the table, treated and taken to the recovery tent— Jane lost count of how many. The weariness had begun to creep over her, her back ached—the smell of blood and either made her nauseous. She looked at Gramps, he looked ready to drop, but carefully treated each man as though he was the first of the day. The orderlies removed another man; Dr. George stood waiting; no more appeared on the table. Jane was at the stove cleaning his instruments. She looked up to find the table empty. "That's it for a while," Dr. Fugate said. "Get some rest while you can. You did a good job there young lady," he said to Jane as she returned to the table. "I'll have the orderlies clean up the table while you rest. Both of you go now; we may have to call you again at anytime." He turned from them, going to his tent to rest also.

Jane almost staggered as she made her way to their wagon. "This sure looks like heaven," she said to her grandfather, as she stretched out on one of the bunks. She had hardly lay down until she was asleep. Dr. George lost no time himself; he lowered himself to his bed. He was so weary he didn't think he could relax enough to sleep, his soft snores were heard in an instant.

🎗 Chapter Twelve 🎗

Jane was sleeping soundly when the sound of screaming jerked her upright in her bunk. Looking around in the darkness she couldn't remember where she was until she heard snoring, and realized that it was her grandfather on the other bunk. She swung her feet to the floor and finding her shoes quickly pulled them on. Being as quiet as possible so as not to waken her grandfather, knowing he was exhausted and needed his rest, she hurried from the wagon and found that the screams were coming from the large tent that held the wounded. Lanterns hung in trees by the tents and threw a dim light around the area. She quickly went toward the light, and as she got closer the screams became loud and urgent. Going into the tent she saw orderlies moving between the cots of the wounded.

Going to the cot where the screams were coming from, she felt the bandaged head of the soldier, "Mom, mom, I can't see, stay with me mom I hurt so, mom." Jane took the young man's hand, "It's all right son. Go to sleep. You will feel better in the morning." Squatting beside the cot she began to hum a lullaby,

"Go to sleep little boy, go to sleep." The soldier quieted; the thrashing and turning stopped as he seemed to relax. Jane tested him for fever. He was warm but didn't seem to have a fever. He's just scared Jane decided. He looked as though he had a head and eye injuries. She didn't remember his being on Gramp's table; if she had applied the bandages she would have remembered. She continued to hum to him until she felt he was sleeping. She placed his hand on his chest and pulled the blanket up to his chin, tucking it in around his body.

Jane walked between the cots, feeling heads and seeing that the blankets were covering the patients; one boy had his eyes open watching her.

"Can't you sleep?" she asked him.

"I hurt so!" he said. "It's my leg and foot."

Pulling up the blanket Jane saw that the leg had been amputated just above the knee. "I'll bring you something that will help you sleep she told him."

Jane went to the operating tent where the medicines were kept. Opening a bottle of whiskey, she poured an inch in a cup, added some honey and water and stirred it till it was dissolved. Taking it back she lifted the young man's head and held the cup to his lips, "Drink this, you will sleep like a baby and the pain will go away; now that wasn't so bad was it?" she asked smiling as she lowered him to the cot and tucked the covers around him.

"God bless you; are you an angel?" he wanted to know, "I was thinking of my mother and wishing she were here; she would make the pain go away; and there you were—you must be an angel!" Jane giggled softly, "I'm afraid not, just someone who wants you to get better. Now close your eyes, I'll sing to you till you're asleep." She knelt and began humming the lullaby as she had to the other young boy.

Jane made the rounds of the other cots not seeing anyone else who seemed to be awake; she pulled up a blanket or two on the way; then silently left the tent going back to the wagon where her grandfather still slept.

There were no more interruptions and Jane slept till the stirring of the camp at daybreak awoke her. When she looked over, she saw that her grandfather had already gotten up and gone. She hurried out of bed, washing her face in cold water from the bucket that sat on the little stove; they hadn't needed a fire yet and she was used to cold water for morning washing anyway. Combing her hair and braiding it, she was soon ready for the day. Just as she finished, Zoll knocked on the door of the wagon.

"I've brought your breakfast Jane; Dr. George is in the tent checking the wounded. He says for you to eat and come to the operating tent as the wagons are arriving with the night's wounded." Zoll handed a plate and steaming cup of coffee to Jane.

Pushing the bucket of water to the back of the little stove, she set the cup of coffee on a corner; sitting on the bunk she held the plate on her lap as she hurriedly ate the scrambled eggs, hot grits, and bread. When she was finished she took the tin plate and cup with her to drop off at the cook tent.

When Jane arrived at the tent she saw that her grandfather was already working at the operating table where a young boy lay with blood running down his face, and whimpering like a small hurt animal.

121

Jane hurried to clean the blood from his face and head, with a cloth dipped in warm water.

Dr. George said, "I don't think he's hurt bad. Looks like a bullet grazed him on the temple; he's a little out of his head though. You can put a dressing on, and pour some carbolic acid on the wound; there is a jug diluted over there." Jane hurried to do his bidding and the orderlies removed the patient.

From the look of things, today wouldn't be any different than it had been yesterday; each time a wounded man was removed another took his place, seeming to come in spurts. Jane was surprised that they hadn't had to work through the night; she was sure the time would come when that would be the case.

Another table had been added to the tent. Those who just needed cleaning and dressing of wounds were lifted to it. The orderly could help the doctor, and Jane was put in charge of cleaning and bandaging and deciding if the doctor was needed. This made for a quicker, more efficient, turnover and more men could be taken care of faster.

There was a lull around two in the afternoon; Jane and Dr. George went to the mess tent for hot coffee and something to eat. When they were through Dr. Connolly said, "You go rest Jane, I'll take a look at our patients." He went to the recovery tent to make the rounds of the cots; it seemed that all the patients had made it through the night. The orderlies kept a watch over them, and would call the doctor if it was necessary. The men were all brave, and didn't want to bother the doctor when they knew how busy he was saving lives.

Dr. George soon joined Jane in the wagon. Removing his shoes and the linen coat he wore over his clothes, he stretched out on the cot. The wagon was cozy, with the sun shining down warming it, and he soon slept.

There was no work for them for about three hours. Jane was washing out a pair of her woolen stockings when Dr. Connolly awoke.

"What time is it, Jane?" he asked as he yawned and stretched.

"It's six o'clock; there hasn't been any wagons for a while. I'm glad you had a nice rest; do you feel rested, Gramps?"

"I feel much rested; how about you?" He looked at his granddaughter thinking, "I'm certainly glad I have her with me; she has helped to save many lives; I couldn't have done half as much without her. She seems to know just how to take hold and do what was needed without being told. "Have I told you today that I love you, granddaughter?" he asked with a smile.

"As to your first question, I'm fine; feel refreshed and ready to go again. And no, you haven't told me. Thank you very much; I love you too, Gramps. Now I have a question; are you sorry I came along?" She looked at him with a teasing smile.

"I was just thinking Jane, you have helped save many more lives than I could have alone; I'm glad you are along, I would miss you more than I can say if you weren't here. Thank you for insisting on coming " He gave her an affectionate smile.

Suddenly, the sound of cannon booming in the distance stopped the flow of their conversation.

"Looks like we'll soon be busy again Jane," Dr. George said as he tilted his head listening to the cannon. "Let's go by the mess tent and get something to eat, at least some hot coffee; we may not eat again tonight." Dr. George left the wagon as Jane hung her stockings to dry, and followed.

When Jane reached the Mess, her grandfather had a plate of food for her and a cup of coffee. They sat at one of the long tables and ate, knowing that soon there would be blood and suffering before them.

They sat sipping their coffee and talking for perhaps half an hour when the sound of wagons careening into the compound brought them to their feet and they hurried to the operating tent.

The first two patients that were laid on the table were mangled beyond recognition. It took only a moment for Dr. Connolly to motion the orderlies to remove them; they were beyond help. Tears sprang to Jane's eyes as she watched them being removed.

The tub at the end of the operation table had been emptied twice of the ravages of war, before the night was through. Dr. Connolly, and Jane were pale with fatigue. Jane was weak with exhaustion as she looked toward her grandfather. He was so old she knew he was worse off than she was. "Gramps, you must rest; you go on to the wagon, I'll finish any bandaging and cleaning up there will be. The cannons have stopped, there shouldn't be any more tonight."

"You come as soon as you finish with the one you're working on now; I don't want you fainting during an operation." he told her, staggering slightly as he left the tent.

Jane placed all the operating equipment in the big pan on the stove to boil, and straightened up the medical supplies. Going over to the orderly, "We need more bandages and ether from the supply wagon; will you bring them and just lay them on the table? I'll put them away when I return," she told him as she went to the recovery tent to check on the patients. She hurried along the cots feeling heads, checking bandages for bleeding; finding things in good order she went to the wagon to rest.

The sound of cannon brought Jane upright in her bed. Either the wind was blowing the sound toward them or the cannon were nearer; she heard a commotion in the compound, hurrying to get dressed, she saw that her grandfather was awakening, too.

"Gramps, I think the cannons are getting closer, hurry Gramps, I think we may be in danger." Jane told him as she rushed outside to see what was taking place.

A corporal galloped into the compound, "The Rebels are coming," he said to Dr. Fugate who met him. "The hospital will have to be moved to a safer location right away the Sergeant said. Are there enough men here to get you to a safer location?" he asked looking anxiously around.

"How far away are the Rebels?" Dr. Fugate calmly asked.

"Not far; I think not more than five miles; you can hear the cannon." He turned in his saddle looking wildly back the way he had come, as though expecting to see them on his heels.

Dr. Connolly, just arriving heard the news. "Have you had to move before Dr. Fugate, What are the procedure?" he asked.

"We've only moved once before; there weren't as many wounded as we have now, and we had plenty of time. I'm afraid we don't have much time now; of course the Federals may hold them for a while. We best get rolling however." Dr. Fugate sent the orderly to bring the others for instructions. "Jane, you go to the recovery tent; any who can walk, get them up; one of the orderlies can take them on ahead while we load the others. Get the wagons ready," he called. Doctor George you and I will pack the medicines and implements." Dr. Fugate began wrapping and packing the things into large wooden crates that stood around the tent. After watching Dr. Fugate for a minute, Dr. George saw how things were done, and hurried with the storing and packing as fast as he could.

Jane entering the big tent asked, "How many of you feel up to going for a walk?" There were groans from some of the beds, while others began getting off their cots knowing what was coming. "Each of you take your blanket, wrap it around your shoulders, put your shoes and socks on, and any extra clothing you have. I don't know how far you will have to walk; in fact I have no idea how far we may have to go. Don't say you can walk if you can't; We have enough heroes now. If you get too tired, or sick, some of the wagons will pick you up; get ready as soon as you can. If you are still bleeding from a wound let me know and I will take a look to make sure you can walk. When you are ready, go to the front entrance of the tent; an orderly will accompany you, starting ahead while the wagons are being loaded; if you have to drop out they can pick you up. Does everyone understand?" Several nodded as Jane was called to one and then another of those who were showing blood on their bandages. "You, and you can walk; your wound won't be bothered by movement; you, stay for the wagon," she told a tall blond young man with a leg wound. Soon the occupants of the tent were separated. About forty were able to walk without problems; there were well over a hundred in the tent altogether. She wondered how they could ever get enough wagons to carry them all with the tents and equipment too.

The wagons began to line up. The worse cases were lifted and carried to the wagons. Jane saw that there had been platforms built to make two layers in each wagon; canvas was stretched over the hooped wagons. They were loading the big wagons from the front and the rear, four men fit tightly together in the wagon bed, feet to feet, their heads toward the outside. She saw that each wagon took sixteen men. The first wagon rolled out on the route that the walking wounded had taken; the next wagon was in position. The sound of cannon-fire seemed to be getting closer. "Hurry men," she told them as she quickly checked each soldier, before they were loaded, making sure they were as comfortable as possible, with folded blankets under the amputees. There wasn't much she could do but comfort them.

The big tent was being struck; the hospital tent was already down. Dr. George had taken some of the medicine and his bag of instruments to their wagon. Zoll was helping load and take down the tents; he had the mules hooked to their wagon ready to go. The cook tent was stored on a big wagon; the camp began to look deserted as the last wagon was loaded.

"Dr. George, you and Jane pull out before the tent wagons do."

Dr. George decided to mount his riding mare for the trip; "I'll go on ahead to the wounded convoy," he told Jane as he took off after the forward wagons. He wanted to look after the wounded and make sure they weren't injured any worse than they already were.

Jane was glad to sit on the wagon seat beside Zoll, and let her hands rest in her lap. It had been a worrisome task, seeing all the wounded lifted aboard the rough wagons. "I'll be surprised if half of them live; it would have been doubtful even in bed, without being jolted along this rutted track," she said with tears in her eyes just thinking about it. She looked at Zoll who sat watching the road and skillfully handling the mules; what a blessing he had been to them.

Jane could hear the boom of the big guns which seemed to be getting closer and closer even with the wagon train moving as fast as it could; she was worried they might be overtaken. If they were, what would happen to all the men and boys who were just hanging on to life by a thread? "It's so unfair." She told Zoll. "The soldiers have fought gallantly and now have to run for their lives; there will be some who won't make it; they are so sick." There were tears running down Jane's face which she wiped angrily away with one hand.

"Don't you worry missy; we'll get them all safe. If this keeps up I may have to take a gun and roust the Rebels myself," he said as he smiled at her, trying to lift her spirits.

Over the rattle and creak of the wagon, Jane thought she heard a fast approaching rider; turning she tried to see around the house that was built on their wagon. She couldn't lean far enough around the side to see anything. Soon a sergeant came alongside on a large roan horse, "Speed it up he called; the Rebels are advancing; move up, don't straggle," he called as he went ahead at a fast clip.

Zoll slapped the reins on the mules's backs, urging them to a faster pace. They soon were close to the tail gate of the wagon in front of them; the wagon train picked up speed, heeding the sergeant's warning. They had been on the trail for an hour or more. Jane judged they had traveled more than five mile. However the sound of cannon seemed to be advancing as fast as they were.

Suddenly, the wind picked up and it began to get colder. Looking up at the sky, Jane could see slate-colored clouds scuttling overhead, seeming to be settling in the northwest; in the direction they were headed, and she knew that the clouds were full of snow. She thought of the sick men ahead and hoped that the orderlies had put extra blankets over them when they were loaded. She would miss her guess if they wouldn't end up with some of the wounded with quick consumption; if they did, there wasn't anything anyone could do especially under these conditions.

The wagons kept to a steady pace, traveling faster than when they had started out. Zoll couldn't go any faster than the wagon in front. He had settled back and didn't seem to mind, guiding the mules and keeping a safe distance from the wagon ahead. Thank God for Zoll; what she and her Gramps would have done without him looking after them, she didn't know. There was little conversation; the sound of cannon and the noise of so many wagons, one had to almost yell to be heard. Jane sat thinking to herself and her concern on the welfare of her patients. They hadn't seen her grandfather since starting out; she hoped that he wasn't in any trouble up ahead. She smiled to herself, thinking that she seemed the older as she tried to see that he didn't overwork. She was like a mother hen where her Gramps was concerned.

The wagons had been traveling for several hours. Jane's back had begun to ache from the bouncing and swaying of the wagon; She was tired and wondered when they would find a safe place to set up the tents again. It seemed that they had traveled miles. "Do you think we will stop soon, Zoll? Seems that the cannons sound farther away now, don't you think?"

"They do seem to be farther away, or they just aren't shooting them as often; I would say we have come at least ten miles. We can't get too far ahead of the fighting men or it will take too long to get the wounded to the doctors. I would imagine that we will stop soon. The sergeant hasn't returned; he'll probably help find a fit spot; it would be nice if we could hit a railroad and send some of the wounded we have to a hospital. We'll have snow tonight; there's no heat in the recovery tent; that isn't good for sick people." Zoll cracked the lines on the rump of the mules seeing they had a space between them and the wagon ahead.

Zoll had hardly stopped talking when the first snowflakes began to fall in a thick shower.

"Oh, how pretty," Jane remarked, as she lifted her face toward them.

"It won't be pretty long; this will make the roads a quagmire in a short time; Maybe wagons getting stuck, too. I'm sure the drivers aren't looking forward to a deep snow; We are close to the mountains; it could be a big one; it's coming down in earnest now." Zoll looked around at the snow clinging to trees and bushes.

Jane shook the clinging snow from her shawl and pulled it closer to her neck crossing the corners across her breast. She couldn't afford to catch a cold—then she couldn't help with the sick if she were sick herself. She pulled a toboggan cap she had brought over her head; at the rate the snow was falling she knew it wouldn't be dry for long.

It took no time at all for the snow to cover the downed leaves in a thick layer—only the wagon tracks ahead remained clear; the wet snow soon began to turn the trail to mud as the wagons churned it into a quagmire. The front wagons were beginning to slow, and suddenly ground to a halt. After a few minutes Zoll said, "I think they may have found a camp, I hope so; it won't be easy to get the tents set in this weather. We will have to have a fire for the wounded even if we have to find a farmhouse and raid it for a stove; they'll die on a night such is coming on us." Jane nodded knowing he was right.

The wagons moved slowly on; finally they came in sight of where they were going to set up the tents. Zoll pulled to the side so the tent-wagons could pass him. He looked around and found a place close to some trees where he would put the Doctor's wagon.

"As soon as I can, I'll pull in over there. I think we will be out of the way, and the wind won't be so strong under those trees. You're lucky, you have a stove. Thank God, Dr. George thought to get one in Charleston before leaving."

Jane sat watching the big tent being raised; as soon as the poles were set, the orderlies started to set up the cots. There was snow over everything; one of the men was trying to sweep the wet snow-covered leaves from the tent area without much success. The wounded were beginning to be brought in. Jane turned to Zoll, "I'll have to get into the wagon; I want to change into warmer shoes, and I think it is a good time for my new outfits." She smiled at Zoll as she climbed down; he could hear the door open in the back and hear Jane moving around in the wagon house.

Jane brought out the boys clothes she had bought at the store; they were warm flannel-like material, with the heavy bloomers her mother made her underneath—she would be kept warm. She also put on extra wool stockings and the pair of boys shoes she had bought. She came out of the wagon and Zoll gave her a second look before he was sure it was Jane.

"I sure do feel comfortable; I may never wear a dress again— I'm warm as toast. I'm going over to see if I can help with the wounded; they are freezing I know." She went sliding along, the boys shoes awkward on her small feet. The tent already had an inch of snow on it as she approached; they had the sides anchored down and the flaps closed. Pulling the door flap open, Jane entered. It was a sorry sight before her; there was a stack of blankets on an empty cot. She took one look at the shivering men, and going to the first cot she tucked an extra blanket in around the soldier, he was the one with the bandaged head and eyes that she had comforted the night before. She brought another blanket and folding it tucked it around him. Going from cot to cot she covered the shaking men with the extra blankets until they were all gone. She saw her grandfather at the other side of the tent—he was working over someone it seemed. She saw him tuck the blankets around his patient and head toward her.

"They're freezing Gramps; what are we going to do?" She had tears in her eyes as she looked at her grandfather.

"Is that you, darlin'? I thought for a moment that one of my patients had gotten up." He smiled at her as he put an arm around her shoulders. "I'll send Zoll and some men out to the closest settlement; they'll have to find a stove for in here. It won't do much good to operate on them and then have them freeze to death." He had hardly finished speaking when Zoll came toward him.

"Dr. George, do you want me to go forging for a stove? I'll need to take someone with me, and I need a wagon." Zoll looked intently at the doctor.

"I'll find someone; you wait here." Dr. George went to the back of the tent where he talked to one of the orderlies; they saw him nodding his head as Dr. George motioned for Zoll to come to him. Jane was checking the sick and didn't see Zoll leave. She knew that somehow they would take care of all the wounded who lay depending on them.

The men who were well enough to walk had built a big fire outside the tent. Jane could feel the warmth through the tent when she went over on the side where the fire was built. "Now why didn't I think of that? Mamma always put stones to our feet when we were sick," she said out loud to herself as she hurried outside. Going over to one of the stronger-looking ones; with bandages she said, "Would you boys go along the stream over there and pick up some good-size rocks and heat them in the fire? Our wounded are freezing; we have to get them warm. All the men who felt able headed for the creek, some carrying large buckets that the horses drank from. They were soon back and laying the wet rocks onto the coals sending steam up through the trees overhead. It was nice to stand close to the fire, turning to warm each side. Jane's hands had been so cold she could hardly hold anything; she was beginning to thaw out; she had been moving around and must be warmer than those who were on the cots. The wind could go right through the canvas bottoms and there was no way they could keep warm no matter how many blankets were piled on them.

The rocks were soon hot and one of the men brought a bucket full into the tent.

"Miss Jane, what should I do with these?" he asked.

"Do you think you can find some feed sacks? We will wrap them and put them in the cots—that will get the cold ones warm soon enough." She smiled as the young man hurried out and was soon back with an armload of sacks.

"Can you wrap them for me?" He brought her several at a time where she stood by the cots. Jane placed a stone at the feet and a couple up about the waist of the ones who were shivering the most.

"Have more heated; we will put buckets of hot stones all through between the cots; that will take the chill off. We'll have it comfortable in here in no time." Several were working with her now. The boys that she had placed the hot stones around were beginning to drop off to sleep. Steam was rising from the wet ground where the buckets of hot stones had been set.

The wagons that had transported the wounded to the new compound had returned to the battle area, and were returning with wounded. Dr. George sent for Jane; the wounded were numerous and badly in need of care. When Jane entered the operating tent, she could see that everyone was working as quickly as they could. Gramps had a bleeding soldier on the table; blood was spurting almost to the next table.

"Help me clamp off this artery—it just broke loose." Jane hurried to help. The patient was unconscious; Dr. George worked quickly suturing the wound; Jane poured the ever handy carbolic acid over the wound, and wound a bandage around it. The orderlies removed him and placed another onto the table. Some Dr. Connolly waved aside—it was no use to spend time on the ones who wouldn't live regardless of what he did; he would work on the ones that had a chance. They worked for what Jane thought was hours; ·she had lost count of the time as one after another bloody man was laid on the table.

The flow of wounded ground to a halt. Dr. Connolly washing hands said, "I think that will be it for a time, Jane. Did men return with a stove yet?"

"No, not yet Gramps. I've been heating rocks and putting around the worse cases. I've had the men bring in buckets of hot stones to set around inside the tent—that seems to be warming and drying it."

"Good girl! I should have thought of that myself; that's how the Indians tend their ill; "I'm afraid we will lose some if we can't get them to a hospital soon. I've sent the Sergeant to see if we can get a train to ship them north."

The snow was still coming down as Jane left the operating tent. She and her grandfather together went to the recovery tent where it seemed much warmer.

Zoll and another man were setting up a big pot-belly stove toward the center, a stovepipe was put in place, and a hole cut in the tent top for it. "Keep a wet sack or something around that pipe Zoll, we don't want a fire," Dr. George told him. "Yes sir, I'll do that," Zoll answered.

The pipe was hardly in place when two men came with two shovels full of live coals and another with an armload of wood. In no time a fire roared in the big stove, sending out heat throughout the big tent. Jane nodded, "they will be warm now." She went around each cot, touching, saying a cheery word to those who were awake. Dr. George took her arm. "It's time you got warm yourself and had some food and rest. You can't keep this up or you will be a patient. Come, I'll go with you; things seem under control here; the orderlies can manage now.

The snow was still coming down. The roadway where the wagons came and went was becoming a mud-hole—getting deeper with each trip; snow lay on the tent roof three inches deep. Going to the Mess Tent, each ate a bowl of hot soup and then went to their little house on their wagon; to sleep while they could.

❧ Chapter Thirteen ❧

The sound of activity throughout the compound awoke Jane. She listened for a few minutes, and then decided to get dressed and see what was going on. She seemed to recuperate much faster than her grandfather. She knew that he still slept when she heard his gentle snoring; glancing toward him she quietly opened the door and went outside.

As Jane walked toward the lantern-lighted tents, she saw several wagon teams pulled in close to the big tent. Holding her shawl around her as she stood looking, she decided it was early morning—no more than four o'clock. She wondered what was going on as she walked toward the tent. Entering she saw that the wounded were being wrapped in blankets and loaded aboard the wagons.

"What's going on? Are we moving again?" she asked one of the orderlies, who was helping get the wounded ready to be moved.

"There's a train due early this morning which will take the wounded to a northern hospital, and we don't have much time to get them to the pick-up area." He continued working as he talked.

"What can I do to help?" she asked.

"If you will you can check the bandages, see if any are bleeding too much to move, and replace what bandages you think need it—you will find plenty over on that bunk in the corner." He finished wrapping a wounded man and the orderlies took him to be loaded aboard the wagon.

Jane worked as fast as she could, motioning to the orderlies that certain ones were ready. It was a God-send that they were being sent to a hospital and there wouldn't be so many to look after; it was a problem just seeing that they had hot food. The orderlies and the soldiers who were well enough to helped; Some of the orderlies were taken from other jobs to hurry the loading.

As the last man was loaded, the Sergeant who supervised the moving before came hurrying into the compound on his horse.

"Now what?" Jane said to herself as she saw him dismount.

"What is it Sergeant?" the orderly who was in charge asked.

"The medical compound has to move. The Rebels have been

driven south and we have to have the hospital and medical tents closer to the battlefield. I see you are moving the wounded out. That's good; we certainly couldn't cart them back toward our lines again; are they going to a hospital?" He looked around as he talked, watching the end wagon pull out with the last of the wounded.

"Yes, five wagonloads are headed north. We have a train coming into the next village where the wagons will meet it. It's a blessing; there were so many that we couldn't keep up with the feeding and treatment."

"Are there any who are ready to return to combat?"

Jane's heart lurched when she heard this. To send those who had been wounded back into the fighting was something that she hadn't thought about. To have the young men go through the battles again and maybe not live this time brought tears to her eyes.

"There's about twenty-five or thirty that I think could return; the Doctor will have the last say as to that. Some have been up and around for a day or two," the orderly answered. He started toward the back of the tent where the cots had to be folded and loaded, motioning to some of the walking wounded to help. A stack of cots were soon piled by the opening.

In the next thirty days the army of the north and the Rebels of the south surged back and forth across the Carolinas and Virginia, leaving destruction and ruin in their wake.

The medical teams moved first one way and then the other. They had moved so many times that they could pack and move in a matter of hours, and be ready for the next wave of wounded.

Jane packing the medicine and surgical materials, began to worry as she counted the boxes of bandages and medicines which were depleted until they were in short supply. She went to the orderly who was in charge of the supply wagon. "How much ether do we have? I will need another canister of it, and bandages, turpentine, and carbolic acid. Do we have a good supply? If not send for more." She looked at the orderly who just stood looking at her.

"We have two canisters of ether, one of carbolic acid and a gallon of turpentine. I have no idea when we will get a replacement of supplies; I'll send someone to wire the main supply office and see if we can get more; I wouldn't count on it. From what I hear there is a shortage of all medicines."

"What are we going to do? We can't operate without ether, or treat the sick without medicines;" She looked crestfallen at the orderly. "Send someone immediately for replacements. Hurry! We are heading into battle again and must have supplies."

"I've heard that in some of the areas they are having to operate without ether or any antiseptic, and washing used bandages to use again." As he looked at Jane, tears filled her eyes.

"What do they use? surely they can't chop off someone's arm or leg without anything?" Fear showed in her blue eyes. It was hard enough to see the suffering even with the help of medicine.

"Whiskey helps some; I'll see what I can do to lay in a supply of that." He turned from Jane, not wanting to see her distress, knowing what she had been through as she tended the wounded.

There must be something; think, think! she told herself. What does Mamma do for pain? What can we use for disinfecting? There's bound to be something; I'll ask Gramps, he should know something. I'll jog his memory on what the Indians use." She hurried back to the wagon.

Dr. George was just getting up from his bunk when Jane came rushing in. "Gramps, Gramps, we are moving again; they have taken all the wounded out in wagons to meet a train and be sent north to a hospital. Gramps, we are running out of ether and medicine! What are we going to do?" Her face crumpled as tears came.

Dr. George took his granddaughter in his arms, holding her and patting her back. "There, there, haven't I told you that you waste energy crying? We will find something; the thing to do in an emergency is think. Somewhere in our brain there is an answer; now think! I don't want you to try to solve a problem with tears." He gently dried her tears with a towel that lay close by.

Jane sat on the bunk; she couldn't help her sniffling as her tears abated. "I've tried to think what Mamma does for pain; can't you think of what the Indian's did?"

"Let's not cross our bridges till we have to; I'm sure we will get enough supplies. The best thing I know to do is go get a big cup of hot coffee before the pot is on its way back down the trail." He smiled as he ushered her toward the door.

Jane had to smile at her Gramps. What would he do without his hot coffee? He would think of something to use for medicine. He always seemed to know the answers and come up with a cure. The cook was pouring the last of the coffee into cups for whoever wanted it. Dr. Connolly and Jane were just in time to grab a cup; as usual the cook tent was the last to be struck. The men were dissembling it as the cook slung the last of the coffee grounds out. Dr. George and Jane went back to the wagon where Zoll was just finishing hooking up the mules ready to move out.

"All aboard" he called to them, "Get yourselves comfortable; we will be on our way in a jiffy."

Dr. Fugate had gone on ahead with the medical supply wagon, and would be there when they reached their destination to supervise the hospital tent set-up. Dr. George was thinking of what Jane had told him about the medicine shortage. He would talk to Dr. Fugate as soon as they arrived to see what was to be done. The fighting had been fierce for months now, and where the medicines were coming from to treat so many he had no idea. There was no doubt that it was getting low as much as had been used. He began raking his memory of what he had heard on wagon trains and about what the Indians used to cure their sick. There were herbs, barks, and roots, but how could they find them when the ground was frozen and no plants were up. They might get some barks, but that would be the extent of it; not knowing where plants grew, they would never find the roots that would heal. The wagon lurched and the mules lunged to draw them from the pot holes and mud that was left behind by so many wagons and horses churning the roadway. Clouds scuttled across the sky and a weak sun filtered through the leafless trees as they made their way toward the next campsite.

Suddenly Zoll brought the wagon to a halt; the wagon they were following had topped up ahead. The mules slung their heads, snorting and sending steam from their nostrils. Mud splashed on the front of the wagon as they stomped their clumsy hoofs in agitation. Zoll leaned side ways trying to see up the trail to find out what the hold-up was. The wagon ahead was piled so high with tenting that he couldn't even see the driver; they waited. The cold seemed to seep in more when they weren't moving, and they pulled their mufflers and cloaks more closely about them.

"Why don't you go inside the house, Jane? It will be warmer in the enclosure and there may still be some coals in the stove; now would be a good time while we are stopped," Dr. George said as he looked at Jane.

"I think I will; that wind is bitter. I think you should come too.

There is no reason for you to be out in the cold either Gramps."

"Would you hold the reins first?" Zoll asked looking at the Doctor. "I'll go up a ways and see what the delay is."

"Good! Maybe there's been an accident; if we're needed return and tell us." Dr. George took the reins from Zoll and held them firmly, trying to quiet the stomping restless mules.

Zoll took Jane's arm and helped her from the front wagon seat where the three had been crammed in together. "You'll be comfortable inside Jane. I'll have the Dr. join you when I come back; he doesn't need to take any more chances of becoming sick than he has to."

The first wagon ahead of Zoll didn't know any more than he did. He hurried down the line and had passed five wagons before he found what the problem was. They were fording a wide sprawling, creek and had to use two teams on some of the wagons that were heavily loaded to get them across. This took time as they had to hook and unhook each team and take the wagon across the stream and then return for the other wagon. There was nothing to do but sit and wait. All the wagons didn't need two teams, and the ones not loaded so heavily could make it on their own. The wagon driver Zoll talked to said maybe an hour or less would see them safely across.

Zoll hurried back through the mud to his wagon, and explained to Dr. George what the delay was. "Dr. I think it best you go inside and join Jane; they seem to think it will take an hour or more to ford the stream. No use you sitting out here in the wind. I have a blanket I'll put over myself, but no need for you to take the weather."

"I guess you're right, Zoll; there are enough sick now without one more," he chuckled as he climbed down the wheel and went back to join Jane in their snug little house.

"Here I am darlin'; couldn't let you back here all alone." He smiled at Jane as he saw the twinkle in her eye and a smile light her face.

"This is where you should be Gramps; no need to take chances of coming down with a cold when you don't have to. Why don't you stretch out and have a little nap while we wait? You never know what we will find when we arrive." Jane looked fondly at her grandfather, as she busied herself spreading out some rain gear for his feet to rest on so he wouldn't have to remove his muddy shoes.

She fluffed a pillow for her Gramps, and smiled as he eased his tired body down on the bunk. She covered him with a blanket and in seconds it seemed she heard his soft snoring. Looking at his relaxed features, she said, "Poor Gramps, I know how tired you must be; have a nice sleep," she kissed his cheek.

Jane opened the stove door and saw a few live coals in the ashes. She carefully placed some chips inside, just enough to keep the fire going; it would keep the chill off and she didn't think there would be any danger of catching the wagon on fire. The stove was securely bolted to the floor, and it would take a big jolt to loosen the stove pipe.

She then wrapped a quilt around herself and leaned back onto her bunk. She could hear Zoll talking to the mules to keep them under control as they waited. The chips caught and she could feel the warmth coming from the little stove; she suddenly couldn't hold her eyes open another minute and she fell into a deep sleep.

The lurch of the wagon starting up awoke Jane. For a minute she couldn't remember what had happened. Sitting up she looked at her grandfather, worrying that he might topple from the bunk. His eyes opened, and looked around the cozy little room. Seeing Jane he smiled, "That was a good nap; seems we are moving again. I feel much rested and I could use some food; how about you?" he asked.

"I doubt we will be fed soon. We have just started to move, and we still have to ford the stream ahead. Do you think we will be all right back here?" she asked.

"I don't know why not. We'll have to brace ourselves—we may be jolted around a bit. If there is danger, I'm sure Zoll will inform us. It may be a little strange not being able to see where we are going—the small windows over our beds don't give us much of a view, but I'm sure we will be just fine." With that he grabbed the leather strap that went from the fold down bunk to the ceiling and motioned for Jane to do the same.

It wasn't long before they could hear the yells of the men who were up ahead at the ford and the crack of whips as the animals lunged and pulled to clear the stream. Zoll eased their wagon over the edge of the creek which had been worn down by the other wagons. They could hear the water as it slushed through the wagon wheels and splashed the flooring; so far none had found its way through the floor. They could tell when they had reached the center by the sound of the swiftly rushing water through the wheel spokes. Jane closed her eyes and felt the pull as the mules began to clear the creek bank and were on solid ground. Opening her eyes she looked at her Gramps, "That wasn't so bad; I knew Zoll would make it easy for us." She smiled her sunny smile at her grandfather.

"No, not bad at all; Thank God for Zoll."

"I thank God every day for him and for you too, Gramps. The soldiers don't know how lucky they are to have you looking after them." Jane stretched a hand toward her grandfather touching him on the knee.

"And having you too darlin'; your smiling face has healed many of them I'm sure."

Jane looked out the small window; all she could see was lonely empty woods, barren and cold. "Wherever we're headed it doesn't look too promising. I can't even see a barn or field; it certainly is rugged desolate country." She sat looking out as the wagon lurched from side to side—sometimes over a stone buried in the mud that seemed to jar their teeth.

The time passed slowly; all they had to do was hold on while the wagon moved along behind the others. They could hear muffled voices as the drivers called to each other or gave their team commands. Sometimes Jane heard the drivers cussing their animals for stumbling or for laying on the traces and not pulling their share of the load. She saw that her grandfather was relaxed and swayed with the wagon as it moved along.

Jane's stomach had been growling for some time when the wagon train began slowing, then moved ahead again. Hearing loud shouting she looked out the small window and could see the Sergeant riding toward them giving the wagon drivers orders. She turned to Dr. Connolly, "I think we have reached where we are going; seems there is a cleared space ahead, and looks as though there have been troops here." She craned her neck this way and that to watch what she could as their wagon moved toward the side of the main row of wagons.

Dr. Connolly was also looking from the other window on his side. "I think you're right; we have arrived. They are already staking out the tents and I can see wounded laying in the woods on pieces of canvas. Get ready darlin', our work is about to began." Dr. Connolly heaved a sigh as he told her.

Zoll maneuvered the wagon under a large tree; big rocks stuck up where he was headed—some as tall as a house. He took the wagon as close as he could to them—always trying to find a place where he felt was safe for his charges, and where he could have the wagon as level as possible.

Dr. Connolly opened the door as soon as the wagon came to a stop and tilted out the step that was attached to the back on hinges and was lifted inside when the door was closed. He stepped from the wagon and looked around at the work going on as the tents were hurriedly assembled. He saw that Dr. Fugate was supervising the operating tent. In minutes the tables were removed from a wagon and carried inside. The two doctors met and began getting ready for the wounded that were soon to be brought into their work area.

Jane could hear the sound of a saw and knew wood was being cut to start the big stove in the tents. The cook tent would soon be in working order; they wouldn't get food for a while and would have to start on the wounded before eating. "Oh well, we will live. I doubt the wounded have been fed either," she said as she prepared to go to the operating area.

Jane hurried across the area between their wagon and the operating tent. How thankful she was for her boy shoes and the warm britches she had thought to bring. The stove was up and a bucket of water brought as the fire was started. Jane found the sterile instruments she had wrapped in a clean sheet before packing them. She would have liked to boil them again, but from the looks of things there wouldn't be time. She mixed a few drops of turpentine in a pan of water for the doctors to wash in. The wounded were being brought in to the tables. Jane didn't turn to look but could hear the moans of those who would be first. She held out a towel for the two doctors to use. She turned to Dr. Connolly and he motioned for her to cut away the soiled bandages that had been applied in the field. A gaping hole as big as her fist, full of clotted blood and dirt, high in the right shoulder was what she found; no doubt a musket ball was still embedded in the wound. Quickly cleaning it with warm water containing a few drops of carbolic acid, she stepped back for the Doctor to examine it. He took a probe and soon dropped a half inch lead ball into the pan she held. "Move him to the next table; Jane, wash the wound and bandage it." She followed the two orderlies and began applying the dressing.

One after another bloody soldiers followed for what seemed hours—some in such bad shape that nothing could be done to save them; they were moved where they could be covered and kept warm until the end. Jane's heart went out to each of them. When her duties let up she washed faces and held hands, talking softly to the condemned young men.

It was getting dark when her grandfather came to take her away to the cook tent for their evening meal. "I can't eat Gramps, I'm so tired and sick over those we can't help," tears streamed down her face.

"Come darlin'; you need hot food; you're making yourself sick— it won't help them. You have to keep your strength up to help those we can." He led her to a table and had someone bring her a plate of food. His cure all was hot coffee, and he drank a cup before touching his plate of food.

The hot beans and cornbread tasted wonderful, and Jane thinking she couldn't eat soon was on a second helping. "That sure tasted good Gramps, thanks. You always know what is best for me." Jane's face now had some color in it.

"I want you to go to the wagon and have a hot bath and go to bed—you've earned it; I'm sure Zoll will have water heating for you. Now scat, I'll be there in half an hour." He looked fondly on his granddaughter as she rose from the table.

Jane washed herself in a warm sudsy pan of water, and put on one of the long flannel night dresses that her mother had made for her. "Oh, that feels delicious," she said as she climbed into her bed, so weary she could hardly cover herself with the blanket; in minutes she was sound asleep.

The rumble of the big guns had halted; after a conference with Dr. Fugate about the lack of medical supplies, Dr. Connolly took himself off to the wagon to snatch some sleep while there was a lull in the fighting.

* * *

Dawn broke to the sound of field artillery; the distant roar of the big guns jarred the ground where the wagon sat. Jane awoke to the distant rumble. "We must be close to the front," she said to herself. "I hope we don't have to move again today; I'm just too tired," then felt ashamed of herself, thinking of the young men out in the cold crawling through mud with no place to sleep even when they had a chance. Some weren't even dressed for such cold weather. Tears dimmed her eyes; her heart broke over the soldiers. "Why can't this war be over! I'm so weary of it; when will it end? When can we go home?" Jane wanted her mamma more than anything at this moment.

The big guns continued, seeming to be nearer. At times Jane thought she could hear the shells when they dropped near by. "I must be mistaken; we couldn't be that near the front lines," she said to herself.

Suddenly a rider came rushing in, his horse splattered with mud as he raced to the hospital tent and skidded to a stop. Throwing himself from his horse he hurried inside. "Dr. Fugate Dr. Fugate, you have to move, the lines are surging this way; we can't hold them; I doubt you will have time to get the wounded out. Hurry! Hurry!" He turned and headed back to his horse, mounted and hurried away.

Dr. Connolly looked toward the table where Dr. Fugate was in the middle of an amputation. "What can we do?" he asked.

"You and Jane head out with whoever is going to a safe area. I can't stop now—this man will die." He continued the operation seeming unconcerned by the confusion around him.

Zoll, always close by to help Jane and the doctor, hurried away to hook up his team to the doctor's wagon. In ten minutes he had the wagon beside the operating tent; he hurried inside; Jane was directing the removal of some of the wounded. Wagons had been readied as quickly as possible; only a few were loading wounded and going at a spine jarring rush toward safety.

"Jane, take the ether and medicine as quickly as you can and put in our wagon. Hurry!" her grandfather ordered. Jane handed the medicines that she had haphazardly thrown into boxes to Zoll who stored them in the wagon. The instruments were rolled quickly into towels; as fast as she got things ready Zoll took them to their wagon.

"What about our patients? They will be taken prisoners if we leave them." She looked at her grandfather.

A shell exploded nearby, not far from the tent. "You go with Zoll; I'll ride the mare and be along directly." He motioned for Zoll to leave with Jane.

Turning to look at the soldiers that had just been operated on, Jane shook her head. The wagons weren't being loaded fast enough to get them all out. Turning to an orderly she said, "take that young man and that one; load them in our wagon." At least she could save two of them. Seeing that Jane was determined to save them Zoll hurried to help; he got into the wagon and helped to lift the two wounded soldiers and lay them on the bunk beds. He tucked the blankets that covered them under the mattress hoping that it would hold them firmly for the mad dash he knew he would have to make to get Jane out of harm's way.

The mess tent which usually was left till last was almost down. The tents would have to be saved or there would be nowhere for them to work and take care of the wounded.

Jane looked over her shoulder and called to Dr. Connolly, "Gramps come with us," as she rushed toward the wagon with Zoll holding her arm hurrying her along, half carrying her as he lifted her into the wagon and lifted the step and slammed the door.

In seconds the wagon was jolting along the rutted road following the wagons that had already left. Zoll talking to the mules encouraged them to all the speed that he could.

Jane could still hear the big guns rumbling in the distance; they sounded too close for comfort. She sat on the edge of one of the bunks trying to hold on to both of the soldiers to keep them from rolling onto the floor from the narrow beds. Both of them had either fainted or were still out due to the ether administered for their operations. She took their pulse as they careened along in the jolting wagon. One seemed to flutter now and then—the other seemed fairly strong. "Oh, God I hope they make it. I've done all I can for you, she said as she patted the tightly wrapped young men; please don't die on me." She thought of her Gramps; why didn't he come with them? He could be killed staying behind, then who would look after her? She knew he would be sensible and leave before it was too late. Tears ran down her cheeks. Gramps always told her that tears "wouldn't solve anything," but she just couldn't help from crying. She was so tired of the war, the cold, the pain she saw the young men suffering. She had been with Gramps for over three years, with one trip home to see her family. Gramps hadn't gone even one time. How could Grandma stand it so long without him?

Jane carefully raised up to peer through the small window. She could see only a small stretch of the road behind them. There were wagons piled haphazardly with tents rocking from side to side over the muddy road. There was no sign of her Gramps.

Suddenly there was an explosion, so near it rocked the wagon. "Oh, God! Don't let Gramps be hurt!" She tried to look back again; she could see smoke in the distance toward where their camp had been. "Oh, No! It looked as though the camp was being shelled; they couldn't all have gotten out in time. Zoll yelling at the team speeded them up if that was possible. Jane was sure that the wagon would overturn. The bumps that were in the road threw it from side to side in an alarming way. How she kept the patients on the bunks she didn't know. She just braced her feet on the floor and hung on.

There was no chance that Jane could look out the window with the mules going so fast. "Where is Gramps?, he should have been along by now." She realized that she couldn't tell even if he were outside. It seemed ages that Zoll had been traveling at this high rate of speed; surely the Rebel army behind them couldn't travel as fast. How far would they have to go to be in a safe zone? Jane listened to the shelling—it didn't sound so close now. Suddenly she heard shelling coming from a different direction. Oh, God! we are wedged in between two lines; we will all be killed!" She strained to listen; taking a chance she halfway raised up to peek through the window. She saw a Union soldier riding along the line of flee-ing wagons, "It must be our army I hear in the distance meeting the Rebels. Yes, I'm sure that that is what it is; those guns are firing on the Rebels." She felt better to know that someone was still looking out for the fleeing medical staff. "Where is Gramps?"

One of her charges started to moan and move about. "You are safe, she told him, I'll take care of you." She started to sing softly to the wounded man which seemed to quiet him; it was hard enough to keep them on the bunks without them tossing about and fighting her.

She felt the wagon slowing; hopefully they were out of harm's way and out-of-reach of the firing. Jane could tell that the wagon was moving away from the main road, and was hoping that they had found a safe camping sight. Soon the wagon came to a stand-still. She got up to look through the small window and could see the wagons spreading out in sparse woods. The site for the tents were being selected and the wagons unloaded. "Where is Gramps? Where can he be?" she was very worried about her grandfather. She checked on the soldiers and opened the door and looked out. The wagon seemed to be level; she dropped the step down and alighted. Zoll was working at the front of the wagon.

Going toward him she asked, "are we camping here? Do you know where Gramps is?" She was becoming alarmed that something had happened to her grandfather.

"Yes we're stopping here; a rider came up a bit back and said that the Rebels had been shoved back, they seem to think we can settle here for a while. I asked about Dr. Connolly, but all they knew was that he was still with the hospital unit. Don't worry, he'll show up soon."

Jane returned to the house on the wagon and began to build a fire in the little stove. Their flight wouldn't allow a fire sooner; soon the little stove was sending out heat. She checked the men again; they were sleeping she thought. It was hard to tell sometimes if they slept or were unconscious. Jane put a pot of water on the stove and got out the small can of coffee that she kept on hand for emergencies. If Gramps came he would welcome a cup of coffee she knew. The smell of coffee filled the little room; when it had boiled enough she poured a tin cup full, adding some hoarded sugar and took it outside to Zoll. She knew he must be frozen from being outside in the cold so long. He was still tending the team, covering them with their blankets to keep them from the cold; they were sweaty from the long run to get away from the gunfire. He would take care of his team even if he were cold. Jane came up to him and handed him the steaming cup of coffee.

"Just what I needed; ummm—that tastes good." He wrapped both hands around the steaming cup, sipping it slowly. "Thanks Jane; I think you may have just saved my life. It was getting a little chilly up where I was. I hope my mules will be all right; they got overheated during our run; we'd be lost without them." Finishing his cup, he handed it back to Jane.

Looking all around, Jane could see no sign of Dr. Connolly or Dr. Fugate. The big tent was half up, the wagons with the wounded waiting to be unloaded.

Where are they? they are needed; I can't take care of all the wounded alone. She walked this way and that peering into the distance.

A rider came rushing up from the direction they had vacated. Seeing Jane he came toward her, pulling his horse in as he came near. "Is there a doctor here?" he asked. One is needed badly; a doctor has been hit.

Jane staggered; Zoll caught her before she could fall. "Oh, It's Gramps, we have to go to him Zoll; we have to save him. Look for Dr. Fugate he must go with us; hurry Zoll."

"Easy missy; your Gramps will be fine. He was on horseback, and could easily be anywhere, we can't go chasing back toward the battle. He would never forgive me if something happened to you. Jane broke down with the news, tears ran down her face as she walked back and forth looking down the trail.

The hospital tent had just arrived and was hurriedly being raised. Wagons were waiting with wounded from the shelling of the camp. Jane went toward the workers. "Have you seen Dr. Connolly? Did you see him leave the area?" she questioned the workers and the wagon drivers. One driver said, "I saw a doctor working on a soldier on a table where the operation tent was, after it was loaded on a wagon. He was out in the open. The shells were coming in all around. I had to get out of there with the load of wounded I had. I didn't see him leave."

"Oh God! Zoll what are we to do?" I just know Gramps is hurt." Zoll put an arm around the trembling girl. He was beginning to be afraid also.

"Miss Jane! Miss Jane! Come quickly; we have some badly wounded on the tables. Hurry! The orderly who helped in the operating tent grabbed her by the arm and rushed her to the tent that had hurriedly been erected.

Zoll turned to a couple of the orderlies; come and help with the medicine and instruments; he loaded each with armloads of the things that had been brought in their wagon.

Jane entered the operating tent; looking around at all the wounded lying on the ground and on cots waiting for the doctors. There were no doctors around. She went to the table that had been set up where she and Gramps usually worked. There was a young wounded soldier, his hand wrapped in a bloody rag.

"This is the worse one Miss Jane," the orderly told her. "He needs to be worked on first."

She unwrapped the bloody rag, and saw that his arm would have to be amputated—the hand and half way up the arm was

146

almost gone just hanging in bloody shreds of bone and flesh. "This man needs a doctor; his arm must be amputated."

The orderly brought the needed equipment to the waiting stand beside the operating table. "There is no doctor, Miss Jane; you'll have to do it. I'll help as much as I can. I have helped Dr. Fugate many times." He looked at her with an unflinching trust. You have to do it! He'll die otherwise; you've helped with so many you could operate with your eyes closed."

Jane took the rubber apron from the table and pulled it over her head—removed the bloody wrappings, and began to clean the wound. The orderly had been given a swatch of cotton with ether which he held to the patient's nose. Jane examined the arm to see where the cut should be made, allowing for firm skin to fold over the stub. She took a scalpel and ringed around the arm clamping the arteries and veins, "Saw" she demanded. The flesh was pulled away so she could make a clean cut to the bone; the hand and half the arm below the elbow thumped into the empty tub at the end of the table. She quickly sutured the veins, folded the extending skin over the bare stub of bone and flesh and quickly sewed the catgut through the overlap as she had seen Gramp do time and time again. She couldn't work as quickly as he did but the arm looked professional. She bandaged it and motioned for the patient to be removed.

"That was as good as Dr. Fugate could have done, Miss Jane; you did a fine job." Seeing that she was weak and shaken he put an arm around her until she steadied herself, and took a deep shuddering breath. "I'm all right," she said as she turned to the pan of water that waited and washed the blood from her hands.

When she turned back, another soldier lay on the table. There was nothing she could do but try to help those who would otherwise die before they could get help from anyone else. She worked as quickly as she could—making the decisions that she must in order to save lives. She began to get in the swing of things and took care of all the worse cases. Looking around she saw that they were all taken care of. "Thank God!" She was so exhausted she wasn't sure she could reach the pan to remove all the blood without collapsing onto the ground at her feet.

Zoll had been standing behind her keeping an eye on her all the time. He had helped with the wounded being removed. She was too busy to notice him. When she had washed, he was there to take her arm and had a hot cup of coffee ready with a dollop of whiskey and sugar in it. "Oh Zoll, you are a sight for sore eyes; you knew just what I needed. The first sips had brought color to her cheeks. "If I have to do this many times, I'll become like Gramps about your coffee. Have you heard from him?" Tears stung her eyes as Zoll shook his head.

"Come you need to rest." He helped her toward the wagon, where he deposited her on the bunk, the wagon was warm and Zoll had tidied it after the two soldiers were removed. He eased her down and covered her with a quilt. She was so exhausted that she had fallen asleep. Zoll checked the stove and finding it to his satisfaction, quietly left the wagon.

❧ Chapter Fourteen ❧

Jane awoke with a start; suddenly remembering that her grandfather had been missing for several hours, she hurried from the wagon to the operating tent; after looking around saw there was no sign of Dr. Connolly. The tent was empty of all the activity that usually went on. Going toward the big tent where the wounded were kept, Jane rushed through to the back where an orderly was who had helped her with the operations. "Has Dr. Connolly or Dr. Fugate showed up yet?" she asked anxiously.

"I haven't seen either since we moved here Miss Jane. I don't think they have come yet." He looked sadly at Jane, as he turned back to the job he was working at.

Jane hurried away, "Oh, God, where can Gramps be? I've got to find Zoll—" She ran to the first soldier she saw. "Have you seen either of the doctors?" she asked as she kept looking all around. "No, Miss. I haven't seen them since we moved here."

Jane hurried back to her wagon; no one was there. She could hear wagons and horses coming from the direction of the battlefield and hurried to where she could look down the trail. She saw a horse and rider accompanying the wagons; the horse broke into a canter and the rider came quickly toward her and she realized it was Zoll; dismounting he joined her.

"Zoll, where is Gramps? Have you seen him?" she grabbed his arm shaking him as she asked.

"I've been looking for hours it seems; he is no where to be found. The enemy didn't overrun the last campsite, but it was shelled. I couldn't find anyone who could give me any information on either doctor. I don't know what to think. If they had been captured I think someone would have known. They were last seen at our old camp which was three miles from enemy lines. Dr. George knows how to take care of himself. He may have been called somewhere to see to one of the officers. I just don't know. There's a wagonload of wounded coming—some in very bad shape. We will have to do what we can. Pull yourself together Jane; Doctor will be all right. Come along, we have to help the men." He took her arm and steered

149

her toward the operating tent.

"Oh God, Zoll, I can't. I have to find Gramps; I have to! When they entered the tent and Jane saw a wounded soldier on the table she removed her shawl and slipped the rubber apron over her head, automatically beginning her examination. One after the other she administered what help she could to the wounded. Zoll watched over Jane saving her all he could; but looking at her knew she was exhausted and ready to drop. Where could Doctor George be?

Dr. Connolly had started to mount his horse when the shells began to find the camp. Looking toward where the operating tent had been he saw Dr. Fugate working by a table setting out in the open, shells dropping all around. He saw the table fly into a million pieces and Dr. Fugate drop to the ground. He mounted his mare and hurried over, He saw that the soldier who had been on the table was blown in two. Seeing movement from Dr. Fugate, he knew that he was alive but badly wounded. Dismounting he grabbed Doctor William throwing him up over the saddle and managed to climb on behind; whipping the mare he raced from the area. The shells were bursting all around as Dr. Connolly leaned over his friend and guided the mare through the thick woods along the trail and hurried away from the shelling. He was soon out of range and the shells were dropping harmless behind him. Coming to an area where large rocks projected from a cliff he halted. Sliding from the horse he gently lowered Dr. Fugate to the ground close to the rocks where he would be somewhat sheltered. Taking his black bag that was tied to the saddle and a blanket and rain gear that he kept tied behind the saddle, he spread the rain gear on the ground and covered the doctor with the blanket. He was covered with blood and bits of flesh from the soldier he had been operating on when the explosion occurred. Dr. George could see that Will's left arm was hanging limp and bleeding profusely; opening his bag he quickly cut away the doctor's sleeve; the arm was mangled beyond description. "It'll have to come off, Will. It can't wait; I'll have to do it here." Taking out a clean cloth he laid out his instruments, saturated a small swatch of cotton with ether and held it under the unconscious doctor's nose. He didn't dare give him but a couple whiffs. He saturated another cloth in carbolic acid and wiped the arm the best he could and used it on his hands, and followed the procedure he had done dozen of times. He carefully selected the area for the cut, saving as much of the arm as he felt was safe. Kneeling on the ground beside his patient was awkward for him to do such a delicate operation; but working as quickly as he could, he finished and wrapped the arm in a bandage and made a sling tying the arm close to the body and covering it with Will's torn clothing as well as he could. Dr. Connolly didn't know how far away the camp would be; he had to get Will to cover and get him warm if he was to live, and soon. Heading in what he thought was a northwest direction where the camp was headed, he walked along beside his horse holding Dr. Fugate across the saddle with the blanket and rain-gear wrapped tightly around him to hold his body heat. Dr. Fugate was still unconscious. Doctor Connolly had trudged through the wet leaves and over fallen trees for what seemed miles to him. The weak sun was sinking toward the horizon, and the chill air found its way down the doctor's coat collar and caused shivers to course up and down his back. Every step seemed to be harder to make as he dragged his feet through all the obstacles. "I must find shelter, but where?" suddenly he smelled smoke. "There's a fire somewhere near; I don't know where but wherever it is I intend to share it." Making his way around a thick clump of scrub pine and green-briars he saw a log cabin in the distance, and headed toward it. It could be enemy he realized but it was better than freezing to death and letting Will die of exposure. As he neared the cabin, a young boy about eight or nine came through the door, a pitchfork in his skinny hands.

"What're you doing here?" he called out in a scared voice.

"I'm Dr. Connolly; I have a patient that has to have shelter; where are your folks?" he asked the scared little boy.

"Mom!" screamed the child as he looked behind him at the closed door. A tall skinny woman in her thirties came out wrapping a ragged shawl about herself.

"What can I do for you?" she asked in a meek voice. "We have very little left, the soldiers have taken everything."

"I'm a Union doctor, I have another doctor here who has been wounded; if I can't get him warmth and shelter he will die. I have just cut off his arm out there in the woods. May we come inside to your fire—I don't mean you any harm. I have no weapon, and could your boy house my horse somewhere? Please Mam, as I say I'm a doctor."

"Come in doctor, you are welcome to what we have; John take the doctor's horse to the shed and tend it."

The boy hurried to help remove the wounded man from the horse, and carry him inside as the woman held the door open.

"Thank you son, and for caring for my horse." They laid the wounded doctor on a small bunk which was against one wall, as the woman hurried to add wood to the meager fire.

"My man is out there somewhere; I haven't heard from him for over a month. He managed to get back to us once but had to go out again. He's fighting for the Union too. We skimp on our wood as it's so hard to get, with just John and me. The other youngins are too small to help much. I'll make some tea, all I have is Calomel; I still have some honey for sweetning. It will help to warm you up." she said as she hurried toward a small lean-to in the back. Glancing in the direction she took, the doctor saw three pairs of eyes watching him from a bed on the other wall.

Seeing a wash pan by the hearth and a kettle of water on the hopper, he dipped out a pan-full and brought it over to the bunk and using his handkerchief he washed away the splattered blood and grime from Dr. Fugate's face and removed his outer clothes. Looking at his arm bound close to his body, decided that hanging head down on the saddle had caused no harm. It didn't seem to be bleeding, due to the cold no doubt he decided. Making Dr. Fugate as comfortable as he could he covered him with several quilts, and sat watching his friend. He had very little pain killer with him and knew when he regained consciousness the pain would be unbearable.

"Here is your tea, doctor, my name is Margaret Mitchell, I hope this will help some. Is there anything I can get for you or help in any way?"

"When Dr. Fugate that's my patient's name—comes around if you have any broth you could fix for him, I would appreciate it. And have some of this tea ready; it is delicious and has already warmed me; and the honey goes directly to the blood and gives energy.

"We have very little as I told you, but what we have we will share. I have managed to hang on to one cow; there is little for her to eat, but we have a field far back on that mountain where we have a couple of small hay-stacks. I go at night and bring all I can carry in a sheet to feed her so the soldiers won't find it. The boy managed to kill a rabbit today; It will make broth, and I'll have it ready when the doctor awakens.

"Thank you, Mrs. Mitchell when I get back to our camp I'll see if I can get you a little help. Do you happen to know where the Union camp moved to."

"We could hear the wagons passing in that direction, she pointed toward the north. They must have gone some distance; we haven't been able to hear anything since they passed earlier.'"

"I'll have to find them soon, I'm the only doctor now to help the wounded. I have left my granddaughter in the camp; she is my nurse and a fine one but she won't be able to cope alone."

"I'll be glad to do whatever I can to help. I could look after your friend until you think he is out of danger, if you tell me what to do, while you find your camp."

"That is very generous of you Mrs. Mitchell, with all you have to worry about now. I don't think I can take the doctor any further with his head hanging down over the horse, and it is impossible to hold him upright and ride through this rugged area.

We'll see how he fares in the next few hours." A moan sounded from the bunk as Dr. Connolly finished talking; he picked up the wrist of his patient to check his heart-beat. It was strong and steady, maybe he would pull through; he was a tough old bird as was proven by the long hard hours he had been working.

Dr. Connolly sat watching as Will made faces and began to move under the pile of covers. He tried to move his amputated arm that was wrapped tightly to his body. "Will, can you hear me?" the doctor asked. Another grimace washed over his face and a deep moan escaped his bruised lips. His face was swollen and Dr. Connolly knew there must be numerous bruises about his body from the exploding shell; he had checked for broken bones and hadn't bothered with anything else as the arm was his main concern. He was pleased with Will's reaction so far to the surgery that was done under the most primitive conditions. If they could get him to take nourishment and he had good care he felt he would pull through.

The woman was busy at the fire; she had added another pot to the hopper and seemed to be adding a few vegetables to the rabbit stew she was working over. The smell penetrated the small room and caused the doctor's stomach to growl from emptiness. She pulled the pot to the side of the fire to simmer and wrapping herself in the ragged shawl left the house, soon returning with a small bucket of milk. The three children still sat on the bed against the wall and quietly watched every move in the cabin. Dr. George wondered how a mother could expect to feed so many small children on what she could gather from the land. And how long it could continue. He saw her mix a small amount of meal for bread and add it to a Dutch Oven and bury it in the coals of the fireplace.

He doubted she would have done so if the two men hadn't been there to feed. She would share even though she had so little for her family.

Mrs. Mitchell finished at the fire and came over to inquire about Will, "how is he?" she asked.

He should rally soon, his heart is holding up well—he's a strong man." he replied. "There will be considerable pain when he does rally, I have little I can give him for it." the doctor shook his head sadly.

The children were lined up on a bench beside a rough table in the corner beside the hearth. The mother dipped out bowls of the stew and broke pieces of the cornbread into each bowl for them. "Doctor, would you join us, the food is ready." She had placed some of the rabbit and vegetables in a larger bowl for him; he knew there was hardly enough for her and her children but he ate what was presented to him. "I've saved plenty of the broth and some of the vegetables for your friend when he comes to. I know he will need nourishment."

Thank you Mrs. Mitchell; you have a fine hunter there to be able to provide for your family." he saw the proud look the mother turned on her son, as he squirmed in embarrassment.

The doctor finished his meal and returned to the cot; suddenly Dr. Fugate opened his eyes, squinting toward the doctor. He turned his head from side to side. "Where am I?" he mumbled. "What happened?" he asked as he focused on Dr. George. "My arm—it hurts, am I wounded doctor? What happened to the young man I was working on?" he said as he tried to raise himself up on the cot.

"Lie still Will; you've been hurt bad. When you feel like it, I'll prop you up; I want you to take some nourishment as soon as you feel you can. We were out in the weather longer than I would have liked, when I happened on this cabin and Mrs. Mitchell took us in. You're warm and dry now, but need food to fortify you for your recovery."

Dr. Fugate lay for a few minutes, his face scrunched up in pain, as he raised his right arm and brought it across himself to inspect his left arm that was wrapped tight against his body. Dr. George watched his eyes, knowing he wouldn't have to tell Will that his hand and half his arm was missing. Being a doctor he would realize soon enough. "Help me up George and bring on that nourishment you are talking about. Seems I need it, I feel as weak as a kitten."

Dr. George lifted his friend and placed several pillows behind him that Mrs. Mitchell brought from the other bed. She then brought a small bowl of the stew and broth, and a cup of the hot calomel tea laced with honey. She sat on the edge of the cot and fed Will. Swallowing several mouthfuls, he motioned for the cup and drank half the tea as she held it to his mouth.

Sighing, he turned to Doctor George, "Tell me about it," he said. "I remember the shells were coming closer and closer and I was hurrying to finish the operation I was working on. Then I seem to have blanked out."

"That you did, your table got an almost direct hit; I picked you up and slung you across my saddle and took off as fast as I could with the Reb's shells bouncing off old Babe's heels. I had to perform one of my famous surgical feats beside a rock on the trail; I imagine you are sore all over or will be soon. You have all kinds of bruises and lacerations, which I haven't treated due to things beyond my control. How do you feel?"

Even though Dr. Will was in pain, he managed a faint smile after hearing the doctor's triad about what happened. "You make it all sound like you are the Hero; I'm the one who is hurting, he smiled weakly at the doctor. If it had to happen I'm glad you were there to pick up my pieces, even though you didn't get them all put back together like they should be. I guess I owe you my life, friend. Thank you; now do you have anything in that little magic bag that will stop the pain and let me sleep a while to regain my strength?"

"I have some opium, you may have some erotic dreams, but that should make you feel better," he smilingly told him as he prepared a needle. In a very short time Dr. Fugate was sleeping soundly. After checking his amputation to see if it was bleeding he covered his friend and heaved a sigh of thankfulness that Dr.

Fugate had taken it so well; he didn't know if he could have accepted the loss of an arm with such good grace.

"Doctor, I've a pallet I will place by the hearth as soon as I get the children down, and I'll watch over your friend while you get some rest." She hurried off toward the small children that needed to be put into bed.

Dr. George was sitting beside the cot nodding by the time she finished. He could hardly hold his head up and was grateful that she had volunteered to spell him for a while. The warmth of the fire and the hot food had done him in and he was in danger of going to sleep and falling onto the floor.

* * *

The cabin had a faint brightness illuminating the small window when the doctor awoke; he was stiff and sore from the previous day's activities. He lay for a moment listening to the quiet breathing of the sleeping cabin. He was thankful there was no moans of pain from the other side of the room where Dr. Fugate lay. Rousing himself he went to the cot; he saw that Mrs. Mitchell was still at her post—she had leaned forward onto the edge of the cot and was sleeping. The slight bump to her chair as the doctor approached awoke her.

"Good morning doctor; forgive me for dozing. There has been no change. Whatever you gave your friend, he slept all through the night. He moved very little; under the circumstances I guess that is what he needs. I always think that sleep is the greatest healer."

"You are absolutely right". He picked up Will's wrist and felt his pulse. I am very pleased with the progress he is making. Do you think I could leave him in your hands until I find my unit and send someone for him? I must reach my unit; many soldiers may die if they don't have a doctor. We were the only two in the region. I must start at first light to find them as soon as possible. I'll try not to burden you for long."

"I'll be glad to do all I can to help. It could be my man who needed care. When he wakes I'll try to get food down him."

"I'll leave some drops for pain. Don't under any circumstances give them to him unless he is in bad pain, and then never more than three drops no closer than four hours apart. Can you remember that? It would be very dangerous to his heart for him to have more. I'll send someone to you as soon as I can find our unit. I want to thank you for all your kindness. I won't forget. I'll go now I know I'm not needed. That night's sleep has revived me. Thank you again." He silently opened the cabin door and went to the shed to find his horse. He led her out of the stall and put the saddle on and left toward the north. He had traveled for two hours or more easing northwest when he heard the neigh of horses. Hurrying toward the sound he soon came in sight of the compound. Some of the wagons were lined up facing south, with mules in the traces, ready at a moment's notice to go forward to collect the wounded. He began to pick up the sound of explosions far to the south, still so faint he strained to hear, not sure he was right, until the front wagons began to pull out. Hurrying forward he found the smaller operating tent. He rounded the tent to the front and handed his horse to an orderly. Hurrying inside he saw that the tables were clean and ready for action. No one seemed to be around and he walked through the tent toward the big one in back. Going in he saw cots with wounded—going from one to another he checked on the occupants. He could see amputees and bandaged wounds of all sorts which appeared very professionally treated. Maybe they had gotten another doctor while he and Dr. Fugate had been out of commission. An orderly came rushing from the rear, not recognizing the doctor in the dim light. "Dr. Connolly.' We've been searching everywhere for you; are you all right? Where have you been? Have you seen Dr. Fugate?"

"Hold it, one question at a time. Dr. Fugate was still operating when the Rebels shelled the compound. He was almost in a direct hit. The shell hit close to the table where he was working and killed the soldier he was working on and knocked him down, shattering his left arm. I luckily rescued him, throwing him across my mare and took him to safety. I had to remove his arm in the woods where we took shelter. I found a cabin close by where he is now. He is doing well and has someone to look after him for the present. What about my granddaughter? Where is she? Is she hurt?"

The orderly smiling said, "One question at a time, sir." Look around you. She has been a busy girl. She is resting in her wagon with Zoll standing guard."

"You mean she did all this? No doctor on duty?"

"She sure did; we had to almost force her to take over but once she got in the swing she did wonders, saved many a soldier's life.

She is an angel in disguise, sir. I've never seen a more efficient operation (begging your pardon, sir) than she performed. She was wonderful; no doctor could have done better. We'll bless her forever." The orderly looked a little confused after his outburst but proud nevertheless. "The shelling has started again. We haven't had any wounded for several hours. The wagons have gone out now they will be returning soon. I think the mess tent is open, maybe you want to eat now before we get busy," he suggested.

"I think that is a good idea; I need a good wash too. I'll head right out. Don't call my granddaughter, let her rest. One of you can assist me when the time comes. Tell Zoll not to wake her, will you?"

"We're sure glad to have you back, sir. Yes sir we sure are!"

Dr. George had been working for more than an hour when Jane came bursting into the tent, "Gramps! Gramps! You're here, I've been so worried," she grabbed him around the waist and gave him a big hug. "Oh, Gramps don't ever leave me again.

"Miss, are you aware I am in the operation theater and at work on a patient," he pretended to glare at her, "This is no way for another professional to behave in time of emergency."

"Oh, Gramps I'm so happy to have you back—I felt like I was shipwrecked and all alone. I have had a good rest; why didn't you wake me when you arrived?"

"I wanted you to rest while you could; I had a good night's sleep, too, and felt able to take care of whatever came in. I think we will be busy soon; we may not get much time to sleep tonight. From the sound of the firing there must be a big battle going on. How I wish this would be over and we could go home; I'm becoming weary." The sadness in his eyes overwhelmed her.

The wagons were hurrying into the compound; the orderly had set up another table where Jane would work. Soon wounded filled both tables. Jane looked over at her grandfather, then said to the orderly— "tell Gramps this is an amputation, I'll change tables with him."

When the orderly approached Dr. Connolly and told him Jane's message, he looked toward his granddaughter— "tell her to proceed—if she needs me let me know, I have a serious internal problem here that needs my attention."

Jane saw her grandfather nod in her direction—he wants me to go ahead—I can't believe this—I'm doctoring with Gramp's approval. A smile flitted around her pretty mouth— "what will mamma say?" she whispered. Being a doctor had always been her ambition—and she worshipped her Gramps—but it wasn't as much fun as she had imagined—there was too much heartbreak and hard work to it. However, she felt like a doctor; she was anxious to know what her Gramps thought now.

Jane and Dr. George worked for several hours before the influx of wounded slowed. They were both weary when they finally took a break and went to the mess for hot coffee. Jane finished her coffee and turned to her grandfather— "I'll go check on the patients from yesterday. I haven't done that since I came in this morning." She left toward the recovery tent.

❧ Chapter Fifteen ❧

Jane entered the recovery tent and went from cot to cot checking her work of the previous day; she marveled at how well everyone was doing. She saw the orderly at a cot near the back and noticed he was wrapping one of the patients in a sheet; hurrying toward him she asked, "What are you doing? What's wrong?"

"Miss Jane, why don't you have a cup of coffee? We are just rearranging the beds in this section." Another orderly had joined him.

Jane continued toward him and soon saw that the soldier they were wrapping was one she had operated on the day before for a head wound. "What's wrong with that patient? I want to examine him; move over." She forced herself between the cot and the orderly, "What is this? What is wrong with him? He was doing so well." She looked perplexed while she took up his hand and felt for a pulse; the orderly didn't know what to do. He saw her face blanch, "oh my God! He's dead! How could this happen?" Jane turned almost knocking the orderly over in her haste as she rushed from the tent.

"No, no, no she was sobbing and mumbling to herself. Going over to a log nearby she miserably fell down upon it.

The orderly had followed her outside and seeing her in this dejected state knew she was becoming hysterical; he sent the other orderly to bring her grandfather while he stood watching her, not knowing what to do.

Angrily pounding her fist against the log where she sat—"I can't stand it! I can't! I want to go home. I hate war! Hate it! Oh God, I'm so weary I can't stand it another day. I can't." She slumped over her head in her lap, shaking with sobs. "Mamma, I want my Mamma. Oh God! I want to go home, "I've killed a poor wounded soldier. What did I do wrong? Oh, God! I can't stand it." Her sobbing could be heard all through the compound.

When Dr. Connolly was told what had happened he hurried from the mess tent toward where his granddaughter sat on the log. Seeing her hands laced through her hair pulling handfuls, and tears flowing in rivulets, a look of the demented on her face, he hurried to her. Taking her in his arms, he patted her back murmuring soothing words to her. "It's all right, darlin' don't cry; you did a wonderful job. We all do our best; even that isn't enough sometimes; don't blame yourself." He kept patting and soothing her.

"Gramps, I can't stand anymore, I want my Mamma; I want my Mamma." She was sobbing as if her heart was tearing into little pieces. "I want to go home, I can't stand it another minute; please take me home to Mamma, Gramps. Please."

Dr. Connolly had tears in his eyes listening to his distraught granddaughter. What should he do? Jane continued to rant and rave sobbing until she was hoarse; putting his arm around her he lifted her up and walked toward their wagon. Zoll seeing Dr. Connolly holding up the limp Jane, almost carrying her, came to help. "Help get her into the wagon, and then bring my bag. She's hysterical, I must give her something to make her sleep; she has been working too hard and the shock of having to take over and operate has been too much for her."

The doctor placed her on her bed and covered her warmly. Zoll soon returned with his medical bag and the doctor quickly gave her a small shot of opium. He sat by her side until she quieted and slept soundly. "She'll sleep several hours. What am I going to do with her? I can't take her home. I have to stay here; there is no one else to take care of the wounded."

"Maybe she will be better after a rest, Dr. George," Zoll said. "I have been hearing that the fighting is almost over. There is a rumor going the rounds that peace is being negotiated. Maybe we'll all be going home soon."

"Zoll, find out if you can, how far we are from Charlotte. See if the roads are open. I have a good friend I could send her to for a few days if we can find a way to get her there." Zoll nodded and left.

When Dr. Connolly returned to the operating tent, Zoll came with the information he had asked for. "The roads are under Union control at this time. They have held Charlotte for the past month; it's about sixty miles from here by road; if you cut through the country, about forty; I've found a young private who lives in Charlotte, and knows all the country around and he could guide us in and back by the closer route. We could make it there and back in say three days and nights. We would have to go by horseback and travel hard I don't know if Miss Jane could travel that way. It would be a hard trip in her condition.

"I don't think we have much choice. If we keep her here she may become permanently disabled by her experiences. My friends are southern to the bone. I know they would take her in even though they know my sympathies are with the Union. It would be a touchy project at best. I'll write them a letter to send along. See if you can locate some horses; Jane can ride Babe, if we decide. I promised Mrs. Mitchell we would try to help her. How about rounding up some food, potatoes, rice, beef if possible, whatever you can get hold of, and take a load of feed for her cow; when you have it ready I'll give you directions how to get there. And see if she can keep Dr. Fugate a few more days till he is out of danger; take an orderly to change his bandages. That shouldn't take but about three hours there and back. Get on it right away. By the time you're back I'll have decided what to do about Jane." Dr. George turned back to the work that was before him.

Zoll checked on Jane—she was sleeping soundly. He approached the young private and found that he had his own horse. Zoll remembered that Dr. Fugate had a horse and went to the rumanda and found that it was there and in good shape; he could ride it. Making arrangements for the Private to stand by and be ready to travel, he started rounding up the things he could take to Mrs. Mitchell. Potatoes and rice were plentiful; he included a half bushel of apples, some beef and a slab of bacon, and sack of chopped corn for feed—if she had chickens, it would come in handy. He sorted through some canned stuff and fixed a box of assorted goods. A bag of sugar and a bucket of honey was included. He picked up a couple of clean sheets and a blanket and added those to the crate; she might need them since she was tending the doctor. He and the private loaded the things onto a wagon and covered them with hay filling the wagon as full as they could travel with it.

The orderly that Dr. George was sending waited in the operating tent until Zoll went to get directions, and they were off.

Dr. Connolly couldn't believe how much he missed Jane. She had been such a help. He would just have to get used to it—he doubted she would return. He would talk to the Private while Zoll was gone and see if he knew the Barrlettes—they had a big plantation close in to Charlotte, and before the war had been considered a wealthy southern family. He wasn't even sure that they were still alive, there had been a lot of fighting close to Charlotte. He decided he would have to send the private to inquire first before sending Jane so far.

* * *

Zoll found the Mitchell's cabin without any trouble. When he pulled into the yard with the wagon, the door opened and Mrs. Mitchell came out onto the porch. Zoll and the orderly climbed from the wagon and went toward the cabin. I'm Zoll, Dr. Connolly sent me. We want to check on Dr. Fugate and change his bandage. "How is he?"

"How do you do," Mrs. Mitchell said, nodding to both the men. "Dr. Fugate is coming along well, he is a good patient; come in and make yourself at home." She held the door as the orderly went first with the bag that held the dressings.

"Well Dr. Fugate! I see you are taking a vacation." The orderly who had worked so long with him smiled at the doctor who was propped up on the cot. "You look good, how do you feel?"

"I'm pretty fit considering. Mrs. Mitchell has taken good care of me. You're a sight for sore eyes, how are things at the compound? How's Dr. George?"

"Things are moving along—not too busy when we left; seems the fighting is slowing some. Dr. George has a problem on his hands," He explained how Jane had taken over and what had resulted in her getting overtired.

"That's some girl; she has worked like a beaver and always an eye out for her grandfather's welfare. She needs a rest."

The orderly was busy unwrapping the bandage from the doctor's arm. When the wound was exposed they both examined it professionally, "Don't look too bad considering that it was done out in the middle of the woods. What do you think Orderly?" the doctor asked.

"It's healing nicely; no bleeding or proud-flesh; I'd say you were very lucky; course you had an experienced surgeon." He smiled at the doctor as he wiped the wound with a sterile swab, covered it with ointment and replaced the bandages with a fresh one. Mrs. Mitchell stood by holding the pan of hot water she had brought to cleanse the wound. Turning, the orderly asked, "Do you think Dr.

Fugate could remain here for another few days? Things are a little hectic at the compound, and Dr. George wants the best for his friend and colleague."

"There's no reason why he can't remain; we don't have much food but we can manage," Mrs. Mitchell replied.

"We're going to remedy that; we've brought food and hay for your animal; you should be well-fixed for a few days. Dr. George said to thank you for all you've done. He appreciates it more than you know."

When the orderly finished, he went to help unload the wagon. Zoll had the food piled up on the porch ready to take it into the house. "Where do you want this, Mrs. Mitchell?"

"Bring it into the lean-to if you will; my, look at all that stuff, you have out-done yourself. I'm so grateful to the doctor; I never expected so much and such a variety. We have a hidden 'hidey-hole' under the floor; John and I will stash most of it there, so if the soldiers return they won't take it. They don't seem to care that there are small children to feed." She was smiling as she looked through all the food.

As soon as the hay was unloaded into the shed, the two men said a last good-by to Dr. Fugate and waved as they headed back to the compound.

* * *

As he worked, Dr. Connolly went around and around in his mind about sending Jane off. Maybe he should keep her where he could keep an eye on her. He called in the private who was from Charlotte. "Private, are you acquainted with the Barrlettes who have a plantation east of Charlotte?"

"Yes sir, I don't know them personally but I know the plantation Barrlette House—it's well known in Charlotte."

"I'm going to write a letter to Charles & Elizabeth Barrlette. Could you by any chance, find their plantation and deliver it and bring back an answer? You could also have time to visit your family since you are from Charlotte," the doctor asked the young soldier.

A big smile lit the young man's face, "You bet I can sir. If you will clear it with my commanding officer I'll be more than glad to. I can leave anytime. I know the country like the back of my hand

and could even travel in the dark. But there will be a moon to-night—I can be there by tomorrow morning. Just say the word sir."

There was a letup in the tent activities, and Dr. Connolly hurried to his wagon for writing paper. Checking on Jane he found she still slept; Careful not to disturb her, he collected his writing paper and pen and went to the mess tent to write the letter; he could indulge himself with a cup of coffee while he completed his writing. He soon had a letter to his friends explaining the situation and asking for refuge for his granddaughter; it wouldn't do to send her all that way and maybe the Barrlettes' somewhere else. Who knew in this situation where people would be. Lots of plantations had been deserted with the slaves leaving for the north and no one to keep them going.

The private waited inside the operating tent for the doctor's return. Dr. Connolly returned with his letter and went with the private to his commanding officer where he explained the situation to him.

"The private is at your disposal doctor; whatever you want, he will have sufficient time to perform. You understand private what the doctor wants?" The sergeant who was over the soldiers and helped with the hospital detail commanded.

"Yes Sir! I do Sir."

"Thank you Sergeant, I'll have him back as soon as possible."

"Private, take some food for the trail from the mess tent. You can start anytime you have a mind to. Take this letter and give it to either Mr. or Mrs. Barrlette in person. Go to the Plantation first, then a short visit with your family. You may spend a night with them and then return with the Barrlettes answer. Be careful and make sure you travel carefully and keep your eyes open. I don't want you a captive. Return as quickly as you can." The doctor slapped the young private on the back and said, "God Speed!"

As Dr. Connolly returned to his patients, he heard the sound of the private's horse leaving the compound on his mission.

The operation tent was busy all day; the orderlies bringing in wounded and removing them as the doctor finished. Zoll would routinely check on Jane and report that she was still sleeping soundly. Poor little thing, she was completely exhausted. "I should have seen that she was ready to collapse," the doctor said shaking his head at his neglect.

Late in the afternoon, Jane slowly opened her eyes looking around her. She saw light at the small windows and wondered why she was in bed in the daytime. She and her Gramps sometimes lie down for a nap if there were no wounded, but looking around the small room saw that Gramps wasn't with her. She noticed that her pillow was wet, "I've been crying in my sleep," she said to herself; then it all came back to her. The death of the soldier she had worked on, and how she had fallen apart afterwards. "Gramps must be worried sick," she said as she swung her feet over the bunk; she felt dizzy and weak, and slightly nauseous "What's wrong with me? I must be coming down with something." Smiling she continued, "and I'm talking to myself, that's not a good sign she said shaking her head. She sat until the dizziness passed, "I'm hungry that's it! I'll have something to eat and go back and help Gramps." She washed her face and tidied her hair, then went toward the mess tent. Helping herself to a cup of coffee, she asked the cook if there was anything hot to eat.

"I can give you a bowl of hot vegetable soup, Miss, if that will do?" he dished it up at her nod.

"Thank you, that will do nicely." Sipping the hot soup, Jane began to feel much better. Thinking back on what had happened, Jane said, "I did the best I could, and that's all anyone can do Gramps says. He loses a patient occasionally and doesn't go into a tailspin like I did." Gramps would say— "Not too professional young lady!" Jane smiled to herself, thinking of just how he would look as he said it. "I'm a good nurse and doctor—Gramps said so. No more tears, Gramps says they don't solve anything."

Finishing her soup Jane went back to the operating tent; removing her shawl she picked up her rubber apron and pulled it over her head. Going to the table where she usually worked she motioned for the orderly to bring one of the soldiers who sat waiting. He had several bandages bloody and dirty—one on his hand and another wrapped around his head. He was sitting up so she knew he couldn't be wounded too badly. She cut away the bandages, seeing that he had a deep cut on his head that had bled a lot; cleansing it she cut away some of his hair and sterilized the wound and decided that a couple of stitches were needed. She gave him a couple whiffs of ether while she got the catgut ready; he closed his eyes and she picked up a hand to find he was relaxed and limp. It took only a couple of minutes to suture the wound—only three stitches were needed. Hurrying, she applied a dressing then treated the arm where a slight laceration needed only a cleaning and bandage. She motioned for him to be removed. He could have a nap and would be ready to return to combat in a day or two.

Doctor Connolly was busy with an operation when Jane came back. He hadn't even noticed that she was there, he was so used to seeing her at her post. Looking up, he saw her as the patient was removed from her table. "Darlin' are you all right? Do you think you should be here?" he came closer to see how she looked.

"I'm fine Gramps; I had some coffee and hot soup and I feel better; I'm sorry I gave you a scare. The rest did me a world of good. I'll be fine now." she smiled her beautiful smile at him.

"We only have a few more and we will go have another cup of coffee; I could do with one. With you helping, we'll be out of here in no time."

The two left the messy tables for the orderlies to clean. The rubber aprons were also left; they would be washed and ready for the next influx of wounded. Jane did take time to gather all the instruments and deposit them in the big pan of boiling water on the stove.

Doctor had his arm around Jane as they went toward the mess. "I was so worried about you darlin'; I know you are worn out—I am and I'm a man and have been doing this for ages. I should have kept a better watch on you. I have something to tell you. I have sent the private to a friend of mine in Charlotte. If they are still in their home, I want to send you there for a rest and get you away from this for a while. You won't be any help if you come down sick; I'll just have another patient to care for. I've requested another doctor to come; Dr. Will won't be much help with only one arm. He'll be sent home now. I don't want you to put up a fuss; you have to get your strength back and heal your nerves, then you can come back and help, or go on home whichever you decide." The doctor looked at her expecting her to refuse, but he knew it was necessary for her to have a long rest if her health wasn't to be sacrificed.

"I know you're right Gramps, but I do hate to leave you with no one to watch out for you. I am tired. And I know I couldn't work as much as I have been. It's been a long time; I'm so sick of all the blood and pain; the poor boys and what they are going through. I feel ashamed that I'm complaining; it's them that are hurting. I'll do whatever you think best Gramps, I don't want to cause you any more worry than you already have."

"Good, that's my sensible girl. A good professional knows their limits. That's what you are a Professional. In the areas you have worked in you are as good as most doctors are, and even better than some. I'm sure you know I'm proud of you." He reached over and gave her a big hug.

"Oh, Gramps it's so good to hear you say that. I'll be ready whenever you say."

"I gave the private leave to visit his family; he's from Charlotte; he should be back in a day or so. Then I'll arrange for someone to escort you to the Barrlettes. You will like them. I've known them for years. They are about my age but they have one son I know of, and I'm sure there will be some young people around. They have a big plantation and used to entertain a lot. They are southern to the bone, so be careful with them. Charlotte is under Union now and they have to conform, but you may hear things differently. I don't think I have ever told you about them. They have an enormous plantation, they raise cotton, corn, tobacco and lots more. Charles Barrlette was crazy about Pears—he worked for ages trying to produce a better-tasting pear. One carries his name; I'm not sure if it was him that developed it or someone else, however, the Barrlette Pear is widely known. He is a fine family man, and a good businessman. At one time I think, wealthy. I don't know how they have fared in this conflict. He had a big investment in slaves to work his holdings; they all seemed happy, but as you know I didn't approve.

Jane smiled at her grandfather, "I'm always amazed at how many people you are acquainted with and with the area your friendships cover, Gramps you are amazing, and I love you to pieces.

* * *

Jane worked beside her grandfather for several days waiting for the Private to return. Dr. Connolly insisted that she take a long nap every afternoon regardless of how busy they were. Jane's color had improved and she didn't tire as easily as she had been. She was trying to eat regularly and not get overtired.

In the afternoon a few days later, a small one-seated rig drew up at the operating tent. A big black man with gray sideburns peeking from under his old slouch hat sat high on the seat driving the team. He brought the rig in smartly and pulled the team to a stop beside the tent. The Private riding alongside dismounted and entered the tent looking for the doctor or Jane.

Dr. Connolly spotted the Private as he was removing his apron for a break; throwing it aside, he went toward the Private. "I'm back with you a letter and another surprise doctor." Dr. Connolly looked quickly at the Private, "Let's go have a cup of coffee while you fill me in on your trip," he said as he started toward the tent opening; looking up as he stepped through, he spied the rig; squinting his eyes against the sun, he said, "As I live and breathe, Sam! You old buzzard, you. It is you, isn't it? I never expected to see you!"

"It's me sure enough Mr. George. I've come to fetch that granddaughter of yours back to Ms'. Barrlette; she saiz I was to tell you to come, too—that she knows youz need a rest. I'z watch over her real good. Ms.' Barrlette made arrangements for stopovers going back to Charlotte so 'z she don'z get too tired." Sam had a grin from ear to ear; he was fond of Dr. George and was glad to see him.

"Get down Sam; rest yourself; are you hungry? Come on we'll get something to eat and some coffee." The doctor took Sam's arm and led him to a corner table in the tent, then went to the cook and soon had a plate of vittles for them all and big tin cups of coffee delivered to their table. Looking at the Private the doctor remarked, "Didn't have any trouble finding the place I see. Have a nice visit home? Folks all right?" The private nodded with each question.

Turning to the black man Dr. Connolly asked, "Do you want to spend the night here and rest a bit before starting back, Sam?"

"It's pretty late, guess that would be best, I'z don'z like much bein' on the road after dark. I sure don'zt want anything to happen to Miss Jane. No sir I don'z I'z find a place to bunk down and spenz the night if you think it'z all right, Dr. George, and get an early start tomorrow at sun-up. We' z can make iz in to Perry Junction where we are going to stop off at The Rafferty Plantation for the night. W'z have one other stop az the Ball House; then we can make it back to Barrlette House the next day."

"That sounds good, Sam. I'll have Jane ready to leave. How are things in that direction? Are there any goods for sale? Jane only brought work clothes and may need to buy a few things," he said.

"If you have gold, there are things for sale," the Private spoke up. "Just about anything you want but it's costly. I think Charlotte has some stores that are fairly well-stocked. She should find something there; lots of people hoarded dress goods, Mrs. Barrlette may have done so and have material. Some of the women whose menfolk have been killed are selling their clothes to survive. That's a possibility. I wouldn't worry, I'm sure the women can work out something if she needs things."

"You make it sound simple; I'll not worry then. I just want her away from all this where she won't have to smell blood and unwashed bodies. Where she can smile and set of an afternoon on the veranda and have a glass of lemonade, and where she can smile again. She has worked every day practically for three years. It's time she had a rest. I want to thank you both for what you are doing for her. And Sam, you old dog you, take care of yourself. I'll hold you responsible for my granddaughter—she is very precious to me." The doctor shook Sam's hand and clapped him on the shoulder. "Private, I wonder if I could impose on you again and ask you to see that Sam has a place to sleep and help him with his team. I'll appreciate it."

"You bet doctor, it's as good as done. Come along Sam. I'll show you where we bunk. See you doctor."

"Doctor George youz takez care of yourself; don'z you worry none about Miss Jane, I'z see to her, don'z you worry."

🎄 Chapter Sixteen 🎄

Jane felt ashamed of herself that she was so anxious to leave, and poor Gramps, he would be left to cope all alone. He had sent word to headquarters about Dr. Fugate being wounded and had requested another doctor, but so far none had arrived. Zoll was bringing Dr. Fugate back to the compound at the end of the week; a train north was due then and she was sure he would be on it and heading home at last. He had recovered and seemed to accept his fate, she was told. A wonderful surgeon who wouldn't be able to continue his profession; however, he could still practice medicine. But surgery would be out of the question for him.

Jane washed her hair and got her few dresses together. She wouldn't take the boy clothes that she worked in—they wouldn't be needed; Gramps was giving her some gold to buy some new things when she reached Charlotte. Her hair hung to her waist— the red highlights glistening in the sunlight that was peeking through the small window to the west. They were to leave at daybreak. She felt she would be safe with the big black man, Sam, who would be driving her, but her grandfather had asked that the private go as an escort, and he had been permitted leave to go with them.

Gramps had sent her to the wagon to do the necessary things it took to be ready; when he finally came to fetch her for supper, she was ready. Her hair and face shining and with a big smile, she greeted her Gramps. They talked through the meal and when they returned to the wagon they talked well into the night.

"Gramps, thank you for being so good to me, and for letting me try my hand at doctoring; I love you and will be back to help soon." Jane gave her Gramps a big hug and kiss as she was helped aboard the rig for the trip to Charlotte.

"Take care of her, Sam, I'll see you soon, granddaughter," he waved a kiss at her as Sam flicked the reins and the rig left the compound.

Jane waved to those who looked up as they drove away. Tears came into her eyes, thinking of her grandfather. She soon became interested in the wayside, as they traveled along. The main road was in bad shape in places but Sam maneuvered the small rig around mud holes and obstacles that were in their way. Jane's cheeks were pink, her eyes shining, as she looked around. The crisp air smelled so wonderful after being closed in with the smells of the operating tent, and she relished the freshness. She was wrapped in a warm wool throw and was very comfortable in the rig as it raced along.

The three reached the Rafferty Plantation just as the sun slid behind the far mountain. The Raffertys welcomed Jane; they had three daughters—one prettier than the other, who came out onto the veranda to hug and fuss over Jane, while they all cast sly glances at the good-looking Private who accompanied her.

"Come in, come in, Mrs. Rafferty hurried to invite, you must be frozen; come in to the fire, you too, private; Sam, go around back and one of the boys will take care of you and help with your team. We weren't sure just what day you would come, but you're welcome," she hurried ahead her long dress swinging as she walked.

Someone took Jane's shawl and handed her a hot spicy drink; the girls were all trying to help the private with his great-coat and seeing that he had a steaming cup, too. "You'all come sit by the fire and thaw out. Supper will soon be served," the pretty girls informed them.

Mrs. Rafferty hurried off to the kitchen; returning after her check, she looked at the oldest daughter. "Chloe, take Jane up to her room and let her freshen up for supper—it will be ready directly; Private, come this way; you can wash, and you will sleep in the library—we are limited for space for gentlemen."

"Thank you, Mrs. Rafferty, I can bunk anywhere. Don't put yourself out. I'm used to a tent or anywhere," he told her.

"Come back to the foyer when you are ready. We'll be eating when you're finished," she hurried away back down the long hall.

The supper was a lively affair with Mrs. Rafferty apologizing for the lack of more variety in their food, which to Jane and the Private seemed a banquet in comparison to what they had been used to at the compound.

Mr. Rafferty was a tall distinguished man who walked with a limp; he had been in the fighting early on in the war, and had been wounded. The conversation was about the war and the waste of lives and homes. He seemed to think that it would soon end.

"There is nothing more left, no more young men so much destruction, the south will never recover. This should never have happened," he shook his head as the sadness crept into his eyes. The guests were encouraged to go to their rooms whenever they wanted, knowing that they had to be on the road at daybreak. Jane could see the threadbare of the carpet down the hallway as she went to her room. This had been a proud plantation, she could see, but four years of war had taken its toll.

* * *

The Ball house where they stopped the second night was much smaller than the Rafferty Plantation. Jane only noticed one old Negro who help Sam with the team. Their welcome was just as warm and the best given them as the guests of the Balls.

Jane had discovered it was tiring to sit all day even in the comfortable rig that had been sent for her. She was glad to go to bed early, to be prepared for the following day's travel.

When they left the Balls, the road seemed to be wider and to have a rock base; after a while, the look of the countryside changed. Wide fields lay along each side of the road. Houses were in a bad state of neglect, and some had been burned to the ground. Large barns had been burned and ravaged. You could see the broken trees leading to what had been beautiful plantation houses. Jane had tears in her eyes, thinking of her home and thankful that the ravages of war hadn't reached it.

Sam finally turned up a long curving driveway lined with oleanders, with mimosa beyond them, their bare branches rattling in the winter wind. Jane could see neglect here too—gardens overgrown, down fence rails and a barn roof sadly in need of repair. When they came in sight of the house, she was amazed at how big and rambling it was. Big round pillars held up a rounded roof that reached out to cover the many stone steps that led up to the double-door entrance way. An old lady waited on the piazza standing tall and proud, a worn shawl over her head and wrapped around her shoulders.

"There's Ms' Barrlette, Miss Jane, she will show you in; I'll bring your tote;" he took Jane's arm and guided her to the old lady. "Ms' Barrlette, this is Miss Jane; doctor sent his regards." Sam went to stable the horse and rig.

"Come in child, you must be frozen the cold gets to me nowadays; come, I'll have a hot drink brought. She led her through a mammoth foyer down a long hall way to a setting room toward the back that boasted a big open fire, and deep comfortable chairs. "Take your things off; the girl will be here momentarily to take your wraps—she's busy fixin' drinks. We spied you coming down below as you rounded the bend. Welcome to 'Barrlette House', it's not what it used to be, but we still have a roof over our heads which some don't. Our grandson says we are one of the lucky ones. It's hard to feel so when we have lost so much. Here's Lucy with our drinks. This is Jane, Lucy; she is going to be our guest for a time. Lucy dropped a small curtsey Ms' Jane, I've brought you a hot drink." She handed one to Mrs. Barrlette and one to Jane. The mugs were daulton blue and nice and hot—minty steam wafting from them scented the air.

"Thank you Lucy, ummm that smells so—good, and such pretty cups. It's nice to meet you Lucy; I'll try not to be too much trouble during my stay," she smiled at Lucy who smiled a big toothy smile back.

Mr. Barrlette has took to his bed with the gripp. He's been failing for some time. I think worry has took its toll. There isn't a doctor around and we just have to do the best we can with what we have. I'm afraid his age is telling on him. I'm not well either but try to stay on my feet. Lucy douses us with whatever she thinks will help, it usually just has to run its course."

Jane could hardly keep her eyes open. After all the cold fresh air she couldn't stay awake. I'm sorry Ms. Barrlette, I think this hot drink is making me sleepy; the air was so fresh and sweet smelling after being around ether and disinfectant for so long I had forgotten how nice it was to breathe fresh air," Jane laughing told her.

"I'm sorry, I should have realized how far you have traveled today; I'll call Lucy and she can see you to your room; you can freshen up and have a nap before supper." She walked over to the fireplace and pulled on a tasseled pull to call Lucy.

"Did you ring Ms' Barrlette?"

"Lucy, would you show Jane to the blue room—she needs a rest before supper; and would you please look in on Mr. Barrlette while you are above stairs, if you will. I think I may rest awhile myself—getting excited over our quests has tired me too." Mrs.

Barrlette smiled at the girls as they started up the long winding staircase.

"This is a beautiful old house. I'll bet it has seen a lot in its day. It's so sad to see it neglected." Jane was looking at the carved banister and the beautiful chandeliers with their prisms throwing off light as they turned.

"This was a house full of laughter, music and good talk. The Barrlettes only had one son, Eric—he was killed at the beginning of the war; their only grandson, Lance, is fighting now. He makes his home here. His mother, Ealnore, died shortly after Eric was killed. Ms' Barrlette is still grieving for her only son and she loved Ealnore as she would have a daughter; Losing them both so close together told on Mr. Barrlette too; I'm afraid for him. We can't get the proper care for him, as all the doctors are with the army. Lance is due for a leave; I hope he comes soon even though I don't know what he would or could do." They had reached the long hall as Lucy finished telling her this.

"As soon as I rest a little I would like to examine Mr. Barrlette; I've been doctoring with my grandfather for four years, and treated most everything—maybe I can do something. But I'm so tired now, I just have to rest and have my wits about me before I could form an opinion." Jane smiled at Lucy as she opened the door to a beautiful room. "Oh, how pretty," Jane remarked as she entered the big airy room. The big canopy bed had peacock blue curtains tied back—sheer embroidered batiste curtains underneath. The mulled windows had the same Sheers with tied back drapes. An Autobusom rug covered the shining wood floor and a small fire burned in the grate. Two pale blue wing-chairs faced the small blaze. A tea service sat on one of the tables beside the chair. Lovely pictures adorned the walls and a chaise filled with pillows was in front of the double windows. Books were on every table and chest. "This is certainly not what I'm used to." Jane proceeded to tell Lucy about their house on wheels where she and her grandfather shared. "Are you the only maid, Lucy?" she asked.

"No. There's Flo the cook, and her boy Getty, and Slazze the house maid—she does the cleaning; we all pitch in with that. There are several still left in the fields and at the barn. Sam—he has been here for ages—he was married once. His wife died with birthin their first baby. There is a young white boy come here. That's Andy; he has no kin; Sam took him in; he does a little of everything around the barn and yard. He's a good boy about eight or so. Used to be over three hundred workers; most took off; they don't knows when they are well off. The Barrlette's are good masters. They never mistreated no one." Lucy shook her head, "I don't understand what is happening, we have all been happy here. Now everything is so unsettled. I'll look in on Mr. Barrlette and go help with supper; I'll call you when it's ready—you have a nice nap."

Jane washed herself and changed into another dress—the one she had on needed airing. She then decided to stretch out on the chaise and threw a coverlet over herself and was soon asleep.

It was more than an hour when Lucy came and knocked on Jane's door. She had begun to awaken when she heard the knock She swung her feet over the chaise and went to the door. "Yes?" she said as she opened the door.

Lucy stood there, "Dinner is almost ready to be served. You can come down with me if you are ready. It's easy to get lost in all the turns up here if you don't know your way."

"I can see that; how many rooms are there?"

"There are thirty counting the downstairs with the ballroom. It's a big house—lots of the rooms are closed off now, of course. Some of the beautiful things were taken to sell for the cause, so some aren't as beautiful as they once were. All the valuable silver and paintings are gone. We still have some things that were Ms' Barrlette's mothers—she refused to let those go, but not many."

"How is Mr. Barrlette? Is he showing improvement?" Jane looked at Lucy as she asked and saw a fleeting look of worry on the black face.

"No better I'm afraid; I took him some broth; he doesn't look good and not eating enough. I'm very worried and I know that Ms' Barrlette is too. I do hope you can do something." Lucy looked hopefully at Jane.

When the dinner was over, Ms' Barrlette and Jane went to the small sitting room where they had been before and had their tea. After seating themselves Mrs. Barrlette said, "We don't have the food to do our cook justice. She does well with what she has, and I long for a real cup of coffee or tea. There's been none for months. We make do. Lucy explained that you have been doctoring with your grandfather for almost four years. Have you been with him all the time he has been with the army? That seems a rugged life for a bit of a girl, especially one as beautiful as you. No wonder you need a rest away from it."

"Yes, Gramps and I came from home together; I had helped him in his practice, more as a nurse. When we got into the thick of the war and wounded piling up, we put up another table for me. I would take the less serious cases and tend them. If I needed help he would come. Then one day he disappeared. We looked and looked. We had moved the camp and he stayed behind, Doctor Fugate was still operating; Gramps had old Babe and usually rode her when we broke camp. It gave him a change. Anyway, while Doctor Fugate was operating they took down the operating tent and sent it on ahead. He was out in the open finishing an amputation when the camp was shelled. A shell found its way in and hit the table where Dr. Fugate was working, it killed the soldier and wounded the doctor.

Gramps picked him up from where he fell and threw him across old Babe, and headed away into the woods. He had to stop and amputate the doctor's left arm out in the woods. He ran onto a cabin in the area and took Dr. Fugate there; he stayed to make sure the doctor was going to survive—you see they are very good friends. When Gramps didn't show up for two days, I had to take over. The orderlies said I had to operate or dozens of soldiers would perish. I had helped Gramps for so long— I started in—after the first one it seemed as though I had always been doing it. Out of all the operations I performed, I only lost one patient; I still don't know what happened. It was a very bad head wound; there could have been a fragment of bone that worked its way into the brain. There is no way of telling. I did my best and Gramps says sometimes that isn't good enough." Tears were streaming down Jane's face as she relived that terrible experience.

"I never realized you had gone through so much. Some of our women volunteered in the hospitals here, but I don't think they had to witness things like this. You poor child, try not to think of it. You must guard your health." She smiled at Jane.

"I guess I'm different. I have always wanted to be a doctor even when I was little. I started helping Gramps at about eight years old, you know keeping things picked up, cleaning and sterilizing his instruments. I was ready for it but there was too much all at once, and I was so worried about Gramps; we didn't know where he was if he was dead or alive. I was the only female for miles; the men had gone searching for him and not a sign anywhere. We didn't know if he had been killed or captured or what. I was just sick with worry, but still had to go on. I kept thinking what if he doesn't show up. The wounded just kept coming. I couldn't keep up where three had been working before and still not able to keep abreast of the wounded at times—only I was left. It was a scary time—I get weak just thinking of it." Jane wiped her eyes and looked toward Mrs. Barrlette.

"What a brave girl you are. I doubt even a man could have held up under all of that. I would appreciate your looking at Mr. Barrlette when you feel up to it. There's little medicine anywhere. Maybe when Lance comes home on leave, which we had word would be soon, he can get anything you need. He's a Major now. I worry and pray for him every day. We have lost them all but him. I'm so afraid for him. If only this awful war would end. It'll take fifty years for each side to build back what has been destroyed— if then. I know the south will never be the same again.

Jane felt so sorry for the Barrlette family. They had lost so much but still held themselves with dignity. "I'll go now and see if I can do anything for Mr. Barrlette." Jane had a small black satchel with her things—her grandfather had given her a few things to equip it with. She asked Lucy to guide her to her room and go with her to the room where Mr. Barrlette was.

Lucy opened the door to a room along the hall closer to the staircase. It was, if anything, even larger than the one Jane occupied. Massive furniture crowded the room; a fire burned in the grate and the room was stifling hot. Jane could see the sick man propped up on numerous pillows. His face pale as he watched them enter.

Lucy took her hand and led her to the bed. "This is Jane Jarvis, your friend Doctor George's granddaughter. She has been doctoring with him for four years in the war, and even helped him before. Ms' Barrlette has asked her to have a look at you and see what can be done to get you up and around. Your grandson will be here in a few days and she wants to have a small 'sorea' to give him some fun while he's home and a chance to see some of his friends. You have to be better to take part in the fun."

Jane took hold of his hand; feeling it hot and dry, she took his pulse. "It's so good to meet you sir. Gramps has told me so much about you." His pulse was racing, he definitely had a fever. "How do you feel? Do you have pain anywhere?"

"Yes, I have pain here," he touched his side under his left arm at the beginning of the rib-cage. "It hurts when I breathe and my head hurts; I am hot one minute and cold the next. Lucy has given me all sorts of awful tasting brews—nothing seems to help. I have no appetite, and even though I force some broths down I grow weaker and weaker each day." He stopped describing his symptoms and looked long at Jane.

"That's a good description of your ailment; now we will see what we can do to make you feel better. I'll consult with Lucy and see what she has given you so far and if anything helped. I would like to air this room out some. Let's cover you good and let a little air in to clean out some of this foul air that's here now. I think that may make breathing easier for you." She and Lucy opened a couple of windows that wouldn't blow directly on the old man. "Five minutes no longer", Jane told Lucy. While they waited Lucy told her the teas she had brewed for him. Jane could see why he thought they were foul and why they hadn't done any good.

The five minutes were up; as they closed the two windows that had been opened, Jane could tell the room didn't smell so stale. She firmly believed in a lot of fresh air for the sick. Some didn't— even doctors.

"I'll be back directly," Jane told him as she and Lucy closed the door. Jane wanted to gather some willow bark and branches before dark, and she needed some mint and mustard seed. Hopefully, the house would have some. If there had been mullein she would have used that. She had some of her mullein cough medicine with her that she had made before leaving home.

She would give him that— it would help as an expectorant and bring up the phlegm that kept his breathing shallow and helped to bring on fever. A mustard plaster would help loosen it too, the willow tea would bring the fever down and make him sleep and help the headache he had complained of. Yes, she nodded her head he should be feeling some better by tomorrow.

Jane saw Sam in the back and asked him about willows—where she could find some. "I'll fetch them Miss Jane. Do you want small ones or older ones?"

"Peel some of the bark from about an inch growth and bring me a handful of the small twig-branches—I don't need a lot. And I thank you Sam. They are to treat Mr. Barrlette."

Going to the kitchen to find Lucy, Jane asked, "Do you have mustard? And do you know how to make a mustard plaster?" Lucy smiled. "I've made mustard plasters since I was eight years old. I'll have one ready for you in a short time. Anything else you need.?"

"Yes, I'll need flat irons heated and wrapped in something to put at his feet. We have to break this fever he has, and get the phlegm up that is hampering his breathing. I have something for that."

Jane found her way back to the sickroom. She had brought a tea kettle and put it on the hopper at the fire to heat, and a mug for the tonic she would mix with hot water. The water was soon hot and she mixed the drink for him and held him up in bed to drink it. It consisted of steeped mullein leaves, honey, a small amount of whiskey and some mint to flavor it.

"That tastes a lot better than Lucy's concoctions—I hope it works." He smiled at Jane.

"It'll work. But I'm not through yet. I still have some tea and a mustard plaster for you; by tomorrow you will be feeling much better, I promise." She smiled at the gentle old man—he reminded her of her Gramps; tears stung her eyes when she thought of him.

Jane went back down the long stairway. Sam should be back with the willows; they had to steep for some time for the tea for headache and fever. She wanted to get that started. The mustard plaster could only stay on for minutes and then she would give him the tea and he would sleep, hopefully, most of the night.

The mustard was about ready and Sam had brought the willow bark and twigs. She rinsed them in a pan of water and cut the stems in lengths that would fit the cooking pot. Pouring enough water over them to cover them well she set them where they would simmer on the back of the stove.

"I think you had better take the pot of mustard and spread it on the material when you get upstairs—that way it will stay hot," Lucy said handing Jane a square of folded flannel.

"You're right. Would you keep an eye on the willow tea for me? I'll take this right up and get it on our patient. The sooner he is treated the sooner he will be well."

Minutes after the plaster was applied Mr. Barrlette seemed to be breathing easier. "How's the pain?" Jane asked.

"My chest feels better, and the pain isn't so severe. I can begin to feel the tightness going; Your grandfather had better watch out, you may take all his patients," he smiled at Jane.

Jane sat watching him. She could see he was suppressing coughs; soon the phlegm would be coming up. Even a little would help his breathing and make him feel easier. Jane felt the plaster; it was cool enough that it wouldn't burn him while she went to make the willow tea. "I'll be back directly," she told him. She could see he was much more relaxed than before as she left the room.

Checking the willows that were seeping she asked— "Do you have honey Lucy?"

"I'm sure there is some. Let me look. Here's a small amount, I hope its enough."

"That's more than enough; where can I find a strainer? Lucy handed her a small one that Jane held over a stoneware pitcher to catch the tea. While it was hot she stirred a spoonful or two of honey into it. Taking the pitcher and a cup she went back to the sick room. She removed the mustard plaster and put a pillow behind her patient's head and held the cup while he drank a good amount of the tea. When he finished he started to cough; Jane held a pan for him to dispose of the phlegm, then removed the pillow from behind him. "You'll soon sleep, and I think you will sleep through the night. How do you feel?"

"I can't believe how much better; my head still aches, but I don't have so much pain, and I do feel sleepy," he told her.

"The tea will take care of your headache. I'll sit till I know you are asleep. One of us will watch through the night in case you need us." His eyes had closed before she finished telling him.

Going back down the stairs she explained that someone should be with him throughout the night in case he had a severe coughing spell and couldn't get the phlegm up, they needed to lift him up in bed. I'll sit with him for the next few hours. I feel refreshed after my nap. Then I'll call Lucy, if I may."

❧ Chapter Seventeen ❧

Mr. Barrlette slept for about three hours. Jane seeing him stir, mixed another tonic and raised him up holding the cup to his mouth. She decided to apply the mustard plaster again. It could only be left a short time or there would be blistering due to the previous application; in eight minutes she removed it, and heated the willow tea and brought a cup for him. He should sleep the rest of the night in comfort; his color had returned and he seemed to have slept a natural sleep.

When morning came Jane, hurrying to the sick room found Mr. Barrlette sitting up in bed and having poached eggs on toast. He smiled at Jane's surprised look.

"Good morning! Don't tell me I no longer have a patient. You look ready for a morning stroll," she said with a quick smile.

"I'm feeling so much better; I would have gotten out of bed but Elizabeth forbade it. Whatever you gave me has done the trick. You're a fine doctor; I hope all those soldiers appreciated you. I can see where Dr. George will miss your help. I'll just take it easy today but tomorrow my feet will be on the floor."

"Is the pain in your chest gone?"

"Even my headache is completely gone. I still cough a little but nothing comes up; you are a remarkable girl."

Jane looking at Mr. Barrlette was well pleased. She had been so afraid he had pneumonia and it was almost always fatal. "I'm so pleased with your speedy recovery; I'll have breakfast and look in later." Jane left the room and headed toward the downstairs. When she reached the kitchen there was an air of excitement among the servants. They all seemed to be busy—she looked around for Lucy—not seeing her decided to go to the small dining room where she and Mrs. Barrlette had their meals. There was food set out on the buffet; Jane took a plate and began to fill it with hot food. She had just poured a cup of tea when Mrs. Barrlette came in.

"Good morning," Jane cheerfully called."

"Good morning child; oh, Jane, I can't tell you how pleased I am with Charles' progress. He hasn't looked so well in weeks. And seems to have energy enough to leave his bed, but I told him it wasn't advisable. You have worked a miracle! There should be more doctors like you."

"I thank you Mrs. Barrlette, but I'm not a doctor. I would love to be but I'm not."

"Well, you should have the title; just because you are a female I know it's not allowed; but I know some people I'm going to talk to about that situation. We have wonderful news. Lance is on his way home. I plan to have a little party to welcome him, now that his grandfather will be up to join us. I've sent word to several of the plantations for Saturday night. We are going to roast one of the few steers that are left; the girls are doing what they can in the baking and cooking department. I have Sam and the boys hanging lanterns in the trees to make it look festive. We will all be together again; after all the things that have happened, I don't believe in wasting a moment." she smiled at Jane.

"What can I do to help? I'm afraid I don't have anything to wear to such a doings. Is there anywhere I could buy suitable clothing? Gramps gave me some money for things. I brought very little clothing with me. I wore boy's clothes most of the time for work. They were warm and comfortable," she explained.

"My word, they would be more suitable among so many men I dare say. As soon as things settle a little I'll send Lucy with you to some of the stores. I'm sure you can find something to your liking. I have yard-goods but there's no time for sewing."

"If there's something I can do don't hesitate to tell me, I would like to help," Jane replied.

"The steer will be roasted outside and brought in sliced for the table. We will have a buffet; perhaps you would like to help me arrange it. The girls are all busy now and we could do that. Come along, I've had tables set up in the ballroom on one end. There will be plenty of room for the music and dancing in the other end. I'm having chairs arranged between the tables and dance floor where people can sit if they desire. We'll get some greenery and arrange a center piece for the table. I'll let you do that, when we are ready. I've eaten but will sit and have a cup of tea with you while you eat."

One of the servants had brought a big glimmering cut glass punch bowl leaving it on the long table in the ballroom, and soon returned with a tray of matching cups. An armload of different kinds of greenery was brought into the work room and Jane selected what she needed to decorate the buffet table. After arranging the greenery she shined some red and yellow apples, added a few, then cut carrots into rosebuds, there were plenty of turnips and she made those into open roses which looked very attractive, she finished with a circle of greenery and roses where the punch bowl would set.

"My that looks nice,"Mrs. Barrlette said as she came with napkins and rings. "You did a lovely job; I would never have thought of the fruit and vegetables for color—wherever did you learn to make roses from turnips? That adds a nice dash. Flo is bringing the plates and silver; it hasn't taken long at all. Thanks to your help we're almost finished." As soon as the ballroom was done to Mrs. Barrlette's satisfaction, she sent for Lucy who was to take Jane to look for a dress. It would have to be done today; if any alterations were necessary, she would have time to do them.

* * *

Sam fetched the light rig to drive the girls into town to do their shopping. Lucy shyly told Jane that she was seeing a man from the neighboring plantation his name was Londo and she hoped to marry soon, and that she would like a new dress for the festivities too. Lucy said that she wanted to look in a shop where some of the southern ladies were selling their clothing and they might find a bargain. Jane decided it would be a good idea; she might find something that wasn't too costly that she would like; she didn't mind that they were used. She would probably never see the owners anyway.

The big storeroom was full of racks of dresses, and tables held other accessories. "I don't know where to start," Jane told Lucy. "We'll find someone to help us who knows what sizes and where; wait, I'll get someone." Lucy spotted a youngish woman who came with a smile to help. "I'm Hester," she said as she looked at Jane. "I think your size will be over here—I know just the thing; it will look wonderful on you." She selected a dress from the long rack; it was a peacock blue velvet with long slim sleeves, rounded neck, a tucked-in waist and full graceful skirt. It looked awfully plain to Lucy, but she could see it would be what Jane would like. "You'll need some pearls to go with it, and there are slippers to match that I think are your size. Would you like to try it?"

Jane's eyes lit up—it was beautiful; she had never seen such soft lovely material before. She could see that the severe lines of the dress would look well on her and she would be comfortable in it. "How much will the outfit cost?" she asked.

"Let's pick out a couple more and you can try them." She selected a daytime dress of silk material. "This is called ashes of roses; isn't it pretty? And there's a pale green I want you to try too. Here it is. Come along, we will try them; we have plenty more if you aren't satisfied."

When Jane saw herself in the blue dress, she couldn't believe it was her. Her blue eyes looked enormous, her hair looked almost red, and the dress fit as though it was made for her. Hester hurried away and soon returned with the shoes and a lovely string of pearls. When Jane stepped into the slippers, the dress just brushed the floor, the shoes adding two inches to Jane's height. The pearls were all that was needed to set off the dress; Hester tucked a beautiful lacy handkerchief into the cuff of one sleeve. "You need your hair up," she lifted it slightly from Jane's neck, "With a couple of curls in front of the ears; "you look lovely."

"That you do Miss, Jane," Lucy seconded.

"Let's try the others; the ashes of roses was next; it gave Jane a completely different look. She couldn't believe that dresses and color could make her look so different. It was removed and the pale green was next, Jane saw it shimmered and change colors to a golden green when seen in different light. She looked like a wood nymph that she had read about in a fairy story; her hair looked lighter, her skin seemed to glow and her eyes changed to a green-blue. The way the dress was cut her small breasts seemed to stand out and appear larger. "Oh my," she said with a blush.

"You're beautiful," Hester told her. "I could try dresses on you all day, and enjoy each one."

"I'll have to have shoes to go with the other two dresses." Jane remarked.

"Just a minute, I have the very thing," she returned with a pair of bone-colored pumps and a small bag to match.

When Jane tried them, she could see that they were perfect with both dresses too. "I only have a hundred dollar gold piece; will that be enough?" she looked worriedly at Hester.

"It will cover them and a few other things that you need. She hurried to the accessory table and selected a lacy handful of undergarments, a set of combs with several pearls in them and a small leather bag to match the blue-gray shoes that went with the peacock blue dress. "There you are, you don't need anything else. Oh, yes you'll need a wrap; she searched through another table piled high with things and selected a long gray wool wrap that had threads of gold and a deep fringe on each end; placing it around Jane's shoulders it hung to her knees. "That's it; now you have everything you need. My! The first gentleman you meet is going to propose to you." she smiled at Jane's blush.

"I'm so pleased; thank you Hester; now, could you find Lucy something for the party too?"

Hester took Lucy to another rack and soon found a dress for Lucy; she liked a soft yellow with violets splashed over it. I'll have shoes and things to go with it," Lucy told them.

"Lucy you look lovely; that man of yours is going to want to marry you immediately," Jane told her.

Lucy was embarrassed from Jane's compliment. Hester nodded, you do look lovely Lucy; may I suggest you leave your hair curl a little more around your face—you're a very pretty girl."

* * *

When the girls returned to the plantation, Jane hurried to check in on Mr. Barrlette. He was sleeping soundly; someone had raised one of the windows an inch and a cool breeze made the sick room fresh smelling. Jane couldn't wait to try on all three dresses again, and put her hair up like Hester had suggested. When she opened the package with the accessories, she discovered that Hester had tucked in a packet of sachet that smelled of lavender. The material of the dresses had picked up the scent. She felt absolutely glamorous with all her new attire as she tried them—swirling in front of the mirror. Smiling to herself she said, "if Timmy Miller saw me now he would faint dead away," she giggled as she gave another twirl.

* * *

The household settled down to an early night. Jane had checked on Mr. Barrlette, gave him a hot cup of the willow tea and tucked him in. Someone had closed the crack of the window and the fire had been banked for the night. "I think you will have a good night tonight; sleep tight," she smiled.

"And don't let the bedbugs bite," came from the half asleep Mr. Barrlette.

* * *

Jane slept so soundly that even the weak sun that shone on her big four poster bed didn't awaken her. She had been dreaming of the operating tent. There were piles and piles of wounded and she was the only one around to help them. She heard moaning and knew someone was crying out— "Miss Jane—Miss Jane" a knock on the door and Lucy entered. "Is something wrong, Miss Jane? I heard you cry out."

"I'm sorry Lucy, I've overslept; I was dreaming of the hospital tent where I worked. I was all alone and the wounded were everywhere; they were crying out for help—tears ran down Jane's face as she raised up in bed. I feel so bad leaving my Gramps to cope with everything. I must go back as soon as I'm rested."

"Try not to think about it," Lucy handed her a robe and poured warm water into the basin for Jane to wash. "When you're finished Ms. Barrlette said to tell you she's in the small sitting room and she would like to have you join her for tea."

"I'm sorry I'm so late. I'll be right there." Jane quickly dressed and rushed down the long flight of stairs to the small room in back.

"Good morning Jane, I hope you slept well. Charles slept the night through and is wanting up this morning. I've told him to wait a while, that we are all busy and he should rest; I don't want him to have a backset. You look lovely as usual; I've asked Lucy to bring you a plate here so we can talk. I miss having someone close to talk to. Here's Lucy now."

"I've brought you some scrambled eggs and toast and a little preserves. I know you eat lightly." she placed them on a small table by Jane's chair. "Thank you Lucy," Jane said as Lucy left the room.

"I hope you and Lance like each other. He is old enough to take a wife. There'll be more than one girl here tonight that will be using all her charm to be that person. So far he hasn't favored any of them. He likes to tease them all. He is very special to his grandfather and I, and will be our heir—all the rest are gone. At one time he would have been a wealthy man; as things are now, there are only the land and house. And it will take years to get things back where there will be a profit from it. We all love this old house—I'm afraid it will be too costly to keep it up; most of the darkies are gone; we treated them well but that didn't seem to be enough. Charles' health isn't good even though he pulled through this. I'm afraid each time he takes to his bed will be his last. I'm strong, but at times it's hard for me to carry on and keep things moving; the place needs a man's hand to manage it. I'm anxious to have Lance meet you, I know you two will like each other. Who knows."

The color stained Jane's face as she looked at Mrs. Barrlette. "This is a lovely old place; I love the house, but I can see it needs care. We saw so much devastation on the way here, and I know there are worse areas where the fighting has been more intense. I'm anxious to meet your grandson, maybe being away will make the young ladies of his acquaintance more attractive to him. Who knows, you may have a wedding before he has to return to his unit," she smiled at Mrs. Barrlette.

* * *

The beef had been in the roasting pit since early morning—the smell made everyone hungry as it wafted toward the house. All the cooking and baking was finished. Lucy had told Jane to go to her room and have a nap and she would have warm water brought for her bath in an hour. "I want you dressed and ready to help Mrs. Barrlette in the receiving line when people arrive; I'll be up to help with your hair and help get you dressed. You have to look special tonight." She smiled at Jane as she bossed her.

"Thank you Lucy; I am a little tired. Those stairs are long and I've been up and down them several times today. Mr. Barrlette is napping and so is Mrs. Barrlette; I guess it will be a long evening. I'll go right up. Don't let me oversleep."

A slight knock on the door awoke Jane, "I'm coming," she called. When she went to the door, Lucy stood there. "Time to get up and get dressed. Lance and his friends have arrived, and have gone to their rooms to rest. I'm surprised they didn't wake you. I'll come in half an hour to help you dress and fix your hair. Ms. Barrlette wants you to help her receive." Lucy hurried off, and Flo's son Getty came with buckets of water for Jane.

"Thank you, Getty; just bring a couple of buckets of cold water and that will do." Jane sprinkled some dried lavender leaves into the hot water to seep a minute while she waited for the cold water to cool it enough to get into. The dried lavender scented the room as the steam rose from the tub. Getty soon returned and the bath water was ready. Jane had laid out on her bed the things she would wear. Jane sat in the tub of scented water thinking what a luxury it was after the three years she had lived in a house built on a wagon with her Gramps and took her baths in a wash pan; she smiled to herself as she hurried out of the tub and started to dress. The lacy things she put on seemed weightless; she had never worn anything so flimsy before and she felt as though she had nothing on. "What would Mamma say?" she smiled to herself. Lucy came and helped her lift the blue velvet over her head; it was heavy and gave her the feeling of being dressed; the fabric had absorbed the sachet and also smelled of lavender. "Mmmm, you smell good; let's start on your hair."

Jane sat at the dressing table as Lucy spread out the skirt of her dress so it didn't become wrinkled. She brushed Jane's hair till it crackled and popped, rubbed some brilliantine on her hands and lightly stroked her hair. There was a curling iron lying across a cast-iron container with hot coals in it. Lucy tested the iron, and picking up strands of hair here and there made curls letting them drop until she was ready to pin up Jane's hair. She tried it first one way and then another. Jane's hair was natural curly and thick and easy to work with. Lucy brushed most of it to one side and let several curls trail down onto her neck; raising the rest to the top of her head, she pinned it and inserted the combs, letting the pearls show. She pulled enough hair out of the upsweep to add curls in front of each ear—patted it here and there. "That's it; how do you like it?" Lucy asked.

Jane sat speechless; she didn't know the beautiful girl who looked back at her from the mirror. "Oh, Lucy you have made me beautiful. I never knew I could look like this. What did you do to my hair? It looks almost red." Thank you, Lucy.

"You are beautiful, Miss Jane; you just needed the clothes to bring it out. We have to hurry now, people will be arriving any minute." Lucy was tidying the room as she talked.

Jane swirled in front of the mirror admiring herself. She took one more look and swirled the full skirt until it stood out in graceful fullness. "I'm ready." Picking up the skirt with one hand so she wouldn't accidentally step on it, she followed Lucy down the long staircase. Londo, dressed in a black suit with white linen, stood at the big double doors ready to open it for the guests. He had been borrowed from a neighboring plantation to butler for the Barrettes. Lucy, in her new yellow dress, would stand beside him ready to show the ladies to the dressing room beside the ballroom to remove their cloaks, and see to any last minute grooming.

Jane entered the ballroom by herself; she saw that Mrs. Barrlette was all ready there. She went toward her and when Mrs. Barrlette saw her she looked with astonishment when she recognized her.

"Jane! I didn't recognize you; you are positively beautiful; there isn't a girl around who will be dressed so lavishly or as beautiful. You are a sight to behold; what did you do to your hair? It shines with red highlights and you don't look like the same girl. You're going to break a lot of hearts tonight. I know Lance will be overwhelmed, I certainly am." Her eyes sparkled as she stared at Jane.

Londo came to the door, bowed to Mrs. Barrlette, and announced— "Mr. and Mrs. Lane and daughters;" "Welcome come in, how are you? Sueann, Cecile, you both look lovely. I would like you to meet our guest, Jane Jarvis, who is staying with us for a while." Jane bowed to Mr. and Mrs. Lane and smiled at the two girls; there was no time for small talk as the Ferrells were right behind them to be welcomed. Several young gentlemen were introduced to Jane; she couldn't keep count of names and was at a loss to remember even one. The room began to fill; Getty was passing through the room with a silver tray of drinks, nodding to this one and that one as they said hello to him. The musicians began to play softly, and the room buzzed with talk.

"Where can Lance and his friends be? I suppose they want to make an entrance; that's just like that bunch of boys," Mrs. Barrlette smiled as she thought of them.

No one had come for a few minutes and Jane had time to catch her breath and look around. There was suddenly a drum roll—

Jane looked toward the door—her eyes met the biggest pair of brown eyes fringed in long black eyelashes that she had ever seen. Her heart skipped a beat. There were five tall handsome soldiers, dressed in gold braid, and sashed Confederate uniforms. She glanced at the handsome men but her eyes quickly returned to the brown eyes which were still locked on her. They traveled from the curls atop her head to the dainty slippers on her feet, then back to her lips. A slight flush swept up Jane's face, as she tore her eyes away in confusion.

"Here they are at last," Mrs. Barrlette announced; as the men came to her she scolded— "you naughty boys, where have you been, the party can't start until you're here. Jane, I would like to introduce you to my grandson; Lance, this is Jane Jarvis; going on she said Jane, Major Rex Hargrove, Major Ron Blankenship, Captain Walter Rice, Captain Rick Long." Each took Jane's small hand and bowing placed a light kiss upon it. Jane blushed prettily as she acknowledged the young men.

Several of the girls gave little squeals as they rushed toward the soldiers. Each of them soon had a female on each arm as they were ushered toward the dance floor, laughter and a few tears, greeting them.

"Grandma, you never warned me that our guest was so beautiful; I thought you said she was a doctor or nurse or something. She is neither—she's a fairy princess," Lance glanced around and spotted Sueann rushing toward him; turning he took Jane's arm. "Let me get you a drink; come." He steered her through the crowd away from the approaching Sueann. He handed Jane a drink, and taking one for himself, he looked into her eyes, "here is to the most beautiful girl in the room, and to a long and pleasant acquaintance." They sipped their drinks for a few minutes when Lance said, "let's dance, I can't wait another minute to hold you in my arms." The top of Jane's head came even with his mouth, where he proceeded to plant a kiss. Jane knew she was blushing again. "You're the most beautiful woman I've ever seen; you're light as a feather, and smell so—good, you know I'm never going to let you go, don't you?"

Jane was weak-kneed and speechless; finally getting her wits about her she said, "I doubt I will be able to find a suitable horse to join your cavalry in time to go back with you, Major Barrlette, however, it sounds exciting."

Lance let out a loud laugh stopping in the middle of the dance, his arm still around Jane as she looked up at him. "A sense of humor too." He grabbed her to him and whirled her away as all eyes turned toward them. He danced in silence for several minutes. "I guess you know I have to be polite and dance with some of the other girls? I don't want to let you go, you know that too, don't you?"

"That never crossed my mind," Jane remarked, a faint smile on her pretty mouth. Just then the music ended. Rather than being left alone when Lance left to do his duty dances, Jane went toward Mrs. Barrlette where she sat with several of the older women; she proceeded to introduce Jane to the others. Lance bent to her ear, "I'll be back!" he whispered as he melted into the crowd.

Mr. Barrlette, seeing Jane sitting alone while his wife and friends gossiped, came and asked Jane for a dance. "Are you sure you should?" she asked him. "Just a short one my dear," He led her to the floor and waltzed her around the room a couple of times, "You are a wonderful dancer, and so beautiful half the men in this room are falling in love with you. You know that don't you?" he asked as he smiled into her upturned face.

"Oh, Mr. Barrlette you are as bad as your grandson; you're an excellent dance partner yourself you know; I think we should stop now—you aren't as strong as you should be." She headed back to the seated group. "Thank you my dear," he said as he joined some of his friends. Someone else claimed Jane and off she went to mingle with the other dancers. She notice whoever she danced with that Lance's eyes followed her. Even when she wasn't looking in his direction she could feel his eyes on her. She suddenly wondered how the five officers made their way through the Union lines to come to the dance. When she thought of all those young men being taken to a prison camp she shivered with apprehension.

At eight o'clock dinner was served, the big table filled with food; laughter and talk echoed throughout the big ballroom. Announcements were made for various things and causes the women were working on. The musicians started the dance tunes and partners were chosen and the dancing began. Jane had her back turned to the room when an arm went around her waist, "oh," she said startled. "It's only me—your betrothed; you are going to marry me aren't you? How about tomorrow at ten?" Lance's smiling eyes looked into hers. "Let's dance, you can decide while we dance," he smiled at her again.

Jane didn't know how to answer him. Her heart was quivering in her chest, and her legs almost refused to hold her. She saw Sueann, giving her murderous looks from across the floor. "I think Sueann would be more your type" she answered. "She seems to be very interested in you."

"I grew up with Sueann; if I had wanted her, I would have already been married. She's like a sister to me; you are the one I want—you're my mate; did you know there's only one mate for each person on this earth?" he whispered into her hair, "of course you know, you can feel it that we were meant for each other." Shivers were running up and down Jane's back, and she started to shake. Lance raised her chin with his finger, looking deep into her eyes, "Come let's go somewhere we can talk."

❧ Chapter Eighteen ❧

Jane wasn't sure that her legs would hold her up as Lance led her from the ballroom. When they were out of sight he circled her waist with one arm and guided her down the long hallway to the back setting room where he placed her in an armchair and knelt on the floor at her feet. Taking both of her hands he tenderly kissed each one as he looked into her eyes, his big brown eyes full of feeling. "Jane, I know you think this is sudden, but I've been waiting all my life for you. I have loved you forever—I just hadn't seen you before. I want you to be my wife, tonight. Say you will marry me. I don't know how much time we have. I might have to leave at any moment. There are a lot of Confederate officers in that ballroom. We could all die tonight. Our cause is lost, we all know that, it is just a matter of time. We are gathering our forces for a last big battle. I don't want to think of that—just of us. Say you will be my wife, Jane, I'll come back I promise you and we will rebuild Barrlette House and raise our family here. You belong here, Jane; you make a perfect Lady of the Manor." Lance pulled her into his arms, raising up from the floor, holding her as if he would never let her go. He kissed her hair, eyes, and finally her rosebud mouth, murmuring love words all the while.

Jane could scarcely stand, she was so weak-kneed; she had heard of southern girls swooning, she had never been so close to that in her life. She wanted to be held forever in this tall handsome Major's arms; "Lance, Lance, we have just met. You don't know me. We are even on different sides in this war. When you hold me my mind refuses to function; I seem helpless to make a decision; you sweep me along on a wave of love; I have to admit I've never had the feelings I have at this minute. Marriage is a big step; I will soon have to return to my Grandfather's unit; maybe when its over—."

"Jane, I love you so." He rained kisses on every part of her flushed face as Jane tried to keep her wits about her. "Please Jane, marry me now."

Jane frowned, knowing that they couldn't be married tonight;

there were license and things to do to make it legal, and by day-break he would be gone. She nodded, "All right Lance; I can't re-sist you any longer; I will marry you as soon as it can be arranged."

Lance kissed her long and hard, "Wait here just a minute, I'll be right back."

It was minutes when Lance returned with his grandfather and a heavy set man who was beaming at them both. "Jane, this is Judge Winthrop; he has the power to marry us tonight," Lance smiled from ear to ear, his eyes shining as he looked from Jane to his grandfather and then at the Judge.

Judge Winthrop took Jane's hand in his, bowed and kissed it. "It will be a pleasure, Miss Jarvis; you couldn't find a finer up-standing man than Lance, from a fine family, I've known him and his family all his life. These are unsettled times, we don't know from minute to minute what they will bring. I just happen to have Special License, for marriages of this sort. I carry special official papers with me now a days; as I said, you don't know what will be demanded from hour to hour."

Jane was shocked; it never occurred to her that a marriage could be performed on such short notice. Her knees were knock-ing together; she wasn't sure if what she felt was love or just the excitement and newness of all that was going on. She knew she had never felt this way in her life before. Her mind was going this way and that. What would her grandfather think? What would her family think? What was she to do?

Lance saw the panic in Jane's eyes and went to her, and placed an arm around her waist and pulled her close to him. "Don't be frightened darling; I know it's what we both want."

Mr. Barrlette came and took Jane's hands in his. " Jane, I want to tell you how pleased both Mrs. Barrlette and I are to have you in our family. Lance couldn't have picked someone more suitable, or someone we welcome with as much pleasure as we do you. I hope you both will be very happy my dear," he kissed her on the cheek. "Do you want me to announce the ceremony and arrange to have it in the ballroom where our guests can be part of it?"

Lance looked longingly at Jane, "Will that be what you want Jane? Or would you rather have it private? I would like for all the world to be at our wedding," he smiled into her eyes.

Jane was so numb she couldn't utter a word; she nodded her head, whatever they took it to mean was all right with her.

Lance's arm was around her and he was leading her back to the ballroom. Mr. Barrlette and Judge Winthrop led the way. As they neared the doorway, they all stopped. "Wait here, I'll make the announcement."

Mr. Barrlette went to his wife and whispered in her ear, "Oh," she said, as a smile lit her face; together they went to where the musicians were. Mr. Barrlette whispered to the leader and the dance in progress was played to the end. The Judge had followed them in and stood to one side. A few had noticed them and wondered what was going to happen. Maybe some announcement about the war; a few whispered to each other.

A drum roll — Mr. Barrlette looked around the room as all eyes were turned toward him. "Friends, neighbors, as you all know these are trying times with everything as we have known it all out of kilter; Mrs. Barrlette and I want to thank you for coming tonight and sharing with us the happiness we feel having our grandson and his friends with us, for even a short time. We have wonderful news to share with you tonight which I'm sure will be a surprise to all of you as it has been to us. You are invited to witness the wedding of our grandson in a few minutes, to someone near and dear to our hearts." Several looked toward Sueann, as she blushed and looked around for Lance. "Jane Jarvis is the granddaughter of a dear friend of mine, and has been visiting us for some time. Lance has informed me that they wish to wed here tonight; our dear friend, Judge Winthrop, has issued a special license and will perform the ceremony. Another drum roll as the Judge stepped forward, the band struck up the wedding march–.

Lucy rushed up to Jane all out of breath, handed her a small white Bible, "It's Mrs. Barrlette's; since you don't have a bouquet, you can carry it." Jane turned to Lucy, nodded as Lance took her arm and started into the ballroom. An aisle was opened as people stepped to the side to let them pass. Lance walked slowly up the length of the ballroom, firmly holding onto Jane; when he glanced at her he could see she was white as a ghost; he smiled at her, "don't faint on me darling, it will soon be over." Jane lifted her head and smiled at him.

As they reached the Judge, the ballroom was so quiet you could have heard a pin drop.

"Dearly beloved, we are gathered here this day of our Lord to join together this man and this woman in Holy Matrimony; is there anyone present who objects to this union?" the Judge continued with the rest of the ceremony; when he asked for a ring Mrs. Barrlette stepped forward and handed Lance a circle of rubies and diamonds that matched the beautiful necklace she wore. "I now pronounce you man and wife," the Judge intoned as Lance placed the circlet on Jane's finger. "You may kiss the bride." Lance wasted no time taking Jane into his arms, kissed her deeply, then turned to the Judge who shook his hand and wished him happiness; his grandfather and grandmother both hugged him and wished him happiness. His comrades gathered around the happy couple, "You dog, you! Why didn't you tell us?" Lance just brushed the questions aside and accepted the claps on the back and all the good wishes that were directed toward him and Jane. He still had an arm around her as Mr. Barrlette directed the musicians to begin the dance music again. Lance whirled Jane into the waltz that was playing. He swirled her around the dance floor as others began to dance. "You are the most beautiful bride I have ever seen, Mrs. Barrlette. You are the light of my life, and I love you to distraction," he kissed her hair and whispered into her ear. Tell me you're happy and that you love me, my sweet adorable wife."

Jane had to tilt her head back to look into Lance's eyes, "of course I love you; I'm still numb but I'm sure I'm happy; it's just that I've never had feelings like these before. Oh, Lance, I hope I can make you happy and be a good wife; to tell you the truth, I'm scared to death. This was so fast and I hardly know you; I love your grandparents, and I love this old house, and I know that is all part of you. I do love you."

"That's all I need to know; let's dance toward the doors and when no one is looking we will disappear, I want you all to myself." Lance was as good as his word and soon they had escaped into the hall. As Jane glanced back she saw Sueann glaring at her. "I'm sorry to hurt Sueann," she said as they hurried down the hall toward the stairs.

"Don't let it worry you; Sueann and I have talked about this many times and I've told her she and I weren't meant for each other. I doubt it's me she wants as much as she wants a husband. I saw Rex was showing her a lot of attention; she'll soon forget about me."

"Where are we going?" Jane asked in a small quavery voice.

"To a little hide-a-way on the second floor. Don't be afraid my darling, nothing is ever going to hurt you while I'm around."

Lance opened one of the many doors that lined the long hall; they entered a dimly lit room with glowing coals in the fireplace. Looking around Jane saw that the room had massive, leather furniture and shelves lining the walls held books and trophies of bygone days. She saw that it was a man's room.

"Come sit, we'll have a sherry; that will get rid of the shivers you've had all evening." The brown-fringed eyes looked at her lovingly as he saw the blush travel up Jane's face.

"How do you know I have shivers?" Jane asked as she accepted the stemmed glass Lance was holding toward her.

"I knew; you don't think I could hold you and not know, do you? Come, let me hold you", he slid his arms under her hips and lifted her up and carried her to one of the big chairs; he sat down with her on his lap, and picked up the wine glass where he had set it. Clicking her glass to his he said, "to my darling wife, and to us forever till death do us part."

A chill went over Jane that numbed her for a moment. "And to you Lance, may you return safe to those who love you."

Lance kissed her warm lips, tasting the sherry that matched their color. "My darling," he said as he continued to kiss her ears, her neck and her eyes. They talked about what Jane had been doing and how she came to be at the Barrlette's. How fate had intervened to bring them together. Jane told Lance of her threat to marry Timmy Miller to get her way. They both laughed and laughed. Never having had even a beau, Jane was amazed at the things they could talk about and how close she felt to Lance, even though they had known each other such a short time. They finished their glass of wine; each beginning to relax, "pour us another glass darling," Lance said as he helped her from his lap. Jane did his bidding; when she finished and turned away he grabbed her hand and pulled her back onto his lap again. "Oh no you don't, I want you close to me." He kissed her again; running his hand up her back caressing her he could feel her shiver. "You're mine now, you know", he kept raining kisses over her neck and shoulders, up to her dainty ears and across her face finding her beautiful warm lips. "I never knew I could love someone as much as I do you; I've had many girls, but none of them were right. You are, and I love you with every breath, I breathe. I love you, my Jane." As he kissed her again, they both became aware of a commotion outside toward the stables. "Everyone must be leaving at once from the sound," Lance said. "I didn't think it was that late; how long have we been up here?"

Jane got up from his lap, and they both went toward the window; it didn't look out in the right direction of the sounds, and they couldn't see what was going on. They heard footsteps running down the hall toward the library. Someone pounded on the door, "Major! Major?"

Throwing the door open Lance was surprised to see one of the soldiers they had left on guard. They had stationed several around the plantation to keep watch in case of enemy movement; however, they didn't expect it as the Union Army was gathering to the southeast forty miles away readying for a last push south.

"Major, we're being surrounded by a company of Union soldiers; hurry, your horse is ready; where are your arms? The others have gone on ahead; they said you know where to meet them. They plan to scatter so if they are captured it won't be all of them.

Jane grabbed Lance's jacket he had removed, and held it for him. Grabbing Jane in a fierce hug he said, "I'll be back; I love you my darling." He and the private raced down the hall to his room where he collected his duffel bag and his arms. They raced down the stairs and away. Jane hurried downstairs, her legs so weak she could hardly find the stair treads. When she reached the floor below, Mr. and Mrs. Barrlette stood, tears running down their faces. She went to them and put an arm around each.

"Did the others get away?" she asked. They both nodded as they turned to their guests who were hurrying to leave. "Maybe it would be better if you stayed", Mr. Barrlette suggested.

"No, we had better take the back roads and get home as soon as possible" they all said. "They may decide to burn the city—you never know what may happen. Our thoughts and prayers are with you." The drivers whipped the horses to get as far away and as fast as they could. Some had already left before the alarm had sounded. Jane didn't know what to think or expect. Lance had been alone when he left; his friends were long gone when he got started. Maybe that would be for the best. The Union soldiers would follow the others who left together and might think that was all of them. Lance had grown up in this country and would know every stone. "Lance will be safe", she said hopefully, trying to quiet his grandparents' fears.

"He shouldn't have taken such a chance, even though they thought there was no danger; he told me they had scouts out for days checking on the Union troops. They all felt they would be safe. All those officers. If they are caught, they will all be hung." Mr. Barrlette, began to shake; Jane could feel him leaning on her. "I think we had better get you upstairs," she said as she called, "Getty, get Londo to help you; we need to get Mr. Barrlette to bed." Jane went on ahead to turn the bed down and put the flat-irons to heat. By the time they got him up the stairs they were almost carrying him. Jane knew he wasn't as strong as he thought he was and that the shock of the evening could do him in. She covered him and raced down the stairs to the kitchen. She had stored some of the willow tea in the cold room and had gone to fetch it. She put it in a small pot to heat in the coals, the flat-irons were hot and she wrapped them in a towel and slid them to his feet. He was shivering and Jane knew he was going into shock. Lucy had arrived. "Get more comforts, Lucy, tuck them around his body to hold what heat he has; put another set of irons to heat and build up the fire. He is going into shock; if we don't get him warm he could die." Jane tested the tea and decided it was hot enough— poured a cup and raised Mr. Barrlette up and held it for him to drink. "Drink it all, you'll soon feel better." When the cup was empty she laid him back and tucked the covers close about him.

All the lights had been put out below stairs except the one in the kitchen and a dim one in the hall. Loud pounding sounded on the front doors. "Open up! We want to search the house."

Londo was spending the night at the plantation and came to open the big double doors. "Yes sir?" Londo asked. Stand aside, we are going to search the house. "I hear there are five Confederate officers here. Where are they? You will save us and yourself a lot of grief if you lead us to them." The burly Lieutenant demanded as he pushed Londo aside. "I beg your pardon sir, the master is very ill—he's upstairs in bed; there are no soldiers here that I know of." "You're a liar," the Lieutenant said as he hit Londo in the face with his fist, knocking him to the floor. "Where are they? Tell me if you know what's good for you."

"I told you sir, I don't know of any soldiers that are here." Londo cringed on the floor not trying to get up.

"Come men, search every room; start with this floor; one of you guard the door so no one can escape. They went through to the kitchen; pots and pans were being thrown about and the commotion could be heard upstairs.

Jane came downstairs, "What's going on here?" she came on down the stairs; seeing the bunch of soldiers, they weren't as ragged as most she had been dealing with, but she had been with them for so long she had no fear of them. "Who's in charge here?

The burly Lieutenant stepped forward. "I'm in charge, Miss; may I ask who you are? and what you are doing here?"

Jane had changed to her calico dress while she waited for the irons to heat. She drew herself to her full height. "What is it you want in this house, Lieutenant? And why have you hit this man? she glanced at Londo still on the floor. "One of you help him up. You are a disgrace to the Union army. I'll ask you again what are you doing here?"

The Lieutenant didn't give an inch, even though he had motioned for one of the soldiers to assist Londo to his feet. "We're searching this house; we have information that five Rebel officers are here. I want to know who you are and what you have to do with this?"

I'm Jane Jarvis; I'm the granddaughter of Dr. George Connolly of the Union Army, I'm his nurse; I've been sent here to look after Mr. Barrlette, an elderly patient, who is a friend of my grandfathers. He is gravely ill upstairs. I doubt five Confederate officers would be hiding in this house, sir! Unless you remove yourselves from these premises, you will be reported to the right authorities." Jane's stubborn chin was in the air as she demanded they leave. She had been ordering soldiers around for four years and she wasn't about to back down now.

"Round up the boys," he said as he motioned a soldier toward the kitchen. As he went in that direction he yelled, "Let's go men, it's all over; seems we've made a mistake."

Londo stood at the door and held it open until the last soldier left. The Lieutenant turned, "You had better be telling the truth; if we have to return, you'll be in big trouble."

As Londo closed and shot the bolt on the door, Jane sank to the stair tread, "Are you hurt, Londo?" She looked at the bruise on his chin that was beginning to turn blue.

"I'll have Lucy come and apply some cold packs to help keep the swelling down. That looks like a pretty good wallop; I'm sorry you had to get hurt. I came as soon as I knew there was trouble; I

doubt we will see them again; Gramps is known far and wide."
Jane smiled as she started back upstairs.

"You're a brave woman, Miss, and think fast on your feet. I'm
sure you saved us all a lot of work. If that bunch had gotten into
the main house they would have caused havoc. It's hard to say
what they might have done if they became riled up."

"Well they're gone now. I hope we kept them long enough for
Major Barrlette to get away."

* * *

Sam had saddled Major Barrlette's horse Cherokee, and stood
holding it in readiness when he came racing toward him and flung
himself into the saddle; he was kicking his horse before his feet
was firmly in the stirrups. He raced through the field behind the
barn and headed for a thick stand of timber a few hundred feet
away. He could hear shots in the distance; as the wind whistled
around his ears he wasn't sure which direction they were coming
from. He was headed north, and soon he could tell that shots were
being fired to the east and also to the west. He raced deep into
the woods. He knew they went for about ten miles and curved
somewhat toward the west, then thinned out as another plantation with cleared fields took over. He kept to a slight trail he knew
went through the trees, never slacking his pace. He and his horse
had been over this area many times before. After a half hour,
Lance stopped to rest his horse and listen. He heard shots which
sounded closer now. Why would there be Union troops so close
when Charlotte was already in their hands. It must be the company that was looking for him and his friends. I hope they got
away; if they didn't, it will all be my fault. He walked his horse for
about a mile while he tried to figure out where the Union soldiers
were and where his friends were. He was still protected by the
shadows the trees made, even though they were bare of leaves.
Some evergreens were mixed through the woods which would
confuse anyone who searched—they even confused him. He
couldn't be sure someone didn't lurk in their shadow. "Oh, the
Hell with it," he said as he kicked his horse into a lope, heading
southwest toward the rendezvous with his friends. They were
going to meet at an old mill on a small creek about fifteen miles
from their lines; he felt if he could make that he would be safe.

When he came to the edge of the wood, he stopped to search the area; for a moment he thought he saw movement over close to some buildings where tobacco used to be stored; as he watched he decided he was mistaken and started toward a road he knew was beyond the plantation house just ahead. He trotted his horse toward it. Suddenly he heard several horses racing toward him from the tobacco barn. He kicked his horse to a run giving it its head and lay low over the saddle as he approached the road heading south. His big bay stallion made the dirt fly with the long stride he had. Soon the sound of the horses seemed farther behind. He couldn't decide if he should stay on the road or cut across the fields and try to find cover. He heard shots as he raced ahead. "This is going to be a close one," he said to his horse. He saw some trees coming up a thick grove of pine, and he swerved into them. He dropped from his saddle, and led his horse deep into the clump of trees, his hand on his horse's nose to keep him from making any noise. Soon his pursuers came racing toward him. He counted six of them as they slowed and milled around on the road looking and listening for him. "Maybe he is in that clump of trees" one of the soldiers said as he raised his rifle and shot several times toward the trees. Lance didn't think the distance was close enough for the rifle to reach but stepped behind a tree to shield himself anyway. "You fool, now he'll know just where we are", one of the soldiers said. "Don't you think he knows, with us racing behind him as far as we have? I think the Lieutenant got one of them. They scattered when they knew we were after them. We will get them all before they make it back to their lines. We have people all along every major road for ten miles out from their lines. We'll get them. Let's be on our way, keep your eyes and ears open."

Lance's heart dropped to his boots on hearing the strategy they were planning. He knew now that he had to keep to the rougher route through fields and woods. Open fields were a hazard; he could be sky-lighted crossing them and it would be dangerous. As soon as the six were out of hearing down the road, Lance mounted and headed west again. He circled as far as he dared toward the west. He wasn't as familiar with the countryside in that direction as he was the area closer to home. His horse picked his way around the obstacles in his path. He stopped a couple times at barb-wire fences, where Lance had to look for a gate or down fence; not finding any, he followed the fence for several miles. Finding a gully where the fence had been washed out he followed it, maybe it would lead him to the creek where the mill was located. The gully finally played out and he was on higher ground; there was some scrub that he casually guided his horse through. He soon got his bearings and headed south where he knew the mill was located. He finally located it in the distance; there was some cover he could take advantage of until he was almost there. The fields were overgrown surrounding the old mill. Lance topped a small hillock and stopped to listen and look around for any movement. Deciding it was safe he circled around and came in from the back. He dismounted and walked his horse slowly toward the mill. There was no movement or sound that he could make out. He stood with his horse as close to the building as he could and listened. He couldn't hear anything, and kept a hand on his horse; if any animals were around he felt sure that Cherokee would alert him; he carefully opened a door, and entered the darkness before him. He stepped to the side and led Cherokee inside; suddenly the stallion began to stomp and throw his head around. Lance knew something wasn't right; he cocked his pistol, dropped the bridle reins and moved to his right keeping close to the wall. His eyes began to adjust to the deeper darkness; his horse still seemed to be nervous. Lance stopped and leaned against the wall; a window was a few feet away, and a faint light filtered through the vines that covered it. He stood still, waiting. He heard nothing but the breathing of his horse. He took a couple more steps; as he did his foot touched something soft. Lifting his toe he gently nudged whatever it was; his heart leaped into his throat—it felt like a body. Kneeling he felt around where the object was. He felt the belt and sash of a soldier. One of his he was sure after his careful examination. There was blood on the jacket—he had been shot. "Which one?" he asked himself. Feeling the face and head he knew it was Rick; he had long blond hair tied back with a thong which he was proud of and all the girls seemed to admire. Poor Rick. There wasn't anything he could do for him now. "Where the hell are the others?" he asked in a whisper. He knelt beside Rick for a couple of minutes trying to make up his mind what to do. His knee was touching the ground and he felt a slight vibration. Horses! Traveling fast; he jumped to his feet and grabbed the bridle reins, rushed out the door and flung himself into the saddle and took off through the scrub toward the south. Lance heard shouting and shots behind him as he desperately tried to put distance between himself and those chasing him.

❦ Chapter Nineteen ❦

Lance forged ahead through the undergrowth forcing his stallion to race over dangerous terrain—dodging large rocks and fallen trees—which forced the gallant horse to make sudden leaps to clear the obstacles.

Lance had decided that after killing Rick, the Union soldiers had lain in hiding to see if any others showed up and he had walked into their trap. He asked himself why they hid themselves so far from the mill—could this be a different bunch that was chasing him than the ones who had killed Rick? It's my fault, I should never have asked them to come along and take such a risk. We all knew it was dangerous to go into Union territory. Lance's mind was tumbling this way and that—blaming himself for his friend's death. Cherokee's long stride was lengthening the distance between the soldiers who chased them. Lance could feel the sweat along the stallion's neck and knew he was tiring. "Just a little further fellow; I see a grove of pine ahead, maybe we can lose them if we can make the woods." Lance was laying low along the horse's neck, making himself as small a target as possible and making it easier for the horse to fight the wind-pull. He could still hear the pounding hoof beats behind him; they seemed to be fainter than before—he certainly hoped so. It was hard to judge in the darkness—but the Rebel lines couldn't be far away. Another hundred yards and they would be in the darkness under the trees. Shots rang out behind him; he urged Cherokee on, sure that he could feel the hot breath of the bullets as they sang overhead and all around. Cherokee gave another lunge and they were under the trees. Deep pine needles deadened the sound of the hoofbeats; there was no undergrowth here to hamper their way— pine branches grew to the ground in places—Lance realized there could be a whole regiment hidden in the shadows as he let his horse have his head. Continuing on deep into the wooded area, Lance was undecided what action to take. He pulled Cherokee to a halt; dismounting from the heaving horse he guided him into a close cluster of pines and tried to rub some of the sweat from the over heated horse. Lance could hear no sound of the pounding hoofbeats that had been behind them for so long; Cherokee was breathing normal again—his sides had stopped heaving with the effort brought on from running so far. Lance waited and waited— perhaps fifteen minutes passed; he couldn't hear a sound only of night birds in the trees above him. They weren't disturbed and Lance knew there was no movement in the dense trees. He waited a while longer then decided that it was safe to travel. Mounting up he slowly made his way toward the south. It wasn't long until he came to the edge of the piney woods; he halted again to listen—no sound of pursuit came to his straining ears. He had only gone a few steps from the safety of the trees when four shadowy figures rose from the grass spread out all around him. A volley of shots rang out and Major Lance Barrlette, without a sound, tumbled from his horse—a mass of mangled flesh; blood saturated the dried grass beneath the mound of broken bones and flesh that was once the handsome Major. Cherokee stood still as he had been trained—beside where his master fell—.

The Union soldiers rushed forward, "That's another one boys— this time a Major. A Captain and a Major in one night, that's a good haul, I'd say," the lieutenant slapped one of his men on the back. "Good work boys." Without examining the fallen soldier, the order was given, "Let's go home." Taking the reins of the Major's horse they started back to where their horses had been hidden. Mounting they headed back toward their camp near Charlotte. The four soldiers had raced ahead around the piney forest and way laid the lone Major beyond; it had been a gamble as the Confederate lines were within yelling distance of the ambush.

* * *

Jane sat beside the bed where Mr. Barrlette slept; the willow tea had done its work again. She began to think of the night and all that had happened—she was now a married woman, she wasn't quite sure just how it had happened. She felt as though she was in a dream—nothing seemed real. Suddenly she had such a queer feeling—sweat broke out onto her forehead—then her teeth began to chatter—"what's wrong with me? I must be coming down with something." She pulled a throw from another chair and wrapped it around her. Suddenly she knew, "It's Lance!

Something's happened to Lance! What should I do?" She got up and went downstairs and toward the kitchen; she knew Lucy slept in a room beyond. Picking up a lamp in the foyer she made her way in that direction. Jane called as she went—Lucy—Lucy?

"Yes, Miss Jane, what is it?" Is it Mr. Barrlette? I was just getting ready to come spell you. Is he worse?" Lucy held the lamp up to look into Jane's face; she was white as a ghost and tears streamed down her face. "Tell me, Miss Jane, what is it?"

"It's Lance; I think he's just been killed; Oh Lucy, what have I done?" Jane began to shake again swaying toward Lucy.

Lucy grabbed Jane around the waist; taking the lamp from her she set it on a table and helped Jane to a chair. "Whatever gave you that idea? He's halfway back to his unit by now." Jane was sobbing as she tried to tell Lucy what had happened. "I was sitting beside Mr. Barrlette's bed; he was sleeping soundly when suddenly I had this queer feeling—it was as though Lance kissed my cheek—he often did in a certain way—I became hot, and then a chill took me—my teeth were chattering—and I knew. What are we going to do Lucy? Can we get Sam to look for him? What can we do?" Jane's tears wet Lucy's shoulder as she leaned against her.

"We can't do anything tonight. Come, I'll walk you back upstairs and put you to bed; I'll sit the rest of the night with Mr. Barrlette. You're just tired; you've been through a lot today; I don't blame you for being afraid. Nothing's going to happen to Mr. Lance; he knows what he's doing; after all he wouldn't be a Major if he didn't; you're just tired. I'll make you a cup of your famous willow tea and you'll be asleep in no time. You'll hear from your new husband soon telling you he's back with his unit safe and sound."

Lucy made it sound possible to Jane; maybe she was just having an attack of nerves. It had been a long day and night; she was so tired that she wasn't sure she could reach the top of the long flight of stairs; her legs were weak and shaky by the time they reached her room. Lucy helped her into her night things, and tucked the quilts around her. "I'll be back with you a hot cup of tea in a few minutes." Lucy returned with the hot tea, held it while Jane drank, kissed her forehead, and left the room.

* * *

Jane went to sleep in seconds it seemed and slept through the rest of the night and well into the morning—she awoke to Lucy's voice as she entered her room with hot coffee. "How'er you feelin' this mornin', Miss Jane?"

"I'm rested—I feel better. I don't usually go off in a tizzy like last night; I'll bet you thought I had suddenly lost my mind. I really don't know what came over me—it seemed so real. Has there been any word—?"

"Nothing I've heard; Mr. Barrlette wanted to get out of bed, but so far we have managed to keep him there. Ms. Barrlette says he has to stay until you give him the word that he can get up." Lucy laughed when she told Jane.

"Well I had better get up myself, and let him up too if he's better. He seems to get these fevers so suddenly.' I don't understand it. Of course, I'm not a doctor." Jane smiled.

"I'll make you some breakfast; you had better have something to eat before you face the dragon—he's as mean as a bear this mornin'" Lucy giggled as she went back to her work.

Jane made sure that she was dressed neatly and she fussed over her hair braiding and pinned it in a figure eight on the back of her head, before going for her breakfast. The longer she took, the longer Mr. Barrlette would stay resting in bed. She sat sipping her second cup of tea; looking out the window at the barren trees and dull garden, she felt very depressed—everything was dead and so dreary—I wonder what made me have such a strange experience last night? I've never had anything like that before. It was so real.

Lucy came to the door of the small sitting room where Jane had eaten her breakfast. After knocking, she came in with Sam; that's strange Jane thought to herself; she had never seen Sam in this part of the house before; she looked from one face to the other—Lucy looked scared, "What is it? What is it, Sam? Oh God, is it Gramps?" Sam had his hat in his hand, turning it around and around. It's not your grandfather, Miss Jane. Jane hadn't realized she had been holding her breath until she let it out with a sigh.

"I'z afraid it'z bad news; maybe youz should have Ms. Barrlette with youz before I tell you." Sam looked at Jane with apprehension. "Out with it Sam; I'll judge if Mrs. Barrlette should be here; she's with her husband and they are both in frail health; I don't think they should have to be worried unless it's necessary."

"It'z about the Major's horse—iz came in sometime in the night. I was up till sometime after midnight—, iz was after that, I'z not sure just what time. Iz didn't hear anything. That old Cherokee can sneak around and not make no noise a'tall when he wantz to."

Jane's hand went to her mouth as if to stifle a scream, gall rushed into her throat, her heart almost jumped from her bosom. "Take a deep breath," she could hear her Gramps tell her, as he had many times. "You need a clear head to solve problems."

"Is the horse all right—is it lame or anything? Or any messages with him? Maybe he threw the Major." Jane watched Sam and knew there was more

"Miss Jane, thz saddle and gearz are covered with blood—lotz of blood— "Sam had tears running down his weathered face, "Cherokee haz been run—run hard, I think they got the Major— somehow old Cherokee gotz away from them and come home. I'z sorry Miss Jane, iz don't look good—Iz don't know what to doz— —."

When Jane heard this she knew she had been right—that's when Lance died. He wouldn't be coming back like he promised. Jane started to shake, Lucy went to her and put an arm around the frightened girl— "Miss Jane, pull yourself together, we'll send a scouting party to find the Major; he probably just ran into a tree limb, in the dark; no news is good news they say. Miss Jane, you'll have to be strong; the Barrlettes need your strength."

"Stay with her, Sam, I'll get something to give her, she has to pull herself together. She'll be needed when the family finds out. This could kill them both," Lucy hurried from the room, returning soon with a cup of Jane's willow tea. After drinking it, Jane sat staring into space. Sam and Lucy stood watching her, not knowing what else to do.

"Sam, do you know which way the Major went? Or where they were to rendezvous?" Jane asked as she tried to pull herself together and think clearly.

Sam scratched his head, "I'z heard the Major say somethin' about an old mill; the only mill I'z know of iz about ten miles over on Little Creek; I'z been by there a few times huntin'. I'z could have one of the boys go over and see could they find somethin'; guess I'z better stay here case somethin' else comes up."

"Jane rose from her chair, "send someone to the Judge's and have him come here, and send someone who can read the signs at the mill, and have them hurry. The more information we have the sooner we can get to the bottom of this. I don't think we will tell the family until the Judge gets here; maybe he's heard something in the city, or will know how to contact the Major's unit. Hurry Sam, you go for the Judge, and tell him the details. I'll go up to Mr. Barrlette and keep him in bed as long as possible." Sam already had left the room. In minutes Jane heard a horse leaving at a fast pace from the barnyard.

Thank God for Lucy she seemed to be level headed, and had done the right thing giving her the willow tea. It soothed the nerves and had brought her back to some form of sanity. When she entered the sick room Mrs. Barrlette was setting with her husband as he finished his breakfast. "Good morning, how's our patient this morning?" She smiled at them both putting up a cheerful front for them.

"This confounded bed—I'm beginning to hate it; I want up— Elizabeth won't let me stir a foot until you say so."

"Well—Jane acted undecided—if you're good you can get up in about an hour—it will be warming up by then. You can go to the library on this floor; I'll see there's a good fire burning. You can watch out the window at all the winter birds; we'll scatter some bread, that will bring a lot of them. I saw a couple of cardinals a few minutes ago. Then maybe I'll read to you. I don't want you to get a chill," she smiled as if that was the biggest worry she had.

"That's a good idea, Charles, I'll even bring some lap work and sit with you and look at birds too." Mrs. Barrlette looked at Jane and could see the strain on the girl's face, and wondered if there was something she was keeping from her. She had a feeling that all wasn't as it should be. She was so worried about the young officers that had to go through the Union-held territory before being safe. She had heard a fast-moving horse leaving the yard and wondered why. "Was there someone here?" she asked looking toward Jane, "I thought I heard a horse leaving."

"Yes, you did, I sent one of the boys on an errand, I hope you don't mind." Jane turned her back straightening the bed covers. She couldn't look Mrs. Barrlette in the eye just now. "I'll go see if the fire has warmed the library, so we can get our patient to his bird watching." Jane hurried from the room, she wanted to regain her composure before returning.

"Bird watching! my foot, you're both trying to make an invalid out of me. I'm fine today. I just may decide to go to the barn and inspect things; the boys need supervision and I saw some fences that need repair. I can get them working on that."

"You know Charles that it's too cold for you to be outside. You don't want a cold on top of what you already have," she looked sternly at her husband.

"Hurmf!" he said as he settled himself to await Jane's return. She seemed to be taking her good time.

When Jane entered the room where she and Lance had set on the big overstuffed chair drinking toasts to each other she couldn't control the tears. They had so little time—he couldn't be gone, he was so full of life and loved her so much—they had made plans for a family—Jane fell on her knees to the floor in front of the chair; resting her arms on it she laid her head down and cried, great sobs from deep inside wrenched her body and tore at her heart. It can't be—no,—no—no Jane knew she had to pull herself together, as the Judge would be here soon. He would help; he had seemed to take to her and she knew he was very fond of Lance; if anyone could do anything, he could. She returned to her room and washed her face with cold water before going back to the sick room.

"What were you doing? catching some of those birds you so admire?" Mr. Barrlette asked in a grumpy voice as he looked at Jane.

"My, you're anxious to bird watch I see. Let's get a warm robe on you and we will get at it." Jane smiled at Mr. Barrlette as she helped him out of bed. "Lean on me," she told him.

"I'm capable of walking on my own. You forget just last night I was waltzing you around the ballroom; I'm not going to wear a robe, I want my clothes; if you don't mind you can leave the room Miss and let me dress." He glared at Jane, which made her giggle.

"If you don't behave I'll have Lucy make a brew for you. You know how well you like those," she smilingly left the room, waiting in the hall to help him if he needed it. She was anxious to be downstairs when Sam and the Judge returned. She wanted to talk to the Judge before telling the Barrlettes anything. Jane waited sometime before the door opened and both of the old people came out. Mrs. Barrlette started down the hall; she had give up on trying to help her husband. "I'll leave him to you Jane as you seem to be able to manage the old grouch better than I can."

"Come along," Jane tried to take his arm but he shrugged her off. "I can manage, thank you." Jane brought up the rear; when they reached the room she maneuvered him toward the big comfortable chair she had pulled to the window. He seated himself where she indicated, but was still in a bad humor.

"I'll go scatter some bread to bring the birds, and I'll bring you a hot tonic when I return." She leaned over and planted a kiss on his cheek. That brought a faint grin to his lips.

"I can't wait," he said still trying to be grouchy. He adored Jane; he could see why Lance had fallen head over heels for her; they couldn't have asked for a more suitable wife for their only living relative. The two made a handsome couple, and their children should be something to see. I hope it's soon he thought to himself; I won't be around much longer. There's something wrong; I shouldn't be getting these spells so often.

Jane hurried down the stairs and sent Getty with some grain and bread crumbs for the birds. She told him where to sprinkle the feed so that Mr. Barrlette could see the birds from the window where he sat looking out. She then looked for Lucy to see if either of the men had returned. Lucy didn't seem to be around. She could be anywhere in the big rambling house doing the morning chores. Jane took a cup of tea and went to the small setting room and sat by a window sipping the strong brew. What am I to do? If Lance is dead, that leaves only me to look after two old people. I'm the only living relative they will have. I have Gramps; I must go back and help him, and look after him. He's old too, and overworked. Oh, God, don't let it be so. After all the heartbreak the two old people had been through Jane doubted if they could survive losing their grandson and only relative. Jane sat for some time, then remembered that she was supposed to take a hot cup of tea to Mr. Barrlette. Going to the kitchen, she took the small teakettle that she had the willow tea in. It could be put on the hopper in any of the rooms to heat; taking two cups she headed upstairs. When she entered the room both pairs of eyes turned to her. "Well! How's the bird watching coming?" She placed the kettle on the hopper to warm and walked to the window. "Oh," she exclaimed, "that looks like a robin, and there's the pair of Cardinals I saw this morning. How many kinds have you spotted?" She turned to Mr. Barrlette with the question, a big smile on her face.

"Bah!" he said as he gave her a sour look. " Can think of a lot of things I would rather do than bird watching."

"Remember you're to be good or one of Lucy's tonics will be on its way." She poured a cup of the tea for him. "How about you, Mrs. Barrlette, would you like a cup? Come, I've poured one for you too. It will warm you and be good to ward off a cold." Jane couldn't believe she could keep up such drivel; she was so afraid of what the news would be and had to keep talking to keep her sanity.

Jane heard horses in the yard—she wasn't sure if the Barrlettes had heard or just thought it was the men at work. "I'll be right back, I want to talk to Lucy a moment"—and hurried from the room. Mrs. Barrlette wondered what was wrong with Jane, as she seemed to be so flighty—Jane's not like that; something's up, now what I wonder."

Jane made it to the front door as Judge Winthrop entered. Wide-eyed she stood looking at him as he took off his wraps. "This way" she said as she took him toward the small setting room. "Is there any news?" she asked as the Judge went toward the fire and held his hands toward the flames. Pulling a chair up he motioned for her to do the same. Jane sat down by the crackling blaze, her eyes still on the Judge.

"I'm afraid this will be a grave shock to you Jane," he said as he pulled a newspaper from his pocket and handed it to her. There were big headlines—REBELS ROUTED FROM BURNING SPREE—A rebel force slipped through our guards into the heart of the city planning to burn Charlotte. Our brave Union soldiers routed the Rebels chasing them on horseback for several miles. We have it on good authority that two of the scoundrels were killed during the chase. Several of those whose sympathy are known to be with the Confederate forces are being questioned. It is thought that those in question will be found to have had a part in this wild scheme, and may be hung for treason. The Union forces are still scouring the countryside looking for the rest of the Confederate soldiers, who dared to commit such an atrocity. The Union announces that they will be caught and hung.

There was more, but Jane couldn't read any farther; she looked at the Judge—tears stood in her eyes, "what are we to do?"

"Sam has told me you have sent someone to the mill; they may find some answers there. I've put in some calls and have sent a wire to the friends I have in the Confederacy; we have to be careful—as you know they weren't here to burn Charlotte but we could all be caught up in this and someone come to harm. Caution must be used in our investigation. "How are the Barrlette's this morning?"

"Mr. Barrlette had another one of his spells, I'm very worried about him. I don't understand the recurring fevers he has that come so suddenly. I'm not trained to diagnose something so fleeting. Mrs. Barrlette seems to be well, although I think she knows something is in the air. I gave both of them something for their nerves before coming downstairs. They are both frail."

Sam entered the room, "Doz you want to talk to Elmo the man I'z sent to the barn, Miss Jane? He's back."

"Yes, bring him in." Elmo was a big young Negro, who had an intelligent look about him.

"Elmo, did you find anything?" the Judge asked the question.

"Yes Sir, I'z found a dead soldier; he was laying in the mill and had been dead for long time; he'z been shot a lot. I'ze brung him back tied to saddle; rode behind; he'z one that was here for Mr. Lance's party. Wazn't Mr. Lance but one of his friends. We have him layin in the barn now. What you want we do with him, Mr. Judge?"

"Did you find any other sign Elmo, how many were there?"

"Yes sir, I'z track around some—found a bunch of horsemen coms from a hill above mill, theyz was ridin' hard. I think this was after the other one was shot. Therez was another horse in the barn and it took off throwin' mud; looks like they chased him toward the south. That'z all I could tell, Mr. Judge. I come home and bringz Mr. Lance's friend."

"You did a fine job Elmo; I'll take care of the corpse; have someone stay around and I'll go back to town and send the undertaker to arrange burial. Do you know the young man?"

"No sir, Mr. Judge; hz' young one with light hair tied behind with a thong, I'z don't know his name."

"That's Rick," Jane said; my God, he was so young and full of life, and now he's gone." a sob caught in her throat.

"Sounds as though the Union knew they were to meet at the Mill and lay-in-wait—shot the first one to arrive and watched for the next ones to show up—at least one got away, but who knows

215

how far if a bunch chased him toward the south. That may be the second one they are bragging about killing. We still don't know about your husband Jane; I'll go back and send someone for the body and see if there are any answers to my messages I have out. I suppose I'd better see Charles while I'm here or if he sees me leave he may cause you problems."

Jane took the Judge to the upstairs library to talk a few minutes with the Barrlettes.

"Good morning Charles—Elizabeth; I was passing and thought I would look in and see how the new bride was faring and see how both of you are. This is cold weather we are having—you had better both stay in by the fire. There's a lot of sickness around. I'd better be on my way; take care of yourself."

It was late afternoon, and Jane had lain down for a short rest. She slept for some time when Lucy came for her.

"Jane you'll have to come; Mr. Barrlette sneaked out to the barn and found out about Rick. He made Elmo tell him everythin— now he insists he is going to take a horse and track the other rider south—that he's sure it's Lance. In fact, he has already taken Elmo and gone; I just found out."

Jane was half asleep—she jumped from the chaise where she lay and grabbed a wrap and hurried after Lucy toward the barn. She saw that the Judge hadn't sent for the body—it still lay wrapped in a blanket on some hay. "Where's Sam? she asked the boy, Andy, who was working in one of the stalls.

"Here's I am Miss Jane, what's you want?"

"Sam, I want you to go after Mr. Barrlette and bring him back; he's not well and can't be out in this weather. Hurry Sam, he'll catch his death."

"I's sorry, Miss Jane; there ain't no more horses. They's took both of the one's we has. I can't catch them afoot no way."

"Lord what are we to do? What about Lance's horse?"

"We'z just wait Miss Jane, nothin' we kin do. I'z doubt that old stallion will ever be any good again, his head is hangin' to the ground," Sam told her.

"Let me know when they return Sam. Right away."

"I'z do that Miss Jane." ·

🍃 Chapter Twenty 🍃

Jane had returned to the house. What in the world was she to do, if Mr. Barrlette didn't survive this? Mrs. Barrlette had been napping and didn't realize that her husband was missing until she went to the small sitting room and demanded to know what was going on. Jane decided it best she was told; the longer she waited to inform her the harder it would be on them all.

"Mrs. Barrlette, please come and sit down. Mr. Barrlette has left to go looking for Lance; he took Elmo with him—they went on horseback. The Federals caught up with Rick in the mill where the boys were to meet after leaving here; Rick has been killed. Elmo found him and brought him here; we don't know about the others. I'm very worried about Mr. Barrlette, as he isn't well enough to be out in this cold weather; but there doesn't seem much we can do. There's no horses for a search party to go after him. We'll just have to wait."

"Oh, my heavens! That stubborn old man. He has signed his death warrant; he'll never survive this Jane dear, try not to worry, as you say there's nothing we can do. It seems to be the fate of wives to wait—and wait some more. I've done enough of it in my time; and I'm sure Lance can take care of himself."

Sounds of a wheeled vehicle was heard arriving in the barnyard. Jane rushed to see who or what it was. When she went to the kitchen Lucy said, "It's the Judge, come to fetch Rick; he has the undertaker with him in the death wagon. I'll put on a fresh batch of tea—he's coming in."

Jane held the door as Judge Winthrop came in; he was almost frozen, his nose red and runny. "Come in to the sitting room to the fire," she hurried him down the hall, "Mrs. Barrlette knows about Rick—I've just told her; have you heard what Mr. Barrlette did?"

The Judge hurried to the fire, and after a few seconds he removed his greatcoat. He turned to Mrs. Barrlette and said, "I've heard about Charles, he's a stubborn fool; a man his age won't last long out there. I'm frozen and I just came from the city and was wrapped in blankets. I've some news, for whatever it means; there hasn't been any more reports of capture—since the two— that's encouraging."

"Two? What two? Jane has told me that Rick has been killed; who else was captured? Are they alive?" she was growing excited as she threw questions at the Judge.

"It's rumored that two were killed. We have no proof of that, or a body—there were five officers, you know. We'll have to wait for further information. I've wired a friend of mine to try and contact Lance and have him send a message. We should hear any-time. I'll return to town with the undertaker and Rick's body I'll see if I can get someone to look for Charles—I know the boys here can't do anything. Damn, this war; it's time we had peace. He drank the tea that Lucy brought and was struggling back into his greatcoat. I'll let you know anything I hear." He hurried back to the barn and the waiting men.

I can't believe that wonderful boy is lying dead, and now on his way to be buried. Just last night they were all having such a good time in this house; and now Charles, gone to his death." Mrs. Barrlette sat shaking her head.

Jane couldn't think; there must be something she could do be-sides, as Mrs. Barrlette said—just wait and wait some more.

Jane looked toward Mrs. Barrlette, "Don't worry about me Jane, I'm all right. I'll weather this. I have to—to be ready to take care of Charles when he's brought home."

They all waited in the sitting room—even Sam and little Andy had come in with Lucy and sat beside the fire, waiting. The wait-ing stretched into the night and still no word. Jane said, "Mrs. Barrlette, I think you should be in your bed."

"Not until I know that Charles is in his," she shook her head.

"At least come over and let me cover you on the sofa; you won't be much help if you've worn yourself out before we hear any-thing or they bring him home."

"You're right, I'll nap for a while; I'll need to be alert when they fetch him." Jane helped her to get comfortable and tucked a warm comforter over her, and she closed her eyes.

It was midnight and still no word—Lucy had brought sand-wiches and tea for them and they had all eaten as they waited. Mrs. Barrlette had been sleeping and they could hear her soft snoring. Jane turned to Sam, "I think you and Andy might as well go to your beds; we may need you tomorrow to help with Mr. Barrlette when they find him. We're not doing any good waiting up for him. We may not hear anything for hours. I doubt anyone will come with word before daybreak. The weather's too bad for them to venture out in the dark."

"You'z right Miss Jane; have Lucy ring the bell if you needz us. Come along Andy, you'z asleep on your feet," Sam put an arm around the boy as he stumbled along, glad of Sam's help.

Jane sent Lucy off to her bed and pulled another chair close to hers and put her feet up; leaning back into the soft chair, she waited for Mrs. Barrlette to awaken.

* * *

Elmo led the way as he and Mr. Barrlette headed in the direction of the mill—it was about ten miles toward the south. Elmo was concerned about Mr. Barrlette who had insisted that he was going to find his grandson and no one could stop him. Elmo had on his warmest clothing and had brought along a blanket that he had draped around his shoulders. Mr. Barrlette had long boots and a greatcoat, but the wind was fierce. Elmo was comfortable; he was used to being outside. He knew that Mr. Barrlette wasn't well enough for such a ride, especially in winter—there wasn't anything Elmo could do but his bidding, as they started at a fast clip from the barnyard. There was no conversation as Elmo kept ahead; he had just been over the route when he fetched Rick's body back, and knew it well. An hour went by—Mr. Barrlette had kept up so far; Elmo kept looking back to make sure he was still all right. By the time they came in sight of the mill he knew Mr. Barrlette was tiring, and he hoped he could get him to return to the plantation. When they reached the building, Elmo opened the mill doors and dismounting guided the horses inside out of the wind and where it was warmer. Mr. Barrlette dismounted and Elmo pointed out the dark spot in the dust where Rick's body had been discovered; then took him outside and showed him the tracks of the horse that had raced from the mill splashing mud that still stuck against shrubs along the path.

"There's not much to be learned from this; we'll follow the tracks south—that could be Lance." Mr. Barrlette turned back and went inside. Elmo suggested they rest the horses a spell which Mr. Barrlette agreed to. Elmo would have liked to build a fire but it was too windy outside and too dangerous to build one inside the old weathered mill. They both stomped around beating their hands against their arms to keep warm. Nothing was being gained and Mr. Barrlette said, "Let's get on with it. We'll have to travel as far as we can while it's still light, we can't track in the dark." They started at a fast pace following the clear trail where dead weeds had been tromped down and mud thrown up. They sometimes lost sight of the tracks but kept going in the southerly direction and soon found more sign as they traveled ahead. It was late afternoon and getting colder with snowflakes born on the wind, peppering them about the face and head. The weather was becoming worse by the minute and Elmo knew that they couldn't spend a night in the open without food or camping equipment. Mr. Barrlette was weaving in the saddle and he was afraid for him; worried that he might fall under the horse's hooves.

"Elmo, how far do you think we've come?" Mr. Barrlette had pulled his horse in beside Elmo's.

"I recon' boutsz fifteen or eighteen miles, sir; I'z hear the boys say it'z forty miles to their lines. I thinks we better find a place to stay the night; it'z goin' be dark soon."

"I think there's a small plantation beyond those hills yonder; we'll see if we can warm up there—belongs to a family called Meade; we'll ask anyway."

As they advanced they saw a small weather-beaten house that stood beneath some liveoaks—it looked dismal and lonely; no lights showed in the evening shadows; however, a spiral of smoke lifted from a back chimney, indicating that it was occupied. The two frozen men rode toward the back of the house. Their horses were tired and their heads drooped toward the ground as they dismounted and made their way through the yard clutter toward the door. Mr. Barrlette knocked—it was several seconds before the door was opened a crack by a young black girl, "Yes sir, whatz you want?" she asked in a scared voice.

"I'm Charles Barrlette—is Mr. or Mrs. Meade at home? My man and I are almost frozen and seek refuge by your fire; may we come in.?"

"Mr. Meades' a fightin' and Ms. Meade's poorly; I'z recon' you can come to the fire ifs you want." She moved aside for them to enter and pointed toward a room beyond—they had entered through the kitchen—it was so dark they were in danger of running into furniture and not much warmer than it was outside.

"Mam, this is Mr. Barrlette and his man; theyz most frozen and ask leave to warm themselves—this is Ms' Meade," she went to a woman who sat in a worn rocker wrapped in a quilt; she looked as though she hadn't had a good meal in weeks.

"Mrs. Meade," Charles said as he shook the claw-like hand she extended from the folds of the quilt, "we're searching for my grandson—he's Major Barrlette of the Confederate army; have you seen him?"

"My husband's out there fighting for the south—no, I've not seen a Major around here. A few nights ago we heard some riders going through—making considerable noise, singing and yelling. I'm sure they were Yankees back from their killin'. We've not heard from my husband in nigh a month now—I expect he's dead—there's so many—almost everyone we know—everything's gone—there's no food or even wood to keep warm by—we'll all be dead soon—there's only Mary and myself now—" she had started to ramble.

Mr. Barrlette looked around the room seeing worn furniture filling every corner. "Find a place Elmo where you can put the horses out of the weather—then come back and stretch out on the floor close enough to the fire to get warm. We'll spend the night and then start out at first light." He pulled a large arm chair closer to the fire for himself and leaned his tired aching frame back and closed his eyes.

Mary poked at the fire and added a small stick at a time Mrs. Meade went to a couch and stretched out and Mary piled several ragged covers over her. No food had been offered and Mr. Barrlette asked for none.

Mr. Barrlette had slept fitfully for several hours. Elmo shook him awake as dawn showed through the dirty windows. "It'z time we' z on our way—how you feel this mornin'?" he asked.

"I'm not sure how far I can travel Elmo, maybe it's best if I wait here while you scout around and see what you can find.

If you see any houses, ask questions. Be careful, we don't know which side we're talking to. The yankees that Mrs. Meade heard could be the ones that were chasing the man from the mill. They've probably killed him to be in such a jolly mood. Don't be gone more than a couple of hours. See if you can find anything to eat while you're at it—don't look as though they have anything here; go."

Elmo went to an old half-fallen-in shed where he had tied the horses for the night. He mounted quickly and started south again. He swung around and picked up the trail where they had abandoned it to go toward the house. He saw some tracks but they were so churned up in the mud that he had trouble telling anything about them. He kept to the trail for several miles. Seeing woods in the distance, he headed toward them. It would break some of the wind as he tried to follow the hoofprints south. He could tell that a single horse had gone into the woods too—and felt sure it was the one whose prints he had seen at the mill. He became excited as he casually followed the trail, not knowing what or who would step out from behind one of the dense pines, and he stopped every little while to listen. He couldn't hear a sound as he waited and watched. Moving deeper into the woods, his horse started throwing it's ears forward and shying at every branch that stuck out in their path. Elmo knew there was something making it nervous and decided to dismount and walk his horse while he decided what to do. Suddenly he heard squawking birds; crows—overhead, he hurried forward—the woods ended just ahead and he spotted the crows circling around and around— a sure sign they saw something dead or dying to feed on. Elmo eased ahead looking in the brush for whatever the crows saw— soon he saw what looked like a bundle of rags; when he got closer, he saw it was a body in an officer of the Confederacy uniform. He could tell it had been there for some time and when he went closer he saw that he had found what they had been searching for—Major Barrlette lay in a crumpled heap, his uniform full of bullet holes and saturated with his blood. He was torn up bad from several shots. Hearing a wagon, he looked up; a young black boy came toward him with a load of wood stacked on a beat-up cart, and a sway-back mule pulling it. Elmo raised from the squatting position he had been in; the boy looked scared as he watched him raise up from the dead weeds and grass.

"Over this way boy—I got a job for you—"

"I'z got a job—I'z gonna' take this here wood over to Ms. Meade's. She han't got no wood and she'z need it—I'z don't want no job. No sir, I'z got a job to do."

"I happen to be'z goin' to the Meade's place too—come on over here—you'z can help me with something." Elmo motioned for him to come to him.

The boy turned the cart in his direction and coaxed the old mule along—"Lord God Almighty-e-you'z killed a soldier—I'z don't want nothin' to do with that. No sir I'z don't." The whites of his eyes showed as he pulled back on the reins scared to death.

"I didn't kill no one—this is Major Barrlette—we'z been huntin' him for two days. The damn Yankees done killed him—I'z got to get him home—you'z gonna' help me. Now get on down here—we'z make room a top your load of wood and heft him up there. Climb down boy and help me. Come on I says." Reluctantly the scared boy climbed from the cart—started to rearrange the wood, pushing some down as stakes along the side and leveling the top. He turned his head trying not to look at the corpse as he took hold of the clothing and helped lift the Major to the place he had fixed—sticking more pieces of wood on the other side, fencing in the Major so he didn't roll from the cart.

"That'z a good job you done fixin the Major so he will ride easy. Now let'z be on our way. Do you'z know where we can find somethin' to eat around here?" as Elmo asked he thought to himself that the boy didn't look like he had been feeding too well for some time.

"There' a Post just beyond the forks where the Meade's place is—sometimez they have somethin' there—if you'z got gold money. We don'tz never have any ourselves." He swallowed several times as though he was thinking of something to eat himself.

"You helpzs me with the Major—when we getzs' back to the Meade's place you and me'll go find out—Mr. Barrlette has gold money—I'z hungry as a bear."

The journey with the cart was slow and difficult; the boy knew shortcuts where there were trails of sorts which helped some. The sun was almost down by the time they arrived at the Meade's place. Elmo went inside to see Mr. Barrlette, and found him now on the sofa covered with a quilt.

Mrs. Meade looked up as Elmo entered. Your master's in bad shape; we had to pick him up from the floor—he fell from his chair; we managed to get him to the sofa and cover him. He's burning up with fever. Mary made some tea and we tried to give him that. We have no medicine, and he wouldn't drink the catnip tea that Mary made. We have warm irons at his feet and try to keep him covered. That's all we can do. I don't know what ails him, but he isn't getting any better."

Elmo tried to think what to do—"howz far do you think it is to Charlotte?" he asked.

"It's more than ten miles, about twelve maybe. Is that where you come from?" Mrs. Meade asked.

"No we'z come from Barrlette House, that'z about six miles from Charlotte on the tother side. I'z guess I'z better go back there and getz a wagon to fetch Mr. Barrlette; I'z can't take him on horseback—ken Mary look after him while'z I go? I'z be back as quick as I'z can. If'en you do that I'z try to get you some food. I can't promise but I'z try. If you and Mary wants to come back to Barrlette House, we'z got food there and wood to keep warm. I'z know they take you in, I'z take you with me if'en you want."

"We couldn't do that. My husband may be home any day or hour; he wouldn't know where to find us. No, we couldn't go. I thank you anyway. We would accept some food if you can get it."

Elmo and the boy unloaded the body of Major Barrlette and placed him in the shed on a pile of old sacks. Elmo ripped his blanket in two and tucked half of it over him. It was so cold that the body would be all right and Elmo would move him when he found a wagon. He took the other horse—he might have to use them in a wagon when he found one. Elmo motioned for the boy to come with him to the post to try to find food. Mr. Barrlette had given him a gold-piece before sending him to look further south for the Major while he stayed behind.

It was a short distance to the Post, Elmo went in to see what he could buy. The merchant looked on him with suspicion as he wasn't known in the area. "Where you from, boy? I don't think I know you."

"I'z from Barrlette House. Mr. Barrlette's at the Meade plantation and sent me to buy some food; what do you'z have sir?"

"I've potatoes, eggs, turnip greens, flour and meal—you tell me what you want and I'll tell you if I have it."

Elmo looked around—the place was small but merchandise lined the shelves, more than most small places had—I'z like a slab of bacon, eggs, flour, dry beans, turnip greens, apples—how much that comes to?" Elmo asked.

"That's close to a twenty gold piece; you have that?"

"Put in enough meal to make it twenty, I'z has that.

Elmo started to pack the things into a couple of sacks that could be tied together and thrown across the mule the boy had ridden to the Post. Elmo didn't want to return to the Meade's place; he wanted to be on his way. He handed an apple to the skinny boy and stuck a couple of them into his pocket; that's all he would have to eat, and he hadn't eaten since Barrlette House. "You'z take this back to Mary, and tell them I'z be back as soon as I can. Thiz do them for a while." Elmo mounted up and leading the other horse headed north to Charlotte.

Elmo decided to try Judge Winthrop's house for a wagon; he was sure if the Judge didn't have one he would know where he could find one. When he talked to the Judge and explained that they had found the Major and that Mr. Barrlette was in bad shape, the Judge sent a servant to the undertakers and had him prepare to fetch the Major and Mr. Barrlette. The Judge didn't think it necessary for him to go and told Elmo to guide the undertaker and his driver and help bring the two Barrlettes back. Elmo left one of the horses in the Judge's barn and gave it some much-needed feed. "I'z run up and down this here road so much I must own part of it." Elmo said to himself. "I'z wants' to go home to Barrlette House and has me some hot food and a good sleep. I'z doubt Mr. Barrlette will be alive when we getz there—he'z that sick."

The deathwagon pulled in at the Meade's. The wagon was filled with straw, and extra blankets were put in to keep Mr. Barrlette warm. Elmo helped wrap the corpse of the Major and load it against the side of the wagon and cover it. Then they put Mr. Barrlette in with heated rocks around him and wrapped him tightly in the extra blankets. He had a high fever and looked as though he wouldn't last till they could get him home. "I'z back Mr. Barrlette; it'z me, Elmo." Elmo tried to talk to him but got no answer. He turned to Mrs. Meade—"thank you mam for looking after the Master; we' z appreciate it."

"Thank you for the food; we would have died without it. There was nothing to eat in the house. If things don't get better, we may have to take you up on Barrlette House. Thank your master for us and I hope he gets better—he's a very sick man. Thank you, Elmo."

Elmo nodded and closed the door behind himself as he hurried to the wagon so they could be on their way.

* * *

Snow was coming down in earnest as the wagon entered the outskirts of Charlotte. The undertaker took the corpse directly to his establishment and unloaded it—Mr. Barrlette was taken inside to warm up and wait for a servant to heat the stones and try to get some hot broth into him. Elmo hurried to the Judge's home to retrieve the other horse and give him the news that the Major had been brought back, and how sick Mr. Barrlette was.

"I suppose I should come along with you and see if there is anything I can do for my old friend. I'll ride Charles' horse and come back with the wagon. Go tell the undertaker that we'll start on ahead; make sure he keeps Charles warm. We'll ride slowly so they can catch up."

* * *

The deathwagon pulled in close to the veranda in the front of the house. Jane had walked miles looking out first one window and then another watching for Mr. Barrlette and Elmo. Seeing the wagon coming she hurried to the veranda to await them. "Oh, God he must be dead," she whispered to herself. She heard Mrs. Barrlette behind her; turning she put an arm around the frail woman, holding her close.

"Is it Charles?" she asked a quiver in her voice.

"I'm not sure, Jane answered, seeing Elmo dismount and began helping the undertaker to remove a body from the wagon.

Lucy now stood on the veranda with the other two women, her hand covering her mouth.

"Lucy, prepare Mr. Barrlette's bed—they are bringing him home," Jane told her as she led the way holding the doors for the men with their burden. Mrs. Barrlette trailed behind as they mounted the staircase to the upper floor.

Lucy stood at the doorway to the bedroom where Mr. Barrlette was to be taken. "In here Elmo," she stood aside and hurried in after them. She and Elmo began to take the Master's boots and greatcoat off; his outerware also was removed as they got him settled into bed and covered well. Lucy hurried to bring the flat-irons that were heating to be put to his feet. Mrs. Barrlette went to her husband—"Oh Charles, you've done it this time." He was burning up with fever and unable to answer her. Jane hurried forward to see what she could do. She took his pulse, felt his forehead and hurried to the hearth where she had a kettle brewing. Pouring a cupful, she mixed in honey and hurried to the bed—lifted her patient and tried to get him to drink—she only got a few sips down nodding to Lucy she said "the mustard plaster—quick!" Jane and Lucy worked frantically over Mr. Barrlette. Mrs. Barrlette pulled a chair close to the bed and sat holding the burning hand of her husband. Looking at Jane as she stepped back said, "you've done all you can, it's in God's hands now."

Elmo had stood at the door watching them work on Mr. Barrlette; shaking his head he said, "Miss Jane, could you comz downstairs—the Judge wants to talk to you."

"Jane put her hand on Mr. Barrlette's head and looked at Lucy; "time the plaster—only ten minutes please." She followed Elmo down the stairs and to the sitting room where the Judge waited.

"How is Charles?" the Judge asked.

"He's very bad; I've done all I can with what I have to work with. He was bad before he left here and worse now. I doubt he will live the night. If we can't get the fever broke—and I think it's too late—he'll die. Mrs. Barrlette hasn't rested or eaten properly since he left and she isn't in the best of health either; if he dies—I just don't know if she can stand it." Jane sat down on a chair suddenly her knees weak and shaky.

"Jane I hope you can be strong; I have more bad news—I don't want to break it to Elizabeth yet, not with what she is going through now—" he bowed his head, then looked up at Jane "they've found the Major—". Jane sat up straight looking the Judge in the eyes—"is he?"

"He's been shot—several times and was killed about five miles from his lines, and left where he fell. We brought him back to Charlotte. He's being seen to now; I'm sorry to have to tell you Jane. He was a fine young man and the last of a proud family.

When he's prepared, we'll send him home to Barrlette House; you'll want him in the family plot I'm sure."

Jane started to raise from her chair—she fell back into it nausea and dizziness overcoming her as sobs rose in her throat choking her; she leaned forward onto her knees her face buried in

227

her hands, "I must be strong—strong," she mumbled to herself. "Oh, God—he was so young and full of laughter—I'm so sick of war," she looked at the Judge her eyes empty and blank—"what are we to do?" she asked in a little girl voice.

"We do the best we can, Jane; I lost my only son sometime ago. I didn't want to live but life is precious and we survive somehow. He was all I had; my wife was gone when all this started; I'm somehow glad she didn't have to face what is before us now. Be strong Jane—there's more to come. I'll have to be going—tell Elizabeth when you can. I'll return with Lance when he's ready. Bless you my Child."

She heard the wagon going from the yard. She never knew a wagon rolling away could sound so mournful. Suddenly everything was quiet and she heard the soulful call of a dove in the trees outside the window. It was as though Lance called to her— telling her how lonely he was without her.

🎄 Chapter Twenty-One 🎄

When the Judge left, Jane went back upstairs to see about Mr. Barrlette. Lucy had removed the mustard plaster and had replaced warm irons at the feet of their patient. Jane went to the bedside and felt his pulse—it wasn't good, strong for a few beats and then strung out with fluttering between. Get a pan, Lucy, with some hot water and cloths—I have some turpentine in my bag—we'll try turpentine packs. I think from what I can tell, that he has pleurisy—make some ginger-tea as quickly as you can—that will loosen the phlegm which is building up. If we can clear his chest of the congestion, we may be able to help him. Jane could feel that Mrs. Barrlette was watching her.

"Jane, you can talk honestly—I know he probably won't get over this. I didn't expect him to be brought home alive. If he has pleurisy, it could go into pneumonia and he will die. I'm sorry he took such a chance as this—he couldn't have helped Lance even if he had found him. And it puts you under a greater strain trying to take care of him—he'll be eighty years old next month— he's lived his life; just as long as he doesn't have to suffer, I'll be able to accept it."

"Mrs. Barrlette, would you please go and lie down for a while? I'll call you if there is any change; you need your rest; you haven't had a good night's sleep for two days."

Mrs. Barrlette nodded, "I don't want to worry you more than you are all ready. I'll go into your room—there's a fire in there, and lie on the lounge—call if I can be of help."

"Lucy, see that she's covered; I have to talk to Sam. Keep a watch on Mr. Barrlette and I'll take over when I return." Jane left the room and started to the barn. Sam came toward her leaving whatever he was working on.

"Miss Jane, whatz you want? You wantz old Sam?"

"Yes Sam, we have to get the grave started for the Major. Do you know how to dig a grave?"

"Lord, yes, Miss Jane, I'z dug a' many a' one. Let's walk to the burying place and you show old Sam where you' z wantz it."

229

They walked to the grove of trees where an ornate iron fence wrapped around the family graves protecting them. Jane saw that some dated back to seventeen hundred—there must be some a hundred years old she thought—"where are Lance's parents?" Sam walked a few steps further and stood head bowed and his hat in his hand. "There, Miss Jane. I'z helped to bury both of them; poor little Lance he wanted to climb into the coffin with his mamma. They had to hold him back and him fighting them all; how he loved his mamma—now he'z with her."

Tears stood in Jane's eyes as she read the inscription on the tomb stone—'A mother's love never dies'—"Do you know how to measure the grave and lay it off, Sam? We'll put him beside his mamma."

"Miss Jane, don'zt you worry; the funeral man will send someone to help and there'll be plenty around in the mornin'. The word goes out and theyz come. I'z do what has to be done. I'z spect the Judge will take care of things at that end."

"Thank you Sam, I'll go back to Mr. Barrlette, I haven't told Mrs. Barrlette yet—I'll have to do that—I don't know how, but I have to."

"How'z Mr. Barrlette? Is he doin' all right?"

"I'll be surprised if he lives through the night. I've done all I can."

"It'z a blessin' youz here Miss Jane, I'z don't know how Ms. Barrlette would manage without you."

"Thank you Sam, I feel helpless, just too much happening for anyone to cope with."

* * *

Jane went to her bedroom to see if Mrs. Barrlette was sleeping. When Jane entered, she sat up on the chaise-lounge. "What is it, Jane? Is Charles worse?"

"It's not your husband I have something I have to tell you— I've been putting it off—I don't know how but it has to be done, Elmo found the Major—he was just five miles from his lines when he was shot by the Federal soldiers. Several of them had chased him from the mill where he was waiting for the other officers, and set a trap for him—he's in Charlotte and they will be bringing him home soon" Mrs. Barrlette seemed to shrink before her eyes—Jane put her arms around her.

With tears streaming down her face Mrs. Barrlette said, "I had a premonition that he was dead. He was so happy when you two were married. Charles and I both were very pleased—maybe there is still hope that there'll be another Barrlette to carry on the name. It would be so wonderful if he has left an heir."

"There's not much hope of there being an heir; we were married for only a few hours when he had to leave. I've told Sam to put him next to his Mamma—I thought that would be where you would want him. The grave will be started in the morning."

"That's the best place for him—he loved his Mamma so." Mrs. Barrlette wiped her tears. I must go to Charles; I won't have him long I'm afraid."

Jane had tears running down her face too, "I do wish you would rest but I know how you feel; there seems to be so little time—so little time," she whispered as she left the room. Mrs. Barrlette was a few years younger than her husband but now looked much older. Jane didn't know what to do. She felt old herself as she slowly made her way back to the sickroom. Mr. Barrlette was struggling to breathe through all the phlegm that had built up. The turpentine packs had loosened it and with trying to cough it up he was becoming weaker and weaker. Lucy looked toward Jane— "he isn't any better—is there anything else you want?"

"Bring a couple more pillows to prop him up, maybe that will help." Jane was so afraid he would drown in his own fluids. "I wish Gramps were here, maybe he could do something," she sat down beside the bed, tears standing in her eyes as she watched.

"And I was supposed to be getting away from pain and death," Jane mused, "it's only hitting closer to home".

Toward midnight Jane coaxed Mrs. Barrlette to go to bed. "I'll call you if there is a change she promised." She removed the pillows from behind her patient's head; he seemed easier and had stopped the terrible coughing. She felt his pulse and it was steadier; maybe he's improving she thought to herself. She had given him a large cup of willow tea and he seemed to be sleeping normally now. Jane sat beside the bed; Lucy had brought in a high-back rocker and she leaned her head back and dozed—waking off and on to check her patient.

The chirping of birds and the sound of horses arriving woke Jane from a sound sleep—.

* * *

For a moment Jane thought she was back in the compound with soldiers arriving—she looked toward the bed—Mr. Barrlette looked as though he was dead. She went to him and felt for a pulse, it was very weak and thready. That's not good she thought—she leaned her ear on his chest—she could hear the congestion as he drew each breath. I'll give him more of the willow tea, it keeps the fever down and maybe if he sleeps he will be able to breath without so much effort. Going to the hearth she poured a cup from the kettle on the hopper. Looking out the window, she saw several horses in the yard; whoever had arrived would be working on the grave.

Mrs. Barrlette came in to see how her husband was. Jane just shook her head— "He's no better, but has made it through the night; I've done all I can."

"I know you have Jane; if you keep him comfortable, I'm grateful; I'm going below; they will be bringing Lance home soon; we'll put him in the ballroom. I'm sure Judge Winthrop will bring the minister and have things under control; we'll have a short service before the burial. Does that meet with your approval?"

"Of course—whatever you do will be fine with me; you know more about these things than I do. Please don't overtire yourself."

Lucy came into the sickroom, "Will you set with Mr. Barrlette? I would like to freshen up and put on another dress; people will be arriving soon. I don't have a black dress; I'll just have to wear one of the dark ones I have. Do you think that will be permissible?" Jane asked.

"I think it will do, people don't have the means to buy a new dress for funerals—there have been so many; it'll do fine."

When Jane reached her room she sat a moment on the chaise by the window looking out at the dreary landscape; there were clouds scuttling overhead—she heard the mournful cry of the doves in the tree outside. "What am I doing here? I've seen so much death—so many young men—now my husband whom I never knew; he was so young and full of fun and loved by so many—she wasn't sure if she had loved him or not— "I can't even remember what he looked like," she murmured to herself. "How did I manage to get married so quickly? It was too fast—and now it's over—all but burying a man I didn't know. How could I have let this happen—what will Gramps say?" Jane sat talking to herself. Tears ran down her face as she thought of it all. She heard more horses going toward the barn, and knew she must hurry. She brought out a dark brown calico with a black print. Looking at it she said," It'll have to do." She took a black scarf to drape over her head later when the funeral started. As she finished she heard a wagon coming to the front veranda and knew that Lance had come home. I must go down to meet him—it's the hardest thing I've ever had to do in my life. Jane draped the scarf over her head and descended the beautiful staircase—Mrs. Barrlette stood beside the doors to the veranda, Jane went and stood beside her; she reached out a hand and patted Jane's arm. Tears stood in her eyes as the casket was brought in and taken to the ballroom. The two women followed—Jane was surprised to see so many people setting on rows of chairs waiting. She hadn't known they were there. The Judge was sitting where the family would sit in front close to the flag-draped casket. The servants came in and stood with bowed heads and the minister began—.

The service was short; Jane couldn't have told you one word that was said—they all stood and Jane put an arm around Mrs. Barrlette as they slowly followed the casket out and to the cemetery—it had turned colder and soft flakes of snow came down around the mourners. In minutes clods of earth fell on the wooden box with a hollow sound "strange—Jane thought just like my heart—hollow with nothing left in it—empty and hollow."

The few neighbors who had come came by and shook hands with the two Mrs. Barrlettes. Some came back to the house but most started home before the weather worsened. The Judge walked along holding onto Mrs. Barrlette's arm on one side and Jane on the other. When they arrived at the house, the Judge said, "Elizabeth, I have some papers for you to sign; let's go into the library.

Jane hurried back to the sickroom. Lucy was with their patient—"Is he any worse?" Jane asked. "About the same," Lucy told her.

Jane sat beside the sickbed thinking, all the Barrlettes except one—gone—and she was sure he would be gone soon—all that would be left would be the two Barrlette widows. "I must get back to Gramps—he needs me. What about Mrs. Barrlette? Who would look after her—Jane's mind went this way and that not knowing where her loyalties lay. She wrung out some cloths in the turpentine and placed them on Mr. Barrlette's chest. The fumes rose from the hot cloths and brought tears to Jane's eyes. Mr. Barrlette seemed to be trying to throw off the hot packs—moving from side to side. Jane tested them on her wrist to make sure that they weren't too hot. "What is it Mr. Barrlette, what do you want?" Jane leaned down close to be able to understand him.

"Elizabeth—Elizabeth—where's Lance?—We must find him—find—him—," he was tossing from side to side. Just then Lucy came in.

"Bring a cup of the willow tea; we must quiet him or he will wear himself out." Jane held the tea to his lips and got most of it down him. "He should sleep for awhile now. I hope throughout the night. I don't want Mrs. Barrlette staying up another night or she'll be down too."

"I'm going to bed now. Call me when you want a break and I'll set with him," Lucy said as she went back downstairs.

Jane sat in the rocker dozing on and off; she had gotten Mrs. Barrlette into bed to rest. Her patient had slept for some time. The house was quiet, and at first Jane didn't notice there was no sound from the bed—the raspy breathing had stopped; she went to the bed and leaned over her patient, taking up a wrist she felt for a pulse; not finding one she felt below the jaw on the large vein—there was no pulse. She tested the eyes lifting each eyelid—no reaction—poor Mr. Barrlette, he had followed his grandson peacefully and quietly. Jane removed the packs that were still on his chest, straightened his night clothes, removed the covering and left only a sheet that she pulled over his face. She looked at the clock on the dresser—four o'clock—she could see light clouds tinged with pink in the east—and she thought she heard the mournful call of the dove as she sat—waiting until dawn to send Elmo to the city for the death wagon.

Mrs. Barrlette came slowly into the room where Jane sat beside the body of Mr. Barrlette. Seeing the sheet-covered form she asked—"when?" as she dropped into another chair beside Jane's.

"He went quietly about four o'clock; he had been sleeping peacefully most of the night. I don't think he was in any pain. Are you all right?"

"Yes, I'm fine, you go do whatever is necessary—I'd like a moment alone with Charles. And Jane, thank you; I know you did all that could have been done."

Jane went to her room and washed her face and combed her hair. Then went below stairs and to the barn to tell Sam and start the preparations for another Barrlette's final departure from Barrlette House. When she told Sam he stood with bowed head tears coming to his eyes, "he'z a good master, we'z get the wagon ready and take him to be readied for burial."

"I'll have Mrs. Barrlette decide where she wants his grave. Bring a board or door to carry him down to the wagon. He will be ready when you are." Jane slowly walked back to the house, dreading the days ahead.

Mrs. Barrlette still sat beside her husband. Her tears had all been shed, and she sat with eyes closed.

"Are you all right?" Jane asked.

"I'm all right, Jane; I was just thinking of our long life together—sixty years—we'll bury him next to our son, Eric, with a space between for me. I'll be between the two men in my life. Lance my only grandson came later and was a joy to us both; you two would have been very happy given the chance. I'm sorry Jane that you have to lose a husband before you could know him. Your stay with us has not been pleasant for you; especially when you wanted to escape all the death and sickness you have been exposed to. But I'll be forever grateful you were here—you're like the daughter I never had—Charles loved you too. Thank you, Jane." She rose from her chair and put both arms around Jane

"Come, Mrs. Barrlette—let me put you to bed—you've done all you can. The boys will be coming for Mr. Barrlette soon." Jane poured a cup of the willow tea and guided her to the bedroom where she wanted her to rest.

The body was taken from the bedroom and on its way to be prepared for the funeral—two in three days at the plantation.

Jane had the bedroom aired and cleaned and the bed made up fresh, she was sure Mrs. Barrlette would rest better in her own bed. Jane was worried about her—she was an old woman and had been through so much.

* * *

The funeral was over. A few close friends kept Mrs. Barrlette company in the parlor, talking of all the things that had taken place in the last few months and of the long life the Barrletts had enjoyed together. Talk of the war was always foremost in their minds; rumors were flying that the war would be over soon. Their hopes had been shattered so many times that no one believed them anymore.

Jane had gone to the kitchen to see if some sort of refreshments could be served to their guests. Lucy was busy making some small sandwiches and cutting a cake that was ready. Flo was making a big pot of tea; Getty was getting the trays ready with napkins and small plates for serving. Jane wasn't sure that provisions allowed the courtesy of refreshments and was glad to note that there would be a good show of things served appropriately with the silver tray and teapot.

Jane entered the parlor and quietly seated herself, listening to the gossip around her, hearing of more deaths and so much sickness. "I want to go home, away from all this; if only Gramps would come, I would go and not have to think about death again." Looking at Mrs. Barrlette, she knew her conscience wouldn't let her go and leave the old woman in her grief. After all she was now her grandmother and she felt in lieu of another relative, she should look after her. Jane let her thoughts wander not joining in the conversation around her.

"Jane, what do you plan to do? Will you stay in Charlotte?" one of the neighbors asked.

"I'll have to go back and see about my grandfather soon. I never intended to be gone so long. He needs me to help him. He's old and I worry about him." Jane looked around the group as they all turned toward her—she felt they were all wondering if she had lost her mind—going back to where the fighting was.

"How can you stand living in a tent and seeing so many wounded? It must be terrible, what do you have to do?" one of the younger women asked as she looked at Jane.

"I do just about everything the doctors do. When doctor Fugate was hit by enemy shell and lost his arm my grandfather took care of him and found a woman who looked after him after removing his arm in the woods. He didn't come back to the compound for a couple of days; we didn't know where he was. Searchers were sent out—they couldn't find a trace of him. There wasn't another doctor to be had— I had to take over. There wasn't any-

236

one to treat the wounded—some had to be operated on—there was no one but me—I had to do what I could or many would have died. I've helped my Gramps for three years on the battlefield; I have helped with all sorts of emergencies—so I just did it; I was forced into it by necessity. When we had two doctors working, I only did cleaning of wounds and dressing and assisting with more serious operations where help was needed." Jane dropped her head as she thought of all the pain she had seen.

There were gasps from the women present, as they all turned to look at Jane. "That must have been very hard for you, although you appear to be very strong," one of the matrons commented.

After the refreshments, wraps were gathered and the guests began to depart; offerings of help if needed and invitations to visit extended. Soon Jane and her new grandmother were left alone. The servants gathered the refreshment clutter and removed it to the kitchen. The two women left the parlor and went to the small setting room where they both sank into chairs—drained of energy and emotions.

"Mrs. Barrlette, I've had your room aired and made up fresh; I think you should spend the rest of the day in bed. You are sorely in need of rest and I'm worried you will come down with something from being so tired and worried and from lack of proper rest. Would you please let me put you to bed? You must rest." Jane looked toward her noticing how she had aged since she had been there; Jane's heart went out to her. Going to her she took her hand, "Come, I'll take you upstairs." Mrs. Barrlette slowly rose; Jane put her arm around her and guided her toward the long flight of stairs.

Lucy had made a fresh kettle of the willow tea, helping get Mrs. Barrlette into a warm flannel nightdress Jane gave her a cup of the hot tea and settled her into bed. Jane sat beside the bed until soft snoring told her that the old lady was sleeping soundly. She pulled the covers close around the sleeping woman and left the room.

Jane returned to her room, and sat down on the chaise-lounge by the window. The day was cloudy and dreary; the mournful sound of the doves could still be heard. It was getting late in the day and the dirty clouds that scuddled overhead warned of snow. Jane's heart was dark and heavy as the clouds above. Her mind didn't seem to want to face the reality of all she had been through.

As she sat she wanted to cry a flood of tears and wash away all the ugliness that had haunted her for so long. "Gramps says tears never solved anything; you have to keep a clear mind and work it out." How many times she had been told that from the age of five. She knew he was right and squared her shoulders to be ready to face whatever the future brought.

ASHES OF ROSES AND WAR

BOOK TWO

❧ Chapter Twenty-Two ❧

Jane sat looking out the window of her room at the gray landscape. Nothing moved in her line of vision until snowflakes began to fall. She watched as the dreary landscape began to take on a coat of soft white watching mesmerized thinking; it's God's way of washing away all the ugliness. If only her heart could be washed as clean of all the sadness that she had been through.

"What am I to do?" she asked the emptiness around her. "I can't go off and leave Mrs. Barrlette; she needs care and I'm the only one left to do that." Jane sat with her head propped in her hand mumbling over all her choices. She was exhausted and finally leaning back in her chair, she dozed.

Lance knelt beside her chair holding her two hands in his, as he looked into her eyes. "Darling, you're worn out; you must take better care of yourself. You've done so much for my family and I'm so grateful that you were here during all their problems. The war is almost over and everyone can get back to a normal life. "It won't be what we knew before, but hopefully it will right itself and become an even better one. It's going to be an uphill struggle for all concerned. Promise you will dry your tears and get on with your life; if only we could be together—I love you so," His arms went around her and his warm lips covered hers, in a long loving kiss.

Jane awoke, and with a smile she touched her finger tips to her lips. She looked around the room. Lance was here—it was all so real. "Oh, God! He's dead and buried," she whispered as her thin over-tired body began to shake, and tears streamed down her pale cheeks. Sobs shook her for several minutes. Drying her eyes, she rose from her chair to go check on Mrs. Barrlette.

Jane slowly made her way down the darkened hall of the big house to Mrs. Barrlette's room. She quietly opened the door and entered. Seeing that the old lady still slept, Jane walked aimlessly around the room, thinking of time spent in this room nursing Mr. Barrlette until he died. She sat for a few minutes beside the bed, then rose and went from the room toward the down stairs.

She wanted Lucy to have a tray ready when Mrs. Barrlette awoke, not wanting her to get out of bed even to eat. She must rest if she wanted to regain her strength and be well again.

As Jane went toward the kitchen, she heard several excited voices. She recognized one as Sam's. He rarely came to the big house unless there was an emergency or it was mealtime which he ate in the kitchen with the other help. They seemed to be excited about something. "What now?" she wondered, as she opened the door and looked at all of them gathered there.

"Miss Jane Miss Jane the war's over. It's shor's over. Dats' what de man said." Sam had a smile from ear to ear, and all the others looked toward Jane not knowing if they should smile or not.

"What man, Sam? When?" Jane asked looking from one to the other.

"I'z don't know his name. He came through and I'z shoed his horse for him. Said he's on his way to Charlott' he been where the fightin' goin' on and now it's done over."

"I didn't hear anyone. Why didn't you call me?"

"I'z didn't want to disturb you Miss Jane. I knos' you parful tired and all."

"It's all right, Sam. We'll send someone early in the morning to Charlotte to find out if it's true or not. We must not get our hopes up too much. As you know we have had false rumors before. Let's all pray that it's true. All the states North and South are worn out with the fighting, and I'm sure will be celebrating if it is true. I, for one, surely hope so.

"Lucy, will you please prepare a tray for Mrs. Barrlette—some hot soup or something light. I don't want her to get out of bed. She must have rest; can you do that?"

"I'll have something ready when she awakes, Miss Jane. Can I'z ask you sometin' ifin' the wars over are we's free? And what do it mean? Do we have to leave Barrlette House?" she looked anxiously at Jane.

Let's not count our chickens, I'm sure Judge Winthrop will inform everyone when the time comes. I'll send someone early tomorrow to have him come here and explain what is going on. He is a very learned man and should know everything. We will just have to wait a little longer. Is dinner ready? If not I will return upstairs. Jane looked toward the table and saw it was prepared for the meager meal she knew would be served.

"Youz' sit Miss; everything is ready; we's just waiting for you." Flo began dipping the thin stew over some rice. It smelled delicious. She had also stewed dried plums which were served for dessert.

"It smells wonderful Flo, and I'm hungry." Jane smiled toward all the Barrlette people as she seated herself at the big round kitchen table where they all ate since the household had diminished.

After Jane finished the filling dinner she went back to the sick room to sit with Mrs. Barrlette while she had her tray. Soon the household became quiet, even Mrs. Barrlette fell into a sound sleep after she ate.

* * *

Jane was up early; she could hear fires being tended and the household awakening. She hadn't slept too well, waking every little while thinking of the news that the war was over. She hoped it was true—it had lasted much too long. She hurried to check on Mrs. Barrlette, and found her still sleeping. The room was comfortable as one of the help had stirred up the fire.

Hearing a horse entering the courtyard, Jane went to a window and looking out she saw a bundled figure dismounting. She recognized the Judge. "My, it's early to have company. I wonder what's wrong now. Seeing him brought to mind all the bad news that seemed to surround the Judge. Glancing into a mirror to see that her hair was tidy, she hurried from the room and down the long stairway to the front door where Lucy was just welcoming the dignified Judge.

Going forward, Jane extended her hand, "Do come in Judge Winthrop; you must be frozen. Lucy, please bring some hot tea to the small sitting room for the Judge. Lucy took his heavy greatcoat shaking the snow from it and hung it to dry. "I'll bring it directly, Miss Jane."

"How are you Jane? and how is Mrs. Barrlette? I've been worried about you both, there is so much influenza going around."

"I have been keeping Mrs. Barrlette in bed to rest. I'm fine—a little tired but it will go away in time. Thank you for asking. Now I have a question. What brings you out so early on such a cold day?" she smiled as she looked at the dear old man.

"I need you to gather the household; no need to awaken Mrs. Barrlette— she already knows what I have to tell you. Bring the people in from the out-buildings. It concerns them all; right away if possible as I have other calls to make."

Jane looked perplexed as she said, "I'll call them immediately. I think they are all up and dressed; shall I bring them in here?"

"Yes please," the Judge said as he took up a satchel that rested at his feet and began to riffle through a stack of papers spreading them out on a table nearby.

Jane hurried toward the kitchen to inform Lucy to call everyone in for the Judge's announcement—whatever it was to be.

All the 'people' except what field hands that still remained came, even little Andy, each looking at the Judge wondering if they had done something wrong. The men especially kept shuffling their feet on the worn carpet in their nervousness. The Judge sat behind the table where all his papers lay. He rummaged through the clutter and looked up as Sam finally came into the room; all the others were assembled.

"Good morning to all of you. I have Mr. Barrlette's will here and each of you have been named by him with his bequest. Mrs. Barrlette knows everything in the will and signed it the day her husband was buried. She and Charles had me write up their wishes in legal form and I have those wishes before me now. Sam, you're first on the list having been here so long." Sam stepped forward, his hat in his hand, and stood before the Judge. "Sam, these papers have been made up for some time; in fact even before the war. Mr. Barrlette never gave them to you—he seemed to be afraid—thinking that you might go away and leave the family. I will present them to you now.

"What papers iz they, Mr. Judge? I ant' heard of no papers."

"They set you free, Sam, free to do as you wish, go where ever you want, live wherever you want. There is also some cash— Charles left you one hundred dollars in gold. Here it is," he reached out an envelope and a small bag toward Sam.

"Gold! Lord God Almighty! Iz never had any gold, never in my life. Doz' that means' I have to leave Barrlette House, Judge?"

"No, Sam, you can stay if you wish; from now on you will be paid a fee for your work."

"Lucy, you're next," the Judge announced as he picked up another envelope and a small bag.

Lucy stepped forward—whatz' mine say, Judge?"

"It says you are free, too Lucy; and also you have fifty dollars in gold."

Lucy stepped back with a look of amazement on her pretty black face, she had been educated by Mrs. Barrlette and understood better than the others, what this meant. She didn't talk or think like the other servants.

"Flo, you're next—she stepped up to the table and held her hand out. "You're free too; these are the papers to that effect, and twenty five-dollars in gold."

"Getty?" He hurried up to the table not waiting to hear that he was next, no doubt thinking of the gold he might get.

"You also have your freedom affidavit, and a five dollar gold piece." Getty stepped toward the back of the room a big smile on his face.

"Slazzy?" She hurried up. "You are a free woman, too, and have five dollars in gold.

The Judge started to gather up the papers before him. "That is all that is required of you people; guard your money and papers—they will both be very useful. Be careful of your gold, there isn't much of that to be had in the South today.

Little Andy looked around at all the happy faces; he looked ready to break into tears. Finally getting up enough nerve he went up to the table shifting from one foot to the other, he stood before the Judge., "Don't Iz' get free too, Judge?"

The Judge looked Andy straight in the eye, "You've always been free boy—you're not Barrlette 'People'. I want you and Jane to remain; all the rest of you can get back to your work.

When they had all filed from the room, he turned to Jane. "Jane, you now own Barrlette House and the plantation. You are also trustee for the young lad, Andy, and are to see to his upbringing until he is old enough to look out for himself. Mrs. Barrlette will have widow's rights here for as long as she lives. You, as their Granddaughter-in-law are the only heir of the Barrlette's. Besides the land, there is some money; I'm not sure just how much—Mrs. Barrlette will inform you of that. You will do whatever you wish with the field hands; I don't know how many are left. At one time the Barrlettes had around fifty people. I know some have gone North and a few joined the Rebel army. These are the papers freeing them. You will have to fill in their names, and sign them. If you care to give them some money that's up to you.

Jane had a shocked expression on her face as she looked at the Judge, "I can't accept all this. I have to go back to my grandfather—he needs me. I can't take the Barrlettes property, I don't deserve it."

"They both thought that you did. I would suggest you send someone to your grandfather and tell him the situation; let him come here now that the war is ended. Yes, they signed the treaty several days ago. There will be no more fighting. You or your grandfather will no longer be needed in the capacity of doctor. I know that Mrs. Barrlette still needs you. She could die at any time, and she loves you as the daughter she never had. They both loved you and are grateful for all you have done in their time of need. I'm sure things will work out given time. Thank you for the refreshing tea. I'll leave copies of all the 'people's' papers for you. This was a fine plantation at one time housing many souls, now there are so few. Perhaps it will right itself and become prosperous again. Have hope Jane, things seem to work themselves out. I'll be going now, I have several stops yet on my journey. I'll check in now and then to see how things are progressing."

Jane sat down on the chair behind the table that the Judge had occupied, too stunned to even see him out. She stared straight ahead trying to compose herself, and her thoughts.

"Miss Jane, what you want I do now?" Andy looked at Jane with a half scared look on his little face.

Jane had forgotten that the little orphan boy sat in a corner of the room—she thought everyone had gone. "Andy, I'll be your Guardian now, I would like for us to get to know each other. I've never had a chance to talk much to you. How would you like to move into the big house, and maybe we can spend some time together and I can start you on some lessons. How does that sound?"

"I'z don't know; Sam needs me in the barn; I have chores to do, and stuff. Won't I see Sam now? Will I have to stay in the house all the time?"

Jane smiled as she looked at the serious little face, "Oh, you'll have plenty of time for your chores; in fact we will all have to work to keep the plantation going. You run along now and see Sam. I expect they are all celebrating and you should be part of it. Gather your things, and this evening we will move you in here. Is that all right?"

Andy hurriedly left his chair and said, "That's fine with me," as he almost ran from the room.

Jane was in shock, as she sat thinking of all that had occurred in the last few minutes. What was she to do with a three hundred acre plantation and a passel of freed slaves? She had no idea of where to start. Who would she ask? Sam knew about what was to be done around Barrlette's barn, but would he know about the plantation? I can't do it, I just can't. I do know something about farming but a plantation—I know nothing. She sat thinking—there must be records—suddenly rising from her chair she started from the room and went down the hall to the library.

She knew that Mr. Barrlette had his office there and all the records should be there. Jane opened the door; a cold blast of air greeted her making goose-bumps rise and sending a shiver down her back. Since Mr. Barrlette's death there had been no fire in the room. Looking around she saw a large ledger lying on the desk by the window. Quickly gathering the heavy volume into her arms she hurried from the cold room. Going back to the small sitting room that was warm and cozy, she placed the large volume on the table that was being used as a desk. Warming her cold hands at the fire, she was soon ready to tackle the large ledger.

Jane sat for a few seconds, her hands on the big book thinking of the many times a Barrlette had held the information of the plantation in their hands. Opening the volume she found it dated back to eighteen hundred and three. The information of several generations bound in leather. Jane was overwhelmed at the responsibility she was facing. As she read she become so engrossed that time escaped her. She raised her eyes as Lucy entered the room.

"Would you like a dinner tray in here, Miss Jane?" She looked at Jane and the big book she held, wondering what she found in it to make her forget the time.

"Oh, is it noon already? Has Mrs. Barrlette awakened? I'm afraid I've neglected her. How is she?" Jane looked confused as she asked Lucy all the questions.

"Ms. Barrlette had a tray and is sleeping again. She didn't take much notice, and didn't even ask about you. I'm not sure her mind isn't wandering. She wanted to know about Lance—said he was here last night. I knew then she was flighty. I'll bring you a tray right away," she said as she left the room.

"I wonder how Mrs. Barrlette knew Lance was here last night? I'll ask her as soon as I can. I knew he was here, but how did she know? Maybe I'm losing my mind," she sat thinking, then started to read again, becoming absorbed in the big volume. It was all here, written in a neat hand, explaining the breeding of the animals, the crops, and how they were rotated. Even the breeding of the 'People'—who belonged to whom. It wouldn't make much sense now. There were no 'people' to carry on all the tasks that had to be done. She decided that instead of the plantation, they would have to go back with the basics of farming, raising a few head of cattle, pigs, and chickens and a large garden to provide the food necessary for them to survive. Cotton and fields of grain would have to be abandoned, at least for now. The ones who would remain on the plantation would be busy raising enough food to survive. She closed the book, as Lucy entered with her dinner tray.

Jane's mind was traveling at a great rate of speed, going over everything she had read and trying to absorb it all and convert it to everyday use. She didn't know how much money was to hand. There were a lot of repairs that must be done or the house would fall down around their heads. Fences had to be rebuilt to hold any animals that were left. Sam seemed to have kept the barn and shop in repair—after all he slept in a room at the back and spent all his time there. At present, Andy shared his room. Jane had decided to move Andy into Lance's room. She didn't know how Mrs. Barrlette would like the idea, but Jane thought it might have a great influence on the young boy. All Lance's boyhood things were there and all the books he had collected as a man. It would be something for Andy to live up to. He had known Lance and admired him, she knew.

Jane decided to see Mrs. Barrlette; if she was awake, she would ask how she felt about it. Then she intended to seek Sam out and go over whatever still remained on the plantation in the way of livestock, and how many field hands were about. She wanted to know how many wanted to remain in their quarters, and how many wished to go.

When Jane entered the room, Mrs. Barrlette was sitting up in bed. Lucy sat in the rocking chair beside her with mending on her lap. Mrs. Barrlette's face lit up and she smiled her welcome.

"Jane, how are you child? Come sit by me and tell me."

"I'm fine," turning to Lucy she said, "I'll sit with Mrs. Barrlette for an hour, if you have something to do."

Picking up her basket of mending Lucy left the two women alone.

"I'm so much better now that Lance is home. Have you talked to him, Jane?"

"Mrs. Barrlette, are you all right? Lance got killed, don't you remember?"

"Oh, yes! I remember. But he came last night and talked to me; he said when he left that he was going to you. Didn't you see him?"

"What did he say to you Mrs. Barrlette? Do you remember?"

"He said I was to take care of myself—that I was in danger of being seriously ill. Also to see that you rested and took care of yourself. He said that Charles had joined him, and that Rick was near too. You do believe me don't you? You don't think I'm round the bend do you like Lucy and the rest? They get so scared thinking that the dead can return. Do you think they can, Jane?"

Jane smiled at the serious expression on Mrs. Barrlette's face. "I might think you were, if it hadn't happened to me too last night. If the dead can't return, then we're both—round the bend.

"Tell me what happened. Was it Lance? Did he visit you?"

"I was dozing in my chair, Lance came and knelt beside me and took my hand in his. I could even feel the warmth of his dear hands. He seemed to be concerned about us both. He said he wished he could be with us, and that he loved me; then he kissed me on the lips, and was gone." Tears were slowly running down Jane's face as she talked. "He asked me not to cry—to get on with my life."

"I knew he would go to you. I knew he was here—I knew it. Jane, I feel so good knowing that Charles is with Lance and that Rick found his way too. I'll not cry anymore, I'll soon be joining them myself. I don't want you to worry about me. You must guard your health—you're a young woman with lots of life before you. She patted Jane's hand and turned to the wall and soon she was snoring softly.

Jane left the room and returned to the small sitting room where she wanted to pursue the information she had found in the large plantation Ledger. Where the entries had left off she entered the information of Lance's being shot, the date and the circumstances of his death and burial, also that of Mr. Barrlette. She wasn't sure what date the treaty was signed between the states, leaving a blank and just filling in the year of 1865. She thought this should be made known to whoever or wherever the big ledger would go. She thought of Sueann, and knew that if she had married Lance she would treasure such a memento. As it was, if she had married Lance, she would now be his widow. She had married Major Rex Hargrove soon after Jane and Lance were married. He was now in a northern prison and no one knew if he was alive or not. Word had seeped through the southern lines that he was gravely ill, and had lost a leg while fighting in Virginia somewhere. Sueann had aged before her time, as had many young women having to face the heartache of war.

Jane sent Getty to the blacksmith shop where Sam was busy on the farm equipment to ask him to come to the house—that she wanted to talk to him.

She was still pursuing the information in the ledger when she heard Sam coming down the hallway, and looked up when he entered.

"Good morning, Sam. I hate to take you away from whatever task you were at, but I need some information."

"Good mornin' Miss Jane; I'z not too busy this mornin'; I come as soon as I can. Whats' you want to know that old Sam knows?"

"I've been going over the Plantation ledger. I know it isn't correct now as to the stock, people and etc. What I want to ask you is—how many workers are still here? Do they plan on staying or do you know?"

"Thez' about ten I recon'; how many will stay—that I'z don't know.

"Could you give me a run-down on what stock we have, and where it is. Also what supplies there are on the plantation."

"Well now lez' see—there' the Major's stallion—it's comm' back some from when the Major run it so hard. I think it will be fine in a little while. Then ther' Mr. Barrlette's mare; she' not too young, but still goin. We got some pretty good mules—I think five or six. There' four cows, two with calf, some chickens, I'z don't know how many. And several pigs running wild down to the swampy. We'z got three bags of salt, some corn for the animals, a little hay; I'z have to think on it Miss Jane. I'z do know we don't have much. Mr. Barrlette gave to the army all he could and some he shouldn't. Not that I'z mean to say something I'z shouldn't."

"Thank you Sam, you think of how much you missed, if any, and we will go over it together tomorrow and I'll make a list. We have to know what we have to work with. Can you have the workers come to the shop house about three o'clock today, and try to think what should be done first around the plantation? I'll come to the shop and make a list of everyone. We have to start somewhere. Thank you Sam, you can get back to your work now."

Jane still studied the ledger trying to piece together what had been. She knew that nothing in the ledger would apply now. But some of it might still help. Her back ached and her eyes had begun to blur as she finally closed the heavy volume. I'll have to talk to Mrs. Barrlette, "I really don't know where to start," she mumbled as she went to her room, "I've got to have a nap, my brain seems numb." She stretched out on her bed and pulled a blanket over herself; she no more than put her head on the pillow until she was asleep.

❧ Chapter Twenty-Three ❧

When Jane awoke she went to Mrs. Barrlette's room, and found her sitting in a chair by the window. She looked up when Jane entered— "Good afternoon Jane, Lucy told me you were napping. I'm sure you needed it you look rested; do you feel all right?"

"I'm fine, how about you? You too look better, a stay in bed works wonders." Jane pulled a footstool close and sat down by Mrs. Barrlette.

"Yes, I do feel rested and have finally accepted the fact that Charles, and Lance are both gone; I'm much more content now that I know they are together and happy."

"Mrs. Barrlette, I didn't tell you that Judge Winethrop was here while you were bedfast. He brought the legal papers that you and Mr. Barrlette had him prepare. We called in Sam and all the house people and he explained everything, he gave them their freedom papers, plus the moneys allotted. They were all concerned that they might now have to leave the plantation. He explained to me that you both wanted me to have all you own. I didn't want to accept it, but the Judge convinced me that that was the way you both wanted it. I have to tell you now, I don't know if I can stay in the South. It doesn't have very pleasant memories for me."

"Promise me Jane that you will stay as long as I'm alive, which as you know can't be long. Then you can sell the plantation or do whatever you want. I know you don't feel as if you belong here, and that is your privilege; if Lance had lived it would have been different. The plantation is so run down, I doubt anyone would want it, but someone will come along who does when the time comes. I want you to know that I love you as a daughter, as did Charles, you're a fine young woman, Lance would have made you happy," She turned toward the window as the mournful call of a dove sounded in the tree outside.

"Mrs. Barrlette, is there anything you want me to do concerning the people and the up-keep of the place? I've ask Sam to call all of them for a meeting at three this afternoon. I want to know how many are left and their intentions."

"Jane, the Plantation is yours, to do with as you see necessary. I'll come down soon and give you some of the money that is left to run things on. There's about ten thousand in gold and silver, and several thousand in Confederate money that of course isn't worth anything. I don't have the energy to even help you plan. I want you to know where the valuables are so if anything happens to me, you will know. No one else knows but me."

"I'm going to the barn to meet with Sam, and take inventory of what there is left, and try to decide what we should do first.

I know as far as fields of cotton, tobacco and grain are out of the question. I think large plots for gardens, to grow food, and some livestock, will be as much as we can manage. I do know how to farm but running a plantation is a little out of my experience, and knowledge. I'll check back with you at supper time and tell you what we have accomplished. Don't stay up too long and tire yourself again. If you take care maybe you can come down stairs tomorrow, ' Jane kissed her cheek and gave her a squeeze.

"You can help me to bed, before you leave dear. I'm going to be good, I surely don't want to spend more time than necessary in that bed." Jane took her arm, helping her remove her heavy robe and in to bed. Patting Jane's hand she closed her eyes.

Jane went back to her room and pulled on another pair of heavy woolen socks, and the heaviest shoes she had, added a woolen sweater, tied a shawl over her head and throwing a heavy cape around her shoulders, she was ready for a prolonged stay outdoors.

Jane arrived at the barn, a small ledger and pencil in her hand, Sam was waiting for her, Andy at his elbow.

"Good, Andy I'm glad you re coming along, I'll explain as we go so you will understand what we are about. We're going to take an inventory, you say it."

"Inventory," Andy repeated. "What doz' it mean?"

"First it's does, not doz'" he repeated it after Jane. It means making a list of everything we have on the Plantation. The old lists aren't accurate anymore. We have to find out what we have to work with and how much we can do with what we have.

"Doz' you want a list of the things in the barn?"

"Everything Sam," Jane started to write as Sam called off the equipment—6 set harness, two oxen yokes, six sack grain, saddles, bridles, check rains, extra cured leather for repairs and for new, two anvils—the list went on and on. By the time they had finished in the barn and shop, the 'people' had assembled outside.

Jane looked them over, there were twelve adults, and three youngsters. Most of them were too old to have children and too old to do much work it looked like.

"Good afternoon, I'm Jane, Mr. Lance's widow. Mrs. Barrlette is resting, everything has been turned over to me. My purpose is to get things working on the plantation again so we can all eat, and live as comfortable as possible. I've never had any experience running a big Plantation and you will all have to help me, for all our benefit. First would all of you line up facing me, I will go down the line and write down your name." Jane opened her ledger as the line formed. Going to the first-a tall well built middle age man, "Iz' Tom."

"How old are you Tom? do you know?"

"Iz' thirty two, Miss Jane, Iz' born here on Barrlette Plantation, Iz' good worker."

"You know you are free, and can leave if you want, do you want to leave?"

Doz' I have to?"

"No, of course not. You can stay and will be paid a wage; but I can tell you now it won't be much. You will be fed and housed. Many who leave won't have that. Many are living in the woods without a warm place to sleep or anything to eat. Are you married?"

He pointed to the woman next to him.

Turning to her Jane asked," Do you agree with Tom?"

"My name's Ella; Iz' want to stay in my cabin. Iz' don't want to go nowhere. These' my grand childs—their mother died when last was born; their pappy went to war and was killed."

"I'm sorry to hear that." She went down the line, asking questions—if they knew the name of their parents and etc; how long they had been Barrlette 'people', getting all the information she could. "I'll have your free papers written up in a few days and you will have them. We will have to organize work crews to start getting things in order before planting time. If we are to eat we will have to raise food. Tom, could you check the fences and see what needs repaired to keep our livestock in. There's going to be a lot of hungry people roaming the area and we have to protect what we have. Could you do that?"

"I shore can Miss Jane; I'll have a crew working on them come mornin; Iz' think the pens close to the barn first and so we can lock them in the barn at night."

"Thank you Tom; I think that is a good place to start. You can all go now; if you need anything let me know, and be here early in the morning if it's a fit day to work we will get started." The 'people' returned to their quarters.

"Sam, thank you for your help. I'll go over this tonight and have some things lined up tomorrow. From now on we will charge for your work. I'll make up a price list for how much to charge and you can post it in your shop. I know the Plantation was very generous and did for people who were traveling we can no longer afford to do that. I'll see you tomorrow and we will work up a list." She turned back to the house, saying to herself, well, that's a start.

Jane went back to her room and removed the layers of clothing she had worn outside. Her chair was close to the small fire in the grate and she sat down to go over the inventory, and the list of people. She could remember most of them as she looked at their written names. She would start organizing work crews so all would be useful. It seemed that they all wanted to stay on the place, not wanting to take a chance of not having something to eat or a dry place to sleep. Most probably thought they were too old, and they were right. The cruel northern winters would take their toll on southern born Negroes, especially old ones.

After studying the list she decided that four of the men could be sent to cut wood, while four more worked on fences. As soon as it warmed up, she wanted the front yard cleaned and trimmed and some repair to the house done. She would see if Sam would do that. The place had a run down look that she wanted to remedy at once. She had seen an old shed that needed to be taken down, the boards saved to use on some other project. The money would have to be stretched. Ten thousand dollars seemed a fortune and would be, now that the war was over; but she didn't want anyone to know there was gold on the plantation. No telling what would happen if the drifters even got a hint that gold was to be had. She would talk to Sam about taking his gold to the bank and let everyone know that it was there. It certainly wouldn't be safe on a free Negro; and he could be hurt or killed for that much gold.

Jane checked on Mrs. Barrlette, and noted she had eaten, and fallen asleep again. She decided to let her sleep through the night and turned the lamp low as she left the room. Lucy had brought her a tray too so she could get at her book work without being disturbed. She had most of the plans worked out in her head, and had made lists of who worked where.

Little Andy had settled in nicely into Lance's room and seemed to be awed by all the wonderful things he found there. Jane had cautioned him to be careful of Lance's things. "Will Lance come back to haunt me if I break something?" he had asked Jane. She told him that Lance would be very disappointed that he had some of the things for years and treasured them. They had decided that as soon as the work progressed to her satisfaction that she would start his lessons.

Jane finally laid aside the ledger she had been working on and went to bed. If it was a fit day she would be up early and start the work crews at their allotted jobs. She didn't know how well they would work without an overseer.

* * *

When Jane opened her eyes it was to beautiful sunshine, a welcoming sight after all the dreary days they had been having. This morning looked almost like spring. She hurried with dressing and went down to the kitchen to find all waiting for her.

Andy left his chair and held hers for her. She had told him that was what gentlemen did. She hadn't expected him to remember with just one telling. "Thank you, Andy," She gave him a big smile, and all around the table smiled too. They had seen the Barrlette men extend that courtesy to all the ladies who came to Barrlette House.

"Mr. Andy, you remind me of Mr. Lance; he seated his ladies just like you did Miss Jane." Lord O' Mercy he was a charmer." Lucy chuckled as she saw how pleased Andy was.

Jane looked around the table at the 'people' seeing the questions in their eyes.

"I've gone over what we have to work with. We won't be growing cotton or tobacco. It takes too much work. Our main purpose is to feed everyone and what stock we have. I'm going to send a crew to cut wood and haul it in. Another group will be working on fences around the barn. Andy, I want you and the other young boys to bring in the livestock in the evenings. We will keep them all in the barn at night with locks on the doors. Sam you see to the locks. There's going to be scavengers coming through looking for easy pickings. We don't want to lose what we have to them. Remember you're all free; keep something handy to protect yourself. It could be that you will need it. I don't want anyone starting trouble but we don't intend to hide from it on our own place. Sam, will you saddle the mare that Mr. Barrlette rode. I'll need to check around to see what else we need to do first. One of the wagons will have to be readied for hauling in the wood. The three boys can go along to load it. We will put it in ricks, easy to get to. We don't want it against any buildings; in case of fire it would go up like a tinderbox. And we never know who might get the idea to burn us out. As you know our capital—Columbia, was burned and no one seems to know for sure if it was the north or south who did it. Seems we can trust no one. Sam, I want you to go to Charlotte, as soon as we get everyone started; I think you should put your gold into the bank. If any of these ruffians that will be coming through here got wind that gold was to be had they would let nothing stand in their way to get it. You might be hurt or even killed. Let everyone know that it is in the bank. Will you do that Sam?"

"I'z' been wondering where I could keep it. It be safe in the bank; Mr. Barrlette always say so."

"There is going to be land for sale cheap; maybe in future, you will want a little parcel of your own. That gold could be the means of your owning your own home." Jane looked around the table at the awed faces. They had none ever dreamed of such grandeur.

"Miss Jane, can I have Sam take mine too?" Lucy asked.

"By all means, Lucy. I'll write a note to the Judge; he will know just how to go about it." They were all nodding their heads.

"Flo looked at her son, Getty. "We send our gold to the bank too, she said with a satisfied look on her wrinkled old face. My Getty will be marryin' someday; maybe it will buy them a home."

Getting up from the table Jane said, "I'll go and write the letter to the Judge. When you're ready, Sam, let me know."

Andy followed Jane into the small sitting room where she had gone to write; she looked up and saw him watching her.

"What is it, Andy? did you want something?"

"I wish I had some gold, Miss Jane. I'd buy me a big saddle-horse and go out west and build me a cabin. That's what I'd do." The longing in his eyes almost made her cry.

"Come here, Andy." She put both arms around the little boy— "I'll tell you what. I'll see you get paid when you work. And to-night we will find a book in Mr. Barrlette's library about the west. We will read all about what to expect when you do decide to go. How about that?"

"Oh, Miss Jane that will be almost like going. Thank you," he shyly kissed her cheek and ran from the room.

"Jane sat, a smile on her face. She was beginning to love the homeless little lad. And she wanted more for him than the 'people' expected in their life.

Sam came to the door; Jane had the letter to the Judge writ-ten; she needed to add the names for the bank and how much each sent. "You be careful Sam. Don't stop for anyone, even if you know them; people change when there is gold involved. And hurry back; I'll worry until I see your face again."

"I'z do that Miss Jane; I'z feel a little skittish carrying all that money. "I'z never seen that much at one time before."

Jane hurried outside to get everyone on the job allotted. Some of the women came to help too, which surprised Jane. They were told to go back to their cabins; it was too cold for them to work outside, and they weren't needed today. She put Tom in charge of the crew to work on the fence. "Do you know how to do this, Tom."

"Yes, I'z do Miss Jane. I'z built lots of fences. I'z build it good you see."

"Thank you Tom; could you send a couple of the men to tear down that shed back there." she pointed to where it was falling over, back in the paster field. "I can't stand to look at it another day. Have them save all the boards that can be used; whatever else is left we can use for firewood. Can you get your fence crew started then start the others on it?"

The wood crew was standing by—with saws and broad axes, ready to cut. Jane started them off toward the woods about half a mile away. She mounted the mare that stood ready for her and turned her toward the wood-lot. She wanted to see what could be cut and if anything was valuable for timber that should be left. She could see there were lots of downed trees that had fallen in storms and been neglected. Jane smiled to herself, everything that was down must be taken up and cleaned up and everything would look better. She was ahead of the men somewhat. She rode into the woods, and saw that the down trees would be several days work to cut up into lengths. She sat looking around waiting for the crew to catch up. She noticed one of the men looked around and seemed more knowledgeable than the rest. She went over to him., "Is your name Jeb?"

"Yes, Miss Jane; what youz' want cut?"

"What do you think, Jeb?" She wanted to see if he could look over the trees and work out a plan.

"I'z think ifn' we start say over there," he pointed to a large wind blown tree on the ground. "Ifn' wes' start there and work ourself on into the woods, the wagon can follow and the boys can throw it in the wagon as we cut."

"That sounds fine Jeb; I'm going to put you in charge; keep your men clear of the axes so no one gets hurt. Do you all hear— Jeb's in charge of the cutting; those who don't do a good day's work won't be paid." Thank you all. I'll see you have a hot meal at noontime." Jane started back toward the house and decided to swing by the shed where the sound of hammers and prying boards could be heard. When she arrived she noticed a pile of sound boards being piled neatly, and scraps or broken boards thrown into another pile. "You're doing a good job," she told the men as they stopped to look toward her. Jane waved her hand as she started riding away. She was thinking of the startled look on Andy's face when she told him he was in charge of the wagon loading. "Keep your workers alert so they don't get hurt." A big smile showed every tooth he owned as he squared his shoulders and began directing the two other boys helping him.

When Jane arrived at the barn she took the saddle off the mare and put her into a stall. She didn't know how long Sam would be gone and didn't want the horse to be uncomfortable until he arrived.

* * *

It was still cool, and Jane was glad to get inside again. She went to check on Mrs. Barrlette and found her sitting by her window looking outside.

"Good morning, Mrs. Barrlette, how do you feel this morning."
Jane went toward her with shining eyes and pink cheeks.

"Good morning, Jane; you look about fifteen years old—your
cheeks all rosy. I saw you come in on Charles' mare. Did you have
a good ride?"

"The air was invigorating, but I was out seeing that everyone
got started on their jobs. They are all working, and I think happy
to have something to accomplish. I warned them if they didn't
work well there would be no pay. Even Andy has his crew and
will get paid if he does a good job. You should have seen how
proud he was."

"It's so good to see things being done, and someone taking
charge. I think you will do just fine. I saw Sam going off toward
Charlotte."

Jane explained about the money, and not having it around. "We
just don't know who we can trust anymore. There are going to be
a lot of scavengers around—the people drifting back from the war.
They will all be hungry; we can't even offer them food without
wondering if we will be robbed. It's going to be a difficult time. I
think all our 'people' are loyal; they seem happy to have someone to direct them."

"Would you like to go down to the setting' room for a short
time?" Jane looked at Mrs. Barrlette and saw how aged she had
become and her heart sank. She was right she wouldn't be around
much longer.

"Why don't you get on with your work. I'll sit here for a while
then have a nap. I don't want to have to climb the stairs after
such a short stay."

"Do you need anything before I go?"

"I have my Bible—that will keep me occupied if I run out of
things to look at outside; you go along; Lucy will be bringing tea
soon."

Jane said nothing more as she left the room. She must see to
food for the men. Flo would know what to do about that. If she
needed help she could have some of the women from the quarters come. She had sent them all back to their cabins—it was too
cold to have them out without proper clothing. She didn't want
sickness; there were enough problems now.

Jane heard the wagon coming; going to the kitchen door she
saw that Andy's crew was approaching with a heaped-up wagon

of cut wood. She had Sam put down two sturdy posts out from the kitchen door a short pace—the wood would be stacked between them. Going out as they arrived, she pointed out the posts to Andy; he came toward her. "Make sure it's stacked so it won't fall over; how's it going?"

"I have a good work crew; we loaded as fast as they could cut. We have to hurry and unload so they don't get it piled up on us. You, Moe, start throwing down; Boe and I will stack. Sorry, Miss Jane I'll visit another time." He turned to show Boe how to make a layer for the foundation of the stack. The two boys worked with precision and the stack started to form.

Seems I'm not needed here, Jane thought to herself. She was so pleased that everything was progressing so smoothly. She knew that Mrs. Barrlette could see the wagon come in, although she couldn't see the stacking going on. There was at least some activity she could watch.

As Jane returned to the house she saw that preparation was in progress to feed the men, and knew that was one project she didn't need to worry about. She decided to walk through to the front of the house and look at the outside to see what could be done to make the house less un-kept looking. She noticed that some of the shutters were loose—those could be repaired, and needed painting. It was basically a strong sturdy house of red bricks and natural stone. The front pillars were of wood and there were wrought iron railings; which needed to be scraped off and painted. That alone would make a big difference. She would start Sam on that as soon as possible. The shrubs were overgrown, and needed trimmed—that would help. And, of course, no raking had been done for some time. There were leaves and twigs all around which made for a messy appearance. She would put that on the list. These things could be accomplished before plowing and planting time came.

Jane went back to the kitchen, seeing big buckets of the soup were being toted back to the cabins for the workers. The women had come for it and the big pans of cornbread. She heard the big dinner bell ringing and knew they would be coming soon to eat---several in each cabin. She sat down at the table and Flo dipped her a big bowl of soup and handed her a thick slice of cornpone with a big dab of butter on top.

"My, that looks and smells delicious. I didn't know I was hungry until now; thank you, Flo," Jane gave her an appreciative smile.

"It makes a body hungry runnin' a plantation. We'ze sure glad to see some work being done on this place. Seemed the only ones workin' were me and Lucy. We running all the time."

"If you need help, with washing or whatever, have some of the women in the quarters help. I'll leave it to you and Lucy. I didn't think there was much they could do outside and I don't want them sick on us. So do whatever you think best." Jane went back to work on her lists and looked over her inventory again.

The cellar still had turnips, some apples, potatoes, and there had been a turnip patch planted and the tops were coming up, green and inviting for greens. The hens, even though several had been taken by the soldiers, were laying enough eggs for the big house. Jane wanted to start saving them for hatching as soon as some of the old hens started setting. Chickens could be smoked, put down in grease, and prepared fresh in so many ways for food—and didn't take long to raise. There would be little beef, if any; some pork; the wild game had been deleted by the hoards that roamed through during the war. It would be years before deer, and even rabbits would flourish again.

Jane thought about her grandfather, wondering if she should send Sam to fetch him to the plantation. She must get off a letter to him and her family, explaining why she hadn't returned. It seemed her life had become so complicated, that she wasn't sure what was important and what wasn't. She knew that she had to stay with Mrs. Barrlette. There were people around her grandfather, and Zol was there to take care of him. So he would be all right, even though she worried about him.

Sam had returned and came to tell Jane that the gold had been taken by the Judge, and would be deposited for them. He brought a letter to her from her grandfather. As he handed it to her he said, "Iz' unsaddle, and see how things are going, Iz' know you want your letter first. If'n you want me to do anything you'z send Getty for me, Miss Jane."

"Thank you, Sam; I have crews working; they are getting along fine. I'd like for you to look at the front of the house; there are some loose shutters, and see what you will need to scrape the loose paint, and paint the trim. I'll talk to you about it later." She had slit the envelope while she talked, anxious to read what her grandfather had written.

Dear Granddaughter,

These few lines finds an old man as well as can be expected in respect to his age and the long bloody time we have been through.

Thank God the fighting is over. There are still some wounded here, but most will be on their feet shortly. The serious cases have been sent North to hospitals. It's a relief not to have the sound of pain around us night and day. Now that things are quieter I find myself so tired I can hardly put one foot after the other. The fatigue of war is catching up.

I received your letter telling me of my old friend Charles demise. I will miss knowing he is there. I know Elizabeth is devastated; give her my sympathy and best wishes. She and Charles were so close I know she will take it hard.

Zol and I are leaving here the first of the week. We are coming to see you before we take a train north, and hopefully home. I want to make sure that you are all right before I leave you so far from home. We can get a train in Charlotte, that will take us into Charleston, and then have someone pick us up there for the rest of the journey.

Keep your pretty chin up; we will see you before you know it.

Lots of Love,
Your Gramps

When Jane finished the letter she started reading it again, a big smile on her face. Oh, how she loved that old man. She was so excited that he and Zol would be stopping by before leaving, and how she longed to go with them.

Looking at the date of the letter she knew they could arrive anytime. She hurried through the house looking for Lucy. She needed to have a room prepared for her grandfather and for Zol. She found Lucy with Mrs. Barrlette; she was sitting visiting with her while she drank her tea.

"What is it, Jane? You looked excited enough to burst. Have

you had good news?"

"I have had a letter from Gramps." She waved the letter she held. "He's coming to see us, then he and Zol will take a train home from Charlotte." Pulling a chair closer she sat down, "I'll read it to you."

After she had read the letter, Mrs. Barrlette said, "Jane, I'm so happy for you, and I will be so happy to see Dr. Connolly; Charles thought so much of George; poor man he must be exhausted, doctoring through all this dreadful war. I hope you can get him to rest a few days before taking such a journey."

"I hope so, too." Jane turned to Lucy, " I was looking for you, could you see that rooms are prepared for the two men; they will be tired and cold by the time they arrive, and from the date on his letter it could be anytime." Jane couldn't keep a smile off her face as she talked.

Lucy gathered the tea things, and said, "I'll see to it Miss Jane."

Jane sat talking with Mrs. Barrlette for some time telling her about the work that was in progress, and that Sam had returned safely from Charlotte. And that he told her about all the ragged, crippled men who were on the streets.

"It's so sad; there are so many homes that will be broken due to the terrible disaster that has befallen so many." A tear rolled down Mrs. Barrlette's weathered cheek.

Jane couldn't keep the tears from her eyes too, as they sat thinking of Barrlette house, and its tragedy.

🎄 Chapter Twenty-Four 🎄

Three days passed before the beloved little house on a wagon came into sight. Jane's heart skipped a beat as she watched it coming up the long avenue toward Barrlette House. Zol was sitting on the high seat wrapped in a blanket—her grandfather beside him—also bundled against the cold. She saw that Zol intended to go around the drive to the back and hurriedly grabbing a shawl, threw it over her head and wrapping it about herself she rushed toward the back. Going to the kitchen door she waited until they arrived in the barnyard. Sam was there to help her Gramps down and take care of the team. Walking out a way she called—

"Gramps, Zol come in to the fire; Sam will see to the team." They walked toward her; she waited. When her grandfather came near she couldn't stand it any longer and flew into his arms. "Oh, Gramps, I have missed you so much. It's so good to see you," she said as she hugged him to her. "Come inside, you must be frozen." As they hurried through the kitchen, toward the sittingroom she used, she called, "Lucy, could you bring some hot tea? We have some frozen men here."

"Right away, Miss Jane."

Jane had built up the fire as soon as she saw them coming, and it was warm as toast in the room as they stood before the fireplace and began to remove the wraps they had on.

"The house looks the same, only rundown. It's been a long haul through this bloody war. Thank God, it's over. You look well, Jane. How is Elizabeth?" her grandfather asked, as he looked around the room.

"I've been keeping her in bed; she has had a rough time of it, and with the cold and so many people sick, I'm making her rest as much as possible. She is as well as I think we can expect her to be, but has aged so since I've been here. It's been terrible burying two loved ones so close together." Jane hadn't told her grandfather that she had married. She wanted to tell him in person.

As soon as Zol had warmed up and had a hot cup of tea, he

was ready to head back to the barn to see that his beloved team was cared for.

Jane decided that she must tell her grandfather about her marriage before he talked to Mrs. Barrlette——she might inadvertently let it slip, and then she would have a lot of explaining to do—besides hurting her Gramps.

"Gramps, I have something to tell you. Maybe I should have written to you but I didn't want to worry you." She proceeded to tell him of the party and of the young Confederate officers stealing through the Union lines and coming to Barrlette House for one disastrous night of fun. "Gramps, Lance and I were married at the party; when we met, Lance fell in love on sight. He was so handsome and charming and things seemed to rush head long into something I didn't seem to have control over. Mr. Barrlette, Lance, and Judge Winthrope planned everything so quickly that we were married before I realized what was happening. We were both so happy that night as we danced and danced. We had just gone upstairs to be alone when the alarm was sounded. The Federal troops had found them out. The race for survival started. Lance was within two miles of his lines when they laid a trap for him and shot him dead. They had already killed another officer, who was his friend." She told how the search began and Mr. Barrlette went looking for Lance and died from the exposure. Tears were streaming down Jane's pale cheeks, as she looked toward her grandfather.

Dr. Connolly came and knelt beside his granddaughter, taking her cold hands in his. "Oh, my God, Jane, what I've let you go through since I brought you from the protection of your home and family. If I had known, I would have come to you, even if it meant losing more soldiers."

"That's one reason I didn't write you about it. There was nothing you could have done, and I wouldn't have wanted to take you away from those who needed you so desperately. Lance was a fine young man even if he was on the side of the Confederates; he didn't want the war anymore than you and I, and he gave his life for the cause." Jane continued by telling him how she longed for home, but that she was bound more or less to remain with Mrs. Barrlette and all the others who now depended on her. And the desperation of the Plantation, and her obligation—now that it belonged to her. And of Andy, that she had almost come to think of as her own son.

Dr. George sat back down—pouring another cup of the hot tea from the hopper, and refilling Jane's cup as well. "I can see how you must feel honor bound to look after Elizabeth. When Zol and I rest up a few days, we will go north; I'll explain to your father and mother about the situation. I suppose you heard that your brother Thomas was wounded three times—once seriously in the face, braking his jaw and destroying most of his teeth? He survived and that is a miracle in itself."

"Yes, I heard—mom wrote to me. I've never told them I was married. Will you do that for me, Gramps? I know it's asking a lot, but I would appreciate having it over and done with before I come home again."

Dr. George nodded his head, "Of course, granddaughter, I'll take care of it."

Zol came back into the room, going to the fire, and holding his hands out. They talked until suppertime—when they all went into the kitchen for their dinner. Jane had told Lucy not to set up the dining room. Mrs. Barrlette wouldn't be down and they were family. Flo had made chicken and dumplings, with big fluffy biscuits, and had an apple pie for dessert. Dr. George knew Flo from other visits he had paid the Barrlettes, and said, "Without a doubt that's the best meal I've ever eaten, Flo. You've outdone yourself. Thank you on my behalf and also Zol's. If you show me to Elizabeth's room, I'll visit her for an hour before she falls asleep," he told Jane.

* * *

The five days Dr. Connolly and Zol were at Barrlette House seemed to fly by. Jane and her grandfather would ride over the Plantation, with him offering advice about how to bring the plantation back to life. He congratulated Jane on a good start. Keeping the 'people' busy would keep them out of trouble; they all seemed content, and to be ready and willing to do Jane's bidding without any problems.

Dr. George decided to leave the wagon with the little house built on it at the Plantation, and the team of big mules too, saying, "When you want to come home you can drive it or put it on a freight train, or sell it whatever you want to do." He also left a set of his surgical tools, and several of his medical books. "I have more at home; I'm too old to do much doctoring anyway; I'll not encourage patients again; I just want to rest for months. You can use what you want and sell or give the rest away."

Jane stood watching Sam driving Gramps and Zol to the train station in Charlotte, wondering when she would see him again, if ever. She knew how fragile life could be, and at his age his days were numbered. She and Gramps had enjoyed a wonderful visit, and it helped somewhat the craving she had to go home. She could wait a while longer now. Gramps, next to her father and mother, was the most important person in her life. She knew the time had come when she would spend little time with them all. It was a sorrowful thought that brought tears to sting her eyes. Turning, she returned to Barrlette House, and to her many duties and obligations that were before her.

After watching her grandfather out of sight, Jane went to check on Mrs. Barrlette, and found her sleeping. She had begun to worry about how much sleeping the old lady was doing. Turning away she decided to ride out to all the jobs and see how they were doing. She went to the barn and saddled the mare herself. Sam would be gone most of the day as he had been instructed to bring home supplies, if they could be had. And Jane knew he would check in with Judge Winthrop to report on the family.

Jane went to the wood-lot where the wood cutting was being done. She couldn't believe how the cleaning up of the downed trees had improved the area. They now had wood stacked at the compound and at the house to do most of the next year. There were a few more downed trees and as soon as those were cleared and cut, the crew could move on to something else. If the weather held she intended to start them turning the soil for planting. The shed had been torn down, and all the dry pieces that weren't saved for further use had been fetched to the house and compound for kindling. That crew was now working on repairing more fences. Jane rode along the fence until she found Tom. She wanted to send him with some helpers to bring home a couple of the hogs from the swamp to butcher—And try to find out how many were there. She spotted him ahead where several of the men were digging post holes.

"Oh Tom," she called, as she saw him look toward her.

"Yes, Miss Jane, iz' somin' you want?"

"Tom, I would like you to take a couple of the men or however many you need and bring home a couple of the shoates from the swamp to butcher. And if possible try to count the herd to see how many we have. If we can arrange for food, we may bring some and pen them here to fatten. When the planting starts we will need nourishing food and our root crops are diminishing rapidly."

"Yes mam, we'll need to take a gun ifn' there' any bullits. I'z' a purty good shot. Ifin we have no bullits, wetz have to trap them, and that takes time and work."

"How do you trap them, Tom? I've never seen it done."

"We'z have watch them a few days to see where ther' feedin' and dig a deep hole close by on a trail the'z use and run them into it, and then try to cut their throat or club them. Somz them bors are mean and can kill a man." He shook his head, a worried look on his face.

"Well, it sounds as though a gun is the answer. I'll have to see if we have one available. When would you want to try for them?"

"We'z hav to start early when it'z feedin' time for them critters. Thez' a mean bunch." He smiled at Jane.

"I'll see what I can do. You will have to take a conveyance to bring them back to the house."

"Wetz have specil' sled for that Miss Jane; don't youz' worry, I'z get it done."

"Thank you, Tom; the fences you have repaired look good—your crew seems to work well." Jane turned and rode back toward Barrlette House, leaving Tom with a big proud smile on his black face.

When Jane arrived back at the barn, Andy came to meet her. "I'll take the mare, Miss Jane. You're needed in the house. Ms. Barrlette went to the buryin' place and fell and hurt herself bad. Lucy and some of the women laid her on the small ladder and carried her to her bed. You'd better hurry." He took the reins and led the mare back to the tack room to remove the saddle, as Jane hurried toward the back door.

"Oh, my God! what now?" she asked herself as she ran to the house.

"Flo met her at the door. "Miss Jane, thank God; Ms. Barrlette iz' bad. Lucy's with her now; she'z out of her mind—, callin' for Lance, and her husband. We'z didn't know she went outside. I'z

Sibyl Jarvis Pischke

must been in the cellar checking the food supply when she went. I sorry Miss Jane; wetz didn't know she would go out on such a cold day."

"It wasn't your fault Flo. I never dreamed she would go outside either. She's been in bed for several days and weak. I'm surprised she could even walk that far. I'll see bout her. Make some willow tea for me if you will; when it's ready bring it to her room." Jane removed her heavy things, throwing them onto a chair as she rushed up the long winding staircase to Mrs. Barrlette.

As Jane entered the room, Lucy turned from the bed where she had been leaning over the old woman. "Miss Jane, thank God' Ms. Barrlette' bad, I'z don't know what to do."

When Jane entered the room, she saw that Mrs. Barrlette was unconscious. She pulled the covers down and could see that there were bruises on her arms and face. She started to examine each arm and down the body; pulling the covers further she examined each leg. Not finding any broken bones, she placed her hand under each knee and lifted the leg up turning the foot slightly from side to side; the left one was fine, but when she lifted the right Mrs. Barrlette let out a terrible scream, coming to with the excruciating pain. Jane felt up the leg to the hip; when she put her hand on the hip area and pressed, Mrs. Barrlette fainted from the pain. "Bring my bag from my room for me, will you Lucy?" Jane asked as she took up Mrs. Barrlette's hand and felt her pulse.

Lucy soon returned with the bag that had seen Jane through so much pain and suffering in the war. Flo entered with a big pot of the tea Jane had asked her to bring. "Put it on the hopper Flo," it'll stay hot for when I need it."

"Anything I'z can do to help, Miss Jane?" Flo asked worriedly.

"I think she has broken her hip, Flo. There isn't anything you can do now. I'll call if I need you. Thank you, go about your work."

"Broken hip?" Lucy asked her eyes growing wild looking as she looked at Jane.

"I'm not sure yet, but I think so. If it is, there isn't a lot we can do." Taking the stethoscope she examined her chest and heartbeat—finding it too fast and beating too hard. Her breathing was labored. Jane felt a sinking feeling as she continued her examination. If her grandfather hadn't left maybe he could have done something. Jane had helped with a few hip fractures but they

269

were complicated and hard to do anything with. She left Lucy with her patient, knowing that she would be in the feint for a few minutes, as she left the room. Going back to her bedroom she took the book her grandfather had left her and looked up fractured hip information. As she read, she became so frightened she could hardly go on. "Almost always fatal; if patient survives, usually doesn't walk again—only with great pain and deformity." Jane closed the book; there was little treatment to follow in the information she had read. "Oh, God! what am I to do? Will disaster follow me the rest of my life?"

She wiped the tears that had gathered in her eyes and hurried back to the sickroom.

Moans came from the bed where Mrs. Barrlette was coming out of the faint. "Bring some willow tea, Lucy; maybe we can get her to drink enough to help the pain and let her sleep."

Lucy brought a cup and they gently raised her up; the old woman groaned as the stress on her hip brought pain. "Drink this, Mrs. Barrlette—it'll help the pain." The cup was empty when they laid her back onto the bed; Jane could see her body relaxing, but knew the pain must be terrible. She motioned to Lucy, to follow her to the hall.

"Lucy send Getty to Charlotte. I'll write a note to the Judge and ask him to send a doctor to see what can be done. I'm not knowledgeable enough to treat something so serious. From what I've read in the medical book my grandfather left me, there isn't much that can be done—but we must make sure. If one could operate and see what has been damaged in the joint, maybe it could be fixed. To my knowledge it has never been done. I certainly can't do it. Hurry!" As Lucy left to find Getty, Jane wrote to the Judge, also asking him to come. She didn't feel that she wanted the responsibility if Mrs. Barrlette didn't survive. Her heart might give out, or a number of other things could happen that was caused by the fall. "Why would she go out on such a day when no one was about? Why?" Jane shook her head as she went back to the bed and sat beside the old woman. She went over in her mind the information in the medical book she had read. Keep immobile; strap leg to board with splints; keep in one position for at least six to eight weeks; Pulling leg to length of uninjured limb; some shrinkage expected as break heals; some lameness after healing. "How could one strap a hip? you would have to go beyond the waist or bending would not let the healing process work. How could a person lay on his back for such a long period of time?" Jane sat looking at the old lady as she talked it over to herself.

It was late afternoon when Sam drove the wagon to the back door to unload the supplies. Lucy went to fetch Jane as the wagon was being unloaded and the sacks of rice, beans and other supplies brought into the pantry.

Getty had followed Sam back but without bringing the doctor he had been sent for.

"Miss Jane, the old doctor Noe, iz' down with the enfluzenia, and tother' doctor hez' with a birthin' that hez' can't leave. The Judge said youz' do best youz' can; he'll bring the doctor az' soon az' he can. Judge says, not much hope for somethin' like zat. Espacelly in old person. I'z' sorry, Miss Jane, I'z' do best I ken'."

"I know you did, Getty; thank you." Jane stood a thoughtful expression on her face as she watched the bags being brought into the house. "Sam, could you come into the sittin' room a minute? I need to talk to you," turning she started to the small room where she usually sat, expecting Sam to follow her.

Jane sat down and opened the medical book to the chapter of fracture, and broken bones, looking at the diagrams and reading again the recommendations for treatment. Sam came in and stood before her waiting until she finished.

"Sam, Mrs. Barrlette went to the cemetery when no one was about. She fell and has broken or fractured her hip. It is very serious, and very hard to treat. I want you to look at these diagrams, and we will see if we can duplicate the splints and board that we need to try to bind her leg and hip so it won't move. It has to stay that way for six to eight weeks. I don't know how we can manage it but we must try. She will probably be lame—maybe a stiff joint in the hip. But there is so much pain that we have to do something. Do you think you can cut me some splints, as thin, and firm as you can? I'll need about three for the top, and a wider board for the bottom. The board for the bottom should be about two and half feet long—the splints for the top about two feet. I don't know if it will work—we'll just have to try. Make them smooth, and as soon as possible. Bring them to her bedroom. You'll have to help in lifting her. I hate to think how painful it will be I have some morphine left but I'm so afraid it will affect her heart.

Go now and hurry." Sam hurried from the room, a worried look on his face.

Jane went to look for Lucy, finding her she said, "Lucy can you find some cotton-batten and strips of soft cloth we can use to pad the board and splints? We are going to try to splint Mrs. Barrlette's hip and leg. It'll have to be in one position to heal. Sam is making the splints now; get things ready please." Jane went back to the sickroom to wait for the supplies. She found that Mrs. Barrlette seemed to be sleeping; taking up her hand she felt her pulse; it seemed stronger and not skipping as it had before. Maybe she would be strong enough to stand the ordeal she would have to put her through.

* * *

Jane had splinted the leg and hip with the light-weight boards that Sam had so carefully prepared for her. She gave Mrs. Barrlette a few whiffs of ether to put her out while it was being done. Cup after cup of willow tea had been given to her and seemed to keep her comfortable enough to sleep. Jane sat until midnight with her, then called Lucy for a few hours to be with her, while Jane went to bed.

The second day, Jane became worried as Mrs. Barrlette started to sneeze, and cough—she seemed to be coming down with a cold. No wonder after going out on such a cold day with wind blowing from the north. "Oh, God! if she gets pneumonia, she will die; there's nothing I can do but pray."

The second night, Lucy came to Jane's room about four in the morning gently shaking her awake she said, "Miss Jane, you'd better come; she' worse, I've been givin' her tea but she' not breathing good. I don' know what to do."

Jane pulled on a warm robe and hurried back to the sickroom with Lucy. As she entered she could hear the wheeze that told her the old lady had pneumonia, and she doubted anything could save her now. "Get some towels, and a bowl of hot water, we'll try turpentine packs—it may help. At least we will be doing something." Lucy hurried from the room and was soon back. There was a teakettle of hot water on the hopper in the sickroom ready for use. Jane poured a few drops of the precious turpentine into the bowl, dipped in the towel, and wrung it out fanning it in the air to cool enough to put on the chest of her patient. She moaned and moved away as the hot towel covered her chest. "It's all right, I'm trying to help you breathe easier, Mrs. Barrlette. How do you feel? Does your hip hurt?" Jane asked. She moaned but didn't answer. Covering her, Jane sat by her bed. "Lucy, go to bed, you can get a couple of hour's sleep. I'll call you if I need you."

The room was quiet as Jane changed the turpentine packs several times, dozing in between. Mrs. Barrlette didn't cough as much and seemed easier. Jane couldn't tell if she slept or if she was in a stupor. Her pulse rate was very slow and sluggish. Jane still kept a watchful eye on her as daylight began to show in the windows.

Lucy came in the sickroom before going about her work. "How is she, Miss Jane? Is there any change?"

"She isn't any better as I can see; however, she slept most of the night. I've examined her leg and it's swelling, which isn't a good sign, but a broken bone usually causes swelling. Her heart doesn't sound too good. It's sluggish, which could be caused by so much of the tea. I do hope that the Judge will bring the doctor today. I've done all I can, which isn't much. I'm very worried about her. You go have your breakfast, then come back so I can get something to eat. We need to have someone with her all the time."

* * *

Jane sat at the kitchen table, drinking her second cup of tea as she listened to the talk around her. She was so tired that nothing registered as she listened, when suddenly Lucy rushed into the room calling her.

"What is it Lucy; calm down and tell me, is Mrs. Barrlette worse?" Jane took her arm and gave her a shake.

"Miss Jane, she stop' breathin'. I been settin' watching her and she just stop' breathin'. She never make a sound. I don't know exactly when," tears were streaming from Lucy's eyes and she began to shake from head to toe.

"Here, sit down; Flo get a cup of hot tea for Lucy—see that she drinks it. I'll go see what has happened." Jane hurried from the kitchen and toward the sickroom.

When Jane entered the room, she could smell death, and knew that Mrs. Barrlette was gone. Going to the bed she felt for a pulse or heartbeat—there was none. Her old heart had just given up—the pain, and shock were too much. Jane pulled a sheet over the old woman, and going to the window, opened it a crack to let some fresh air into the room. As she stood looking out at the snowy landscape, she heard the dove in the tree outside the window. Jane realized suddenly that she was all alone in a household of free slaves. Fear came over her as she stood there alone. What was she to do? She was free of her obligations to the Barrlette's and could leave, but what would become of the 'people'? They were good people, in her estimation, and loyal to her and the plantation. She became calm as she weighed the choices she could make. First, there would be another funeral to get through. Jane couldn't even bear to take the splints from the injured leg. She would have Mrs. Barrlette wrapped in the bedding as she was and taken to the funeral home—the people there could cope with it. "I've done all I can," she said to the empty room as she picked up her medical bag and left closing the door behind her.

🎋 Chapter Twenty-Five 🎋

The funeral had been held in the family plot on a dreary day with intermittent rain and snow. It was a hurried affair with very few attending; the influenza was raging through the country side, hundreds sick and there had been several deaths. As Jane turned for the last look at the piled up mound of wet dirt, she said with a tear in her voice, "That's the last of the Barrlettes." Elizabeth Mary Barrlette now rested between her son, Eric, and her husband Charles, as she had told Jane—the two most important men in her life. Those that had attended hurried inside for a hot drink before going home.

Jane wearily removed her dark wet cape, and led everyone toward the fire that was now lit in the big living room next to the library. As they all sipped the hot tea, muted voices could be heard in conversation. Jane sank onto a chair, and rubbed her cold hands together as the conversation went on around her. She couldn't for the life of her comprehend what was being said. Weariness made her shake uncontrollably. One after another, seeing the distraught girl, hurriedly said their good-by's and left. The Judge saw them out, as Jane sat with bowed head and vacant eyes.

"Lucy, the Judge called, see to it that Miss Jane goes to bed immediately; give her some of that willow tea to make her sleep. She is exhausted and may be coming down with the influenza herself. She has had too much for a young lady's shoulders to hold. I'll be leaving, Jane; I'll be back in a few days when you've had time to rest." The Judge was putting on his great coat that had been draped over a chair by the fire to dry.

Lucy sent Getty for a hot-water bottle and helped Jane to her feet and led her to her room. Getty arrived with the water bottle wrapped in a towel, as Lucy tucked the warmed blankets around the shaking girl.

Jane's brain seemed vacant, as Lucy ministered to her tired body, and she fell into a deep dark area of sleep.

* * *

275

Jane slept the rest of that day, and all the following night without waking, as the wind whistled around the chimneys, and the trees switched their frozen branches in the icy air. She awoke to a slight noise as Lucy lay a cloth over a table by the fire and placed a tray of food on it. Raising her head from the pillow Jane asked, "What time is it, Lucy, have I slept a long while?"

"You've slept all afternoon and the whole night without moving; I com' to see if you all right a couple times. You were dead to the world. I've brought food; you must eat somethin' you make yourself sick. Come now, I've brought hot water for you to wash."

Jane sat up in bed looking around, seemed as though she still didn't know where she was, but soon recognized her belongings and taking her warm robe from the foot of her bed she put it on, and went to wash her hands and face before eating. The smell of the food Lucy had brought made her stomach rumble in hunger.

"I didn't know I was so hungry, Lucy; I'm starved. And whatever you brought sure smells good," she said as she sat at the table.

"Hot biscuits, scrambled eggs, and apple butter—Your favorite—now you eat every bite." Lucy stood smiling at Jane as she began eating. "Take your'er time; every body hole up at the fire; It's too cold to work outside. So you might as well eat and get back in your warm bed. You could stand a week's rest, way you've been going."

"Maybe I'll do that; I have a lot of important thinking to do, and that's as good a place as any." Jane took a note pad and pencil with her to the bed after she had finished eating. She would make lists of what she needed to do, and how to go about it. She wanted to talk to the Judge about the 'people' and the plantation before she would decide anything. Jane leaned against the pillows Lucy had piled behind her. She couldn't seem to get her mind in order to make the lists she had in mind, and slowly scooted down into the warm, cozy covers and fell asleep.

The cold spell finally broke after a week of undecided weather, with rain, snow and blusterly winds. Jane had enjoyed her warm bed, and had been in and out of it for over a week. When the sunshine streamed through her window sending dust motes dancing, she decided it was time to get on with her work and dressed accordingly. As she finished dressing she heard a horse coming into the barnyard. Going to the window she saw that the Judge was arriving, and hurried down to the sitting room where she knew he would be taken by Lucy.

Jane straightened the papers on her writing table and went to the window, to look toward the burying place. It looked tranquil in the bright sunshine, the new grave blending in with the others. As she turned, the Judge entered.

"Good morning, Jane; how are you today? It's good to see the sunshine after the inclement weather we've been having," he remarked as he removed his coat and looked at Jane.

"Good morning, Judge; It's good to see you and the sunshine. I've been thinking of you and hoping you would come soon. I have so many decisions to make and questions to ask you," she smiled at him.

"I hope I can be of service. I've a whole day to myself for a change and should be able to answer all your questions in that time. What is it I can help you with?"

"As I explained to Mrs. Barrlette before she died, I don't think I can remain in the south; there has been so many tears, blood and death that I can't forget in a hurry. She suggested that I might like to sell Barrlette House and the Plantation. I haven't decided anything. I can't seem to get my brain to comprehend what has happened to me."

"You're not the only one that feels that way, Jane. I saw in the paper this morning that several people from this area are going West. Where—I don't know. Since the war and the Indians being crowded out—there's free land to be had. I personally think they should stay home and help rebuild their lands here. They know what they have now, and there is no certainty of what they would have in the west."

"That's strange; Andy said when he earned some gold he wanted to go West and build him a cabin and homestead land. I was reading him a book about the West and he is even more interested in going than before. I thought it was funny but maybe more people are thinking of it. I'm concerned about the 'people' and what they will do. I've wondered if I could deed each of them a small portion of Barrlette Plantation, to build a cabin and raise a garden. Do you think I would be allowed to do that?"

"Well now—that's a noble gesture, Jane. I'm sure there is a map of the plantation; do you have it? We can look and see if there is a dividing line where it might work."

Jane looked startled at the Judge's remark and hurried to the library where she had seen such a map, and soon returned with it in her hand; going to the table she spread it out, and she and the Judge poured over it.

"Here!" he pointed to a section that made a 'dog leg' off to one corner of the rest of the land—a small creek divided it from the rest of the plantation. "That might work. Looks as though there is about thirty five acres there; it wouldn't support too many— they would want to have a few chickens, and maybe a cow. They would have to have animals to work with. How many were you thinking of Jane?"

"I hadn't gotten that far," she said with a smile. "I'm sure Tom and Ella and their grandchildren would want to stay. There are three married couples, and the rest are all single—I doubt they would want a place to farm. Lucy is going to marry Londo from the neighboring plantation. He wants to go north; she isn't too happy about it but she is a wonderful house maid and can get work most anywhere. Flo wants to go to Georgia close to her married daughter, I think; and, of course, Getty would go with her. Slazzy has a family close and would go to them, I suppose. That disposes of the house 'people'. I'll take Andy with me, and would like for Sam to go with me too. That only leaves the single men. I can maybe place them on another plantation, or if I sell the plantation maybe they could stay with the new owner."

"Sounds as if you have been doing more thinking than you were aware of," the Judge said laughing.

"It does sound like it, doesn't it?" Jane blushed as she looked at the Judge.

Looking at the map again, he said, "The old mill where Nick was killed is over there; a road can be made down through here," he pointed it out to Jane. "It joined up with Johnson Trail, over toward Dawson. There are stores in Dawson and mills. It's just a village, but sufficient for the settlement if you decide. I'll look into the legal aspect of deeding it to them. What about houses? I expect some of the cabins could be taken down and moved from here. I'm sure whoever buys the plantation won't need them all; fifty-some people were housed in them at one time."

"That sounds a good solution; I'll be thinking on it, but as you know I do need some help working it out. It should be soon so they can get a small crop in to feed themselves."

"There's some money; a small amount can be left with you and in an emergency you will have it. I doubt many will be good at handling money as they have never had any in their life. If you have a chance would you feel out the people you come in contact with and see if anyone would be interested in the land? I'm going ahead and sprucing up the manor house and have all the fences done around the immediate area. We have torn down that old building that was fallen in and disposed of the debris; it helped the looks of the area a great deal. We have also cleaned out the wood-lot and cut the down trees into wood. It looks nice now. The shrubs and yard are going to be worked on now that the weather has broke. I intend to have gardens planted that will be an enticement too."

"You're on your way looks like. I wish you would reconsider and stay. I have a feeling you could make a difference in the area. You're high on my list." He started putting on his great coat, "I'll get back with you in a short time. As soon as I contact some acquaintances, and look into the deeding of the land."

Jane followed him to the door, and stood watching him mount his horse; she waved a good by as he rode away.

Jane sat thinking about what she was about to undertake. If I leave a team of mules to use in the settlement, they could use them to work for others and earn some money. The old mill can be used by them all to house a cow and chickens. We'll call it Barrlette Settlement, and I'll leave Tom in charge; he has a good mind and can help them all. I have to remember they have never been on their own before. We have to think about where they can get water. I'll ask Sam. I'm sure he will know if there are springs there anywhere. There would have to be someone figure out the area and how to divide it. She didn't think she was capable of doing that. If tomorrow warmed up she would take Sam and ride over the area and find out what it was like. They would have to have wood, and water, and garden space to survive. Of course with all the slaves going north there would be work for those who wanted to hire themselves out. It can work—I know it can. Jane smiled to herself thinking of the uniqueness of the idea, and the eyebrows it would raise.

* * *

A week went by with Jane spending most of her time in the small setting room working on lists, and figuring out what was going to be best for the 'people'.

When Lucy brought her tea, she said, "Lucy would you send Getty, and ask Tom, and Sam to come in; I need to talk to them."

She continued with her drawings and lists until she heard the two men coming, and laid her pencil down waiting for them.

"Mornin' Miss Jane," they both said in unison.

"Good morning to both of you. Would you pull up chairs; I have some things I want to discuss with you." She smiled encouragingly at them, seeing the surprise on their faces.

Bringing two armchairs close to the table they both clumsily seated themselves, not seeming able to find a suitable place for their big feet, and moving around settling themselves in their chairs. They had never been called in and seated for a discussion of any kind and were uneasy.

"You both know that I am now the owner of the plantation?" they both nodded their heads, "and you know you're all free?" Again they nodded. "I have a plan—I don't intend to remain in the south—I want to go home. It's been a long time, and I need to see my folks." Again they both nodded. "I have a drawing here," turning it to where it could be seen by both, she asked, "Do you recognize it?" both of the men studied the drawing Jane had so painstakenly made.

After a few minutes, Sam spoke! "Thas' the mill over on Little Creek that's where the rondvu' was. I knows' the place. Tom, yoz' been over thar' huntin'," Tom nodded.

Jane nodded, "Good, you both know the place. What I want to know is, are there springs, or water to be had? Has anyone ever lived over there?"

The men looked at each other. "I'z believe there' once a house on the creek, wher' the miller once' lived. I'z know there' a dug well, but the buldin' been torn down."

"What about springs, with drinkable water—do you know of any?" Jane looked from one to another.

"Yes, wez' use to run some cattle over that way once. I'z think theys' several scattered against the hill." Sam was nodding his head. "Doz' we'z have to leave Barrlette Plantation Miss Jane?" A worried look was on both faces as the question was asked.

"I have something to tell you, but you both must promise not to say a word until the Judge brings me the final information." They both gave solemn nods. "I have a plan to start a village on this section. She pulled the map of the plantation over for them to see, then showed the map of the leg of land she had painstakenly made. "You see this section separated from the rest of the plantation by Little Creek? There's about thirty five acres there we think more or less. We have three married couples here. The single men won't care; I know some have left, and others will work on plantations, maybe here, or a neighboring one. The settlement will be called Barrlette Settlement, the Judge thinks we can deed each of the families a plot of land, where they can have a house and garden and space for a few chickens, maybe a pig, and cow. The land will support each family if they use it wisely. I want to leave Tom as an overseer for the families, and to help them all get the most from their section. He won't be a boss but will be available for them to come to for advice. The Judge will also be available if they need him. Do you think it can work?" Jane looked from one face to the other. A look of amazement appeared on both.

Each of the men waited for the other to answer Jane's question. Finally Tom spoke, "Youz' mean we'z have our own land with a house? our own?"

"That's what I plan Tom. And you Sam, I'm hoping you will go north with Andy and me when the time comes. I know you have no ties here, and you will have a choice. If you'd rather stay, then you will be included in a share of the land.

"Miss Jane, yoz' a wonder! I'z go wherever yoz' and little Andy be. I'z be satisfied anywhere. What yoz' being planin' is a hope of Heaven' and a Godsend for the folk'." Tears stood in his big brown eyes. "I'z afraid yoz' go off and I never see yoz' again'. I'z know you can't stay here; it'z a good plan."

"Lordy' Miss Jane, wetz black folk' think we died and go to heaven. Ownin' land iz' somethin' none ever dream of. I'z' see that everythin' goin' along fine as can be. We'z work hard. May the good God bless youz." Tears were streaming down Tom's face as he brought out a big red bandana and blowed his nose.

"I'm not sure yet if it can be done. It will be something new in this area. I have to wait until the Judge sees if it can be done legally. If so, we will get started. In fact, I want both of you to saddle horses for the three of us. We'll ride out and look things over today; its a nice warm day. I'll be ready in half an hour. As you go through the kitchen tell Flo to pack a lunch for the three of us. I'll be ready when you are." She reached out her hand and shook hands with the two smiling men.

Flo had a couple of tablecloth wrapped parcels to go into the saddle-bags. Two containers of tea, sat ready. Sam included those into the saddle-bags, tied a heavy cape behind Jane's saddle in case of rain or she got cold, and they were off. Everyone looked up from the plowing of the gardens as they rode by wondering what was going on. Jane set a leisurely pace. She knew it was less than ten miles to the creek, and that was where they would start their inspection. She had brought the map she had drawn and a pencil to make notes as they scouted around. After the first hour she became anxious and stepped up the pace. She had decided to ride Cherokee. Since the other mare and mule were along, she didn't expect him to be hard to manage. She had been petting him and giving him a taste of sugar once in a while, and he knew her well. He hadn't been rode much only by Sam when he was recuperating from the long run with Lance. Jane intended him as her own mount. He sidestepped, and showed off a bit but had settled down nicely. The travelers were in sight of the old mill as the sun was almost overhead. Jane had noticed that there were woods where wood could be gotten, with lots of downed trees. Even the stream had lots of dry wood along its banks. Sam pointed beyond the mill to where Jane could see a chimney still standing, where the house had been.

"I'z' remember when that house stood there," Sam pointed to the chimney. "The well iz' just tother' side."

They all dismounted, and walked over to the house site. The weeds were dead and brush had grown over the area.

"That chimney looks pretty sturdy; do you suppose it could still be used?" Jane walked around studying it, with both men doing the same thing.

Tom stood back looking at the top, and poking around the fireplace. "I'z can fix it," he remarked. "Needs only little dabbin' with creek mud, it be good as new. It good place for house, garden over there he pointed across the overgrown roadway."

Jane walked to the well and looked in seeing the reflection of water with tree branches and leaves inside the curbin. It looked as though it had been kept somewhat in good repair. "What can be done with the well? Can it be used do you think?" She turned to look at Sam, as he walked over.

"Wells can be bailed out, and someone go down and clean all the stuff that fallen in out. I'z seen it done lots time. Look like plenty water in this one. Wont' take long to fix." Sam was still studying the chimney.

"Tell me Tom, can a cabin be built onto the chimney? I know so little about things like that," she looked toward him waiting for his answer.

"It'z easier to build chemney last, but I'z know I'z can do it."

"If this comes through as I have it planned, I would like for this section to be yours Tom. Let's send some of the boys over to clean off the garden patch and put a fence around it and get it ready to plant. Most of the work at the manor is done; we will still keep some to work there, too. Now let's ride around and see where we can locate the other two families. See if we can find water." They mounted and started toward the small hills in the distance. They hadn't gone more than a mile till they came on a clump of trees with a swampy area near. "I'll bet that's a spring in that clump of trees," Jane remarked. They dismounted and began to look the area over. "This is a lovely place for a cabin," she said.

Tom looked around and remarked, "thaz' spring tail can be ditched out and drain this marshy part dry as bone."

"Well this can be another homestead, and I'm sure we can find another with good water. Remember, not a word. But we will move along as though we already had the authority to do so. Let's get back.," They had eaten their lunch at the mill as they rested the horses and were ready to return.

When they arrived back at Barrlette House, the men were still working on the gardens, in the quarters. Jane asked Tom to go there with her, and told Sam to go back to his work. When they reached the quarters, Jane turned to Tom. Which cabin is yours?"

"That'z one with the rose over the door. My Ella likz' to grow blossom.' That one over thar' iz' Job and thr' iz' Pete and his Rose. Thez' all good people. The tother' men live in that big cabin over thar," he pointed to a little larger cabin some distance.

"What are the two large buildings over there?" Jane asked.

"Thez' cookin' and eatin' when we had a big bunch livin' here."

Jane walked over to the buildings, seeing that some of the windows were broken, and that they could use repair. "Tom, could these buildings be torn down and used to build the cabins with? There's not much money for new material."

"Thez' sure can be. Several of the cabins neez' work and could be torn down. We'z' can sav' most of wood."

"Get a crew that's not busy on these two tomorrow. Bring a wagon and let them load them as they take the boards down, and send them to the chimney for your house. Be careful of the windows—glass is hard to come by. Send Ella up to the house; I want to talk to her about what she needs in a house. She can come in an hour after I freshen up. Thank you Tom."

Ella came to the manor and Lucy showed her in to Jane's sitting room. Jane was at the writing table. "Come Ella, sit down, I want to talk to you."

"Didz I do som' wrong Miss Jane, I'Z surly sorry fiin' I did." She had a frightened look on her face.

"No, of course not Ella; you've all been doing a wonderful job. The yard looks so much better with all the raking and cleaning up you women did while we were gone. I noticed it as soon as I came in. Thank you. I want to ask you some questions. How big is your cabin? do you have enough room?"

"Lord a mercy' no one ever azk me that afore. I'z have the big room where I'z doz' the cookin' in the fir' place, we'z have two big beds, one for Tom and me and one for the three grand childs'. Tom he make me table wis' two settle—one on each side, and shelf' to put thing' on. We'z hav' our own out-house, Tom made. He'z good that way. He'z make anything." Ella stopped, looking enquiringly at Jane.

"Could you use more room? What kind of cabin would you like if you could have a choice?"

"Miz' Jane I'z don' kno' why youz' as' me all thez' questions. I'z fine where I'z is. Youz' not gona' as' me to leave is' youz '?"

Jane had done some drawing while she waited for Ella. She held out the sketch to Ella.

Jane smiled as Ella reached for the paper that showed a good likeness of a small cottage with an attic addition and a large chimney protruding from the roof. The well curbing showed at one side and a porch across the front reaching the well and roofed over.

Ella studied the drawing; suddenly a smile covered her face.

"I'fn' it wer' mine, I'z plant me the purtiest' rose to vine all along the veranda to shade in afternoon." She handed it back to Jane. "I'tz sure purty'."

"It'll have a great room where the fireplace is, for sitting and for eating. Then a separate bedroom here, she pointed to the opposite end of the cottage. A stairway will go up here to a large attic room on top which will be divided for the two boys and the little girl."

"You'z tellin' me I'z have a cottage like thaz'? Where?"

Ella looked so scared that Jane couldn't help laughing. "I only want to know if you like it?"

"I'z like it., I'z might hav' one like it when I'z go to heaven." Shaking her head, "not on thisz earth, Miz' Jane, not on thisz' earth."

"You run along, and thanks again for getting the women to clean up the yard. I'll see you in a few days, and we'll talk some more." Jane smiled as she gathered up the papers into a pile. They were all so good, and like children in many ways. She was so thankful they had all been freed. Many would make it all worthwhile and some would only add to their misery by dalliance. She would give those who wanted to work and have their own home the chance that had been denied them. The others— they would have to make up their own mind.

❦ Chapter Twenty-Six ❦

The days were sunny which everyone welcomed as the dreary days of winter seemed to fade into the background. The work at the compound was going full blast. The dismantling of the slave quarters had begun, and the wagons were filled to overflowing with the boards that were being taken down. Jane could hear the workers singing as they pulled nails and hammered. Jane walked to the compound to check the job that was going on. Saw that the lumber from just one of the larger buildings had filled two wagons, and it looked as though there would be at least two more wagon loads, if not more. Seeing her, Tom walked over.

"I'z goin' good Miss Jane. We'z be leaving for the Settlement soon. W'z gonna' leave the winders' till last, le'z someone take them when we not there."

"I've been thinking on that. Do you suppose there will be trouble along that line? Maybe we will have to have a crew stay over there."

"I'z figure first few days be all right, no one know we'z haulin' over there. Then maybe w'z have to stay nights. I'z dont' knows. W'z about ready for the first haul. One a day will be abouts all w'z can do I'z think. I'z go along to put it where we want it. And maybe get the foundation laid out. And the corner stones set. Whenz' that don' I'z stay and work on building; Job can seez to things here."

"That sounds like a fine idea. I'm glad everyone is so enthusiastic. They are working for themselves now, and they know it. I'm so pleased the way things are going. Sam is scraping the trim on the mansion and will soon be ready to paint it. That will make things look better and Barrlette House will be a welcome sight. It's beginning to look as though someone lives here," Jane laughed. "Let me know before you leave, Tom. Have something to eat before you go. And perhaps you had better take what you need to go down into the well and clean it out—you'll need to have drinking water. Do be careful, we don't want anyone hurt. Make sure someone stands by while the workers are in the well, and keep a rope on them so if anything goes wrong you can pull them out in a hurry. Maybe I'll ride over with you when you start on it. I'm interested in how it will be done."

"We'll be pullin' out in about an hour. I'z sent a crew to clean out the brush where the cabin will be. So'z we'z can put the lumber wher' we'z need it, I'z get back to work now." He turned back to the wagons, and Jane went back to the house.

Jane was working on her drawings when she heard the wagons moving out to the building site. "There they go she said to herself. Won't take them long to get up a house with so many working on it. The first one will be the hardest."

Several days went by when Tom came in to see Jane.

"Miss Jane, we'z goin' to work's on the well today. I'z have Cherokee saddled fer you'z if'n you'z want to ride out with me," he smiled his big toothy smile at her.

"I sure do want to see what you're doing. Tell Flo to pack a lunch for me too, and I'll be right out. I'll hurry so I don't hold you up." She began stacking the papers she had been working on.

"I'z sent the wagon on ahead. You'z dont' need to hurry much, Miss Jane. I'z saddle your horse, we'z can catch up in no time," he said as he left.

Jane went to her room and changed into something warmer. Even though the sun was shining, it was cool yet. She always took her medicine bag and a blanket or heavy cape tied behind her saddle just in case she was cold. Didn't hurt to be prepared. She became excited thinking of the trip. She had been working steadily on things about the plantation and hadn't been out for several days. Even the Judge hadn't been by for some time.

When Jane mounted Cherokee, he did his usual exuberant dance, showing off his energy. Jane smiled to herself; he was just like a child when let out of lessons.

"You've picked a lovely day, Tom. Listen to the birds, they know spring is coming and are as happy about it as we are," she turned and smiled at the big strong man.

"One thing I'z not happy to see iz' snakes, they com' out on sunny days, we killes two at the Settlement, I'z guess when they knows' we around, they find another place to be."

"I hope they weren't poisonous I don't like snakes either., Why God made them is a mystery to me. Maybe they have a place in this world, but I would just as soon it was somewhere else," Jane laughed.

Soon the area became brushy, and overgrown with small scrubby brush. Jane could see where the wagons were beating down a roadway that they could follow. There would eventually be a road with so much being hauled over the route, and would be much easier for hauling. She knew there would be many trips over the area before the buildings were finished. She was excited to know something was being done for the wonderful hard working people from the Plantation who had been so faithful to the Barrlettes.

When they came in sight of the Settlement, Jane was amazed to see that the foundation and framework for the cottage was up. "My, Tom, I didn't expect so much to have been done. It's going to look nice. I'm so proud of all of you." She could see that Tom was as proud as she was of what had been accomplished.

"My Ella want to know every night whatz' been done. She anxious. She dons' believe'z what I'z tell her been done. She gonna' be surprised when she see. Next week I'z bring her. She'z gonna' plant some early stuff in the garden. She'z dyin' to see what this place look' like'z. I'z proud to show her where'z we'z live out our livez.'

"I believe you will all like living here. From what I understand there's a village not too far, where you can go to the store and where you can get things you need. And maybe find a day's work now and then. When you're not busy on your own place, I'm sure others will need help. With so many of their help going North, they will have to hire help. It'll give you a chance to make some money for things you can't raise."

"Thaz' a fact. We'z need some cash, for salt, coffee, and thingz' like that. I'z intend to raise nuff stuff to feed us though. Wetz can hole potatoes, turnips, cabbage and stuff to keep through the winter," he turned to Jane for approval.

"That's right; where I come from we have vegetables all winter—some in cellars and some buried in mounds in the garden. We always hole apples too, they are so crisp that when you bite into one the juice sprays all over," she laughingly told him.

Tom tied the horses out of the way and showed Jane around the building. She saw that it was all framed out and even the framework for the staircase was in. It was a good job; everything looked sturdy and well-built.

The brush had all been cleaned away, piled over on the garden plot and burned. Jane was surprised that Tom knew the ashes would be good for the garden. He was a lot smarter than people gave him credit for. The garden had a nice fence around it to keep animals out. As they walked around Jane could imagine the laughter that would be heard when the family moved here on their own property.

As they neared the well, Tom turned to Jane. "Ella heart gonna' break ifn' we'z don't get to own all this. I'z guess mine will too; it'z sure a dream ifn' it'z come true," he looked at Jane expectantly.

"I haven't heard from the Judge yet. But we will work it out. If I sell the plantation, I'll reserve this portion. If I can't deed it to you, then I'll keep it and you can live here as though you did own it. How does that sound to you?"

Jane could see the relief wash over big Tom's face as he answered, "Oh Miss Jane, you'z make me the happiest man alivez.' You'z dons' know how I's worried about it. Now I feel good; happy; you'z the best master I ever seez." He was smiling from ear to ear.

"I'm not your master. Remember you're free, and I'm your friend. You'll never have a master again, never! That is unless you want to count Ella," Jane laughed as she walked ahead.

"Thatz' right Miss Jane, thatz' right," he gave a delightful chuckle.

The tackle was piled up by the well curbing where all the weeds had been cut and raked and taken away. One of the men was already pulling up buckets of water and pouring it into a ditch that had been dug to run the water down off the building area. "The man who was working said, "Theyz a lot of water down there. Gonna take a lot of dippin' to get it all out." He was working as fast as he could so the water didn't have a chance to build up.

"How long you'z been dippin'?" Tom asked.

"About an hour I'z recon'; it'z goin' down some I can tell; another hour I'z think I'z can try goin' down. Won't takez long to clean it then. You'z gonna' have good water here." He kept a steady stream of water coming up as he pulled one bucket after another to the top.

Jane turned to Tom. "Since this place is going so well, maybe you should send a crew to ditch the other site that we looked at and drain the spring so you will be ready when you want to build there. We want to keep things moving along while we don't have to work on the crops," Jane turned to see what Tom had to say.

"I'z send a crew soon as this well done. I'z don't want to trust anyone but me lookin' after thiz."

"I'm glad to see you are so cautious, Tom. I know I can trust you to look after the 'people'.

"It's a responsibility; I'z try hard; I'z wants to please youz, Miss Jane," He looked at Jane with devotion on his face.

"You'll do fine, Tom; you're a fine man, I'm so pleased to see you're finally going to have something of your own that you can be proud of. And I know you will keep the Settlement in good shape so all of you can hold your head high." Jane watched the water bucket descend the well and with a strong pull of the rope come back in seconds full of water to be dumped into the ditch. Another half hour and it was declared safe to descend the well and start cleaning out the trash that had accumulated in the bottom. A strong rope was tied to Amos as he climbed upon the curb. A pulley had been made by using a log across the well with a handle on one end so that it could be turned and the rope wound around the log as the object at the end could be hauled up—in this case Amos. Tom held onto the handle that had been carefully installed, and lowered the man a bit at a time. When he reached bottom he called, "I'z down, sends down the bucket for the trash."

Tom carefully dropped over the bucket tied to another rope. He dropped in a pair of leather gloves calling, "Use thez gloves---might be broken glass down there. Go az fast az youz can; water comin youz know," Tom reminded Amos.

Amos called back up, "not az much trash az I thinks. Have it out fast. Thez a nice sandy bottom here, be clean, clear water."

It didn't seem to Jane that it took ten minutes to send out the last bucket full of twigs and leaves from the well bottom. Looking into the dark well she could see the gleam of water before Amos declared, "Haulz me up Tom—Iz done, and water comin in fast. Thiz gonna' be a good well with plenty of good clear water. Didn' get muddy witz me workin' on it." Tom hurriedly pulled up the rope with the bucket attached, and then used his powerful arms to turn the crank to bring Amos to the top.

As Amos untied the rope from around his waist, Tom thumped him on the back., "Thaz a good job, Amos; "thanks." The bucket was now attached to the rope on the log arm across the well and fastened to a nail to be ready to lower for fresh water when needed.

Tom had someone reevving boards for the roof from a tree that had been brought in for that purpose. Jane counted eight men working on the project. The lumber had been piled in a neat heap next to the building they were working on, ready to use.

Tom turned to Jane, "Do youz want to go to the other site and see where you thinkz thez cabin be built? I'z take two of the men to do the ditchin, and shoz them where to run off the water."

"That sounds like fun. I'll go along with you; I want to get a better picture of the area in my mind. I'm ready." They mounted their horses. One of the mules had been taken from the wagon for the two men to ride. They carried shovels, and a maddox across the mule in front of them for the job.

The area where the spring was would make a beautiful homestead. Tom got the men started on the project, pointing out where the water had cut out a deeper ditch than some of the ones branching off—telling them to "clean out the spring, then follow the general trend of where the water wanted to flow, and deepen it and fill in the others." Tom came to Jane, "Iffn we'z put the cabin here close to the spring, thez trees be some shade, and water close to getz to. Iz high enough soz the rain drain off too. I'z think a garden over there." He pointed out a spot off to the right of the house, "then build chicken coopz and hog pen over there. I'z have them build a spring house for milk and eggs and things and keep animans out."

Jane looked around her, "I think you have it already figured out, Tom. That looks like a sensible solution. It's a wonderful location. I wouldn't mind living here myself," she laughed as she turned to Tom. "As soon as things move along a little we will have to think of building fence, to keep in a couple of cows for the Settlement."

"I'z rode around and some of it has line-fence 'z already, we'z only have to build down the creek areas, whenz you decide where." Tom looked to see if Jane approved.

"We want enough of Little Creek included to furnish water if needed. However looks as though there will be plenty of water for stock in the springs that exist. I'll go over the map with the Judge when he comes and try to figure out the fence between the Settlement and the plantation. I'll work on it, Tom." Jane smiled at the serious look on the black face.

"When youz men finish, youz come on back; makez sure you get all the branch ditches filled up soz the water knoz where to go." Tom waved to them as he and Jane mounted and headed back to the building site, hearing sawing and nailing from some distance away.

* * *

Several days passed. The Judge came and he and Jane went over the map again to decide about the dividing line between the two places. He informed Jane that she would have to go to a lawyer, and make deeds; but first the Settlement would have to be divided, into parcels—a surveyor would have to do that. But since she owned all the plantation she could do what she wanted. Now that the 'people' had their freedom nothing could keep them from owning property, although the southern states were against it. It had become a Federal law that would be upheld. "I don't think that section will be challenged," the Judge told her.

Jane asked the Judge to send a surveyor as soon as possible. This was something she could do while the building was looked after by Tom. The Judge had told Jane to let the surveyor look at the area and decide where best to put the dividing line to the best advantage, which she agreed to. She was anxious to move along as quickly as possible. If anything should happen to her, she wanted it settled.

Jane was giving Andy lessons in reading, writing, and numbers. She also let him sit in when she and the Judge discussed the business of the plantation. She wanted him to learn first-hand about how to handle business. She knew he was too young to retain it all, but whatever he was exposed to would have some effect on his young mind. He seemed interested in all the work that was going on and could tell Jane in detail what had been accomplished in any one day. Tom would let him nail some of the boards onto the cabin, giving him a feeling of helping build. Sam also put him to scraping paint, talking as they worked about what had to be done. Each thing was a lesson for Andy and Jane was glad there were so many to teach him.

* * *

The day came when Ella was going on one of the wagons, with seeds to plant at her new home. Jane couldn't resist going along too. She wanted to see the surprise on Ella's serious little face when she first saw her new home. Tom had informed her that it was almost complete. The roof was the last thing to be done and it was being worked on now. The windows were to be installed that day. Tom was overjoyed; he felt as though he had just acquired a plantation all his own.

"I'z the purties' thing I'z ever seen, Miss Jane. You'z don't haz to go out in rain—just step out de kitchen door and pull up a bucket of clear cool water. I'z handy as can be. My Ella gonna' love thiz house, you wait and see. She not gonna' be able to talkz when shz see it," he chuckled as he told her.

"I'll be as happy as she is, Tom. You've all worked hard. We'll have to make plans for Amos and his family's house now. You will be able to lay the foundation for it, next week I think."

"I'z don' have much more to do at ours, that I'z can't do as I'z go along. I'z put one of the men to building an out-house, and two more on buildin' a chicken lot and small hut to close them up in. Iffn' you'z agree, maybe Ella and me'z move over here to keep an eye on thing 'z. I'z can ride one of the mules back to the plantation if I'z needed," he looked to Jane for an answer.

"I think that's a good idea. I don't like to let it stand empty— you never know who may stumble onto it and maybe damage it. I expect that Ella will be anxious to move in too."

The day arrived when the last load of lumber from the one building was being delivered to the Settlement. Lucy perched on top of it, her bags of seeds tucked in where they wouldn't spill or be lost. Jane was riding Cherokee, and had a lunch packed in the saddle pockets. She trailed along behind the wagon part of the way and then would ride ahead when the notion struck her. Cherokee was anxious to run but Jane held him to a slow trot a short distance from the wagon. When they arrived where the first sight of the cottage could be seen, Jane pulled Cherokee to a halt to wait till the wagon caught up. She wanted to see Ella when Tom brought the wagon up the slight rise where the cabin could first be sighted. As she waited, she saw that Tom had a big smile on his face as he topped the rise and yelled, "wooh." Jane saw Ella stand up in the wagon—,

"Oh, oh, oh, iz thatz it? I'z dons' belivez that could be where I'z gonna' live. Oh, Tom," she threw her arms around him and laying her head on his shoulder she started to sob.

Tom was laughing, as he patted her shoulder, "Don' carry on so'z wait till you'z see the inside. I'z hurry so you can see, I'z can' go through thiz but one time." He chuckled as he flapped the lines on the mules' backs and brought the wagon in to the porch. Ella's eyes were glued to the cottage. Jane had to admit that it was a lovely home.

Tom jumped down and lifted Ella to the ground. "There' your home, woman," He proudly helped her up the new steps that had been built that day. Ella stood on the porch a few minutes looking around her, then went to the open door and looked inside. Oh, my, whatz a beautiful fir' place. And it'z mine. She went inside and rubbed her hand along the mantel that Tom had worked until it was satiny smooth. She stood, her hand on the lovely wood, looking around her. Her eyes traveled up the new stairs to the second floor. Slowly she moved toward them, mounting the stairs one step at a time slowly savoring the climb to the top floor. When she reached the top, she yelled—"Tom! Tom!"

He had been watching her from below and raced up the steps thinking maybe a snake had gotten in and had frightened her.

"What is it, Ella? What 'z you'z yeller' aboutz? You'z scared me half to death. I'z think a Yankie somers' around and got you."

Ella stood leaning over looking from one of the windows. "I'z can see almost to Barrlette House; I'z can see everythin'; come look, Tom, come look," Ella was enthralled with the scene before her.

Tom chuckled, "you'z like a little gal, so excited' I'z glad you'z likes it, or doz' you?" he looked at Ella, a teasing sparkle in his eye.

Turning to Tom, she wrapped her arms around him and kissed him at least ten times, "doe'z I ever. I'z never seen anything so beautiful in my'z life. Waitz till the youngins seez their rooms. Thez go crazy. Miss Jane sure is wonderful."

"That she iz, that she iz! Let'z get to work, woman," Tom started back down the stairs, a reluctant Ella behind him.

Jane had remained downstairs, looking around she admired what the men had done with used lumber. It was a very well-built cottage, with everything they would need to live comfortably.

Ella went from window to window and touched everything inside the cottage until she suddenly remembered what she had come for. "I'z better get at my plantin." Going outside she saw that the garden had been freshly harrowed and furried out for her seeds. Taking her seeds and a hoe from the wagon she went toward the new gate looking from one end of it to the other, deciding where she wanted to plant each thing.

Jane had brought the drawings of what the other cottages would be like. Job and Amos didn't have children and didn't need the space that Ella and Tom needed. Jane had drawn them with two rooms each. There wouldn't be a chimney on them as it would take too long and be too costly to build. She would look for stoves that could be used for cooking and heating too. If they felt that they needed more space, they could add on a shed kitchen at a later date. What was essential now was for them a house to live comfortably in. At the compound they only had one room, used for everything. They would both have a nice roofed-over porch, which in summer would give them much pleasure. There would have to be a few small out-buildings, and the lumber would be scarce. It would be sufficient and comfortable.

The sun was almost down when things were packed up to return to the plantation—just allowing time to get there before dark. "I'z worry about the place, Miss Jane, I'z maybe have my supper and com'z back and stay the night. Tom said. Tomorro' I'f you thinks it'z alright we'z move some of our stuff and Ella com'z too."

"I have been a little uneasy, too; however, we haven't seen anyone in the area. But maybe you should come back just to be safe. Bring one of the other men with you if you want. Ella can send your breakfast in the morning," Jane smiled at Tom, seeing the relief on his tired face.

🎄 Chapter Twenty-Seven 🎄

Jane had gone to Ellen's cabin with her when they came back from the Settlement, to see what was to be moved.

"Whatz you want me to take Miss Jane?"

"You take everything here—it belongs to you. If you need other things, we can look in the other cabins that aren't used and see what we can scrounge from them. You'll need food for a few days. I can send more when the men come to work, if you run out. Load your wash tubs; it'll be easier to carry and keep things together. I'll look through some of the things at the big house—maybe find something you can use. You can start packing so the loading can begin and be ready for departure in the morning. Your clothes can be put into pillow cases. Don't put anything in the wagon that dampness will bother tonight. You don't want to be bothered with drying things out when you get there. Just get them ready and leave them inside till morning. Do you need any help?"

"No, Miss Jane, I'z do fine. The childrn' helpz me. They good childrn'."

Jane could see that little Moe was taking down his grandma's clothes line in the back of the cabin and carefully coiling the wire to load into the wagon. All the old buckets that were outside were brought to the front. Some were used for picking vegetables and picking up chips for the fire. Everything was needed. They had very little—only the bare necessities as Jane could see. Jane hadn't been used to alot herself and appreciated the way they took care of what they had. "They'll get along," she told herself as she went back to the plantation house, a happy smile on her face.

On moving day everyone was up before it was light enough to see. The kitchen was full of activity as the women cooked and packed a big basket with food.

The men had the two wagons at the cabin and were loading them with Ellen and Tom's things. The young boys were scurrying in and out helping bring things to be packed into the wagons. Jane had suggested that the animals be taken at another time as there would be enough to do just to take the household plunder and food to do on for the time being.

The mules were tied to a tree while the men hurriedly ate the breakfast of pancakes and molasses that had been made, and drank the big tin-cups of scalding tea.

Jane waved to them as the wagons pulled out—Ellen perched high in the front of one wagon with the children hanging onto the back area. They were all so excited—the children calling to each other laughing and waving. Jane longed to go along but had to wait for the Judge and surveyor that were supposed to come from Charlotte that day. She was anxious to conclude the business she had with them.

Everything was ready when the Judge finally came bringing the surveyor. They spread the map of the plantation onto the table as they all leaned over it.

"Seems to me that the practical solution would be to include Little Creek where it joins along the Settlement land. The people will need to fish to supplement their food. There would be plenty of water from the creek before it reached the boundaries of the Settlement, and also beyond, where it ends. That would give the Plantation plenty of water as well as the Settlement. There would have to be two water gaps built, but that wouldn't be a problem with all the trees that are close to the project. Here, and here," the surveyor pointed out where the fence was to go inclosing the section that curved into the Settlement land.

"What do you think, Jane?"

"Seems fair to me; and that curve in the creek looks the simplest way of dividing it. A straight line will solve the problem. I'm satisfied," she smiled at the two men.

"I'll bring my equipment and help, and start staking it off tomorrow. You can soon have a crew fencing it. It should be done before the deeds are drawn up. Looks like a sensible solution to your problem. Then we can start on the parcels, staking them for later dividing fences. You're easy to do business with, Miss Jane." He turned and shook her hand.

"How are things shaping up, Jane?" the Judge asked.

"Tom and Ella's house is finished. In fact, they are moving in today to keep an eye on things. All the gardens are being planted there. The single men will stay here and work the plantation, and the kitchen girls can do their cooking until the plantation is sold. Things seem to be moving along. We are sprucing up Barrlette House; maybe someone will come along and want it," Jane told the Judge.

"I've passed the word around. I may have some interested parties soon. A young fellow who has decided he likes the area is going to settle here. He's from up in the Eastern states—from New Jersey. He seems to have money. I've told him about Barrlette House., When he wants to come out I'll send you word and bring him out myself. Well I had better get going—I'm busy with legal work almost more than I can handle." He left with the surveyor as Jane stood on the Peazza watching them ride toward Charlotte.

Jane stood watching Sam work on the house. He would be ready to paint by the end of the week. She was anxious to see the stately old mansion restored to its original beauty. The lawn had been cleaned up, and the flower beds cleaned out and trimmed back, the fieldstone borders re-alined—it was beginning to look lovely. As soon as the plantings began to fill in, it would look wonderful. Jane nodded her head, well-pleased with the results of her careful management.

Another two loads of lumber had been taken over to the Settlement to start the next cabin. Jane would send Sam to Charlotte to find the stoves that were needed. She was sure there would be some used ones sold from the slave quarters after so many leaving for the north. She had given Sam orders to buy at least three of them. She wanted Ella to have a stove, too, even though she had the beautiful fireplace. The things Jane was helping them with would last them their lifetime.

The big house was still cold inside, but Jane wanted to go to the attic and see if she could find curtains for Ella's new house. There should be things stored in the Barrlette's attic. Jane went to the kitchen to find Lucy, and was told that she was in the upstairs cleaning. Jane went up the long curving stairway to find her, "Lucy?" she called as she reached the upstairs hall.

"Here I am," Miss Jane, she answered as she looked around the doorway from Mrs. Barrlette's bedroom. "I just doin' some dustin'. I don't want Mrs. Barrlette's room to get in bad shape."

"Thank you, Lucy; I know you take good care of it. Could you leave what you're doing and come to the attic with me? If we need a light, would you bring one please?"

"Sure, I'll come right now; there's a lite up there we can use, and matches. No one been since Mrs. Barrlette and I were there some time ago. There's sure a lot of stuff up there, Miss Jane. You looking fer something special?"

"I want to see if we can find some old curtains for Ella's parlor—there should be some old ones somewhere," Jane told her as they went to the attic entrance.

"There plenty of old sheets and linens, and I think curtains too. If not she make some from the sheets, or somethin. She sews good. Ms. Barrlette she give some to the hospital for bandages, but plenty left I think."

Jane hadn't been to the attic and when they climbed the narrow stairs and opened the door at the top she was amazed at the piles of things that were there. "Must be enough things here to start a store. I'm sure we can find useful things to help furnish her new house. And there couldn't be so much stored here. It would be terrible if a fire started for some reason—maybe even from lightning. Where do you think we should look?" Jane looked around her in amazement.

"They're some old trunks over here," she pointed toward a back corner.

Jane hurried over and lifted up the trunk lid. A whiff of atter of roses rose from the fully packed steamer trunk. "This seems to be all clothing," Jane said as she lifted a few pieces, laid them back and closed the lid.

Seeing a bureau against the wall, she pulled out a drawer. It was full of linens; some drapery material caught Jane's eye.

"I think I've found them; these looks like draperies. She lifted several pieces, holding them up to the light. These will do, I think. Laying them aside she began to stack several sheets, a couple of tablecloths, and some folded calico that was new, onto the pile for Ella. "Take these over to the top of the steps, while I see what else I can find, Lucy." Jane spied a small bedframe of white iron over in a corner. She lifted it out and handed it to Lucy as she returned. "This will be wonderful for the little girl's room. Now if I can find the frames, and the bedding that goes with it." She kept scrounging in the piled-up feather beds that were stacked together. "Here it, is Lucy; help me get it over where the men can carry it downstairs." Jane found a small painted white table and put that out too. It would take time to find things useful in all the hodgepoge that was stored, but she intended to put most of the stored things to use for the 'people.' Finding some worn quilts she put those aside too. She didn't want to give everything to Ella—the others would need things too. She stacked six towels that were worn around the edges on top of the other things. "I think that will do it for now; the men can take it over in the morning as they go to work. Thank you, Lucy for helping me. We will carry a load down as we go—we can pile them on a sheet and tie them to put on top of the lumber." They carefully made their way down the narrow stairs with armloads of linens.

Jane decided to write to her family, telling them all that she had been doing and asking about her Gramps. She went back to the small sitting room and stood looking over the map of the Settlement that still lay on the table. They hadn't decided where the third cabin was to be built. Maybe she would go over tomorrow and she and Tom could ride around and find a suitable place with a spring big enough to provide water for the homestead. She thought it best not to locate them too far apart in case of trouble—they should be at least in sight of each other. That would have to be worked out. She marked the place where the two cabins now were, then folded the map and got out her writing paper and pen and began her letter.

* * *

The days had gone by quickly with the building and the moving of the three families. They all seemed pleased with their new homes and were working diligently at planting gardens, and cleaning off areas for meadows where they could cut hay for their animals. Each family had a dozen hens and a couple of roosters; each had built housing for them and fenced in a section to keep them secure. The gardens had been fenced, and two cows had been taken over for milk for all the families. Until the line fences were built they had to be watched and brought in at night and fastened into the barn which were used by them all. Ella had shortened the drapes, and had them up at her parlor windows— she was so proud of her new home. The little girl's room looked sweet with the white iron bed and table. The white curtains with pink ruffles that Ella made and hung at the one half-window that looked out toward the garden, and up the road toward

Barlette House.

Ella was so proud of her house and kept it spotless.

Everything was so much handier than it had been in the crowded slave cabin that she had been used to. She loved the cooking stove that Jane had found for her; but the fireplace was a miracle that she would never get over.

The other two cabins had been provided for too and the people very pleased and happy with everything they had. Jane had been worried that the other two women might be jealous of Ella's bigger house. But to them they seemed to think that their location and house was the better of the others. Having lived together and worked together for so many years without being allowed their opinions, they were content.

The land had been surveyed and duly deeded to them. Everything had moved along smoothly, and was finally recorded and finished. Barrlette House had new paint on all the trim, the beautiful old red brick and stone had all been scrubbed down and glistened in the spring sunshine. All the shrubs that had been cut back were showing new growth; the daffodils were plentiful beneath the big oak trees like pools of sunshine. Forsynthia, sent graceful sprays of yellow blossoms toward the blue sky. Birds sang and built nests in out-of-the way corners—their songs heard all day long. Jane was restless as she walked the paths breathing in the sweet air of spring. The Judge had promised to bring the young man who was interested in Barrlette Plantation on Monday of next week. Jane had mixed feelings of parting with the old plantation, but she still wanted to go home to her family. She knew she would never be happy here, even though she did love the old house. She often asked herself, "What would it have been like if Lance had lived. I really think I loved him, although she knew, not like he had loved her. She thought she could have, if given time. He was so dashing and full of laughter, she seemed to hear him still. At times she felt him near and would look around expecting him to materialize at any moment. He had come to her only that one night when Mrs. Barrlette saw him too.

The Judge brought the young northerner to look over the plantation on Monday as he had promised.

"Miss Jane, this is Jacob Fallridge, from New Jersey, that I told you about. Mr. Fallridge, Mrs. Jane Barrlett. Jane almost swooned when she heard herself called Mrs. Barrlette. Never before had she received that name, when introduced. As he reached out a slim well kept-hand to Jane, she shook hands looking him over. He was tall and slim, his features were sharp, with a long hooked nose that gave him a look of a learned man. His hair was dark, tied back in a neat que on his neck. He was dressed in a long black coat, and wore a stovepipe hat. His boots looked hand crafted, and shined. Jane quickly decided that she liked him; he seemed to fit into the large lofty rooms that she showed him through. He was surprised and delighted with the library, going and taking down volume after volume; as he replaced them his hand lingered lovingly on the leather-bound books.

"Do these go with the house?" he asked.

Jane looked at him and saw the admiration in his eyes as he looked around the room.

"It can be arranged. I had never thought that someone would appreciate Mr. Barrlette's collection and had thought to give them to the college here in Charlotte, but I see that you are a connoisseur of good literature, and I would be willing to sell them—but separately from the Plantation." Jane smiled at the strange man.

After the prolonged inspection of the inside of the house, Jane led the two men outside toward the barn and blacksmith shop, pointing out the new fences, and other improvements the men had done. Mr. Fallridge seemed impressed, as he looked over the fields, and the woodlot in the distance.

"I'm impressed, and I like the property; however, I've made commitment to look at other properties before deciding. I'll want to ride over the plantation, before I declare myself. If you will permit me I'll think it over and do my calculation. I would appreciate your not selling any of the furnishings, especially the library, until you hear from me. I'll return in no longer than five days to make you an offer or release you from your obligations. Will you agree to that Mrs. Barrlette?"

"That is a suitable arrangement, Mr. Fallridge; I'll wait to hear from you." Jane shook hands with the two men and watched them ride off. "It's as good as sold," Jane said to herself. "He won't find anyone who has fixed up their places as we have here at Barrlette House. I knew it would pay off," she smiled to herself as she went back to the house to think on what she should ask for the place. "I'll talk to the Judge before I see Mr. Fallridge again. I'm not sure what I can get but nowhere what it's worth, I'm sure."

* * *

Jane sat on the wrought-iron bench in the cemetery, looking around at all the Barrlettes who had lived on the lovely plantation in days gone by. Imagining the happiness, sorrow, and pain they had all endured. And the many slaves who had known it as home. She knew that the Barrlette's had treated their 'people' well but still some were in a hurry to leave—and did—many to their sorrow, she was sure. The ones that had remained loyal now were well off; better than lots of white people who were struggling to survive after the drawn-out cruelty of the four years of war. Most were thankful to have food and a roof over their heads. Many had just given up—Especially the ladies of some of the once prosperous plantations—too coddled to take responsibility for themselves; some not knowing how to do for themselves, without their slaves. While others lived on pride, and survived by pure determination.

Judge Winthrop rode into the plantation yard two days after bringing Jacob Fallridge to Bartlette House. Jane went to the big double doors to meet him anxious to hear his opinion of the encounter.

"Good morning, Judge Winthrop. How are you this beautiful spring day?" Jane held out her hand to her visitor.

"Good morning, Jane; I decided I had better come over and we would go over what you need to know about the selling of Barrlette Plantation. I have a feeling that Mr. Fallridge won't find anything more to his liking. I'm so glad you've had the 'people' working and restoring and sprucing up the house, inside and out. It looks good in the spring sunshine." Lucy appeared to take the Judge's hat and riding gloves.

"Come into the setting' room Judge where we can sit down. I'm so glad you have come. I had began to worry a bit; I have no idea what to ask for things. I know there are many rare books in the library; if they were to be sold for their value, there would be a fortune in them alone. I'm also aware that money is scarce even in the north, even to those who have the name of being wealthy. What do you think?" she asked the Judge as he sat sipping the tea that Lucy had brought to them.

"You're very wise to recognize the value of the library. The Barrlettes collected that library over three generations, in this country and also in Europe. However, not many have the means today to indulge themselves in such luxuries."

Jane nodded, "I'm well aware of that. Do you have any idea what is being asked for similar plantations in the area?"

"I'm sorry to say that I don't. At one time this place would have been worth a quarter of a million dollars. But now—I don't know, the Judge shook his head as he looked around him.

"I think the best thing to do is see what Mr. Fallridge will offer—let him decide what he will pay then I can come back with a counter offer if I think it is too little." Jane looked at the Judge to see what he thought.

"I think that's a good solution. He will offer less than he thinks he can get it for, so keep that in mind. He will contact me when he wants to come back. I suppose you'll want me with you while you are dealing with him?" the Judge asked.

"Oh yes. I want you by my side. I know very little about business. I would never know how to go about writing up options or whatever has to be done. Thank you Judge for your concern. I do appreciate it very much." Jane shook the Judge's hand and impulsively kissed his cheek, as he collected his things to leave.

* * *

Four days after looking at the property, Mr. Fallridge and Judge Winthrop returned to the plantation. Jane took it as a good sign that he hadn't waited the allotted five days they had agreed on, and welcomed them with a smile, as she guided them to the small sitting room that she used as her office.

They had hardly gotten seated when Lucy came with the tea service and served the aromic tea that she had prepared; some small cakes had also been added to the silver tray she offered.

"Mrs. Barrlette, I've been to several other plantations, but this one intrigues me. I somehow feel at home here, and would like to make you an offer, for the plantation, land and whatever catches my eye of the furnishings. If you wouldn't mind I would like to go through the house and make a list of the things to be included. I don't know your circumstances, however, I know that money is scarce everywhere. I fully intend to make you a fair offer. I understand that most of your workers have already gone. How many do you have on the plantation that plan to stay?"

There are eight single men, they work for wages and at present the house girls looks after their cooking and such. They live in the quarters, and I think would remain as is if you like. I've made arrangements for the married couples. There were three left who had been with the Barrlettes all their life since they were born here. They are all honest, hard-working people, who you can trust. I've deeded them each a homestead and helped build each a home, not far from here. They are reliable and will be available to work on the plantation, when needed. Most of the house help have plans—they could change if you wanted to talk to them. That is—some of them would change their plans. They all have their freedom papers all legal, but they like Barrlette House, and I think perhaps would like to remain. I can't speak for them myself."

"If you like we can tour the house again and you can choose what is to remain—the rest can be disposed of. Some perhaps used in the quarters as you plan to have workers there." Jane rose and led the way through the rooms. As they finished with the downstairs, with lists being made by Mr. Fallridge, he turned to Jane, "Mrs. Barrlette, would you consider staying on as housekeeper to oversee Barrlette House? I know Judge Winthrop said you are a doctor and wanted to visit your family in Virginia, which could be arranged, and you could return after a visit to them." he looked expectantly at her.

Jane colored under his intent gaze, embarrassed that he would ask her such a personal question, and was at a loss to know how to answer him without her anger showing.

"Mrs. Barrlette, I'm sorry; I never intended to embarrass you in any way. I don't mean strictly as housekeeper, but as hostess to Barrlette House. You see, I plan to do a lot of entertaining—people from Washington, and the north where finesse is needed to handle the situation. They will mostly be gentlemen who will bring their wives and stay here several days at a time. I can see I've shocked you. I'm truely sorry if I've made you uncomfortable. I meant it as an honor to you, Mrs. Barrlette, you are an excellent hostess." He looked her in the eye and repeated, "I'm sincerely sorry if I have offended you."

Jane gathered all her willpower, looked at him and answered, "I would have remained at Barrlette House as its owner if it had been possible; however, too much has occurred here of a personal nature to allow me to remain. I love Barrlette House; but must now leave it to others for my own well-being. Thank you for your gracious offer, Mr. Fallridge." Jane turned and started up the long winding staircase to the floor above.

The two men followed her slowly up the stairs. Judge Winthrop wisely kept his thoughts to himself.

The upstairs finished, she asked him if he cared to see the attic, and they proceeded up the narrow stairs, to view the now almost empty space. Jane and Lucy had moved all the collection of years, into one side, furniture setting idle for years was taken to the new houses to be used. Mr. Fallridge glanced around without comment, as they descended the stairs again.

They reached the small sitting room-office and he presented his list to Jane. She saw that all the lovely pieces that she loved had been meticulously included. He had an eye for good well-made things, and she knew he would cherish them as she did. "You have a liking for lovely things I see," Jane said, smiling at him.

"There are some lovely pieces here. They have been taken care of by someone else who likes lovely things," he said. "What about the potraits of what I assume are family?"

"I would like to ask you a question before answering you, if you don't mind. Do you intend to change the name of the plantation?"

"Absolutely not! I love the name of Barrlette House and as it is famous, more or less, I intend to keep the name. Is there an objection in doing so?" He looked almost shaken by Jane's question.

"No. I would like to have it remain Barrlette House. All the Barrlettes are buried in the cemetery behind the house. And if the house retains its name, I would like very much for the images of the people who built it to remain too. I'm now a Barrlette, but hardly knew them. I was married to Major Lance Barrlette for only three hours when he was ambushed and killed—if the Judge hasn't already told you. That is the reason I must leave." Again Jane was embarrassed telling her personal life to a stranger.

"I didn't know, Mrs. Barrlette. I'm so sorry—it must be terrible for you. Rest assured that I'll treasure all the things that the Barrlette family collected and cherished. And as long as I live it shall remain Barrlette House. Would you like me to come another time to talk business and make my offer? I know this has been painful! for you." He started to take Jane's hand but thought better of it as he looked at her.

"No, Mr. Fallridge, I think it best if we conclude our business; it will take time to get the papers in order and I want to make my plans as soon as possible." Jane gave him a faint smile.

"Very well, I know the Plantation was worth a lot in its prime, when it was a working plantation. Things have changed drastically due to the catastrophe we have just gone through, and I cannot offer you what you may value it for. I've gone over everything carefully, and can offer you in United States currency the amount of $25,000.00 dollars for the list of things and the plantation itself. I think at today's market that is a sound evaluation."

Jane caught her lip between her teeth, her heart was pounding; she never dreamed that she could receive that much cash if she sold the plantation. However, the Judge had said that a counter offer would be appropriate. She shook her head thinking, knowing that Mr. Fallridge was watching her. She looked up and caught the look on his face, and made up her mind, "I had thought that it might be worth more like $50,000.00 Mr. Fallridge. However as I feel that you do really appreciate what the Barrlette Plantation stands for, I'll be willing to let it go to you for $30,000.00, and I think that is a fair price for both of us; if there's a problem, I'll be glad to take a mortgage, say for five years on the other five thousand." She held her breath wondering if she had come on too strongly.

Mr. Fallridge, shook his head. He did feel terrible, making the mistake he had, offering a housekeeping job to a Barrlette—but that was a lot of money. However, there wasn't a lot that had to be done, as she had repaired most of the mansion. "Done! I'll give you the thirty thousand, as I said, in United States Currency." Turning to the Judge, he said, "Will you be handling the paperwork for Mrs. Barrlette?"

They both turned to the Judge. "I've been taking care of Jane's business, and will get started on the paperwork at once. Jane stood and shook hands with both the men. "Then that's settled. I can get on with my plans. Congratulations, Mr. Fallridge, I'm sure you will be happy here. It's a wonderful old place. I'm sorry I feel compelled to leave.

"Good-by Jane. I'll let you know when I have things ready for signing, Judge Winthrop said as they mounted and rode away.

❧ Chapter Twenty-Eight ❧

Jane had to smile to herself as she watched the two men disappear out of sight. I do believe Mr. Fallridge was flirting with me. He seems a nice man, she mused to herself; he'll have no problem finding a suitable wife among all the girls of Charlotte. Going back into the sitting room, she sat down by the window thinking. I have to pack what things I will take with me, and make arrangements for the journey. She had sent a big barrel of fine china to her mother some months ago. She, at least, wanted her to have that from her Barrlette family.

When Lucy came to see if Jane wanted tea, she said to her, "Please call Sam and Andy from the barn and have the rest of the help come to the kitchen. I have something to tell everyone."

Lucy looked quickly at Jane, seeing the serious expression on her face. Everyone knew that the Judge had brought a stranger to look over the house; there was speculation as to why he was there. They all thought him a fine-looking gentleman and thought what an appropriate match it would be for Jane—after all it had been almost a year since Lance had been killed and they had been married for such a short time. They all knew that sometimes marriages were arranged for business reasons and thought perhaps that Barrlette House had fallen on bad times, although there seemed to be plenty of money for the repairs and sprucing up that Jane had arranged. There could have been a purpose in that too, to draw in the right gentlemen.

Jane patted her hair and started toward the kitchen. This wasn't something she would enjoy doing—although most of the 'people' had known that Jane planned to leave for home at some time in the future. She could hear the murmur of voices as she approached the big kitchen. All the help, excluding the field hands, were on hand. "Won't you all sit at the table. Flo, could we have some of that fragrant tea I smell?" Jane smiled at her as she herself sat down.

When the tea was served, Jane said, "I have some news to tell you. The plantation has been sold to Mr. Fallridge—the gentleman you saw looking around. He has taken a great liking for

Barrlette House, and has promised that it will retain the name. Also that the Barrlette family cemetery will be kept up and honored; and the Barrlette's portraits will still hang in the hall, as they have for many years. He is anxious to have all of you who want to stay to continue as before. I'm sure he will need more help as he plans to renovate the mansion, and as he has announced, do a lot of entertaining. I think he will be a responsible, caring custodian of the Barrlette heritage. I feel confident that he will restore the plantation to a productive, proud plantation once again. Those of you who wish to remain, I feel sure will be treated with respect and consideration. I'll be leaving soon; the papers are being processed now, and as soon as the business is taken care of, I will be going to my home. It has been a long time since I've seen my family. Sam, and of course Andy, will be going with me. Arrangements have not been made yet as to how we will proceed. Do any of you have any questions?" Jane looked from one to another, seeing tears in Flo and Lucy's eyes, as they all shook their heads.

We have several days before we will be ready to travel. I haven't decided if we will be going by train or by horse and wagon. There is very little I expect to take. Mr. Fallridge wants everything concerning the Barrlettes, left in the mansion. It will, in fact, be a sort of museum to them. I think it appropriate, as there are no heirs, besides myself. I was a Barrlette for such a short time that I don't feel that it applies to me. I loved the Barrlettes and think they would approve my decision. While you are all together I would like to thank all of you for your respect and caring since I've been here. I do appreciate all you've done for me and the Barrlettes." Jane rose from her chair and left the kitchen, going toward the front of the house where she detoured toward the big library; her eyes followed the tall book cases and trophy cases that lined the big room. What memories were held inside these walls she thought to herself. She then went to Lance's room and stood there for several moments. I'll let Andy select some of Lance's things if he wants a reminder of Barrlette House, she thought. She knew it would be hard to leave Barrlette Plantation, but it was a page that had to be turned.

The Judge had brought her several newspapers when he and Mr. Fallridge came. She sat by the window with them on her lap. She had time now to read some of the news that was happening around the country. She sat reading about the restoration of the cities and what was being done about all the shortages that had occurred, and the lack of money the people were feeling.

As Jane read, an article caught her eye about the lands in the West being opened up for homesteading. The Indians were being pushed westward and those who could be rounded up were placed on reservations in Northwest Oklahoma and in Arizona. There had been some killing on both sides, as the soldiers collected the wild red man and took his land. Jane's heart ached for the untamed men of the plains who were trying to keep their heritage, but knew they could never win, as the white man moved further west in their quest for gold, and more land. As she read, she saw a small announcement about a group that was meeting to consider forming a wagon train to head westward in search of the free land. The meeting was to be held two days from now. Jane laid the newspaper aside as she sat staring off into the distance. "I'm going to that meeting she said to herself; I want to know what they plan; it sounds interesting." She picked up the paper and read through the announcement again. It seems that a railroad company was going to hold the meeting and show maps and pictures of the area and give people a description of the surroundings. The government had given large sections of the newly acquired lands to the railroad. They wanted to have it developed and the railroads were essential for that purpose; and the railroad companies would benefit by the lands, which they would sell to emigrants. The more populous—the more freight would go by rail to the cities and to the seacoast to be shipped to foreign countries. The land was going for a bargain price to those who were brave enough to buy in a remote area and face the hazards and hardships that would no doubt be a part of pioneering. There was a sketchy map of parts of the area in question that Jane sat studying it. She wanted to learn all she could about the land before going to hear the promoters who would speak on the subject. Jane knew that the Judge as well as her family would think her foolish to even consider such an idea—a woman alone without a husband. It was even doubtful if she would be allowed to homestead or buy land, as a single female. She remembered all she had gone through by wanting to be a doctor. Smiling to herself she said, "I won out on that one—this will be no different." Looking at the date for the meeting, she saw she only had two days to be ready to go. "I'll be there," she said with determination, as she left the room.

Jane went toward the barn the paper tucked under her arm. She wanted to discuss the article with Sam and Andy. She found them both sitting on nail kegs in the tack room repairing a bridle. They looked up as Jane entered.

"Youz want old Sam, Miss Jane?"

Jane pulled another keg over and sat next to them. "I have something to read to you that was in the newspaper the Judge brought." Jane unfolded the paper and started to read the article. Glancing toward the two she could see the surprise on both faces. Andy's face glowed as she read, she knew he was imagining himself on that wagon train, going west. She smiled as she finished reading, and looked first at Sam and then at Andy.

"Are we going on the wagon train, Miss Jane?" Andy wanted to know. Not waiting for her answer he said, "Let's. Let's go Miss Jane, can we?"

Sam smiled at Andy, and shook his head, waiting for Jane to answer the lad's questions.

"Well, I have just read the news about this. I'm not at all sure that there will be a wagon train. It's only in the talking stage. I did want to know if you two would like to go with me and listen to the railroad people talk about it. I'd like to hear what they have to say." She smiled at the excited look on Andy's little face.

"I, for one, wants to go, Miss Jane; when can we go?" Andy asked looking anxiously at Jane.

"What do you think, Sam?" Jane asked the old black man.

Sam pushed his old straw hat back and scratched his head; "Well now, I'z heft to think on it a spell; no harm in going to hear the talk az I can see. Every thinz changin' so fast makz a man wonder what next. I'z go with youz ifn' you wantz. When It'z gonna' be?"

"Day after tomorrow at one o'clock. We'll go into Charlotte early as I want to talk to the Judge before the meeting. We can have dinner and then attend the talk at the railroad station. Have the buggy ready to leave about eight in the morning, I think, to give us plenty of time. If you think of anything else, let me know," she said as she left the barn.

Jane returned to her sitting room and re-read the newspaper article again. "Most interesting," she said out loud.

"You talkie' to me Miss Jane?" Lucy asked as she entered with the tea service, and set it down beside Jane.

Jane laughed, "I guess I was really talking to myself, Lucy. I've been reading something in the newspaper that has caught my interest."

"Whets that Miss Jane?."

"It's a talk at the railroad station in Charlotte about the westward movement—new land opening up for homesteaders. I've decided to go and see what it's all about. Would you ask Flo to pack a basket of food for Sam, Andy and me. We plan to leave here about eight o'clock in the morning. I want to go by the Judge's house and speak with him first, oh you had better include food for him too."

"You don't mean you're goin' go out there where the wild men are do you Miss Jane? Lord Almity, I'd never want to go out there. They take all that pretty reddish hair of yours and hang it on their belt," her eyes rolled back in her head as she looked at Jane in horror.

Jane laughed. "I doubt it is all that bad, Lucy. There's a lot of soldiers out there keeping an eye on things. Besides, I just want to listen to what the Railroad people have to say. Now that Barrlette House has been sold, I only have about a month to leave. I want to go home, but like the south it will not be the same after all the things I have seen and been through. I know I don't want to stay in the South, I may not want to stay in the North either. I have found that I do have a choice and can do whatever I choose. I've been on my own for some time and it hasn't turned out too bad. Jane looked toward the door as she heard someone coming down the hallway.

Andy came bursting into the room. "Miss Jane, Miss Jane, are we gonna' go out West? Let's! I sure want to go. Can we?" He went over to Jane looking into her face, his face glowing with anticipation "Will there be Indians? And buffalo? Will we see the 'Bad Lands'? When can we go, Miss Jane? When?"

"Whoa! We are just going to the Depot in Charlotte to hear what the men have to say about lands being opened up for pioneers—that's all I know. We will just have to wait and listen carefully to what is said. I want you washed and dressed in your good clothes, ready to leave in the morning. It should be an exciting day for us. We'll find out, I'm sure. Now run along and help Sam get the buggy cleaned up and ready for our trip.," Jane gave the excited little boy a push toward the door.

"All that excitement!" Lucy said, shaking her head.

"I'm sure the people who are promoting this project will have everyone riled up ready to throw down whatever they are doing and rushing off to the unknown. Some won't even question what to expect, thinking that someone will look after them. I myself want to know what the prospects are, and what can happen if you aren't satisfied when you get there. How much cash is needed. How one is to live until crops can be raised. I have a lot of questions to ask and want honest answers. If I were to go I would want to be sure of what I was getting, and what to expect. I've been working on a list of things that I will ask. I expect to have to fight my way as I always have, being a woman. So far, it hasn't worked out too bad. But I do know what to expect in that direction."

Lucy just shook her head as she left the room.

Jane sat thinking, going over in her mind what she would ask, and how she would ask it, knowing that she was on shaky ground to say the least. It was an exciting prospect, and she had nothing to lose by going, and who was to say what she could gain by getting involved?

Jane went to her room to decide what to wear. She had completed her list of questions she intended to ask, and would want to look her best when she asked them. She went to the big walnut amoire and opened the double doors. She had quite a selection of dresses to choose from—not like when she arrived on the plantation, with nothing but a couple of calico dresses. Tears stung her eyes as she removed the beautiful blue velvet that she had been married in. She doubted she would ever wear it again. There was the lovely 'ashes of roses' daytime frock that she had only worn a few times. Most of her dresses were dark due to all the deaths that had occurred in the family. She and Lucy had recently made her a blue paisley print, that would be suitable to wear to the city. It was a bright blue and she had trimmed a black straw hat she had found in the attic with a band of white, and a contrived white rose of stiff white fabric. It looked stylish and suited her, matching the white piping on the dress. She had a suitable pair of black shoes that finished the ensemble. Laying them all out onto a chair for easy access in the morning, she checked her doctor's bag, making sure that all the emergency equipment was in place. She chose a small ridicule in black and folded her list and put it into the bag, as well as a considerable amount of money, and was ready to dress for the trip in the early morning. It had been a long time since she had gone to the city without the worry of the plantation on her mind. This would be a pleasure trip, more or less, and she was becoming very excited about the prospect. A day just to enjoy herself was a rare event, and she meant to make the most of it.

* * *

The buggy rolled out of the barnyard on a beautiful sunny morning. The big basket of food was carefully stored under the buggy seat. Sam and Andy had shined and polished the buggy and curried the mules till their reddish coats glistened in the sun. Jane sat back in the comfortable seat ready to enjoy herself on the ride.

Birds singing and the jingle of the harness lulled her into a passive mood. She looked at the roadside but didn't clearly see anything they were passing.

Sam suddenly broke into song. The vibration of his deep voice could be felt through the buggy seat as he sang— "I'm goin' to that promised land, away beyond the mountain' top I'm goin' to that promise land." Jane noticed he had a deep, mellow voice that carried the tune of the old hymn well. He only sang a few lines absentminded and then clucked to the team that had begun to lag a little.

Andy looked at Sam—waiting—seeming to expect more; when he didn't pick up the melody Andy asked, "I'z that the land we'z going to hear about," he turned to Jane, a gleam in his eye.

Jane looked down at the boy who sat between Sam and herself; she loved him as though he belonged to her as her own flesh and blood. "Andy, ask me properly and I'll answer you. What has happened to all the lessons we have been having?"

"I forgot; Is that the land we're going to hear about?" he said in proper form.

"The song that Sam was singing is a religious song, speaking of the land beyond this life. I hope none of us will be going there for a very long time in the future. I think it best if we wait until

315

we hear the details of what the railroad is offering then we can discuss it. Don't you agree?" she asked him as she gave him a squeeze.

He nodded his head in answer as something else took his eye. He laughed as a striped ground squirrel made a hasty retreat from beneath the buggy wheels, escaping into the brush along the roadway. "He made it! Boy! I didn't think he would." He laughed again.

"He is one of God's creatures, and was running for his life. Somewhere in the underbrush, he has a home and a family that would miss him if he were killed. Always remember—don't kill for the sake of killing—every living creature has a place in God's plan. The Good Book says God knows when even a little sparrow falls."

"How could he know that when he's up in heaven?" Andy asked anxiously.

"Oh, he knows—he's God! God knows everything," Jane answered him.

"Does God know we're going to Charlotte?" he asked.

"Oh, he knows all right and will keep us safe while we are there."

There was silence, while Andy mulled that information over in his mind.

"Look at that lovely garden, looks as though they have plowed up part of the plantation's lawn to put in vegetables. I guess they didn't want to go so far to tend a garden. There are lots of beautiful flowers too, but they need tending. They are getting wild." Jane's heart broke each time she saw a lovely old plantation house going to rack and ruin. And so many were doing just that. There was no one to take care of them, and no money for repairs. Most of the owners didn't know how to do anything themselves—they had always had servants for the work. Jane, thinking of them thought, I never want to be at the mercy of others, not knowing how to do things. Jane could do most everything, although housework wasn't one of the things she had been exposed to like her sisters. She had learned to sew, and could cook some, and of course make a bed, but the finer things in cooking she didn't know, but knew she could learn with a little help. When she went home she meant to spend time with her mother in the kitchen. She would learn to be a good cook if it killed her.

Jane could see that they were nearing Charlotte; the roadway had become smoother and there was more traffic in evidence. The buggy seemed to be making better time now as Sam expertly maneuvered it between other traffic and turned down a boulevard. Jane recognized that it went to the Judge's house. She knew they would soon be there and sat up straighter in the seat, smoothing her skirt around her. Sam quickly drove into the curved drive in front of the big pillored portico, and brought the buggy to a halt; hurrying around, he helped Jane to the ground. She went toward the wide steps that led to the front door where the housekeeper waited to show her into the Judge's quarters. Sam had found a wide area along the curving drive and pulled the buggy into it. He removed the bits from the mule's mouths and brought a bucket of water from around the house to give them drink while they waited.

Andy sat in the buggy watching Sam water the mules and any other activity he could see from his perch. He finally got tired of waiting and climbed from the buggy and strolled around the big mansion toward the back.

"Don youz go too far boy, and staz out of trouble," Sam called after him. It wasn't long until Andy came strolling back to the front of the big house, his hands deep in his pockets, a bored look on his face.

"Tant' no one around here; wonder where everyone is? I don't even seez a barn or shop to work in, he told Sam.

"Your' in town now, boy. Theyz don' have shops by fancy town houses. Make too much noise. A driver coms and take Mr. Judge where he want to go. Or people walk—everything is so close together. He laughed at the look on Andy's face, which he didn't appreciate and he went and climbed up into the buggy and stretched out on the seat to wait for Jane. After the mules were watered, Sam took an old saddle blanket from the back and throwed it down on the grass and stretched out on it.

Andy could soon hear Sam snoring and drifted off himself, the birds singing above him and the sun filtering down through the trees making him drowsy.

The Judge received Jane in his cluttered office; coffee was served to them as they talked. Jane asked several questions about the closing of the plantation business, which the Judge informed her was coming along as expected. "It takes time you know," he told her. There was nothing more to learn about the transaction.

"Have you heard about the Railroads giving open land, and are giving a talk on it today, showing maps and such?" Jane asked.

"I have heard some talk; seems several people are interested. I think it best if they stay home and try to repair the damages from the war, and get on with what they know. Don't tell me that you're interested in going West?" he looked at Jane in astonishment.

"I've come to Charlotte especially to hear the speeches, and see what they are offering. As I told the 'people', I know I don't want to stay in the south, and when I get home I may not want to stay there either. I would like to get away from any reminder of the war—all the blood, pain and suffering that it caused. I don't know if I would like to go West, being a pioneer does have its charm—like my going into doctoring. It's a challenge. And I know in all likelihood, I will be told it's not for a female, which I must say is an enticement in itself," Jane smiled at the Judge, causing him to smile himself.

"Well, my dear, I know how stubborn you can be, and my friend, your grandfather Dr. Connolly, would certainly double that statement. I can't decide for you, but do advise you not to fall into something that you will lose all your money in. There are lots of fast-talking scoundrels out there just waiting to fleece the innocent—so be very careful. In fact, I think I'll go along to see just what is going on. It might be useful to know; I'll tell the household that I'm going. Just a moment."

Jane rose from where she had been sitting. She felt cramped from sitting so long and she stretched and walked around the room as she waited for the Judge.

Judge Winthrop soon returned and they went out to the buggy. Andy made himself comfortable on the blanket behind the seat, and the Judge climbed aboard and they were off to the depot.

Jane and the Judge had talked for some time and they neither said much on the way to the train station, as Sam drove at a fast clip. They could see that several people had already arrived ahead of them. Sam scanned the area looking for a spot for them to pull into and have their dinner. He drove around the side of the building and found an oak tree and pulled in under it. After helping Jane and the Judge to alight, he tended the mules. Taking them from the shaft, and putting feed bags around

318

their necks, he gave them some grain, and would then lead them to the watering trough. They would be comfortable while they waited.

Jane had spread a blanket on a grassy spot out of the way of the team and proceeded to lay out the food. Flo had made a big pan of fried chicken, fried apple fritters, several biscuits with butter and jelly between. "I don't think we will go hungry," she said as she motioned for the Judge to be seated. They all ate hungrily, and then taking a tin-cup went to the well for a cooling drink of water.

After eating, they sat watching the people coming and going—looked as though there would be a crowd to hear the talks. Jane finished putting the leftover food into the basket and tied the cloth over the top; they might want to finish it on the way home.

"I think I'll go inside and look around," she said as she smoothed down her skirt and adjusted her hat. She walked across to the building nodding to people as she went. She hadn't seen anyone she knew yet, but everyone seemed friendly and in a festive mood as they moved around jostling each other. There were several people inside milling around and Jane found herself blocked by a family—husband, wife and three children. She looked them over and saw that a boy was the older and a girl—about Andy's age, and another boy about four-and-a-half. They were well-behaved and seemed to be enjoying the crowd. Since Jane couldn't move, she looked toward the raised platform. There was a blackboard behind it with some drawings and figures on it where the speakers would be. She looked at the drawings but decided that they would have to be explained; she couldn't seem to understand the symbols that were displayed. Looking back toward the door, she saw that the others were coming toward her. Motioning toward them she followed the family that had begun to move toward the rows of benches up ahead. By the time they had pushed their way to the seats, the Judge and Sam and Andy had reached her. Sam leaned toward her—

"I'z stay in back Miss Jane. I'z be close ifn' you needz me."

Jane nodded; she seemed to feel someone's eyes on her; glancing around, her eyes met the biggest pair of brown eyes fringed by golden curling lashes, that she had ever seen. He was a tall lean-looking man, dressed in western garb, leaning casually against the wall, his arms folded across his chest. He held her gaze a moment, smiled and nodded. Jane knew she blushed as she nodded back and dropped her head. She felt weak and shaken. My heavens, could a glance from a stranger do that to someone? Trying to regain her composure, she turned to the woman next to her and introduced herself.

"I'm Mrs. Barrlette, and this is my son Andy, and Judge Winthrop."

"I'm Mrs. Thompson, my husband John, my son Mark, my daughter Sarah, and little Matthew the baby, which he doesn't like to be called," she said with a smile. I'm Mary, you can call me that," she reached over and patted Jane on the hand.

"And you can call me Jane. Is your family interested in going West? Of course you are or you wouldn't be here," Jane smiled in embarrassment.

"Oh, yes. We're very interested. My husband has always wanted to live in the West and this is a 'golden opportunity' as he puts it. And the children are excited—all but Sarah—she has friends here and it's hard at her age to go where there may not be many people. Our home was burned during the war, and most of all we possessed destroyed or taken, as John says, it's time we moved on."

"I suppose that is a good philosophy especially after so much hardship. At least you have a lovely family."

The speakers were about to mount the platform where they would start their program, and the two women turned their attention to them. Out of the corner of her eye, Jane could still see the tall man watching her; he had moved down the wall a space and stood as he had before with his arms crossed.

One of the men, dressed in a business-suit, walked to the center of the stage and cleared his throat. "Good morning! I'm Thomas Morgan, representative for the Western Railroad. It's good to see that so many of you saw our advertisement. Thank you for coming. This may well be the luckiest day of your life! It's a golden opportunity for those of you who have dreamed of the West, and are now reaching out for that dream. Rich land awaits the plow, and tall trees await the saw to be made into homes. It will take a certain type of man and women to tame this land that we are going to tell you about. It will take hard work and perseverance. If you aren't interested in hard work, then you aren't the person we are looking for. I will be showing you maps of the area. If you know what you want, you may want to make your choice today, before someone else snatches your dream away. Most of the land is suitable for farming, and for grazing lands. There is plenty of water in every section. The winters are mild—about six months of bad weather. The temperatures gets hot with plenty of breeze in the summer. The rainfall is plentiful.

The Western Railway goes through the center of the territory, with opportunity to ship beef, grain, and other products. You'll have access to the Eastern cities if you would decide to travel by train." With that, the tall man came over and helped to roll down a large map behind them. "This is a map of the area, those of you who are interested study it a few minutes. We are also going to give you a smaller version to take with you. We don't expect you to decide right away; there will be time for all of you to choose, and there are many many acres for all." With that, he stepped aside, motioning for those in the front to come up. John, Mary, Jane and the Judge followed toward the front.

The Judge took Jane's arm, "Not a bad speech; I don't see how anyone can choose a homestead by looking at a map though. I would want to see the land itself. Can you imagine the squabble there is going to be over who gets what?" They had reached the map and all stood looking. About all that was shown was the rivers, lakes, mountains and wooded sections. Everyone was looking confused—the Railroad people watching.

Mary walked over to Jane, "Mrs. Barrlette, wouldn't it be nice if we could choose a section joining? Our children seem to like each other and we could be neighbors?" She was smiling from ear to ear.

"I'm not sure that I will be going, Mrs. Thompson. Or if a female alone will be eligible. I've run up against this before." She smiled at Mary, Turning slightly, she saw the tall man was still watching her. She couldn't understand the effect he was having on her. She had seen much more handsome men. But somehow the shock of sandy curly hair and those big brown eyes with the golden fringe of lashes touched her in some way she didn't understand.

"We will take a break and come back in half an hour to discuss what you have learned. We also want a list of those who are interested; how many in the household and ages and etc. I'll tell you more in our next session—In half an hour then," he said.

❧ Chapter Twenty-Nine ❧

As soon as Mr. Morgan left the stage, people surged forward. Some seemed very anxious to choose—without what Jane thought was proper consideration. Of course, that was their business. The Judge had walked to the side of the room with Jane. The Thompsons were still studying the map, and talking to those who were interested.

"What do you think, Judge Winthrop? No mention of monies has been made. Maybe we will get that information in the next segment," Jane looked expectantly at her friend.

"From the map it looks prime land—lots of valleys along nice streams. Timber to build and fence; but I still think I would like seeing it before deciding."

"Perhaps, one could choose a location, with stipulation that it could be changed if there were a more desirable location available upon arriving. I'm like you—it's too much like buying 'a pig in a poke', as they say where I come from." She smiled at the Judge as he smiled back.

There was a touch on her elbow, and she turned; the tall man stood by her side, and up close, was even more devastating than before; there was a crooked grin on his face as he said, "Excuse me Mrs. Barrlette, I would like to introduce myself. I'm Jason Turner; I'm a scout for the railroad and know the area like the back of my hand. If there is anything I can help you with I'll be glad to try." Jane extended her hand and they shook hands.

Jane turned to the Judge. Judge Winthrop, may I present Jason Turner, a scout for the railroad; The two men shook hands and the Judge looked the young man over, "You're a tall one Mr. Turner. You say you work for the railroad? Do you expect to get rid of your land in this sort of campaign?

"The answer to your last three questions, is yes!" There was an amused smile on his face as he answered, "I'm tall, six-one in stocking feet. Yes, I work for the railroad as a scout. And yes, we do expect to 'get rid' of the land. It will help lots of people who have lost so much in the war. If you don't think there are those who are interested, look at them gathered to select their land. It will be a fresh start for many and for those who have little money; however it will take a strong back to conquer the territory."

Jane looked up and their eyes met, "Just how much money is involved? and what is the catch?"

"There's no catch; the government in Washington gave the land to the railroads, to entice them to build the line through the territory. In return, they want settlers out there—strong healthy families to work the land and use the rails to transport grain, cattle, hogs, and such to market in the East. Everyone will gain by this arrangement. As for money, it will take some. There is a stipulation that the homesteaders must improve the land and live on it. Building a place to live and fencing areas for livestock is improvement. Also, clearing and tilling the soil. So improvement is no problem as anyone going there will be doing just that. It takes farmers to till the soil. It will be up to each individual to spend what he can. If he doesn't have it, then he will have to do it with his own two hands. There will be the need of some cash from the beginning—to file their deeds, and pay the small fee that is charged per acre. They will have to live until crops can be harvested. I think most of those who are seriously considering this move will know and understand that, any more questions?"

"Shall we sit down, Mr. Turner, so we can look at the map?" Jane spread it out between them on the seat. "Where would you choose if you were in the running," Jane asked him.

"Any of these river-bottoms is top quality soil; however, you have to watch for flooding. The farther you go to the source of the river the less likely flooding is. The further down the streams you go, there are other streams feeding into it and flooding is possible. Also depends what you plan to use the land for. Some of these streams will be good for mills, which will be needed. The plains will be good to run cattle on, the hilly area for sheep, and etc."

"How many acres will be allowed each family?"

"One hundred sixty acres can be homesteaded; and the law states that every adult over twenty one-years of age, head of family, or has been in the service of their country for fourteen days will be qualified—but they must live on it for five years. The cost is somewhere around thirty—three dollars, and the improvements. Everyone will have to have a house to live in, and a barn for their animals; anything counts as improvement."

"That sounds almost too good to be true. It will be a life saver for people like the Thompsons—they had everything burnt or taken. I don't blame them for wanting to take their children there. Now, the next question, How are they to go? and when?" Jane waited holding her breath as she looked at the tall stranger.

There will be some railroad cars furnished, but it's a long way before they are available. In fact, only part of the trip can be taken by rail. There are some water routes, depending on where they are coming from; and, of course wagon trains will be the main conveyance. We have experienced wagon masters who do nothing but put together the trains, who know the routes and who can take them through safely. There's a lot to plan before starting. In fact, they won't be starting before early spring. In this section, they could leave the last of February, or early March— Maybe even before that. It will take three months or more to arrive in the area where we are going. Most people want to get there in time to plant a late crop. It's best to count on buying food for yourself and your animals for one season upon arriving.

"That will incur a big expenditure for some. Of course they have to eat wherever they are. As for the animals, will there be any sort of roughage that—say mules could survive till grass?" Jane asked, all business.

"There is buffalo grass that they could survived through the winter with, but I don't recommend planning on it. If it's been a hard winter, the deer, elk, and moose, and still some buffalo will have been wintering on it. Hay and fodder can be sent by rail from areas that sell it to where the eimigrants will be. They would have to go to the railroad to collect it—but it can be done. There will be government people keeping an eye on things, as well as the army. In an emergency, help can be gotten." He smiled at the serious expression on Jane's face.

"That makes me feel better. I wouldn't want to be in the center of no where with neighbors in the same fix as I in case of emergencies. It sounds as though the government is doing everything they can about helping the homesteaders make a go of things. I want to thank you for making everything so clear."

The meeting was about to be called to order again, and everyone was asked to take their seats.

"I'm sorry, I have work to do now; please excuse me; I have

something rolling around in my head I would like to talk to you about after the meeting." He nodded to them both and said, "I'll see you later."

There were questions from every direction. Mr. Morgan asked that he call on each one separately so everyone didn't talk at once. "The question you are going to ask may be the same as your neighbor wants an answer to. We will get to everyone. Please make your questions as brief as possible, so that everyone has a turn. You, in the brown coat, what is your question?"

"My name is Brown; when do you plan to leave? How much money is needed? How long does it take to get there?"

"That's three questions, Mr. Brown, but precisely put, and here is your answer. We will leave from here, picking up other parties along the way, sometime in February. Without too many problems, it will take between three to four months journey. Anyone who is twenty one-years of age, a head of family, or has served at least fourteen days in the service of his country will be eligible to homestead. Each will receive one hundred sixty acres. The cost of closing deeds and etc. will be thirty-three dollars. There are rules to be met. You must live on the land for not less than five years, make improvements of fifty dollars minimum—that can be in fencing, planting, houses and such." He looked around the room seeing that most of the questions were already answered. "Anyone else?" he stood waiting.

"My name is Boothe; is there a limit on what can be taken with you? I'm a merchant and expect to open a store."

"You will be given a list of what you will need; however, in your case you must have qualified drivers. Get with Mr. Turner—he will inform you how to pack your wares and the charge for additional wagons."

"Each person will have an inspection of the final load they are going to take; if it is over our maximum limit, then it will cost you. When we reach the railhead, it will not be a problem as it can be shipped aboard the freight cars. If it is on a wagon, it may become a problem. Mr. Turner will see that you all have maps, lists, and other information that you will need. Go home and look it over carefully, then all meet back here on Monday of next week. We will then distribute the parcels. Please choose at least two, in case the first is already gone when your time comes. We want to please everyone; however, that is usually impossible, so instead of fist-fights, we will draw if there is a certain parcel that more than one wants. We'll see you next week."

Thomas Morgan stepped down and hurried away, not wanting to get into a lengthy conversation with anyone.

Jane turned to the Judge, "What do you think, Judge Winthrop?"

He looked at Jane a minute then said, "I think there is a man to be reckoned with, who knows where, when, and how. Sounds as though he knew his business. This will be a life saver for lots of people, but with hardships they have never dreamed of before. Looks as though most of these people were not slave holders, but worked the land themselves. There will be some who will start businesses and not want to work the land. Like your Mr. Turner said, build mills, stores, and such," the Judge smiled at Jane.

"My Mr. Turner, as you call him," she smiled impishly at the Judge, "seems to be headed this way. I'm anxious to know what has been 'rolling around in his head', aren't you? Sounds ominous." Jane turned to watch him approach.

"I'm not sure we can get all these pilgrims to wait until February. They're all anxious to get on the trail, start choppin' down trees and building. Some can't seem to decide where they want to locate. It might be better just to draw parcels. If they don't like what they draw, they could swap with someone." He smiled at the Judge and then Jane.

"Are the Thompsons friends of yours, Mrs. Barrlette?"

"I just met them when coming here. They seem a very nice family. I like them and the children. Andy has made friends with the children. Why do you ask?"

"I heard Mrs. Thompson remark that it would be nice to have joining parcels, and thought that you might have been acquainted with them before. I have a reason for asking—as I told you, I know the area like the back of my hand. He waited for Jane's answer.

"No, I don't really know them, but if it was convenient to do, so I would welcome them as neighbors; however, I've not decided that I want to go West. This is something that will take a great deal of thought and planning." she smilingly told him."

"Oh, I think you will be one of those going, Mrs. Barrlette. I can see the bug in your eyes. You are a born pioneer—I can plainly see that. I think you know it too in your heart."

Andy sat listening to the conversation, "I for one want to go, Mr. Turner. If I was old enough you can bet I'd have my hundred and sixty acres. I'd raise horses, and cows and make a lot of money. Besides, I like horses—I like to ride and be around them." As an afterthought he said, "I sure like the Thompsons too."

"There, you have your answer; your son is a pioneer too," Jason said with a laugh.

The Judge spoke up, "I can see that you read Jane rather well. I, too, think she is a maverick that wants to see the other side of the hill." He smiled affectionately at Jane and patted her hand.

They were sitting in the back of the room away from all the noisy conversation at the front where people were still looking and pointing at the big map. Mary Thompson turned and saw them in the back and began to make her way over to them.

"Jane, have you decided on your location yet? John has almost decided on two places—actually any place suits me as long as we can farm and be close to a stream with fish. We will all be happy, she laughed. We all love to fish and that is a must. It looks like any place will be nice. Looks like beautiful country. We're all anxious to start as soon as possible. It will be nice to have a home again, even if it's under a rock cliff," she laughed, and sat down beside them.

"I'm not sure that I want to decide so quickly. I think I'll have to sleep on it and give it some serious thought," Jane answered.

"Ah, Maw, I know you want to go like Sam and me. Why don't you decide and we can go with the Thompsons, and Mr. Turner, and like Mrs. Thompson says, get near a stream where we can fish. You don't have to worry, we can live. If we have animals and fish, we can eat. Can't you decide now? We've talked about it before, remember?" Andy looked at Jane with longing.

Jane was shocked to hear Andy calling her maw, and smiled— a wonderful feeling of belonging going through her. Her son! If he had been born to her, she couldn't have been more proud of the little boy. Looking at his adoring face, she at that moment couldn't have denied him anything. She turned to Mr. Turner. "I'm ready to listen to what has been 'rollin around in your head'. It sounds ominous, but all this is something that is unexpected and out of the ordinary for me," Jane smiled at him.

Mary turned to him, "Shall I leave, Mr. Turner?"

"No. This concerns you and your family, too. Perhaps you'll want to have your husband hear what I am going to tell Mrs. Barrlette." He waited while Mary went to fetch him.

When Mary returned with her husband, John, Mr. Turner stood and shook his hand. "Jason Turner; it's good to meet you and your lovely wife; you have a nice family, John; you should be a proud man."

"That I am, Jason; and I'm overwhelmed at what the government is doing for folks like us. I'm ready to leave tomorrow, and roll up my sleeves and get to work making a home. I'll be glad to leave all the bad memories behind. I'm not a young man anymore but I can do my share of a day's work, you can bet on it."

"Are you a farmer, John, or do you have other trades?"

"I'm a fair carpenter; can do blacksmithing; and, of course, I'm primarily a farmer. I love the soil. I can do a little of whatever needs doing. We, my wife and I, didn't believe in slavery, although we lived in among them. That was why we lost our home and everything we owned. I've sold the small farm we had, and have a little money, enough for us to get by. So we're ready to choose a parcel and be on our way," he slapped his leg and his hearty laugh rang out making everyone smile.

"You're the kind of man we like on our trains, who can see humor in things that other folks find intolerable. I understand that you have picked two parcels that you're interested in. Could you show me on the map where you have picked?"

"Right here—and here."

Jason looked and shook his head. "Remember, these maps are small scale; this section here—see all the small lakes and waterways—that is a very low-lying area. It would not be suitable for farming; and in my opinion, not a healthy place to live. There is a lot of swampy area—good if you expect to tadpole farm. You would have a bumper crop for that."

John let out a roaring laugh, making everyone in the room turn to look. "You sure took care of my new farm Jason. I'm not into tadpole farming. What about the other parcel—is it as bad?" he asked with another chuckle. Mary had a worried look on her face as the two men talked.

"The other parcel isn't bad—would be tillable. However, you're in a very rocky area in that location. As I said, I know the area like the back of my hand. I have a map here that I've carried with me for some time. It's an area that I've always thought I would some day homestead myself. As long as I can't live on it, I can't homestead it. I've even marked the boundary. It is choice— it's two parcels. That is why I've had you come to hear about it. Your wife said that she would like to be neighbors with Mrs. Barrlette, and Andy wants your children as friends. There is a nice stream separating the two parcels, a branch of the Cimmeron. I can assure you, Mary, that there is good fishing. I've had many a supper out of it when I was scouting. There is good timber close, and cleared meadow where buffalo grass grows half- way up your horse. This can be harvested for fodder in winter. There is good soil for farming. I named it "Peaceful Valley" and it is. There is game, and in my opinion, just about the best in all the territory. You could build just about anywhere and have good water and high ground. I want Mrs. Barrlette to have the par- cel—east of the stream; and if you are willing, you and Mary, west of the stream. There is even a rock cliff with a big cave where Mary can make her home, since I heard her say she would live in one if she had to. It can shelter your family until you can build. I've slept in it many a time. You are close to the Oregon trail where emigrants will be coming through. Anything you have to sell, I'm sure you can sell to the people going further West."

Mary was still chuckling—a cave. "You sure do look after your pilgrims, Jason, even down to furnishing them a cave for a home. I'll be careful what I say around you, from now on," she chuckled again.

"I can't believe that I couldn't see that one parcel was too swampy. I should have known with so many small lakes, they are probably just puddles. Tadpole farming! You're one for the books, you are. So what is the catch on this other Pleasant Val- ley thing? Are the woods full of Indians and bears? Tell us about it. What do we have to do to go to this paradise."

"Well, there is a slight catch. You will have to travel farther. A lot of the train will want to stop as soon as they reach the terri- tory. You'll all be tired, maybe some sick, your animals sore-footed. It's at least another week of travel to the Northwest. Take my word it's well-worth your while. The only reason I'm telling you is, I can't homestead it myself; and if I don't, someone else will grab it as soon as they see it. With the influx of trains coming through, it won't be long. I've taken a liking to you people, and want you to have it if at all possible," he looked at Jane, and back to John.

Jane couldn't help the blush that crept up her neck to her face, and dropped her head so that her hatbrim would cover it till she got her composure back.

Mary noticing, said in her hearty voice, "Mr. Jason, you can put my name over that cave this very minute, and have all the rattlesnakes out when I get there. We're on our way, wouldn't you say, John?"

"John let out another rollicking laugh. Looks as though you have said it all wife. I don't know why I spent so much time studying that old map over yonder, when you can do better than I can. I'll like living in a cave better than tadpole farming." His laughter again shook the building.

"And what about you, Mrs. Barrlette?" his crooked smile undone Jane, making her knees turn to water.

"I believe in fate. Seems it has took over for me. I seem to be outnumbered—by Andy, Sam and the rest. I am planning on returning to my home, in Virginia—well, now West Virginia, to see my family. I'll need your advice if I should return here, or go on from there? I'll want to go over the list that we are to receive, and also take care of the paperwork and transfer of monies."

Jason looked at them all, "So it's settled, I can proceed with the plan. Is that satisfactory with you, Mary and John?" They both nodded. "I'll register this with my company. It may be breaking the rules just a little, but I doubt anyone here will choose that far north anyway. I'll arrange it. When we meet back here, I'll have your contracts all written. You will need the thirty three-dollars in hand to seal everything. Leave everything to me." He shook hands all around and left.

The three sat as in a daze, "Whew! that was fast; I can hardly believe it was so easy. That is some man! What would we have done without him? Don't answer that—tadpole farming." John let out another roaring laugh.

Jane smiled, "He is rather surprising. I'm not sure how I got into this, but I'm getting more excited by the minute."

The Judge sat nodding his head. "I knew it; you couldn't resist. I have only one regret—that I'm not young enough to go along. You're going to enjoy every minute of it, Jane. You people don't know how lucky you are having Jane along. She worked with her grandfather Dr. Connolly, who is my best friend, all through the war as his nurse, and even as a doctor when necessary. She's a very talented young woman."

"Oh my, I didn't know,." Mary said as she looked at Jane with new respect. "And you so young, and to lose your husband, too. You've been through a lot. I'll not feel sorry for myself from now on. What we lost can be replaced—we have all our family. Oh, my!" Mary shook her head back and forth.

The crowd still studied the large hanging map. Suddenly there was a commotion. Jane stood up to see what was happening. Someone seemed to be on the floor and people moving back to give room. Jane grabbed her black bag from under the seat where she sat, shoved her handbag at Mary, "Take care of this, please," and hurried forward. She saw that it was a young woman she had noticed before who looked pale, and peaked. Jane pushed her way through the crowd and knelt at the side of the young woman, lifted her eyelids, and felt the pulse in her neck. Getting out her stethoscope and listened to her breathing, and heart. Her heart rate was slow and sluggish. A worried young man knelt on the other side of the girl.

"Are you a relation?"

"I'm her husband. We've been married six months. She has been feeling poorly for about a week. Is she bad, doctor? What happened to her? she isn't going to die is she?" His worried face looked at Jane.

Getting out smelling salts, Jane waved them beneath the girl's nose. She moaned as her head started to turn from side to side to get away from the smell.

"She just fainted; she's going to be just fine. I'll bet she didn't have dinner—she needs to eat something," Jane told the new husband.

"I told her she should eat, but she was so excited about homesteading. Now it seems all a waste. We won't have money to get a wagon, and the money to go. We don't have anyone to help us—her pa died in the war, and her ma, shortly after. I've been on my own since I was ten, working here and there. Now there's just no jobs to get. The slaves work for almost nothing, and take all the jobs." He had tears in his eyes as he told this to Jane.

"I think your wife is able to get up. Let's take her in the back away from the crowd. What's her name?"

"I'm Nat, and her name is Laura. How do you feel, honey," he asked, his arm around the pale girl.

"I'm sorry I caused trouble; I know you told me to eat, but I just didn't feel like it. I'm sorry, I know you are ashamed of me falling down on the floor like that, in front of strangers," tears were running down her face.

"You just sit still for a few minutes. You couldn't help fainting, but the next time you feel faint, sit down and lean your head over to your knees—that will bring the blood to your head and you won't faint." Jane smiled at the shaken girl.

"Are you a doctor? Thank you for knowing what to do—I feel so ashamed," she wiped her eyes with a tiny handkerchief.

Jane noticed that they were both dressed in clean well-ironed clothes. Laura's hair was clean and neat, and Nat's hair was trimmed. "Where have you two been staying? Are you working?"

"My name is Nathanial McDowell. Laura and I have been working in Charlotte. She helps in the house; she's a real good cook; and I help on the farm that's out from town. The people we work for lost all their slaves; they all ran off but a couple too old to go. I'll not mention their name, but I can see why. That's one reason Laura is sick. They keep her busy in that big old house every minute; and I work from daylight to dark. We get our keep, and the Misses has given Laura some of her clothes to cut down and make for herself, and some clothes that her son who was killed in the war, to me. We only have five dollars in cash, but do have a place to stay and food to eat. I like farming; we thought somehow we might be able to go West and homestead a farm for ourselves. We are both hard-workers, and honest. I see now it's hopeless." He dropped his head, Jane knew, to keep her from seeing the tears in his eyes.

The Judge sat listening to the conversation. How sad to be so young and so hopeless. And so in love. He knew what Jane would do. The young couple were as well as on their way out West. He knew she would want to take more than one wagon and it would be a perfect arrangement for the young fellow to drive one for her.

Andy had been outside with the Thompson's children; he came in to tell Jane where he was. "Maw, I'm out by the buggy, with John and Mary; is that all right?"

"It's fine, just behave yourself." Turning to Laura she said, "Laura, this is my son, Andy I have a food basket in the buggy;

there's still food from our dinner; you and Nat go with Andy and eat. You'll feel better. I need to talk to Mr. Turner. Go along, that's an order. Andy, show the McDowell's where it is. I'll be out later."

Jane knew that Jason Turner had been watching everything that went on—she could feel his eyes burning into her from across the room. Replacing the things in her bag and taking her reticule from Mary, she walked across to where he stood listening to the people trying to decide where they wanted to homestead.

"Mr. Turner, I have a few more questions. Is there a limit on wagons? Livestock and such? and how is it managed? Is there a fee? I suppose there has to be."

"You surprise me more and more Mrs. Barrlette. I wasn't told you were a doctor; what else haven't I been told?" He smiled as he showed her to a seat nearby—away from all the chatter at the map.

"I'm not a doctor—I worked with my grandfather, Dr. Connolly of Virginia, through the war as his nurse. There were times when I had to do doctoring—in an emergency. I'm sorry, I never intended to mislead you. It's just something you don't go around bragging about to strangers. When there is an emergency, I do what I can. I don't think there is a doctor handy now," she smiled saucily at him.

"I suspect that young couple has a problem—one that you plan on solving. Am I correct?" The crooked smile flashed at Jane.

"You helped me solve mine, and also solved the Thompsons so, don't you think it is time I paid back in kind? That's why I've been asking so many questions. They are only married for a short while, and want desperately to go West to make a home. They neither have any family, I will need another driver and it seems fate has slammed into me once more." She had to giggle at the look on Jason's face.

"Do you plan on picking up all the strays along the way? Are you asking my opinion, or telling me? If you want my opinion, I had my eye on them from the beginning. They didn't look as though they had any funds, but they are neatly dressed, polite, and in my opinion hard-working, I saw that little girl's hands. She is a hard worker—take my word for it. And Nat's hands has calluses that will last a lifetime. I think you've made a good choice. Anything else?"

"The only other thing that I have to decide is, do I come back here or go home and leave from there. I have sold my home and have to be out of it within a month. Do you have any suggestions?" She smiled up at him as his forehead creased in concentration.

"We will have to sit down and see just where you are located in Virginia, and where you can meet the train from there. It would be quite a leg on your trip and you would have time to rest in between. We'll have to think this out carefully. In fact, we may be going in that direction when the rally here is over. Show me on the map where you are in Virginia and I'll study it out and see you next Monday. Make whatever arrangements with the young couple that you want—you have my hearty approval. I have work to do; I'll see you on Monday."

Jane and the Judge went toward the buggy after telling John and Mary where to get in touch with them in case of an emergency, and that otherwise they would see them on Monday.

Laura and Nat sat on the blanket under the tree. Laura, Jane saw, had some color in her face and looked much better.

Nat jumped up and said, "That was mighty fine eatin' Mrs. Barrlette. We sure thank you. Laura is feeling much better."

"What do you two plan to do?"

Nat shook his head, "It's hopeless, we'll just have to go back to the Webbers—oh I didn't want to mention their names. We don't have anyplace else to go."

"That old skinflint! He was hard on his slaves. No wonder they all ran away," the Judge said, as he looked at the young couple.

"Do you think you could trust me?" Jane asked.

"Oh, yes, we sure could. Laura?" she nodded.

"Try to hold out till next Monday. I've talked to Mr. Turner; I may have a job for you driving a wagon West. I can't promise what will happen then, but I think we can work something out. What do you own, any household plunder?" Jane asked.

"No. just a couple old trunks, with our clothes and some pictures," Nat answered.

"Have everything packed and ready next Monday. We'll have everything worked out by then. Don't forget, Next Monday." Jane smiled at the two anxious young people.

"Don't you worry, we won't forget; and Laura will eat breakfast, too, if I have to feed it to her myself. Thank you, Thank you more than you know." Ned and Laura both finally smiled.

🌿 Chapter Thirty 🌿

Jane took the Judge back to his home. She had talked to him about her finances; the money from the plantation was being sent to a bank in Charlotte where the Judge seemed to think it would be safe. He could send her cash as she needed it by rail or telegraph. She would take the money from the hiding place, where Mrs. Barrlette had shown her, with her to West Virginia. And maybe, at a later date, have part of the Plantation payment sent to a bank in Charleston. She didn't trust having so much in one bank.

"We'll see you next Monday," Jane called as the Judge left them.

Sam made good time back to the plantation. Jane was anxious to begun packing what she wanted to take with her. She had saved two trunks from the attic to store the things she would need. She wanted to keep a couple of the fine linen tablecloths and napkins, and some of the bed linen, a small picture of the three Barrlettes in a silver frame, a porcelain dove that Mrs. Barrlette had given her, and a small porcelain vase that Mrs. Barrlette had always kept a rose in, in summer. Those were wrapped in towels and packed between the linens. Jane finished filling the trunk with the best towels, wash cloths, and linen dish cloths. Several of the best blankets and coverlets were stacked, ready to load. Her clothing had all been washed and ironed. Andy's clothing was in with hers, and Sam had taken care of his things. Jane expected to buy them all new clothing when she arrived at her home. Things were more plentiful in that area than here in Charlotte where there were so many shortages. They would all need rugged clothing for the trail. So many things to think about—She sat down with a large writing pad, and began a list of medicines she must take. She would try to get those at the Pharmaceutical in Charleston where Gramps always dealt. "Let's see—ether, turpentine, alcohol, quinine, morphine, carbolic acid, belladonna, charcoal powder, cinnamon, ammonia, caster oil, ginger, two sets of splints in different sizes—broken limbs and fractures were always happening. She would have to add things as

335

she thought of them, but wanted to have medicine for any emergency.

Jane went to the barn to see Sam—finding him doing just what she had come to tell him to do.

"I'z know you'z want to take your house on wheels. I'z putting on new wheels, and replacin' the tongue, adding some braces and new brakes, I'z have it in fine shape when we'z go."

"Thank you, Sam. I see you are way ahead of me," she laughingly told him. "We'll need another wagon but will wait till we get home. I think we can get one cheaper and not have to haul it so far. We'll go by train to Charleston, then make our way to my home from there by wagon and horseback. Do you think the team of mules will do? Or should we sell them here? I'm going to take Cherokee. I won't leave him behind," she looked at Sam.

"I'z think thez mules do fine. Thez had good treatment, not overworked any, and maybe the mare willz do for Andy, iffn' youz want to pay the cost to take them. You'z want to get nother team for the new wagon, and maybe a spare. I'z talk to some of the others; they take cows and extra horses in herd."

"I haven't gone over the list yet, but there's lots of things we must take. There'll be no place to buy when we get there. And whatever we have left that we don't need when we arrive, I expect we can sell to those going further. You'll need your tools, and whatever you think we can't replace. Go over everything very carefully. Whatever you think you need, we will make a way to take them. I'll go now and look at the list; I want to write to my folks and make sure we can buy things there. I'll talk to you later." Jane hurried back to the house, suddenly wanting to study the list she had.

It wasn't as long as she had thought it might be. Farming tools were the top priority, followed with cooking equipment, bedding, and medical supplies. For those who could afford to take them, were suggested two of each. And then your teams were to be top notch and the equipment of wagons, feed and food, and water. Jane could see that each thing was a must for a journey of that distance. How could they ever take so much, she wondered. With feed for the animals and themselves would mean that the farther they went the lighter the load would be. She would like to take three wagons; but didn't see how she could. If Sam drove one, and Nat one, maybe she and Laura could drive the house wagon; she would have to think on that. So much to be done. But first, a letter home, to see if they could all go there for a few days to wait to meet the train, and also to ask about buying supplies. She would do that right away.

Dear Ones,

I am writing a most unusual letter to you, I'm sure you will be as surprised as I am at this time. I am well; since Mrs. Barrlette passed on, things have been moving at a remarkable rate. As I wrote before, everything was left to me in the Barrlette's will.

All the freed 'people' have been taken care of, by deeding each a small portion of the plantation and building of cabins to house them. They now have animals, cow, chickens, and pigs and a team between them for plowing gardens. They are all wildly happy with their good fortune.

The plantation has been sold for a much better price than I ever dreamed I would get in these perilous times. Even Judge Winthrop was amazed that I got a worthwhile price.

The single men will remain with the new owner, a Mr. Fallridge from New Jersey, a fine gentleman who wants to keep the plantation name and the people who want to remain. He has also bought the furnishings. I am pleased with the new owner, and the renovation that he plans for Barrlette House.

I will be coming home in the near future. This is hard to word so that you will understand. There will be some people who are to join a wagon train coming with me. They will have to remain there for a few days or weeks, but will be self-sufficient, until the train leaves for the West. What we want to know is if there are animals— mule teams, or cattle teams, milk cows, wagons, and supplies available for sale, or should we supply them here?

Supplies of all kinds are scarce and very costly in this area which has been ravaged by war. And the cost of bringing them that distance is also a factor. We will be coming by train and rail-car to Charleston from Charlotte. Some wagons and animals will be brought by rail with us—also our personal belongings. Can you put us up in the barnyard, and find what we need in the way of wagons and animals? I hope you can understand what I am asking, as we need to know as soon as possible.

I'm looking forward to seeing everyone. I hope all is well with you, until I see you. All my love, and devotion,

Your daughter, Jane.

* * *

The time flew and Monday rolled around before they knew it. Jane had Sam got the house wagon ready this time for the trip to the depot. Flo packed a basket of food and some sassafras tea in a big jug. Tin cups were put into another basket with a throw to put out to set the dinner out on. Andy could hardly contain himself, having never traveled in the house wagon. He was excited and asking a million questions about it. Sam and Slazzy had cleaned everything—even the little stove had been polished till it shone. The bedding had been washed and aired and the little house smelled clean and fresh. Looking at it, all the memories came back to Jane and she was getting as excited as Andy.

The mule's coats were shining, and they were well-fed. The wagon was ready to roll out of the plantation gate. They all sat up on the high seat in front. When they picked up the Judge, Andy would ride on Jane's lap for the short distance to the depot. It would be crowded, but they could manage.

The Judge was ready when they arrived. He had some trouble getting up to the high seat but finally made it, with Jane giving him help by pulling on his arm. "My, this is some contraption. And what a view one has from up here. Do you intend to travel in this to the West?" he asked with a smile.

"I certainly do. In fact we may make another one for the young McDowell's if my Mr. Turner will allow it." Jane said with a laugh.

"You seem in a fine mood; that must mean you have finally decided that you will be going?" the Judge looked at her shining eyes and smiled.

"I'm sending my folks a letter today, telling them to look for a wagon train to come to the barnyard for a few weeks, and to locate supplies for us. I can't wait for an answer. I'll be surprised if they don't faint dead away when they get it. I'm getting more excited by the minute. And Andy just can't wait; he doesn't know how tired he is going to be. I know what it's like to travel in the cold and rain with mud so deep you think you'll never get through it, and the waiting to cross swollen streams—the dangers and frustrations of traveling, and how tired your bottom can get from bumping over the trail."

"That should discourage you. You, at least, have some trail experience; but you never had to cook at the end of a hard day or take care of your animals. That will be a new experience." He looked at her with alarm.

"I'm sure we can all adjust to trail life—it has been done by many before us. I only hope everyone stays well. That is the big problem going so far—the threat of sickness and accidents. I've been making a list of medicines to take along. One never knows what will be needed," Jane said, her mind racing ahead to the trip.

They arrived at the depot seeing lots of wagons and buggies—more than were there before it seemed. Everyone seemed in a holiday mood, with lots of talk and laughter. As they turned in under the tree where they had been before, Jane saw that Mr. Turner was out welcoming everyone. She saw Nat and Laura standing beside the door. They both waved, and smiled as they saw her arriving.

Jane and the Judge dismounted from the high seat. "I think I may ride with Andy in the back; that's some trick getting up on the front. How about that, Andy? Do you want company?" the Judge asked as Andy waved to the Thompson children, and hurried away to join them.

Jane called a happy good morning to the McDowell's as they joined the Judge and her as they entered the depot. "How are you two this morning?" she asked.

"We're fine; Laura had a good breakfast. We are so excited, and hope that things will work out for us. Even if we can't homestead land, we can work and save and maybe buy some land later; but we do want to go if we can," Nat looked at Jane, his heart in his eyes.

Jane reached over and patted both their hands, where they were interlocked holding each other. "You'll be going; I promise," she said with a smile.

"You children don't know how lucky you are having Jane to look out for you. She is a fine example for you to follow," the Judge told them.

After nodding to the people they recognized from the week before, Jane and her group went to the back of the room and sat down, where they could watch the crowd and wait for the meeting to begin. Soon Mary and John came and sat on the bench in front of them. They were all excited and were laughing and talking.

"How is your tadpole farm coming along, John?" Jane asked with a laugh.

"Oh, I gave that up for something better. I'm going to be neighbors with the famous doctor Barrlette; hadn't you heard? She's a big land owner in the Oklahoma Territory—very famous." He let out his bellowing laugh that startled the whole room full of people.

Jane couldn't help laughing too, as did all those around her. Just then she saw Jason Turner coming toward her.

"Good morning," he shook hands with all of them, his eyes taking in Jane as he did. "How are my pioneers today? Mrs. Barrlette, it looked as though you came in your house; I've never seen anything like that before. Where did you get such a contraption?" he asked looking at Jane with a smile.

"It belonged to my grandfather, Doctor Connolly; he and I lived in it all through the war, following the hospital tents. It's very comfortable. He had it built special for us. I hope it isn't against the rules to take it in the wagon train?" she looked anxiously at Jason.

"Well, we've never before had one on the trail; however, that is your decision. It does look practical, and you'll have a home wherever you are. I'll have to inspect it and also the wagon master will have to give us his thoughts on it. I don't see any thing that might make him object. It may be a little heavy—I don't know." Jason shook his head.

"As you know, in Europe the Gypsies have traveled for centuries in just such homes. However, I know the rugged trails we will be following are no comparison; if it becomes a problem we can abandon it, although it would break my heart.

Will the wagon master be here today? I would like to talk to him about it; and if he approves it, we may have another one built for the McDowell's." She looked anxiously at Mr. Turner.

"Well, we don't intend to break any hearts if we can help it. I'll investigate it for you. It's good you brought it along so he can have a look at it. I'll have your papers ready in a while, and be right back with you," He said as he went into the office of the railroad, and closed the door behind him.

Mary and John turned where they could talk to the group, "I can't wait to get on the road, Mary said. I know there will be hardships but we are all so anxious. We've gone over and over the list. I think we have everything we will need; just a few things John thinks we may need. We have to watch our finances, as we may need things worse later on."

"I have something to ask you two. I want you to come with me to West Virginia. I've talked to Mr. Turner about it, and we can join the train from there and have a head-start on our trip with time to rest up in-between. "Don't make any unnecessary purchases here; I've written to my folks, and I think we can get what we need there at a better price, as the land hasn't been ravaged like it has in this area. I plan to buy all my food and staples, clothing that we will need, an extra wagon and team, and also will get milk cows to take. I am waiting to hear from my family. I'll let you know when I hear. John, do you have your wagon?" Jane asked.

"I have a fairly good wagon. I've been working on it, and I think it will make the trip," he answered.

"How far are you from the plantation? If it isn't too far, you could bring it out and have Sam go over it. He just replaced the wheels on my house on wheels, and the tongue showed some wear—he replaced that too. He is very good at things like that. Did you drive it here today?" she asked.

"Yes, it's the only vehicle we own now, as we've sold everything. I'll ask him to inspect it today and see what he says."

The meeting had started, and they all turned their attention to Thomas Morgan who began the talk as he had last week.

"Good morning! I see we still have an audience. Those of you who were here last week—have you read all the stipulations, and are you still interested?" There was a roar of voices. "Yes! Yes! We're ready! When can we leave?" one man yelled.

"Do you all have your selection ready?" The map had been sectioned off with numbers on each of the one hundred sixty acres; it seemed the only fair way to allot the land. If so, we will begin. A young man sat at a small desk with a large ledger in front of him, ready to take names and the number allotted and collect the thirty-three dollars needed for ownership. "Each one of you will draw a number. When your number is called, the head of the household will come forward, and we will take your selection, money, and name. That will give everyone an even chance. There may be some disappointments; remember, everything works out for the best. You may have to use your second choice, especially if you have selected the first land as we reach the territory; but you will get your land—it's all good land. Some may have sections that are not desirable, but there will still be workable land for your use. Choose your number from the basket that our clerk is now passing among you. The numbers will be called at random, as soon as you all have a number." Mr. Morgan walked to a table with a pitcher of water on it and had a drink while the numbers were being drawn.

The clerk soon had all the numbers distributed. Jane didn't know if they were to draw a number or not, but since they hadn't been told not to, the Thompsons and she drew their number.

The basket was taken back to the stage. Jason stepped forward, "Number twenty-six." A couple stepped forward, and went to the clerk. The wife had their money tied in a handkerchief and presented it and their selection. For the first half hour, everyone seemed to get their first selection. Then a number was called where two people had the same selection. They had to draw from another number box if they didn't want to decide on their second choice; but they compromised and one took the second choice and everything moved along. Finally Jane's number was called. She stepped to the clerk; he had her selection and she paid the money. Then the Thompsons were called and they did the same. Jane wondered how it had been arranged. The attendants stuck a pin with a flag onto the big map as each section was taken. There were no squabbles about two wanting the same section and everything moved along smoothly. Then a break was called for dinner. Everyone moved outside—some going to stand at the necessary—waiting their turn. Others went to their wagons or buggies and brought out baskets of food.

Jane turned to Nat and Laura, "I've brought enough for all of us." Turning to Mary she asked, "Do you have food?"

"We brought a basket; we'll join you if we may?" she answered.

"Come along, I want to show you our house on wheels too. We can all eat together. I'm so happy that our sections were no problem. They seem to know how to organize something like this. I wouldn't have known the first thing how to go about it;" Jane smiled as she went to the wagon.

They all admired the house on wheels, and spread the throws and sat out the food, with everyone sitting around talking and laughing. They were all excited and thrilled with what they were receiving.

Jane turned to Andy, "Would you do something for me, dear? Go ask Mr. Turner to eat with us if he wishes." Andy jumped up and headed to the depot. Soon he returned with a beaming Jason, "Do sit down, Mr. Turner," Jane invited, handing him a cup of the sassafras tea and a plate of fried chicken.

"My, it looks delicious. Thank you for asking me; I would have had to eat one of the terrible sandwiches the depot brings in otherwise; this is a real treat." He smiled at them all.

John said, "Things seem to be moving smoothly; I'm surprised that there hasn't been more with the same parcel. We sure are pleased with ours, thanks to you"

"You're lucky. The others who will be selecting won't have the choices you've had. However, all the land is very desirable. There just may be someone who wants to tadpole farm, John; then just think, there goes your first choice," Jason turned and slapped John on the back and laughed.

John let out his bellowing laugh. "There you go causing Mary to cry because she won't have her cave to live in and will have to built an otter house."

The picnic dinner was a joyous time with everyone laughing and poking fun at John. The food disappeared, as they all sampled both baskets. People had begun to filter back into the depot for the next session. Those who hadn't received their parcel—anxious to select, and be sure they had their promised farm.

When everything was stored away, Jane's party returned to the back of the room where Jason soon brought the deeds to both tracts. "Here's your future, Mrs. Barrlette, John—Mary, may you always be as happy as you all are now. Good Luck! And congratulations on your new acreage." Hands were shook all around as

Jason hurried back to help with the program.

Jane noticed Ned reach over and take Laura's hand and raise it to his lips. She would have to work out something for the two. She would talk to Jason when she got a chance. Maybe she could put down the money for a section for them and let them work for her until it was paid, and then they could make the improvements. The rest of the afternoon went quickly, and seemed smoothly, only at one time was there a heated discussion; but soon it was settled satisfactorily, with everyone shaking hands and being friendly.

John listened to all the debating going on, taking in everything. "Did you hear Jane? seems Mr. Boothe who spoke last week is going to locate not far from where we are and put in his store and a mill. That is lucky for all of us. I had wondered how far we would be from a grist-mill; it's a real necessity, and being near we have lucked out again. I think you have brought this family luck, Jane," he gave her a big smile.

Jane noticed a rugged-looking man standing on the sidelines, watching the proceedings. He seemed to be studying each couple as they advanced to claim their tract. She turned to Mary, "I think that must be the 'wagon master' —he seems to be very interested in each family. He looks very rugged, and I think I would trust him to take us there."

"I believe you may be right," John said, having overheard the conversation. "I'll go along with him any day too," he commented.

The meeting was coming to an end when Mr. Morgan announced that they were to meet the 'wagon master'. "I would like to present to you someone who you will become to know well before you reach the Oklahoma Territory—Zachary Smith. He has taken numerous wagon trains safely across this great country of ours. He knows what he is doing and it's to your advantage to listen closely to what he will be telling you. Zack, it's all yours."

He stepped to the stage as Mr. Morgan stepped down, and looked out over the room. "Good afternoon!" He paused till everyone became quite. "It looks as though we have an anxious bunch here," he laughed, "I want to go over your list; I hope you all have it with you." He paused as the rustle of paper was heard as they all unfolded the list ready to go over it with him. "First on the list is a good strong wagon. Every board and bolt in it has to be in tip-top shape. Next, is your team. We find that the best

344

bet is mules or oxen. However, if you only have horses, they also have to be in good shape, and not too old. There will not be anyway to replace them if one should be injured or die. For those of you who have the means, a spare team is advisable. There will be times when two teams will be necessary to pull one wagon. It delays the train if the wagons have to wait for help. There will be herds men who will be taking a herd of cows and horses. Your initial fee will cover them; however, there will be shifts for each man to help—especially at night. We don't want to be surprised and lose our herd; also, there are renegades out there looking for easy pickings. Some kind of feed will have to be provided for your animals. Grass will soon be available, but it is kept cropped low due to other wagon trains. If we should happen to be unlucky enough to be following another train, we won't have much grass. However, we plan to be first in line, and let them follow us. Those of you who are leaving from here need to tell the clerk. I understand that a group will be going into Virginia and picking up the train that comes through that area. Let Mr. Turner know about that so he can make plans for you. Next on our list food; take staples, dry beans, potatoes, pickled food, things that can last; hopefully, we will have wild game enough to furnish meat, although there will be times through settled areas where we won't be allowed to hunt. A large water barrel is a must, and should be mounted toward the front of your wagon. Cooking supplies—I suggest an iron spider and a Dutch oven and cast-iron pot. A wash tub is handy, pack your food in it, and if we get into water that should reach the floor boards, it will be protected. Any medicines that you have to have; also bandages of some sort; and don't forget your animals. Bedding, several blankets, and a straw or feather bed for sleeping. A tent if, possible; you may have to live in it for several months till a cabin can be built. Good strong shoes, for the whole family, there will be times when you may have to walk. Head wear, too, for sun and rain. Ponchos or foul weather gear. A good gun and plenty of shells. Plenty of salt—you can preserve your meat with it. Anything you take and don't use I'm sure someone will come along who is going further West and will buy it from you. Say you take an extra team, you can probably double your money on it there. Keep as much of your cash as you can; you never know how much you will need and the farther West you go the more costly things are. You should have rugged clothing that will stand up on the trail. You ladies—don't forget your sewing boxes," he smiled toward the room." Take as much food for you and your animals as you can. Remember they are fresh when we start and the farther we travel the lighter the load will be. You should have at least two good broad axes. A cross-cut saw can be fastened against your wagon bed, as can your plows. These are musts. Don't forget axil grease for your wheels and, if possible, a spare wheel. If you have extra leather, take some for mending broken harness and etc. You'll need at least one large bucket for carrying water. Two lanterns, if possible, and oil for those. Try to remember the things you use for everyday life and take as many of these as you can—but also keep your load as light as possible. Remember you'll be on your own, and must take care of yourselves. If there are any more questions, Mr. Turner will be here a few more days and will be available.

We are fortunate that we have a merchant traveling with us. I understand that he intends to take ten wagons of merchandise, And will be putting in a grist mill. We are lucky in that respect. We will also have a doctor from Pennsylvania with us. I understand that Mrs. Barrlette is also a respected medical person. We must consider ourselves twice-blessed. There will no doubt be sickness and accidents. So be careful of your health and be safe. I'm sure things seem confusing to you now, but it will all iron itself out; we will be organized and fit when we pull out. Thank you for your attention, I'll see you on the trail." There was clapping of hands as he left the stage, and headed out through the depot.

Jason Turner went to the front. "Are there any questions? I'll be staying here at the depot, and anyone wanting to get in touch will find me here. We will arrange for everyone to camp for one night in the park here before we pull out. I'll let you know, so you have everything ready. Thank you."

"Jane turned to John and Mary. Why don't you pack your wagon and come out to the plantation in—say a week. I should have heard from my family by then. We can get our arrangements made on the train for ourselves, wagons and livestock. Do you plan on taking a milk cow?"

"We haven't decided; I think if you say we can buy at your home, we'll sell ours here and get one farther north. What do you think?" John asked.

"I'm sure we can get better cows there. My father always has good livestock; that's his business. I think everything will be cheaper. And I do think milk is a must. If one has milk and bread, they can survive. I've seen people who only had that to eat, and were healthy. If I hear sooner, I'll send someone to let you know. We want to leave as soon as I hear. And I have to be out of Barrlette House in a month—which one week is already gone. Time seems to be flying. Do you have the tarp to cover your wagon? I think if possible we should carry a replacement; I've read where storms sometimes damage them. Maybe Sam can help you make the staves you'll need. I want him to put a roll-up tarp on the side of my house so in rainy weather we can have shelter. There are so many things to think of." Jane turned to look for the McDowells, and saw they had gone outside and stood talking to an older man. She saw them turn and point in her direction. "I wonder what that is all about she asked?"

"I saw that man in the depot, listening to everything. He didn't do a drawing though—I'm sure I would have noticed if he had. He must be around thirty or so, and he came alone. Or at least I've not seen him with anyone," John said as they stood talking and looking toward Ned and Laura.

"Have Sam look at your wagon John, and I'll see what Ned and Laura are doing. I'm going to take them home with me. We'll pick up their trunks and they can help me get organized for the trip. I'll keep in touch." Jane went towards the couple. As she approached, Ned came to meet her.

"Miss Jane, that man over there wants me to talk to you. He wants to go West—not to homestead, but will work. He seems like a nice man. His wife died in childbirth during the war while he was gone. He is very sad and lost-like. Will you talk to him?" Ned looked at Jane with doubt in his eyes, thinking maybe he would jeopardize his standing by bringing in another.

They walked toward Laura and the strange man. Jane looked him over as they approached—he was tall, muscular, with a weathered skin showing hard work. His hands were big and calloused. He looked her straight in the eye as he tipped his hat, "Mam."

"Miss Jane, this is Ed Conley; he's a little down on his luck and looking for a job," Ned said, then taking Laura's hand.

"How do you do, Ed Conley. What sort of work do you do?"

347

"As I told the youngster here, my wife and I had a little farm about twenty miles out; we farmed, raised some livestock, and such. I went to the war—I was driver of wagons, and took care of the teams. My wife died with our first child. When I came home—there wasn't anything to come to. Everything had been stolen—even the boards on our house. I don't have good memories of this place and want to go West. I thought of the gold fields, but I'm a farmer—I like the land. I can drive a wagon and pay my way, working. I thought of Mr. Boothe, but it seems he has all his drivers. Ned here said to talk to you, Mam."

"Why didn't you homestead?" Jane asked.

"Well, Mam, since I lost my Rosa, I don't have any heart to start another home. I never intend to put another woman through what my Rosa went through alone." He hung his head, but not before Jane saw the tears that sprung to his eyes.

"We've all been through some trying times." Jane smiled, "Seems fate has caught me up again; I've been wondering how I could get another driver. If you want to join us, you will have your keep, I don't know about pay, but we will work something out. Did you bring your things today?"

"I have my gun and some clothing there in that pack. It's about all I own. I sold my little farm but didn't get much; but I have a little cash. I'm ready for whatever happens," he looked hopefully at Jane.

"Good. I live on a plantation out from town. Ned and Laura will be coming out there too. I've sold it and have to vacate in a month which is flying by at an alarming rate. You bring your things; you might as well join the rest of us. We plan to go to my home in West Virginia and leave from there. We will be ready to go and collect Ned's things—and be on our way."

Sam came over, "When you ready to leave, Miss Jane?"

"You can get the team hitched. This is Ed Conley—he will be going with us; put his things on the front; he can ride up there with you; the rest of us will ride in the back. I have to see Mr. Turner for a minute, and we will be ready to leave. Did you look at John's wagon?"

"Yes'um he'z gonna' bring it to the plantation in a week and we do some work on it. Yes'um."

Jane saw Jason Turner headed her way and walked a few steps to meet him so she would be out of hearing of the rest. "Mr. Turner, is there some way I can put a deposit down on joining acreage for Ned and Laura, and hold it till a little later? I know it's asking a lot, but they want a home so desperately. I'll need them for a while to prove my land, and maybe till they are a little more experienced."

"When are you going to call me Jason? I'm tired of Mr. Turner," Jason said with a smile. "I'll take care of it for you. There's a nice section joining—so far, no one has taken it. I see you've found another stray."

Jane blushed, "He has had a hard time—like so many, losing his wife and farm. I think fate has come my way again as I needed another—driver, I want to take three wagons. What do you think of him?"

"He also looks like a rugged worker; we can use him. I see he has a gun, and a good shot is always welcome. I'll see you soon; good luck," Jane watched his long stride as he returned to the meeting room.

The Judge stood watching everything. He could see that Jason and Jane were attracted to each other.

"All aboard," Jane said as Sam finished with the team, and opened the door and turned down the steps. Andy wanted to be the first in. Jane waited till the Judge mounted the steps and found a seat. "Ned, maybe you will have to sit with Sam and direct him to the house where you will pick up your trunks. Tell Ed to put his things in here so you will have more room." As soon as everyone was seated, they started on their way to pick up the two trunks and head back to the plantation.

❧ Chapter Thirty-One ❧

When the wagon picked up the trunks of the McDowell's and dropped off the Judge, they headed out of town toward the plantation. Everyone seemed to be enjoying their ride in the house on wheels. Andy was in first, peeking out of first one small window and then another. Jane laughed knowing it would get old in a very short time.

When they arrived at the plantation, Jane hurried toward the kitchen to tell Flo to expect three more for supper.

"I'z have plenty, Miss Jane; I'z make the chicken I didn't use for frying with big fat dumpling' and I'z have a big bowl of turnip greens and corn pone. We'z eat fine; don't you'z worry none."

"Thank you Flo, is a room ready for the McDowell's? This is Mrs. McDowell. Which room have you made up?"

"I'z had the one next to Mr. Andy made up with clean linen; they'z be comfortable there," Flo answered.

Jane turned to Laura, "Have the trunk you need brought in.

If you need them both, have the men bring them in, and I'll show them where to go." Jane hurried away to remove her wraps and hat.

As she came back to the kitchen she asked Flo, "I've gotten another driver. Where can we put him for a few days? Maybe we will make up the couch in the library for him. He should be comfortable there. I feel bad about putting anyone in Mrs. Barrlette's room," Jane said.

"You'z and the other lady go sit in your livin' room and I'll brinz the tea for you; it'll be a little time for supper. I'll be right there." Flo hurried around getting the tray ready.

Jane and Laura did her bidding. As they sat, Jane said, "I'll welcome a hot cup of tea; I didn't realize I was so tired. You look a little pale too, Laura."

"I am a little tired. It did seem a long day and I was worried about the Webbers and what they would say when we left. The Judge went in with Nat seems he knows them, and told them the opportunity that we have. They surprised us by giving Nat a five dollar gold piece. He is so excited, we now have ten dollars in gold. I know it won't buy much, but it's a start," She smiled at Jane.

"You bet it's a start. There'll be more along the way, but everything good has to be waited for. I'm glad you young people are going with me. You'll be such a help; and you being a good cook—that'll sure come in handy. I haven't cooked since I left home, and I wasn't very good at it then," Jane smiled at the young girl, seeing a pleased blush creep up her face.

Flo brought in the tea service, with fresh-baked cookies on a small plate. That'll hold you till supper, Miss Jane."

"Thank you Flo. I'm going to miss this old tea service and tray; it holds many fond memories," Jane said as she poured a cup and handed it to Laura.

"Thiz old Willow Ware, setz been in the Barrlette family fer as long az I'z be here. Miss Jane why don't you'z pack it and take it along. Therz another one in the cubbord you'z can leave, I'z think Ms. Barrlette would like you to haz it."

"You know, I think I will. I'll wrap it in towels and put it in one of the trunks. Get out the other one to use and I'll take this one; thank you again, Flo."

When Flo left, the two women sat in silence sipping their tea when Laura began to speak—

"I've cooked over a fire, like Mr. Turner described, and I like doing it; it's not so hard and things taste so good."

"Wonderful. I thought I would have Sam make us a spider; only instead of making it to fit one pot, have him make it oblong where we can set pots, or lay meat to sizzle; what do you think?"

"That's a wonderful idea. We'll need a Dutch oven to place in the coals to make bread. Do you have cooking pans?" Laura asked, getting more talkative all the time.

"We'll spend a day in Charleston and find everything we need. In fact we'll get some things we may not need right away," Jane said as she smiled at her. "When I hear from my folks, I think I may have them bring a wagon and meet us when we get off the train. We have to take the extra set of harness, saddles, and bridles, and beds. We can't get it all in the house on wheels, and have a place for all of us too. You and I will get busy and make some ticks and fill them with what feathers that are left in the attic; we'll have to have sleeping equipment. There are some

351

stoneware churns and jars I want too. No use buying them when I already have them. I didn't intend to take anything much from the plantation, but now that I'm going on a wagon train, we'll sort out what we need. It wasn't included in the sale, so I feel no obligation to leave it."

"I'll help you when you're ready. It sounds like fun," Laura said, her eyes shining, seeing that she could be useful.

Flo called everyone to the table for their supper. She had put an old cloth on the dining room table and had them sit there, since so many had been added to the usual group. The men had washed, and combed their hair and looked at the food with anticipation. Jane turned to Ed, "We'll make up a bed in the library for you. It will be on the sofa, but I think you can be comfortable there for the few days we will be here."

"Thank you, Miss Jane, but Sam has an extra bed in his quarters and has invited me to share with him. I'd just as soon be out there, if you don't mind, and save you some work besides," he smiled shyly at Jane.

"That's my old bunk," Andy spoke up. "You'll sleep sound as can be out there, Ed."

"That'll be fine, if you prefer. I know what it's like sleeping in a strange house. I hope you will be comfortable," Jane smiled at him.

* * *

The time flew by. The feather-beds and several pillows had been made and sunned—the ticks fluffy and inviting. Jane sorted out more linens to take and found the stone jars she wanted. One small one had a lid and dasher for churning butter—she would take it. If they wanted butter, they would have to churn on the trail. Laura had gone through her trunks and packed one to use from for their clothing and the other could be stored during the trip and not have to be dragged out. Jane did the same for her and Andy. She found a couple of large carpet bags that would do for Sam and Ed to hold their things. She set them out to sun and air for a day before giving them to the men. They were pleased to get something weather-tight, for their belongings.

The awaited-for letter from her folks arrived the following week:

Dear Daughter,

We received your letter with surprise, and a million questions going through our minds—you never cease to amaze your family.

We were pleased to hear that you are well and that you are coming home.

A wagon train???? What are you going to get into next? When your grandfather read your letter, he laughed till the tears ran down his face. I've never seen him in such a jovial mood. "That's my Jane!" he remarked. Whatever that's supposed to mean.

I've inquired about wagons; they are being built again, in this area, and there are some teams available. The McGlothlin boys still deal in horseflesh, and I'm sure have access to mules, and oxen too. I've spoken to the Brown brothers who still build wagons; A new one is being made now. They have some on hand it seems if more than one is needed. I have some cows who will be calving soon that will be desirable, and some who will drop late spring calves. Chickens and pigs are no problem as lots of people are trying to raise money on such. Feed is cheap as so many people have little livestock. Charleston should have plenty of whatever your group needs.

If you let me know what train you will be arriving on, I can meet you and help bring what you need here. I'll have your wagon and team ready. Until I hear from you,

Your loving family.

* * *

John, Mary and their family showed up at the plantation in their covered wagon in a week as they said they would. The men started on the wagon, which had to be unloaded, before they could replace the wheels and do what was needed. Everything was put in one of the cabins that had been scrubbed out and ready. There were bedsteads to spread their bedding where they could sleep. Jane had told them that they could eat at the plantation, so cooking wouldn't be a problem. She had bought potatoes and beans

353

from a farmer that brought things in to Charlotte. Two of the pigs had been butchered to use while they were waiting to leave. Big pots of soup and stew were simmering to feed the hungry people. Everyone would cook for themselves when they headed out on the trail, but it was nice having servants now to do for them.

Jane went to Charlotte and talked to Jason Turner, getting the date when they would be coming through for them to join the train. She had made the arrangements for everyone aboard the train. They would be on the road for two days and two nights, and wouldn't have to change trains. The animals would be taken care of and the wagons put aboard. A section was set aside for the men to stay with the animals and see to them. A compartment was engaged for the womenfolk. The men would travel in the animal car. There were two large beds where the ladies could stretch out and get some rest. Baskets of food would be prepared, and if they ran out, food could be bought from huskers who met the train at stops it made along the way. Their plans were made to leave the last of the week, as Jane wanted to spend as much time with her family as possible before joining the train—and there wasn't that much time in between to meet the rest of the group.

Saturday arrived—much too quickly it seemed to Jane. Flo had been up half the night cooking and baking. Jane had bought extra supplies and the kitchen help enjoyed having something to work with for a change. There were several baskets prepared—some with baked goods for the children to snack on, and the regular meals for the rest.

Sam had declared, "Mr. John youz wagon good as old Sam can make it. It'z go along fine now. And last you'z many years."

"Thank you Sam, you saw things that needed repaired that I didn't see and might have been a big problem on the trail. I thank you," John shook his hand as Sam beamed with pride.

The wagon was carefully loaded. Mary kept out changes of clothes for the children. They had loaded the bedding so that John and the boy could sleep there on the train trip. The other wagon on wheels was loaded, with the trunks put under the bunks and under the seat up front. Everything else was stuffed in wherever it would fit. The space between the bunks was piled full and all around the little stove was jars, and farm equipment. Jane had asked Sam to make a slat shelf up above the bunks to put linens and blankets out of the way, he built them with thin lightweight pine strips adding sides slats so things wouldn't fall off. Jane had made a row of pockets from heavy material and tacked that against the wall. She packed some sewing things in that and added some of her shoes in another pocket. It would be easy to get to, and hold many small things she needed. One she saved for Andy's stockings, where they could be easily found. She knew it was necessary to keep warm dry feet.

The two bunk beds in the tack room had been rolled up and tied with rope. The blankets folded and added to the house on wheels, as they could be unrolled in the train for Ed and Sam to sleep. Jane added all the old quilts to use on the way.

Everything was ready to go to the depot. The train was leaving at ten o'clock and all had to be aboard. Cherokee and Mr. Barrlette's mare were saddled and ready. Jane and Andy planned to ride the animals, leaving more room for the others. Jane had put her black bag and important papers and money in the saddlebags under her. Day was breaking as they all gathered to leave.

Jane shook hands with all the servants. Thanking them, she gave each a gold piece in appreciation of all they had been doing for the extra people. Jane glanced toward the Barrlette cemetery; she had gone at dusk last night and said her good-bye. All the servants stood in the barnyard—"Good by," they all called as hugs were given and a few tears shed. Jane looked once at Barrlette House, tears running down her face as she and Andy rode ahead of the two wagons. "We're on our way Andy," Jane called to him.

"Hooray! I'm on my way West. Look out, buffalo, I'm coming to get you!" He took off his hat and waved it above his head. They rode steadily wanting to be in plenty of time to get loaded without having to rush.

They arrived at the station at eight o'clock. Jane dismounted, giving Ed her bridle reins, and went to meet John and Mary. They started to go inside the depot, when Jason met them at the door.

"Good morning, ladies, and John." They shook hands. "It's good to see you're early. Come this way, ladies; we'll get you settled and John and I will see to the loading of the rigs." Jane was so glad to see that he would look after things. He took them aboard the train and toward the rear where he pulled open sliding doors and took them inside. He showed them how the two long seats pulled out with the backs folding back to make a bed. "You'll find bedding above. The wash room is two doors down for your use. I'll leave you now and help outside—it will take a while to load."

The women sat down and began to relax, now that their part was done. Soon the baskets of food were brought in and placed beneath the seats. A window was opened a crack to let in fresh air. The women still had on their heavy wraps, and sat comfortably watching what they could see of the loading from the window. People started coming aboard the train. Being in a closed compartment, they could see or hear little. Little Matthew leaned against his mother until she got up and took a pillow and blanket from the rack above and put them on the seat and removed his shoes and told him to lie down and go to sleep. They had all been up for hours and she knew he would soon fall asleep.

It seemed no time at all until they heard the bell and the shout, "All Aboard!" The train started slowly, steam billowing alongside blocking the view from the windows. The clickety-clack of the wheels on the steel rails, sent a thrill through them all as they watched the buildings begin to whiz by as the train picked up speed, leaving the steam cloud behind them.

"It's a shame we can't travel this fast all the way," Mary said.

"If that were true, there wouldn't be any land to homestead— it would have all been taken a long time ago. We have a long tedious journey, but I'm looking forward to it. I've been on a train, but not on a wagon train. We went south to the war by train, taking the mules and house on wheels," Jane told them.

"I've never been on a train before," Sara said. "I think I like it, but it's so noisy and goes so fast," she laughed.

"I've never been on one either," Laura said. "I know I like it. I could go and go forever, if my Nat were with me." She blushed after telling them that.

The novelty began to wear off, and they all started to nod. Just when they were about to fall asleep, the whistle and bell would sound, jarring them awake again. And their attention would again be on the small towns and hamlets they were going through.

They had been on the train for what seemed hours when Jane looked at her watch, seeing it was going on one o'clock. Just then the door slid back and the men-folk had come to join them for dinner. The men picked up the baskets and told the women to follow them. They went along the aisle to a room where some tables were and set the baskets down for the women to distribute the food. There was one baskets full of biscuits with roast pork between. Jane brought out a jug of sassafras tea and gave each a cup. The men ate four biscuits each and drank the tea, munching on homemade cookies that were passed around.

"The wagons and animals seem in fine shape," John remarked.

"The mare and Cherokee have both traveled by train—also the mules. I'm so glad we are on our way at last, said Jane. My letter should have reached my folks and they will be at the depot with another wagon to meet us. We will have to do our shopping in Charleston. We only have about a week or ten days till the other people will be joining us from Pennsylvania. We must be ready, if we are to meet the main train on the Ohio. I hope we can be ready. I'm getting more excited by the minute," Jane told them. They all talked and laughed until the men said they had better get back to the animals. The baskets were packed and taken back to the compartment. There would be more meals to be eaten from them.

By the second day, everyone was getting a little weary of the continuous noise. Sarah and Laura decided to go for a walk through the train. Mary lay down by young Matt, and dozed. Jane at last decided to do the same. Her legs were tired and she thought she would feel better to stretch them out on the seat.

Laura and Sarah walked from one end of the train to the other, that is—as far as they could go. They went as far as the car that held the animals and waved to the men. Then slowly made their way back to the compartment. Seeing everyone stretched out, they decided to go sit at one of the tables in the other section, and wait till they had their naps before returning. The two girls sat talking about different things. Sarah wanted to know how long Laura and Nat had been married and about the wedding. They had soon talked themselves out and returned to the compartment where the others were. Jane was sitting looking out the window—Mary still lay beside Matt.

"Come sit, girls; twilight is beginning to fall. From the look of those clouds over that mountain, we may have rain tonight. Fortunately it won't hinder our train travel, however, it won't be the same on the wagon train; rain is always a problem with every one wet and miserable." She smiled as the two girls sat down beside her.

They all sat looking at the lights beginning to appear in houses they passed. Soon the conductor came by and lit the two lamps that were on the wall beside the sliding doors. "Now you ladies can see each other. Is everything satisfactory?" he asked, looking at Jane.

"Yes, we are all very comfortable, thank you," Jane smilingly answered him.

* * *

The two days and nights seemed a lifetime for those crowded together in the compartment. They were all becoming weary when the conductor came through, and announced:

"The train will arrive in Charleston in one hour—be ready to depart." They could hear him going down the aisle announcing the news to each compartment.

Mary hurried Matt down the aisle to the wash room and washed his face and combed his hair. While she was gone, Laura folded the bedding and put it on the rack above, tidying the compartment.

Jane took the saddle bags she had brought with her from under the seat. They held her black doctor bag and the money from Mrs. Barrlette's hidey-hole still remained in the tin box, where Mrs. Barrlette had stashed it. There was over ten thousand dollars in gold in it, and it was a little heavy to lug around but she wouldn't trust it anywhere other than in her care. She put her redicule in the saddlebags too and carried it to the wash room when Mary returned.

"I'll comb my hair and freshen up; I'll be right back." She had put her hairbrushes in the saddlebag too. She wanted to transfer some of the money to her redicule to have ready for her shopping, and she certainly didn't want anyone to know she had all that gold.

The train finally reached the outskirts of Charleston. Everyone was glued to the window looking at the town. Jane saw some things she recognized, but it did look different than when she was there before. There were no soldiers for one thing. And the shacks along the tracks full of Negroes were different. They all looked ragged and poor. She had never seen so many here before.

The whistle and bell sounded, as the train began to pull into the station. Several people stood around the platform.

"There's my dad, and my mamma!" Jane cried as she began to wave frantically, knowing it would be a miracle if they could see her.

"Where's my grampa?" Andy wanted to know.

"Right there! See the two people standing by the post? That's your grandpa and grandma. See the lady in the pretty hat—that's my mamma." Jane had tears in her eyes as she looked at her dear parents that she hadn't seen for two years. Her knees were weak and they all sat for a few minutes letting those in front disembark first.

Nat and Ed came into the compartment to help carry out the baskets, and help the females find their way to the train steps.

When Jane's feet hit the platform she rushed toward her parents— "Mamma! Dad!" she called as they in turn rushed toward their daughter. She hugged first one and the other; by that time, the others were near. "Mamma, Dad, I would like to introduce my son, Andy." Andy was at a loss as what to do, until his grandma leaned down and hugged and kissed him. His grandpa held out his hand and shook Andy's little hand.

"Howdy Son; my, you are a fine-looking grandson, welcome to West Virginia, and to our family," Mr. Jarvis said. Andy beamed as he studied his new family.

Jane introduced the others. They all walked down the platform and stood watching the wagons and animals being unloaded.

"I see you still have your Gramp's house on wheels—it still looks good," Jane's dad remarked.

"It's been overhauled and in good shape. What did you come in?" Jane asked looking around. She saw a buggy and a covered wagon sitting down in the parking area where she and Gramps had stayed in an army tent when she left Charleston four years ago.

"We came in the buggy; your mother didn't want to ride in a wagon; Zol drove it. We found you a fine team of young mules, and Zol and the Browns made the framework and covered your new wagon," her father told her.

"I appreciate that so much. Could I see you privately for a few minutes, dad?" She took him aside. "I'm carrying over ten thousand dollars in these saddle bags, and it's heavy," she laughed.

"Could you help me put at least half of it in a bank somewhere?"

"I use Peoples Union Bank here in Charleston. I'd say you had better get rid of part of it, at least, before someone gets rid of it for you. When the men get your rigs hooked up, and parked over there where I've made arrangements for you to spend the night or two if necessary, I'll take the buggy and we can go to the bank."

"Wonderful, that will be a load off my mind as well as my arm," Jane giggled as she gave her dad another hug.

Her dad went to the men and told them where to park. There was a necessary close for them to use—also water and places for them to build fires if they wanted. They would stay the night, and do what shopping they needed to do. The wagon had to be loaded with the extra things that were to be bought for the trip.

Jane told the others that she would be gone for a little while to take care of business. "You can wait in the train station or over where we have parked. There are tables under the trees. It may be too cool, so do what you think best. I won't be gone long."

The Thompsons arranged their wagon where they wanted and unhooked the animals from it. There was a stable where they could be fed and watered and kept for the night.

Jane and her father found the bank and deposited her gold. She was told that it would draw interest and that it could be sent by bank draft to anywhere she was. Jane was satisfied. She had talked to her father and he thought five thousand would be more than she would need to get settled and pay for the things she needed. They had a long talk about her short marriage, and how she had inherited the Barrlette House and plantation, and that she had thirty-thousand dollars in a Charlotte Bank.

"You're a wealthy young woman; I would keep it to myself, if I were you," her father warned her.

"You can bet I intend to. I have to do a lot of shopping. I need to get medicines where Gramps used to go. Do you know the place? And food, and other things. The Thompsons also want to buy some things. Should we get it here or at home?"

"Potatoes, apples, turnips, and I expect cabbage, can be gotten around home. Dry beans and rice, if you want, you should get here; coffee and sugar are high yet, but you'll get the best buy here, I expect," her father told her.

"Could you take Mary and me or should we take the new wagon before it's loaded? What about serviceable clothing?"

"Yes, I can take you where you can get everything. They are friends of mine and you may get a good deal. If you think things too costly, than wait and get them at home."

"Could we go now and get it over with?" Jane asked.

Her father nodded, and Jane hurried off to fetch Mary and get her list ready.

* * *

Her father wheeled the buggy into a spot in front of a big general merchandise store, and helped the two women down. When they walked inside they both let out gasps—the store was so large one could get lost in it. Aisles went in every direction with racks full of clothing, and many things that were new to both women. Her father went to fetch his friend, and introduce his daughter and Mrs. Thompson.

"I don't know where to start," Jane remarked.

"If we can't find it here, it can't be had," Mary laughed as she answered.

Soon her father was back. "This is a friend of mine, Jane. Warren Baily—my daughter, Jane and Mrs. Thompson. Where do you ladies want to start?"

"We want staples; where are they?" They were led over to a corner where sacks were in piles everywhere.

"You name it, we have it, young lady," Warren said with a laugh.

Jane brought out her list. "Shall I go first, Mary, while you look around?"

Mary nodded. "Two sacks beans—are they hundred pound?" She looked at Mr. Bailey as he nodded. "One white northern and one brown. Two hundred pounds of coffee beans: four twenty-five pound bags of salt, six bags twenty-five pounds of sugar, one barrel of flour, and one of meal; a fifty-pound can of lard, four cans of baking powder, four packages of soda, large jar of cinnamon, one of nutmeg, one of pepper. I think that will be all in this department. I need six lanterns, one box of long lasting-candles, six boxes of matches, three fuel cans of oil, two Dutch ovens— one large, one medium, two skillets—one number ten and one number eight; a fish fryer, two brooms, a coffee grinder, a sieve, and a milk strainer; two washtubs, two wash boards, two dozen bars of soap, two cans of lye, two hundred feet of clothes line, five dozen clothes pins, two cans bluing. I need two good rifles with shells, and one pistol with three boxes of shells; two large buckets, two small ones, a coffee-pot large.

While you sort that out I'll look at some clothing." After looking she decided to wait and get them at Minnora, at home.

"Can you send that out to the depot for us?" Jane asked. "Sure can—we'll have it out within the hour."

Mary came and named her order. She didn't order nearly as much as Jane did. After all, they would only have one wagon.

Jane's order came to just under sixty dollars. "Are you starting a store, Jane?" Mr. Baily asked.

Jane laughed, "No, I'm going West on a wagon train. I'm taking three wagons and I hope I can get all that on them. I still have to go to the pharmaceutical, Dad," she reminded him. "We'll go right now daughter. Jane worked with her grandfather, Doctor Connolly all through the war. She is now a doctor herself," her father told his friend.

Jane blushed; hearing her father say that she was a doctor was the proudest moment of her life.

Telling Mr. Baily to mark her order with a red marker, Mary said, "I'm ready now."

They went to pick up the medicines that Jane wanted and then back to the depot. As they arrived the merchandise was arriving in one of the wagons with the store's name on the side.

It was all packed into the new wagon. Some of the trunks were removed from the house on wheels and put in the back of the buggy to give room for some of the sacks under the bunks. They would have to sleep any way they could on the way back to the Jarvis farm—but one night wouldn't kill them. There would be many when they would have to make do. Jane couldn't believe what a pile the things she had bought made. They had to be divided up so all the weight wouldn't be on the one wagon. When they loaded the three wagons it would be fine.

They were up at first light, had coffee and a hurried breakfast of drop biscuits and scrambled eggs that Laura had whipped up. She had fried some ham that Jane had bought and made sandwiches of ham, eggs and biscuits to take along for their dinner. They would have to cook or find a place to eat for supper. The Thompson's wagon and Jane's two with the buggy leading them were soon on their way out of the city.

🎇 Chapter Thirty-Two 🎇

Jane was riding Cherokee, and Andy had decided he wanted to ride with his grandpa and grandma, who were taking the lead out of town. Laura and Nat drove the house on wheels. Mary and John came after it, while Sam, Zol and Ed brought up the rear.

It was a cheery group who were starting out. Jane could hardly wait to see the rest of her family. As she rode along she went over in her mind all the things that had happened in the past five years. It didn't seem real that she had been through so much, and could still keep a cheerful outlook on life.

Jane's father and mother traveled along at a nice clip some distance from the wagons. The sun came out and warmed the air as they left the houses on the outskirts of Charleston and entered the countryside. The birds were singing, adding to the excitement of finally being on the road in their wagons.

Jane looked around her. She couldn't see too much difference in Virginia than it had been in the Carolinas, but she felt different being in her home state. The trees were starting to bud, and a breath of spring seemed to be in the air even though it was the middle of February. She was glad they had hit a warm spell because at times February could be bitterly cold. They traveled for about three hours when her father pulled into a cleared area along the road, and motioned for the wagons to take a break.

They all pulled over and when the men got down they began to go over their rigs seeing that everything was secure. The women climbed down from the high seats and walked about to stretch their legs.

Laura came over to Jane. "It's pretty through here. I hope we always have trees—I can't abide no trees."

"I feel the same way. I want my house built in lots of shade trees. I love to hear the birds, and like you, couldn't do without trees. I understand that Texas is homesteading but I don't think there are many trees there. It's more plains and some desert, I think. I couldn't stand that."

They all walked and stretched, and the men gave the horses

water, and they were ready to move on again.

"We'll stop for noonin' in about three more hours," her father told them. Unless we have problems, we won't be stopping before that." The men nodded as they picked up the reins and urged the teams on.

Jane enjoyed her ride but decided she would try the wagon when they stopped at noon. Cherokee was frisky and would have liked to run, but Jane held him to a slow trot; at times, it was hard to keep him in sight of the others.

When they stopped for noon dinner, John built up a fire so they could all toast themselves and also to make a big pot of coffee, Jane got out the big pot she had bought and told Mary to use it so there would be coffee for everyone. The horses were taken from the wagons and fed and watered while they waited for the coffee to boil. Jane brought out the baskets of food and spread it out on a throw, so everyone could help themselves. "Those biscuits and ham and eggs sure taste good," John said as he was handed a couple. Tin cups were passed around for their coffee. They all ate standing up as the ground was too cold for them to sit on. They took an hour to eat and for the animals to rest and then hooked them to the wagons and headed out again.

As the day wore on, the wind picked up and the sun disappeared behind clouds. The men kept an anxious watch to see if a storm was building. The women folk wrapped shawls around their heads to keep the cold wind off, and had their feet and legs wrapped in quilts. They were warm enough but wished the sun had remained out to cheer them.

The road they were traveling was in fair condition, with some pot holes and mud but mostly dry from the winter winds. They made good time, and as the clouds grew thicker, and the wind seemed colder, they arrived at the farm where Mr. and Mrs. Jarvis had spent the night on their way down, and knew they were welcome with all the wagons to spend the night again with their friends, Sharden and Ninnie Hunt.

Sharden hurried from the front porch to welcome the travelers.

"I see you made it, Thomas, Ailsey. And who is this young man," he asked as he saw Andy coming from under the quilt.

"This is my new grandson, Andy, that Jane has brought me. And a fine one he is too," Mr. Jarvis said as he lifted him from the buggy and gave him a hug.

Sharden bustled about showing where the wagons could be parked—in a circle so they could block some of the wind. The horses could be stabled in the large barn close by with lots of hay to feed them.

"There's a wood pile—help yourselves," he pointed to a mountain of cut wood.

"We'll be just fine, "John told him. "We sure thank you."

They took the animals to the barn and tended them while Ed built up a good fire between the wagons.

The spider was brought out and put over the coals when the fire died down some. One had been made for Mary too—she was so pleased with it.

"Do we need the other spider?" she called from her wagon.

"I think one will do, Laura called, unless you want to bring it to work from; that will be useful." She soon had biscuits ready for the two Dutch ovens, and the big fish-fryer full of sizzling ham. Everyone was getting hungry just from the smell. They would have sandwiches again. Jane had forgotten to buy plates, but would get some when she got home. They still had a basket of eggs and fried some of those. They could get by for the two days they would be on the road.

The Hunts brought out a pitcher of milk for the youngsters, which they enjoyed. The Jarvis' ate in the farmhouse and would sleep there. The others would have to do the best they could.

"Sam, Zol, and I will take our pallets—I see that Zol brought his—and put them in the hay in the barn, and Ned and Laura can have the wagon". Ed said to Jane.

"Take plenty of blankets; there are plenty in the house on wheels—that will make it easy for all of us to sleep."

"I think we have plenty from our beds before; if not, we'll come get more. We'll be just fine; in fact, I expect we'll have the best bed of all," he said, as the two men went to the barn.

"Will you have room for everyone?" Jane asked Mary.

"We'll be just fine, don't you worry none. We'll sleep like logs or hogs, all piled in a pile," she laughed her merry laugh.

"We are getting broken in. Our wagon is so full we'll have to climb in the end of our beds, but we'll make out."

"It's just for one night," Jane said. "Nat, come and get a feather tick to put down for you and Laura; I know we aren't going to get undressed tonight." She took him to the house on wheels and pulled out one of the feather beds she and Laura had made. The pillows were in new cases made from some of the old sheets. She took two of those and handed them to Laura, "You'll need some quilts." She stepped up so she could reach the rack above and took two of the heaviest ones and gave them to Nat who was back. They soon had their bed made cozy and warm.

It was dark and only the fire shed some light over the area. The fire was banked and they all retired for the night. Jane would be glad to stretch out, and Andy was asleep before she got him tucked in. She closed the door to keep the wind out and snuggled down into her bed. She had removed her dress, to be more comfortable and not wrinkle it too much.

* * *

Jane awoke to the sound of the horses being led out to water. She hurried and put on her dress and outer clothes. When she stepped down from the wagon, she saw that one of the men had stoked the fire and added more wood. She could see steam coming from the coffee pot. She picked up the bucket of water that was under the wagon, poured a wash pan full and washed her face and hands in the icy water. When she dried on a towel hanging close by on the door, she felt refreshed. Just as she finished, Laura and Nat came from their wagon. Laura took a pan of water and washed too, and soon was at her cooking. She would have to make enough for them to have something at noon; they should be at the Jarvis' farm by evening.

The men fed the horses and had them harnessed ready to hook up while the women put away the cooking things. As soon as Laura finished with the spider, it was removed from the fire and turned upsidedown on the cold ground to cool enough to store away. The sandwiches Laura made for their dinner was put into one of the buckets and covered over with a towel and a quilt laid on it to keep the food from getting too cold. By the time everything was stored away, the wagons were ready to move; and they all climbed on and wrapped themselves ready for the cold morning travel.

They came to a small creek with thin slivers of ice along the banks. They forded it without difficulty, even though the mules were reluctant to get their feet wet in the hock-deep icy water. No problems occurred and they continued on their journey, fording several other streams, and splashing through mudholes. They stopped to rest the teams for a half hour in midmorning. Then again at noon, letting the teams rest an hour or longer, while they had hot coffee and food.

They were soon entering an area that Jane was familiar with and everything interested her. As she craned her neck to see the houses and to look for anyone who would be outside that she could wave to, she was becoming excited knowing that they would be home very shortly. She could hardly wait as she began to fidget on the wagon seat.

"Are we almost there?" Laura asked, as she looked around her noticing more fencing and houses closer together.

"We'll be home in about an hour—I just can't wait; and to think I was just as anxious when I left home," she laughed at herself.

"I haven't had a home for so long that I'm looking forward to being where I can call home. I know I won't have one of my own for a while, but being with you seems like being with family." Laura, blushed as she looked at Jane.

Jane put her arm around the frail girl, "I'm so glad you feel that way, I couldn't have had a sister that I feel closer to than you. I think we'll make out just fine," Jane smiled at her.

The horses seemed to know they were nearing home and picked up their pace, slinging their heads and acting anxious.

They finally hit the West Fork road and Jane knew at anytime they would be able to see some of the Jarvis land.

"Oh, how wonderful to be home again after so long," Jane said to Laura and Nat. Just then she saw the twin chimneys of her Uncle Patrick's house. "That's my uncle's house; he is my mother's brother; I just love him. They'll all come down to Dad's tonight to welcome us." As they came nearer, they saw people standing on the front portico waving. They were some distance away from the road, with the West Fork between them. Everyone in the wagons waved back.

The next thing Jane saw was the old cedar tree standing tall at the back door, then the big, majestic white house. "That's it! That's it!" Jane called out, almost standing up in the wagon. "I'm home at last, it's been so long." Tears were streaming down her face as she took in every building and fence post.

Someone stood at the big red gate ready to swing it open to let the wagons into the spacious lot surrounding the oversize barn. There were several people in wraps standing on the portico ready to welcome them. Jane couldn't tell who they were, as they were so bundled against the cold. They were waving as were all those aboard the wagons.

"What a wonderful welcome," Laura said. "I think I'm going to cry too."

Mr. and Mrs. Jarvis drove to the house where he helped his wife down, and lifted Andy to stand beside her. He turned the team and went back to help the travelers set up camp. Since they would be there for several days, he showed them where to place their wagons close to the water supply and where they could get wood. The Thompsons were going to set up their tent and he suggested a spot for it, and told them to bring hay from the barn to put down if the ground was damp, and to put their bedding on. Everyone was working to organize the camp before it became dark.

Jane left Laura and Nat to set up things, and she hurried to the house. She just had to say hello to all her relatives. They didn't intend to unload the wagons until she got another one and then things would be organized in all of them. She would spend the night with her family, and Laura and Nat could have the house on wheels which would be warmer, even though it would be hard to get into bed.

They hadn't bought anything much to cook in Charleston and biscuits and ham were beginning to get a little old as their only meal. The family sent out two big pots of food. There were spare ribs, with sour kraut and potatoes, and a big pot of turnip greens and corn bread. It finished off their tiring day with a lovely supper for them all. They only had to make coffee. Jane and Andy ate with the family. Some dry boards were brought from the barn and put on blocks of wood at the wagons and they all sat around the fire, talking, until they started to nod, and first one and the others went to bed. The three men slept in the barn loft again in the hay, declaring they wouldn't trade their bed for all the featherbeds.

The Jarvis clan stayed up late catching up on the years apart, until Jane couldn't hold her eyes open a minute longer. She slept in her old room and a pallet was made for Andy on the floor beside her. It was something new for him and he, too, was exhausted and slept as soon as his head hit the pillow.

The household was up at the crack of dawn as usual. Jane couldn't resist snuggling down in her bed for a few more minutes. She knew everyone was expected to be at the big table in the dining room for breakfast, so that they could all eat together.

A pitcher of water and a wash bowl sat on the wash stand with clean wash rags and towels folded beside it. She washed and dressed and hurried down to breakfast with the family before they scattered for the day, leaving Andy still sleeping. She knew he was worn out with traveling and needed to sleep.

Everyone was chattering away as she came in, "What's on your schedule for today, Jane?" her mother asked.

"I have to find another wagon and team. I hope Dad will help me select one. When we get it, everything has to be taken out and arranged for the long trip to the Oklahoma Territory. I have several things to buy yet, and we need food to cook for everyone. I'm not sure what day the other wagons from Pennsylvania will be here. We'll move out soon after they arrive, as we have to be at the Ohio, to meet the main body of the train. Then we will cross the river on barges, then on to where we meet the Mississippi—there we will turn north again. We want to be ready to move out when the time comes. I wish I could take another wagon, but I guess we can do on three. I also want first pick of the milk cows, before they are picked over. John and Mary want at least one cow, too. I think he may want to buy another team. It's recommended that we have a spare." Jane laughed, "Oh, I have plenty to do."

When breakfast was over, Jane went out to the camp to see if everything was going well. She wanted to take Laura with her to the store when she went. But first she would get the extra wagon and have the covering put on it so they could separate the things in the other wagons and organize them so they would have living space in each wagon.

"How are things going?" she asked.

"I've given them breakfast," Laura said; they are tending the animals now.

"I have a job for Sam." as she said that, he came toward them from the barn.

"What'z you want done, Miss Jane," he asked as he approached.

"Sam, we need some building done. I would like you to make a larger let-down table on the side of the house on wheels. Find some light weight wood. Make it here, between the wheels; we can put the water barrels on the other two wagons. Build it out enough to match the hubs, and leave room to store the plates, cups, and such, and hinge the door so it will make a work-table when it's open. Take out the ones Gramps put in to hold medicine, it's too small for what we need. Do you get the idea?" Jane asked as Sam stood studying the plan she had presented.

"That'z a fine idea, I'z get right at it, Miss Jane; doz your dad havz wood I can use, you think?" he asked.

"I'll ask, I'm sure he does. There is always dry boards handy. I'll find out right away. We'll also need a step-stool for Laura to get into the back of their wagon. When I get the other wagon it'll have to be covered, and then we can sort things and store them properly. I'll be right back." Jane hurried toward the house to ask about wood.

"Dad, do you have some light-weight wood I can buy from you or should I get it at the mill? We need a piece to make a table to let down to work on as it's so unhandy to try to make biscuits and cook and have no place to put things."

"I'll come now and see what you need. Do you want to go by buggy or ride horseback to the McGlothlins to look at a team? I've had them hold one you may like; they have several, but I picked the one I thought would do," he said.

I'm sure John will want to go, too. We can ride; he can ride the mare, then we can all go. I want to get Sam started on the table first. He will know how to do it, I've just given him the idea. He is very good at things. If you have any shoeing or shop work, he can do it while we are here," Jane told her father.

Mr. Jarvis went to the shed beside the barn taking Sam with him and they were soon back with a nice wide poplar board, and some strips they would need and shelving.

"Thaz do nicely; makz good table; light too. I'z get right at it. I'z has extra hengez I make before leaving. Thez do fine. You'z go along Miss, Jane; I'z know what you'z want; I'z have it done in no time," Sam smiled his big toothy smile at her.

"Thank you Sam; I know you'll do it just right." Jane smiled at him as she went to Laura, "I'm going to buy pewter plates or enamel whichever is available. Have Sam fix the shelf where we can stand them up and be handy and put the tin cups, and a place for the forks and knives, you'll know what you need. I'll trust you two to get it done so it will be handy. We may have to live this way for some time before we will have a house. We are going to look at a team, and buy a wagon to get started on, covering it, and sort things out so we have more room. I'll be back in time for us to go to the store, I think, and find something for you to cook." Jane smiled as she left to see if John wanted to go and get a team too.

"John," Jane called as she went to their tent. "Do you want to go with Dad and me to look at teams? Seems he has picked out another one for me; he says they have more. You can ride the mare if you want. We'll be leaving shortly."

"I'll help saddle the animals, and be ready. I guess the sooner we buy, the surer we will be of getting the best. What about feed?" he asked.

"As long as you select the ones you want, I'm sure they can keep them a few days till we leave. But those coming may want teams too; so best you get yours, I'm thinking."

The three were soon off toward the McGlothlins to buy their teams. The men were all busy at the camp; some were chopping wood; they didn't want to use up all the Jarvis' had cut. Zol was helping Sam with the building. He had built the house on wheels, and knew what to do.

The team of mules that her Dad had selected suited Jane; they were young and healthy-looking, and she gave the McGlothlins, fifty dollars in gold for the two. John went over the others that were in the fenced-in area by the barn. "What do you think of these two, Mr. Jarvis?" He held two by their halters. The two men looked at their teeth, felt their legs, looked at their hooves and decided that they were sound, and would do. John had his eye on a small healthy-looking mare when he priced the mules they wanted—the same as Jane had paid; John thought they should be less and offered seventy dollars for the three. After wrangling for some time they decided to trade, and would keep the animals till he was ready to leave. Jane took hers along, as she wanted to pick up a wagon in a few days. They left the McGlothlins and headed for the Browns to look at wagons. They had soon selected one, and the Brown brothers would build the framework for the canvas top and install it, saying it would be ready in two days.

On the way back, they stopped at a farm where they asked about buying potatoes and apples. Jane's father had thought to bring some sacks, and they filled one with potatoes and one with apples, another with turnips, and one with cabbage. They were tied together and put over the horses. Jane inquired about honey or molasses. She bought a gallon of molasses, and John bought a gallon, too. After their purchases they started back home. Jane intended to buy more just before they would leave and told the people she would be back.

When they arrived back at the farm, the men left whatever they were doing to inspect the team—announcing that it was a fine one. The mules were taken to the barn and stabled and fed.

Jane saw that Sam was coming along fine with the table and cupboard she had him working at.

"Laura, here are some things to cook. We will have to store them in the house on wheels and cover them to keep them from freezing. Have Nat, move the extra set of harness and bridles to the barn. The wash tubs can- be put in a corner to set the sacks in. The plows and farm things can be taken and stored in the shed till we get the other wagon. We'll move 'things around so we can get in the house and have some room. Do you know of anything that you think you will need? You and I will take Dad's buggy and go to the store after dinner and buy what we need. The other wagon will be ready in two days, and we can begin to get organized. I think we're making headway," Jane smiled at Laura.

"I'm so pleased with what you are doing with the work table; "I would never have thought of it. It'll make everything so much easier And handy to get to. I'm so happy to be with you; and Mary and John are so nice, too," Laura smiled shyly at Jane.

"What are you making for dinner?" Jane asked.

"Your brother brought over a big bucket of fresh milk. Now that we have apples, I'm going to make apple dumplings—I think everyone will like that," Laura said.

"Oh, that sounds delicious. Why don't we ask John and Mary's family or will it be too many to cook for?" Jane asked.

"We're going to have to borrow some of her bowls, so I think it is only right and I can make a few more; I'm going to cook them in our biggest pot; it'll be no trouble at all." She smiled, pleased that Jane wanted to invite the others.

"I'll get right at the apple peeling, Jane said, while you do the rest. I bought cinnamon and nutmeg too.

Laura set the big pot on the spider, and had Nat bring water to fill it and put more wood on the fire for her. She put a couple of the boards together to have a place to work.

"I have to borrow some things from Mary, and will invite them at the same time." Laura hurried off and came back with a big slit spoon to handle the dumplings with., Mary came back to help with the peeling. She and Jane soon had a large bucket of apples peeled washed and ready. Laura was making dough in the biggest Dutch oven. Jane could readily see that there were lots of things she would have to buy.

"The children are excited about apple dumplings, and my John can eat his weight in them. Thank you for inviting us. We want to make a list and get some things to cook before we leave this area. John said he got sargums—we sure like them on our biscuits in the morning. I like honey, too. We'll buy some as soon as we can. John is excited about the team and a riding mare—we'll need that I'm sure. As they told us, we will be able to sell them when we are through with them. He says they are fine horseflesh—and priced right." Mary talked as fast as she peeled apples.

"I think that will be enough, ladies," Laura told them. "If one of you will watch the fire so they don't boil over, we'll soon have some ready to eat.

Mary volunteered to clean up the dishes so that Jane and Laura could go to the store. Jane's brother Caleb had the team and buggy ready for them. Jane would drive them herself. They were soon on their way.

Mr. Chenoweth was surprised to see Jane but readily recognized her. "Jane! How are you? You look fit and well. I hear you finally became a doctor as you wanted, and that you did a fine job." He shook her hand up and down.

"I'm not really a doctor, although I had to take over the duties of one. I loved the work of trying to save lives, but at times it was very discouraging. This is my friend Laura McDowell. We have come to look over what you have for sale."

Jane smiled as he shook Laura's hand.

"You ladies just look around and I'll help when you're ready."

Jane started piling things on the counter. She picked up two chamber pots, with vines and flowers on them and one in a blue speckled enameled. Two dish pans, two big pewter mixing bowls, a large teakettle, a dozen tin cups, and a dozen enameled coffee cups, several knives a set of pewter flat wear—consisting of a dozen settings. "Laura, pick out the wooden and stirring spoons you want," Jane told her. "Get plenty as we won't be back this way very soon," she laughed. Jane spotted a lovely milk glass lamp, with a fancy hand-paintedglobe.

"Can that be packed so it won't break?" she asked.

"I have one packed by the company. It's come all the way from Philadelphia; it should be safe," Mr. Chenoweth told her.

"I want it if I have to carry it on my lap all the way to the Oklahoma Territory," she laughingly told him.

Jane saw Laura over by the dress goods, feeling and looking at the material. She walked over, "Do you see something you like?" she asked.

"It's all so lovely—I like the calico; I have several dresses, but none suitable for everyday wear on a farm," she answered.

"You pick out three lengths for you and three for me, with thread and trimmings. And something for underthings, too. You'll have the pleasure of making them up when we get home. Laura, find some soup bowls—about a dozen, and a couple of small cooking pots. I want to buy Andy some clothes too. Oh, yes, we all have to have sturdy shoes, so look for those too. Get a pair for Nat if you know his size, And sox too, and for you. Don't be stingy," she smiled at Laura knowing how much she was enjoying picking out things. She found shoes and clothes for Andy and shoes for herself with cotton stockings. She would let the menfolk come and buy their own.

"You know, Jane, you remind me of your sister-in-law Mammy Jane, when she was first married—how she chose the things she needed at Tom's house. She was just as choosy as your are, but she did good," the storekeeper told her. "Have you seen her yet?"

"No, but I'm going over just as soon as we get organized. We aren't sure when we will have to pull out and want everything ready. I can't wait to see their big house, I've heard so much about."

"It's a far cry from what she had to go to as a bride. They are known as one of the finest families around. You can be proud of her as well as your brother who has had a hard time recovering from the wounds he received-in the war."

As everything was loaded in the buggy, Jane called, "We'll see you soon." They were off—Laura beaming with pride, at having been asked to choose what she liked.

"I think we have everything now other than livestock—our cows, a couple small pigs, and some chickens, and the men some serviceable clothing. When we get our wagons sorted out we are ready to homestead land. How do you feel, Laura?"

"Oh, Miss Jane, I feel wonderful; you are so good to us," she said as tears stood in her eyes.

"No more of this Miss Jane stuff; we're family. I'm just Jane, as you are Laura. Let's go home." She flicked the reins and they were off.

Mary came over to oh, and ah, at all the things Laura and Jane had selected at the store.

"What beautiful material," she said as Laura showed the dress lengths she had chosen.

"We're going to be the best-dressed farm women in the area when Laura gets them all made up," Jane said with a laugh. "Clothing isn't so costly here, if you need anything. Do you have sturdy shoes?" Jane asked. "If not, you should get them here as there's a good selection."

The women talked over all the things and compared, and decided another trip to the store would be in order before the wagons pulled out.

❦ Chapter Thirty-Three ❦

Laura and Jane went to examine the new cupboard-table that Sam had been working on while they were gone. They were surprised that it was finished—and also the step-stool for Laura.

"My, isn't this nice!" They both said as they examined all the details, "Even a place for the coffee grinder so we don't have to look for it." The wash pan was in a slot made for it, with a hook for the towel below. "The plates will just fit here, and all the cups on the top; a drop-down holder for the flatware, and it pushes up when the door is closed. I can't believe that Sam built everything so nice," Laura's eyes shone with happiness, looking at all the conveniences she would have to aid her in cooking.

Mary stood by watching the two girls' reactions. "Sam borrowed a plate so he would be sure just how big to make the compartments. I think I am going to have John make a smaller one for me. We have so much piled in our wagon, it's hard to find anything. I'm beginning to look forward to living under my rock cliff," Mary said with a hearty laugh.

Jane and Laura laughed too. "This is the nicest thing I ever saw built" Laura said, "I love it. I have to find Sam and tell him right away."

"I saw the men going off with the teams. I think they are going to haul in some logs for wood as we don't want to use up all Mr. Jarvis has cut while we're here. The other wagons, when they arrive, may use some too," Mary told the girls. "I think I will do a little wash while I have the time. The children need some clean clothes, and I don't want to let them pile up on me," Mary said as she headed back to her tent.

"I'll go back to the house. I want to go see my sister-in-law tomorrow. I'll see if she has anything for sale; might as well give her the money as strangers. I want to talk to Dad, and choose the cows I want. Do you want to go along, Laura?"

"Thanks Jane; I'll stay here and wash all the plates and things and arrange the cupboard, and get everything ready for the evening cooking. I'm going to put on a big pot of beans and make cornbread. I'll make a big bowl of cold slaw too. Oh, I don't think we have vinegar—what will we do? Maybe Mary has some; I'll ask."

"Don't bother, Laura; I'll get some from Mamma for today and get a jug when we go back to the store; don't let me forget. I'll be back shortly—certainly in time for your slaw." Jane laughed as she went toward the big house.

Jane found her father sitting by the fireplace, "Dad, where are the cows you were telling me about? I would like to choose the ones I want. How much are you going to charge me for them?" she smiled at the startled look on his face.

"Well now! I know you're a rich woman now, so it'll be costly for you." He smiled at his daughter, with pride in his eyes.

"I think I know two you will like, one is with calf, and the other has a month old calf. She gives lots of milk—enough for the calf and your family too. The other will drop her calf in May; you should be at your homestead by then. I have another one that is fresh, for the Thompsons. Her calf can be put to another cow if they don't want to take a chance of driving it with the herd. I'll keep those three for you. I have others if anyone in the group that is to join you want any. I think Jane and Tom may have some too. Jane has lots of nice chickens, and a new litter of pigs. They need to sell some of their livestock, if you care to look," her father told her.

"I plan to visit them tomorrow if I may use the buggy. I may want to bring some things back—or should I leave them a few days? I hate to impose on you with all my animals, although I want to be ready when the wagons arrive to leave with them and not cause a hold up."

"You might as well get things together. There will have to be crates made for the chickens and pigs. How do you plan to take them?" he asked.

"I think on the wagon Ed will drive. They can be stacked at the back and taken out at night. I haven't discussed it with him yet but he won't mind I'm sure. Most of the farm equipment will go in his wagon and the food stuff will go in the house on wheels and in Laura's and Ned's wagon. About feed, I don't know what to do about that. I'll get a few bags of shelled corn or oats for the teams and put them wherever there is room. I may have to buy some hay along the way. Thank God I have the money to do so,"

Jane looked at her dad for approval.

"Until grass comes, it will be touch and go to feed so many animals. The train may provide some feed, but I'm not familiar with what they do. You'll know when they get here. Your milk cows need to be fed some if you expect to get milk," her father told her. You can load a little heavy as you start out. Your wagons will be getting lighter as you use things."

I'll have to wait until the other new wagon comes, then we can start loading things correctly. The extra harness I brought will be in use, and we can always put the saddles on the horses, and even some of the sacks of feed, if necessary, to lighten the load in the wagons at first." She looked at her father for approval.

"That's a possibility; you'll just, as you say, have to wait until the other wagon is loaded."

"I'm thinking about an extra team. The wagonmaster suggested everyone should have a spare. He also says we will be able to double our money on them out there—that people going farther will need to buy teams. I'm thinking of horses for the spare.

I think I remember some young-looking horses at the McGlothlins; do you remember?" Jane asked.

"Yes, I do remember some nice-looking horses, but I don't know if they are broken to harness. I expect any animals they have are broken for hauling. When John goes to pick up his team, we can look around. What time do you want to go to see Tom and Jane?"

"I'll go right after breakfast in the morning," Jane told him.

"I'll have the cows put in the lot at the barn, and have the buggy ready when you want to leave tomorrow. I want the Thompson's to see the cow I have for them, and I know you're anxious to see your two," her dad smiled.

"Yes, and I want to pay you for them. There are so many things to think of and do before we leave. I'll go back and help Laura, now that is settled; I doubt she will want any help though; she is so pleased with Sam's handiwork, he did a wonderful job. I'll see you later, Dad," she said as she started back to the wagons. She could smell the beans cooking as she neared the camp. Laura was busy putting the plates in their rack and standing back to see how they looked. Jane smiled to herself. She saw that Mary was hanging out clothes; she had stretched a line from a fencepost to the wagon wheel, and clothes were blowing in the slight breeze;

the sun was out and would soon dry them.

"Your beans smell good, Laura. My! Look at your beautiful cupboard; that looks nice and so handy," Jane smiled at the proud look on Laura's face.

"I love it. And your idea for the spider is wonderful. It's big enough that I can put the big pot and the coffee pot on at the same time. Will you be eating with us?" she asked.

"No, it will be the same while we're here. I'll spend as much time with my family as I can. I'll be going to see my brother's family early in the morning, and you do whatever you want. I would take you, but I'll be gone for a while and be bringing back a load of things.

"I think if it is a fit day tomorrow, I'll wash what clothes we have dirty; like Mary, I don't want them to pile up," Laura told her.

* * *

As soon as the sun came up the buggy was brought to the gate for Jane. She left Andy with his grandpa, who he was forming quite a liking for, and started off to see her brother's family.

As Jane came to the forks of Beech, she could see a beautiful, big ornate white house sitting on a knoll with an apple orchard in the front. The road winding up to the house passed between a lot of outbuildings, where she saw some people at work. As she made her way toward them, she looked first one way and then another. She was amazed at the beautiful home and surroundings that belonged to her brother and his wife. "I'm so proud of my brother and Mammy Jane. A lot of this is her doing, I'm sure."

As Jane came to the front gate, her sister-in-law came out onto the veranda, where Tom sat in a rocking chair, in the sun.

"Good Morning!" Jane called as she wrapped the reins around the gatepost.

"Well, just look who's here," her brother called.

"Come in," Mammy Jane invited, "Tom, I think it's too cool for you to sit out here; come Jane, maybe we can get him inside as that wind is a little cool yet," she said as she led Jane into the big vestibule.

"I wasn't sure I was in the right place; this is a big house; sure looks like someone has been busy while I've been gone," Jane said as she sat down by the fire.

"Mammy Jane built it while I was away during the war. She did most everything you see around the place," her brother told her.

"Tom, you know I didn't do it all. You've worked very hard, even with your war wounds hurting every step of the way. You won't listen to me about doing too much," She looked fondly at her frail-looking husband.

"Sister, you look fit. How did you make out in the war? Did you get to be a doctor like you wanted?" When Tom smiled at her, she could hardly see his lips for the beard he had grown after being wounded in the face.

Jane proceeded to tell them about Dr. Connolly disappearing for two days and what she had to do until her grandfather was found.

"We've heard most of this from the family. We heard about your marriage and the loss of your young husband. We were so sorry to hear of that," her brother said sadly.

"We were married for such a short time—only hours. He was a fine man, and a Major in the Army. He lived with his grandparents where I was visiting. His grandfather contracted pleurisy and pneumonia when he went looking for his grandson, and he died. I did all I could; he was old and feeble and should never have gone out in the dead of winter. Then Grandmother Barrlette, fell and broke her hip. Again, there was little I could do. I buried three of them in a very short time—the last of the Barrlette family. I found I couldn't stay there after that, So here I am," Jane smiled as she looked at her brother, (thinking he won't be around long either. He has consumption or I don't know my medicine.)

"What's this I hear that you're going West to homestead. Is that true?" Tom asked.

Jane laughed, "Yes, it's true. I inherited some money and I have a lot of help. A young couple is going to drive one of my wagons and will stay with me and I'm taking a black man who was born on the Barrlette plantation. He is an exceptional man and wanted to go with me. I also have a widower who wanted to go and offered to drive a wagon. I feel well-taken care of. Another family, with three children, will homestead next to me and came here with me. We all seem like one big family. Of course, there's my son—and she explained about Andy. I'm getting things together.

The wagonmaster went on into Pennsylvania to bring part of the train through here to pick us up. We will then meet the rest of the train on the Ohio and go on from there. I'm very excited about the venture."

Her brother laughed, "You wouldn't be planning on taking Timmy Miller with you this time, would you?" he chuckled at seeing the horrified look on his sister's face.

"I don't think I'd want to go that far away from familiar surroundings her brother said."

"I'm so excited; it's like one big party. I know we will have hardships, but there are enough of us to help each other. Mammy Jane, do you have anything you want to sell? I'm in the market for some chickens and pigs to name a few."

"I have a new litter of pigs—eight of them, and another sow due anytime. How many do you want?" she asked.

"How much are you selling them for?" Jane asked.

"They're eight weeks old; old enough so they can be weaned. How about two dollars a head?" she said.

"I'll take three—two females and a male, and I need some chickens; what kind do you have?" Jane asked.

"I have a mixed breed; they're good layers and still have meat on their bones for cooking. I can let you have as many as you want."

"I would like a dozen hens, as young as possible and two roosters. If you have potatoes or root crops and a churn of sour krout or pickled beans you want to sell, I'll take those. How about honey, or molasses?"

"I think we can fix you up. You'll want some oats, and corn, for your animals and for the chickens. I have that, too. Do you want to start picking out your chickens and pigs? Or will you spend the night with us?"

"I think I would like to pick what I need and be on my way as soon as I can. Do you have crates I can borrow and leave at Dad's? How about a young team of horses? I need one broken to harness; do you have any for sale?" Jane asked her sister-in-law.

"I have several young colts, but none that would do for a team yet. Wish I had—you could have them. I have sour-krout and pickled-beans in three-gallon churns; will that do? I have molasses but no honey."

"I'll take both the churns. Count the price of replacing the churns, as I can't empty them. Do you happen to have vinegar in jugs? If so, I'll take two jugs of vinegar and two of molasses. Have someone put the things in the buggy as I want to get back. I aim to go to the McGlothlins and try to pick up a spare team; the wagonmaster recommends that we have one," Jane told her.

Jane soon had the buggy loaded and was ready to leave "I'll write the folks, and you can share their letters. I'm so glad to see you both." She had told her sister-in-law to try to keep Tom separate from the family and about boiling his dishes and clothing. It seemed that Mammy Jane knew that her husband had a fatal disease and had already been taking precautions about it.

"Good luck!" The two called. Come back soon."

"Come visit me," Jane called laughingly, waving as she wheeled the buggy out the gate to the main highway. She had the buggy as full as they could pile things. They might come back for more potatoes. Jane said she would fix her a packet of seeds to take for her garden as she had saved plenty and could share them. As she left Mammy Jane handed her a small bucket with a lid on it, telling her to keep the seeds from getting damp till she planted them. Jane's eyes lingered on everything as she left, knowing she would never return or see them again. She knew she would never see her brother, and would hear before long that he was gone. Tears stung her eyes until she could hardly see to drive the buggy.

Jane arrived back at the barn with chickens squawking and pigs squealing, to the delight of the men who were in the barnyard sawing wood. She brought the buggy to a halt close to her house on wheels where they could unload the churns of sour krout and pickled beans. Ed hurried over and lifted them into the wagon, and moved them up to the front where Jane indicated she wanted them.

Laura stood watching the unloading. The chickens were put into a small shed close by the barn.

"You're sure collecting a lot of stuff, Jane, but we did forget one thing at the store—I need a rolling pin for pie dough," Laura told her.

"I got your vinegar, and more molasses; you can make the men pancakes for breakfast; they may like a change.

Mary couldn't stand not knowing what Jane had brought and came to look and comment. "How are you ever going to take so much, Jane? Will you have room?" she asked.

"I'll have three wagons; and as we use things, the wagons will get lighter. The further we go, the less we will have. I have three men and a boy to feed, and that takes a lot of food. When we get into the wilds we will be able to hunt. Do either of you know how to use a gun? she asked as she turned to look at the two women.

"I've done some fishing and a little hunting when I was at home; my pa taught me how to shoot," Laura said, "I've not hunted in some time though. Nat is a good shot, but he doesn't own a gun."

"I've shot snakes a few times," Mary said. "If I have to I can kill things. Do you think we will need to use guns?" "I think it best to be prepared. We are going to a wilderness, and there are renegade Indians and scavengers from the war still out there. I bought two guns, and I know Ed has his own. I'll get shells for it and get a couple more guns to take along. We will be hunting to eat before long. I hope I can remember everything," Jane laughed at the worried look on the two women's faces. "It'll be a while before you need to start looking over your shoulder," she told them.

"Laura, have you ever used a sewing machine? My mamma has one. You could make one of your dresses while we're here. It will go so much faster on the machine, if you want. You'll have some time as soon as we get things organized. The men can load the wagons; you'll have little to do there," Jane told her.

"Yes, I've used a machine. I would love to start sewing. I may have some time tomorrow if you think she won't mind." Laura said looked pleased.

"Oh, she won't mind. I'll tell her you will be up to use the machine. She has it in a room where there is a table to use for cutting I hope you can get a lot done on them, while we're waiting," Jane told her.

* * *

The next morning Jane spent a lot of time making lists of what was to go where. She had begun to think she had too much to take. She wanted to get a piece of canvas for a roll-up above the cupboard, in bad weather it would make a covering for them to be under, when working outside. She could get that at the Brown brothers when the new wagon was picked up. Sam would know just what she wanted done. "I wish I could take a rocking chair," she said; "but I know I just don't have room for one. I'll bet Sam can make me one when we get to the homestead.," She smiled thinking of Sam, and how much talent he had. If he had been a white man, he would have gone far.

In the afternoon when Laura was settled at the sewing machine, Jane asked Sam to hook up the buggy for her. She wanted to go to the store and get the rest of what she needed, and wanted to take Sam and get clothing for him. She asked Ed what size shoes he took as she could see the ones he wore were old and wouldn't last much longer. He gave her a strange look when she asked him. He was about the size of Sam, and she was sure she could find other things for him.

"Mary, do you need anything, or do you want to come along?" Jane asked.

"I'll see if John can keep an eye on the children as I would like to go with you. I still need to get shoes for everyone, and John could use some heavy work clothes." Mary hurried over where John was stacking wood. She came went to the tent for her reticule and was soon back. "I'm ready," she announced.

Mary hadn't been away from the camp and enjoyed the ride to the store, which was about a mile away. Sam tied the buggy and horses under a tree and went in to the store with Jane, as she had already told him she wanted him to come with her.

"Sam, do you know what size shoes you wear?" she asked him.

"No, Miss Jane, I'z never knows; they just buy me big ones once in a while," Sam said as he shook his head.

"Well, we're going to get you a pair that will fit your feet as you may have to do some walking. Come," she said as she went toward the counter where Mr. Chenoweth was standing.

"Good afternoon, Jane; what can I do for you today,?" he looked Sam over as he gave Jane the greeting.

"This is Sam; he's one of my drivers. He needs shoes and some other clothing; can you fit him?" Jane asked as she looked Mr. Chenoweth in the eye.

He stuck out his hand, shaking hands with Sam. "Good to meet you, Sam. I'll fix you right up. You're a lucky man to have Miss Jane here to work for," Mr. Chenoweth told him.

"That'z true enough sir. Yes Sir! Miss Jane a fine lady."

"Sit down, Sam and see if you can get your feet in these. They're size thirteen wide; they should fit."

Sam sat down and soon slid his big foot into the shoe. "My, that feel good; thez fit fine sir." Sam had a big smile from ear to ear. "Old Sam never had such a fine shoe before, never."

"I need another pair for another driver, in size twelve wide—just like this pair will do, and six pair sox—each size, and some sturdy work-clothing two pants, two shirts, and two Jimmisons; I'll need two repeating rifles, with about twelve boxes of shells. Do you have any hand guns—one of those, if you have them, with shells. Oh yes, I have orders for a rolling pin—to make pies. I guess four pie pans too." She smiled when she gave that order. "This is Mrs. Thompson," she said as Mary came over where they were. "I think she wants some things too when you get mine counted up and ready."

The shoes were soon ready. Sam had picked out two shirts—one in a blue plaid and one in red. Jane then selected a different pattern—one in blue and one in brown for Ed. They were all wrapped in brown paper. The guns were brought out for Jane to select what she wanted. They were soon finished, Sam took the things to the buggy while Mary was waited on. She soon had shoes for them all, and some sturdy pants and jackets for the boys, and for her husband.

When the packages were finished being wrapped Mary said, "I'm ready to go; I think I have everything." Turning to Jane as they left, she said, "We were wise to wait, as things are of better quality and less costly here than they were in Charleston. I didn't spend nearly as much as I thought I would."

"Good, you can buy potatoes for fifty cents a bushel and apples and turnips. My sister-in-law said she had plenty she could sell. The pigs were only two dollars each, if you want to take one along," Jane told her as they settled themselves in the buggy for the trip back.

As they traveled along, Sam broke into song. He had a wonderful voice and Jane loved hearing him sing the old gospel songs. Even the mules perked up their ears seeming to be listening. Sam entertained them all the way back to the farm.

"That was wonderful, Sam; I sure do enjoy hearing you sing. You have a good voice," Mary told him as she gathered her packages and said good-by.

Sam took the buggy to the barn and took care of the team.

The men were still cutting and stacking wood and her father would have enough to do all next winter if they continued. They felt it was the least they could do in return for staying on the farm, even though they felt more than welcome.

Jane saw Laura coming from the house where she had been sewing on her dress material.

"How did you get along?" Jane asked.

"I cut out one dress and have the main seams sewed, I will be able to finish it tomorrow, after I get things done here. I'm so glad you suggested it. Your mother and sisters are so nice, and they have a beautiful home. I wonder what it would be like living like that on so much land," she smiled shyly at Jane.

"We'll be going to pick up the other wagon tomorrow, and then to the McGlothlins to look at another team I want to get. Then we can get our wagons loaded properly, and can begin to see the end of buying and loading. I think we have enough of everything. Here, I brought you something" Jane handed the rolling pin and pie tins to her."

"Thank you, I'm not sure how I can bake pies yet, but I'll find a way," Laura told her, a big smile on her face.

"That'll be no problem when we get the house on wheels cleared out a little. The little stove in there has a small oven, and it will hold one pie tin, maybe two. We can use it for baking when necessary, or when it is raining," Jane told her

"I know that it has an oven. Laura's eyes got big when she remembered. That's wonderful, I'm sure we will be using it a lot on the trip."

"I'll see you in the morning., Do you need me to help with anything before I go up to the house? Can you cook for everyone? I'll help if you need me," Jane told Laura.

"You go ahead and enjoy your family as much as you can. I'll be just fine," Laura answered.

Jane started to the house. She was tired and would love to have a nap, but didn't feel that she could. She should visit with her mother and father as much as possible, knowing she might never see either of them again.

❧ Chapter Thirty-Four ❧

As usual Jane awoke when she heard the household coming to life. Today was going to be a very busy one, and she hurried with her toilet and went down to the dining room where everyone had begun to gather for breakfast.

"Good Morning!" she called as she went to the chair where she usually sat.

Good mornings were heard around the table. Some, she noticed, were in a grouchy voice. It took some people more time to get the sleep out of their eyes and voice than it did others.

"Today is the big day, Dad—we go for the new wagon. Maybe with another wagon, I'll have space to get to my bed in the house on wheels," Jane laughed. "When I was over at brother Tom's, he wanted to know if I planned to take Timmy Miller with me this time? Wasn't I awful to use poor Timmy to get my way? I wouldn't trade the time I spent with Gramps for anything. There were lots of tears but lots of laughs too. I want to go and spend some time with him, I miss him even yet." No one seemed to want to carry on a conversation this morning, so Jane began to eat in silence.

Her father cleared his voice, "What time do you want to leave? We'll have to take the team to bring the wagon home. If you plan to go on to McGlothlins to get horses, I think we should have Zol come with us and drive the wagon back."

Jane nodded, "Yes, I think we should. The wagon may not be ready by the time we arrive, so we can go on ahead. I'm anxious to get things sorted out and loaded, then I'll know how much feed and extras can be taken. Do you think I have too much already, Dad?" she asked looking anxiously at her father.

"I haven't gone over everything. As I said before, you can load a little heavier at first; as you are using things, the weight goes down; however, most of the supplies you have weigh in at a considerable amount. Salt, sugar and etc. are heavy. They all ate in silence for a while. Jane was going over in her mind the things maybe she could do without. Each item she pictured in her mind that she had bought was a necessity though, and she would have to find a way to take it. She turned to Zol, "You wouldn't want to go West, would you Zol? You could drive another wagon for me and maybe homestead some land when you get there." She smiled at the old man she had been through so much with, and who had brought her and her Gramps through the war safely.

"If I were twenty years younger, Jane, you wouldn't even have to ask. I'd be ready to join you in a minute. As it is, I don't think these old bones could stand much more jolting in a wagon. Dr. George would want to go too. We went to the Oklahoma Territory back in the twenties; it was a wild country then. It's tamed down some now; however, keep your eyes pealed for the Redskins. We didn't go as far as you plan. I understand that up around the Cimmeron it's a beautiful place with rich soil and plenty of trees. You'll like it there." He had a sad look on his weathered face as Jane looked at him.

"Oh, Zol, if you really could come along, how wonderful it would be. And Gramps—he hasn't been feeling well; I'm going to see him and have a long visit, maybe tomorrow, if I get a lot done today. I'll be ready in a minute, Dad, and then we will be on our way to pick up the wagon. I'll hurry," she said as she left the room and went back upstairs to get whatever she needed. Her saddlebags with her reticule and money would go on Cherokee, with her black doctor's bag. She never went anywhere without it.

She would leave Andy at the house as it was quite a ways to the McGlothlin's place and they were in a hurry.

Zol had the horses saddled and the team harnessed. He would ride one of the mules, and not have to take another saddle horse.

Jane went into the kitchen and fixed several sandwiches of ham and eggs to take along. They wouldn't be back for dinner, and there could be problems that would keep them well into the afternoon. She hurried to the front veranda, giving her mother a hug, "We'll be back soon. Thank you, Mamma," she called as she mounted Cherokee, "Keep an eye on my son."

"Andy and I are making hen's nests today; he's looking forward to it," Her mother called to her.

They rode at a fast pace, with Zol bringing up the rear with the mule team, and were soon at the Brown brothers where they could see the newly covered wagon sitting in the front of the shop.

"Looks as though they have it ready," her dad commented.

"Yes, it seems so. I want to get a tarp to put over our kitchen of the house on wheels. I'll have Sam put it on so it can be rolled up and tied to make a shelter if we need it to cook," Jane told him.

"That sounds like a good idea. You sure are going to have a modern covered wagon to travel in. Everyone will be envious," her father remarked.

Jane let out a joyful laugh, "I'm going to miss my family; I don't know when I'll be back; if the railroads get better, maybe sometime. But we can keep in touch by writing. Promise me that you will; I know I'll be lonely," she looked at her father her eyes bright with tears.

"If I know you, you'll be too busy to be lonely. You have a long row to hoe in front of you, daughter. I know you'll do well. You have a good start, and when the right man comes along, you'll be raising a family. Your Andy is a fine boy, and smart. You have enough people around you that we won't worry too much. Your Sam worships you, and he is a fine man. I'm glad you brought him along. The Thompsons will be wonderful neighbors to you. You were wise to decide to share the land that was next to you, and I'm sure you will all work together to help each other. You don't know how proud your mother and I are of you."

Jane couldn't keep the tears from standing in her eyes. She loved her mother and father and was so glad she could share this time alone with her dad. They had talked for hours, and she had learned just how much they had worried about her and how much they cared.

Jane dismounted and looked the wagon over. She was pleased with the canvas covering. They had done a good job putting a draw string in each end that could be closed when the weather was bad. I'm very pleased, you've done a wonderful job. If you have a couple of squares of tarp throw those in too, I need something to go under my chicken coops." The price was decided on and Zol was hooking up the team. He would return to the farm; only she and her father would go to look at the horses.

When they reached the McGlothlin farm, they saw two of the men at the corral working with some colts—putting bridles on them and walking them around; then next placing saddles on their backs and walking again. One colt tried to run with the saddle, but they held him firmly by the bridle, stroking him and talking softly to quiet him. This routine would go on for several days, then a heavy sack of corn or something would be tied to the saddle to add weight before they would try to ride the animal. By that time, usually there would be little difficulty in mounting and riding them a short distance. Taking time with the breaking in always made for a better riding animal.

Jane and her father dismounted, tying their mounts to the fence, and stood watching the men work. Jane's eyes went over all the herd that was in a pen next to where the men were working. There were several nice-looking mules. She also noticed a couple of horses that she liked. They were both bays, with black manes and long black tails, well-matched and looked young and healthy. If they were broken to harness she wanted those two.

"How about those two bays, Dad?" she asked.

"That would be my choice if they will pull; you'll want to try them here. You don't want to get on the trail and have a problem with them. I don't think the boys would tell you wrong though, but it's best to be sure."

Just then Hurshel came to the fence to talk to them. "Are you in the market for more mules? We just got in five fine animals yesterday, from over in Roane County. They're broken and gentle. As gentle—as a mule ever is," he said with a laugh.

"They look like a fine bunch, but Jane says she wants horses this time. She needs a spare team to take along, just in case they are needed. The wagon boss recommends it. What about those two matched bays; are they broken in?" he asked.

"Let's go take a closer look; come around this way," he led them along the fence to another gate. "They're a fine pair of mares, four years old, and, yes, they're broken to harness, and saddle too." He went over to them, and catching them by their halters, brought them toward the two.

"Easy to catch," Jane remarked.

"That's a good feature. The boys are easy with their stock and handle them with gentleness. I like that; makes for calm animals and easy to handle," her dad told her.

"Do you want to see them work, Tom?"

"I think Jane wants to know what they will do. How much are you asking for these two?"

"I can let you have them for a hundred and a quarter. They're fine mares. I'll harness them and let you see them pull." He hollered for his brother to come help. They soon had them harnessed and hooked to a large cut tree that was outside the lot for that purpose. They pulled together without any problem—both straining into the traces together.

"They look good, daughter," her father said.

"I love them. Andy wants to raise horses. Maybe we will be able to breed these." Jane had a pleased look on her face.

Hurshel came up to them while his brother unhooked the team from the tree. "They're just as good on wagons or buggies too," he said.

"Is that as good as you can do on the price? I was hoping to get a team for not over a hundred. I've bought one from you already, and brought you another buyer. I may have some more buyers for you in a few days," Jane told him.

"Let me see what my brother says." He walked over and the two men talked together for a few minutes.

"We'll let you have them for a hundred. Are you taking them today?" he asked.

"Yes, we'll take them with us," her father said. "Mr. Thompson will be over to get his team of mules and mare in a day or two."

Jane went to Cherokee and took her reticule from the saddle bags, and gave him the hundred in gold. "Could I have a bill of sale please?" she asked.

Her father went to his horse and took some rope he had brought and went to the mares. "Can we leave the halters on and I'll send them back by Thompson?" he asked as he looked at Hurshel.

"That'll be fine; we have plenty. Be sure to send us some more buyers as we have a nice bunch of animals here," he smiled at Jane, his snow white teeth looking even whiter in his tanned face.

"I'm sure some will want animals," Jane told him. "Thanks for taking such good care of us; and good luck," she said.

They headed home. After riding some distance they stopped in a cleared space, tied the animals to trees, and ate the sandwiches Jane had made.

"My, they are beautiful; I'm so pleased; Andy will have a fit. I think I'll let him name them," she told her father.

"You got a good buy on them, I would say; they are fine mares," he rubbed his hand down the one nearest to him. "And they're gentle as can be. You can ride these horses as well as work them," he told her.

They arrived back at the farm in the early afternoon. Everyone seemed to be busy with the men still cutting and hauling wood. Jane turned over the mares to Ed and Nat who both looked them over, admiring them.

"That's a fine team," Ed told her. Walking around them, rubbing first one and then another, he said to her, "This one is in foal or I don't know my horse flesh."

"In foal? Oh, my, I'll bet the McGlothlin boys didn't know that. If it's true, I got a real bargain. I was telling Dad I wanted to breed them. If possible, I would like to use Cherokee if we can. I love that animal."

"He would make a fine stud for them. And yes, he is a fine animal. It's wonderful that he recovered from the run from the soldiers, Sam told me about it. Not many do, they're usually never any good again," he continued petting them.

Jane could tell that Ed loved animals and would take good care of them. "Put them in the field with the cows. They should be all right there. When you finish could you help us rearrange and load the new wagons; since you will be driving this one, you'll know what to do. She went back to the wagons; they had parked the new one close to the others so they didn't have to carry things far.

She looked for Laura and not finding her, she went to Mary, "Do you know where Laura is? She doesn't seem to be around," Jane said.

"She went up to sew at your mother's, while Sam did the canvas overhang for you. He just finished and went to put his tools away; I wish we had one on our wagon too. We may put one on. It would be a big help when we don't set up the tent, but canvas is heavy; it may be too much." Mary looked doubtful. "Looks as though you found a fine team of horses. If you needed Laura for something, maybe I can help," Mary told her.

"We're going to rearrange the wagons. I think maybe the men can do that with me bossing." Jane saw where a small platform had been added on the other wagon to set the water barrel on, and she saw Sam coming with his tools and boards to add one to the wagon they had just brought in. He didn't wait to be told, but just went ahead when he knew what was wanted.

"Sam, you sure are busy. That platform looks like just what is needed, and I see you finished the canvas cover for the kitchen. It looks good. Thank you," Jane smiled at him.

"I'z gonna' do the platform on this wagon, you'z gonna' load it now,?" he asked.

"Yes, but you go ahead with your job. Nat and Ed will do that. We'll have to bring everything out and see how we can load it. Do you want your anvil under the seat in front? Will that be the best place for it and for your tools?" she asked looking at him.

"I'z expect that be best. I can get them out easily there." He scratched his head while he thought on it.

Ned went to the shed and begun to bring the farm implements over to put into the wagon. It took both men to manage the anvil and to lift it up and put it under the wagon seat. Next they fastened the plow along the bed of the wagon, removing the handles so it would fit flat on the opposite side from the water barrel. The hoes and shovels would go through slots of leather nailed on the wagon bed. They would be held firmly but easy to remove if they needed them. There was a place for the broad ax too. Both wagons had the same things along the sides. That took care of some of the things that had taken so much space. Two extra plow blades were put under the wagon seat. The sacks of grain were laid down both sides, crosswise the wagon with a small walk space between. They were piled two deep. The two beds for Sam and Ed would be put on top of them, with the chicken coops and pig coop toward the end where they would be lifted off at night. Jane hoped that the smell wouldn't linger in the wagon. They would put hay under the coops and the canvas she had gotten would cover it. The hay could do for one feed for the animals. One bag of the salt and one of sugar were put in the house on wheels, also, one of the four sacks of coffee grains. The two barrels—one of flour and one of corn meal were put in the McDowell's wagon. They were placed up at the front. One of their trunks was placed under the seat with the two big iron pots used for cooking, where they could be gotten at easily. The other trunk put by their bed. A load of hay would be put into the wagon and their bed put on top of it. A few more sacks of feed could be added to their wagon. The churns of pickled food, the apples, potatoes, cabbage, and other food stuff would go into the wagon on wheels. After taking out the two trunks, there was room for the other cooking and root vegetables in the tubs under the bunks. The only thing Jane was concerned about was the flour and meal, but Laura assured her that she could get at them without difficulty.

Jane called, Ed and Sam—how about going over the wagons to make sure they are loaded equally, and not too much in either wagon. Do you think the barrels are stable?" Jane had had a rope put around the barrels and tied to the front seat so they couldn't slide out of place. She had wedged the churns in together putting other things around them and they seemed solid. The only thing left to store was the spider. "Where can we put that she asked?" She noticed the big wooden buckets were hung on the back swinging from the wagon bed, with a lantern hanging in each bucket to protect their globes from breaking.

Sam looked around, "We'z hang it on Laura's wagon in the back." I'z make a hook and tie it down so'z it don't clang."

After looking everything over, Jane was satisfied that everything was as tidy and secure as they could make it.

"Ed, do you think the chickens and pigs will smell up your wagon till you can't sleep in it?" Jane asked anxiously.

"Don't you worry about it; we'll leave the back flap open and plenty of air can get in. I expect Sam and I'll be smelling worse than the chickens by two or three days," he laughed as he looked at Sam, knowing how he liked to keep clean. "The tarp can be washed every night and it shouldn't get that bad. It'll all work out. I'm sure we will be making changes as we go along. It'll take a day or two on the trail to get settled in.

Everything will be fine, Miss Jane. You've got plenty of everything and much more than most will have. If we can hang on till we get some grass for the animals, we'll be in good shape. I think we can relax for a few days now till we leave," he smiled at the worried look on Jane's face.

They were all finished and Laura had come back and was getting things ready to start cooking.

"I hope you can find things," Jane told her. "If you want to know where things are, just ask, I'll tell you. What do you plan for supper?" Jane asked.

"I have beans from yesterday. We'll have beans and cornbread, and I'll make some apple dumplings. Ed said your calf can't drink all the milk your cow gives, so he started to milk her this morning and will milk her again tonight. We should have enough milk. Is that all right?" she ask.

"It sounds fine with me," Jane said. Who is that coming into the compound?" she asked as she watched a man riding through the gate. Suddenly she recognized him.

"That's Jason Turner! I didn't think he would come so soon. I wonder if something is wrong? I'm glad we had that mess cleaned up before he got here. I'm so smelly and dirty, but it can't be helped." She stood her ground and waited till he rode up.

"Howdy, ladies," he said as he doffed his hat. "Looks as though we have a wagon train ready to go here," he smiled at Jane taking in her rumpled attire.

"We just now finished loading the extra wagon. I think we have everything we need and have the wagons evened out so the teams can manage them. Get down, Mr. Turner. I'll have someone attend your mount," she smiled at him as Ed came and took his horse.

"Don't worry, Mr. Turner. He will be rubbed down, and fed, and watered," Ed told him.

"Thank you, Ed. I appreciate that," Jason told him.

"Excuse me, Mr. Turner. If you would like to look around, I'll be with you in a minute and take you up to meet my folks." Jane didn't wait for an answer and hurried into the house on wheels. She opened her trunk and took out the 'Ashes of Roses' silk dress. She intended for Jason to see her looking like a lady tonight after seeing her the way she was now. She took out clean underclothes from the scented trunk, her bone shoes, and the things she would need; putting them into a pillow case lay them across her arm and was ready to go.

She went over to the tent where Jason stood talking to John and Mary, "You see we're all right at home, Mr. Turner. I'm ready if you would like to go to the house and meet my family," she smiled shyly at him.

He turned, "I'll see you two later," he said to the Thompsons. Turning to Jane, his eyes sparkled, "I thought you had agreed to call me Jason. Looks as though you have been busy, I knew you wouldn't waste any time. Are those your animals over there?" he asked looking toward the pen where the cows and horses and mules were.

"Yes, we just bought the team of bays today for a spare as we were advised. The cows I've gotten from my father, as well as the mule team for the extra wagon. I have grain for the animals, and I think everything we will need. I'll show you everything tomorrow." She hurried her steps toward the house not wanting to answer any more questions.

Jane's father was on the veranda when they reached the house. "Dad, I would like to present Jason Turner, who is the scout for the wagon train, and who managed for me to get a choice piece of land for homesteading. Jason, my father, Thomas Jarvis. And here is my mother—Mamma, Jason Turner, scout for the wagon train."

"Come in, Jason. I feel as though I know you since I've heard so much about you from everyone," Mrs. Jarvis said in her sweet voice.

They took him into the living room, and they all sat down by the fire. Jane turned to them.

"Would you excuse me while I get cleaned up for supper? I've had a busy day."

Jason stood as she left the room. "That's some daughter you have there Mr. and Mrs. Jarvis," he said with a proud smile on his face.

"Yes, she is a fine young woman. She's been very stubborn about this war thing, but I guess she doesn't take after any strangers. She did very well and we're proud of her. I don't think we will worry so much at her going West. She has a fine bunch of people to help her."

"Excuse me," Mrs. Jarvis said, "I'd better see how supper is coming along. Tom, show Jason where to wash up, and we'll have a bed prepared for you tonight. No excuses," she said as she sailed toward the kitchen.

"I see you're surrounded by determined women, Mr. Jarvis," Jason laughed as he said that.

"I can see that you figured it out fast," Tom said. They both laughed together.

"Jane looked at herself in the mirror and thought to herself, "what a bedraggled looking person," she blushed to think Jason saw her looking like that. She said to the mirror, "Well, I'll remedy that; he'll see the greatest transformation he has ever been witness to in his life!" She smiled to herself as she took her hair down and poured water into the wash basin. Removing all her clothing, she washed from top to toe with her lavender-scented soap, pouring one pan of water into the chamber pot. She poured out another and washed and scrubbed until her skin tingled. She put on the flimsy under garments she had bought in Charlotte before her marriage. She shook the wrinkles from the silk dress, and pulled it over her head, and stood looking at herself as she fastened the tiny buttons at the front. Picking up her hair brush she brushed and brushed till her hair crackled and glistened. She rolled it up and placed the combs where the pearls would show, and pushed pins in here and there till she was satisfied. Some of her hair that had gotten wet was curling around her face and neck making a soft halo. She stood looking at herself, remembering when she bought the dress— 'Ashes of Roses' was the color the saleslady had told her. She turned in front of the mirror, looking over first one shoulder then over the other. "Ashes of Roses and War!" she said as she looked. Stepping into her bone slippers, she was ready. Picking up a lacy handkerchief, she went to the stairs. She took a deep breath as she started down, knowing her family would be surprised to see her dressed in silk for supper, but she wanted to look nice for one evening at least.

Her father and Jason still sat by the fireplace. She saw Jason had washed and changed his travel soiled shirt for a clean one. His hair gleamed in the firelight and he looked up as Jane was about half way down the stairs.

His face glowed, and he was smiling as he got to his feet. Then her father stood and turned; they both stood looking at her. "What a beautiful daughter you have, sir," Jason said to her father.

"I have several beautiful daughters; but Jane is special, as is her mother, who is also beautiful."

Jane knew he was confused to see her so dressed when most wore silk only to funerals or weddings. Her mother came into the room as she walked to the fireplace and caught her breath as she looked at Jane.

Going to her, she gave her a hug, "My you look nice; it's good to see you in something besides dark, work clothes. Come, supper is ready." She stepped to her husband and took his arm and proceeded to the dining room.

Jason took Jane's arm and followed, leaning over to whisper, "You're lovely, and smell so nice," he smiled into her eyes.

Jane blushed; she knew she looked different than usual and she felt pretty.

The table was set with a snowy white cloth and with the dishes Jane had sent from Barrlette House. It looked lovely. "Mamma, you're using Barrlette dishes; thank you I'll remember this always," tears had welled in Jane's eyes as she looked around the beautiful table.

There was lively conversation around the supper table. Jason was telling them some of the things that happened on wagon trains, and how helpless some were who went West. "It's no place for greenhorns. This wagon train that we are putting together is a hearty bunch; I think they can all pull their weight."

"Are there any other females going alone?" Jane's brother, Caleb asked.

"No. However your sister isn't exactly alone; she has a young couple who will be living with her, plus two other very big and brave men. I'd say she was better protected than she'd be as just husband and wife. She has also been through four years of war and lived in very primitive conditions. Your sister is much stronger than most females, as you put it." Jason answered.

"I'd hate to go up against her," Caleb hurried to say, with a laugh.

Turning to her father, Jason asked, "Do you have any beef cattle you want to sell? I'll need to locate about twelve—one or two-year-old for beef.

"I have eight two-and-half year old steers, that I plan to sell this spring. They're in good shape; been grain fed all winter. My son Tom and his wife live close. I think he said he had four; that should fill your needs. Do you need any feed? or horseflesh? We'll look at the ones Jane has bought in the morning. The McGlothlin boys have some nice animals yet. I'll be glad to take you to see them," her father told him.

"I want to go see my Gramps tomorrow; would you like to go along Jason? I would like you to meet one of the finest men that ever walked this earth," she smiled up at Jason.

"I'd love to meet him. If we could go early, then I can look around and see what is for sale in this area. I don't know how many will want food or such. There are ten wagons and several animals that will be here by the end of the week. We will spend two days and then head out. I'm hoping I can find space for them to camp for that time. Do you have any suggestions Mr. Jarvis?" Jason asked, looking toward her father. "We'll need a pen for the herd if possible. We'll be coming through some rough country and need to rest up. I'll also need some hay for the animals as the grass isn't up enough yet."

"I think we can fix you up. Jane has several animals penned, and there's room for more. They will be together for the trip so they might as well get used to being together. I can let you have feed for the time you're here. If you need more, we can find some for you," her father told him.

"I appreciate that." Jason seemed to be pleased that everything could be taken care of in one place.

Everyone turned in a couple of hours after having supper, getting ready for a busy day ahead.

Jason thanked Mrs. Jarvis for a lovely dinner and Tom for all his help, and was shown to his room. He was looking forward to a good night's sleep in a real bed.

❧ Chapter Thirty-Five ❧

Jane was up early; she wanted to get an early start to her grandfather's, so she and Jason could be back to go with her father to her brother Tom's place. Jason was interested in beef cattle, and it would be an opportunity for Tom to sell what he had.

Nat had saddled Jane's and Jason's horses and brought them to the front gate, ready for when they wanted to leave.

Jane had dressed carefully and put on her best riding habit (which was a medium blue with a purple trim,) and a hat to match. Jane had refused to ride side saddle, even before she had left home and had rode astride all through the war. In her opinion it was just too uncomfortable to ride in a twist on a side saddle. Besides, she liked a spirited horse and liked to run them. She knew she was looked at by some of the so-called ladies as being ridiculous riding astride. She would give her nose a twitch and do it anyway.

The breakfast table showed some vacancies as she sat down; however, Jason was there. When she came in, they were both served a hot plate from the kitchen of pancakes, sausage, fried apples, and eggs. There was a big pitcher of sargum molasses on the table and steaming coffee by their plates.

Her mother came in and sat down. "Good morning, Jane, Jason," she said, a smile lighting her face.

"Where is everyone?" Jane asked.

"Your father was up most of the night. There were two cows that dropped their calves last night and there was some trouble; he just got to bed. Said to tell you that he would be ready when you get back from your grandfather's to go to Tom's to look at the cattle."

"Jason and I are leaving right away so I can spend some time with Gramps, if he feels up to it. We will be back before noon." Jane looked at Jason and saw he had finished his breakfast.

"My, that was good, Mrs. Jarvis, I'll be so spoiled that I'll starve on the way West. I love pancakes, and those were the best apples

I've ever eaten. Thank you for having me here."

"I'll be right back; I have to get my bag from upstairs." Jane hurried off and they soon heard her coming back down the stairs. She was carrying the saddle-pockets that she took everywhere with her. "Ready, Jason. Let's hit the road."

Her mother followed them to the ~veranda and stood watching as they both mounted; she waved to them and they both waved back, with Jane blowing her a kiss.

"You have a wonderful family, Jane; such a lovely mother and a wise father. They seem very much in love even now."

"Yes, they are very devoted. I think if anything happened to my mother, my dad would just fold up and blow away. They're never away from each other."

They rode in silence, each deep in their own thoughts. Jason glanced at Jane now and then not letting her know he was watching her. She seemed deep in thought as they rode along.

"We're almost there; right around that next bend in the road you'll see their house. I can't wait to see Gramps. I do hope he feels well. Do you have family, Jason? You've never mentioned anyone."

"No. I don't have anyone that I know of. I was an orphan, raised in a home till I was old enough to be on my own. I don't even know my name. They gave me the name of the home when I was small, 'Turner Home for Orphans'."

"Oh, I'm sorry. I didn't mean to bring up unhappy memories on such a lovely morning. I'm truly sorry, Jason."

"Don't be; it doesn't bother me; it's been a long time ago and all I have ever known. I did enjoy the loving feeling in your home though since I never had it myself."

"Believe me, it wasn't always loving. When we were growing up, there was always some of us fighting, and when my brother Joshiah joined the Confederacy during the war, there was almost a war in our front parlor," she laughed, as tears came into her eyes, remembering losing her brother. "He was no longer recognized as a member of the family, even to this day."

They rode into the yard and tied their horses to the hitching rail, and went toward the front door. The door opened and there was her lovely gray-haired grandmother waiting with open arms.

"Gram, oh Gram, I've missed you, This is our wagon scout, Jason Turner. Where's Gramps?"

"He's not too good, Jane; he's in by the fire, come on in. Nice to make your acquaintance, Jason." They shook hands and she led them into the room where her husband sat in a rocking chair bundled in blankets.

Jane ran over to him, "Gramps, Gramps," she knelt on the floor, her head in his lap as he patted her shoulder. Tears were streaming from her eyes when she raised her face to look at him.

"Now! Now! Jane; remember tears never solve anything." He leaned forward and kissed her forehead.

"How many times you've told me that," she said, as she kissed his cheek. "How are you, Gramps? I've come to take you with me out West to homestead a farm. This is Jason Turner, our wagon train scout. I'm going in our wagon on wheels, and Sam put on new wheels and a new tongue, so it's like new again."

"You're a little late, darling. I've been West and homesteaded land in the early twenties. It was wild then; it's tamed down a lot since that time. Didn't Zol tell you about it? We had us a time, old Zol and I. Your grandmother never forgave me for dragging her all that way and then turning around in five years and coming back. I made my money—a lot of it. I hope you will be as lucky as I was," he sat thinking. Jane noticed his hands starting to shake, and knew she was tiring him.

"I've missed you, Gramps. I wouldn't have missed the four years we spent together for anything. It was rough at times, but I loved watching you work. And I learned so much. Thank you grandfather for letting me tag along."

"I don't know what I'd a done without your help. I'm just about done now. I'll soon be joining some of those who I tried so hard to save. Remember, no tears; that's my girl," he said as Jane smiled. He turned to Jason, "Young man you take good care of my granddaughter; she's been through a lot and deserves to be looked after now. Thank you for coming—I wanted to see you. I'll have to get back in bed now. Good-by darlin'." He kissed her forehead as he pulled himself up from the chair.

"Good-by, Gramps, I love you." Tears streamed down Jane's cheeks. She turned blindly to Jason and he opened his arms and held her close, as she sobbed against his chest.

Her grandmother soon returned after helping her husband to bed. "I'm glad you caught him when he knew who you were, he has bad days. Sometimes doesn't know who I am; he can go anytime now. His poor, big loving, heart has worn out. Don't cry, child; he wouldn't want you to." Jane went from Jason's arms to her grandmother's, holding on to her and sobbing.

"I love you, Gram. Take care of yourself; I'll write to you. Is there anything I can do?"

"Just say a prayer that God will take his hand, and he will cross the river without pain. It'll be soon. Good luck to you, child. And know that we love you wherever you are. Thanks for bringing her, Jason." She walked them to the door, seeming to want to get back to her sick husband.

* * *

Jane's father was ready to go when they returned. He had the buggy hitched and ready waiting out by the hitching rail. "I wasn't sure if you would want to bring something back; knowing you, you'll have another pig or more chickens to bring," he smiled at Jane, seeing she had been crying. "How were things at your grandfathers?"

"Gramps knew me; we had a nice talk, but he isn't well. Gram is very worried about him; said some days he doesn't know her." Tears sprang to Jane's eyes as she told him. "Pick me up at the wagons, as I want to see if Mary wants anything, and we have to take their crates back." She mounted Cherokee and rode to the compound.

"Mary? Mary? Did you decide if you wanted a pig or not? The coop Sam made, I think, will hold another one. I don't know how much they'll grow in four months; it may be a little crowded then." Jane smiled at Mary as she came to see what she was yelling about.

"Bring me one—a female; and if you have room, a bushel of potatoes, and one of apples. Are you leaving now?"

"Yes. Where's Nat?" Just as she asked, he came over.

"Do you want me to take Cherokee?" he asked. "Please, and bring the two crates that I brought the chickens and pigs in; I want to return them. The buggy is coming and we are going in it. Thanks Nat.

Jason and her father kept up a conversation discussing everything under the sun. Before they knew it they were at her brother Tom's place. He was on the piazza in his rocking chair, with a throw across his legs.

"Good morning son, how are you today?" his father asked. By then Mammy Jane had come out on the piazza.

"Good morning Mr. Jarvis, Jane," she nodded to both and looked questioningly at Jason.

"This is Jason Turner, our wagon scout. Jason, Mammy Jane and my brother Thomas." They all shook hands.

"What brings you out, Jane? Do you want more pigs?" she asked with a smile. "I have another ten today—a new litter. I'm being overrun with pigs. If you know anyone who wants any, I have them."

The two women left the men to talk and went to the pig pen. "I've brought your coops back. My friend, Mary, wants a female, and a bushel of potatoes, and one of apples if you have them, and I'll take a bushel of each. I think Jason will buy your steers for beef, and maybe some grain. You can get rid of whatever excess you have. I brought a sack to put the pig in till I get it back."

Jane stepped into the pig pen and chose a female pig and set it down over the fence. "It'll follow us, I think. I'll have one of the boys go to the mounds where the apples and potatoes are holed and get them for you. When will you be leaving? That's a fine-looking man you have in tow; is he yours?"

"He is a fine-looking man. No, he is the wagon scout; he advised me to homestead the acreage he had picked out for himself. He had chosen two sections, and the Thompson family took one section and I took the other. It's choice land he tells us, but with so many going out, he was afraid someone else would grab it. As long as he is working, he can't improve it so he can't homestead it now. I appreciate it a lot. He knows the area, as he said 'like the back of his hand.' He's been very helpful."

"You'd better grab him," Mammy Jane said. "I see a spark there—the way he looks at you." She saw Jane blush when she said that.

As they returned to the house they entered where the water well was. Jane glanced against the wall and saw the big black-snake whip that Mammy Jane always had handy.

"Is that the whip you taught me to use when I was growing up?" Jane asked her sister-in-law.

"The same one. I have a newer one now. Here, take it with you, you'll maybe need it with all your animals. Can you still use it?"

Taking it down they both walked back out into the yard.

"Let's just see." Jane moved her wrist around and around getting the feel of the whip, snaked it out and gave a quick pull cracking it till it sounded like a gunshot. She let out a chuckle as she looked at her sister-in-law, "I haven't forgotten, and I'll bet neither have you."

"It may come in handy to you; it did to me once. I'm never without it when I'm on horseback, even now. You've not forgotten what I taught you. Keep it with you, as there's lots of rattlesnakes where you're going. I've taken the head off many a snake with that whip, and never had to get off my horse.

Let's go see what the men have done about the cattle."

When they went toward the front of the house, they saw the men over at the barn, and the two women started over to hear what was going on. The four steers were milling around in the lot that surrounded the barn, as they all stood watching."

"Those are nice looking beef," Jane said.

Jason spoke to Tom, "I'll take all four, and if you have some grain, about five hundred pounds of that. What are you asking for grain?"

Mammy Jane spoke, "Three dollars a hundred for oats or corn, she told him, and forty dollars each for the steers."

"I'll give you a total of one hundred sixty dollars for everything; that's a little over thirty-five dollars a head for your steers, Jason said."

"You drive a hard bargain," Mammy Jane told him. "Since you're taking them all, and a friend of Jane's, it's settled."

"I thank you, Mrs. Jarvis. We may want a load of hay if you have it; we'll be over tomorrow to get the beef; I'll know by then. I'll have a bill of sale and your money when I come. It's good doing business with you." Jason tipped his hat to her.

Mammy Jane went to her husband, and said, "Tom, you shouldn't be out here so long. Let's go back to the house. The girls have dinner ready, and we'll eat before you leave." She took Tom's arm and led him toward the house.

"After they had eaten, Mammy Jane said, "I have something to show you, Jane, that you may be in the market for. While they load the buggy, we'll go look." She led Jane to an out building, where from a pile of hay in the corner a bunch of fuzzy puppies came tumbling toward her. Jane stooped down and gathered a lovely white and lemon spotted one into her arms.

"Oh, you sweet thing. My heavens how many do you have? They're beautiful."

"My collie, Old Nell, had ten; they're ready to wean, ten weeks old; I have to get rid of some of them. What do you say? You'll need a dog, and they won't be easy to get where you're going." Jane knew she would take one. She had already fallen in love with the female she had picked up. It was licking her face as Jane tried to hold it far enough away that it couldn't reach her. She was laughing at the rambunctious puppy.

"I'll take two; give me that black and white male for the Thompsons; if they don't want it I'm sure I can find someone who will. The yonguns will go crazy over them. "Jane took the other one Jane handed her, and with a puppy in both arms started back to the buggy.

The buggy was loaded with the pig squealing in the sack as Jane came toward them laughing, with an armful of squirming puppies. Mammy Jane had a pleased look on her face. Jason smiled as he called, "I'll see you tomorrow Mr. and Mrs. Jarvis; thank you. Those are beautiful puppies. Does she have more she wants to be rid of?"

"Yes, eight more, if anyone wants them." Jane answered.

"When they drove into camp, Andy came racing toward them, "What have you brought, Maw?" When Jane handed him the puppy, she thought his eyes would bug out of his head. He was speechless for once. Sarah came up and she put the other one in her arms. Her big smile lit up her whole face, as she took off running to show her folks, with Andy tagging along.

"I'd say they liked them, wouldn't you?" Jason asked with a smile.

* * *

The time was flying by. Jane was in and out of her house on wheels rearranging her things to make more room. Nat and Laura had moved into their own wagon. Jane had shown Laura how to make the strip of pockets and nail them down the wall beside her bed to hold small things she would need. Mary made some for herself and fastened them to the staves that held the tent covering on the wagon. She also made one for Sarah, so she could keep her hair ribbons and girl things in them.

Jane took one of the pretty chamber pots and gave it to Laura, leaving one for herself. The darker one she put into the wagon that Ed would be driving. He saw her and his face became flushed. "That's in case you have to throw up in the night and can't get outside. It'll come in handy," she smiled at Ed as he nodded in acknowledgment.

The day arrived when the rest of the wagons were supposed to come. By early morning the children were watching for the wagon train, so excited that they said, "I can't wait another minute."

Jason hearing them said, "I'm afraid they won't arrive before late evening. They have some bad area to come over, and hills take longer. But they will be here. Just think in two more days you'll be on your way too. What an experience for you at your age." He smiled at the eager children. Andy was the most eager it seemed.

Laura went up to the house to work on her sewing as soon as she finished with breakfast and put things away. She had made two of her dresses and was working on one for Jane, and wanted to finish it for her to wear on the first day of the their trip. Everything was ready for the wagons when they arrived. Her father and Jason had made plans where they were to be put and where the herd would be penned for the two days they were to be there.

Jane thought something should be done about making food for them when they arrived. She remembered how thankful they all were when her folks had something made for them when they came in tired, dirty and hungry. But what could they make for ten wagons? There were bound to be more than two to each wagon, probably fifty people. She asked Jason what they could do.

"Don't worry, Jane; our chuck-wagon will be with this group; they'll feed them this first night until they can get settled in. Usually they only cook for our crew. Some cook the night before so they won't have to wait when they are tired and late arriving at a campground. It'd be too much for you girls to handle, but thank you for concerning yourself. These two days have been very enjoyable for me. Your family has treated me wonderfully, thanks to you," he gave her a glowing smile.

Jane's heart did a flip-flop when he looked at her as he was doing. What's wrong with me she asked herself, as her knees got weak.

Everything was done that could be done. Sam had made cages for the chickens and for the pigs, and fastened hooks on the wagon bed where they could be tied down. The wagons all looked neatly packed with some room to spare. Jane was contemplating adding a few more sacks of grain. She wanted her animals fed well so they would stay healthy.

* * *

It was after three o'clock in the afternoon when Andy came running to the house to find Jane. "They're coming, they're coming," he yelled at the top of his voice as he dashed up on the veranda and slammed open the door, his puppy 'Goldie' in his arms. "She's worth pure gold," he had told them about why he had named her that.

Everyone rushed to the outdoors. They all became quiet as they listened, and in the distance they could hear the wagons, as they rattled along the roadway, and the sound of cattle and horses and men's voices as they called to one another shouting directions.

Jason's horse stood at the rail. He mounted and rode toward the train to bring them into the compound. They had cleared space down along the fence for the ten wagons. The teams would be tied on the other side of the fence and fed hay and grain. The extra horses and cows were herded into the corral next to the barn where the others were. Jane's two cows and calf were in one of the large stalls in the barn. It didn't take long for Jason and Smith, the wagon master, to get everyone organized.

Andy was beside himself; there were children in some of the wagons; they were calling out to each other, and causing more excitement. When the wagons stopped, they were sent out of the way where they would be safe. There were too many teams being moved about, and danger of being stepped on.

Jane, Mary, and Laura stood watching as the tired women and children came from the wagons.

"If there's this much commotion with ten wagons, just think what it will be like with fifty," Jane said with a laugh. She had her eye on Jason as he sat his horse going from one wagon to another giving directions. He's some man, she thought as she watched; each order he gave was well thought out, and soon the train was settled, each with his own space and a look of neatness and order to the camp.

A wagon pulled in close to a big maple tree and stopped. The women watched for a minute. "That's the chuck wagon; I want to see how one man is going to feed this group; maybe we can learn something. His team was taken away by a young man and tended. The cook began opening up the wagon by rolling up the covering and tying it in a roll toward the top. The side of the wagon let down forming a shelf between the wheels. The young man who had taken the horses came and helped lift down a big metal contraption. It was in pieces and was soon assembled on legs and set up a short distance from the wagon, and a fire was being built under it. While this was done the cook was busy counting potatoes; he had a big kettle that he threw them into. Jane noticed that the fire was much bigger than a normal campfire would be. As soon as the coals were formed, he went to the back and raked out part of them, forming ashes for a bed and laid all the potatoes in a flat layer and covered them with more coals and ashes and pulled the fire over to cover them. He next brought out several heads of cabbage, dipped them into a big bucket of water his helper had brought, and laid them on the shelf; next a thick board cutting block was brought out. The cook started to chop and soon filled two very large bowls. He climbed up into the wagon and threw a tarp covered something over his shoulder, and climbed down and brought it to the fire. When he removed the tarp there was a metal rod through the biggest beef roast anyone had ever seen. It was partially cooked and he arranged it over the grilling area of his makeshift stove, and placed a flat pan under to catch the drippings. Next, he brought out two very large Dutch ovens and proceeded to mix up corn bread. When that was done he raked out coals on the front of the fire and placed the bread in and covered them with coals and hot ashes not disturbing the potatoes in the back.

"Did you ever see anything like that in your life? He sure knows what he's doing. That should be a good supper," Mary said. They watched him fill a big bucket, that must hold at least twenty gallons, with water and set it against the fire at one end where the other things were. Only one side was in the fire.

"Now what will he do with that?" Mary asked. "He wouldn't be heating dishwater now I wouldn't think."

"I have a suspicion that will be coffee when it's hot," Jane told her. "He's making me hungry just watching."

"He brought out a stool and sat down, filled his pipe and started to smoke as though he didn't have a care in the world."

"I don't believe this. He acts like everything is so easy, and that it will cook itself," Mary remarked. "I think I can learn something from him," she laughed.

The cook smiled to himself. He knew the three women were watching him expecting him to fall on his face. He had been cooking for wagon trains for ten years. He had gotten his start coming from France on a boat when he was thirteen and had to cook for the crew. They would have thrown him overboard if the food hadn't been good. He had learned the hard way but had learned his lesson well.

There was quite a run on the spring; some of the women were washing their younguns, and themselves. Some putting clothes to soak in tubs for washing the next day. "I guess it's about time for me to start my supper," Mary and Laura said to Jane, as they went toward their wagons.

Jane collected Andy and they went to the house. She went to her room and washed her hands and face. She had changed from her riding habit into a dress before going to her brother's. She had Andy wash and comb his hair. The two went down to the parlor, where Jane sat down at the pianoforte, and began to play. This was something new for Andy and he was fascinated by her playing, and soon edged his little behind on the bench next to her. Jane opened a book of some of her favorite songs and began to play and sing. Jane didn't realize she had collected an audience—all her sisters and the woman who helped in the kitchen; and she suddenly felt Jason's presence behind her. He reached over her shoulder and turned the page when she finished the song she was singing.

"That was lovely, Jane; how about some more?"

"She smiled and started 'Barbara Ellen', a haunting ballad that she had played and sung many times. Her sisters and her mother moved over behind her and they all sang together as they once did long ago. Jane had tears in her eyes from the memory of her childhood home that she was soon to leave.

"Mamma, I sure wish I could take this old pianoforte West with me. I could cry every day as I played it; I'll miss it; think of me when you all gather around to sing." Her heart was so full she couldn't talk, as her mother put her arms around her.

"Come, supper is ready; maybe we'll play and sing some more after we eat." They all went in to another good meal.

"When supper was over, the stars had begun to come out, "Let's walk down to the compound, and see what's going on," Andy suggested. They all grabbed wraps and started out; even Jane's mother decided to go. When they got close they could hear a mouth organ playing, and suddenly several broke into song. They're singing too, Maw. I think everyone is happy tonight just like we are; just one more day and we'll be on the trail." Andy grabbed her hand and held on tight.

Jason managed to walk on the other side of Jane. She didn't know why her knees got so weak when he was near her. He had a strange effect on her and she hadn't figured it out yet. I'll ask Mamma tomorrow; she'll know, Jane thought to herself.

The children were running and playing in the firelight; the older people sat on whatever was available and some stood as they all sang, 'The Old Rugged Cross,' some with tears in their eyes, When Jason stepped forward.

"I have an announcement to make. He waited till things quieted down and those off a ways came up where they could hear. We have tomorrow here, we will be leaving on a long difficult march to the Ohio, where we will meet up with the rest of our train. Mr. Jarvis, where we are staying, has some cows yet for sale. He has fine cattle, and there are root crops available in the area at reasonable prices; also some fine teams. The general store has most anything you need in clothing and etc. at reasonable prices. Molasses are plentiful, as well as chickens and pigs. Decide if you can take more and what you want and get it tomorrow. Make sure you have grain to give each of your animals at least a quart a day, to keep them healthy. Hopefully, we will find some grass further west. Check your wagons and make sure every bolt is tightened and every wheel is in good shape. Check harness for breakage; you women who want to wash clothing, Mr. Jarvis says to string lines, and do so, as you may not have an opportunity for some time to do these chores; and you don't want to be left on the trail due to carelessness. Make use of your day;

if you can't find me, talk to Mr. Jarvis or Jane here; they will know where to send you for what you need. Now that you're weathered travelers you should know if you're missing some necessity. Is there any sickness among you? If so, go to Doctor Myers, and he can help you. If he is busy, find Mrs. Barrlette; she is a doctor too. Are there any questions?"

"My name is Offitt. Will it be possible to take cattle—say yearlings—on the drive?"

"They will have to be fed. You're all allowed three animals extra, without charge, and they will have feed. Other than that, there will be a charge of five dollars a head, including feed to the end of the drive. As you were informed in the beginning, each man will spend so many hours on guard duty helping to guard those animals, it will be mostly at night. Our regular drovers will manage the drive by day, unless there is an emergency where you are called on. If you're called on, please respond immediately. Most of your womenfolk can manage your wagon for a short while. That is all; we'll have another meeting tomorrow night before pulling out the next morning. Good night all."

Jason, Jane and the rest from the house started back; everyone would go to bed early and be up early in the morning. Jane was tired and ready for bed. Andy was almost asleep while walking, as she asked him, "Did you have a nice day?"

"I had a good time; Gramma and I made twenty hen's nests. I went to look and they already laid eggs in them. I'll make you some when we get to our ranch; I know how now." He looked at her, a smile on his face.

"I'm so proud of you; you've been a big help." Jane put her arm around him as they reached the house. She called "Good night all," as she and Andy climbed the stairs to their beds.

🎋 Chapter Thirty-Six 🎋

The commotion of the barnyard awoke Jane. Glancing at the alarm clock next to her bed she saw it was six-thirty. Going to the window she saw three teams at once were being taken to the creek to be watered. Blue smoke was billowing up where breakfast fires had been started.

"Time to get going," she said to herself, as she dashed cold water onto her face. Andy was still sleeping, his puppy snuggled against him.

When Jane finished dressing, she picked up the puppy and took her down to put her outside before she puddled on her mother's carpet. When she set her on the ground she went NOW. "That's a good girl, Goldie, you're a good girl, she told her as the puppy looked at her as if to say thanks." She wouldn't be hard to housebreak if they paid attention to her, and took her out when she needed to be.

She saw that Jason's horse had been saddled and was being brought to the hitching rail out front. Several others were saddled and stood outside the barn. He had his crew well trained. This morning they were going for the cattle, and whatever else had to be brought to the compound for early departure the next day. Jane saw Ed coming toward her.

"Good morning, Ed. Looks as though we have lots of action already at the compound." She gave him her ready smile.

"Yes, everyone is up and at it. We'll be part of it starting tomorrow. Do you want Cherokee or the buggy today?" he asked.

"The buggy, please, I want to pick up some more things at the store; I forgot alarm clocks, can you believe that?" she said with a laugh.

"I'd say that was a necessity; but I never need one, I wake with the sun."

"What if we don't have any sun?" Jane teased him.

Ed chuckled, as he went back toward the barn to harness the team and bring the buggy. He seemed happier than when he had first joined them, for which Jane was thankful.

Jane took Goldie back into the house where she made an effort to get up the stairs to Andy. She would go up two steps and slide back three; Jane stood laughing at her as she watched.

"What's so funny?" Jason asked coming down the staircase. When he saw Goldie he laughed too. "Wait little one, and I'll help you up," he said as he came and lifted her up and took her to the top of the stairs and set her down watching her make a bee line down the hall to Andy's room.

Jane's heart did it's usual flip flop seeing him so gentle with a small animal. She remembered crying on his chest at her grandfather's and blushed.

"Have you had breakfast?" he asked her coming to stand with her at the foot of the stairs.

No. Come into the dining room; I'll see if anyone is up yet." She went to the kitchen and soon returned with two cups of steaming coffee. "Our breakfast is on the way." They sat and chattered while they waited.

"I see the horses are ready for the men to go for the cattle; you'll have a busy day today. Are you going for horses? John has to pick up his team and his riding mare. I'm sure Dad will go with you if you want. I'm going to the store, and I want to pick up more apples; those apple dumplings that Laura makes melt in your mouth, and it's an easy meal, and filling. I'll see if any of the ladies want to go for anything."

"Good, that will help out. Do you plan to take any more cattle?" Jason asked her.

"I don't think so. I have one cow and calf, and another that will have a calf about the time we arrive, and the extra team of horses. That's thirteen animals I will have to feed. I would like to take a couple of the yearling heifers, but think I had better plan on getting what I have there in good health. I'll think on it, and see what my father says."

"Two wouldn't be too costly to take, and be a start of a good herd with the little heifer calf you now have. You won't have to worry about feed when you get there. I have to run; have a good day." He smiled at her as he left.

Jane's father came to the table, "You're up early; everything all right?" he asked.

"Everything's fine; I just had breakfast with Jason; his crew are ready to fetch the steers. He thinks maybe I should take some of your heifers; what do you think? I now have thirteen animals, plus the calf I'll have soon," she looked at him for an answer.

"I have four real nice Hereford yearling heifers; from what I understand, it will only cost you twenty dollars for feed and including them in the herd. If you plan on raising cattle, it might be a good idea to include them. You'll always be able to sell them out there," her father said.

"What will I do for a bull?" Jane asked her face slightly pink.

"Well! That would be a good investment too. There won't be many out West and you can charge for his services. Let's go look at one I have; he's a year and half; he'll be ready for action in another year. Come along."

Jane went with her father to another lot over beyond the barn where several cattle were penned. They stood hanging over the fence looking as he pointed out the beautiful red with white face cattle.

"They're beautiful; I think I'll take the five of them. I've got the money and might as well. I want to settle up with you today, and get a bill of sale for everything, so get it ready. I hope it's all right for me to take your buggy again. I want to go to the store, and thought I would invite a couple of the ladies who want things to go with me," Jane told him.

"You know you don't have to ask, daughter. I don't think you'll be sorry for deciding on the cattle."

"I have a herd of my own already," she laughed. "I expect Jason will think he started a snowball rolling when he hears." She laughed again.

"Jason is a fine man; you could do worse. What's the story there?" her father looked at her under his eyebrows as he asked.

"I don't think there is a story. I have just met him and he has been very kind to me and to the Thompsons. I have to admit that he has a strange effect on me when he's around, and I like and admire him."

"Yet you married a man you had just met for a few hours? What about that?" he asked.

"Dad, I don't know what happened; it was all so fast, and everyone deciding for me. I think I would have been happy if given a chance, but we didn't have a chance. I loved Mr. and Mrs. Barrlette, as they said they loved me. I do know that Major Lance Barrlette loved me as much as any man can love a woman. He came to me after he died, and the same night he also came to Mrs. Barrlette, she told me. He told me to get on with my life and shed no more tears. That's what I'm doing. Who knows what the future holds. I hope—happiness for me. Although I have never been happier than right now. I'm doing something I really want to do. And my Andy—I love him as though he were my own child." She looked at her father and chuckled, "It's a long trip, who knows?"

Her father looked at her, and smiled his crooked smile, "That it is, daughter. Write and let us know what happens. I'll say this, I couldn't want for a finer husband for you than Jason. So if it does happen, you have my wholehearted blessing." He walked over and gave her a loving hug.

"I want Ed to see the cattle, just to let him feel part of the decision. He knows cattle and horses better than anyone I ever saw, but you. Do you know he says one of the mares I bought is in foal; says he's positive. Do you want to wait, and I'll go and fetch him," When her father nodded, she started toward the barn-yard where all the men seemed to be gathered. Jane picked Ed out from the group. Just as she did, he looked her way and she motioned for him and stood waiting for him to come up to her and then they went back to where her dad waited.

"Ed, I need your advice;, I'm thinking of taking a beginning of a herd from dad's choice Hereford's; I have the money now and may not have it later. Look at them and tell me what you think."

"Mornin', Mr. Jarvis; that's a fine bunch of yearlings you have there, and that little bull, just watch him strut. He's a fine animal." He smiled as he watched him. "How many you plannin' on, Miss Jane?"

"The four heifers, and the bull?" she held her breath for his answer.

"You can't go wrong; wish the choice were mine." Ed said keeping his eye on the cattle in question.

"Then that's it, dad; write it up and give me the total I want to get everything settled today. Don't sell my herd," she said with a happy laugh.

"I'll go see if anyone needs any help," Ed said a happy look on his face.

"Ed's going away feeling ten foot tall," her father said.

"I know. That's what I wanted. He lost his wife while in the army, and all he had was stolen, as he said even the boards on his house. He's another fine young man. I want him to be happy, as he's now part of our family. I have a fine bunch of people around me, Dad, no use of you and mamma worrying; and I'll keep in touch." Jane hugged her father. "I'd better get going before Worth sells everything in his store." she said as she hurried away to the Compound.

She found Mary busy washing out some clothes, and tidying her wagon for the morning departure. Laura had gone to the house to finish Jane's dress. The children were playing.

"I'm going to the store; anything you need? Did you get a chamber pot? How about an alarm clock?" Jane asked.

"I have a chamber pot; it's old and ugly; I would dearly love one of the pretty ones you got, but I'd better not; and I have the alarm clock from our home. I just know when we arrive at my rock-cliff, I'm going to wish I had bought some things; thanks, anyway." She smiled as Jane went to talk to the others.

She saw a bunch of women talking together, and walked over, "does anyone want to go to the store? I have room for two if anyone needs to buy something; I'm ready to leave now."

One of the older looking ladies spoke up, "I've been wondering how I could get there; I would love to join you. I'll get my reticule and be right out." "I'd love to go too," a girl who looked like she was pregnant said.

"That's all I can take; if more want to go, maybe later; or I have a mare one can ride; I don't know about the stallion I ride. But I'm sure we can get some horses if you want to ride."

Two more held up their hands. "We'll ride horseback if we may." "Get ready and I'll have some saddled for you." She saw Nat coming toward her. Oh, Nat, could you saddle Andy's mare and one of the new ones I bought; put saddlebags on them please, as soon as you can, and bring them over.

"I'll have them ready in a jiffy. I'll put in a couple of sacks and string in case you need them," he said as he hurried away.

He was soon back; Jane had turned the buggy, and the two ladies who were going to ride with her, were in. Nat came with the two mares and held them by a block of wood where the girls could mount.

"Thanks Nat, we'll be back soon. Tell Laura for me."

* * *

The store had a lot of people hanging around out on the porch, as Jane and her troupe went inside. They stood a moment till their eyes adjusted to the dimness.

"Mornin' Jane, I see you've brought a lot of pretty ladies with you this morning," Mr. Chenoweth said nodding to them all.

"This is part of our wagon train; we leave in the morning; I found I had forgotten some things I will need. Do you want to wait on me while they look around? I need three alarm clocks. What do you have? he brought out several sizes, and one fancy one with flowers painted on it. "I'll take that, that, and the one with flowers. I need another chamber, too; a pretty one." She went over to the yard goods. Knowing that Laura would likely be having a baby before long she bought fifteen yards of white flannel, six of soft batiste, and some lace, all in white. That would be a start for a layette, when the time came. She decided to get another pair of overalls for each of the men, and two more pair for Andy. She bought a couple pair for herself, knowing how she liked boys clothes to work in, and a couple of chambray shirts. Might as well get me a straw hat too while I'm at it she thought as she picked one up and tried it on. She laid it on the pile she was accumulating. "And a box of peppermint sticks. That'll be all for me."

By that time there were other piles on the counter, as each woman brought what she chose and stacked it up saying, "They have a nice selection, and good prices," each showing the other what they had chosen. They were soon finished, going around the store again to make sure they hadn't forgotten anything.

Jane finally got them outside, and their packages stored away, as many as possible, in the saddlebags.

"I want to go by a farm and get a few things; I hope you don't mind. They have a lot of root crops and good molasses—I got some the other day. They sure are good on biscuits or pancakes," she laughingly told them.

"I'd like some of those myself; it's hard to get something sweet for breakfast," one of the ladies said.

They soon arrived at the farm. Mrs. Ellison was in her garden and when she looked up and saw so many women she looked startled.

"Good morning, Mrs. Ellison—I've brought you some customers. I would like a bushel of those delicious apples like I got before."

"Tommy?" she called, "he's over in the shed; go on over and tell him what you want. He'll get them for you."

Jane walked over and saw Tommy puttering on some sort of equipment. The prettiest cats she had ever seen were all around him—some on the bench and some at his feet; they were all long hair angora, it looked like. "What pretty kittens," she said as she picked up a snow-white one, that was perched on the window sill.

"Take your pick; maw's threatening to drowning them all if someone doesn't take them, and I don't want the job."

"Are you serious? I'll take this one then, and I'll bet some of the other ladies will take one too. I need a bushel of apples, Tommy. Here's a sack for them. Do you have turnips?" He nodded, "Give me a bushel of them too. Sack them and put them in the buggy for me, but don't charge me for the kitten," she said with a giggle.

When the buggy pulled out, the kitten population was greatly reduced, and the buggy full of sacks of vegetables and jugs of molasses. The women were all happy with what they had gotten at what they declared a bargain price, and they chattered all the way back to the compound.

Jane saw that in the pasture field was a bunch of cattle and horses standing around a wagon load of hay, pulling mouth fulls from the pile—that was the herd, no doubt. She saw the five yearlings she had just bought and the cow that was with calf. Her bay mares were there too. What an accumulation of animals she was getting. Looks as though they were getting them all together to move out in the morning. She saw the two-year-old beef steers from her brother's farm too.

Jane took the buggy to the compound to unload. The women went to their wagons—some having to make two trips to take all they had bought. There were ohs, and ahs, over the beautiful kittens—wanting to know if there were more of them to be given away. Jane took the material in and put it in the trunk where the linens were. The box of candy she set on the overhead blanket shelf and covered it with a blanket. She gave Laura the turnips and apples and an alarm clock for their wagon. She put the chamber in her wagon with the other clock. Knowing that soon Mary would be bewailing the fact that her chamber pot had sprung a leak and she wished she had bought one, Jane would have one ready for her.

Everyone arrived at the house for supper, and there was much washing on the back porch. Jason changed into a clean shirt as he had been gone from early morning till now, getting everything collected.

Jane had gotten a sack of corn and one of oats from her father and put those in Nat's wagon.

Jane could see that everyone was tired; Jason looked beat. "How did it go?" her father asked Jason.

"We bought most of the available mules and horses from the McGlothlin brothers, two wagons from the Browns, all the cattle your son had big enough for beef, and the rest of Mammy Jane's ten-week-old pigs were sold too as were all the potatoes and apples she could spare. All in all, we made a pretty good haul, and will be ready by sun up to travel. Are you all set, Jane?"

"I think so. There's no danger of you getting my heifers mixed up is there? I'd hate for your hungry men to be eating on them. That's my future Hereford herd. I'm mighty proud of my cattle," Jane said, with a smile. She had found out that her father had already informed Jason of her purchase.

"You don't eat horses do you, Jason? I don't want my horses to disappear; I'm starting my herd. Ed said that one is in foal now, so soon I'll have four with my riding mare," Andy told him.

"That's a good start young man," Jason told him with a big smile. "And Jane, I think you made a wise choice in taking well-bred cattle to stock your acreage with. You'll have a herd to be proud of in no time. Those are two fine mares of Andy's too. We put them all together to get used to each other before starting out. They all seem well-behaved so far. We have plenty of men and should leave on time and without much trouble. Till they get trail-broken, sometimes we have problems; hopefully, not this time."

After supper was over, Jane sat at the pianoforte again and started to play. She played and sang "Danny Boy," and everyone had tears in their eyes. "Sing something cheerful, her father advised. Jane played "Cindy", and "Old Jo Clark" and finished with "The West Virginia Hills." Getting up she said, "Let's all walk down to the compound and see if they are singing there before we go to bed." They took one of the lanterns that was sitting on the front veranda and walked down toward the area, hearing singing before they arrived. Sounded as though everyone was joining in and having a good time.

Jane walked between her father and mother with an arm around them both. "I sure hate to leave you two. I had gotten used to being without you, but now I have to go through it all over again.

"You be sure and write and tell me everything that's going on—who has babies, who, got married—everything, you hear." Her mother warned her. "You'll be so busy you won't miss us at all. I envy you going somewhere so wonderful to start a new life.

You'll hear often from us, and you'll be coming to see us in a year or two," her mother told her. "I know how your Dad and I were about coming into the Wilderness of Virginia to homestead. My parents, and I both were like we are now, hating to leave each other; but we've never been sorry. I don't think you will be either. You have so much more than we had to begin with. We had a lot of help, from your uncle Patrick and the Browns. They are all family to us."

"We won't have much time in the morning, but I want you both to know that I love you no matter where I am. I'll think of you every day. I guess you know that brother Tom won't be around much longer as he is very ill. Mammy Jane knows; we talked about it. See him when you can, and tell him I love him."

They only stayed a short time. When the singing came to an end and every one began to go to their wagons to go to bed, they returned to the house and to their beds too.

* * *

Jane had set her alarm clock to awake her at five o'clock. She wanted to have time to wash herself all over, and to pack Andy's things and her own. She had taken everything they didn't need to the wagon and put it away. She was soon dressed; she would let Andy sleep another half hour and then he must get up and dress and have his breakfast.

When she took Goldie and went downstairs, she heard someone in the kitchen. She knew her mother would have breakfast ready and would be packing them a basket to take for their dinner meal. When she brought Goldie in and took her to the kitchen to feed her, she saw that Jason was having coffee at the dining room table. She poured herself a steaming cup and went to join him.

"Good morning, Jason; I hope you slept well. This seems to be the big day for us—anyway, our first day on the trail." Jane smiled at him, noticing he had shaved and was clean and tidy.

"Good morning, Jane; yes, I slept like a log; I was tired from yesterday's many projects that had to be taken care of. Did you sleep well? You look fresh as the morning dew," he said as he gave her an enticing smile.

"I'm so excited. I know Andy will be too; he can't wait to get started. I hate to leave my home, but I suppose I've outgrown it. My family is so dear to me, and I may never see them again," she said sadly.

"It's not as though you are crossing the sea like many immigrants do. The railroad will be spanning the country directly and traveling will be made easy. You'll be back to see them. I'll have to go now and see that everyone is getting ready to move out. Don't be late; we'd hate to leave you behind," he said with a chuckle.

"Not likely. I'll be right up-front helping direct this train. I'll see you shortly. Would you like to have dinner with us this first day? Mamma is packing enough for the whole train, I just know," Jane laughed as she told him.

"I sure would; I'll save you a space; you'll want all your wagons together with the Thompsons, I assume." He waved to her and was gone.

Jane went back and awakened Andy and got him washed and dressed. He could hardly keep his eyes open. She picked up the pallet and folded the blankets, did the same to her bed, putting the sheets aside to be laundered. Gathering up Andy's things and her own, she took them downstairs.

"Come along, sleepy head." Andy hadn't missed Goldie yet—he was too sleepy. When they came down the stairs, she was waiting at the bottom.

"Goldie!" he yelled as he picked her up and cuddled her and took her with him to eat breakfast.

Andy didn't want to eat, but Jane told him it would be a long time before they would stop for dinner, and that he couldn't get anything to eat while the train was going.

Jane's mother came carrying two baskets of food. She had asked Jane for baskets when they were at the compound last night knowing she didn't have room to keep so many in her house on wheels.

"Good morning, daughter, and Andy. It's going to be a lovely day to travel; I'm so glad it is. The mist is hanging over the tops of the mountains, and the sun will soon be up. It's an exciting day for you." Jane knew tears weren't far away as her mother tried to make pleasant talk.

"Grandma, thank you for teaching me to make hen-nests, and for cooking so good. It's going to be mighty quiet when everyone leaves; but no tears, Grandpa says they never solve anything. I'll be saying good-bye all the way home to our ranch; then I'll be saying hello. I'll write to you." He ran over and hugged her around the waist. "I love you, Grandma, and I'll miss you." He was on the verge of crying when he turned and picked up Goldie. "We'd better get going, Maw."

Jane's dad was waiting on the veranda—he hadn't come in for coffee. Jane knew he was hating to see them leave and wouldn't be able to eat for a while.

"Good morning, Dad; I guess we're ready." Her mother handed him the baskets. Jane had her saddle bags and Andy's and her clothes; both arms were full. Andy carried Goldie. They all started to the compound. They could hear the cows bawling, mules braying, and a general sound of confusion as everyone began to harness their teams and get them hooked to wagons. The women were busy putting away the breakfast clutter and each was packing something for their dinner on the trail. When they got to their wagon, Laura and Nat seemed to have everything under control. Jane saw that Ed had his wagon ready; the chickens and pigs were in crates on the back. Sam was hooking up the mules to their house on wheels. Jane went into the little house and found a place for the baskets, and put away the other things she had. She took a heavy quilt down and took it out to fold to put on the seat to sit on. She took a throw in case it was too cool. Her mother had given her an old rug for Goldie; she put that down on the floor, so when Andy got tired of holding her she could lay there.

Jane's eyes searched the area for Jason. She saw him wheeling his horse this way and that checking every wagon. Zachary Smith, the wagonmaster, was starting to line up the wagons. The group from Pennsylvania was to be first in line. Sam was directed to fall in behind them with the house on wheels. Jane had asked if she could tie her cow behind Nat's wagon and was given permission. Cherokee was tied behind her wagon; he was saddled, with the stirrups looped over the saddle horn so they didn't flop around and maybe frighten him. Jane saw that several with milk cows had them tied to their wagons. All the men, once they were in line, came down from their wagons and circled them seeing that everything was in order—nothing hanging loose or clanging to cause problems. Jane got back down too, as she wanted to take a last look around. She couldn't believe that everything had been left so neat—even the burned wood from the fires had been put in a pile and the ashes scattered and raked level. You could hardly tell that so many wagons had been there—only where the ground was cut up from the animals hooves. One rainstorm and the tracks would disappear.

Jane was standing with her parents when Jason came up, dismounted, and walked over to them.

"Thank you, Mr. and Mrs. Jarvis for having us here. It has been a real pleasure. We may want to use your place again if we may. We'll be coming through here next spring, I'm sure. I'll keep in touch, and if it's convenient for you, we will see. And thank you, Mrs. Jarvis for such a good bed and wonderful meals. You can rest assured that your daughter will be well-taken care of on the trail." He shook hands with them both and walked over to Jane's wagon, leading his horse to wait for her.

Jane hugged first her mother, then her father and then back to her mother. She kissed both their cheeks. Her heart was so full she could hardly talk. "Take care of yourself; I love you both; good by, I'll write soon, I love you." She hurried to the wagon where Jason waited to help her up into the seat.

"I'll be by from time to time to see that all is well." He mounted and hurried toward the front. The first wagons were starting to roll; slowly the whole string of wagons were moving. Jane turned to wave one last time, tears streaming down her face. She could hear the cattle being brought out and herded to follow the wagons.

Andy was waving and yelling, "Good by grandpa; good-by

grandma; we're on our way home. Hooray! Buffalo, look out, here we come!"

The wagons began to spread out, some with more space between them, as they went down the West Fork. They were passing houses where people stood in the fields and on their porches waving. Jane could see Chenoweth's store where several people came out to stand and watch the wagons, waving and calling, "Good Luck!"

The road followed the creek where the mist still hung over the water. They were on their way!

❧ Chapter Thirty-Seven ❧

The wagon train moved along slowly at first until everyone found their own speed—not too close but not lagging behind. The sun had begun to shine, and the air was spring-like making it pleasant for the travelers as they started their journey. They were making good time and had left the West Fork and came to the first hill at mid-morning; the road never became very steep, but was a steady hard pull as it wound its way through the trees in switch-backs. Some called the area Liberty Hill which referred to old man Moses Hill who had a log shack on top of the hill during the War and said he would have liberty on his hill if he had to fight the whole Confederate army. He didn't have to prove himself as he died soon afterward. All that remained of his shack was a pile of half rotten logs in the woods, and the story of his stand on liberty. Jane recited this story to Andy who wanted to know why it was named Liberty Hill.

After crossing the hill, they were now following a small stream where there was little land between the hills for them to travel on. Jane watched Jason riding ahead of the train at a trot looking for a spot where they could stop for the noon hour. That was his job to scout out places to camp and where feed for the animals was available.

"I expect Jason is looking for a spot big enough for us to stop for our dinner and let the animals rest," she told Andy and Sam.

"There's not very many level spots," Andy remarked. "We may not get to stop for some time. I'm getting hungry, too."

"Good, then you'll enjoy the food grandma packed for us," Jane told him with a smile.

"Sam let out a chuckle, "You'z won't starve boy." To take Andy's mind off eating, Sam started to sing softly in his deep voice, "We all gotta' travel that lonesome valley, we all gotta' travel it by yourself."

Andy listened for a few minutes and said, "Sam, sing a happy song. I sure wish we had us one of them pianoforte. I'd like to learn to play one myself. Do gentlemen play them, Maw?"

"I expect so, although all I've ever seen play were ladies. We just may get us one when we have a big house and fields full of red cows with white faces and a lot of bay horses galloping across a big meadow. I'll teach you to play; we don't care if ladies or gentlemen do or don't play, you and I will."

"Could you teach Sam to play?" he asked.

"I expect Sam could learn too; but I think we'll keep him busy singing happy songs." Sam had switched to "Froggy Went a Courtin.'"

It was getting on to one o'clock before Jason was spotted up at the head of the wagon train conversing with Zachary the wagonmaster. He came back down the train—sometimes having to wait till a wagon passed him before he found footing on the narrow road for his horse. He came up to Jane's wagon, turned and rode beside it for a short distance.

"We'll be stopping soon. Pull in where you're directed. Sam, unhook and water and feed your animals. We'll eat and rest for an hour or more. I'll see you later," he called as he went back to the front to help direct the wagons.

In about half an hour Jane saw the first wagon pulling into a field following Jason who rode ahead in a wide circle.

"What are they doing, Maw? Why is Jason riding out in such a big circle?" Andy wanted to know.

"You watch, I think we are going to 'Circle Up' it's called. They're making a pen for the herd. You just watch; this is something none of us has ever seen before." Jane watched fascinated as the first wagon came back almost to where it started from and another wagon followed close on its tailgate. A complete circle was formed with the horses overlapping the wagon next to it, so that the wagons when stopped were at a slight angle and close together. It was quite a feat to be able to judge just how big a circle could be made out of the wagons available.

As Sam slowly took his position, he turned to Jane, "Ain't thaz somthin', I'z never seen a fence built so fast," he chuckled as he watched the other wagons. As soon as the wagon behind him stopped, he got down to tend his team.

"Here comes the herd, Maw, they're bringing in the hay wagon for them to eat. Just look at my beautiful mares and your heifers. We've got us a fine herd, Maw," Andy said with satisfaction.

"I think we can get down now. I'll find a throw if anyone wants to sit down. I think the ground is too cold myself, and I want to stand after all that sitting." She got down and had to climb over the wagon tongue of the next wagon to get to the door of the house on wheels to bring out the baskets. Laura was down from their wagon and came to help. She let down the drop table on the side and put out the basket of food. There were hard-boiled eggs, pickles in a small lard bucket, big fluffy biscuits with ham and eggs between. And another bucket of sassafras tea, nice and sweet. The other basket had fresh made cookies, several apples shined and polished and some dried peaches. Jane helped place everything on the table in an attractive array

"What a feast," Laura said. "We're ready when the men come." Taking a bucket she went to the creek and brought back a bucket of water for them to wash. She put it and the wash-pan on the step she used to get into her wagon, and brought out a towel, just as Jason came toward them.

Seeing all the food he said, "Thanks for having me for dinner. That food looks wonderful and I'm starved." Seeing the wash-pan, he went and washed. The others were there and dived into the wash-pan when he finished.

"I'm starved too; tomorrow I'm going to bring something up front to eat," Andy informed them.

Laura poured out cups of tea, and told everyone to come up and help themselves. They all stood around eating sandwiches and munching on pickles. Some walked while eating, getting the kinks out of their legs.

"It won't be so bad when we get to more open country, It's hard to find a place through here for all the wagons to stop. We're going to stay at the fairgrounds outside Spencer tonight. It's not such a long haul from here; we do have one more hill to get up that'll take a little work, but we'll be there before sunset. There will be wood provided for our fires which will be helpful," Jason told them.

"This is a good solution for controlling the herd," Ed said. "It was a picture to watch how you did it. This sure is a good picnic, Miss Jane, Laura," Ed told them.

"This is my mother's doing. She was up at five o'clock when I came down stairs this morning fixing this for us. She and my dad were homesteaders themselves when the area where they now live was all wilderness, covered in trees and wild animals.

She knows how it is." Jane had tears in her eyes thinking of her mother's love. "There's plenty—help yourselves."

"Bless her!" Jason and Sam said in unison, with Ed and Nat both saying, "Amen."

"Maw, can I ride with Ed? It won't be so crowded then, and Goldie will have more room," Andy asked.

"Ask him if he says yes, it'll be fine with me," Jane said.

"You don't even have to ask young man. I'll enjoy the company and having Goldie to guard us," Ed told him.

"I'll get a bucket of water for the cow," Nat said as he took the wooden bucket hanging on the back of his wagon and went to the creek. The cow and calf both drank deeply.

There wasn't much time after eating, cleaning and storing everything, till the order came from the wagon master.

"Let's saddle up; we won't be stopping till this evening." Jane saw several going into some bushes—the women on one side and the men on another. She and Laura went in the direction the women had gone. Nat took Andy with him; there wouldn't be time to relieve themselves until they camped for the night.

The wagons were soon ready to move out; they were all amazed at how the first wagon could pull out in front and one after another followed. The herd was then directed to the stream where they all had their fill of water before being driven in behind the wagons. The next stop would be the fairgrounds.

* * *

There was a good road the rest of the way to the hill Jason had mentioned. At the foot of the hill, Jason came trotting his horse and announced" a ten-minute stop—let your team blow before we tackle the hill." He went on down the line so everyone knew what was going on.

"What does he mean, "Let your team blow?" Andy asked Ed.

"You just wait and watch; see what my old mules, Mo and Jo do, you'll see."

"Whoa!" Ed called, pulling on the check-lines; the mules stopped and began slinging their heads, snorting and blowing; one did some pawing in the loose dirt and gravel. They both snorted and blowed again and then stood with heads drooping, half asleep.

"They really do blow; why did old Mo dig in the dirt?" Andy, all eyes, wanted to know.

"They do that sometimes; maybe he has an itchy foot; could be it's a way of saying thank you for stopping," Ed smiled at the curious little boy.

Jason came through at a cantor waving them up the hill till all the wagons were moving. It would be a steady climb without stopping; otherwise, they would have to use brakes and sometimes it was hard for the team to hold a loaded wagon after the brakes were kicked off to go again. It was better to keep moving at a slow steady pace. The drivers all knew this and moved slowly.

Toward the top one team lost its momentum and started to lag. Jason saw what was happening and hurried his horse to the team's head and took hold of the blind-bridle and yelled to the driver, "Give them the whip."

The driver pulled his whip from the slot in the dashboard where it was kept and flicked the backs of the team. He only had to touch them until they both leaned into the traces and reached the top of the hill and went over. The west side was graded more gradually and the team only had to walk and keep the wagon from rolling too fast down the other side. Jason let go the team's bridle giving the driver the go ahead sign.

Jason stayed where he could see the stream of wagons coming up the hill, and to make sure there was no more trouble. Soon all had crested the hill and were on the down side. They only had about five miles more till they would be at the fairgrounds, where they would stay for the night.

Jason waited at the entrance to the big open field till the wagons reached him. He gave the signal for the first wagon to follow him, as he led them into a wider circle than before giving enough room between wagons for people to get out comfortably to build their fires and cook their suppers. When all the wagons were situated, they brought in the herd—the hay wagon coming in first with the animals following close behind. There were two watering troughs that were filled from a spring—one was inside the circle for the animals, the other was left outside where the men were taking their teams to water them. There was a pump for drinking water and necessaries, one for men and one for women, which made it better for the privacy of the travelers.

Fires were being built; children were sent to the woodpile where they returned with arm loads of wood, while mothers began to bring out cooking pots.

Jane had Sam make them another spider while at her dad's. The one he had made at the plantation was twenty-four by twenty-four inches. She had him make one twelve by twenty-four to fit at the side of the other one. When Laura and she had discussed it. They decided that on the trail another one would save on wood by putting it beside the larger one, and starting a pot of beans for the next day while they cooked supper—or for heating water while they cooked. They brought it out and set the teakettle on it to heat.

"What are we going to have tonight, Laura?" Jane asked.

"I'm going to make a big pan of fried potatoes, pickled beans, a pot of turnips, and, of course, cornbread. I'll cook the leftover dried peaches and make a thickened sauce over them for dessert. If you would like, you can wash some dry beans to put on to cook for tomorrow night. I'll get them from my wagon. We'll need a bucket of water to wash them in.

Jane went to the pump to get water. She had to wait for a few minutes as those ahead of her pumped their buckets full.

The fire was hot enough for the pots to go on. Laura had the turnips sliced and on in a big pot with seasoning in them. She was making up the cornbread as it would have to bake almost an hour. When Jane returned, she peeled and sliced the potatoes for frying. She peeled two large onions and sliced them on top of the potatoes, mixing them with a big wooden paddle. She set the two skillets on the spider and added lard when it was hot. She added the potatoes, salt and a sprinkling of sugar; soon the potatoes were sizzling, sending a mouth-watering smell wafting through the camp. Laura went to her wagon and took out enough pickled beans and carefully replaced the stone in the churn to keep the rest down in the brine. There was a wooden lid that fit over the top of the churn. She then tied a cloth over it. She had to rinse them quickly with a little water so they wouldn't be too sour, and put them beside the tea kettle with a little seasoning to simmer. They didn't have to be cooked, just heated nice and hot.

Nat had taken care of his team, had the feed bags on with grain for them. He came to get the milk bucket to milk their cow. Jane had saved the potato peels, sprinkled a smidgen of salt over them and she gave them to Nat for the cow a treat.

"After she eats that, give her a handful of grain; see if the calf will eat some too, as we want to put it with the herd soon so we'll have more milk. When they eat, put them in the circle so they can eat some hay and get to the water. Have you taken care of Cherokee? Give him a handful of grain too."

"It's all taken care of. I'll have your milk directly."

"Andy, bring a load of wood from the pile. In fact, bring a couple before it gets dark so we will have it for morning," Jane said. He was showing some of the children his Goldie. Jane had fixed a basket for her kitten in the house on wheels; it seemed content when she went to see about it. She set her down on the ground so she could feed her when Nat brought the warm milk. It stayed beside her, rubbing against her legs.

Good smells were coming from the wagons along the line. Mary called back and forth as she worked. Her children brought water and wood, and helped her. Her son, Mark, milked the cow; he had plenty of experience, and could milk as well as a grown up.

Jane took note and would have Nat show Andy how to do that core; He would have to learn how to work on a farm.

Sam helped Ed set the chicken coops out on the ground, and fed and watered the chickens. The pigs were fed some milk that was left from yesterday and the turnip peelings;, any scraps were kept to feed the animals.

The men soon came over to the fire. The wash pan had been set out with a bucket of water. There was hot water in the tea-kettle if they wanted to shave—which they usually did at night to save time in the morning.

The supper was ready. Jane filled the tin plates, heaping them up with potatoes, pickled beans, and turnips, a big hunk of cornbread on top and handed them to the men who went to sit on the wagon tongues, their tin cup of coffee beside them. "If you want more, come back and get it," she told them. Laura dished out the peach dessert into the enameled cups so that they would be ready when they finished eating—then she filled her plate.

"This sure does taste good," they all remarked. Several people had finished eating and the men began to form in groups talking. The women folk took care of cleaning up of dishes and making something for their noon dinner the next day, and also starting their pots of beans for supper the next night. It took some time for dry beans to cook and no one wanted to wait in the evenings for them to get done.

Laura would wait till morning when she made biscuits to make their sandwiches for noon. There were some left from the basket Jane's mother had fixed. They had a big basket of eggs that would do for several days; by then, Laura hoped they would have some meat. She planned to give everyone pancakes with molasses for breakfast. She brought the flour in a bowl, tied a clean rag over it and put it on the drop-down table to have ready for morning. The milk was strained into a stone jar and she turned a plate over it. She left it on the table as it would be cool enough for it not to get blankey before morning.

Jane's mother had given her a slab of fat-back, which Laura sliced a few slices and dropped them into the bean pot, and added hot water. She didn't want them to get too dry. They were cooking and sending out a good smell; soon they would be done enough to let cool, and would only need to be brought to boil for supper the next day.

As the women finished with their cooking chores, they too began to visit those close to them. Some had small children and were washing them and getting them ready to put into the wagons to sleep. The camp became quiet, and the fires were banked with ashes so they wouldn't go out and could be started easily in the morning—also saving on matches.

As Jane said good night and everyone started to their wagons, she noticed that even the animals had quieted, no doubt tired as were all the wagon people.

* * *

Jane and Laura had set their alarm clocks for five o'clock. As the alarms went off, they could hear the men tending the teams. Nat had slipped out before Laura awoke. She hurried and dressed for the day, folded the comforts, and straightened the bed. She hated things untidy to come back to at night. Going outside she hurried to the necessary, then back to wash up. She saw that Nat had started the fire for her. Jane came out as Laura started to fill the water bucket at the pump.

"You do whatever you were doing—I'll bring water." She left her bucket at the well while she made use of the necessary. They didn't realize what a luxury it was, and would surely miss it when

433

they were out on the plains where there wouldn't even be a tree to hide behind. Jane poured hot water from the tea kettle into the coffee pot and added coffee, while Laura was making the pancakes. Ed and Sam came in from their chores; the coffee was boiling sending fragrant steam blowing through the camp. By the time they had washed, Laura had a heaping stack of pancakes piled on plates for them and handed them the molasses. They doused them with the sweet sargums, grabbed a steaming cup of coffee, and headed for the wagon tongue. Nat brought in the cow and calf, gave her a handful or two of grain in the big wooden bucket and began milking her. He was soon finished and tied her to the back of the wagon and came in for his breakfast. Jane had to awake Andy or he wouldn't get any breakfast. Laura fixed him a plate of pancakes and poured him a cup of foaming milk, while Jane got him dressed. The men all had seconds of pancakes and several cups of coffee. When they finished, they stacked their plates on the table and went to harness the teams. The wagon train was coming awake with children crying from being dragged from their beds to eat. Some of the smaller ones were left in their beds; they could sleep while the wagons rolled, and would have to make do on a biscuit with jelly, for their breakfast when they awoke. The necessary was having a full house; the ladies had four holes, and could accommodate four at a time. Jane made sure she sent Andy to the men's telling him there would be no more stopping until noon. She gave him an apple to take with him to Ed's wagon. He had asked Mark to ride with them too and took an apple for him.

Jane had named her kitten "Angel" She set her down on the ground, gave her a small pan of milk which she lapped up hungrily, then went under the wagon and dug her little hole and squatted over it. Everything was stored away and the drop table closed and latched. The spiders cooled and stored. Jane lifted Angel into the house on wheels, and went in and brought out the folded quilt to sit on. She had taken it in at night so it didn't get damp from the dew, grabbed her throw and was ready to mount the wagon. One of the crew of the train came around with a rake and scattered the fire and ashes that remained. Jane had stacked a small load of wood inside the house to have the next night to start their fire. Laura had gone to their wagon. Most of the women and children were in ready to go, as the last of the teams were hooked up. It was just getting light as the first wagons pulled out. Jason came back to say good morning and was then off to his duties, They soon left Spencer behind and followed a stream through the sparsely-settled area where trees lined the road. Soon most of the dwellings were left behind. The wagons moved along up one small hill and then down another, still following a stream. Jane couldn't tell if it was the one that ran through Spencer or not. She doubted it could be.

They reached a level area where they could stop for noon, and followed the procedure as before—resting for a little over an hour and then heading out again. Things were going smoothly with everyone following the direction of the wagon master.

They came to a larger stream where the one they had been following met it. Following the joined streams for a short time, they came to a place where the water became wide and shallow and they could ford the stream. It took over two hours to take the wagons across. Those with cows and horses tied behind had to untie them and have a rider lead them across. Each wagon had a rider at the horses' heads to keep them in line and make sure there were no mishaps. Only two wagons at a time were allowed to cross. After crossing they were directed up a small valley where Jason waited a mile away to circle the wagons up and wait for the herd to be brought across. The train had left the main traveled road that went to Parkersburgh and headed in a slightly southwestern direction. The wagons were in a wide circle end-to-end. The chuck wagon had pulled to one side, leaving an opening for the herd to enter. Then it would pull in and plug the hole. The hay wagon was in the circle to entice the animals inside. Everyone had been told to stay in their wagons until the herd was secure. Soon the herders had all the animals rounded up and safely penned.

Dusk was falling and everyone was tired and irritable. Jason came by the wagon to inquire if everything was all right and see if they had flooded anything. The wagons had been warned to drive very slowly to keep the water from flooding the wagons.

"I was worried about my calf, but she came through with only getting a wetting," Jane told him with a smile. "No water came in the wagons; I'm certainly glad it wasn't any deeper."

"We'll have some that will be deeper, but you'll be warned; we'll try to ferry across those." Jason tipped his hat and went back to his chores.

Everyone had lighted from the wagons and were getting on with the work of building their fires and getting supper together. The men folk were tending the animals. By the time the men came to eat, they had to light a couple of the lanterns, it had gotten so dark. Nat did his chores of milking and feeding the cow and calf. Sam came and took care of Cherokee, giving him a small portion of grain and then turned him in with the rest of the herd for the night.

After supper was over, everyone was ready for bed. It had been a long hard day, and they didn't expect tomorrow would be much better. There was a cool breeze blowing and everyone was shivering as they stood close to the fire. Laura checked the bean pot and saw there would be enough for another meal with something else added, so she wouldn't have to cook anything for tomorrow. Everything was closed up for the night and the camp quieted.

It would take at least two more days to reach the Ohio,—maybe three. There were several hilly areas they had to travel through and the crossing of the Kanawah river before reaching the Ohio where they might have to wait for the rest of the train.

Jason came and told Jane that they were making for Grimm's Landing where they were supposed to be able to cross the Kanawah river; there was a ferry at this point, but only in use when the river was flooded. They would then head north to the Gallipolis Ferry where a decision had to be made to go over land or by water.

"We're having a meeting in a little while—I'll let you know," Jason told her.

The men were waiting; they had to decide where they would go; overland through the lower Ohio valley, through the northern section of Kentucky in to Missouri where they would follow the Oregon trail for several hundred miles into Oklahoma. It would be costly to try to go by water on the Ohio and then down the Mississippi and cut across to Oklahoma. They weren't sure of how many wagons would be at the Ohio. There were James Boothe, with his merchandise wagons which he had said would be at least ten or twelve, and could easily be twenty-five, and all the pilgrims from Western Pennsylvania, the Northern panhandle of West Virginia, and some even from Ohio. The estimate had been fifty wagons, but could easily become seventy-five as they gathered them along the way. Thomas Morgan, Jason Turner, Zachary Smith, and two of their top drovers sat talking it over; it wouldn't be long till they would have to make a decision, one way or another. Thomas Morgan expected to go only as far as St. Louis where he would board a train and return to the east to form another wagon train for late spring, leaving Jason Turner, the scout, and the wagon master Zachary Smith, in charge to see that the wagon train reached its designation.

After hashing it over for half an hour, they decided to wait until they knew for sure how many wagons would be involved, and how many cattle and horses there were going to be.

Jane was waiting up until Jason returned. He rode in and dismounted to talk to her. "Nothing has been decided, although in my opinion it looks like an overland trip. They want to wait and see just how big a train there will be. With even what cattle and horses we have now, we might have to split up and take them overland, while the wagons went by water. Some won't like that idea and some will want to get out of driving and want to go by water." Jason could see that Jane was thinking it over.

"I would rather keep what I own together, even if it does take a little longer. As I see it, we've come along fine to here, and it should be easier when we reach less-populated areas." Jane smiled, "You really didn't ask my opinion, did you?"

"No, I didn't, but I'm glad you gave it; your thinking is exactly mine. And there is a chance of some grass along the way for the animals. It is a dangerous situation if you run into bad weather and you're on a barge. On land you can always hole up for a few days. It's not all my decision; I'll let you know as soon as it's decided. You'd better get to bed, as it's late; see you in the morning; good-night, Jane." He wheeled his horse and headed back to his wagon as Jane entered the house on wheels and went to bed.

✣ Chapter Thirty-Eight ✣

The wagon train came awake to a cloudy sky and a cold wind blowing. Everyone was slow moving, still tired from the day before. The men had heavy jackets on as they tended the animals getting ready for another day of travel.

When Jane came outside, she saw that Nat had started the fire and Laura had put the big coffee pot on. She stood at the table making biscuits with a heavy shawl wrapped around her.

"Good morning Jane," she said as she continued to work.

"Good morning Laura, how do you feel this morning? It's sure cold; this wind goes right through you." Jane had bought her and Laura jimmisons; she went into the house and got hers and put it on to break the wind. Then she wrapped a shawl around herself and brought out the one she had gotten for Laura.

"Laura when you get a minute put this on under your shawl. It will keep the cold from penetrating to the bone; you can wrap your shawl over top of it. I found when I worked with Gramps in the bitter cold that I kept warmer with one. It's what the men wear to work outside in."

"I am freezing; I'll stop right now and put it on. I can tell the difference already, she said when she washed her hands of dough and put the jacket on and wrapped her shawl over top of it. Thank you, Jane."

Nat brought the cow and calf and tied the cow to the house on wheels and milked and fed her some grain. He brought the pail of milk to Laura.

"You're up early, Nat. I see you put your jimmison on. I bought Laura and me one and it sure feels good this morning. Be sure to keep your rain gear so you can get at it. If this wind dies down we may get rain." He nodded as he left to take care of the mules.

"What are you fixing for breakfast this morning? And what can I do?" Jane asked.

"We have some of the fried potatoes left. We'll warm those and fry some eggs, and have biscuits and molasses; that should fill them up. I'll have to make egg sandwiches again for our dinner.

I hope we can get some meat soon; I know the men crave meat more than we do," Laura told her.

"When we get to a settlement, I'll try to buy a ham or some sausage; at least something we can make sandwiches from for our dinners. I know it's hard but some on the train have a lot less than we do," Jane told her, as she got out the skillets and put the potatoes on to warm in one and melted lard in the other to fry the eggs.

"I'm going out a ways and see if I can find some firewood. I'll take it in the house with us as we may have to build a fire in there if the weather worsens, and cook there. At least we could have a warm place to eat; we could all crowd in. Do you have enough blankets in your wagon?"

"So far we're fine." Laura had the Dutch ovens ready for the fire. "You go ahead with your wood gathering; I can do the rest."

Jane went out from the camp looking for down limbs. She had to go quite a way as everyone else had been gathering wood and it was scarce. She was glad she had hoarded some in the house for them to make the morning fire.

The men were all standing around the fire when she got back, warming first one side and then the other. Laura was frying the eggs; the basket was going down at an alarming rate. They might be like the rest and have to resort to bread and molasses sandwiches for their dinner. They, at least, had plenty of beans they could cook and warm at noon or even eat cold.

The camp was rather quiet as mothers let their children stay in their warm beds. They would make biscuits for them and wrap them in a cloth till they awoke and they could eat on the way. They would have to use the chamber-pot inside the wagons, if they weren't up in time.

Jason came by with his cheery hello. "Good morning all, we're about ready to form up. This will be a rough day; we have some mountains and woods to go through. We may not be able to cross the Kanawah today., and have to camp on this side till morning, especially if the weather gets any colder. It'll take most of one day for the crossing, and we don't want to start it late in the day when we won't all have time to cross. We'll be taking it easy this morning. Stay warm," he called as he rode away.

"That's one fine man," Ed remarked.

"Youz can say that again," Sam seconded.

The wagons began to pull out. The overcast sky got darker and darker till it looked almost like evening. Jane had decided to stay inside the house with Andy—he still slept. She had built a tiny fire in the little stove to take the chill off. She removed her jimmison and now sat with just a light shawl around her. Angel was on the bed curled up against her. Goldie lay next to Andy on her rug on the floor. The wagon moved slowly, without many bumps. They were traveling across country not following a road at this point. Jane kept looking out the windows as the sky darkened and the wind seemed to pick up. She could hear the animals in the distant herd. The cows were bawling, and the mules braying. They know we are in for bad weather Jane thought to herself. When she looked up again she saw drops of rain on the little windows. Andy still slept snug and warm in his bed.

The wagons were on the move for over three hours when they slowed and came to a stop. "I wonder what has happened?" Jane asked herself, looking out the windows, trying to see what the trouble was. She waited for several minutes then opened the door and stepped outside. Going to the front she asked Sam, "Do you know what the problem is?"

"Noz I don't Miss Jane. Somethin' must be wrong in one of the front wagons. You'z best not stray out in the damp, Miss Jane; we'z can't have you sick on us," he told her with a big smile. She saw that he had his rain gear on.

"I'm going to Nat's wagon and bring Laura back here; there is no reason for her to sit out in this weather." She hurried up to the other wagon. "Laura, come down and come back to the house. It's warm inside and you're not doing any good up here. Nat are you all right?"

"Go ahead, Laura I'm fine; this rain gear over my jacket you bought keeps me good and warm." Laura climbed down and they hurried back to the little house on wheels and went in out of the bitter wind.

"Oh, this feels good; I didn't realize I was so cold. I went in under the wagon cover for a while but it wasn't much better in there."

"If this keeps up for long we'll have some sick people on our hands I'm afraid. I'm glad the mothers are keeping their children inside at least. Andy is still sleeping. I've begun to think he will sleep all day. Jane had set the coffee pot with what coffee was in it on the stove when she went outside. It was now hot. I'll jump out and get some cups and cream she said as she grabbed a small basket to put things in.

She yelled at Sam, "let me know if you're going to go Sam; I'm outside. She hurried to the cupboard and got cups, the sugar and cream and hurried back inside. She filled one cup with coffee adding sugar and cream and went outside again, handed it up to Sam. "This will help warm you up. Hold up till I can give Ed and Nat one." She hurried back and Laura reached out the other two cups of steaming coffee. She went to Ed first and handed him a cup and then back to Nat. The wind was so strong she had trouble opening the door to get back in.

Jane stood drinking her coffee and looking out the window. She saw Jason riding down the line of wagons. "Is there any more coffee, Laura?"

"About two more cups."

"I see Jason coming; fix him a cup will you and add plenty of sugar—that will help ward off the cold." Jason had stopped to say something to Sam, then came to the back and knocked on the door.

"Can you come in, Jason?" He shook his head and she handed him the steaming cup of coffee.

"My God, you don't know how I needed that." he said with a smile. One of the front wagons hit a rabbit-hole and cracked a wheel; we're trying to repair it enough to get to our noon stop, then it will have to be replaced. Just a freak accident; we'll be moving soon. I see you and Laura are comfortable; your house on wheels may replace the covered wagon," he laughed.

"Thanks for letting us know what's going on. I hope we can get to our noon stop with the repaired wheel. We don't seem to have made much progress this morning."

"Everyone does seem in slow motion. We'll get there though."

He handed the cup back. "That was a life saver, thanks." he waved as he hurried away. Jane closed the door on the cold. Soon the wagons began to move along, and Laura set the big coffee pot into one of the galvanized buckets on the floor.

* * *

It was over two hours before the wagons started to slow again and then swing out into the 'Circle Up'; Jane saw a small stream in the distance and a heavy stand of pines; seemed they had chosen a place where they could find plenty of wood. As soon as their wagon stopped, Laura hurried up to her wagon with a basket and got potatoes and onions; she took a big kettle and put it on the little stove. Jane had filled one of the churns inside the door with water to use in case they weren't where any was handy. Laura dumped the potatoes into a pan of water and peeled them cutting them into small pieces and adding those to the water on the stove; then peeled three big onions and added those. I'm going to make some hot soup; it won't take long to cook and they will be working on the wagon wheel so we should have time. Jane saw that the men had built two big fires and were gathered around, thawing out. Some of the women had brought coffee pots and set them onto the coals to boil coffee. Jane filled the big coffee pot and set it on the stove, adding some small sticks of wood to the fire. She saw the men tending their teams. While she stood looking, she saw Sam take the ax and go toward some down trees. He soon had a sizable pile of wood cut into short lengths, and she knew he was getting a supply for the little stove; Ed went to help and came toward them with an armload. Jane kept waiting for a knock on the door but none came. "Now what happened to him?" she asked as she looked out one window and then another.

"Who?" Laura asked as she stirred the soup kettle.

As Jane stood watching, she saw Ed going for another load; as she watched, he brought three loads of wood and took it where she couldn't see. Who is he giving the wood to, she wondered. Then he and Sam each brought a load to the house on wheels. When Jane opened the door, they stacked it in the corner at the end of her bed. Jane looked questioningly at Ed.

"I filled in front of the seat in my wagon with wood. If the boys ride with me they can put their feet on it. We may not be able to find wood when we reach the river, especially if the other wagons are there," Ed explained.

"Something' smells good," Sam said.

"Laura is making some hot soup for dinner to go with your sandwiches; It'll be ready soon," she told them.

"Watch the soup for me, Jane; I'm going to get some beans ready so we can cook them a while for tonight's supper. Might as well make use of the nice fire we have. If they start the wagons, I'll just set the pot in one of the buckets." "That's a good idea," Jane answered as she stirred the soup which was almost done. Andy had gotten up and dressed some time ago, telling the girls not to look. Jane rolled the two beds up and put them in a pile on one end, making space for the men to come in and sit and have their dinner.

"Andy, go see if the men are ready to eat," Laura said. She had washed the cups, ready for coffee and got out the enameled cups from the cupboard for the soup; It was ready when they came.

Jane opened the door when they came and bid them all to come inside; they asked for the wash-pan first; Jane handed them a small bucket of water from the churn and told them to get the pan from the cupboard, When they had all washed, she invited them to come inside to have their food.

The three men came in and sat on the bunk. Laura dipped out the soup and handed them cups and an egg sandwich. "It sure is comfortable in here; I wonder why more people don't build houses on wheels to travel in?" Ed asked.

"Not everyone is as smart as my Gramps; it's his idea, although the Gypsies in Europe have traveled for centuries in houses such as this; it's the only home they know. I've read about them.; they paint all sorts of designs on their houses; some to keep the evil spirits away it seems," she smiled as she told them.

"If I decide to go to California to look for gold, I'll want to borrow your house on wheels," Ed jokingly told Jane.

"You'll have to make your own as I'll be living on my ranch in mine," Jane told him with a laugh.

"Whew! With hot soup and the fire in here I'm getting too warm," Nat said as he opened the door and went outside. The others drank the remainder of their coffee and all went to see how long they would be stopped.

Jane and Laura had set a pan of water on the stove, and as soon as it was warm they washed the cups and stacked them in the basket with the container of sugar and cream. They soon had the house tidy again and ready to go. The beans had begun to boil and they left them as long as they could to cook.

Jane, looking out the window, said, "I think they are getting ready to pull out." Andy had wanted to go ride with Ed but Jane wouldn't let him, so he sat on his bed playing with Goldie. Sam called out and knocked on the front of the house, "We'z pulling out." Laura hurriedly removed the pot of beans from the stove and set them into the bucket on the floor, as the wagon jerked into motion.

* * *

The wagon train moved slowly over the uneven ground. The wind continued with rain and sleet beating on the canvas covers of the wagons, and making the animals sling their heads in protest. It seemed to be getting colder as the wagons made their slow way forward. Jane, Andy and Laura were all very comfortable in the house on wheels, but Jane knew the women and children would be cold and miserable in the wagons with just the canvas cover between them and the elements.

"Maybe we could have taken some in with us but would have overloaded our wagon," Jane said as she watched the cold rain beat against the window.

"Everyone knew there would be hardships." Laura said; this is just part of them I suppose. I just hope they all keeps warm and dry and don't get sick." The men are warmly dressed and the rain gear you got them keeps the bitter wind out. I saw some that didn't look as though they had warm enough clothing on; as you say, we are better off than some of the rest."

"I'm going to stretch out; you lie down on Andy's bed and sleep if you want. If he wants to lie down, he and Goldie can take a quilt and lie on the floor; it's nice and warm in here. I think I'll put in another stick of wood as I don't want the fire to die on us." Jane took a rather heavy stick of wood and crammed it into the stove, knowing it would burn slowly. Laura had stretched out and closed her eyes, and Jane did the same. She gave Andy a heavy quilt for a pallet and he and Goldie curled up on it by the stove.

Jane didn't know how long she had slept when the rhythm of the wagon changed awaking her. She sat up and looked out the window, seeing a village ahead where several weather-beaten buildings nestled together at the foot of a small hill. She could see the river in the distance, knowing they had come to Grimms Crossing, where they would spend the night. She looked at her lapel watch and saw it was three o'clock as the wagons started to circle on the banks of the river. Turning, she saw that Laura was awake. "We're there," Jane told her. The rain had stopped and the wind died down some. Andy still slept on the floor, close to the stove where he was toasty warm.

Jane kept looking out the window, watching as the circle came full swing where she could see the other side of it. The front wagon had reached its space and had stopped. Their wagon would be almost on the river bend when it stopped. She could see nothing but woods and mountains on the other side. Looked as though they had reached the wilderness area, and the wagons finally came to a halt. She sat down on the bunk and said, "I guess we're there. It's early, and the weather seems to have settled down some although there are snow clouds hanging over us yet."

The cattle could be heard as they were brought into the circle, Jane didn't open the door until she was sure it was safe. Andy slowly opened his eyes, looked around and asked, "Where are we?"

"We're at Grimms Landings where we'll stay the tonight; tomorrow we cross the Kanawah River, then on to the Ohio.

"Let's see how far we are from the village; maybe we can see about getting some meat there." She opened the door seeing that they were a good distance away from the ramshackle buildings which didn't look too promising anyway. Laura came to stand beside her. "Maybe on the river there would be fish. Do you think?"

"I think the best thing to do will be wait and ask Jason," Jane said. They saw Mary and her children coming from their wagon.

"How are you?" Jane called out to her as Mary started toward them.

"We had to go to bed, we were so cold. John was wrapped like an Eskimo to keep warm. I'm glad the rain and wind have stopped. I wonder how long we'll be here? I sure don't like the looks of that river, and it's not near as big as the Ohio or Mississippi, I understand, and we have to cross both of them," Mary said.

"I think you should get out your fishing gear and get us a mess of fish for supper. I'll bet there's some big ones in there." Jane told her with a smile.

"You know, I just might do that; I'd love a good mess of fried catfish," Mary looked thoughtfully at the wide stream.

Jason came down the line of wagons and stopped to talk to the women. "Good afternoon, Ladies; I see everyone is in one piece. There'll be a load of wood coming in soon for fires. The damaged wagon is being worked on now, and should be repaired by tomorrow morning. We will ford the river then if the weather holds. If you want your wagons ferried across, it will be a dollar a wagon. Let me know if you want to ferry or try to ford," he smiled at them.

"I know now I want my three ferried if you say it's safe; I don't want to take a chance of wetting everything I have," Jane told him.

"I feel the same way," Mary said; "but you'll have to ask John. Jason, are there any fish to be had from this river?"

Jason laughed, "Fish maybe, but no tadpoles, tell John. I would think there would be. I don't know if it is too cold or not to fish. I'll ask the natives when they bring the wood. We're going to have some time; why don't you try it?"

"Is there any chance of getting some meat, do you think?" Jane asked.

"As soon as the wood comes, we're butchering a steer, some of it may be for sale; ask cook, he will be the one to decide," Jason told Jane.

"Mary, what do you say we try for some fish; I'll go with you. I'll get my heavy coat on and my fish line. I'll have to cut a pole and we probably can find some worms close to the river bank— I'll get a maddox.

Jane brought a basket and put her line, sinker and hooks in, and a good knife to cut the pole with and clean fish if they caught any. She had found an old cup in the house that had been there for ages. She put that in for her bait. She went to Nat's wagon and took a maddox from the side and was ready. "Andy, you and Mark can go up where they are working on the wagon and look around; don't come to the river as it's too dangerous." she told him.

"All right Maw, we'll do that. Good luck," he said as he went to look for Sarah and Mark.

Jane stood watching for Mary. She saw her coming with pole and line, looking like a true fisherman with her head wrapped in a long scarf. "Let's go; I feel lucky," she said.

They had only a short distance to go till they were on the river bank. Jane set her basket down and went over to an old log and started to dig. Surprisingly, the ground wasn't frozen. She swung the maddox a couple of times and found some nice big worms. "We're in luck, Mary; plenty of bait, and she soon filled the cup she had brought. They went to the log and climbed up to sit on it, leaving the maddox leaning on the other side. Mary soon had her line in the water, and it seemed the bait had hardly touched the water when her line went taunt; with a shocked expression, Mary squealed, "Got one. She gave a jerk on her line to set the hook and began hauling it in to shore. She got up from the tree and went to the bank and began pulling her line in hand over hand. "It sure is heavy; must be a big one." she pulled it out of the water a fifteen inch yellow channel cat fish. "It's a dandy." she said to Jane as Jane let out a squeal too, as she tugged her line in to shore. She had an even bigger one on her hook. Jane had thought to put in an old pair of leather gloves in her basket. "Here let me get the gloves to take them off the hook." They soon had the two fish off and in their basket, and lines back in the water. They continued to pull in one big cat after another.

"Boy, are we going to eat good tonight," Mary said smacking her lips.

"The basket is full; I don't know if the handle will hold with all that weight." Jane was looking at Mary when something caught her eye across the river. She stood looking; there were a dozen beautiful deer, at the edge of the wood.

"Mary, look! across the river!" Jane was whispering and the least Mary thought to herself would be a band of wild Indians.

"Deer! Meat on the hoof. But how can we get across to get one. We'll have to tell the men; maybe they can cross somehow and hunt."

"Mary, you stay and fish and I'll take the basket back and empty it and tell Ed. He and John may still have time to get a deer before dark; just be quiet and don't scare them."

Jane went bent over till she was out of sight and hurried to their wagon. "Laura, do you have hot water?" she asked as she knocked on the door.

Laura opened the door, "Yes I have hot—my God where did you get all those fish?" Laura's eyes were as big as saucers.

"Scheeee—don't say anything; we don't want to alert everyone just yet. Empty the basket and start cleaning them and we'll have a feast tonight. The Thompsons can eat with us. I have to find Ed; I'll get the basket when I come back."

She went up the line and found Ed cleaning the old axle grease from the wheels, and replacing it with new. "Ed," she said, looking carefully around to see that no one heard her.

"You should see the fish Mary and I are catching; and across the river next to those woods over there is a big herd of deer; do you think you and John can find a way to get over and kill us a couple? Take Cherokee if you want, but don't tell anyone until we get a kill. That may be selfish, but we come first. They would all go yipping and yelling and no one would get one. Maybe we should ask Jason if it's all right to hunt over there. Get going before dark; I'm going back to fish so we can salt some down to take with us." Jane hurried away.

When she reached the house, Laura was busily cleaning fish. "These are some of the nicest cats I've ever seen. Get as many as you can as we can salt them down. How I love salt fish.

"Me too," Jane said as she took the emptied basket and grabbed a sack that lay on the steps, and hurried away.

Jane carefully crept back to where Mary stood fishing; "My heavens, you have a wagon load caught already. Laura is busy cleaning fish and we will feast tonight. Jane looked across the water; the deer were still browsing in the edge of the wood. Ed will see if he and John can get across the river and get us each a deer; I'll leave it to them; we're the fishermen in the family." Jane laughed as she put fish into the sack she had brought. Mary still busy flinging them up on the bank.

"I don't believe this, Jane said as she threw in her hook and soon pulled out another fish. The basket was soon full again and the sack too; how will we get it home?" Jane asked.

"Pull it if we have to," Mary told her. "You cut a bushy branch—like from that willow—she pointed, and put the sack on it and pull the branch. That way anything in the sack doesn't drag on the ground and ruin whatever you're pulling. I've done it a many a time."

"Our sack is full and our basket is full; I think we had better quit, don't you?" Jane asked.

I sure hate to quit as long as they are biting." Mary looked so sad that Jane laughed at her.

"You stay and I'll take the basket and maddox back, and send Nat to bring the sack and send the basket for what you catch, in the meantime." Mary didn't waste time talking and just nodded as Jane started back.

"More?" Laura asked as Jane came around the corner. "Yes;

another basket; and we also have a sackful!; I wonder if Nat would go and help bring them back, and bring Mary back too; she would stay out there all night, I think, if we let her," she giggled. "I never in my life saw anyone who liked to fish so well."

Just then Nat came around the wagon having been up where work on the disabled wagon was being done.

"Where in the world did all those fish come from?" he asked in amazement.

"From the river; Jane and Mary have more than they can carry and want you to help," Laura told him.

Nat and Jane went toward the river as she explained about the deer and fish. They were very careful as they approached the river so as not to alert the deer on the other side. When Nat saw the pile of fish and the sackful, besides, he just shook his head, "I just don't believe this."

"Mary, we have to go now;" Jane was filling the basket again.

Mary reluctantly pulled her line from the water and wound it around her pole. Nat grabbed the fish and half carried and half drug the sack back. Mary took the poles, while Jane carried the basket full of fish.

Laura was still cleaning fish. She had almost finished the basketful that Jane had brought. "Nat would you fill the pot with water for me and put it on to get hot to clean the rest of the fish. Mary, I brought out two heads of cabbage; would you make the cold slaw? Jane, you can turn the fish while I make the hush puppies."

Nat put more wood on the fire which Laura had built; and had the spiders on. Jane handed Mary one of the big pewter bowls for the cold slaw. Laura was sifting meal and chopping up onions for the hush puppies. Jane put the coffee to boil; she didn't want to start frying fish yet. She put meal into a bowl to dip the fish in and got out the fish fryer and the lard. She would wait till the coffee started to boil before frying the fish.

They heard horses approaching and looking up saw Ed and John coming in; both had a deer in front of them on the horses. "Oh, my, two deer to work up." Laura said. "Looks as though we are all going to eat well," she said.

"We've gutted them and will finish butchering after supper." John said as they took them and hung them in a tree close to the wagons.

Jane had one of the big bowls piled up with fried fish. Laura had another with hush puppies and Mary came with the big bowl of slaw. They set them on the table and gave out plates telling everyone to help themselves. "Do be careful of bones," Jane cautioned them. "I'll be too full to operate to remove bones tonight," she told them with a laugh.

They all ate till they were moaning about being too full. The three women started to clean-up. The other fish had to be cleaned and salted down before they were finished—then the deer meat had to be taken care of.

Jane brought one of the wash tubs to put their deer meat in and Mary brought hers. Buckets of water was brought to wash the meat, before it was salted down.

"We've got to have some sort of work area, and a place to eat," Jane said. As soon as we get where we can buy some lumber, I'll have Sam make us a table with fold-down legs and a bench to sit on. We shouldn't have to eat standing up."

The lanterns had to be lit to finish up the deer meat and the fish before they could call it a night.

Several of the train had seen Mary and Jane with their fishing poles and smiled. Seeing the fish they had caught they hastened to find their poles and take off for the river.

Word was spread about hunting but some didn't want to have to cross the river. Several braved the river and came back with game. After seeing the results of the hunt some decided to be in the woods by dawn and try their luck. Hunting had been scarce and the lack of meat for cooking was beginning to worry some of the women, and they sent their men to hunt.

❄ Chapter Thirty-Nine ❄

The cattle were being moved out before day light. The noise and confusion woke Jane, and she hurried out of bed and looked out a window; she saw several men standing watching the drovers. I wonder why they are taking them out first? She hurried and dressed, putting on her jimmison, and went outside. Nat was building up the fire. Laura had a leg of the deer on the table slicing big pieces from it. She took a cutting board and laying the meat on it started to pound it with the knife, then floured it and put it into the big fish fryer to fry.

"That sure smells good," Jane said. "What can I do?" she asked Laura.

"Can you slice this and pound and flour it and watch the fryer? I'll make the biscuits. And we're going to have steak and gravy and biscuits, and we'll make enough for sandwiches for dinner. We have beans cooked for supper, and we have some fish left over. Oh, yes you can make the coffee. I have to get these biscuits in to bake."

"I'll take care of the rest," Jane told her, as she filled the big coffee pot and set it to boil. Jane saw several of the women taking fishing poles toward the river. She was glad to see that they were taking advantage of the time they had and maybe would catch enough fish for them a meal, at least.

Jane sliced all the meat from the leg bone and fried it. There would be plenty for breakfast and for dinner. She took the bone to Laura's wagon and put it in the tub. They had taken the meat to her wagon where it would be cool and not spoil by being in the house where there was a fire; the bone would be cooked later for soup.

When the men came to eat they oh'd , and ah'd, saying it was the best breakfast they ever had in their lives.

Ed told them that the herd had been taken up to shallow water where the cows could swim across, and then driven up the river where there were hopes of some roughage they could feed on. They would be held there till the wagon train came.

451

Jane and Laura cleaned up things as fast as they could, putting everything away. Jane decided to take a chance on getting better water at the next stop and didn't fill the churn that was in her wagon, as there was still a little left for drinking. She didn't like the idea of river water to drink.

The men were bringing the teams for hitching to the wagons. Laura made up her bed and changed things around so she would have room for the fish and meat. It was crowded, but they would make do.

Jane didn't build up the fire in the stove, but banked it to save it for heating coffee for dinner. It wasn't as cold as it had been the day before, and as long as the bitter wind didn't blow it wasn't bad.

The first wagons that were to go on the ferry pulled out. It would be a while before Jane's turn came. The cow and calf and Cherokee were tied to the back of the house on wheels. Sam was still checking everything out, and then climbed to the high seat. Jane and Andy stayed inside. Nat's wagon pulled out and Sam slowly followed, it wasn't far to the ferry. Some of the wagons were going to try to ford the river and went on past the ferry in the direction of the ford. Their wagon was in line for some time waiting their turn.

Jason came by, "Sam, pull your brake once you're on board the ferry and stand at your team's head and hold them. Untie the cow and Cherokee—Jane you hold him; and Laura, you hold the cow by the halter; watch yourself, and your feet in case they step if the barge should wobble; hang on to the side railings. Bring Andy outside, and let him stand by the railing and hang on. Does everyone understand? Talk to the animals and keep them calm. We're almost ready to go." He got off the barge and went to instruct the others.

Jane was scared to death as she held on tight to Cherokee; he had been through a lot and maybe wouldn't mind a trip by water. "Are you all right, Laura?"

"I'm fine; it isn't far." A gate was fastened behind them. Jane knew it had been done many times and she shouldn't be nervous. She had hardly made up her mind to that fact when they nudged into the other shore and the opposite gate swung open and the two wagons rolled gently onto land. There hadn't been a wobble of the barge and none of the animals seemed to mind.

They tied the cow and Cherokee to the back of the house on wheels. Jane had decided to ride up with Sam, and told Andy to come up too. He could change at noon if he wanted to ride in Ed's wagon. Jane was anxious to see the country they were going through.

They had traveled some distance up the trail when two men came by with deer across their horses. Jane didn't know them but knew they were with the wagon train. "Looks like they were lucky," Jane said.

"That'z fish and deer meat sure good eatin'," Sam told her.

"It saved the day; we'll have meat for a while—maybe until we get where we can hunt more. We were lucky to stumble onto fishing and the deer," Jane said with a nod.

Jane's wagon followed those in front of them; so far it had taken almost three hours to come this far. She looked up the river as they were leaving it and could see the wagons struggling to cross; it didn't look as though they were having an easy time of crossing. There was a lot of shouting and waving of arms; then all she could hear was the shouting, having passed a turn in the trail, and she could no longer see the wagons.

They kept to the river for a time; the area was cleared and level and easy to travel over. There were mountains and forests to the west of them.

"That was the Indian Chief Cornstock's hunting ground not long ago," Jane told Sam and Andy. We got our deer where he used to hunt deer, and his braves maybe fished in the river.

They seemed to have been on the trail for some time when they came in sight of the herd grazing peacefully to the west of them. The route they were on now was almost directly north. They would be turning west soon toward the ferry over the Ohio River; it was called the Gallipolis Ferry. Jane didn't think they would be there for another day; with the herd so contented she thought they might be spending the night in the valley close to it.

A rider came racing toward them. "Hold up! Hold up! he called waving his arms as he approached Jane's wagon. They need a doctor at the crossing, are you Doctor Barrlette? Hurry, come with me. Hurry!"

"Jane didn't waste time asking questions. She hurried down from the wagon, opened the door to the house, and snatched her saddlebags, threw them on Cherokee, untied and mounted in a

453

matter of seconds, "Lets go!" she yelled as she gave Cherokee his head and he stretched his long legs into a run. She could hear yelling and see a lot of excitement ahead at the crossing. She couldn't tell what had happened; she saw what looked like two wagons tangled together in the water, with horses struggling to right themselves; she saw what looked like a child lying on the river bank, with people standing around pointing and yelling.

Jane jumped from Cherokee, grabbed her bag from the saddle bag, gave the bridle reins to someone and hurried over. "What happened?" she asked as she kneeled beside the young child who looked about Andy's age. She saw he was wet and had a gash on his head but little bleeding; he was ashen, and looked dead.

"He was thrown from the wagon and we couldn't find him. He was in the water some time," someone answered.

Jane had her stethoscope out listening for a heart beat and breathing. She could tell there was water in his lungs, but he had a faint heart flutter. She hurriedly turned him over and patted him hard on the back; some water came out; she then laid him on his back turning his head to the side, and pushed on his chest; water trickled from the corner of his mouth; she kept working his chest, and more water trickled out. She lifted his head, placed her mouth over his and blew a couple of breaths into his lungs. She placed her hand against his neck and could feel a weak heartbeat.

"Does someone have a dry blanket, she asked." Someone ran to one of the wagons that had already crossed and brought back a blanket. She quickly pulled the wet clothing from his upper torso, wrapped him and motioned for some one to pull his trousers and shoes off. She waited a few seconds, and listened with the stethoscope. She could still hear water in his lungs and she turned his head to the side and worked some more on his chest. The boy suddenly moved his arms, and legs, and Jane could tell his heartbeat was stronger; he would be all right.

"Where are his parents?" Jane asked. A young woman stepped forward, "I'm his maw," she said with tears in her eyes.

"Is your wagon on this side?" Jane wanted to know. The girl shook her head no and pointed to the wagon in the river, too frightened to tell her.

"Someone carry him to our wagon," a woman standing close said.

"I'll have to stitch that gash on his head. Please build a fire and heat some rocks to put around him. He's frozen."

Jane followed to a wagon that stood close by, and climbed inside as they laid him on the bed. She covered him with the quilts that were on the bed tucking them around him. Getting out the carbolic acid, she cleaned his head wound which was bleeding more now—being in the cold water had kept the bleeding down. She again felt his pulse which seemed normal. She knew he was woozy from the trauma, and wanted to wait till she knew he was strong enough to give him chloroform and sew up the deep head wound.

The mother asked, "Is he dead?" with a tremble in her voice.

Jane reached over and patted her hand, "He's going to be all right. I'm just making sure he is breathing right before I can give him something so I can stitch up the gash on his head. We got to him quick enough; he'll have a headache, and will probably want to sleep a lot, but he'll be fine." She lifted the pad of carbolic acid from the wound; it was a clean gash, and maybe not even leave a scar. "What's his name?"

"It's Howard; we call him Howie; I don't know what I would have done if he had died. I tried to hang on to him, but it was so sudden, he just flew right out of my arms."

"Howie, can you hear me? Howie? answer me, Howie.?

"What do you want?" he asked in a slurred voice, "I want to sleep; go away."

"We're going to let you sleep in just a few minutes." Jane got out the chloroform and put three drops on a piece of gauze and held it over his nose, Soon he had relaxed every muscle, and became limp. She held it for a couple of minutes longer, then got her equipment and sewed up the gash carefully pulling it together so the ragged edges met perfectly. "I don't think he will even have a scar. I'm going to bind it; just be careful he doesn't tear the bandage off." She took strips and wound them around his head and pinned them with a safety pin. "There, he'll sleep soundly for at least three hours. Keep him warm. As soon as the rocks are heated, put some at his feet and around his legs. Where is his father?" Jane asked knowing that no man came to see about him.

"He was killed in the war. I came with my sister and her family. Her oldest son was driving the wagon; my sister and the rest are still on the other side; I know they will blame me," she had tears in her eyes.

"They shouldn't blame anyone; it was an accident. Where is the driver?"

"They are working to get the horses out; they have the tongue of the wagons rammed together; the horses started to carry on and jumped at the other team, and got tangled together."

"What is your name?" Jane asked.

"It was Mrs. Howard Boggess; now it's Nettie Boggess."

"Don't you worry, no one is going to blame you. You just take care of your son. I have one almost the same age," Jane smiled at her. "I'll look at Howie when we get settled tonight before we go to bed. He's going to be just fine; he had seven stitches; you can tell him when he awakens."

"Oh, thank you, thank you, I don't know how I'll pay you but I will."

"By the way, where was the wagon train doctor? Do you know?" Jane asked looking at the distraught girl.

"He's down with the influenza, I hear; he's pretty old, and he caught cold. I hear he's real bad," Nettie told her.

"That's strange; I wonder who's treating him? I'll see you a little later.

"Jane went to the river bank to see what was happening with the wagons. They had gotten one team out but both wagons were still wedged together. They were tying ropes to both wagons and trying to pull them in with teams on the shore. The one wagon was being washed downstream. She saw Jason in the stream directing the operation. It didn't look good; but as long as no lives were lost maybe it would come out all right.

Jane stood watching for some time. They finally cut the harness of the other team and brought it on shore, leaving the two wagons in mid stream. They had fastened ropes in several places and were slowly pulling them to shore. The fire Jane had asked to be built was blazing up and several of those who had been in the water were standing close trying to get warm. Jane saw someone pick some of the stones out of the fire and wrap them in some rags and take them toward the wagon where Nettie and Howie were. The wagons finally made it in to where men could get hold and pulled and pushed them from the river. Jane saw there was damage to both vehicles and they would have to be left on shore until the damage could be repaired.

Jane saw the young woman who was pregnant standing by the fire; her husband stood with his arm around the sobbing girl.

Jason saw Jane and came over to her. "Jason, you need to get out of those wet clothes right away, or you'll be down with influenza yourself," Jane told him.

"How is young Howie? Is he going to live? We couldn't find him for about five or ten minutes. I doubt he will make it."

"He's sleeping comfortably, He had seven stitches on his head and water in his lungs. We got it all out and he will be just fine. Don't you trust me?" Jane asked with a teasing smile.

He looked at her with a strange expression, "Seems you never cease to amaze me. "Nettle has a hard time of it. I'm glad her little boy is going to be all right, thanks to you; and I'm glad you were close by. He couldn't have survived long the shape he was in."

"You're right there; he was almost a goner, but he will be fine, and Nettie is with him. What about that couple? Was she hurt?" Jane nodded to the couple at the fire.

"One of the damaged wagons is theirs. They were going on the train on a shoestring; I don't know what they'll do now. Everything they owned has gotten wet. Their team is fine; that's a blessing, maybe they will turn around and go back; I don't know." He shook his head.

"Are we camping here tonight?" Jane asked looking at Jason.

"Yes, we'll stay out close to the herd. As soon as I follow my doctor's orders and get into dry duds, I'll be out to get them settled. I'll see you in a little while; thanks Jane." He mounted and quickly disappeared.

Jane walked over to the couple by the fire, noticing that the girl had only a light jacket on, and no one seemed to be paying any attention to them. "Honey, are you all right?" Jane asked her.

Her husband turned as Jane asked, "She got shook up pretty bad. Some one took her on their horse and brought her to shore. Our wagon is in bad shape. I don't know what happened; my mules are young and the other wagon was following too close and washed into mine and caused them to panic. I don't know what we'll do now. The team is fine but all we own is ruined. We can't go back; we have no one. All our family died in the flu epidemic during the war—what didn't die in the war. We wanted to make a new start." He shook his head and held his wife tightly.

"You wait here just a few minutes; keep her by the fire until I get back." Jane took the reins of Cherokee from the man who stood holding him. "Thank you so much. I appreciate your taking care of my horse."

"You're welcome doctor; that was a grand thing you did for the little tyke. If I'm ever sick I'll send for you."

Jane mounted and smiled at him and was off toward the house on wheels. She spotted Sam pulled over and waiting.

Jane got down, went to the back of the wagon and opened the door and got a blanket, went to the front and said, "Sam, untie the cow and hook her to a tree here, and then come over to the river bank please; I'll be over there." She mounted Cherokee and hurried away as Sam started to turn the wagon.

She rode up and dismounted and went to the shaking girl, and wrapped the blanket around her.

"My wagon will be here in a short time, and I want you to lie down. You've had a shock and you could lose your little one. I won't let that happen if I can help it. Do you have any friends on the train?" Jane asked thinking it strange no one had offered to have the girl lie down in a wagon.

"We don't know anyone; I saw you at the depot; I thought you were so pretty," the girl answered smiling shyly.

"I want you both to stop worrying; it's not good for you in your condition. We'll get things cleaned up and your wagon repaired; my driver, Sam, can do anything. As soon as we get settled he can come and look at the damage and get some help to fix it. We'll take your things out of your wagon and get them washed and dried for you, and you will be as good as new, and be on the wagon train when it pulls out.

Sam drove up and pulled over so he was heading out toward the trail. Tying the reins around the brake, he came over.

"What 'z you want Miss Jane?

"Sam, this is, Mr. and Mrs.—" laughing she said, "I don't know your names."

"We're Ray and Caroline Hayse, from Charlotte; we're the ones who were in the accident.

Sam stuck out his black hand, "You 'z both not hurt; You'z lucky, the wagon can be fixed. We'z get right on it as soon az we get the woman folk settled." He took Caroline's arm, "Come this way little lady; Miss Jane take fine care of you."

Jane opened the door of the house on wheels and Sam almost lifted Caroline inside. "Az soon az I get the wagon settled I'z be back, Ray;" he closed the wagon door on the two women.

Jane straightened Andy's bunk and told Caroline to lie down. Here, let's put the blanket over you. When she lay back on the pillow Jane removed her shoes and tucked the blanket around her. "We can't do much until the wagon stops; then I'll see where we're at. Just lie still, Caroline; you're safe now.

Closing her eyes she whispered, "Thank you;" she had been at the river for some time and with being shook up she was completely exhausted. Jane was furious that no one had seemed to pay attention to her needs. Jane sat holding her hand as the wagon moved over the trail toward where they would be camping for the night. When the wagon stopped, Jane found the fire was still smoldering in the stove, added some small pieces of wood and set the flat irons on. She took a cup and poured out a cup of milk and set it to warm on the stove. Taking her stethoscope she listened to Caroline's heartbeat; it sounded strong; she lowered the stethoscope to her stomach and listened for the heartbeat of the baby she carried. She kept moving the stethoscope around until she heard the faint little thump telling her that the baby was all right. Caroline had been watching what she was doing all the time.

"Your baby is fine; its heartbeat is normal," Jane told her.

"You can hear its heartbeat? Oh, my! I'm only five months along. I never knew you could hear a heartbeat of an unborn baby." She smiled happily, "I'm so glad, Ray has been so worried."

Jane removed the cup of milk from the stove and took the pillow from her bunk and put it behind Caroline. "Here, I want you to drink this and then take a long nap. You'll stay with me tonight, and we'll find a place for Ray to sleep in one of the wagons. Things will look better after a good night's sleep and a good meal." Jane turned and wrapped the irons in an old towel and put them under the covers at her feet.

Jane went outside to see if they were situated for the night. He saw Jason coming toward her.

"Another stray, Jane?" Jason asked with a chuckle.

"How did you know?" Jane asked with a smile.

"Word gets around. Sam told me that he and Ed were going to

help fix the wagon, and that you had taken the girl in to doctor."

"I was furious when I saw no one paying any attention to a woman in her condition after what she had been through. She was shivering and no one seemed to care. She'll be fine, and the baby is all right, I have her in a warm bed. Mary, Laura and I will go see what we can salvage from their wagon. Is this where we will camp tonight?"

"Yes, we'll not circle up tonight as the cattle are contented and will be fine with a few men patrolling them. If you need help, let me know," he said as he road off.

Jane waved as he rode away. Laura came over and Jane told her about the accident and about Caroline.

"I think Mary and you and I had better go see what we can do about their wagon. Everything is wet and we'll have to dry things out before they can use it. I expect their food is all ruined. Get Mary and I'll let Caroline know."

The three women walked the short distance to the river's edge where the wagon was being worked on. Sam, Ed and Ray were removing the broken parts. Jane explained to Ray what they were going to do and told him that his wife was sleeping and that she and the baby were both fine.

"It's a mess he told them. Help yourself," he said as he returned to help the men.

Laura and Jane climbed into the wagon. The first thing they did was open up both ends of the wagon tarp and let in light and air. Jane saw that their bedding and everything was covered with river mud. They began to throw out all the wet clothes, quilts, and bedding. There was a trunk which they opened and found it was dry inside, and put it aside. A wash tub had all her cooking utensils in it, but the sacks of flour were wet as were a couple sacks of meal. We'll get something to put that in and we can make gruel for the pigs and chickens—I'll give them some dry for it. They found a couple of stone jars that had beans, salt, and coffee in bags; they were fine.

"First we have to get everything out, and then I'll scrub the wagon floor," Laura said.

Jane asked the men to come and remove the trunk to the front seat and all the cooking pans. She then took the wash tub and put it out on the ground and threw all the wet clothes into it. "We'll have to bring our tubs and heat some water, wash everything and hang it up to dry," she said, "It'll take forever for a feather tick to dry, but we'll try putting it by the fire; if it doesn't get dry we'll put a line across the wagon and let it dry as we travel, and put it in the sun when we can. It's the only thing I know to do. We have hay in one wagon which we can give them for a pallet."

Laura and Mary made another trip to the wagons and came back with washboards and two tubs, and a bar of soap.

Soon there was a tub of water heating. The clothes were sorted and the mud rinsed from them and ready when the hot water was. They set the churns outside, and all the flatware and dishes were packed in a large kettle. The couple didn't have a lot they were taking with them. The three women picked up the feather tick as best they could and took it to the edge of the river and swished it up and down several times—also the two pillows. The mud came off the ticking better than they thought it would. They squeezed it as much as they could and took it back and laid it close to the fire on some dead tree branches they drug in to hold it. Soon they could see steam rising from the bedding. The water was hot and they fixed two tubs of sudsy water and Mary and Laura started to scrub, while the tub was removed from the fire and Jane was bringing cold water to finish filling it for rinsing. She had brought her clothes line and pins, and she tied it from tree to tree; soon there was clothes hanging flapping in the breeze. Jane went and washed while Laura took some of the soapy water and scrubbed the wagon. Soon the women had everything washed and out drying. They kept shaking and turning the feather bed.

When Laura finished with the floor, she brought all the pots and pans and dishes and got a clean bucket of water and washed, dried and stacked them neatly ready for use. She took the small bags of food from the big stone jar to make sure it was all dry, then replaced them. The wind was drying the floor; they would just have to leave it for a while. It was early yet and it should be dried by dark, and then they could put everything back. The heavy quilts and blankets would take a lot longer; they had put them on branches close to the fire as possible. At least all the mud was out of them.

They stacked the tubs and wash boards ready to take back. Jane called Ray over.

"Can you watch the feather bed, Ray, and not let it get too hot on one side? Keep shaking it and turning it so it will dry. "We're going home now. I want to see if Caroline is all right, and I have to see to the little boy. You come with the men; you'll eat with us and we'll go from there." He nodded.

"Thank all of you," he said.

* * *

Caroline slept the night on Andy's bunk; Andy on a pallet between the beds. Ray had slept on a pallet in Sam and Ed's wagon. The couple had eaten dinner of deer sandwiches and had eaten supper with Jane's group. The wagon had been repaired to some extent. Sam still had to hammer a couple of iron pieces to re-enforce the tongue, but everything looked better than it had before. One wheel had to be replaced as the rim was bent.

They had a new one tied to the side of their wagon and it hadn't gotten damaged. The other wagon only had minor damage—one spoke in a wheel was replaced, and a singletree had to be repaired. The harness was being repaired in several places from cutting it loose to free the team; everything was almost done. Jason had decided to leave about ten o'clock the next day and that would give them time to put things together.

The feather bed would be dry in a short time. They were still turning and fluffing it. It looked fluffier than when new. All the clothing had been folded and put inside on the stack of clean quilts and the wagon was clean and neat. Jane had hay brought and put down for the feather bed to rest on. When Caroline came to look she had tears streaming down her face.

"You two come and eat with us until you can get some game, or somewhere or get your own food," Jane told them.

"You have all been so good to us. I hope we can repay you sometime. We'll sure try," Ray told all of them. "It was fortunate that my rifle and shells were tied to the roof and didn't get ruined; I'll be able to kill game," he said.

The train was ready by nine o'clock and the lead wagons pulled out with Jason going ahead showing them the route. The herd was left till all the wagons were lined up on the trail. Then the cattle were held in a close group; they didn't want to leave the feed they had enjoyed in the valley, and it was hard for the herders to get them headed in the right direction.

The wagons and herd were soon settled down to their usual pace, and moved along the trail in a smooth line. The sun was shining for a change and everyone seemed to be in a good mood after all that had happened.

Ray had asked permission to pull in behind the Thompson's wagon and he and Caroline were on their own wagon. Caroline, after a good night's sleep and food, was in good shape. She had stopped crying and was stronger. They would be able to sleep in their own wagon tonight. The feather bed had dried and their wagon smelled fresh and clean. Ray had told Jane that besides their team they had two cows with the herd, and both were with calf. He wanted to give her one of them for helping them with food and fixing the wagon.

"You keep your cows; if you have milk and bread and occasional meat, you can survive. You must have some greenery and fruit once in a while or you can get sick," she told them. "Especially Caroline." Jane was having her eat an apple a day while she was with them, and drink milk for the development of the baby.

The train turned due west, toward the ferry across the Ohio. Jason had told them they should be there by noon. He wanted everyone to have a rest before trying to cross the river. They might even lay over for a day. Zachary Smith, the wagon master, and the rest had decided they would go by land and not try going on the river, thinking it safer, and less costly for those who had little money which seemed to please the majority of the travelers. Thinking of the near disaster at the other crossing, it could just as easily been any one of them, and maybe loss of a loved one.

❦ Chapter Forty ❦

The wagons were rolling along at a good pace, and were passing through the edge of Chief Cornstock's hunting ground. Jane was sure that if the wagons had to lay over at the crossing that some of the men would come back to hunt. It looked wild and untamed; most of the trees were evergreens, and packed close together they resembled a wall of green. Jane was watching the forest closely; she saw several birds fly into and out of the thick trees along the edge of the woods. Once she saw movement and thought it might be a deer, but it was too far away for her to be sure.

Jason came by the wagon right after they had started out.

"How are things going?" he asked. I hear you had a bang up fish fry," he chuckled as he looked at Jane.

"Mary sure likes to fish. She caught so many we had to make several trips to bring them all back to the wagons. We both have a churnfull put down in salt for later. I think I caught my share too. Too bad more people didn't try it," Jane told him.

"I hear your men got a couple of deer. That helps out the eating department. We sure enjoyed steaks from the Jarvis steers," he said with a smile.

"I don't want to hear about that. They were pets, to look at—not eat. I could have told you that." She gave him a flirty smile.

"If you need anything, there's a good-size store at the crossing; you may want to try it. Sorry I have to be on the job; I'll see you later." He urged his horse into a trot as he went down the length of the train, speaking to first one and then another.

Jane turned to Sam, "Sam, do you think you could make us a table with fold-down legs or detachable legs and maybe a bench to go with it? It doesn't have to be fancy, just serviceable It's a long way to Oklahoma Territory and I'd like to enjoy my meals, as I'm sure the others would too. I've been thinking—we could carry it on top of the house on wheels if it would lay flat. What do you think?"

"I'z have to think on it. I'z don't know why not. I'z thought iffin we haz time, I make that little Caroline lady a small cupboard, and let down-shelf, as she'z don't haz nothin' to work with. She'z need a spider too; all she got is a grate to lay on the coals."

"We'll try to help them get a few things they need. I don't know how much money they have—not much I expect. It won't be long till she can't bend over a fire to cook. I was so afraid she might lose her baby, but she's fine."

Andy sat between them and when the talk lagged he broke into song— "You ough-rer see my Cindy, she lives way down south; Git along home Cindy, Cindy, get along home." He had his puppy, Goldie in his arms and was singing to her. He had suddenly run out of words.

Sam chuckled, "Now that'z a happy song, and that'z a happy dog iffin I ever seed one."

Jane noticed a few farm houses along the route; they were set back in fields, too far to see much. Most of them were 'Genny Linn's' built out of cut boards, up and down with smaller boards covering the cracks. All of them were small, and didn't look too prosperous. She saw a couple of fields that had seen the plow recently. Potato planting time was coming up. She knew they would never reach the Territory in time to plant potatoes, but she certainly meant to try to plant as much as she could even if it was late. There were lots of crops that would grow in a short time, and according to her calculations the Territory was farther south than West Virginia and the season should be longer. She would find out before planting things, and what would grow well there.

Jane glanced at her lapel-watch; it was getting on to noon; they should be coming to the river soon. She was getting restless waiting to see the river, and scared to cross it—and they still had the Mother of rivers to cross, the Mississippi. The Ohio was a big river and they would be lucky if no one was hurt crossing it, or they had loss of animals and belongings.

Jason came by once more. "Doesn't look as though the rest of our train is here yet, unless they have moved to the other side already. We're almost there; just wanted you to know," he called as he rode on.

Jane could now see the river. There were barges and some boats tied up along the shore. She could see a long row of weather-beaten buildings along the river, which looked like storage sheds.

There was one larger building farther up—it was on higher ground above the river, which she thought might be the store. She could see several people working at various things, but as far as she could see there was no wagon train.

"I wonder what has happened? I don't see the wagon train; I hope we aren't held up too many days," Jane said as she scanned the area, stretching to look in every direction. As far as she could see there were no wagons on the other side.

Sam pulled the mules to a halt, as the wagons in front had stopped. They sat for a few minutes and then the wagons moved again; they were going east away from the river making a deep circle into a big field following the other wagons, and soon came around the circle toward the river again. They didn't overlap the wagons as they did at first, but left them farther apart with the tongues filling in the space between. Jane surmised that the cattle were trailbroke enough that they could be managed without such a tight enclosure.

Sam finally pulled on the check lines and brought the mules to a standstill; they slung their heads and stomped, blowing and snorting.

"They're not supposed to blow now," Andy said, "only when they are going up a hill." Jane and Sam both laughed.

"They know they are not going again soon, and that food isn't far away. They are used to getting unharnessed after stopping behind the other wagons and they're happy," Jane told Andy.

They all climbed down, and Sam began to tend to his team. Jane wanted to find the fresh water they would be using and fill her churn. She saw a small stream on the other side of the circle, and walked in that direction. There were two water boxes, and she went back to get her bucket, asking Laura to fetch a bucket and come too. When she got to the first water box it didn't look like it was meant for humans. They went on to another which she saw was close to a spring with a water trough pouring clean water into it. They both filled their buckets and went back to the wagon.

"I'd like to get a couple more buckets before we have to wait in line," Jane said as they poured out the water still in the churn into the big wooden bucket, and poured in the fresh water. The churn was almost full.

"Let's go get two more buckets while we're at it," Laura said, and they went back for more. They saw women coming from their wagons toward the spring as they filled their buckets and started back. Mary and Caroline were among them.

The churn was full, and Jane turned a plate over it to keep dirt from falling in. They had an extra bucket to use in cooking. The table was let down and the bucket set on it, with cups by it for anyone who would want a drink. The camp was coming alive, some getting ready to eat their dinner, some building fires for coffee; everyone busy. Laura and Jane had sandwiches made for the men when they came to eat. She took the coffee pot and put it onto the stove in the house on wheels, and made a small fire. The coffee would be hot soon.

Andy with his Goldie were over playing with Mark and Sarah. She had named her puppy 'polka dot'. It was black and white spotted where Goldie was a gold and white. There were never two puppies as loved. Jane's white cat was content to stay inside most of the time. She would set her out morning and night and she was happy otherwise lying on Jane's bed.

Jane walked back to talk to Mary and Caroline. "I'm going to the store after dinner; do you want to go along? Or are you going to fish, Mary?"

"I don't see any reason I can't do both; I think I'll buy some more hooks while I'm where I can get them. I'll go look around; I don't think I need anything that I can't do without," she laughed. "Might as well get used to doing without."

"I could use some things. I'd like to try fishing; we could start cooking for ourselves then." Caroline said.

"Are you feeling all right Caroline?" Jane asked noticing that her skin looked pink and healthy, and her eyes clear.

"I'm fine. We're going to spend the dollar to cross by barge on this river; we won't take a chance like last time."

"You know what the old saying is, 'penny wise and dollar foolish.' Sometimes it's wise to spend to save," Jane smiled.

"You and Ray come and eat when the others come. I want you to drink some milk. I'll let you know, Mary, when I'm ready to go to the store. When we come back we'll try our hand at fishing the Ohio," she laughed as she went back to her wagon.

Jane saw Ed at his wagon. They had set the chickens and pigs under the wagon, and poured water into the little pan he carried for that. "Ed, do you have any plans? I know Sam plans to do some work on our wagon and he is going to try to make us a table, and he wants to make a small cupboard for Caroline. Would you like to take Ray and try to get them a deer? They want to get back on their own. Mary, Caroline and I are going to try to get some fish. We'll be here for a time, looks like. You'll need to take the horses. Take one of the team and Andy's mare," Jane told him.

"I'd like that; I love to hunt. Could you use a turkey if I see one?" he asked.

"You bet we could, or anything else eatable. We will be ready for another deer soon. Do you think we need to get more shells? I think all the guns we have take the same, only my pistol." I'll get more just to be safe, she decided. "When you men are ready, we'll eat; the coffee should be hot by now. Then you can be off on your hunt. And do be careful."

After they had all eaten and things were put away, Laura, Jane, Mary and Caroline all walked to the store. It was a good walk for them. If they bought much they would have to come back with a horse to get it. The store was a big sprawled-out affair with a good assortment of merchandise. They were all looking around when Jane saw some small stone jars that would be perfect for milk. She selected two of those—one white with a blue stripe around it and one pale blue with a white stripe. They looked just right to set on the shelf in the cupboard. Then she got six more boxes of shells for the guns. She bought a big jar of petroleum jell. She noticed the men's hands were chaffed and cracked; it was for them. She bought six bars of naptha soap. Looking around she didn't see anything else that she really needed.

Caroline was looking at some soft flannel and Jane knew she was thinking of the baby. She should be making baby clothes at five months; there wasn't that much time to do it in.

"You really need to be making things for your baby; have you started yet?" Jane asked.

"No, I thought I would wait, but this seems reasonably priced. We need so many things, I don't know," she said undecided.

"One thing you do need is another bag of salt; if we catch fish, or the men get a deer, you'll need it to salt the meat. And you'll need clothing for your baby, which has to be made; maybe we all can pitch in and help you sew. The farther you go into the wilderness, the more costly things are going to be. I'm going to replace your meal and flour that got wet as we used it for the chickens and pigs. Do you have baking powder and ingredients for bread? You'll need lard for frying meat and fish. Do you have money?"

"Yes, I have some. Ray said I can spend ten dollars. That's a lot of money. I have to be careful, and get all I can for it. Could you help me? I've never done much buying."

"All right." Jane said, "lets start with the material—twenty yards would be eighty cents; then you need two spools of white hand thread; do you have needles, scissors and such?" Caroline nodded. "Two twenty-five pounds bags of salt—that's another fifty cents. Two five pound buckets of lard—that's fifty cents, ten pounds of sugar—that's fifty cents;" Jane was writing the total on a brown bag on the counter. "Baking powder—two small cans; It's better to get two small cans and one can stay sealed and stay fresh. These little jars I bought are only twenty cents a piece; they are good to keep milk in; see how tall—you can set them in water to keep the milk cool. You'll have the lard buckets to milk in but you must not let milk set in them as they'll rust. You'll need a strainer, but you can always use a rag, and scald it each time. You have a sieve, don't you?" Again Caroline nodded. Jane had seen everything in the wagon when they were cleaning it. "A strainer is only ten cents," Jane added that. You'll need soap for the baby's clothes—four bars will be twenty cents.

"I want you to buy some apples, cabbage, and potatoes. You'll need vinegar—a small container to make slaw. You need these things to stay healthy and have a healthy baby. Can you think of anything else you'll need to keep house?" Jane asked.

"So far we've spent three dollars and sixteen cents. You'll be able to get apples, cabbage, turnips, potatoes, and maybe another bag of flour and still have five dollars left over."

"Oh that's wonderful; thank you for helping me. I could never have gotten so much," Caroline said a big smile on her face.

"Now the next thing is getting it home, and then finding the vegetables." The merchant was waiting on Mary; she had a pile of things on the counter, and Caroline's would be even bigger. Jane looked around; she wondered if he would have a way to deliver the things. Or she would have to get Cherokee and some sacks to take it back. She waited till Mary finished; looking around the store she saw a couple of wooden boxes in a corner; I'll ask if I can have those she thought.

Mary was finished buying and the merchant came over to them. Jane had the list ready.

"Do you have any way of delivering?" she asked.

"I'm afraid not; most people take their packages on horseback," he said. "You ladies walked over from the train, did you?"

Jane nodded, "I'll go get a horse and come back when we're through. Could I have those two wooden crates over there?" she asked. "I'm tired of standing up to eat; I want them to sit on," she gave him her most radiant smile.

"What else do you want?" he asked before answering her about the crates.

Jane started to give him the order. As she called it off he piled the things on the counter. Jane paid close attention to everything, making sure it was all there. "Is there anyplace where we can buy potatoes, cabbage and apples?" she asked. "By the bushel, at a reasonable price?" she added.

"I don't keep much in that way, but there's a man I sent word to about the wagon train; he'll be by, I think, with what you'll need. In fact, there he is now." Jane looked toward the window, seeing a wagon coming.

"I think that's all; could you tally it up?" He started to count. Jane had added it and knew to the penny how much it was.

"That will be three dollars and sixteen cents." Jane smiled; to the penny—she trusted him. "What about the crates? she asked again.

"I guess I wouldn't want to eat standing up either," he said. "You take them," they're yours. We just use them for kindling." "I'll go find you some kindling," she said with a smile. Thank you so much." Caroline you and Mary stay with the packages; Laura and I will walk back and I'll bring Cherokee and get our things." Jane went over and picked up the two crates. She and Laura would carry one between them back to the wagon.

"Let's go see what we can buy from the wagon of vegetables," Jane said. The four women walked over and Jane took the two crates, with her.

The farmer threw back the tarp and showed them what he had. It was choice vegetables. Jane hoped they weren't too high.

"What do you get for apples?" she asked.

"I'm getting sixty cents a bushel—same for potatoes; cabbage—

six heads for a dollar; turnips fifty cents a bushel. You ladies from the train? Where are you headed?"

"Oklahoma Territory. We're all farmers and ranchers," Jane said. "Could you drive over to the wagons? I'll guarantee you'll empty your wagon. We don't have any way to get the things over. Only remember we're first," she laughed.

Turning to Caroline she said, "With what you've already bought, if you get one of everything you'll have spent just under six dollars. You'll still have four dollars. If the men get a deer you'll have food to last you almost the whole way."

"Get one of each," Caroline said."

"What about you, Mary?" Jane asked.

"Save me one of each till I get there, or tell John to pay. We'll wait till you return." The two women went and sat down on a bench against the wall, their packages piled beside them.

The girls each took one of the crates to carry to the wagon, and started back.

"Here, throw those on my wagon and I'll bring them for you," the farmer said taking the crates and putting them on top of his potatoes.

"Thank you, they are a little heavy." Jane and Laura discussed what they would need. They both decided that the apples were the most inviting; everyone loved apple dumplings, and the potatoes were filling. Finally Jane said, "looks like we had better take one of each, maybe two of potatoes. We eat those every meal, and who knows when we'll find any more."

"I think that's a good idea. We won't have to buy anything else if we can get meat," Laura nodded.

"I'm sure Ed will come back with a deer, maybe more. And I hope Ray has luck too. I feel sorry for that young couple. They don't have much to go on," Jane said.

They were lucky they didn't have a funeral on their hands, with the accident they were in," Laura said.

They were back at the wagon; Jane found some sacks and string to tie them with and untied Cherokee, mounted and headed back to the store on horseback; it didn't seem very far. The wagon waited until she returned before going to the train.

"I'll just take a minute and I can show you where to go," she told the wagon driver.

"Take your time, Miss." he told her, as he sat eating an apple.

471

Jane went inside the store where the girls were sitting waiting with the packages all around them. Jane had brought in the sacks and started to fill them, tying two of the ends together to put over the horse. Some of them were heavy and took Jane and Mary both to put them on the horse. Jane tied the sacks to the saddle; in fact, putting one across the saddle. She would walk with the wagon and the others and lead Cherokee. "We're ready," she announced to the driver.

The wagon followed the women, as they walked as fast as they could back to the wagons. Jane had him park close to where her wagon was. These are our wagons—these four. Laura hurried and brought the big wooden bucket as he measured out the apples, putting some in the bucket. Jane held the crate out for the rest of the bushel; she and Laura took them to the house on wheels; Jane took the things from the sacks and brought them to put potatoes in. Jane told Andy to go from wagon to wagon and tell everyone that the vegetable man was there. The women came hurrying up to buy. Jane asked them to form a line so the first there could be served first, and there wouldn't be any trouble. The farmer was measuring out potatoes, apples, turnips, and counting heads of cabbage. As the line got shorter and shorter, he was scraping bottom, picking up every apple and potato there was.

"If you ladies think you'll need more, I could be here early tomorrow," the farmer said.

"We're supposed to meet a much larger group of wagons here. This is where the main train will be made up. We aren't sure if they have crossed already or if we'll have to wait. If you will contact the wagon master, Zachary Smith or the scout Jason Turner, they may know something. I'm sure you could sell more when they come," Jane assured him. "I told you you'd sell all you had," she smiled at him.

"You were right, young lady; I'll try to see the people you suggested. Lots of luck where you're going, and thank you for helping."

"That's the scout on the black gelding, coming this way. He'll be able to help you. Thanks for giving us a decent price for things. Good luck to you too," Jane said as he turned his wagon and met Jason up the line of wagons.

"Well now, where will we put things ?" Jane asked.

"We'll have to find a place in my wagon, Laura said. "It's too warm in yours."

Mary came with her fishing pole, "Aren't you girls ready yet? Them fish ain't going to wait all day," she laughed her hearty laugh.

"We'll be ready in a minute; I have to find my bait cup, and Caroline wants to go. And I hope you brought a sack if you plan to catch as many as before; I'll get my basket."

They soon had everyone rounded up, each carrying something. They went down river a short distance, away from all the noise and commotion. Looking back, Jane saw three more women coming behind them.

"I think we're starting a parade," Jane told them as they all turned to look.

Mary found a likely spot where she thought might be lucky. Jane went over by a rotting log and dug for worms; soon she had her cup full of squirming fat worms. Mary reached out and grabbed a big one and threaded the fishhook through it leaving the tail wiggling. She went to the edge of the water and threw her line in. She got a bite almost as soon as it hit the water.

Caroline stood watching, "I'm not sure I can do what Mary did she said," looking at the squirming worms.

"I don't like it either, but I'll show you how. Remember we're pioneers and have to do a lot of things we may not want to do, just to eat." Jane baited her hook. "Everyone be careful, and don't slide into the river; make sure you are on solid ground or you'll end up in the Mississippi."

Mary had three fish jumping on the ground behind her. Jane tossed her line out into the water and started to pull and she had a fish too. Caroline timidly threw her line out from the bank and she felt a tug. "Pull it in, pull it in," Mary told her. "I'm pulling; what do I do now?" She had the fish in where she could see it.

"Oh my, I caught one!" she said with an amazed look on her face. Mary went to help her take it off the hook.

"You have to be careful and not get a hook in your hand." Mary put on the leather gloves from Jane's basket and carefully showed her how to take the hook out of the fish. "There's your dinner, Caroline."

"You're officially a fisherman; trained by an expert," Jane laughingly told her.

Caroline carefully put the fish into a bucket she brought; it was so big as she put it in head first, half of the fish stuck over the top.

"Have you ever cooked fish, Caroline?" Laura asked.

"Yes, I've fried fish; but I've never cleaned them myself; if you show me, I'm sure I can do it though," Caroline answered.

"Sure you can, Caroline; you're going to learn a lot of things when you homestead. You grew up on a farm didn't you?" Jane asked.

"Yes, but the menfolk did things like that; we had a couple of slaves too. I never fished or hunted. We were taught to sew and embroidery, things like that; and of course cook and bake; but I'll learn; you girls are a lot of help," she told them.

The other women were down the river a short way and seemed to be catching fish too. Mary had her sack as full as she could carry it. Caroline had six good-size ones in her bucket, and Jane and Laura had a basket and part of a sack full. I think this is as many as we can use," Jane said. "In fact, if Caroline wants to salt down some, she can have part of these. We're about to have more meat than we can use," Jane laughed, "That's a change; we didn't have any for a while."

When they went back to the wagon they saw that the men had returned; they were butchering two deer, and Ed had water on and was cleaning a turkey. Laura went over to look at it. "That's a nice young tom;, we'll make a feast out of him."

Ray was so proud of the deer he had killed, and of the fish Caroline was showing him. "I'll clean them for you as soon as I get the deer finished," he told her.

Jane and Laura helped cut up the deer and salt it down. "I'll make us some steak for supper; we'll eat good tonight," Laura said.

"Caroline, clear out one of your churns and put your groceries in your wash tub. Your flour and things won't get wet if you go through a creek. When Ray is finished he can clean your fish, and we'll show you how to salt them down to keep them," Jane told her.

Jason came by, "Jane, are you busy? Could we talk?" He dismounted and they walked away from the wagon.

"What's wrong?" Jane asked, looking anxiously at him.

"It's Doctor Wayne; I'm afraid he's in a bad way; could you come and take a look at him?"

"Hasn't he had a doctor? I thought he had been sick for several days; someone should have taken care of him before now," Jane told him.

"He's stubborn, and he isn't in favor of a female doctor, I'll tell you now. In his words, "dammit! Women can't be doctors! They're mothers, cooks; they don't know enough to be doctors."

"So, if you will come and see what you can do, you'll know what you're up against; but he needs a doctor and you're all we can get around here for him."

"Wait till I wash up and get a few things I need and I'll be right with you," she said as she went to the house on wheels and to the metal box she had gotten in the pharmaceutical in Charleston to hold her medicines. She washed hurriedly and put in a small bottle of turpentine, some dried mullein leaves, some ginger, and ground mustard. "I'm ready. Laura, I'll be back later; I have a sick man I have to tend."

Jason took her up to where the cook's wagon was parked. They went to the wagon next to it and went inside. Doctor Wayne was lying on a bunk against one side of the wagon; there was a chair that a young man was sitting in watching over him.

"Bill, this is Doctor Barrlette. She has come to take a look at Doctor Wayne. We'll call you if we need you," he told him.

"Before you go, Bill, do you know what he has taken in the last twelve hours?" Jane asked.

"Several drinks of whiskey, other than that, nothing I saw," Bill answered.

"I was afraid of that; I could smell whiskey when I came in, and could see the perspiration on his upper lip." She pulled the chair over to the bed and took up Doctor Wayne's wrist to feel his pulse. It was much too fast and skipping. She took out her stethoscope and listened to his lungs. They were tight and wheezy. He was hot and had a fever; the perspiration on his upper lip was the booze. She would have to get his lungs opened up, and the quickest way was a mustard plaster. She took out a packet of ground mustard, and handed it to Jason. "Could you have the cook mix this with boiling water and make a thin paste with it, and bring the pot while it's hot to me please."

Jason hurried away. Jane took a pan of water and a wash cloth she found and began to put cold compresses on Doctor Wayne's forehead. She found a tin cup, rinsed it out, and put a tea spoon full of ginger into it. When Jason returned she took the got and handed him the tin cup, "Pour this about a third full of hot water and tell cook to stir in two teaspoons of sugar." While she told him this she was coating the square of flannel she had brought with the hot mustard. Opening the doctor's shirt, she placed it over his chest well around under his arms and folded a towel and put on top of it. She timed the mustard plaster for ten minutes. Jason was back before the time was out.

"Help me raise him up, and we'll try to get this tea down him. He's so drunk, I'm afraid it will be useless." But when Jane turned the cup up, he drank it all before he found out it wasn't whiskey. It took his breath away, and he fought to take another breath, wheezing and gasping.

"I can see you're a tough doctor; I think I'll stay well," Jason told her, with a chuckle.

Jane got her patient quieted and covered him. "He has enough fluid in his lungs to drown a steer. If we don't get it out he will die; it's gone on much too long as it is." She removed the mustard plaster. "Would you have the cook fill the wash pan with real hot water for me?" It was handed in and Jane took a piece of clean flannel, counted several drops of turpentine into the pan and dipped the flannel in and out then wrung it as dry as she could and tucked it up under his chin and around his neck and down over his chest. She tented the covers so the fumes would go into his face, and he would breathe them in. She kept cooling his forehead with cold compresses. "Is there a chamber around? See if you can find it and put a little water in the bottom of it. He'll be coughing up phlegm soon, I hope." She took his pulse again. It was rapid, but strong. "He may make it. I've seen people die when they hadn't had influenza for half so long, or half the congestion he has in his chest. He's a doctor and should have known better. And he's an old man; he has no business on a wagon train in the first place."

"I'd hate to see you when you get mad. You're bad enough now, that you scare me half to death," Jason said with a laugh.

"I'm sorry, but it makes me mad to know a doctor would do such a foolish thing to himself, I know he knew better."

They sat and talked for about an hour. Jane removed the turpentine cloth, and listened to his chest with the stethoscope. "It's beginning to break up; he should start coughing soon."

Suddenly the doctor shot up in bed gasping and coughing. Jason held the chamber for him as phlegm came out of his mouth in strings. He coughed and coughed till he was wet with sweat. Jane laid him back on his pillow and covered him. "He'll maybe nap for a while now, till the next attack." She listened to his chest again. It wasn't as tight as before. "He may make it, but I wouldn't have counted on it when I first listened to his chest."

Jane had been in the doctor's wagon for three hours; she was getting very tired and hadn't had her supper; she sent for more hot water and put more turpentine packs on his chest. They gave him another dose of the ginger tea. "He'll sleep for a while," Jane told Jason.

"I'll have Bill come and sit with him; you go get some rest. Do you want him to do anything?"

"Watch him closely and raise him up if he starts to cough again." She removed the turpentine pack and put it in the wash pan. "I am tired. If I'm needed, knock on my door." Jane closed her black bag and left the wagon. She would let Jason tell Bill what to do.

❧ Chapter Forty-One ❧

Jane ate a light supper that Laura had put aside for her and announced she was going to bed. Andy was already sleeping, Goldie on her rug beside his bunk. Jane was so tired she felt as though she was wobbling around as she prepared for bed. Doctor Wayne might not make it through the night; he was very sick and old too. She needed to check on Howie but was just too tired; it seemed as though she had just gone to bed when she was awakened.

The wagon train was up early, and Jane could hear talking and commotion outside. She decided she should get up and see about her patient. She washed and dressed for the day and went outside. Laura was at the fire; Ed and Ray were just finishing their coffee; Laura didn't ask but just poured a cup for Jane and handed it to her, then dished up a piece of steak and opened a biscuit and dipped gravy over it, and set it in front of Jane.

"You didn't eat much last night; I knew you were exhausted. How do you feel this morning?"

"I'm still tired, but it will go away when I eat and move around some. Have you heard anything from Doctor Wayne? I'm still worried about him."

"I've not heard. Several of the men have gone to the woods to hunt; they wanted to get an early start. I guess they are following our lead. I also saw some women going to fish; it's a shame not to take advantage of the plenty nature has put before us.

Jane finished her breakfast and a second cup of coffee, "I'll go check on the doctor, and then I want to see how Nettie and Howie are doing. She seems so skittish; I don't know what her sister does to make her so afraid. Nettie seems so nice. I'll see you later. Are you and Mary fishing today?"

"I think we have enough; maybe we could sell some and go into the business as well as Mary likes fishing," Laura laughed.

"Are you making Ed's turkey for tonight?" Laura nodded that she was. "Would it be all right with you if I ask Nettie and Howie for supper tonight? I feel sorry for her; wouldn't it be nice if she

478

and Ed liked each other? He doesn't seem as lonely as he was when he first came with us. He needs a family, and he's such a nice man."

"I think that's a good idea. Ed is a nice man and should have a family, but I'd tread carefully, he likes his privacy too." Laura said with a laugh.

Jane smiled, "Let's just let nature take its course; we shouldn't interfere. I have to look in on the doctor so I'll see you later,"

Bill heard her as she walked up to their wagon, and he came outside.

"How is he? Did you have any problems last night?' she asked.

"He's one sick man. He coughed all night and threw up once; the phlegm was so bad he couldn't spit it out. I think he is breathing better now. He fell asleep about daylight. Jane went into the wagon; the smell was awful, of stale whiskey and vomit. She opened up the canvas flap to let in some fresh air. The doctor was sleeping, as she took his pulse, finding it strong and regular. Feeling his head she found his fever down, and took her stethoscope and listened to his chest; there was still fluid there but it was loose. As soon as she got some broth down him, she would give him another cup of ginger tea, and bring up the rest of the phlegm. He wasn't out of the woods yet, but if she could keep him in bed a few days, she thought he would recover. Just then he opened his eyes, looking at her curiously.

"Good morning, Doctor Wayne. How are you feeling?!' Jane asked.

"Like someone beat on me. You're that Barrlette woman, aren't you?"

"That's right—Jane Barrlette. You were a sick man when Jason brought me over yesterday afternoon. You've no fever now, and your pulse is good. You still have some fluid in your lungs, that has to be gotten up. I'll have the cook make you some broth and then we'll see what we can do about it."

"Just give me a good slug of whiskey; that's worked so far. That's all I need. You don't have to be here," Doctor Wayne told her.

"Whiskey didn't do you any good—only made you worse. Mr. Turner asked me to treat you. I was here half the night, or you wouldn't have been alive by morning; you'd have drowned in your own fluid. If you're any kind of doctor, you know that. I got it loosened enough that you coughed up most of it. I'm going to give you something to get the rest up, just as soon as you have some nourishment, whether you like it or not." With that announcement, Jane called to Bill, "Could you have the cook fix some hot broth for Doctor Wayne right away please."

"He has it simmering, I'll bring it right away," Bill said as he went to get it.

A large mug of broth, with steam rising from it, was handed to Jane. She took it to the bed. Do you want to drink this on your own, or would you like it done another way?" she asked him.

His hand shook so much that Jane had to hold the cup to his lips, her hand on his as he started to sip the strong hot broth, his eyes never leaving Jane's face. He didn't give her any more argument and drank it all.

"That's good; lie back and rest and I'll have your medicine ready in a minute." Jane took the cup and rinsed it and put a teaspoon of ginger in it and went over to the cook for hot water and sugar; she mixed it well, brought it to the bed and helped him sit up so he could drink it. "Drink it all down at once, and don't breathe," she advised him. He made a terrible face and couldn't catch his breath for a moment.

"What are you trying to do, woman? You'll kill me yet."

"You may still die, but I won't be the cause; it will be your stubbornness that will do you in," Jane told him, as she smiled at him. "I think that may do it, without any more mustard plasters or compresses," she commented as she listened again to his chest. "Stay covered and warm; you'll be coughing up the rest of that phlegm very soon. You'd best go to sleep if you can; I have another patient to see to. I'll drop back later. Good-bye Doctor Wayne." Jane left the wagon with him glaring at her.

Jane finally found the wagon that Nettie and Howie were in. It was parked some distance away from hers. Nettie was outside trying to wash clothes in cold water. Jane stood watching her. She didn't have a washboard and was scrubbing clothes against her hands, and swishing them up and down. She could see the hopelessness on Nettie's face, as she worked.

After watching for a few minutes, Jane went to her. "Nettie, why in the world don't you heat some water to wash clothes in? And why don't you use a washboard?"

Nettie pushed her hair out of her face, and looked at Jane. "My sister doesn't want me to use the wood for a fire, and I don't have a washboard."

"I've never heard anything so asinine; you can use my washboard, and I'll help find wood for you to build a fire. How's Howie?" He came from around the wagon riding a stick horse. He still had the bandage wrapped around his head. "Hello Howie, how's your head? Does it hurt? Can I take a look at it and see how it is?"

He carefully leaned his stick horse against the wagon wheel and came over to Jane. She unwrapped the bandage, which was showing effects of being on a boy. She examined the wound seeing there was no redness or sign of infection. It was healing nicely. It looks good; I'll take the stitches out in a few days. I'll put this bandage back for the present."

"Nettie, I would like you and Howie to come to our wagon for supper tonight. My driver, Ed, went hunting with Ray and he brought home a big tom turkey which Laura, that's Ray's wife, is roasting for supper tonight. Do you like turkey?" Jane asked.

"Oh, I love turkey; my mamma used to make the best turkey and dressing at Christmas; I haven't had any in ages. I don't know, I doubt my sister will want me to go. I don't think Howie has ever had turkey—I know he would just love it. My sister likes me to clean up after the meals. She doesn't let me do any cooking, and I miss it. I love to cook. I just hope I don't forget how; maybe Howie and I will have our own home some day. I don't know how but maybe," she hung her head as though she was wishing for something she didn't deserve.

"Where is your sister? I'll ask her?" Jane told her.

"Her wagon is the next one. Her name is Hazel. I just know she will be mad if you ask," Nettie looked scared as she told Jane.

"Don't you worry; I know just how to do it." Jane walked to the wagon in front. There was a pretty woman sitting on a stool, beside the wagon. She had some sewing on her lap, but seemed to be watching and listening to those around her and not doing much sewing.

"Hello, are you Hazel? I'm Jane Barrlette. I helped when your nephew Howie was thrown into the water," Jane reached out her hand to shake hands.

"That idiot sister of mine; she caused the whole thing we had to have the wagon repaired and the harness has to be spliced and will never be the same. And that Howie, the way that youngin is spoiled I wouldn't put it past him to jump in the water for attention." She seemed to get madder by the minute.

"I was under the impression that your son was driving the wagon, not Nettie, and that his team ran into the other wagon, and they got tangled together. It was an accident. I don't think anyone should be blamed for it. And Howie almost died. I found him a sweet, polite little boy." Jane was losing her patience too, "I didn't come to discuss the accident, but to tell you that I have to have Howie come to my wagon to change his bandage and I've asked Nettie and Howie to stay to supper with us. She is reluctant to do so thinking you may need her. I'm sure you won't mind this once," Jane smiled at her, looking her right in the eye.

"I don't need her; she doesn't do anything but complain all the time; she can go I don't care." She turned her back on Jane and pretended to be involved with a difficult stitch in her sewing.

"I'll tell her you want her and Howie to have a good time and that you won't need her. Thank you for being so gracious." Jane turned and walked away. No wonder Nettie was scared of her shadow; she could see why.

"Nettie, you get yourself all prettied up, and come over to my wagon; we'll make a party out of dinner tonight. It will be special. Come whenever you want; maybe Howie will want to play with my Andy before we're ready for dinner," Jane said. "Are you sure my sister said I could go? That she won't need Me? I didn't think she would let me." Nettie looked doubtful.

"Nettie, you have the right to do as you want; you're not a servant; you're a mother with a little boy who deserves to be happy as you do. I'll see you later." Jane went back to her wagon to let Laura know there would be two more for dinner.

Laura was putting together the dressing for the turkey. She had saved biscuits and cornbread, and was toasting that; and would add onion, and some cut up apples, and the giblets she had cooked and chopped fine; the broth would be used to make gravy. "Do you have sage?" she asked.

"I sure do; I brought some from the Plantation, packed in one of the churns I brought. I put it in the cupboard, here it is in this tin; she took it out and handed it to Laura. I'm looking forward to a scrumptious turkey dinner tonight, and we're having company—Nettie and Howie. That'll be eight just right for our first dinner party," Jane laughed, at Laura's doubtful look.

"What can I do?" Jane asked.

"Peel a big kettle of potatoes; we'll have mashed potatoes, gravy, turkey, dressing, cole slaw, biscuits, and apple tarts. I'll make those while the turkey bakes. How does that sound? We won't have to eat for a week after tonight," Laura laughed.

"I think Ed will be proud of his turkey all dressed up like that; I know I'm going to enjoy it. I'll get the potatoes on right away."

Nettie and Howie came early. She had on a pretty flowered dress, and a heavy shawl over it. She had her hair fluffed around her face which made her look like a very young girl. Her cheeks were flushed and she looked happy for a change. "Howie, how about me showing you my house on wheels, and I'll take a look at your head, and put on a clean bandage; you come too Nettie, if you want." They both followed her inside. "Sit down on one of the bunks. Andy had come in too, wanting to see the stitches in Howie's head. He sat holding Goldie.

"My this is nice; even a little stove; and you have everything so handy," Nettie said as she looked around.

Jane removed the bandage, and let Andy see, as she explained how she had stitched the cut. Nettie also wanted to look, then Jane replaced the dirty bandage with a clean one. "Young man, you have seven stitches; I don't think there will be a scar; if so, it'll fade in time."

"This is my dog, Goldie," Andy told Howie.

"She's pretty; can I pet her? Howie asked as Andy placed Goldie in his arms. "Oh, you're nice Goldie; I wish I had me a dog.

If my daddy had come back from the war, he'd a got me a dog. We had our own little patch of land and our own house, but Aunt Hazel made mamma sell it and go West. I like the wagon train, but I think mamma would have liked to stay in Carolina; she is so sad all the time. I'll grow up soon and then we'll have our own house again." He was stroking Goldie, as she licked his face, making him laugh.

"You boys run along and find Mark and Sarah so Howie can meet them and see their dog too," Jane told them. "That's the Thompsons in the next wagon; they are taking the parcel of land next to mine so we'll be neighbors. They're very nice people with three children," she explained to Nettie. "Let's go out and see if we can help with dinner. Laura is so efficient that she requires little help. When they went outside, Jane saw that Jason was there.

"Good afternoon Jason. You know Nettie, and little Howie, I think," Jane asked.

"How is your little boy, Nettie?" Jason asked, concern in his eyes.

"He's just fine, thanks to Doctor Jane, over there he is" she pointed to the Thompson's wagon where the children were laughing and playing.

"Something sure smells good; Laura you're not cooking fish again? They couldn't smell that good," Jason laughed as he asked.

"We're having roast turkey; Ed killed a nice big Tom, and we're celebrating. Jane, why don't you ask Jason to stay for supper; one more won't be too many," she smiled at Jason.

"How about it, Jason? Do you like turkey? As if I need to ask; everyone likes turkey," Jane laughed.

"That's one invite I won't turn down. I think I'll just stay here and fill up on the smell of it roasting. We're expecting the other members of our train either late this evening or early morning. We have word they aren't too far off. Just so they don't come when I want to eat turkey," he chuckled.

It took most of the day to roast the turkey. Laura made a basketful of apple tarts. She had Jane peeling apples, and she cut a big bowl of them very fine and added sugar, nutmeg, and cinnamon; then made biscuit dough, and rolled rounds about as big as a quart can, dipped a couple spoons of the apple mixture on one side of the round, folded it over and crimped the edges together, punched some holes with the fork tines in the top and fried them in lard till they were golden brown. They smelled so good and looked good. She said she had made three dozen; she put a clean dish towel in a big basket, filled it with tarts and tucked another towel over the top.

Jane saw several men coming back from the hunt—most of them seemed to have game across their saddles. There would be lots of feasts tonight. Jane hoped they would have enough to take on the trail when the wagons started again.

Sam came just as Laura's announcement that the turkey would be done in another half hour. He had been hammering since the day before, and he had a big wide board about five feet long. He laid it aside as they all watched him, wondering what he was going to do. He went around behind the wagon and came back with two what looked like saw horses, leaned them against a wheel and asked; "Miss Jane, where you want your dinner table set?" He was smiling his big toothy smile.

"Right about here, I think; it looks level here. If it isn't, we can move it. He took one of the pieces he had leaned against a wheel and put it under the end of the long board, wooden pieces held it in place; then went to the other end and did the same. "That a beautiful table," Jane said; "Sam, it's wonderful. And just in time for our first dinner party." Jane gave him a kiss on his wrinkled black cheek. He was so flustered he said, "I'z go get the bench for it." He soon had it put together and they were both solid and even looked nice.

"Thank you Sam; I knew you could do it. I don't know if it can make that turkey taste better, but it sure will be a lot more comfortable." Jane brought the two crates she had gotten and the steps from Laura's wagon. Sam had made a step for Caroline and they brought it too. There would be space for them all to sit down to eat the scrumptious dinner Laura had cooked.

There was much laughter throughout the camp with all the good food that was being cooked and eaten that evening, and especially Laura and Jane's dinner party. What a pleasure to sit at a table; Jane had forgotten just how delightful it could be. Everyone declared that it was the best turkey they had ever eaten.

"Miss Jane, thank you from the bottom of my heart. I haven't enjoyed such a meal since my mamma and papa died. And look at my Howie; he loves Andy and Goldie. We have both had such a good time. I think I had better go back; maybe I still can clean up for my sister," Nettie said with that frightened look in her eyes again.

"NO! You're going to sit right here and talk to everyone; your sister told me she didn't need you, and she doesn't; it's time she had time with her family too, " Jane told her in no uncertain terms. Jane had noticed that Ed shyly glanced at Nettie, several times; she was a pretty girl when she wasn't frightened all the time.

"Are you and Howie homesteading?" Ed asked Nettie.

"Oh no! I lost my husband; he was killed in the war. My sister thought I should sell my home and come West with her, and help them when they homestead, and live with them. It's not easy when you've had your own home, but she is my sister, and then the bad luck seems to follow Howie and me; I caused the wagon to wreck, and Howie to almost drown, "Nettie hung her head and a tear dropped into her lap.

"Who said you caused that mishap? Were you driving the team?" Ed asked.

"My, sister's son was driving; but it was my fault you see; Hazel told me it was. I was so sorry and so scared that Howie was going to die, and my sister was out a lot of money to get everything fixed again," she hung her head looking guilty.

Sam spoke up, "Ed and I'z repaired the harness, and helped fix the wagon; ifin there was money spent wez didn't see any."

"There was no money involved, Nettie. It was all repaired as good neighbors. And it's certainly not your fault. How could your sister make you think it was?" Ed said, with an angry note in his voice.

"Why don't we sing some happy songs around the, 'old camp fire'?" Andy wanted to know. "Sam you start out we'll follow," Andy suggested. "Sam has a fine voice,' he informed everyone. 'That soun'z a fine idea." Sam said as he started in.

> You ought to see my Cindy,
> She lives away down south,
> Now she's so sweet the honey bees,
> They swarm around her mouth.
> The first I seen my Cindy
> A standing at the door,
> Her shoes and stockin's in 'er hand,
> Her feet all over the floor.
>
> Git along home, Cindy, Cindy,
> Git along home, Cindy, Cindy,
> Get along home, Cindy, Cindy,
> I'll marry you some day.

Jane looked up; the whole camp seemed to have gathered around listening to the singing and laughing. They had all joined in—even Jason.

"Now that's a happy song," Andy informed then. "Maw and me are going to get us a pianoforte for our big house on our ranch. She plays real good and she is going to teach me, and we'll have parties and sing happy songs."

"That was wonderful! It makes a body feel good to hear people singing, I want to thank you Mrs. Barrlette, for insisting I come; I'll remember this always," Nettie told her.

"Please call me Jane, Nettie; and I'm so glad you and Howie enjoyed the food and the sing. Maybe you won't be too far away that you can visit when we all get settled. You're welcome anytime. "Jane saw Caroline and Ray hand-in-hand taking a walk down by the river, and knew they were touched by the companionship too.

Laura and Jane began to put things away. Nettie wanted to help but they both told her she was a guest and she wasn't to help.

Ed looked longingly at Nettie, and Jane hoped he would have the courage to ask her to go for a walk too.

Nettie sat for a few minutes becoming uncomfortable, and said, "I guess I had better take Howie and put him to bed. He still isn't well yet, " she said looking around for him.

"I'll help you find him and make sure you both get to your wagon safely," Ed said taking her elbow and steering her around the wagon, where they could hear the children laughing.

Jane looked at Laura, "Maybe it's working," they both said at the same time, and then they started to giggle.

"This has been a special time, Laura; thank you for all your work and caring." Jane put her arm around her and gave her a hug.

After giving everyone his thanks, Jason had excused himself some time ago, when one of the drovers came for him.

The camp had begun to settle in for the night, the fires being banked for morning. Andy came tired and dirty, ready to be put to bed, as Jane was herself. Morning would come much too soon.

* * *

Jane woke with a sunbeam shining in her eyes from the little window over Andy's bunk. She sat up and saw that Goldie had a corner of the quilt pulling on it trying to get Andy up. She was becoming a little tease, and loved Andy to distraction.

Jane's alarm clock said five thirty; she picked it up and held it to her ear thinking it had stopped. It seemed all the camp was up because she could hear so much shouting and horses moving around. "What in the world is happening?" she asked as she went to peek out the windows. She saw a lot of strangers—or at least they were strangers to her. She wondered if they were being attacked, and reached under her pillow for her pistol. Then she saw Jason riding among them. "It must be the train has arrived," she said out loud. "Andy? Andy? Time to get up; up Andy," He sat up rubbing his eyes. Looking down he saw Goldie with the quilt corner in her mouth, looking up at him. He reached over and picked her up putting her in his bed while he hurried to find his clothes.

"What's going on, Maw? What's all that racket; has there been another accident?"

"I think it's the wagon train we've been expecting. We'll be on our way soon if it is." Jane had washed her face and hands, and emptied the water into the chamber and poured out some for Andy to wash in.

When they were both dressed they went outside. Laura and Nat were starting the fire for breakfast; Caroline and Ray soon came outside dressed for the day.

"What's going on?" everyone was asking, as they looked around. There were lots of wagons. In the field beyond where their circle was, cattle and horses were everywhere. Riders were trying to control the large herd of animals. The wagons seemed to be trying to make a barricade to help.

"They are certainly not very organized," Jane said. "We've always known what we were supposed to do and did it. We've never had so much commotion. I wonder when they came in? It seems a strange time to be arriving."

Laura and Caroline were getting things ready for breakfast. "Is there anything I can do?" Jane asked.

"I'm making pancakes this morning; I thought it was time for a change," Laura said.

The men had gone to tend the animals. Mat was milking the cow and feeding and watering her. Everyone had worked out a routine they followed and all were done about the same time without confusion. They were soon back and washing and shaving getting ready for breakfast.

"How pleasant it is sitting down at a table," Jane said. There were six of them and they just about filled the table comfortably.

As soon as they had finished, Andy took off to the Thompsons to watch what was going on with the new arrivals.

"Don't you leave our camp. There are too many animals running loose, and you could get hurt," Jane told him.

It was a couple of hours before things quieted down, and became organized. The cattle were now under control, and eating from a wagon loaded with hay. In fact, she could see three wagons from where they were. The horses and cows ate together in harmony.

Jane helped clear up the breakfast things, and said, "I'll go and check on Doctor Wayne, and see how he made out last night. She got her black bag and walked over to his wagon; seeing Bill sitting on a block of wood outside, she went up to him.

"How is Doctor Wayne?"

"He coughed some last night; I think most of the phlegm is out of his lungs; he is still sleeping. He slept much of the night. Cook is fixing his breakfast now."

"I'll come back after he's eaten, and check on him. He needs to be washed and made comfortable, and can sit up in bed some today. I want him to stay in bed and keep warm though. I'll he back later. Jane walked over to see the Thompsons.

"Good morning, John, Mary; seems we have company. There sure was a lot of confusion earlier. Have you heard anything?'" Jane asked as she sat on a block of wood, watching Mary make their breakfast.

" It's the rest of the train. It seems a strange time to arrive; there must have been trouble of some sort," John told her.

Just then Jason came by on his horse. "Good morning everyone; I guess you know the rest of our train has arrived. They had a hard time of it. The farm where they were supposed to spend the night, not far from here, and come on in this morning, had been taken by an Oregon-bound wagon train. Seems there was some sort of misunderstanding. So they had to travel slowly through the night. There just wasn't another place they could stop. They will get themselves together today and rest. We'll be crossing the Ohio early in the morning. Your part of the train will be first, and give the others more time to get organized. We will be moving about three miles into Ohio and spend the night. It'll take most of the day to get across. There'll be someone around telling you when to pull out. Be ready by sunup. I'll see you," he said as he hurried down the line of wagons.

❦ Chapter Forty-Two ❦

Jane and Laura talked it over and decided that maybe they would be better off to wait until they crossed the Ohio to build a fire and start cooking. They asked the men, and they seemed to agree; if Jason said to be ready by sunup, and that they were only going two miles into Ohio, then their camp wasn't far away and they should be there early.

"What if we have accidents, and are held up?" Jane asked.

"I don't think we'll starve to death, even if we don't arrive till noon," Laura laughed, as they said good night, and went to their wagons.

Jane set her alarm for five o'clock; she doubted she would sleep beyond that time anyway. She felt rested; the party seemed to relax everyone, and she wasn't so worried about Doctor Wayne. He would recover if he stayed in bed for a few more days. Jane's head had hardly hit her pillow when she fell asleep; she started to dream—suddenly there was water, rushing by all around her; she seemed to be alone; where was Andy? "Andy? Andy? Where are you?"

"I'm right here, Maw! What's wrong? Are you sick?" He was by her bed, shaking her calling, "Maw? Wake up Maw."

Jane sat up in bed; it was still dark; she looked at the clock and saw it was a quarter till five. "Why are you up so early Andy? The alarm hasn't gone off yet," she looked at him in surprise.

"You were yelling for me. It woke me up and I came over to see what was wrong. You're not sick are you?" he looked worriedly at her.

She smiled at him. "No, I'm not sick; I feel just fine; we're going to cross the Ohio today. I'll get dressed and get busy putting everything in order. You dress too; Jason said to be ready by sunup. We'll be in the first wagons to cross, then the others will follow. Are you scared?"

"No, I sorta' like going across on the ferry; this one will take longer as the river is wider; are you afraid?" he asked looking into her eyes.

490

"Well, I guess a little. So many things could go wrong. But as long as Jason is there to see to things, I feel safe," Jane said as she gave him a hug. "Get dressed."

When they went outside, several were already up. Laura was checking the cupboard, and putting away the wash pan and things that were outside.

"Nat is milking and feeding the cow and calf. I'll take care of the milk. I'm going to throw in what wood we have, for we may not have any handy where we camp." Laura told her.

Jane looked over and saw that Mary had started a fire. Do we have any of those apple tarts left?" Jane asked.

"There were several left. Why? Are you hungry?" Laura laughed. "You said last night that you'd never be hungry again.'

"I see Mary has started a fire. If there is room for our coffee pot, we could give the men coffee and a tart at least to hold them till we get to the camp," Jane said.

"I'll go see if she has room; I have the coffee ready to boil." Laura hurried over and came back in a few minutes and took the big pot and put it on Mary's fire, "There will be enough for all of us and she won't have to make any. It'll be ready by sunup. The men are all up watering and feeding their stock. "I think I'll fetch a bucket of water and put it in the churn. I don't know how we'll be fixed for water tonight." Jane said.

I'll come with you, and bring a bucket too. We can put it in one of the barrels. Mary, do you want to fetch a bucket of water? Jane and I are going to the spring if you want to go," Laura called.

"I believe I will," Mary said as she came with a bucket to join them.

The men had fed and watered their teams, and had begun to harness them ready for hitching to the wagons when the call came to roll out. Ed had put the pig crate and the chickens onto his wagon, and everything was checked to make sure it was secure. He then came and picked up all the wood at the wagon and took it to his wagon, and dumped it onto the rest he had in front of the seat.

When the girls came back with the water, they filled the churn as full as it would take and not slosh out; the rest they added to Laura and Nat's barrel; it was almost full as Nat never let it get below half full. Nat had seen to it that Ray's barrel was full too. Ed always filled his—he didn't have to check.

"Someone took our wood," Laura yelled.

"That someone was me," Ed said with a grin, as he approached the wagon. "Do you want it back?" I didn't think we should waste it. I put it in my wagon."

Laura's face turned red, Thanks, I didn't want to waste it either. Tell the men to come for coffee and an apple tart; it'll hold them till we get settled and can cook. It'll be ready by the time they get here." She turned to get the cups and cream for the coffee, and brought the basket of tarts from the wagon.

Sam and Ed took the table apart and put it up on the top of the house on wheels. Sam had put on brackets where a rope could be pulled through, and through one on the table too so it wouldn't shift. They soon had it secure, and came ready for coffee.

Laura went to get the coffee pot; she poured out a kettle full for Mary and came and poured cups for everyone, and passed the basket around for them to help themselves to the tarts. There were enough for two each.

"These hit the spot, Laura," Ed told her.

"They sure do," Nat seconded.

Jason came by just then. "Coffee, Jason?" Jane asked.

"That sounds good," he said as he dismounted and took a cup, added cream and took a sip.

"Whoever makes your coffee knows how to make a real man's cup-of-coffee," he said with a smile.

Laura offered him the basket with two tarts still in it. "We've all had our share of tarts; you take these; they will hold you over till we can cook."

He took one and crammed half of it into his mouth. "I've never eaten such good tarts. I think I could eat a basketful just by myself," he said as he finished off the last one.

"You're going to have to do on just the two this time," Laura told him. "Are we about ready to move out?"

"You men can start hooking up anytime now. We'll be lining up for the ferry in about ten minutes. I don't want you to lose your place in line. Just remember what you did last time and you'll be fine."

"Do you think we should leave Goldie in the wagon?" Jane asked, concern in her eyes.

"Yes, you never know what an animal will do. If she jumped out of Andy's arms she could cause a disaster," Jason said looking directly at Andy who stood listening with Goldie clutched in his arms. Jason mounted and trotted away toward the head wagon.

The men were busy hooking up the teams to the wagons; there were sounds of low voices, as the men spoke to the teams. The rattle of chains and harnesses were heard throughout the camp as the teams settled themselves.

Mary and John had finished hooking up, and the children were in the wagon as their parents mounted up to the seat high above the team. They were ready. Jane and Andy climbed up beside Sam. Jane could see Laura taking a last look around the camp. She would make sure there were no dropped spoons, or coffee cups left on a stump. She then climbed up beside Nat. Caroline and Ray were behind, and Jane couldn't see them. Their wagon was between hers and the Thompsons. Ed was up ahead of Nat and Laura. Jane could hear the front wagons pulling out.

"Here we go, off to ride the ferry and cross the Ohio. Let's say a prayer that everyone gets over safely." As they came around the curve, it gave them a chance to see the first wagons being loaded. The ferrymen soon had two wagons and teams aboard and let the gate down behind them. It took them several minutes to make the round trip, and two more teams and wagons were carefully led aboard. Jane figured that they would be about the sixth to cross. They sat patiently waiting. They watched the wagons that had reached the other side start southwest, toward where they would camp for the night.

"How in the world are they going to bring all those horses and cattle aboard?" Jane asked Sam.

"I'z never heard, iffin' they gonna' swim them across or try to ferry themz. Hit'z gonna' be bad no matter what way the'z do it. I'z glad I'z don't has to do it." Andy said shaking his head.

Their time finally came. Sam got down and helped Jane and Andy down. He led the team and wagon slowly aboard the ferry. Jane had Cherokee, by the bridle, holding him and talking to him as she held him behind the wagon. Caroline came with the cow, and the calf followed its mother. Ray's wagon was next; he was at the horses' heads, holding onto the bridles. The gate came down with a slight clang, making Cherokee flinch, and toss his head. Jane patted him and talked softly; he settled down as the barge started to move. It was no time at all till they were over and moving off the barge onto solid ground. They all got into the wagon and moved on up the trail behind the other wagons. Jane watched as the barge brought the others over, and they all fell in behind.

Jason had sent one of his men to direct them to the campsite. The wagons slowly moving in a line, drove toward it. Jane looked at her watch; they had been on the trail for two hours. It'll be evening at this rate, she said to herself.

It wasn't long till they saw the wagons in front starting to circle in at a big level field. There was lots of dried grass that the animals could feed- on and save their hay. There seemed to be scattered lakes in the area where the cattle could water. There were several groves of trees and in the distance were thick forests. They moved on slowly following close behind the wagon in front. They had to complete the circle and come back almost to where it started. There were only about ten wagons in front of them. One advantage was that they could watch all the others coming in and circling up. They were motioned to form a tight circle, and Jane was surprised to see the cattle being driven beyond the wagons. Several riders directed them into the meadows where the dry grass was; there must be over a thousand horses and cattle in the herd. They circled and mixed for a time and then began to eat; the riders kept circling and watching that none broke from the main herd. The teams were hobbled and turned out too. Only the milk cows were kept in the circle of wagons. They began to eat the grass and was soon settled and content. Fires were built inside the circle. The table and bench were brought down from the house on wheels and set up ready for Laura and the women to do their cooking. Nat started the fire as the women began doing chores.

"We might as well make this our noon meal—it is so close," Laura said as she brought out the deer meat and sliced it and gave the job of flouring and frying to Jane. Ray and Caroline were now doing their own cooking. There was plenty of wood, not too far off; soon several fires were lit and cooking was going on at most every wagon.

"I think I counted fifteen wagons with a big red B on them; that must be the merchant, Mr. Boothe. They look heavily loaded; most of the wagons have two teams each. They must have discovered a way to swim the cattle and horses over. I wonder where

Jason is?" Jane asked.

Suddenly a rider came racing in, "Where's the doctor? We need a doctor; where's the doctor?" he was yelling as he passed each wagon. Jane stepped out and waved him in.

I'm Jane Barrlette; what has happened? she asked the excited man .

"There's been an accident. We think the man has a broken leg, and his wife is hurt; she was thrown from the wagon when it overturned; if you're the doctor, they want you right away."

Sam was just about to unsaddle Cherokee, when he saw the man approaching and knew something had happened. He tightened the cinch again, and waited.

"I'll get my things. Sorry Laura, you'll have to manage alone. I don't know how long I'll be gone; watch out for Andy."

Jane rushed into the wagon bringing the saddle pockets, and The splints Sam had made for her. She added more medicines to her black bag, and hurried out to where Sam waited with Cherokee, mounted and they took off at a gallop.

"Where are they?" Jane yelled to the rider.

"At the crossing. Hurry, they're bad," he said as he led her in a race toward the river.

It was the first time Jane had ever had the opportunity to let Cherokee run; his long legs reached out and seemed to skim across the ground. He would have outrun the other rider if she would have let him. He seemed to be enjoying his chance to race, as he went on and on. To Jane they seemed to have traveled a great distance when they came in sight of some of the wagons that were headed toward the camp. Then she saw at the river's edge several people milling about. That must be where the accident occurred, as the rider with her headed in that direction. They reached the area and her companion dismounted and came to help her down. He started forward leading the horses.

"They're right over there," he pointed where the crowd was thickest. Jane hurried over pushing herself through the crowd.

"I'm the doctor; give way please." Those standing moved aside; Jane saw a man on a blanket on the ground writhing in pain; he was moaning and turning his head from side to side. She rushed over, knelt beside him and placed her hand on his head; he already had a fever. She raised his eyelids, seeing that shock was setting in. He was covered with a blanket; she raised it up seeing a bloody pants leg. Seemed no one had tried to do anything to his leg, even to stop the bleeding. She took her stethoscope and listened to his heartbeat; it was strong enough; she then took a needle with a small amount of morphine and gave him a shot in the leg, just above the break. She wanted to see how the other patient was; maybe she was needed worse there, the broken leg could wait for a bit.

Jane went and knelt beside the other victim; it was a woman in her early twenties, and from the looks Jane thought she was with child. She had a bluish thing around the mouth; her eyes were closed, and there was perspiration on her upper lip. Jane quickly felt both arms and legs; they seemed to be intact and she moved to the torso feeling her rib-cage and abdomen; she felt no movement. Taking her stethoscope she listened to her heartbeat; it was fast and erratic; she moved the instrument farther down the stomach; she couldn't hear any movement.

"What happened," Jane asked, as she looked up into Jason's face, as he leaned over her.

"They were ready to enter the gate of the ferry when the team became spooked. Both were still on the wagon seat. They were just going to get down when the team reared and came down beside the ferry and overturned. The woman was thrown clear but the wagon pinned her husband. The animals were wild by then. The men standing near grabbed them and cut them from the harness, saving them or they would have gone into the river taking the wagon with them. It took several men to get the man out from under the wheel. We didn't know what to do. His wife has been unconscious all this time. He seems to be in great pain. That's about it. I hope you can do something."

"I suggest getting the wife into a wagon and keep her warm. I think she is several months with child; if so, it may have been killed. Keep her warm. If she regains consciousness give her a warm drink if possible and have her to remain lying down. I'll see if I can set her husband's leg. Would there be boards that we could make a table to work from?"

"I'll see what I can do," Jason said hurrying away.

Soon boards were being put onto blocks of wood nearby. Jane was at her patient's side. "Could I have another blanket please." Someone handed her one and she gently began to work it up under the legs where he could be lifted by the blanket and not by his body. Several men stepped forward and lifted him very carefully, while Jane stayed by his broken leg supporting it. She quickly cut away the pants leg and saw that he had both bones broken and a lot of tissue damage where the wheel had crushed into his leg.

"May I have a pan of hot water please." Someone had a fire going and had put water to heat. They handed her a pan with steam coming from it. Jane poured a few drops of turpentine in the water and took a soft rag from her bag and began to clean the injury. They were all watching carefully; Jane turned and raised his eyelids; he seemed to be fine. She continued to examine the breaks; it was going to be very difficult to set both with a break in different areas. She kept feeling down in the wound, finally deciding that she could only try.

"It's a very bad break, with two bones involved and at two different locations. He'll be very lucky if I can save his leg, but I'm going to try. I'll need two strong men." Two men stepped forward. "One of you hold his shoulders and don't let him get up. The other man down here at his feet; you will have to exert a steady pull on his leg until I tell you to stop; do you understand?" They both nodded. Jane took out a small swatch of cotton and dropped three drops of chloroform on and held it over her patient's nose till she counted ten, then removed it, laying it aside. "Are you ready?" again they nodded. "You hold your hands so," she showed him how to lace his fingers and form them around the ankle. "Whatever you do, don't let up or let your hand slip. Make sure you have a good hold; he can't feel anything, so don't worry about hurting him. It will do damage if you slip. Do you understand?" he nodded. Jane listened to the patient's heartbeat again. It seemed strong; she was ready, her splints and binding were held by Jason who was at her elbow. Jane looked around making sure everything was ready and handy.

"Here we go PULL! PULL!' she was feeling the bones; "PULL! HOLD!" She could feel both bones in place, but would they stay there even with splints? She placed one splint under his leg and two more on the top, and quickly began to wrap them, with a strip of linen. "HOLD," she told her helper, as she worked as quickly as she could. She placed a pad of gauze over the injured tissue and poured carbolic acid over it and wrapped it so it would stay in place. "You both can let go now, thank you."

Jane listened to her patient's heart and took his pulse.

Hopefully it would heal; if not, his leg would have to come off. "Who will be taking care of him?" Jane asked. "He needs to be in a hospital, if at all possible, Jane added, as she saw Jason shake his head.

"I expect Bill will be the best choice," Jason said. "We can put him in a wagon next to Doctor Wayne's.

"He must not be allowed to raise off the bed for the next five days; does Bill know how to deal with that?" Jane asked with raised eyebrows.

"I think so. He has taken care of many sick people as he was an orderly in the army."

"Good, then he will know; a pillow can be put under the leg and foot from the knee to and including the foot. If there is anything he needs to know he can ask. I'll be checking on him regularly. Now I have to see what I can do for his wife. She may be in worse trouble than he is. I'll let you know as soon as I can tell anything; thank you for standing by," Jane nodded as she went to the wagon where the woman had been taken.

She was beginning to moan and move about. Jane took her stethoscope and listened to her heartbeat; it was more normal than before. Laying her hand against the forehead she could tell that she had no fever. Jane began to examine her all over again, feeling each limb and moving it to make sure there was no damage there. She pushed hard on her abdomen. She could feel no movement. Moving the stethoscope to that area, she listened, moving it an inch at a time; finally she heard or felt a very slight movement. She waited; there was more movement, which meant the baby was alive, but maybe injured.

"Do any of you know her name?" Jane asked looking at the women who were helping,

"I think it's Doris—Sam and Doris Witt are their names. They're alone; they haven't been married long and have no children," One of the women answered.

"Do you know if there's a hospital anywhere near?" Jane asked looking at the woman who had answered her before.

"I don't know; I expect Mr. Turner or Mr. Morgan would know. They're not going to like being left behind if there is any hope that they can continue."

"They are both in very serious condition; he could lose his leg

498

and she could not only lose her baby but her own life as well. I'll do what I can, but I don't have the facilities to take care of such injuries as they both have," Jane said as she looked at the concerned women.

"Doris? Doris? Can you hear me? Doris wake up." Her eyelids fluttered and then opened, looking into Jane's eyes.

"What happened? Where's Sam?" She tried to raise up.

"Please lie still Mrs. Witt. Do you have any pain?" She closed her eyes before answering; I hurt all over; my back is burning and hurting. "What happened to me?" she asked as she looked at Jane.

"There was an accident with your wagon; you were thrown out of it, and your husband has a broken leg," Jane said, seeing the emotion wash over Doris' face.

"My baby! Is it all right?" She asked fright showing in her eyes.

"It's alive, I'm not sure if it is injured or not. Can you turn over and let me look at your back," she turned, and Jane raised her clothing and saw that her back had been scraped in the fall and was red and oozing blood; she coated it with a soothing ointment and placed a piece of gauze over it, and let her turn over again. "It's not serious, only uncomfortable. Do you have any pain here or here," Jane placed her hands on her lower body and pushed slightly, watching the expression on her face.

"No, just a sore feeling," she answered.

"I'm going to give you something to help you sleep so the soreness will go away. If you have any mucus or blood showing please call me at once. I'll look in on you later. You and your husband both need to be in a hospital. If that isn't possible then we will have to do the best we can. Stay in bed and rest for the next two days at least." After mixing a small dose of laudamun and giving it to her patient, Jane put her things back in her bag and left the wagon.

Jason had waited to talk to her. "How is Mrs. Witt?"

"They both should be in a hospital. Is there one close do you know? Mr. Witt has two very badly broken bones; he could lose his leg. Mrs. Witt's baby is alive, but it may have injuries; she hasn't been hurt much just scrapes and bruises, and sore all over; I won't be able to know for a couple of days about the baby. She could still lose it."

"There isn't a hospital for over a hundred miles. I don't know what to do. I think it best we continue; if they become worse, maybe we can take them to a hospital further west."

Jane nodded, "You know I'll do my best with them. That's all I can do; there is no guarantee," she smiled at Jason.

"You're a wonderful doctor; I'm truly amazed at your ability. You assess a situation and calmly go about correcting it and winning everyone's respect and admiration. Thank you Jane, I feel confident when you're around to take care of our sick."

"What a nice compliment, Jason. Thank you; I'll get back now; if you need me let me know." She waved at Jason as she mounted Cherokee and headed back to her wagon.

* * *

Jane was exhausted as she had been up most of the night, seeing to the Witts, Doris had become frightened about the baby and sent for her. When Jane arrived, Doris was almost hysterical because she couldn't feel the baby moving.

"Doris, quiet down; let me listen with the stethoscope; I'll be able to tell in a moment." Jane placed the instrument against her abdomen, gently moving it around; she smiled as she felt the baby kick and move. She turned to Doris, "Here, listen for yourself." Jane placed the stethoscope to her ears and gently moved it around.

"I hear it moving; I can even hear a thump, thump; is that its heart beat?" Doris asked so excited she could hardly talk.

Jane smiled as she removed the stethoscope, "That it is; have you had any vaginal discharge?"

"No nothing, but I'm so sore all over; I feel like I had been beaten." Doris told her.

"I want you to lie down as much as you can. I think everything is fine; and of course you're sore, you were thrown from the seat of the wagon; anyone would be sore. Don't overeat, drink plenty of water, and rest the next few days. I've just changed the bandage on your husband's leg; so far there is no sign of gangrene. It will be a while before we know if his leg will heal or not. He should be in a hospital; moving in a wagon isn't going to do his leg any good."

"I know, but we must continue; we have so much at stake. I only hope he doesn't get worse. He's a very strong man," Doris said with stars in her eyes.

"Time will tell; I'll check on you tomorrow; remember stay quiet. I have to check on my other patients." Jane left and went to see how Doctor Wayne was. He was sitting outside drinking a hot cup of soup the cook had made.

"How are you, doctor?" Jane asked with a smile. "I see I haven't caused your death yet."

"I'm a hearty type, and don't succumb to illness. I'll be able to resume my duties in a day or so. Would you like a hearty cup of soup?" he asked as he looked down his nose at Jane.

"I'll listen to your chest and be on my way," she said as she came toward him with her stethoscope. At first she thought he would refuse to let her listen to his breathing, but he held still and let her perform her duty. "Sounds good; take it easy for a few more days, and don't catch more cold. If you need me, send someone for me; Good-bye Doctor Wayne."

Jane went to Nettie's wagon to see how Howie was doing. It was time to remove the stitches which she would do today. Nettie was washing clothes; but she now had hot water and a washboard. "Hello Nettie; busy as usual I see. Where's Howie? I need to remove the stitches." Nettie called, "Howie, come here." He came from around the other side of the wagon. Jane motioned him to come to her. She removed the bandage, which was badly soiled and saw that the gash had healed nicely. "

"I'm going to remove the stitches now, so hold still." She snipped the stitches one at a time and pulled them out with a pair of small tweezers. "You're all better now, Howie; just be careful of your head for a few days as it will still be tender; when you comb your hair be very careful. Good-bye Nettie, Howie; come see us."

Jane felt good about all her patients. She wouldn't have to see Howie and Doctor Wayne again, but would have to see the Witts for some time to come, to make sure they were both fully recovered. "Thank God!" she said as she started back to the wagon on wheels, noticing that twilight was falling, "Where did the day go?" she asked herself.

❧ Chapter Forty-Three ❧

Jane was up as usual long before the sun peeked over the distant mountains. She was soon washed and dressed, made her bed, and left the house on wheels for the outdoors. It was cold so early in the morning and she had a shawl wrapped around herself. No matter how early Jane was up, it seemed that Nat was earlier. He was building up the fire, the smoke swirling around him as the wind picked up.

"Good morning, Nat. I see you're up early as usual," Jane said on a cheery note.

"Well, you know what they say, 'the early bird gets the worm' although I can't say I have a taste for worms," he chuckled as he looked at Jane. "Speaking of early?? seems you are always up too."

"I want to look in on the Witts before the train pulls out. I'm worried about Sam's leg, I would have liked for him to have had some time to keep it quiet and give it a chance to heal. I honestly don't know what will happen if it's jiggled over the trail for days on end. He could still lose his leg; I'll go see if they are up yet," she waved a hand as she walked away.

When she reached the wagon where the Witts were, she saw that Bill was already outside.

"How's our patients?" Jane asked him.

"Mrs. Witt seems much better; she's been helping tend her husband. He didn't get much sleep last night and neither did I. He seems to have a lot of pain. Is there something you can give him to help him sleep?" Bill asked.

"Let me look at his leg, then I'll decide. Are they up?" Jane asked as she went to the step in back of the wagon.

"I'm sure they are, Mrs. Witt? Are you up? The doctor is here," Bill called loud enough to wake several wagons along the line.

Doris came to the opening, and pulled it back, "We're up Doctor Jane; good to see you so early in the morning. Come in," she stepped back still holding the flap of the wagon closing.

"How is your husband?" Jane asked looking at Doris, noticing

502

she had good color and seemed fine.

"He didn't sleep much, just off and on. His leg pains him something awful; I hope you can do something, at least so he can rest," she said.

"Good morning, Sam," Jane said as she went to the bed which was made on trunks and boxes up off the floor of the wagon. "I hear you had a bad night; I'll look at your leg and see what we can do to make you more comfortable." Jane sat down on a wooden box where Doris had been sitting as she unwound the bandage. She saw some swelling of the leg but nothing like what she had expected to see; lifting the swatch of gauze from the mangled tissue, she saw there was some drainage, but no undue redness. "It looks good, I'll change the bandage." She proceeded to pour carbolic acid over the wound, wiping away what seepage there had been through the night and applying another square of gauze wet in carbolic acid, and wrapped the linen strip around it. The splints were holding, and didn't need anything done to them. "I may have to put some stitches in later, but will wait for a few days to see how it's healing first."

"What sort of pain are you having? Can you explain it to me?" Jane asked watching the emotions on his face.

"They're sharp; and then a throbbing sensation, with each heartbeat. The sharp pains seem to be tearing the flesh. I couldn't sleep much through the night," he told her.

"Doris, do you have more quilts? I think you should have them ready; looks as though we are going to have some cold weather. Maybe heat some stones in the fire and put them at his body before we pull out. The temperature seems to be falling. Give him light food, mostly broths, and hot soup for a couple more days. I'm going to trust you to give him some medicine; here's a small bottle; give him only two drops, in a half glass of water, only when he can't stand the pain, or if he has done without it throughout the day; you may give him two drops at bedtime, no more than two drops at five hour intervals. If you give more, it may kill him. Do you understand? Only when he has to have it for severe pain. Be prepared for cold weather, and let him sleep as much as possible. How are you feeling?"

"I feel fine; most of the soreness has gone; my back is all right now. Thanks to you, my baby is fine too and lively," she said with a smile.

"You make sure you drink plenty of milk, and keep warm; have a shawl to tie over your head. Is this your wagon?" When she nodded, Jane said, "Did they save most of your things?" Looking around she saw that all sorts of things were crammed into the wagon, even a rocking chair with pots and pans piled in it.

"Amazingly there wasn't too much lost, just jumbled around; the women helped me straighten things and sort them out. Mr. Turner got someone to drive our wagon, and we are eating at the cook's wagon for now. He's been wonderful, both of you have; I don't know how we can thank you. When my husband is better he will take care of the bills," taking her hand she smiled at Jane.

"Remember to keep warm, both of you; we're going across the flatlands of Ohio and I understand the wind can be fierce. I'll try to look in on you when we stop for noon, till then " Jane turned and left the wagon, and headed back to her own house on wheels.

The wind was so strong now that she had to hold onto her head shawl as she struggled against the strong gusts. By the time she reached her wagon sleet particles were stinging her face. Laura was trying to cook breakfast. She had the big coffee pot on and was trying to mix pancakes, the flour flying around her head, as she struggled to add more to the batter.

"What can I do to help, Laura? Looks like you're having a time of it."

"There isn't much you can do. You might as well get inside out of the wind," Laura told her.

"I think I'll build a fire in the stove in the house. We can at least sit in there to eat and not freeze; I think we are in for a bad storm. We've been lucky so far." Jane went in and laid some kindling in the stove and then came back out to get a shovel full of coals to take in to start the fire with. She soon had a fire going and the little house on wheels became warm and comfortable.

Andy was now awake— "Get up sleepy-head," Jane told him. "Everyone will be in here to eat their breakfast; it's sleeting and blowing up a tempest outside. You'd better hurry and get washed and dressed. Find your toboggan and put that on when you go outside." He was soon dressed and gone to do his morning tour of the bushes. Jane hurried and made up his bed and straightened everything, so there would be room for everyone.

"Laura, do you want me to bring in the coffee pot and what pancakes you have made? The fire is going in here now; put them in a pan and I'll set them in the little oven to stay warm." Laura handed them in to Jane, "Here, throw the forks and cups into this basket, and tell the men to come in when they are ready."

Ed and Sam were soon inside sitting on one of the bunks, their plates filled with pancakes, dripping in sorgums. Caroline and Ray came next, and had a plateful. Each had two cups of hot coffee, and a second helping of pancakes. Ed and Sam were ready to leave.

"Sam, Ed, don't forget your foul-weather gear and extra throw, and get each of you an extra pair of gloves. Andy and I'll ride back here. I think Caroline and Laura should too; no need to take a chance of catching cold when they can be comfortable in here," Jane told them.

When everyone had finished, Jane helped Laura do the dishes and hurry and put everything away; they cooled the spider, and Nat hung it on their wagon. Caroline and Laura both were glad to get out of the wind. They were giggling as they settled on the bunks, waiting for the wagons to began to roll.

"This is so cozy; I don't know why everyone doesn't build a house like this," Laura said.

"It's heavy without much load is one reason," Jane told them. "But I've been more than glad to give up other things to have comfort and warmth. It has come in handy so many times, when Gramps and I were in the war. Once I even loaded some wounded solders in when the wagons couldn't take them fast enough, but it saved their lives." A tear glistened in Jane's eye as she thought about it.

There were sounds of the wagons pulling out ahead and theirs started to move forward. The girls found something to hold on to. Andy had a blanket on the floor over by the stove, and he and Goldie were curled up on it, teasing each other. It wasn't long till Jane could see swirling snowflakes passing the small windows, and knew the storm was worse.

"We're going south west, and will cut across an open area and hit the Ohio again. We'll have to cross it, I think about twice more before we reach the Mississippi. I dread to think of crossing it. It's something we have to do, so we'll have to face it. Thank God we have a good wagon master and scout."

The girls soon ran out of anything to talk about, and became quiet, each lost in their own thoughts as the wagon swayed and creaked across the frozen fields, fording small streams and winding around trees and rocks, on the journey westward.

* * *

The time seemed endless as the wagons lumbered along. Jane could see the snow was coming down so fast and blowing so hard that she wondered how the drivers could find their way. She tried to see out the small window but all she could see was the blizzard, and hear the wind slamming against the little house on wheels.

"Are we ever going to stop," Caroline asked. "Seems it must be five o'clock by now. We've been bumping along for hours."

Jane picked her alarm clock out of one of the pockets she had made, that hung on a strip of cloth against the wall. It's a quarter till twelve; we've not had our mid-morning break at all.

Things must be getting worse, for them not to stop. Maybe they have a location they want to make before stopping. I wish we could see or hear something," Jane said as she again tried to look out of the windows. The snow was laying on and everything was white as far as she could see, which wasn't far. The snow was still blowing and so thick you could hardly see the wagon in front of you. Jane could see Sam, he was bundled up, his head and face covered all but his eyes. He had two pair of gloves on, and the throw wrapped around his legs.

"We'll just have to take what comes; do any of you want to go back? Hop right out and get going," Laura said with a giggle. "I, for one, will stay right here by this wonderful little stove. What a lifesaver it is."

"I wish everyone was as comfortable as we are," Jane said, "but we know they aren't. I hope Ed thought to cover up my chickens and pigs. I don't want frozen ones when we stop.

"I believe we're slowing down," Caroline said. They were all holding their breath to see if she was right. They could hear some of the drivers calling to one another but couldn't understand what was said.

Jane looking out the window could see trees, "Looks as though we are going to camp in among the trees. I see evergreens everywhere. I wonder what that's about; you would think it wouldn't be advisable to build fires among the pine-needles. It will keep off a lot of the wind though. I know everyone must be frozen. I feel sorry for them. But there isn't much that can be done. This storm may last for several days, and how we will be able to cross the river again I don't know. Even the animals couldn't swim it when it's so cold. They would die in no time, or freeze into an ice ball.

They still couldn't tell what was going on. Sam had stopped; they couldn't tell if it was permanent or would he move on in a minute? Jane could see a big pine tree on each side of the wagon, "I hope Sam remembers the stove pipe and allow for it so we don't catch the trees on fire. Pine burns awful fast."

There was a tap on the door. Jane went to see who it was. "It'z me Miss Jane, you all right?"

"I'm fine Sam; what's going on? Are we stopping for noon or what?" she asked looking at him covered in snow.

"I'z thinks we'z stay here a time. Thez storm is gettin' worse. Thez animals are tired, need rest and feed. I'z let you'z know az soon az I find out, you stay warm."

"Come in as soon as you can and warm up, Sam. You look frozen," Jane told him as she eased the door shut.

"Well girls, I guess we sit some more, and wait till we hear what we're supposed to do." Jane told them as she still tried to see out the windows. They were steamed up and she couldn't see only shadowy movements.

Soon there was another knock on the door. Jane opened it and Jason stood looking up at her.

"Come in Jason, and get warm," He turned the step down and came up inside, "Oh, my God I've reached heaven," he laughed,

"You wouldn't want to sell this house on wheels would you?" he asked as he held his hands to the little stove.

"Not for any amount of gold," they all told him at once.

"Looks like we are going to have to 'ride out' the storm; we're taking shelter in this grove of pines. It'll knock some of the wind off. The cattle can be fed in a small clearing in the middle; our wagons are already bringing feed for them."

"What about fires? Isn't it dangerous in the pine needles and among the trees?" Jane asked, concern causing a frown.

"We're going to put up a big tent, and rig some sort of fire inside, so people can sleep in it. This looks like it's going to last a couple of days. They'll have to have heat and be out of the wind.

Even if we have to heat stones and bring them inside in tubs to keep the chill down," Jason told them.

"I remember we had to do that once in the war, to keep the sick warm, It worked," Jane told him. "Is there anything we can do?" she asked.

"Wait till we get organized, then we will know what there is to do. You girls stay inside, and keep out of the wind and snow. We'll have things in order soon; this isn't the first time we've been caught in a storm; our men know what to do. I'll see you later. Thanks for the warm," he hurried out and slammed the door.

Jane poked a couple more small sticks of wood into the stove. "Girls, I think we should fill the coffee pot and get it on as the men will need something warm when they come. I'll get it," she started toward the back.

"You stay put, I'll fetch it, I know where the coffee is; I'll hand it in and you can give me the basket for cups and cream," Laura told her as she wrapped a shawl over her head and one around her shoulders.

When Laura handed the coffee pot in, Jane filled it with water from the churn and sat it on the stove, and added the coffee, Laura had ground quite a lot and had it in a tin, ready for use. She was back in a few minutes, "It's so cold I don't see how the men can work. They are cutting down some small trees behind us, getting ready to put up the tent. I hope they get heat for everyone real soon.

"They can cut pine branches for beds, and bring the bedding from their wagons to sleep on. I hear that makes an excellent bed, and smells good too," Jane told them. "I hope Ed thinks to bring an armload of wood from his wagon when he comes. We don't have much left in here. I think it's time I brought out my special clothes. Jane pulled the small trunk from under her bunk and brought out the heavy boy's pants, shirts, socks and shoes. Please turn your heads while I dress. I'll have to see about my patients, and I need to be dressed for it." The girls turned their heads with a giggle, while Jane was getting dressed.

"How do you like the latest style?" she asked as she stood before them.

They looked and looked, "I don't believe it's you. With that cap pulled down over your hair, you look like a boy. Even boy's shoes; aren't you smart? and a jimmison too," they said as Jane put it on and buttoned it up to her chin.

"I wore clothes like this when I was with my grandfather in the war; they're so comfortable and much warmer than dresses. I'm going to try to find the Witt's wagon and see how Sam is doing; I'm worried about him." She grabbed a heavy cape and her black bag and left the wagon, "Watch the coffee," she called, "I'll need a cup when I return."

The snow was still coming down and the wind was blowing so hard it was hard to walk or see. Jane stopped to get her bearings; looking toward the area that was being cleared off, she saw the cook's wagon and knew that the Witt wagon would be close by, and she headed in that direction. It was difficult to walk; the snow on top of the many pine needles gave an uneven footing, causing her to blunder about to keep from falling. She reached the Witt wagon and called— "Doris, are you there?" she waited till the flap was untied from inside.

"Doctor Jane, come in, we were just talking about you. You must be frozen. My, look at you; I thought for a minute you were a boy. You look like you will be warm in that get-up."

"I learned in the war to wear boy's clothes; they are comfortable and warm. And much easier to get in and out of wagons. How are you, Sam?" she asked as she went toward him. Covers were piled in a heap over him and she saw that Doris had a quilt wrapped around herself.

"I feel pretty good; whatever you gave me helped me during the trip here. And I stayed warm. Doris kept covering me till I couldn't move. I hear we are having a really bad storm," he said.

"Yes, it's getting worse. We've stopped in a grove of pine trees to get out of so much of the wind. It's blowing a gale outside; one can hardly walk the wind is so strong. If I can get to your leg, I'd like to take a look." She lifted one side of the covers to get to his injured leg. After removing the bandages she found little change; "I think the cold is keeping your leg from swelling; that is something in our favor. It's bad when the splints have to be moved before the bone can heal; So far, everything looks good. Don't take any medicine for as long as you can stand doing without it. Then try to sleep as much as you can. It doesn't seem too cold in here. If you stay out of the wind and bundle up you should be fine. Have someone bring some hot stones in a bucket to keep the chill off. She told them about the tent. If you decide to be moved, be careful. I'll check on you again before bedtime." She put her cape on and picked up her bag and left.

I'd better see about Doctor Wayne, while I'm about it she decided talking to herself. Going to his wagon, Bill came to the flap.

"Come in Doctor Jane."

Jane climbed up on the step and into the wagon; she saw the doctor lying on a bunk. "How are you feeling, Doctor Wayne?" she asked, seeing he wasn't inclined to be sociable.

"I'm fine. Why are you out in this weather asking foolish questions? Don't you know to stay inside?" the doctor scowled at her.

"Do you mind if I listen to your chest? I feel responsible for your well-being." She took out her stethoscope as he grudgingly let her listen. "Sounds fine; be sure to stay warm, and eat plenty of hot broths and soup; call me if I'm needed," she smiled at Bill as the doctor let out a disgusted grunt.

Jane made her way slowly back to the wagon. She saw that Laura was outside, puttering in the cupboard.

"What are you doing? Why aren't you inside?"

"I thought I might as well put a pot of stew on the stove and make use of all that heat that's going to waste. We can have it for supper; there's some left-over fried venison steaks that I'll put in the oven and some biscuits I can heat for sandwiches if anyone is hungry before the stew cooks. And I want to make sure our potatoes and apples and turnips don't freeze. I'll be in in a minute. You go in, the coffee is made."

Jane hung her heavy cape on a nail inside the door, and took the cup of steaming coffee that Caroline had ready for her. Nodded her thanks and said, "That tastes heavenly; I never knew a cup of coffee could taste so good," she sat sipping it holding both hands around the cup to get them warm.

Ed came with an arm-load of wood for the stove; Jane motioned for him to put it in the corner at the foot of her bed.

"Thanks Ed. Come in and get a hot cup of coffee. I was hoping you would bring some wood, as we're about out. Did you remember to cover my pigs and chickens?" Jane asked concern in her voice.

"They're fine; snuggled down together; I had put some straw in the coop and they're making use of it. They are toasty warm, and the pigs are growing by leaps and bounds. If they get much bigger we'll have to make a bigger pen for them. This coffee sure tastes good."

Laura had put the meat and biscuits in the oven and they were hot. "Would you like a sandwich? If you do they're hot. You can eat now or whenever you like."

"I might as well have one now, then I won't have to carry in more snow and mud."

"Don't you worry about that; it can always be cleaned up. You get good and warm before you go out again. And Ed—I wish you would see about Nettie and Howie; see if they have enough covers to keep them warm. I'm worried about them. I looked for their wagon but didn't know where it was when I was out. Let us know when you find them," Jane said.

"I think I know where they're parked. I'll see about them right away; if they are in too bad shape I'll bring them over to get warm if that's all right?" Ed asked.

"You know it is; you don't have to ask. I have a soft spot for Nettie, and Howie too. She's such a nice girl; I wish there were room for both of them with me, but we are getting a little crowded," Jane laughed.

As Ed finished his biscuit and coffee, Ray came to the door; "It's all yours; go on in Ray," Ed told him.

Laura had his biscuit ready and Caroline handed him a hot cup of coffee.

"This is what I call real southern hospitality. Thanks Laura, this hits the spot. I'm sure you'll have two more cold hungry men in here in a short time." He finished and put on his coat and opened the door to leave and Nat stood waiting to get in. He and Sam came in together and threw their coats on the floor by the door and sat down on the bunk, took the sandwiches offered to them and the hot coffee. There was little talk as they ate and thawed out.

"I've never seen a colder wind than is blowing out there. My eyes seem to freeze to my eyelids. They have the tent almost up, and several big fires started. People are coming out to get warm, although most of them said they kept warm inside the covered wagons. I think everyone will cook on one or two fires and get along on as little as possible till this blows over. I see my Laura is using her head and cooking supper on your stove while it warms everyone. That's a good idea," he put his arm around her and gave her a hug.

The men finished eating; Sam didn't say much as Nat did most of the talking, "We'd better go see if we can be of help anywhere." They both nodded and left for the outside.

The girls talked and waited to see what would happen. They wondered how many would move into the tent for the night. They peeked out first one tiny window and then the other. The cook pot was steaming them up until it was difficult to see.

"I think I'll take a walk and see who is doing what," Jane said with a laugh. "I'll see how Mary and John and the children are doing. They are so crowded up I don't see how they can stand it. When they can get outside it isn't so bad; maybe they'll put up their tent too." She opened the door and stepped down; she stood a moment looking around—seemed everyone was doing something. Several fires were being built. She walked toward where the big tent was being raised. To the side she spotted Mary and John; sure enough they were putting up their own tent. Jane walked over to talk to them and see if she could help.

"Howdy! Can I help?" she asked as she took a corner of the tent and helped pull it down in place. They soon had stakes in the ground and the tent tied down. It was hard with the gusts of wind that tried to tear it from their hands as they struggled with it. When the tent was up Mary took her broom and swept out as much of the snow as she could and they laid down a square of tarp; John had gone to cut pine branches for their beds.

"You'll sleep good tonight," Jane told Mary.

The children were scrounging for fire wood, and Mary soon had a fire going outside the opening of the tent. Mark and Sarah took a bucket to find stones to heat to bring inside to warm up the tent. Everyone was working to get settled while there was still light and before the storm became worse. Fires were being built everywhere, and cook pots being put on for their evening meal. Soon there were smells of cooking meat wafing through the cold air.

Several had brought bedding and selected their spot in the big tent, meeting new members of the train and a party atmosphere was beginning to build. Children who had been confined all day in the wagons ran around the tent laughing and teasing each other.

Jane finally saw Nettie and Howie, "How are you, Nettie? How is Howie?" she asked.

"We're fine; Howie's head is hardly even sore now. We've been bundled up in the wagon, but kept warm. We have a feather bed and plenty of quilts, so we were fine. My sister wants to move into the big tent, so I guess we will too. I'll use one of the fires already built to cook something for our supper. I'll start it soon," Nettie told her.

All the animals had been tended, and the people settled inside the tent, cook fires going and food cooked for their supper. After eating, several French harps and a couple of string instruments were brought out and the sound of music was heard from the big tent. Those who hadn't moved there soon came to hear the musicians and sing along with those who had. Jane knew her supper would be ready and left the tent to return to her wagon. When she stepped outside she couldn't believe all the tents that had been raised—it looked like a village. "Thank God they are all warm now. I don't have to feel guilty," she said to herself.

The snow was still falling, and the tree tops twisting in the wind as the camp settled down for the winter night.

❧ Chapter Forty-Four ❧

The storm had blown itself out; the wind had quieted and it had stopped snowing. The wagon train had been camped for four days in the grove of pines. The animals were rested and everyone was getting restless, waiting to move on again. It was still bitter cold with the ground frozen solid.

Jason came by in the afternoon, "We'll be pulling out at daybreak tomorrow; we'll be headed south into Kentucky but we will have to cross the Ohio again before getting into Kentucky. There will be barges to aid us. Just wanted you to know and be prepared." He threw up his hand in salute as he went down the line of wagons warning everyone.

Jane and the girls began to go through everything rearranging and sorting. Laura was going to cook a big pot of beans for their evening meal the next day. Their meat would need to be replenished very soon. When she told Nat, he and Ed decided to go out hunting that afternoon to see if they could get some rabbits or other game. They came in with six big rabbits, that they cleaned, and put into water for whatever the girls wanted to do with them. Laura took four to her wagon---hanging them up so they could become frozen and keep for several days. She was going to stuff two and put them in the little stove to roast for their supper.

Everyone was busy getting ready for departure the next morning. Some took down their tents and moved back into their wagons, so they wouldn't have to hurry in the early morning.

At the first peek of dawn, the men were harnessing the horses and hooking up while the women hurried the morning meal. The wagons began to line up in order of their places; the sun looked as though it was trying to shine, as everyone made ready.

"Move them out!" came the order, and the teams leaned into the traces; the wagons creaking and groaning began to move; there was a joyful cheer as they hit the trail again.

"I'm glad we had this rest especially for Mr. Witt; his leg is doing much better than I would have expected. I think it's healing well and he will be able to at least sit up in another week.

The cold weather kept it from swelling. I never heard of any sickness while we were camped—at least no one called me," Jane said to Laura.

Andy was on the floor with Goldie, they were both happy as long as they had each other. Jane's cat, Angel, was right at home in the wagon always finding a place to hide and curl up and sleep.

Laura had the coffee pot full of fresh coffee ready to set it to heat when and if they stopped for a mid-morning rest. She had made a pot after breakfast while they were waiting to move out, setting the full pot into one of the tubs so it would be safe till noontime.

The wagons moved along at a good clip over the frozen ground; when it thawed there might be problems. They were not stopping it seemed for the mid-morning stop, but continued, wanting to make the Ohio crossing by nightfall, where they would camp and be ready to cross in the early morning. They would follow the river south, the Ohio behind them. There would be no more rivers until they came to the Mississippi which everyone dreaded thinking about.

The drovers were pushing the train; now that they were rested, they felt that they must make up for the lost time. It was almost one o'clock before a halt was called for noon. Laura and Jane heated the stew and coffee and had biscuits ready for the men when they came to eat.

Soon they were on the trail again moving smoothly along. Even the herd seemed docile and stayed together without any major problems.

The travelers had become trail-wise as they traveled along, and the river crossing was accomplished without any mishaps. They were headed southwest toward the mighty Mississippi. They would cross it and move into Missouri where there were considerable mountains, and rough country to go through.

Day after day the wagons moved forward—the routine becoming exciting one day and boring the next, as they forded small streams, went around deep ravines, and climbed up mountains. They had been on the trail for several weeks when the heavens let loose with a terrible thundering storm. The rain came down in sheets; it beat on the canvas tops of the wagons as though it might cut right through the flimsy covering. Anything not tied securely banged and clattered. For those who were inside the cov-

515

ered wagons, and couldn't see what was happening, it was terrifying. The children cried and some of the women wept as the vicious storm roared down on the wagon train. It must have been terrible for the men who were driving the wagons, with water running down their faces into their eyes and the lightning flashing and thunder rolling along the mountain tops. The wagons that were in the front of the train fared better than those who brought up the rear. The roads were rutted and worked into a mudhole after the first wagons went through—the more wagons the worse it became. The wagons became splattered, and the horses were mud up to their bellies. For those who had become careless when covering their wagons, rain seeped in. If the front and rear flaps were not overlapped and tied securely, rain came in to run down the floor of the wagon into anything that sat in its way. Everything became damp and dreary—even the bedding seemed to be damp, although most had their beds arranged on top of trunks and storage boxes.

Jane kept checking on the sacks of salt and sugar that were stored under the bunks. Thank heavens the flour and meal were in watertight barrels in Laura's wagon. No water came into the little house on wheels that she could see. The small fire she kept going in the stove kept things dry inside. The three girls were comfortable, and gave thanks that they could be inside where it was dry. There were delays as some wagons had to have extra teams to pull them out of the quagmire they had to maneuver through. After struggling all day through the rain and mud, they came to a rough road that seemed to be mostly gravel. The wagons, were out of the deep ruts they had been traveling through for most of the day. The accumulated mud on wheels splattered along the new route, as the wheels turned freely. The rain had become a drizzle; fog began to raise in the hills; the mud on the horses gradually disappeared in rivulets down their sides, as the drizzle washed it away.

There was little conversation in the little house on wheels as the girls had talked themselves out. First one and then another would stretch out for a nap as the other two sat on the other bunk. Andy had his pillow on the floor where he and Goldie spent much of the time napping, not caring about the country the wagon train was passing through.

Jane, not being use to sitting, walked from tiny window to window, trying to see the area they were traveling through. There were woods, mostly with hilly areas, which gave the land a rough wild look. There were few and far between houses, with no sign of habitation. A couple of times she saw deer in the edge of wooded sections. They disappeared into the thick brush as the clatter of the wagon train alarmed them.

Jane saw Jason ride by and waved to him. She doubted he could see her at the tiny window as he hurried down the train, directing them in the direction of the river landing they were heading for.

The light was dim inside the little house and gave one the impression that it was getting on for nightfall. It seemed they had been traveling for hours, and it became more depressing and boring as the hours ticked by. The girls sat looking at each other with nothing to do or say.

* * *

It took over a week of steady traveling to get them even close to the Mississippi. It seemed the animals knew long before the river was spotted.

When the mighty river came into sight, the train was stopped on a bluff overlooking the water so that everyone could see the challenge that faced them.

"My God! It goes forever. How in the world will we ever cross such a wide stretch of water; it looks like an ocean," Jane remarked as she looked at the river.

"I think I'll go back," Laura decided as she stood looking in awe. "We'll never get over this; all the other times it was just a short distance; this looks like it's a mile or longer from bank to bank. One thing we lucked out on—looks like that storm didn't reach here and raise the water. We'd never get over it then, I have my doubts now."

"Remember trains have been crossing for a long time and they made it. Jason and Mr. Morgan have brought numerous trains across; they know what they are doing," Jane said as she looked at the tranquil flowing river below them.

"Mount up," came the order and everyone scrambled back into the wagons.

The herd had been taken on ahead. As they topped the rise,

they saw in the distance that there was a grouping of buildings, no doubt where the ferry was located. The herd had arrived and was being penned in a large pen out from the buildings. Shortly the first wagons were 'Circling Up' and their wagons followed the lead wagon and made the wide circle where they would camp for the night.

"I'm glad to be here at last; I'm tired, and need to get out of this house and walk," Caroline remarked.

"I'm glad too; it will be nice to walk around; seems we have been inside for months," the others added.

When the girls opened the door to the house on wheels, it seemed a spring breeze greeted them.

"It's not cold anymore," they all said as they walked around breathing in the fresh air. "We can do away with our heavy shawls. That will be a relief."

"Let's look for wood;, I have my doubts there will be any close, but if we are first maybe we won't have to go far,." Laura said as she looked about.

"I saw some dead trees down by the river, probably washed from upstream," Jane said as they took an ax and started out. Caroline, Laura and Jane with Andy and Goldie trailing along behind headed for the river. They found several dead trees and chopped and broke up a good-size pile of wood; Caroline would stay with the pile while the others took armloads back to camp. When Jane and Laura arrived back, they saw several women with axes going toward the woods and river searching for wood for the evening cook fire.

"Let's stack it under the wagon; I'm glad we got a start on the others; let's go get some more; a couple of more trips should be enough for tonight and some to take for the little stove too," Jane told Laura as they turned and went back for more. Andy and Caroline had been picking up pieces of dried wood and had a good-size pile for them to bring; they all piled as much as they could carry in their arms—even Andy brought his share too, and went back to the wagon. They had enough to do for the night and morning cooking; if they stayed longer they would have to get more.

Laura brought out the spider, chose a place and laid the kindling for a fire. She went inside with the shovel and brought out coals from the stove to start it. The coffee pot was soon on. The rabbits were cooked, ready for supper; the pot of beans brought out, and a dish of saurkraut was rinsed off and put on to heat. Jane and Caroline watched them while Laura put on a pone of cornbread in the large Dutch oven.

Sam and Ed came and took the table down from the roof of the little house and soon had it put together and ready for supper. The bench was ready on the far side for the men; the girls used the crates Jane had gotten at the store and the step from the wagon to sit on.

"Ummm somethin' smellz good," Sam said, as he sniffed the air.

"We're having a feast tonight. You should see what Laura has cooking in the little house; it has been cooking all day, and so tender it'll melt in your mouth," Caroline told the men.

When the cornbread was done, it was sliced and piled onto a platter and set on the table; the beans and saurkraut were put on too. Laura went into the house on wheels and brought out the two large rabbits, stuffed with apples and bread stuffing with lots of sage in it. It smelled wonderful and was a golden brown making everyone's mouth water.

"Thatz the prettiest rabbitz I'z ever did see," Sam told Laura with a smile.

"I'm sure glad I married Laura; with my hunting and her cooking we'll get along just fine," Nat said.

"I'm sure glad I latched on to both of you; you make a fine team. We're going to have the best ranch around; and with Ed and Sam, it's an added bonus," Jane said with a laugh. "Now if you just didn't eat so much, we'd be even farther ahead. It's all right though, so dig in, we have us a river to cross tomorrow." Jane smiled at them all. She was so fond of each and every one of them.

"I'z hear'z they been some bad men on the river, goin' up and down cauzing trouble. Yonz all keeps a eye out. And youz women don't go off far by yourz self. Keepz somethin' handy to fight with," Sam told them.

"Does Jason know about this?" Jane asked.

"I'll make sure he knows; as soon as we eat, I'll find him and tell him. He may want to put out sentinels tonight to make sure they don't get into camp," Ed told them.

"Be sure to keep your guns handy, and a club or something close in case you need it,." Jane said as she looked around the table. "Did you hear what they're after, Sam?" Jane asked.

"Noz I'z didn't; just mean I'z recond '," Sam said.

"There's the herd, and all the merchant's loaded wagons, and I'm sure there's money on the train. If they get a woman or child they could demand ransom, and it would be paid," Ed said. "Everyone be extremely careful. Andy, no going off with Goldie unless a man goes with you; and you women, no fishing or firewood gathering alone." Ed looked like he was ready to go looking for the pirates at any moment.

The announcement made everyone quiet as they thought over what had been told.

As soon as supper was over, Ed went to find Jason, and Jane went into the little house on wheels and strapped on her gun belt with her loaded pistol hung on her side. She checked the chamber to make sure it was loaded and in working order. Her rifle was loaded and set inside the door, ready for action.

"Everyone load your rifles and keep shells handy in case we have trouble." Jane told them all.

"Would you shoot someone Jane?" Laura asked.

"You betcha, if they were trying to harm one of us or take what we have. I'd shoot them in a second, and right where it would count. I've been through a war, and I've seen what can be done to those who can't protect themselves. You girls stay inside the circle; use your chamber-pots in the wagon. Don't go to the bushes even to empty them. Think! You could be in danger this minute." They all started looking around them.

Ed was soon back. "Jason knows about them. They're a bunch of renegade deserters from the armies. There's about ten of them and from what we know extremely dangerous. They have raided some farms and taken young girls and women. They trade them to the Indians after they are through with them. They have boats and horses, and roam the area along the Mississippi. There hasn't been a raid for a while and it's rumored they are in Kansas at an Indian reservation. But they could hit at any time. There will be a night patrol—men on-foot and on horses; each man has a two-hour shift, and they want them armed. The herd is being guarded now, and will be all through the night. Jason's men are on the job now, and he is being very cautious. I'm going to the wagon and have a nap as I'm on the midnight shift; Sam, do you want to go with me?"

"I'z might az well. We'z make a good team," Sam laughed.

"Leave Cherokee saddled, one of you can take him to do patrol duty, the other can saddle the other mare," Jane said.

She could see that even the men were nervous. She wanted to warn Mary about the children. It didn't matter if it was daylight or not; from what they said, they were a bold bunch of misfits.

"I'll be right back; I'm going to Mary's wagon."

When Jane arrived everyone seemed in a good mood; their tent was set up and a cook-fire was lit; Mary and Sarah were making their dinner. Young Matt was playing with Polka-dot, the black and white dog, brother to Andy's Goldie. They were having a great time chasing each other.

"Have you heard about the renegades that are prowling this area, Mary?" Jane asked.

"What do you mean, Jane? I haven't heard anything; with all these people around there's no danger surely," Mary said.

"There's grave danger; keep the children in the circle; don't let them even go to the bushes to relieve themselves. They could be stolen and held for ransom. Young girls and women are being stolen and used, then sold to the Indians. Everyone must use their chamber-pots; don't go fishing, or gathering wood without protection of men and guns. There are patrols out even now. Keep your gun handy, but only if you know how to use it, and will use it. Be alert; if you see someone who you don't recognize, be careful and all stay together. I wanted to warn you myself. I know the awful things these renegade soldiers are capable of. So be very careful. I'll see you tomorrow."

Jane left Mary and John's wagon and started back to her little house on wheels. She saw Laura and Caroline washing dishes on the table by the fire. The men had all wandered off somewhere. Jane stepped behind the little house to see how Cherokee was doing. She had saved him some apple peelings that she got from the step as she passed. She stood between him and the house, giving him the tidbits, as he rubbed his nose on her arm and nickered softly. Suddenly his ears perked up. A terrified scream sounded close by. Jane looked around Cherokee and saw a big mangy-looking man on a dark horse. He had leaned over and scooped up Sarah, under the arms; she screamed yeeeeeeee—as she kicked and tried to get away. Jane grabbed the reins loose from the wagon where Cherokee was tied and jumped up into the saddle; as she did, Cherokee gave a lunge, and his long legs reached out in a run toward the other horse. "Get Help!" Jane yelled, "They've got Sarah!" She loosened the hold on Cherokee's bridle rains and gave him his head. He leaped through the air toward the other rider as Jane managed to get the blacksnake whip her sister-in-law Mammy Jane had given her, from the side of the saddle where she had Sam make a special snap-on strap to hold it. She wouldn't dare shoot as she might hit Sarah. "Get him Cherokee!" Jane demanded. The stallion shot away, his lean body laying out flat as Jane leaned forward urging him on. They were gaining on the other horse, "Hang on, Sarah! Hold on, Sarah!" Jane yelled, as her hair came loose from its pins and flew out behind her like an avenging angel. She was three lengths behind, gaining, then two lengths; the blacksnake whip whirled around Jane's head; Cherokee seemed to lengthen his stride, and they were one length behind. Jane called, "Hang on tight Sarah!" The whip kept circling her head as she gained on the renegade. Suddenly Jane let it fly out beyond Cherokee; it passed the abductor's head. As Jane gave a jerk on the leather handle of the whip, it wrapped around the man's neck; he gave a strangled cry as Jane gave a viscous pull on the leather that joined them. His hands flew to his neck trying to get the leather off as he fell from his horse. Jane gave another jerk on the whip embedding it in his neck as he hit the ground. Sarah hung on the side of the running horse holding onto the saddle horn, Jane dropped the whip and raced ahead grabbing the bridle of the running horse, "Hang on Sarah; I'll have you safe in a minute."

Jane had heard other horses running behind her and hoped that it wasn't more of the pirates that were chasing them. Looking around she saw that some of the drovers, with Jason among them had caught up with her. Jane grabbed the hand that Sarah reached out to her and swung her up behind her on Cherokee. Sarah grabbed her around the waist and leaned her head against Jane sobbing. "You're safe now; it's all right Sarah," she told her as she patted her leg.

Jason came over to her. "I've never seen anything like that in all my life. How did you ever learn to use a whip like that? And how did you ever learn to ride like that? We have some fast horseflesh but we couldn't begun to catch you. I don't think he'll want to kidnap anyone else for a while."

"Jason, would you see that I get my whip back; I have to get Sarah back to her mother and give her something to quiet her down. She's been through a terrible experience, but it would have been a lot worse if I hadn't been standing petting Cherokee when it happened." Jane turned and trotted back to the compound talking quietly to Sarah and petting her.

"My mom is going to be so mad at me. I just went around the other side of the wagon for a minute to get some more wood. I looked around, and I didn't see anyone, and he grabbed me. I thought I was going to die right there. Oh, thank you Jane for saving me. I'll never forget what you've done." She sobbed and hiccoughed and sobbed some more.

"Your mom won't be mad at you. I'll guarantee that. Try not to cry anymore; you're safe now," Jane told her as they reached camp and Mary came and pulled Sarah into her arms sobbing as hard as Sarah was.

"My baby, my baby; that dreadful man—I hope they shoot him—trying to carry off my Sarah; She sobbed and patted Sarah with both hanging on to each other.

"Are you hurt anywhere, Sarah?" Jane asked trying to bring the crying to an end.

Other women were gathering from the wagons wanting to know what was going on. It was explained to them and they all looked around peering into the dusk beyond the wagons—wrapping arms around young daughters, pulling them close.

"No one is hurt—that's the main thing to be thankful for. Sarah has had a scare, but she's fine. She's a very lucky little girl. It could have been far worse; that vermin was headed down river probably to join his buddies. The men are out looking for the rest of the gang. If they find them maybe they can save something like this happening again. Just be careful; the rest of our journey will be through rough uninhabited country where there are wild animals and danger everywhere. Just remember that." Jane mixed up a small dose of laudnum and handed it to Mary, "Give her this, and let's you and I get her into bed. She may go into shock if she doesn't rest and keep warm." Sarah drank down the drought and they took her to the tent where her bed had been made up. Jane sat down beside her after she had been made comfortable. "I'll stay with you till you are asleep," she said, as Sarah's, eyes started to droop.

When Jane returned to the little house on wheels, Jason was there; Jane went over to him—

"Can I talk privately to you?" he asked looking intently at Jane. "How is Sarah? Was she hurt?" he asked.

"Sarah's fine; I've given her something to help her sleep; hopefully when she awakens she will have forgotten some of the terror she went through. Did you find their hide-out?" Jane asked looking at Jason feeling he was hiding something.

"Several of the men went down the river; so far they have found nothing. They may have had a barge and put their horses aboard and be halfway to New Orleans by now. I've brought your whip back," Jason said as he handed it to her. "You're quite a woman, Doctor Barrlette; I take my hat off to you." He bowed to her as he said it.

"What about the man who took Sarah? What have you done with him? Wouldn't he tell you where the others are?" Jane asked one question after another.

"We took him to the ferry office, and they'll notify the authorities; and no, he wasn't capable of telling us anything, he's dead." Jason looked closely at Jane, watching for her reaction.

"You mean someone shot him before getting the information?" she asked.

"His neck was broken when he fell from his horse; he was dead when we got to him. He got what he rightly deserved; he did it to himself."

"What!" Jane said the one word, a stunned unbelievable look on her face, as she swayed on her feet toward Jason.

Jason put his arms around Jane and pulled her head over onto his shoulder, "It's all right, my darling," he said softly, as he patted her, smoothing her hair.

Jane raised her face to Jason, "What have I done? What will happen to me?" Tears stood in her eyes, "It was Sarah; it was for Sarah," a sob caught in Jane's throat as Jason held her close.

"You didn't do anything that wasn't right. You must not blame yourself for something that wasn't your fault. And nothing is going to happen to you. When everyone knew what happened, they wanted to give you a medal; and all think he got his right desserts. He was a viper, and like a snake he should be dead, and he is. I want you to forget it. You didn't kill him—he killed himself. And just for a moment, think what he would have done to sweet, little innocent Sarah. And her family. You saved the life of every one of them. I want you to be proud, proud of what you did for us. I'm so proud of you I could bust. And I want you to feel the same way "Jason kissed her hair; she had become so precious to him that he was amazed and overwhelmed by his feelings for this strong woman.

"Let's go back; and I want your head held high. We're all so proud of you, Doctor Barrlette," Jason said as he led her back to the wagons.

🎗 Chapter Forty-Five 🎗

The camp was up late, everyone talking of the bravery of Doctor Barrlette, When the story was told time and again, everyone seemed to agree that it was the bravest thing they ever heard of.

The women were all nervous, knowing there were renegades out there somewhere in the darkness, watching, and waiting to pounce on any unsuspecting person, especially a female. "What if it had been my Katie, or my Flo; I couldn't have lived if she had been stolen," a couple of the mothers said, their arms protecting their girls.

Jane, Laura and Caroline were all sitting around the campfire talking. Jane heard Sam and Ed leave with the horses for their stint of patrol. The girls seemed reluctant to go to their wagons. Ray and Nat finally came, "Let's go to bed girls; everything is safe. The men are riding around the camp and keeping a close watch and will be out there till daylight. We have our guns loaded and ready. Will you be all right, Miss Jane?" Nat asked.

"I'll be fine; I have two guns, and they're loaded and ready. Goldie will bark if there is a disturbance. I'm a light sleeper, and I'll lock the door from inside. I feel quite safe in the little house as it's more protection than just a tent or wagon. I'll be fine. Don't worry about me. Just keep an ear out for anything unusual." The two couples waited till Jane and Andy were inside and the door locked.

There were several lighted lanterns hanging from wagons. Everyone decided it was one time when it would be advisable to keep a light and use their precious oil. The circle inside the wagons was lighted enough to see from one wagon to another.

Everyone went to bed; the sound of the milk cows moving about could be heard—now and then the cry of a small child. Sounds that were not noticed before became distinct now that all ears were tuned for any disturbance.

Jane finally fell into a deep sleep. Lance was there holding her, telling her that everything was going to be all right. Then he turned into Jason who seemed to be kissing her hair. How strange she thought; but she definitely felt his arms around her, and she felt protected and loved. "Why do I feel so strangely when he is near," she asked herself in her dream; she had felt differently with Lance. With Jason she felt so weak and shaken, as though her knees were giving way beneath her. Her heart fluttered at the mere sight of him. The two men were more alike than she wanted to admit. I think I may be falling just a little in love with Jason. But I must not; he will soon be gone. He gave up his homestead because he doesn't want to settle down.

I'll just have to forget such thoughts, Jane reminded herself, as she turned and twisted on the bunk. Suddenly Jane awoke, her night clothes were wrapped around her till she felt strangled by them. She sat up and finally stood untangling her night gown so that it fell in a straight line around her. She could hear Andy asleep on the next bunk. She went to a window and peeked out toward the river and woods. She saw a horse and rider coming toward her, and stood waiting to see if it was the patrol; she began to shake until she recognized Ed, on Cherokee, then she smiled. What one's imagination can do. Jane went back to bed comforted by the men who were giving up their sleep to guard the train.

The sun was shining when Jane awoke; she heard movement outside and decided she had overslept and had better hurry to get dressed. She wasn't sure if the train was going to try to cross the river today or if they would rest a day before crossing.

When Jane came outside, Laura was making breakfast; today she had biscuits, pan gravy and molasses; Sam and Ed already sat at the table eating one biscuit after another. The big coffee pot was getting a workout too.

"Good morning, Miss Jane," they all said, as she sat down with a cup of coffee.

"Good morning all; is there any news this morning?" she asked as she looked at each of them around the table.

Ed answered, "No news that we know of. There wasn't a sign of the renegades. Jason has sent riders upriver and downriver to see if they can find them but no luck. He doesn't want to cross the river until he knows they aren't around to cause trouble. Everyone is busy getting their equipment ready for crossing. Wagons need to be greased and things tightened up. We keep our gear in good shape, because we have an expert here in Sam; he can see things that need doing that the rest of us don't." Sam smiled his big toothy smile.

"We couldn't do without Sam, that's for sure," Everyone nodded. "I couldn't have selected a better crew if I had gone all the way to Charleston," Jane told them. There were smiles on every face. "Just be careful; we can't afford to have anyone hurt and out of commission, we need you all," Jane smiled at the table full of friends.

The camp remained quiet with everyone talking among themselves, and staying close to their wagons. Jason had sent word that they would have a day of rest before crossing the Mississippi. Scouts were out looking for the best place to take the herd across; talk was that there was a shallow place upriver, with sand bars where the cattle and horses would be able to cross. The route would take them through Springfield and then to Joplin, which had been called the jumping off point for all the pioneers going West. The wagon train would start southwest from Joplin and they would soon be in the Oklahoma Territory, but there was still a long way to go. Missouri was full of lakes and streams to cross, and there was the possibility of Indians along the Nebraska/Missouri border. There were several forts—Fort Smith to the south and Fort Gibson to the north, which kept the area mostly free of conflict with the Indians. There had been roving renegades who would pounce on lone travelers, and sometime isolated farms, causing trouble in the newly-settled areas.

Caroline sat sewing on the dresses she had started at the Jarvis farm. She had finished most of them. She still had the one for Jane that she hadn't made. As warm as it was starting to get, they could soon wear the calicos. She had started some of the baby things too. She had two dozen diapers to hem by hand. Jane and Laura were helping her in the afternoons. It was hard to sew when the wagon was moving, and usually too late at night to be able to see to sew when they stopped. But every minute she could, she would work on it.

Laura made a big pot of apple dumplings for their dinner at noon. The men enjoyed them so much, and they made a filling meal. The apples wouldn't last much longer as the weather got warmer. Laura kept an eye on the food and used it to the best advantage. She had a bowl left over, and just as she was wondering what to do with them, Jason popped from behind the wagon.

Jane looked up startled, "Best you come whistling, if you pop out from behind the wagon like that," Jane told him with a smile.

"I'll keep that in mind; I sure don't want to get shot. How are you ladies? I see you're keeping busy," he said as he looked at the sewing they each held in their laps.

"Have you eaten dinner, Jason?" Laura asked, "I have some apple dumplings that are still warm, and plenty of sweet milk."

"Even if I had eaten I'd say no, if they are your apple dumplings. I'd be more than happy to finish them off for you. And if you have some hot coffee, I'll take some of that too."

Laura set the bowl of dumplings on the table and poured a cup of coffee from the big pot that still sat on the spider over the low fire; she poured out a pitcher of milk and set that beside him. "There you are; enjoy," she told him.

"Is there any news about the pirates. Did you find out where they are holed-up?" Jane asked, anxious to know if they were still around.

"We looked ten miles in each direction, but no sign of them. I think they headed out for easier pickings. We're being very careful and guarding our camp and will while we are anywhere near the river. I doubt they would attack a train this big if they didn't have the river for a getaway. But you never know what scum like that will do," Jason talked as he ate. "I wanted to let you know we will be pulling out at sunup. Do you need anything?" he asked looking at Jane.

"I think we're well-supplied, so far," Jane told him. "We'll be ready; the men have gone over the equipment and everything is top shape." They all waved as Jason thanked them and left.

* * *

Breakfast was eaten by firelight and everyone was ready for the big day. The crossing of the Mississippi had been looked forward to with dread and anticipation for several days. Today was the day it would happen. As soon as it was light enough the call, "Move Them Out" was heard and the drivers fell into line as their turn came. Jane was glad that they were toward the front and didn't have to wait as long as those in the back of the train to cross. She and Andy sat up on the front seat; the fire in the little house had been let go out and she had cleaned the ashes from the little stove. The weather had turned mild, probably due to being near the water. There was no wind to speak of and it looked like it was going to be a lovely day for the adventure ahead of them.

Jane felt good; she had checked on Mr. Witt and he was sitting up—still with his leg propped up, but at least was more comfortable. In another week she would remove two of the splints. He would be able to move around with the help of a crutch which Sam had made a rough one for him. If there were any sickness on the train, Doctor Wayne must be in charge of it as Jane hadn't been called. She was glad not to have to be responsible for the illnesses; after all, she wasn't a doctor, and Doctor Wayne was being paid by the train to do the job.

These things were going over in Jane's mind as they waited their turn for the barge that would take them to the other side of the river. There were two barges here—one going over and one returning at the same time. It was so far that it saved time in the crossing.

Sam pulled up waiting for the barge; they all got down from the high seat. Jane unhooked Cherokee, and Caroline came from her wagon to hold the cow. Andy would hang onto the railing. The barge bumped against the bank and Sam led the team aboard; they were getting used to the ferry and went on with no problem. Cherokee rubbed his nose against Jane and followed her to stand behind the house on wheels. Again only two wagons and teams and the horse and cow were taken at one time. Andy was cautioned to stand still and not frighten the animals. It seemed an eternity for them to move across the wide space of water. They all heaved a sigh of relief when they were on solid ground again and away from the water.

The front wagons went on ahead—one of the drovers getting them started in the direction they would take; they drove some distance, taking their time for the rest to catch up. The drover told them to stop when they came to a lake and make camp and to wait for the others as they would be camping there for the night. They were on the shore of a lovely lake; the girls decided to do some washing while there was plenty of water and time, and soon had a fire and the wash tubs on to heat. By the time the last wagon arrived at the camp, there was washing hung everywhere. Several of the women took advantage as Jane and her crew had. The women were cooking and the various smells filled the air around the camp. Several were trying their hand at fishing, bringing big strings to be cleaned and fried for their supper. Laura had the rabbits cut up, breaded and browned, and in the Dutch oven under the coals roasting. She made a big bowl of cut cabbage ready for cole slaw, and she had a big pot of beans cooking. She planned her meals so there was always leftovers for the noon meal, and something started for the following evening.

The news came after supper that the sunup call was in effect. Everyone was getting anxious to reach their land, and each day took them nearer. The herd had gotten over the mighty river without loss, and they were on the last long leg of their journey.

Day after day, they left at sunup and stopped at sunset. The long days left little time for anything but the bare necessities.

"This is beautiful land—this Missouri; plenty of water and wood, wild animals for food, and looks like good farming land. If ours is half as good and plentiful, I'll be more than pleased," Jane told Sam and Andy as they traveled along.

"It do look plentiful; I'z gonna' likez it here, I'z can tell," Sam said nodding his head.

"I'd like a little more open land for my horses," Andy remarked.

Jane noticed how much he had grown up on the train, and leaned toward him and gave him a hug. "There'll be open land; Jason said we have a big meadow—of course that will be for hay; but when we clear the trees to build our house, that will open up the land some," Jane commented.

They had to skirt the mountains; passing between Springfield on the north and the Ozark chain that stretched for miles. Tall, rugged mountains, with deep gorges, and wild-rushing mountain streams and waterfalls. The mountains were beautiful reminding Jane of her beloved West Virginia hills and bringing a tear to her eye, as she looked longingly at them in passing. The scenery in this area of their trip was anything but boring. The men itched to hunt the mountains, and several went out at dusk returning at dark with deer which they divided with neighbors. Since the weather had warmed, the meat wouldn't keep and had to be cooked immediately. Trails had to be found to move the wagons over that were reasonable level, even though at times roads had to be cut into a hillside to move around a deep ravine, or to keep from having to haul wagons up over a hill. The travelers found it was a tedious, slow process to make any mileage in a day. There was sometimes damage to wagons that had to be fixed. Tongues twisted and split when trying to maneuver against a slope; spokes in wheels cracked when accidentally hitting a stone along the trail. Horses became lame pulling over shale that cut like a knife and they would fall behind. The wagon masters kept watch and never left a wagon alone. If the repair couldn't be done while the train moved ahead with the lame wagon moving in behind, then a halt of the train was called. About every five days they spent an extra day of camping to let the animals rest and to do repairs. Every wagon was inspected. They couldn't afford to lose a family or a wagon when their goal was so near.

There was excitement throughout the train; they would reach Joplin in the afternoon. They had seen several people on horseback at a distance, and there were several houses and small farms dotting the wayside as they traveled. They had been warned to fill their water barrels, and store some wood if they could. The pilgrims ahead of them had picked the land bare, cutting every tree and ruining the springs and waterways with their herds, on their way to Oregon, California, and Texas. It would be several days until they would have access to plenty again.

When the wagon train came in sight of the city of Joplin, they couldn't believe what they saw. It was a city of tents and large corrals, as far as the eye could see. Cattle, mules, and horses were everywhere; the noise was overwhelming and the dust blew in every direction. Men and boys raced around on horseback, waving guns and whips.

"What's going on?" Jane asked as she turned this way and that trying to take in everything.

Jason came racing up on his horse, "Keep going, Sam; we'll get to the west of the town away from the dust and stench. Keep going." He raced ahead directing the wagons away from the awful noise and smells of Joplin. They went about four miles from the town. Those who wanted to go into the city would have to do so by horseback.

Finally the 'Circle up' sounded, and the wagons formed their big circle; it was routine now and was soon accomplished with Jane's wagon facing toward the town and east.

"I'm sure glad to get away from there," Jane said, as Sam brought the wagon to a standstill.

"I wanted to see the town and the pilgrims. I've never seen a pilgrim, and I want to see an Indian too," Andy whined.

"I want Goldie to smell one, so she will know who to go after if they come sneaking around; can we go back maw? Please?"

"We'll see how long we are going to be here; maybe you and I'll take Cherokee and ride back, just to see what it's like. I would like to know too," Jane said with a smile; she was as curious as the next one. It looked exciting, and she would never be this way again.

The girls were all outside. Caroline couldn't stand the stench and had been throwing up in the chamber pot. Jane went to her medicine supply and mixed a mild lemon extract in water and had her drink it.

"This will settle your stomach; make a cup of hot tea and sit quietly and drink it. Lie down for a while and I'll help Laura with the dinner." They had found it was easier for Caroline and Ray to eat with them and share all the food, instead of building two fires—and the girls liked working together. That had been decided soon after leaving after Caroline had only cooked a few of meals.

Jason came by soon after they had eaten. "I'm going into Joplin; would you like to come along Jane, and see what a real western town looks like?"

"Me too! Can I come too Jason? I'm dying to see a real western town. "Please!" Andy held Goldie—his heart in his eyes as he pleaded.

"I don't see why not; that is if your 'Maw' will let you. It's time a boy your size saw a western town. In fact, I think it's a must. Anyone else want to come?"

"Can I bring Goldie?" Andy asked timidly, knowing he was pushing his luck.

"If you want to put her in a sack and tie her to the saddle," Jason said, trying not to grin.

"I guess I'll leave her in the house on wheels to keep Angel company while I'm gone," Andy decided.

"I believe I'd like to see the town," Ed said if you don't mind."

"Not me," Nat said. "Nor me." Ray spoke up, "I could smell enough of it just passing, and it made Caroline sick. I'll stick around and guard everything while you're gone."

"What about you, Sam?"

"No sir, I'z happy right here."

"I recond we are all that's going; are you ready, Jane?"

"Let me get my saddle bags and I'll be right back." She went to the little house on wheels and came back with the saddle bags, her black doctoring bag and rediicule were in the pockets. She had stuck her pistol in the other side pocket.

Sam had fetched Cherokee; she and Andy would both ride him.

"Thank you Sam, I'm ready," she said as she stepped up onto the crate and onto Cherokee's back; Sam handed Andy up behind her.

"I'm so glad you asked me. I was dying to see what the town is like. Andy would have walked all the way back to take a look, I think," she laughed.

"You may be disappointed, but I know how curious you are. And who knows, you may want to come this way again sometime. I thought I should report the happenings on the Mississippi to the authorities, and let them wire St. Louis to keep an eye open for them," Jason looked serious as he told her.

The stench from the cattle pens, and the waste from all the wagons reached them long before they came to the town.

"How in the world do they stand it? I don't see how they can sleep and eat in such smell," Jane said.

"Oh, they get used to it. It's almost as bad on the trail with a herd. Andy, if you look close down by those trees, you'll see your first Indian encampment," Jason told them.

"Where?" Andy asked as he craned his neck to see. "You mean those hides stretched over sticks? and brush roofs?" That don't look like much. Where are their horses? I don't see any Indian ponies," he kept stretching to see as they rode on.

"You'll be disappointed in a lot of things, seeing them out of their element. It's like seeing Doctor Jane here in her boy's clothes with a pistol strapped on her side, and seeing her in her ancestral home, coming down the winding staircase in her 'ashes of roses' silk dress. There is a big difference, but it suits the locale where you see them. Now take the Indians—when you see them in their big encampments, with their ponies decorated for war, and them with their colorful war paint you have a different picture."

"We're not likely to see that. We'll just see the hangeron's who follow civilization and look like miss-fits. Which they are. In your mind's eye Andy you will have to remember they are out of their element and would look different if they were where they ought to be," Jane told him. "You have to enjoy each thing in a different perspective."

"What's perspective?" Andy asked.

"That's the location or where you see something. Look around; you'll see lots of people and things that are like that but interesting nevertheless." Jane said as she took in all the strange looking people and wagons that she saw.

"You make it all sound so exciting Jane. You sound like you could teach school and feel right at home." Jason looked at her with a peculiar look, that Jane found disconcerting.

"Here we are," Jason announced as he came up to a hitching rail that held all sorts of riding animals; it was in front of the only respectful looking building that Jane saw.

"This is the hotel, store, restaurant, and you name it. Let's go inside."

Andy grabbed Jane's hand. He saw big burly men with long hair and beard and guns strapped around them. Indians wrapped in fancy blankets. Plain people dressed in homespun with big black hats pulled down over their brows, and long mustache. One man was dressed in deerskin, with long fringe along every seam. A squaw following in a deerskin dress decorated in all sorts of beads, shells, and animal teeth. One tall dark man had on leather britches, an embroidered shirt, a big wide-brimmed hat with silver trim around the sweatband, and silver down the britches legs, silver spurs that jingled as he walked. He had two pistols, that gleamed with silver, strapped on each side of his body. Andy couldn't take his eyes off him.

"That's a caballero from Mexico or Texas," Jason explained as he saw Andy watching the colorful fellow.

Looking around, Jane saw ladies dressed in silk and feathered hats looking like -they had just stepped from a fancy carriage, and gentlemen in suits and top hats, right from the pages of magazines. "Oh, my!" she said as her eyes took in everything.

"They have come by train from St. Louis—probably on their way to California," Jason said as he saw the astonishment on Jane's face.

"I think I'll introduce the ladies to my boy's clothing. They could make good use of it," she said with a giggle.

535

Jason let out a roaring laugh, "That they could, and will be wishing for something as practical before long, I'm sure."

"I like you in pretty dresses too," Andy spoke up.

"The store is through there. While I do my business, you and Andy can go look if you care to."

"I want to go with you and see how you do your business. I want to see what they do with the pirate," Andy informed him.

"All right, little man; you and I will do the business and your 'Maw' can do the shopping; we'll see you shortly, Jane."

Jason and Andy started toward an impressive-looking office.

Jane found her way into the store; it was huge, with shelves stocked to the ceiling with every imaginable thing you could think of. Women were milling around looking at this and that. Jane began to look at the yard goods; there were stacks of silks she had never seen the like of before. Smiling, she thought to herself, I'll not need those where I'm going. She saw some wide brim hats, and went toward them. They were men's hats made for farmers. I wonder if the men would like one? She looked at the prices. My heavens—a dollar-and-half a piece. She had seen plenty at home for fifty cents a piece, she kept looking and pricing—everything was so costly. She would like to buy the girls all something, but what? Something for their hair; they were always losing their hair pins. She saw some fancy combs; they were trimmed in silver and looked expensive; she looked at them closely—they were either Mexican or Indian she couldn't tell which. They were a dollar each; she chose a couple for herself, and decided to get one for Laura and one for Caroline, regardless of how costly they were. She got one for Nettie too, and a pen knife each for Howie and Andy; she went back and chose three hats for the men. Now something for Jason. She looked and looked; finally she saw a leather belt trimmed in silver; it was beautiful, and she knew costly, but she would never get a chance to buy him something nice again. What size? She had bought pants for the men. She thought and thought, and decided on a thirty four-thirty six. The price of it was eight dollars—a fortune, but she bought it anyway. She had everything totaled up, and paid for her purchases. They were all in a way silly but they needed to be silly after the journey they had been on. She wouldn't be anywhere to spend her money for a long time. Just think, I could have bought another heifer for Jason's belt. But it wouldn't have been as much fun she told herself. I won't think about the cost—just the plea-sure of my giving and the pleasure of them receiving. She saw people spending a fortune, knowing that they couldn't find the things further west.

Just then Jason walked in. Andy wanted to look in the pack-ages but Jane told him no—he would have to wait.

"Are you ready? Andy and I have taken care of our business. How would you and Andy like to walk through the Hotel lobby? I think you would enjoy that. And have an ice cream cone after-wards. Come along." They followed Jason; he took Jane's arm and guided her through the plush hotel lobby, all done in red velvet and black leather chairs for the men. "I can't believe what I'm seeing. So much splendor, and I've seen so many who need a bath," she laughed up at Jason.

"Oh they don't stay here; there are flop houses and boarding houses. This is too elegant and costly for mere human beings," he said with a hearty laugh. "Come along," he steered them to-ward an outside area where there was a booth—sort of place with a roof-over where he went and stood. "What flavor do you like, Andy? Jane? I, myself, like Chocolate."

"I like Chocolate," Andy said without hesitation.

"I like strawberry," Jane said as she smiled at him.

"Two Chocolate, and one Strawberry, he told the man who stood behind the partition. Soon a cone was handed out piled up with pink strawberry ice cream, another with chocolate, and the last one as Jason paid for them.

"Oh, how delicious," Jane said as she stuck her tongue out for a lick for the first taste.

All Andy could say was mmmmmm as he licked the cold frosty treat, that he might never have again.

"What a nice surprise! Nothing could have pleased me more, and I'm sure Andy would say the same if he had time," she looked at Andy with chocolate all around his mouth.

They hurried to their horses, mounted, and trotted away, try-ing to beat the darkness that was fast descending.

Everyone was still sitting around the campfire when they re-turned. Jane took her packages and sat down at the table. "First, before we tell you all the wonders we saw, I have a present for you. Laura—Jane handed her a comb, Caroline, got one too. You men get something very useful for a farmer—she handed the hats around; if the color doesn't please, you can trade. And for Jason from all of us—she handed him the silver-trimmed belt, and felt a little embarrassed, and she didn't know why; it was from them all; he had done so much for them. She gave Andy his knife. She decided to give Ed the presents to give Nettie later in privacy.

The men were all trying their hats. Sam and Ed traded as Ed liked brown and Sam wanted the black one. Ray was satisfied with the gray; the girls were admiring their combs.

"These are such beautiful combs; where do they come from? I know I could never afford one like it myself; thank you Jane" the girls both said.

"This silver comes from Mexico and done by fine silversmiths; you have a treasure for a lifetime in your combs. And this belt is beautiful; thank you all for such a treasured gift. And it fits; thank you all." He gave Jane a special look knowing it was her doing. What a woman! He knew he could never forget her. Never!

🎐 Chapter Forty-Six 🎐

"Head'm Up Move Them Out". They were leaving Joplin behind; and most were thankful to leave the evil-smelling place to those who wished to stay there. By mid-day the smell had been forgotten in the spring-like weather, the sun shining and the song of birds in the bushes beside the trail. A prairie hen and her chicks ran across the trail between the wagons and squatted in the grass on the other side hiding her brood of chicks.

"She was pretty with her glossy feathers and her little brown and yellow fuzzy babies," Andy said as he laughed at their flight to safety.

"Just as soon as we can we'll be setting some of our hens and you'll get to make the nests, like Grandma Jarvis showed you. We'll have Sam and Ed build us a hen-house first thing so we can get started," Jane told Andy.

It was such a lovely day that Sam decided to sing, or started without deciding as he sometimes did. They had just topped a rise in the trail and looked down into a lovely valley with a small stream winding back and forth across it.

"I wish I was an apple,
A-hangin' on a tree,
An' ev'ry time my Cindy passed,
She'd take a bite of me.
If I were made of sugar,
A-standin' in the town,
Then ev'ry time my Cindy passed,
I'd shake some sugar down.
Git al'og home Cindy."

Andy couldn't help singing along with Sam and giggled so much you couldn't understand the words, but he and Sam had a lot of fun singing their happy song. Jane thought Sam favored religious songs but Andy had said he was to sing only happy—songs, Cindy surely was that.

The wagons wound their way through trees, forded small streams and up hills and down. They would soon cross over into

The Oklahoma Territory. They had been promised a stop for a break as soon as everyone was in the Territory; they all wanted to savor "their state."

One of the drovers went racing ahead; they came in sight of a level meadow-like park where the drover waited on his horse and he waved them into a circle. Jane couldn't believe it was noon already as the morning had been so pleasant. Jason came trotting by— "Welcome to The Oklahoma Territory!" He went down the line announcing the news, as the travelers came down from the wagons and gathered in the center circle. Some fell to their knees; they all doffed their hats and held them over their hearts, as Jason came in. "We have arrived safely to our destination. John would you lead us in the Lord's Prayer, in thanksgiving for a safe arrival. "Our Father Who art in Heaven". The Amens were heard and a yell echoed through the hills, as everyone in jubilation let go.

Jason walked over to Jane's party, "Well we're here," he told them.

"Thank you Jason for a safe trip, and for the wonderful help you have given all of us," Jane told him. The men all stepped forward and shook his hand.

"Jason, where's my tadpole farm? I can't find it anywhere," John yelled causing a laugh to echo through the gathering.

"We have a way to go before we reach the land you own. It will all be marked and easy to find. Let's have dinner and be on our way. We'll have two more days before reaching the first homesteads, or about that. We'll let you know."

"Thanks Jason, I know everyone was anxious to know," Jane said as Jason went down the line to the cook's wagon for dinner.

* * *

The mood had changed among the wagon train, knowing that they were in the Territory. They all took more notice of the surrounding area, noticing the variety of timber and the way the land lay, the look of the soil; it was going to be their home.

Jane wondered what it would be like when night came and they were out in the wilderness alone; not even a house where they could lock the door in safety. The train passed a couple of homesteads, with small log houses setting in a fenced-in area, with plowed garden spots close by, sometimes with the homey look of a clothesline with fresh wash flapping in the breeze and children playing close by.

The weather held, and the train made good time. The mountains were being left behind with wide valleys spreading out before them. Some of the area was swampy with water standing in the tall grasses for several miles.

"Thiz sure is tadpole farms alonz here," Sam said with a laugh. "I'z glad it'z not ours. I'z bet old John is too now that he'z seen it."

"John never will live that down. It'll haunt him for the rest of his life; it's good he took it with such good grace, or his life would be made miserable," Jane laughed.

The sun seemed high yet when they were called to "Circle up" in a pretty valley with streams running through it and plenty of trees and wood. It was a beautiful place. There was some new grass for the animals and they were anxious to be at it as the wagons came to a stop, and the teams taken out of harness.

Jane looked around her at the beauty, and nodding her head said, "I feel at home in this land." There was a cheerful sound to the camp that night. Just one more day and the promised land would be in sight. Anticipating a long evening, Jane was amazed when darkness came suddenly like a blanket to cover everything; there was very little twilight; it was so sudden, and caught everyone unaware.

Jane checked out Mr. Witt, and found that he was in no pain, and could stand on his crutch. She had warned him not to put weight on his leg yet; the torn flesh had healed, and she hadn't had to take stitches in it; there was a scar but not as bad as she at first thought it would be. She would leave the splint on until she left the train. He was a very lucky man. She stopped in to see Nettie; she had her pretty comb in her hair, and seemed happier than Jane had ever seen her.

"How are you, Nettie? and how is Howie?" Jane asked.

"I'm just fine, and Howie is too, and glad our journey is almost over. I'll miss everyone. I hope we will be close enough to see you and everyone sometime. My sister is anxious to get in a garden and get things started. I'll bet you are too."

"Yes, we are. I'll look on the map and see where your farm will be—it can't be too far away. I wanted to tell you that if you ever need me you will be able to find me. I'll miss you." Jane gave her a hug and said good-bye.

Jane's crew went to bed early, thinking of the early morning that would see them on their way; everyone was anxious to see 'their' land. She could hardly wait seeing it in her mind's eye as Jason had described it to her. She couldn't understand why he had given the land that she knew he loved away to someone else. She didn't want to think of their parting in such a short time.

She would stay on the land and he would be headed out to Oregon.

"I think everyone in the wagon train was up at five o'clock this morning," Jane told Laura as they made pancakes for breakfast.

"It's a glorious morning, and everyone is so excited. I know I am and I don't have a farm to go to—only yours for which I'm grateful," Laura smiled at Jane.

Nat came from tending the animals and milking the cow. "Even the animals seem happier and seem to know they are home," he said. "It's sure a beautiful country. It's just what I imagined it would be. Thank you for making it possible for us to come here. I feel so at home already, and I think Laura looks much better and loves it too."

"I'm so lucky to have you both; and I too think Laura is looking well. I just said last night that I feel at home here. I think our place will be even more beautiful along the Cimmaron river. Isn't that a pretty name?"

Caroline came out dressed in one of her pretty dresses she had made.

"My, don't you look nice; I see you're celebrating," Jane said. Caroline only smiled, as she still looked pale from being sick from the stench of Joplin. "You sit down and have some breakfast. We don't want you sick on the day you're coming home."

Breakfast was over and the table taken down and put up on the little house. The teams stomped and slung their heads as they waited for the 'move them out' command.

* * *

Jason called a meeting the last night out. When everyone had gathered, some bringing crates or stools to sit on, he began; "Welcome to your future home. I know some of you are still confused and wondering 'where do I go from here'—that's normal. As I have told you, your land is marked. There will be markers at each corner, and halfway between each corner. I would advise you if at all possible to put down an iron rod deep in the ground where it can't be pulled out. The markers now are pyramids of rocks, piled up, or a slash on a tree that stands on a corner which should never be cut by you or your neighbor. The criteria for establishing where to build your home is first, of course, good water. That won't be a problem in this country, as springs and streams abound. I would suggest that you find a camp where you will be comfortable for a few days and ride your land till you find the perfect place for your house, garden meadow for hay for your animals, and access to a mill, store and etc. You all have a map with the plots and the names of your neighbors; you have marked where Mr. Boothe will build his store and mill; these are things you'll have to think out for yourself. You all saw the swamps that we came by; if you're lucky enough to have one on your property—don't build near it. Your cattle can get stuck in them, there are snakes, and diseases; it isn't a healthy place to live near. The Collins' will be our first family to drop off at their land. Where are you Ted and Amy Collins? They held up their hands. If you would like we will get a drover to drive your wagon the last five miles, and I will ride out with you and help you select a spot for your camp; you may want to change it but it will help to know where you're going for the first few days."

"I'd like that, thank you," the young man said; Amy had a small child in her arms.

"The trail we are taking will no doubt be where the road will be located; keep that in mind when locating your home. I'm sure you all have been thinking of the perfect place, and of course, the decision will be yours; I'm just passing through. I hope you will all find that the land is what it was told you it would be, and that you have a happy life here. It's beautiful country and can be very productive. Good luck to you all. Till sunup tomorrow."

Jason walked over to Jane, "Are you getting excited?" he asked.

"I sure am. I'm glad of one thing—that I have people with me; I don't think I would want to be out here alone when the night comes down like a curtain," Jane laughed.

"It does surprise you, doesn't it? There's very little twilight like it is back East. You'll get used to it. How do you like the looks of the country?" He was looking at her with that measured look she had seen in his eyes before.

"I love it. As I told the girls, I feel at home in this land. I'm going to love making a home here, and seeing everything flourish. I can see my house now with a big curving staircase, and coming down it in my 'ashes of roses' silk dress." She laughed so hard tears came to her eyes.

"Don't laugh at my dream; that's how I will remember you since I haven't seen you in a log cabin by a fireplace in a rocking chair knitting. I'm sure you'll be just as charming and enjoying life just as much. You're a beautiful woman, and a very rare one. I've been honored to have known you on this trip. I hope you'll always be happy here." There was that strange look in his eyes again, so intent that Jane had to turn her head away.

"You won't have to look for a place to make your home. I have been over every inch of the land and know the perfect place, and the Thompsons will be just across the river and almost in hollerin distance. I feel sorry for some—that's why I volunteered to take the Collins to find a place to camp. They seem a little lost," Jason said.

"I know what you mean; but sometimes with just a little help they can find themselves. Look at Laura and Nat; they have come out of their shell, and look so much better and happier," Jane said.

"You'd bring anyone out of their doldrums. You have a happy disposition that's catching. I'll miss you; but I'll be back," he looked at Jane with that searching look again.

"I'll miss you too. I won't have anyone to say pretty things to me when you leave. I hope you have a nice trip to Oregon; you may decide you like it better than the East. You'll know exactly where I'll be, but I can only imagine you on the trail somewhere." Jane looked at him with sadness in her eyes.

"We're heading out at sunup, so you'd better get to bed; I don't want to see those blue eyes all red when they look on your 'Ranch' as Andy is fond of calling it."

"Good night, Jason; sleep well. Your job with us is almost over." Jane walked away toward her wagon, a deep sadness suddenly overwhelming her, and she felt as though she was going to cry.

* * *

Several wagons had already pulled out from the train. A drover was sent with each one on horseback to make sure they would find their farm. Jason was busy up and down the line telling each to pull out when the time came. Some had to go some distance to their parcels, and two or three would pull out together going in the same direction—everyone waving and calling good luck to those who left the train.

Finally the beautiful Cimmaron River was spotted. Jane's eyes lit up. What a lovely river—just big enough to demand respect but not overwhelming like the Ohio and Mississippi. She knew that they wouldn't be far away now. Mr. Boothe had chosen a spot in the bend of the river for his store and mill. His wagons began to gather to one side of the train; he would be about seven miles from the Thompsons and her ranch. As his wagons formed a line it made an impressive sight. There were fifteen loaded with merchandise and three with his family and household goods. He knew just where he was going and where he would settle. He had plenty of help to build his store and mill and was very organized. One of the drovers went with him to show him the markers although he felt quite sure that Mr. Boothe could have found them himself.

There were fewer and fewer wagons—the Thompsons and Jane's four finally were the only ones left, as she and the Thompsons were going the furthest west of all the train.

Jason came by sometime after the Boothe caravan had pulled out. He rode along beside Jane's wagon. "When we reach the top of this rise, pull over and stop. I want you to see the valley beyond." He told each wagon to pull alongside and stop, including the Thompsons. When they each had topped the rise he had pointed out, they stopped.

Jason helped Jane from the wagon. "There she is, Jane; that's your valley, I named it 'Peaceful Valley' because it is." Mary and John came over; Jason had an old pair of army field glasses.

"Mary, come over here; I want to introduce you to your cave. Look right over the river between those two tall pines," he handed her the 'spy glass'.

"Oh, my word, I love it; what a wonderful cave; are you sure mountain lions don't den there? John come look! It's our new home." John came and stood with the glasses and looked and looked, "Darn, no tadpole farm!"

They all started to laugh; the hills vibrated with John's booming laughter. The children all had to look through the glass to see the cave. They all said how wonderful it was, and that they couldn't wish for anything more.

Jane couldn't take her eyes off the beautiful valley. "Jason, it's wonderful. I couldn't have wished for anything more beautiful," she had tears in her eyes. "It's perfect; I love it and feel so at home in my valley. I hope everyone is as happy with their choice as I am." She looked at Jason with stars in her eyes. She felt like a bride come home from her honeymoon; of course she didn't say that out loud and have everyone laugh at her. The glasses were passed around to all the men and they nodded in agreement that it was the perfect place.

Ray and Caroline had decided to stay with Jane a few days until they located their farm and found a place to settle, which Jane welcomed. She wanted to make sure that Caroline had come through the trip in good shape before going off on their own. Their land was northeast about six miles from Jane's valley.

"Let's go down; we'll get the Thompsons across the Cimmaron;

I know Mary can't wait another minute to see her cave. I'm sorry John is so disappointed in his farm though; then we'll get you people settled on your ranch.

They went to the crossing, finding that the water was shallow and would be easy to cross.

The wagons were stopped and Jane took Cherokee, with Andy on behind her. "We'll be back soon" Jason told the others, as he and Jane rode ahead of the Thompson's wagon, to the entrance to the cave.

"My it's big; they will have a whole house in it." They got down and tied the horses to a tree to await the wagon.

Andy started to run to the cave. "No Andy; wait—there could be animals or snakes in there; the men will have to inspect it first."

"Oh! My, how big; I love it. We'll be cozy in there. We'll just have to tidy it up a bit, and we'll be ready to move in. Where's the spring?"

"Just follow that little path; it's right around there, close enough that you don't have to carry water far, I've drunk from it many a time. I've never seen any snakes here, but be careful till they know you're around. Can we do anything before we go get Jane and her crew settled in?"

John had his riding mare and milk cow behind his wagon. Jason had told them that their other livestock would be brought tomorrow by the drovers.

John and Mary shook hands with Jason, "Thank you, you've been more than generous with advice and giving us your choice of land. I hope you never regret it. And for bringing us together with such a wonderful woman as Jane. We are so glad to have her as a neighbor. I feel like I'm going to explode with happiness, I love this place already," John said, and Mary piped up, "Me too," as did each child, and they all shook Jason's hand. "We'll see you soon neighbor. I think I'll catch me some fresh fish for my supper tonight," Mary said with a laugh as she waved them off.

"I sure do like my neighbors," Jane remarked. "Now for my home. I suppose you have a spot picked out?" she turned to Jason with a smile.

"Close to a spring with plenty of water, and a nice run from it for the chickens and animals. I think you'll like it. I've spent many hours looking and dreaming of a house there some day. And now— it'll be your house; maybe." Jason had a sad look in his eyes.

"Who knows by the time you come through here again you may see a big house and lots of horses and cattle filling the meadow. The latch string will be out you know." Jane smiled at Jason.

Jason directed the wagons to follow and they rode on ahead, till they came to a slight rise with two trees at the edge of the run, and several scattered around. A clump of trees where the run started, Jane knew was the spring. The rise leveled off, with a large level area, and then toward the east was another level spot with few trees that would make a wonderful garden-spot. They dismounted and walked around; the men all got down too and walked and looked.

Andy was beside himself. "There's a corral over there," he informed Jane. She looked and saw some sapplins nailed to trees forming an enclosure. "You?" she asked, turning to Jason.

"Guilty; I told you I had spent considerable time here. Look at the view of the river from here." He turned to look toward the river.

"Perfect for my veranda, where I can sit in my rocking chair and watch the sunset," Jane smiled at him. "I think I'll be wear-ing calico or maybe even my boy's clothes," she laughed to ease the tension she was beginning to feel wondering if Jason was regretting his generosity by giving away his choice of land.

They started to walk toward the spring; she saw that every-one else wanted to look and that they could settle the wagons in later.

"This must be a big spring; there's almost a creek coming from it." Jane was examining the run.

"You'll want to build your house back here where you can have a milk house around the spring, and a garden up there." He pointed to the spot Jane had already allotted for her garden, "That way you can carry water to it if need be."

"My thoughts exactly, I want a two-story hewed log house with chimneys, and a veranda, the kitchen and wash room can be an addition on the back with a door out to the spring house. I hope I can find someone to build it for me. I'll have a big keeping room with an open fire, and a small parlor, and one bedroom down stairs. And will build a bunkhouse later for the ranch hands. What do you think?"

Jason looked a little shocked but answered, "I think that's per-fect, and a barn and shop-house across the run. That should do for the time being. We'd better go back and you decide where you want to put your wagons. Will you put up a tent?"

"I guess we'd better; we brought one and if it rains, it will be handy; and after all we're going to be here a spell. It's not as big as the Thompsons but we can eat inside in bad weather. And if anyone wants to move their beds they can do that too. We'd bet-ter get at it or that black blanket will come down and we'll be up the creek."

Looking around Jane decided, "I think the tent along here with the opening facing this way, so we can get to the spring easily; then the house on wheels facing with the opening, where we can let down the cupboard for work, here. The other wagons over there or wherever you want. As long as they are out of the way of the fire, and where smoke will blow. What do you think Jason?"

"Again, I think you've make a wise decision. If you don't need my help, I'll be on my way; we're all meeting at the Boothe com-pound with the cattle as he has several. We'll stay the night there, and be up here tomorrow with your animals. Till then," he mounted and waved as he trotted back the way they had come.

The girls looked for dead wood for the fire and soon had a pile and built a fire to cook their supper. The men had the tent up and rolled the front up to let air in and moved the table from the house on wheels and soon had it together. They set it inside the tent. Then they left things to the girls while they took the mules and hobbled them and turned them out to graze. The cow was let out too, but the calf was penned in the corral—that way the mother wouldn't wander off too far. The chickens and pigs were brought down from the wagon and left under it so they would be safe. They would unload the plows and etc. on the morrow when they would have plenty of time. Sam took a shovel and soon had a good size basin shoveled out a little ways down the run for the teams and cow to drink from. He went to the spring with a scythe and mowed down some of the small brush that was around the spring being careful to keep the water clean. Tomorrow one of the first things he would do would be clean out the spring and rock it and clean all the brush away, leaving only the larger trees—that way no animals or snakes would be hiding there. If there was some place to get lumber, he would build a spring house that would be safe, and a place to keep the milk and meat cool. That would have to wait.

Laura soon had supper done. She had brought out some of the salted fish they had in a churn, made hush puppies, and cole slaw to go with it and a pot of the apple dumplings. They ate in the tent, and lingered over their coffee and dumplings, with a sense that everything was safe for the night. The talk was of what they could do tomorrow with what they had to work with.

"The first thing I want done is the garden plowed and potatoes planted. I have seed for everything. Don't cut any of the trees till we know what we are cutting, as there may be fruit trees that have been planted by birds. If there are, we want to save them. We also have to have a fence around the garden to keep the animals out. And a pen so we can turn the pigs out. The chickens will have to wait for a hen house, where we can contain them. If we can't get lumber, we'll have to build from logs. When Jason comes tomorrow I'll find out if there is a mill close where lumber can be gotten. If so we will send a wagon for some, for a spring house and chicken house; if not we'll do it out of logs. We seem to have acres of timber not too far away. We'll take a day at a time and make sure we don't make a mistake we will regret. Let's all turn in and see what tomorrow brings." Jane rose and went to the wagon on wheels where Andy had all ready gone to bed.

❧ Chapter Forty-Seven ❧

Jane awoke with a start; she had slept so soundly that she was amazed; the birds chirping had awakened her. She got out of bed and looked out the window of the little house on wheels toward the river, "Oh, how beautiful, and it's my home," she said. Andy began to stir with the sound of her voice. She hurried to dress and went outside, just to stand and admire the land around her. She felt as though she had come home at last.

"Good morning, Jane," Laura called as she came from her wagon. Isn't it a beautiful morning? I love this place; don't ever make me leave," she said with a laugh.

"That's not likely. I said to myself when I awoke, I've come home at last. I love it too and want to see it grow into a prosperous farm or as Andy says, Ranch. Don't tell me that I'm up before Nat? He's always the early bird." Jane looked around seeing that he had beat her again, as the fire was already going under the coffee pot. I see him milking the cow; maybe we can have butter now that we're settled."

"I'm working on it. The men want to get the garden plowed this morning and the potatoes in; what else are you going to plant?"

"Beans, corn, lettuce, carrots, cucumbers, radishes—and going to try tomatoes and cabbage in hills. We always planted the seed in the house and set out plants, but we don't have time for that. I also have some roots of herbs I want to put in the ground, and rhubarb. With all of us working, we should have it in in no time. Then the next project is fencing, and houses for the chickens, and a pen for the pigs. But first, we'll feed the men." Looking toward where the garden was to be, she saw Ed looking carefully at all the trees that had to be cut.

Laura got at the pancake making. There wasn't much Jane could do to help only put out plates and cups for coffee, and flatware.

Ed came to the tent. "I've looked closely at all the trees that have to be cut. None of them are fruit trees so we can use some of them for the fence. I think while we're at it we might as well put down proper posts of locust—they'll last thirty-five years, no use having to do them over in three. These trees can be split and used on the corral, as we need some new ones there. They will do for the time being. I'll start the plowing, Sam and Nat can cut trees. We'll need to keep a bushy top for dragging the garden, till we have time to make a proper one." He looked at Jane for any comments.

"I can see you've been busy this morning. Did you have a good night's sleep? I've never slept so sound in my life before.

When you and Sam get around to it, you can cut pine branches and move your beds in to the tent if you want."

"We may do that when it gets warmer; it'll be hot in the wagons with the tops down."

"Here comes Sam; he has been to the meadow for the mules to plow with—and Nat with his milk pail, he has a big bucket full this morning. I can see butter on my biscuits already," Ed said with a grin.

Sam tied the mules and they all washed up for breakfast, as Laura dished up the pancakes. They all sat talking of the day before them all anxious to make their mark on this new land. The sun was just peeking over the distant mountain to the East, as they all went to the garden, to stake out the size. Jane wanted the garden to join her yard and the gate to open from the yard to the garden. She began showing where the boundaries should be. Ed seemed to know what he was doing and pointed out things that she hadn't thought of.

"I'll start the plowing; Sam and Nat can cut trees. Ed explained about a top for a drag. Starting at the corner where they had driven a stake, Ed began plowing a straight line to the one at the other end. He was soon turned and started back the other way. The soil was turning up rich and black. Things should grow in such rich soil without much work. The other two men were sawing and cutting, dragging the trees out of the way of the plow. They brought them to the camp to chop up for wood, what they couldn't use for rails in the fence. When they were through they began trimming the limbs, measuring and cutting the lengths for railings. They chopped small branches into firewood lengths and threw them onto a pile.

By the time the sun was a few hours high, Ed had the garden

half plowed. He and Jane had measured off almost an acre for the garden. He let the mules rest in the middle of a furrow and came for a cold drink of water.

"Miss Jane, the soil plows easily but do you think I should plow the other way too since it's virgin soil? It'll save a lot of digging later."

Jane thought for a minute, "If you think it needs it then do it. You probably know more about it than I do. It'll go easier the next plowing, and shouldn't take long, as long as we get our seeds in today. Every day counts. For we have a late start anyway."

Ed was back at plowing, and Nat and Ray were helping too—they took the railings and nailed them in place on the fenced-in corral. Andy was stacking the cut wood neatly—close to the cook area where it would be handy. Jane watched, thankful that he had interest in helping without being told.

When Andy finished, he and Jane walked over to see the calf and look around where they should build the pig pen. The corral now looked neater and the calf wouldn't be able to get through the widely-spaced railing. It would do nicely for the calves until they were weaned. Jane worried about her heifer who was ready to drop her calf, and hoped she held out till she was home.

"I think we had better ask Ed as he'll know where it should be—I think close to the water where they can wallow in the mud or where we can channel some water to them. They don't need much of a house—just a shed-over with some leaves or hay for a nest in winter, or when they have little ones; but that won't be for a while. It's getting on to dinner time. Guess we'd better get back. Jason should be coming anytime."

"Why won't Jason stay here on the ranch with us, Maw?" Andy asked.

"He has to guide a train to Oregon; that's his job. He says he'll be back. It'll take a long time to go there and back and he may not make it back till next spring. Just think how many changes there will be in our Ranch by then—our herd will be started, there'll be buildings, barns, sheds, shop-house, and any number of changes; won't he be surprised when he comes back?" Jane made it sound exciting because she didn't want to talk about it.

They had just sat down to dinner when they heard the cattle and horses coming. They were brought around by the creek and turned into the meadow.

"There's my horses and your heifers, and our other cow and Thompsons' cow; don't they look great down by the Cimmaron? Our herd is starting, Maw." Andy yelled as he ran a little ways to get a better look.

Jason and one other drover came up to the camp. "Good morning; is this the Barrlette Ranch? I've delivered a herd that's supposed to go to an Andy and Jane Barrlette. Is this the place?" He smiled as he looked at a wide-eyed Andy.

"You've found the place, mister; won't you get down and have a bite and a cup of the best coffee you'll find in the West? There's no better than the Barrlette Ranch Coffee." Andy carried through like a grown man, making them all laugh; and Jason laughed the loudest.

"We've just eaten; if you like beans and cornbread, you're both welcome. Come sit; if you want to wash, there's the pan and water," Jane invited.

The men both dismounted and washed and sat where Laura indicated and she dished up bowls of beans and brought a platter of cornbread. The coffee was poured and a pitcher of cream set down.

"The herd looks in good shape," Jane commented. "Did you have any trouble getting them here?"

"They're pretty docile; they have been on the trail so long. I see you've hobbled your mules; I expect they will stay close to them, but watch them for a few days. I think your one heifer needs to be penned as I think she just made it to her home in time. The place is looking different already. I see your garden is started. Looks good—nice and big. The soil is rich and loamy. That's a good idea plowing both ways the first time. I'd have done the same thing. You've made progress. Keep that up and I won't know the place."

"How is Mr. Boothe coming along with his store?" Jane asked wanting to change the subject.

"He has set up tents, and has things being unpacked and shelves built from the boxes; he'll be open for business by tomorrow. He's having pens built for his animals. Everyone was out working by daylight," Jason smiled.

"How long are you going to be in Oregon?" Andy asked. "When will you be back? Maw says not till next spring; I think that's too long; you'll have forgotten us by then." A worried frown creased

Andy's forehead, as Jane held her breath waiting for his answer.

"Well, I'm glad you think it's too long; that makes me think you may miss me. It's a long way out there. By the time I get there it will be fall and soon the passes will be snowed in and I can't travel. So that means I have to wait till spring to start back and it's a long way back. But I promise you I'll be back. Just as soon as I can make it. And about forgetting you? Never! It has been an experience I'll never forget. Let's put it this way—I was already committed to take this train or I might have changed my mind, but I couldn't do that. I gave my word. I'll be thinking of you every day while I'm gone." He looked at Jane with that searching look in his eyes she had seen before.

"Thanks for the dinner; guess we'd better hit the trail." The other drover nodded his thanks as they both mounted up and Jason tipped his hat to Jane, and they departed.

"Good by Jason; hurry home," Andy called and tears stood in Jane's eyes.

"There goes a good man and a good friend," Laura said as she wiped a tear.

Jane went to her little house on wheels, for a few minutes not wanting anyone to see her sadness at Jason's leaving.

She was soon back and brought the box of seeds and spread them out on the table. "We'll have to cut the potatoes as soon as Ed starts to mark the furrows. Bring the big wooden buckets from the wagons, Andy," Jane instructed.

Just then a horse and rider came tearing up toward them from along the Cimmaron.

"Who in the world?" All the women stood watching; Jane suddenly went to the little house and grabbed her rifle, not knowing if it was friend or foe. Who would ride a horse at such a reckless pace?

Sam was down at the run and came running toward the girls. "Whoz that?" he asked as he came panting toward them, an ax in his hands.

By then the rider came up, skidded in to where they were, and dismounting, came to Jane, "Are you the doctor? We need you; it's a matter of life and death; Please, are you the doctor? I was told there was a woman who is a doctor at one of the camps. I've been to two already. Are you the doctor?" he was a young man and had tears streaming down his face.

"I'm Jane Barrlette; yes I doctor; what seems to be the trouble?"

Sam had taken off to catch Cherokee and saddle him when he heard a doctor was needed, knowing Jane would go.

"It's my wife! She's dying! We've had the midwife for three days. She up and left saying there wasn't anything she could do. The baby isn't born and my wife is bleeding something awful. My maw can't do anything; please help! Please!"

"You sit down and have a cup of coffee, while I get my things. What's your name?"

"Wright. I live over the hill twix here and the Monrows. It' bout ten miles. Hurry! She's bad!"

Jane went into her house on wheels, strapped on her gun and got the saddlebags, put in some more things she thought she might need and took her cape from the hook by the door, and she was ready. "Laura, I'll be back as soon as I can," Jane called, as Sam held Cherokee for her; she hit the saddle and fitted her feet into the stirrups and turned Cherokee and they were off in a run toward the Wright's place. "You lead; I'll keep up," Jane called to the boy, who was laying low on his horse, going at a fast run. If he continued that, his horse wouldn't be worth anything after this ride. Cherokee had no problem keeping up with his long legs reaching for the ground, in a smooth stretch. Jane leaned over too, not knowing when they would go under a low hanging branch along the trail. She called to the boy, "You'd better slow up or you won't have a horse after this." He slackened the reins and the horse began to slow to its own pace; Cherokee did the same. The boy's horse had lather on its withers and Jane knew he had been run much too far. It wasn't long until Jane saw fenced meadows and plowed fields, and the trail became wider. She knew they must be almost there.

"Up ahead there; that's it, just leave your horse and go right in; I'll see to him."

"You had better rub yours down and walk him till he cools down if you don't want a sick horse on your hands," Jane told him while she took the saddlebags and cape from the saddle.

Jane went to the door which stood partly open, "Hello? The doctor's here! She could hear moaning in a side room and went toward it. An old woman leaned over the bed. There were bloody sheets and towels on the foot of the bed, and a young girl as white as the sheets stretched out; she looked dead.

Jane went to the bed, "How is she?" she asked as she picked up a pale hand to take her pulse. She could barely feel her heartbeat.

"She's almost gone; and the wee one still inside her," the old woman said as she wiped her eyes on her apron.

Jane pulled down the quilt and felt the extended stomach of the girl. She moved her hands around pushing gently here and there, but she felt no movement.

"I need hot water. Make some broth for her and get this bloody mess out of here. Bring me some clean towels or rags. Hurry!

Jane moved to the foot of the bed to examine the girl. She took some turpentine on a rag and wiped her hands for there was no time to wait for the water. She saw more bloody rags when she separated the girl's legs and began her examination. She could see the beginning of the head of the baby, it was enlarged and would never be born. She inserted her hand into the torn, bleeding woman. By then, the old lady and a younger woman had returned with hot water and a pan. "The baby has water on the brain—called a mongoloid birth; they are too big to be birthed. Let me see your table." Jane went into the kitchen, seeing a table cluttered with everything.

"Clean off this table and put a clean sheet over it and bring a small pillow. Where is her husband? We'll need him to carry her in here. I'll have to operate." Jane went back to the bedroom and the husband was there. "Carry her into the other room and put her on the table. The baby, I think, is dead and if we don't do something fast your wife will be too. She can't birth the baby; its head is enlarged and can't be birthed. Do I have your permission to operate? She may still die but she certainly will if it isn't done," Jane looked at the scared young man.

"Yes, do whatever you think will save her. If she dies I won't blame you. Can I stay with her? She has suffered so much." Tears ran down his face.

"I don't have time to take care of you; it's a gruesome thing I have to do; you may faint, and you'll just have to lie there; I have to take the baby, maybe a piece at a time; your wife has lost too much blood already." Jane was working as she talked. She propped up the girl's legs with rolled up towels, poured carbolic acid into the hot water and took a wash cloth and cleaned the external area around the vagina. She laid out her instruments on a clean towel, took a pan that hung on the wall, pulled a chair over and put the pan on it. Jane listened to the girls breathing and heart with the stethoscope; her breathing was very shallow, and her heartbeat slow and weak. "It has to be done," Jane said as she dropped one drop of ether on a swatch of gauze and held it under the girl's nose for the count of five. She grabbed the scalpel and made and incision into the head of the infant; using a towel, she caught the yellow fluid that gushed from the open skull. The head diminished in size as the fluid drained out. Jane inserted forceps into the vagina and pulled the head out and the rest of the body a little at a time, until the baby lay on the table. Its legs were twisted into grotesque shapes, as Jane laid it in the pan on the chair. Taking towels she blotted up the blood and fluid and waited to take the placenta; the girl groaned and a spasm brought the afterbirth that was thrown into the pan. Jane washed her patient, with clean hot water and carbolic acid, and folded a soft cloth and placed it between the legs, bringing them together to hold the pad.

Jane checked the bed; the younger woman was putting clean bedding on. Does she have a clean gown? She needs one," Jane said. A fresh gown was brought—Jane, with the husband's help, removed the smelly, bloody gown and Jane washed the girl and slid the clean gown down over her bruised and battered body. "You may take her in to bed now; I've done the best I can. As soon as she awakens I want her to have some strong soup or broth; will you see if it's ready? She must have nourishment to gain her strength." Jane pulled a chair to the bed and sat monitoring her heartbeat and breathing. She seemed easier after the terrible, stressful situation had been alleviated.

"How is she," the old lady crept in to ask.

"She may live; we must give her nourishment now to get her strength back. I've done all I can. Please bring me a cup of hot water and a spoon."

When it was brought, Jane mixed a strong camomile tea and began spooning it into the gravely-ill girl. She started to swallow the tea and soon had drained the cup.

"In about ten minutes, bring the broth if it's ready, and we'll try to get that down her; she's responding very favorably to the tea. It'll be touch and go for a while. If she drinks the broth and then sleeps, I think she will be all right. I can't be sure at this point." Jane still monitored her vital signs, noticing in a few minutes that her heartbeat seemed stronger.

The woman brought a big bowl of the broth and Jane started to spoon it into her patient talking softly as she gave her each spoonful. The girl drank the broth and gave a sigh, and fell into what seemed a natural sleep. Jane checked the pad and saw that the blood was a normal flow and no excess bleeding had occurred. Listening to her heart and lungs with the stethoscope, she could tell that it was stronger. She sat waiting; the girl slept on. Jane sat with the husband; they talked softly as his wife slept.

"I never want her to go through something like this again; I'll hear her screaming till the day I die. Never again! I love her too much."

"You're both young. There's a possibility that she may never have a baby again. If she has injuries inside, she may not get with child. One thing I want to impress on you—let her rest for at least three months before you come together again as husband and wife. Do you understand what I'm saying? She must have time to heal completely. Not only her body, but her mind. After the pain, she may not want normal relations with her husband; if you were to insist she might turn away in fear and you would never have a closeness again. I hope you understand what I'm saying."

"I understand, Doctor Jane. If I have to stay away from her I will; I love her too much and came so close to losing her."

"Yes, we're not out of the woods yet, but looks as though she is responding well. I'll stay another hour, then I have to go home before dark. I'll tell your sister; that was your sister, wasn't it?" He nodded. I'll tell her what to do and leave some medicine for your wife to wash with as she must be careful of infection. Her flesh was torn with all the straining trying to birth and it has to heal. She must be kept clean and fed broths, soups, and soft foods for at least five days, and plenty of fresh cool water. Can you remember that and see that it's done?"

"I sure will; I'll feed her myself," he nodded his head.

"When she awakens, give her more hot broth. Send in your sister I want to explain to her what I want done. What's her name?

"My wife's name is Maybell, and my sister is Lidia. I'll have her come in."

Lidia soon came, "Lidia, will you be helping take care of

Maybell?" She nodded. "Here's what I want you to do. Twice a day pour four drops of this into the wash pan, and wash Maybell's private woman parts with it; when she gets some strength she can do it herself. Put fresh pads on her twice a day, once in the morning, and at night before she goes to sleep. Sponge her whole body every other day and change her nightgown. For the next three days give her broth, fruit juice, or soup every three hours, and plenty of cool water in between. Help her up and over to the chamber—but be sure to hold on to her; she could faint. Then see that she lays flat most of the time for the first week. If I'm needed, send for me. If not, I'll come by in a week to see how she is doing. Can you remember all that? She almost died, you know, and there is still danger of infection, so follow my directions. I'll have to leave now to get home before dark. Can your brother go part way so I don't get lost? I've only been in this country one night. I'll see you, Jane told her as she gathered her things to leave.

The young man stood holding her horse and his too; he mounted and went with her. They rode along in silence; finally he said, "I want you to know how much I appreciate what you did, and coming at a minute's notice. You said you'd be back in a week? I want you to know I think you're the finest doctor I ever saw."

"Thank you. We were lucky." When they reached the Cimmaron Jane turned to him. "I can find my way from here; you can go back to your wife now. I'll be fine; I have my pistol and I'm a good shot," she smiled at the startled look on his face.

"If you're sure; we're more than half way now. Thank you again. You'll hear from me," he waved as he turned around and went back toward his home.

When he was out of sight, Jane gave Cherokee his head and he started at a trot which soon become a lope and then even faster. He loved to run and she let him go for some distance before pulling him in. She rode along slowly thinking of Jason. He would be headed back to Joplin where he was to pick up the train coming from the East. She might never see him again. He would be going through some rugged country and also through the Cherokee, and Blackfoot nation where there was always uprisings. She remembered Lance's flight for life which he lost in the end; what if the same thing happened to Jason? Jane started to cry—the tears streaming down her face. "Oh, God I love him! Don't let anything happen to him. What was she to do for a whole year not knowing if he was dead or alive? She sobbed as she rode along, and hardly knew that she was back to the meadow. She wiped her eyes and blew her nose and rode up to the camp.

They were still all working in the garden as Jane dismounted and tied Cherokee, Goldie came bounding down from the garden barking a greeting.

"Maw, you're home. I missed you," Andy said as he threw himself into her arms. Jason left, then you; I thought you'd never come home. I looked and looked; Goldie looked too."

"Hay! I'm a doctor, remember? I sometimes have to be away— even overnight. You must not think I've deserted you. How is the planting going?" Jane asked, looking toward Laura who was coming in to start the supper.

"I planted potatoes, just like Ed showed me. And Sam showed me how to make little nests for the tomatoes. I'll bet they will grow like anything. We're just about done. We planted your herb garden in a square by the spring; Ed said that's a good place for them and they won't get trampled on. Wait'll you see what Sam did with the spring. We made a drag—he called it, and he and I brought stones from the Cimmaron and—just wait till you see it. It's beautiful. Come, I want to show you." He took her hand and led her to the spring—it didn't look like the same place. There was a deep well-like place walled up with carefully laid up stones, with dirt tamped down all around. Then up where the trees grew from a large mound of dirt, flat field stones had been careful laid flat side by side so dirt and water couldn't wash down when it rained. Beside the well were more flat creek stones to stand on while dipping out water. About five feet down from the spring, another walled-up box had been made with dirt tamped around it and a cleverly built run for the water in each end where the water could run all the way through. There was a wooden top on it which could be lifted off. "That's for the milk," Andy importantly told Jane. "We'll soon have butter, Laura says."

"It's wonderful and just think all in one day; I can't believe it. Our Ranch is getting to be more and more like a home every minute. The men were coming in. Jane saw Ed and Sam taking their clean clothes and heading for the Cimmaron, to wash. Soon Nat and Ray followed, the girls handing them clean clothes. They put out a wash tub with some water and soap to throw the dirty clothes to soak, when they brought them back.

Laura and Caroline soon had supper on the table. There was a big pot of beans, cole slaw and cornbread, It was filling, but someone would have to hunt some meat. The men needed meat to do the work that had to be done.

The men all sat down to eat; they looked so clean and their wet hair combed to perfection.

Laura sat down across from the men. "What's that I smell?" she said as she sniffed and sniffed. The men started looking around wondering if a skunk had wondered into camp and they couldn't smell it.

"I think it may be clean men," Caroline said with a laugh; after a stunned silence, all the men broke out in laughter.

Jane told them about her afternoon, working to save a young girl's life. She only gave them the barest details, and told them the girl would live.

"You accomplished a lot for one day. I'm so proud of you all. It's beginning to look like a home. You all worked very hard. Thank you." Jane smiled at them. "I'm only sorry I wasn't here to help. I missed my bossin' job." They all laughed at that. Everyone became quiet, when Andy suddenly spoke, "I'll bet Jason is back to smelly Joplin by now. Do you think so Maw?" I miss him I wish he would have stayed here with all of us."

"I don't think he could make it to Joplin so quickly; it'll take a couple days anyway. Then he will be off with his wagon train to Oregon. I'm just glad we don't have to go so far," Jane answered.

"Jason is a good man," Ed put in. "He knows what he's about. He'll be back."

"Ray, do you plan to plant a garden on your place?" Laura asked, as she looked at Caroline and then at Ray.

"Yes; and we have to find our place, and get started. If Miss Jane thinks Caroline is well enough, I thought we would leave tomorrow. I guess I should go and select a place first. If Ed could spare a couple of hours, maybe he could help me. He knows how things should be," Ray looked from Ed to Jane.

"I think that could be arranged. Why don't you just take Caroline with you and Ed can get you settled and you won't have to make an extra trip back and take up time. Your garden must be planted. Did you bring seeds?" Jane asked.

"Yes, we have seeds, and our cow, and some food. I can hunt

and get some meat. We'll be fine once we decide where we want to build. We have a tent; I think everything we need. We appreciate all you've done, and hope sometime to repay you.

"We've enjoyed having you both; you take care of Caroline, and you know where we are," Jane patted Caroline's hand seeing a scared look on her face.

"We'd better get to bed if we're going to be up early and see Caroline and Ray off to their new home. I know they are excited—their first real home. Good night everyone," Jane called as she and Andy went to bed with the others following.

Ray and Caroline had their wagon ready with the cow tied on behind. Ed was on horseback ready to go with them to choose a place to camp and establish their home. Jane knew they were nervous going off alone, but they weren't any different than all the others who had to do the same thing. A couple of nights and they would be fine.

Sam went to the corral; he had brought the heifer that was calving and penned her there last night. He saw that she had her calf in the night and it was another little heifer. He came back to tell Jane that she had an addition to her herd.

Ed came back later in the afternoon. "There's another farm started—the Hayse's. Ray and Caroline found a real nice place to build, with a nice spring and garden space that doesn't have to have much clearing. I helped them put up their tent, cut pine branches for their bed and cleaned out their spring. They both seemed to settle in nicely. I'm sure they will be nervous for a couple of nights, but they'll be fine. Everyone has to make a start on their own. I'll get to our work now," Ed said as he went to help with the building of the pig pen.

❧ Chapter Forty-Eight ❧

The pigs had been turned into their pen, and Sam had split out some slabs from a pine tree and made a trough to feed them in. They were running around chasing each other after being confined in such a small area for so long. Jane expected the Thompsons any day to pick up their pig and cow that was with her animals. Tomorrow was Sunday; she expected they might come then. Ed and Nat had gone hunting after they finished the pig pen and came back with two fat deer. They butchered and salted the meat and put it in the tent where it was coolest. It wouldn't keep long. Jane was going to send a quarter to Caroline, and if the Thompsons came she would give them half of one. Laura was busy cooking a pot full and roasting another Dutch oven full; it could be put down in lard and keep several days. Laura had gotten out the meat grinder and ground up one leg and all the scraps to make sausage.

Sam and Nat went in the afternoon to pick out the pine trees they were going to cut to start the chicken house. They took the cross cut saw, and were going to cut trees till supper time. The men had decided on a ten by twelve house, that wouldn't have to be added on to later. It should hold all the chickens they would have. Mr. Boothe was going to put in a saw mill at a later date, but they needed the chickens housed now. They had separated the chickens and used the crate the pigs were in to give them more room. Andy had insisted on making a nest for them in the coop and one hen had laid an egg that excited and pleased him.

Sam and Nat trimmed the trees and hauled them to the building location before cutting them into building lengths, as it was easier than hauling in short lengths after they were cut. They had brought in six trees which would make several logs the length they had settled on. They decided to cut those up and have them ready for notching; but there would be no work on Sunday, as Jane told them that was a day of rest.

Sunday morning dawned bright and sunny; the birds were building nests and chattering away. They all sat and had a second cup of coffee; the chores had been done and they were just taking it easy, when a wagon was heard crossing the Cimmaron. Everyone was looking—watching it as it made it's slow way toward them.

It's the Thompsons! How nice—our first callers," Jane remarked, "Put on another pot of coffee, Laura. Or better still, why don't I make a pot of the sassafras tea from the roots the men brought; that would be good with some sugar." Jane went to get the big pot,

"Here, let me do that; you can bring some sugar from your wagon, and greet the Thompsons," Laura told her as she took the kettle and dipped water from the barrel that stood by the cooking area.

"Good Morning! So good to see you," everyone called. The wagon hardly came to a stand still when the three children came tumbling out. Sam came over to help John with his team. The children and Andy headed over to see the new calf and pig pen. Andy was showing them all the things that had been done in the few days they had been there.

"Something smells good; I could smell it all the way to the cave—that's why I'm here; I know good things to eat when I can smell them," John said with his booming laugh.

"Come in and we'll have a cup of tea and then show you what we've been doing. How are things going with you?"

"We've gotten our garden in, and John has been plowing for a corn field. We've gotten it about half planted. We're settled in, and love it here. We're going to do some work on the cave, but wanted to get the seed in the ground first so they can be growing while we tackle the other jobs," Mary laughed. "I can see you've all been busy; it's shaping up nicely. Your herd looks grand down in the meadow. I'm sorry we haven't come for our animals, but we have been so busy and we figured you would just turn them out with yours. I hope they didn't put you to any trouble."

"No. They're fine." Jane told them about the Wright girl who had almost died. They walked around, looking at the garden and at the spring, and the cooling box in the spring tail, then over to see the pig pen, and the new calf, and to look at where the chicken house was to be built.

"Don't you just love it here?" Mary asked. "Every morning when I get up and see the wonderful sunshine and my river, I thank the Good Lord. And you, of course, for letting us come here with you." Mary smiled at Jane, with tears in her eyes.

"I feel the same way. I love it here; this is a blessed country," Jane replied, as they walked back to the camp.

"We brought you a present. John, would you bring Jane's present out of the wagon; I wanted it to be a surprise."

"Could you help me, Ed?" John asked as he went and climbed up and rolled up the canvas top of the wagon, and brought out a lovely rocking chair, and handed it down to Ed.

"Oh my! What a beautiful rocker; where in the world did you ever get it out here?" Jane asked as she looked at the lovely workmanship on it.

"Found it!" Mary said laughing. "Yes sir we did. About a mile west of our place is the road where the wagons are cutting through to the Oregon trail, and where they cross the Cimmaron; it's steep and not a very good place to cross. You wouldn't believe what they unload after struggling to cross; it's up hill and heavily-loaded wagons just can't make it. The younguns were hauling in wood and discovered the 'treasure trail' —that's what they call it. You won't believe it, John went with them and found me a beautiful cook stove; we have it set up in the cave and it's a godsend. They've brought back trunks of books that had been set out. I have two rocking chairs and just had to bring this one to you. Tomorrow we plan to go up the trail a little farther as I'm sure some more things were left. I have one trunk full of the most beautiful table linens. I'm going to have my cave full soon with beautiful things. Sarah has started her hope chest. It's a shame that the women have to give up all their treasures, but it's better than giving up their lives. You'll have to come over and see all the things we've found." Mary's eyes sparkled as she told Jane of the wonders they were bringing to their cave. They hadn't brought any furniture with them, but it was being furnished with treasures.

Laura was busy at the fire; she was cooking potatoes to mash, and had cut a big bowl of cabbage for slaw; she put on a pot of turnips to cook. Checking the meat, she figured another hour before making the bread.

They heard another wagon coming from the other direction.

"Who can that be?" They all asked as they watched to see it coming through the trees. "It's Caroline and Ray, coming to call."

Everyone was as glad to see them as they would have been if it had been a year since they left the Ranch.

Ed went to help with the team, and help Caroline down; she had on her yellow-checked calico dress and looked like a sunbeam

"My, you look pretty," all the women told her as she beamed with pride. "Your dress is lovely. You sew beautiful!" "How are you, Caroline?" Jane asked anxiously.

"I feel just fine, and love our place; we are in the tent and I sleep like a log. Ray has our garden in—we don't have as big a one as you, but there are only the two of us. Ray has made a pen for the cow. We bring her in every night, just to make sure she's safe. He milks her before he turns her out in the morning; she gives plenty of milk. He fixed a place to put it in the spring tail to keep cool. I picked us a mess of greens this week; they sure were good. Ray hasn't had time to hunt yet, but maybe this week." She was full of news of their new home, and seemed well and very happy.

"He won't have to hunt for a while as the men got two deer and I've saved you a quarter; be sure and cook it all down and put it in grease; if it's covered it will keep for several days. You can put it in a covered container in your spring tail, if you have a place where the animals can't get to it," Jane told her. "Laura is fixing a feast; I'd better help her. I'll pour us some sassafras tea to tide us over; then we'll show you all we've done. Of course we have a bigger work crew than you do," Jane said with a smile.

They all gossiped and the men walked around, as the women were looking at everything that had been done and talking about what they planned to do. Ed had decided they needed to put in a corn field and had located an area where they could start plowing on Monday. He would plow while Sam and Nat cut the trees for the hen-house. When he was ready, they could help with the planting.

They had all seen everything at least twice and admired the spring construction that Sam had done. Then came back to the tent just as Laura took the cornbread from the fire. She had made two Dutch ovens full. The meat was done as were the turnips.

"Jane, would you set the table, while I mash the potatoes, please." Laura asked, "I have to make the gravy too; you can whip the potatoes while I make it."

Mary came up, "Let me do the potato whipping; it's something I like to do. Is everything in them?" Laura nodded as she filled one of the big pewter bowls with the meat, leaving the drippings for the gravy; she chopped an onion real fine and dropped it into the sizzling drippings, to cook while she made the white sauce for the thickening. It was soon all done and the table loaded; the men were washing up and laughing and talking as they got ready for the good-smelling dinner.

Sam said a blessing before they started to eat. There were groans of delight as they took mouthfuls of the delicious meat that Laura had cooked.

"I swear Laura, if you weren't married, I'd marry you just for your gravy; you make the tastiest gravy I ever ate. You've outdone yourself. If they don't pay you enough, come on over to my house and I'll double what you're getting now," John told her, his laugh echoing in the tent.

"That's very generous, John; but I happen to know you have a good cook already, and she can cook circles around me; she's had more experience than I have. Besides, she can bring home the fish and cook them too." Laura laughed at John's offer.

"Speaking of fish, I've never seen so many as there are in the Cimmaron. If we knew when a wagon train was coming through, we'd sell a bunch, and make a fortune." Mary told them.

They all had a wonderful time and ate till they were stuffed. The men threw down a tarp under a tree and stretched out, while the women put away the victuals and washed up. It was fun when there were so many to help.

"How about everyone coming to our house— "Our Cave" —next Sunday for a fish fry; you and Ray too, Caroline," Mary asked.

"That sounds wonderful, Mary; what time?" Jane asked.

"Oh, anytime; we'll eat early in the afternoon to give everyone time to get home and do chores before dark. I'll look forward to our first visitors," Mary laughed. "Have you heard from Jason? I expect he is somewhere on the trail. I sure do miss him."

"I doubt we'll hear, especially so soon. He did say he would be back, but that will be sometime next summer. It takes almost a year to get to Oregon. And if he happens to get "Gold Fever" who knows?" Jane smiled, but felt shaken up just talking of Jason.

"Caroline, I think we should start back," Ray said. Thank you all for such a wonderful day. Everything looks good here, and it gives me some ideas." Jane went to help with the deer; she took a clean feed sack and helped put the deer leg inside and in the wagon.

"That'll fill you up a few days. You two be careful and we'll see you next Sunday. Thanks for coming—we enjoyed it." Jane watched the wagon go on its way with both the Hayes waving.

The Thompsons gathered their pig and cow and were ready to leave. "We'll see you Sunday," they called. We had a wonderful time." They were all waving as they crossed the Cimmaron home.

Everyone went to bed early to get a good night's rest as tomorrow would be a busy day.

Nat and Sam went to the corn field to fell a couple of trees that were in the way of the plow. And hauled them back to the camp to be cut up for wood when they had the time. They were anxious to cut more of the logs for the chicken house and hurried away to do that. They brought a tree with them when they came for dinner; after eating, they cut it into proper lengths. They went back to the woods and cut trees till it was almost dark and hauled another one home with them. Ed announced that he had plowed about an acre for corn.

Laura and Jane had gone looking for greens and had picked a big bucket full. They enjoyed the fresh greenery for a change of diet. They kept busy, washing and cooking, and keeping things in shape in the wagons—everyone busy with a job.

Jane decided she should go to see about the Wright girl and make sure she was all right. She saddled Cherokee and decided that Andy could come along and saddled the other mare for him to ride. They started out early; Jane didn't think she would get lost, as there was only one trail going to the Wright farm. It took them about an a hour and half to reach the Wrights. They tied the horses, and taking her black bag, Jane and Andy knocked.

Lidia came to the door, "Come in Doctor Jane; we were sort of expecting you today; I don't know why, but we all talked about it. Maybell's in bed, as you told her to be. She's so much better." They walked into the bedroom. Jane told Andy to stay in the kitchen, or walk around outside, while she was busy. She hardly recognized the young woman sitting up in bed; she had color in her cheeks and looked so much better.

"Good morning, Maybell; how do you feel?"

"Thanks to you Doctor Jane, I feel almost well again. I'm still a little sore but I have been eating and sleeping good. I've done everything you told me to."

"Are you still bleeding?"

"Just a little now; it's almost stopped," she said her face turning red.

"Stretch out on your back I want to examine you." Jane felt her stomach, and probed deep with her hand to make sure the uterus was going back where it belonged. It usually took a few days but everything felt fine. "You can start sitting with your feet on the floor; in another two days you can start walking around in the room. When you have strength enough you can do whatever you want, but don't over tire yourself for the next two weeks. No lifting or bending. I think you're going to be just fine," Jane smiled at her. "You won't need me anymore. Come see me when you get well. Good-bye, and take care." Jane and Andy left—Jane with a good feeling about the girl.

* * *

Two weeks had passed when Andy said, "Maw, do you miss Jason? I miss him a lot, and wish he would come home. This is where he belongs, with us."

"Yes, I miss him. But I'm afraid that will be his decision if and when he returns. We just have to wait," Jane looked off down the valley with longing.

The chicken coop had been finished. The chickens were happy to have their own house, and able to be outside and scratch in the dirt, and have a safe roosting place at night. They had been kept penned inside the house for a couple of days so they would know where their house was and then turned outside. They were all carefully counted and penned each night. The corn field had been planted, and the men were now cutting posts to fence in the garden and fields, so the animals wouldn't get in and destroy the crops. The garden was coming up, and looking good. Jane was very pleased with her "Ranch," and with the help she had—they were all working so hard. She had begun to worry about getting her house built before winter and would have to get at it. She intended to make a trip to the Boothe store and see if there was anyone who built houses in the area. She wanted it done just so-so, and wanted an expert at least to oversee the building. She had plenty of money for the work to be done well.

The men had come in from a hard day of cutting posts, and had washed up and were sitting resting waiting for the supper to be put on the table when they heard a wagon coming from the direction of the Cimmaron.

"Who in the world can that be so late in the day?" Jane asked as they all got up and walked around the tent for a better view. A covered wagon with a team of horses and another tied behind the wagon was coming toward them.

Andy was beside Jane watching; he recognized the driver before anyone else did.

"It's Jason! It's Jason!" he yelled as he ran to meet the wagon. "Jason, you've come home. Oh, Jason, I'm so glad to see you." Andy had tears in his eyes, and as soon as Jason came down from the wagon, Andy threw both arms around him, hugging and hugging.

Jane thought she would faint; her heart was racing so fast she began to sway on her feet. Her hungry eyes took him in from head to toe. She went toward him, "Jason, welcome; we've missed you. Is something wrong? Why are you here? We thought you were half-way to Oregon by now. Come, we're just ready to eat."

Jason tied the reins to the wagon and came toward the tent. All the men rose and shook his hand. "Good to see you back," they all said in unison.

Andy poured Jason a clean pan of water to wash up, and steered him to the table to sit beside him.

Jane's eyes were sparkling when she raised them to Jason's.

"I hope you'll let me camp here for a few days. You see, I'm out of a job. The scout that came West with the Oregon train, decided he wanted to go all the way to Oregon. He offered to pay me what he would receive to let him take the train. I couldn't honestly do that, although it meant I would be out of a job. We finally settled on half. So I'm making money by not going. I wasn't too sorry as Andy here talked me into the fact that I was needed here." He smiled around the table, his eyes settling on Jane's with a hungry look. Doctor Barrlette and I will have to do some talking to straighten things out. You boys sure have been busy; things are looking good. I'm starved; can we eat now?" They all laughed and started talking telling Jason how glad they were that he had returned.

"I spent some time in Joplin, contacting some people I had

heard of. They build houses, Jane. I found three brothers who make their living by building houses; they are experts on notching and fitting hewed logs, They also have one brother who works with them that builds fireplaces; I've taken it on myself to ask them to come with their equipment ready to work; they'll be here in two weeks. They say they can put your house up well before cold weather. They don't mind your having a house raising, if you're rushed for time, as they take the building job on contract."

"Oh, Jason, that's wonderful. I was going to go to Boothe's store tomorrow and see if there was anyone in the area that could help. Sam did a really good job notching the logs for the hen-house. They fit till you can't see light through them. He's a little leery of tackling a house with big timbers though." She smiled at Sam.

Andy got up and put his arms around Jason, "I'm glad you're home, Jason."

Jane had gotten over her shock and was smiling so much her face started to hurt. It seemed everyone was glad to see Jason, and had given him a warm welcome.

"Does it matter where I park my wagon tonight?" We'll have to figure where you want your house before I put up my tent, so it won't be in the way of building."

After they had all had second cups of the sassafras tea, they all began to wandered off. Laura and Jane were stacking the dishes for washing. "You go entertain our guest; I'll wash the dishes," she told Jane.

Jason and Jane walked toward the spring, and stood looking at the garden; the corn and beans were six inches high and everything looked healthy.

"Your garden is looking good, Jane; I hope it didn't upset you— my coming back," he was looking at her with that look she couldn't quite make out. "I missed you; even before I got to the Cimmaron, I wanted to turn around and come back to you."

Jane had turned toward the calf lot and was leading him away from the compound. "I missed you too Jason, more than I care to remember. You were in my thoughts and prayers every day," Jane looked up into his face.

"Jane, I have so much to tell you. I've filed on the section that I told you I would reserve for Nat and Laura." They walked on to the fence and stood leaning on it, their backs toward the camp. Jason took her arms and turned her toward him. "Jane, I've fallen deeply in love with you; I've tried to see how you feel about me, but you don't give away much of your emotions. I know you're from a fine family; I have no one; I was an orphan. I do love you and would like for us to make a life together if you think you could ever care for me."

"Oh, Jason," Jane swayed toward him and put her head on his shoulder; tears were streaming down her face as she looked up at him. "Jason, I've loved you almost from the first day I met you. My heart was broken to think of your being gone for a year, or maybe never coming back again."

Jason wiped her tears away and brought his mouth down to meet hers, in their first sweet kiss; they neither wanted to pull away. "I have some money—enough to build the house you want, and the other one hundred sixty acres to add to the Ranch. I've reserved another parcel beyond the Cimmaron for Nat and Laura. I'll love you always. Will you be my wife, Jane?"

"I was so afraid I would never get the chance. I want to be your wife Jason; I love you so very much. Yes, I'll marry you whenever you say. I want to tell you about my other marriage."

"You don't need to if it's painful to you. I love you just the way you are, and you are a rare and beautiful woman, and I'm so proud of you and what you've done."

"Lance was a lot like you in some ways. I only knew him for one evening—the evening we were wed. It all happened so suddenly. He was a dashing, handsome Major in the Southern army with all the suaveness of a southern gentleman. I loved his grandparents and felt very close to them. Everything was arranged so quickly that we were married before I knew what was happening—caught up in the excitement of the moment. I think I could have loved Lance in time. We had just gone up to his study, and were having a glass of wine and talking when the alarm sounded, and he rushed away to his death, I was in shock for days, with everything moving so fast. I was married, then a widow, without knowing my husband. I respected and admired Lance and was charmed by him, but I've never felt toward anyone as I do you Jason. I want you to know that and that I come to you without ever knowing another man."

"Oh, my darling, darling girl. I love you so much that I don't think I can stand it. You didn't have to bear your heart to me but I'm glad you did. It only makes you more precious to me. I've never wanted to marry before. I planned to go on working for Mr. Morgan—that's why I turned the land over to you and the Thompsons."

"I love this place Jason; Andy is crazy about it too. He is like my son, and he adores you. He's an orphan, too, you know."

"Andy is a fine lad; you've done a good job on him. I'm very attached to him but not as much as I am to his 'Maw'. Jason laughed as Jane playfully hit him.

It'll be about two weeks before the crew to build the house arrives. Why don't we have a house raising, inviting everyone. It will give us time to get in touch with them, and my bride time to get ready for her wedding. Could we make it a wedding day too?" Jason asked as he held Jane.

"That sounds like a lot for one day, but I'm all for it if you want it that way." Jane smiled into Jason's eyes her love shining like the stars above them.

"Would you wear your 'Ashes of Roses' dress for our wedding?"

"I suppose it would be appropriate as I don't have anything else except calico," Jane laughed up at him.

"Then it's all settled; I'll take care of everything. Will that be a problem? You're such a doer yourself. If I happen to take over things you want to manage, let me know." He gave her a lingering sweet kiss as they turned back to the compound.

Everyone was in bed when Jane and Jason returned to the camp. Someone had taken care of Jason's team and riding horse as he had forgotten them in the excitement of the moment. They had parked his wagon a little away from the others; since Jason hadn't had time to erect his tent, he would sleep in his wagon that night.

"Good night, my darling. We'll tell everyone in the morning. I love you beyond reason," he told her as he gave her a last gentle kiss.

"Good night my love," Jane said as she entered the little house on wheels, so happy she could hardly stand it.

❧ Chapter Forty-Nine ❧

It was a beautiful morning when Jane awoke and looked out the small window. She hurried to dress and go outside; she couldn't wait to see Jason. She was so happy that she seemed to be floating on air. The sunshine never looked so bright or the birds never sang so beautifully before.

As she stepped outside, she saw Jason come from his wagon. She ran toward him and into his outstretched arms. He held her so tight she could scarcely breathe.

"I missed you. Just knowing you were so close and yet out of reach almost drove me crazy; you're so beautiful; did you know your hair looks red in the sunlight?" he was holding her away from him looking into her face. Lowering his head, he kissed her. "I love you Doctor Barrlette. Oh, how I love you."

"I've never been so happy in my life before. I love you Jason with every thought and every breath. Promise you'll never leave me." Jane had a worried look on her face as she raised it to his.

"How could I leave you? I couldn't wait to get back to you.

I brought you a present, but it will have to wait till I put up my tent, before you can see it. What do you say to a ride over your Ranch and look for timber to build your house?"

"I'd like that. I suppose you know just where to find my house standing with limbs all over it?" she laughed at the picture she was painting.

Nat was building the fire when they walked back. "Good morning, Nat," Jason and Jane said together.

As they sat down with everyone for breakfast Jason said— "Jane and I have an announcement to make; we are being married on Saturday after the house raising, we hope you'll all be happy for us;" Stunned silence greeted their announcement. Andy was the first to react with a— "yeppe!" and ran over and put his arms around Jane and Jason both. "I'm happy!" he yelled as he and Goldie ran around them. The men jumped up to shake Jason's hand and the girls to kiss Jane and wish them both happiness. There was laughter and talk from them all as they ate.

After breakfast the happy couple saddled their horses and started toward the Cimmaron, and followed it down river; Jane couldn't believe the many meadows they passed, until finally they arrived at the edge of a hillside covered with pine and cedar trees. Some of them towered a hundred feet into the air.

"There's your new house Jane. I've had in mind to build a house from those cedar trees for ages. Cedar will last two hundred years. There will be more than enough here for your house. What do you think?"

"I think it's a shame to cut such giants; but they do smell good. And even if I'm not around in two hundred years, I would like to think my house would last that long," she smiled at him.

Nat and Laura seem to be happy with me, but I know they will want their own place someday. They are both such workers. Ed say he doesn't want a farm, but he's been going off now and then. He doesn't say, but I think he is seeing Nettie. You remember the wagon that was in the mishap at the crossing? and her son Howie, who almost drowned? Ed has taken a liking to them both. When we were on the train he kept an eye on her and saw to it that she was all right. We'll have to build a house for them here on the Ranch. I think he would like that. She is a very nice girl and a hard worker," Jane told Jason as they walked beneath the towering trees.

* * *

Three wagons showed up in less than the two weeks they had said. Jason met the men; one had brought his wife, who would do the cooking for the brothers. He showed them where the house was to be built; they drove over beyond the spring, where they would have easy access to it, and parked the three wagons. They had a tent that they erected and carried in a bed and rocking chair, and the wife began arranging things to her liking.

"Looks as though they plan to be here awhile—and like comfort," Jane remarked.

"Their names are Hawkins; they are brothers. Mrs. Hawkins name is Genny, I believe. The brothers are Henry, Harry, and Harvey; come along, I'll introduce you." He and Jane walked over to their camp.

"This is Doctor Barrlette, soon to be Mrs. Jason Turner." Then he named each one to her, as he smiled at her startled expression. "We've just been over the Ranch and have found what I think will be our house. There is a grove of cedar trees—some a hundred feet tall; there's about sixty or seventy trees in all. What is your opinion of cedar logs for a house?"

"Well, cedar lasts that's for sure. It's pretty smelly for a while unless you oil it down or put some sort of sealant on it. It works well, and looks good. Sounds like you have enough trees. I'd like to take a look at them, but I'd say they would be choice," Harvey the oldest said. "We'll start early in the morning on the foundation. I've seen some suitable stones around for that. Do you have a drawing of what you want?"

"We'll make one this afternoon, and have it ready for you tonight," Jason said looking at Jane. They went back to the tent and sat at the table. He and Jane discussed what they wanted in a house. They soon were drawing the first floor—the 'great room' or as Jane called it the 'keeping room' which was southern. It would house the kitchen fireplace, table for eating and chairs for sitting, and a place to gather. The stairs would go up from it—that would take up half the length of the house. The other half would be divided into a parlor, and one bedroom with a chimney on each end of the house. Two fireplaces turned catty corner in each of the two end rooms using the same chimney. Upstairs would be three rooms for sleeping; maybe the room where the stairs entered would become a sort of library. When lumber was available there would be a wash room, kitchen, and mud room on the back made from cut boards. They were both pleased with the looks of their drawing. It would be a large house for the area, but Jane didn't want added-on sections done later. There was money for what she wanted and they would build it now. She expected to live there for the rest of her life.

Jane and Jason took the drawing to the Hawkins for approval. "What do you think?" they asked Harvey.

"Nice, very nice; You'll want a veranda across the front. What about upstairs?" he asked turning to Jane.

"I don't think so; just downstairs the whole length of the house. And the windows have to be spaced in the back so we can add the shed-kitchen when lumber is available. What do you think Jason?"

"I like it fine. I hope we can get lumber soon. It will be so much more convenient with a separate kitchen. Come we'll show Harvey, where we want to start the house. We'll move the camp back a little from where it is now. They all walked over to the spot, and pointed the location out, "We want our yard to go to the garden fence, with one gate dividing. A spring house will be built here—joining the kitchen by a covered walkway. We'll need a necessary which will be built along over there. I think Sam and Ed will be able to build the 'spring house' they did a good job on the chicken house. Those are things that we need now," Jason told him.

"We'll stake it out this afternoon and have the foundation laid by Thursday. If you're going to have a raisin' you should plan it for Friday or Saturday. Have teams brought to bring in the logs, while others cut; we'll do all the measuring and hewing the logs and fitting them. We hope to have the foundation logs in place by then."

The details of the raisin' and the house were worked out and everyone had their job to do. Jane couldn't believe how fast the foundation went in, and how large it looked. She could imagine what it would look like when finished.

The notices were sent out, and it looked as though the whole area would be there bringing tents to spend the night since they had decided on Friday for the raisin'. Jane and Jason would be married on Saturday.

Jane was surprised one day to see the Wright boy bring a six-month-old calf on a rope, "This is to pay you for all you did for us. I hope it's enough, Doctor Barrlette. I'm sorry I didn't bring it sooner but I've been busy with spring planting. I want to thank you again; Maybell is just fine. She looks so pretty it takes my breath away," he blushed with that statement. "Would you like me to take it to the pen where your other calves are?" he asked nodding toward the corral.

"Thank you; that would be nice. And it's more than enough in payment. In fact, the next baby is on me," Jane told him.

"Maybell sure likes you; and if we have a baby, you'll deliver it—no more midwives. We'll be here for your raisin' and your wedding—we wouldn't miss it. Thanks again," he said as he rode away, whistling a happy note.

Jason had put his tent up, back a ways so it would be out of the way. He was working in it, and told Jane to stay away; he

wanted to surprise her. She busied herself helping Laura organize things after having moved back toward the spring out of
the way of the building.

Friday morning the wagons came one after another. Ed was
arranging them over beyond the chicken house, where there were
a few trees for shade and where fires could be built. The teams
were taken from the wagons, ready to go haul logs. Several
brought wide boards for tables knowing there wouldn't be any
available at the new farm. Big pots were handed down and put
on spiders ready to cook or reheat for their dinner. Tents were
set up for those who planned to stay the night.

Jane looking over what was happening said, "My heavens, it's
beginning to look like a city around here. I wonder how many
will come? There must be fifty people here already, and it's not
even noon yet." She shook her head, "I don't know about this,"
she said.

In a very short time it seemed the trees began to arrive; some
with three teams hooked to them, they were such giants. Men
were put to sawing them in lengths as soon as the Hawkins carefully measured the lengths they wanted. They were no sooner
cut than one of the Hawkins' men was hewing and notching. It
was like clock work; everyone knew just what to do. Jane couldn't
believe how fast the logs went into place. They were beautiful—
the red grain showing where they had been hewed smooth.

* * *

Cooking, sawing, hewing and just having fun went on and on
into the night. Most everyone stayed over for the wedding which
was to be at ten o'clock the next morning. Mary was bringing the
wedding cake since she had a regular stove for baking, and had
volunteered to make it.

Jane had washed her hair and spent some time in her little
house on wheels, getting out her finery and pressing it so it would
look nice. Caroline and Laura were down in the meadow, picking
wild flowers. Jason had erected a bower and covered it with dogwood branches for them to stand under to be married. "It's going
to be beautiful Laura told Jane. Jane was to take her bridal attire into Jason's tent to get dressed, He wouldn't let her see her
surprise until then.

Laura, Caroline, and Jane went to get Jane dressed for her wedding. Jane went into the tent first. She was so shocked that she stopped and couldn't move for the other girls to come in too.

There stood the most beautiful bed Jane had ever seen in her life. It was Golden Polished Brass dressed all in white; with a sheer ruffled canopy over the top; white linen sheets edged in lace and a quilted satin spread covered it. Several big fluffy pillows trimmed in lace lay at the head. There was a shiffrobe with a full-length mirror, and a row of drawers down one side, setting against the tent. Her rocking chair sat on the other side of the bed. Colorful Indian rugs were placed on each side of the bed, and another in front of the rocking chair. Tears came to Jane's eyes. "What a wonderful surprise she whispered."

The other girls were speechless, "Oh, My!" they both said.

"Come along; we have to get you dressed; they all laid the clothing they were carrying on the bed; Jane had already put on her under things, and was ready for the dress. They soon had her looking the beautiful bride, her skin glowed picking up color from her dress—there were stars in her eyes with just a hint of happy tears.

Laura went out to see if everything was ready. The minister and Jason were out at the bower waiting. Jason was dressed in fawn-colored deerskin with long fringe on every seam. Andy was dressed in a miniature replica as best man and stood beside Jason a big grin on his face. He stood tall and proud waiting for his "Maw".

"It's time," Laura announced, handing Jane the biggest bouquet of wild flowers she had ever seen. Just then she heard music—someone was playing a fiddle and a mouth organ; seemed she heard a banjo too. The beautiful strains of the wedding march echoed up and down the Cimmaron, as Jane in her 'Ashes of Roses' silk dress slowly walked from the tent. Mummers of surprise and pleasure were heard from the audience, as Jane went to meet Jason. He stepped forward and took her hand leading her under the bower of dogwood blossoms, where the minister joined them in Holy Matrimony, for eternity. Andy solemnly handed Jason the circle of gold that made it official, as Jason slipped it on his bride's finger.

There was such a cheer went up when they stepped from the bower that it rocked the hills. Everyone knew Jason and admired him. Jane was known too, even though she wasn't acquainted with some who attended her wedding. They had heard of the doctor who had done so much for people they knew, and whom she didn't know.

The log house was built up to the roof line, and would be finished by the Hawkins' brothers in due time. The celebration of Jane and Jason's wedding went on into the night, with eating, dancing and music. The happiness on their faces reflected in all those who were there.

Oh, Jason, I'm so happy; was there ever a more beautiful wedding? Your bower was beautiful. And your surprise—breathtaking! I've never seen anything so beautiful. Thank you; I love you my husband," she told him as she stood on tippy-toe and kissed him.

* * *

The house had been finished and Jane, Jason, and Andy had moved in. Laura and Nat decided to stay in the tent and moved their bed and what they needed into it. Sam and Ed remained in their wagon.

Soon after her wedding, Ed had come to Jane and said, "Miss Jane, would you mind if I built a small cabin and brought Nettie and Howie to live here. We want to get married," he looked nervously at Jane.

"Ed, that's wonderful; I've been hoping you two would fall in love. She's a wonderful girl; I like her very much. Don't you want your own place?" Jane asked.

"If we can stay here and help run your Ranch, no. I'll work and Nettie can help you. I know that Nat wants his place when he can afford it, but we would like to stay."

"Let me talk to Jason and see what we can arrange. I want you to stay and welcome Nettie and Howie too. I'll see Jason right away." Jane told her new husband about Ed.

Jason sat thinking, "We could put him on the new homestead, but then he might want to get his own. Why don't we have a house raisin' and build him a house say up there on that knoll; it's about a quarter mile from the main house, and there's a good spring there, and space for their own garden. If they want to be married here, we can arrange it."

"That's the perfect arrangement. In the spring I'm going to give the place across the Cimmaron to Nat and Laura, with a little money to get started. They can put in a garden and have enough to live on. We'll have a raisin' and build them a house too. I hear Ray and Caroline is having a raisin' this Saturday.

Caroline is almost due, maybe they will be in their house for the birthin."

Ray and Caroline's house was put up, ready to move into on Monday. Laura and Jane went to see if they could help with the moving. Caroline was having some discomfort. "I think you'd better come home with me. By this time tomorrow you'll be a mama or I'll miss my guess."

Caroline was brought to the Ranch and put to bed in the guest room and in the night gave birth to an eight-pound son. She and Ray were delighted. Caroline had little trouble for a first baby— maybe Jane made the difference. They stayed for two and half weeks when Caroline declared that she must go home and learn to do things on her own. Her baby was being spoiled.

Nettie and Ed had been married on a Sunday morning without much fuss, as they neither wanted it. Their house was finished and Ed and Sam had been busy making furniture for them. Nettie was one of the happiest of women. She finally had her home and a father for Howie. Ed was so good to both of them and Howie dogged his footsteps, helping him with whatever he was doing.

* * *

The saw mill had opened at Boothe's Corner as it was now called. Jason had taken timber to be cut for a new barn and shed for storing hay that was cut off the many meadows, and to house the animals. There had been a shop house built to Sam's specifications. He had insisted he wanted a room off it for himself, which had been added. It was his domain and he was happy.

Laura and Nat were told that a section of land awaited them. There was a scurry to get a garden in for the summer food and to store for winter. A modest log house of two rooms and a shed kitchen had been built by a raisin'. They moved in with furniture Sam had helped them to build. Jane did what she could to make them comfortable. Nat would still work for the Ranch and be paid.

Nettie was expecting and Ed was beaming with happiness. Everything was moving along in a smooth race of building and prospering. The big meadow was filled with cattle now and the horses were bred and several frisky colts played games around their mothers.

Mary and John had moved from the cave to a big house up on the knoll that overlooked the River that Mary loved so well. They now used the big cave for a barn. Their farm had done well, and their three children almost grown.

Andy had his eye on Sarah, which seemed to be mutual. It wouldn't be long until another wedding would be in progress and another house dot the landscape.

When Nettie delivered, it was a set of identical twin girls. Jane thought Ed would bust his buttons he was so proud. They were very happy together.

Jane didn't think she would ever get with child and she had given up hope. She and Jason had been married a glorious four years; Jane was now twenty seven and at last she was sure she was going to have the longed-for baby. The first few weeks she was so miserable that Jason wouldn't let her out of the big brass bed or turn her hand. The girls came—Nettle with her twins, Caroline with her rambunctious son, and Laura who was showing with child.

Jason went to Boothe's Corners and inquired if there was a widow or someone who could come to stay. He was lucky that a widow had inquired at the store if they knew where she could live and work as her husband had died suddenly and she had to give up her homestead. He went to see her immediately. She was still living in her wagon on the homestead barely surviving. Jason had taken his wagon and told her, "Pack what you want, and come home with me. You'll have a home as long as you want to stay."

Matilda was in her late forties. She looked of German descent—big, robust, with taffy-colored hair and the bluest eyes. "I have very little as I've sold the team. If you can sell the wagon maybe you can get a few dollars from it." She soon had her things tied in a sheet and on the wagon. "I'm ready" she announced, "and I be thanking you for taking me in; I had begun to suspect that in another week I'd be eating the bark from the trees. I was so scared at night. It was so dark, that each time the owls hooted I thought for sure I would die right then and there. I thank you. I'll work hard," she nodded her head and a sigh escaped her.

Matilda captivated Jane. She was always running upstairs to bring a cup of tea, or fetch her a bouquet of wild flowers, or tell her about the beautiful blue bird that was building a nest in a rotten limb. In days she had Jane back on her feet feeling that life was worth living again. Poor Jason had gone out of his mind worrying over Jane.

Matilda was a wonderful cook. She could sew and keep house with what seemed little effort. The kitchen had been built on along with the wash room and another room that was kept for a bedroom for farm help when needed. Matilda decided that was to be her room and had put all her things—away, her little keep sakes she had brought from her wagon. What clothing she had was neatly folded on shelves against the wall. She and Sam got on well and he was making her a rocking chair for her room that was to be hers. The big porch across the front of the house now had six rocking chairs setting invitingly for anyone who needed a rest. This was a token of Sam's affection for his family.

Jason was a busy man. He rode from one section to the other supervising the workers he hired. The cattle and horses had grown into a thousand head. He was a good manager and found markets for whatever they had to sell. Many of the homesteaders came for his advice, which he freely gave. He was a happy man waiting the arrival of his first son.

Jane was healthy through the rest of her pregnancy. Matilda told her she would deliver her baby, and Jane was inclined to have her do so. There were no doctors around, and only the one midwife she knew of.

When time came for Jane to deliver, she and Matilda were a close team and the baby was born without much trouble. "A fine healthy son!" Matilda announced, laying the new infant into his worried father's arms. When Jason realized that Jane had fallen asleep, he felt relief, knowing that she was going to get well. He was so fascinated with his new son that he sat for hours just holding him and talking to him. Then Matilda would take him, telling Jason that he must not spoil the child.

Jane was soon her cheery sparkling self to the delight of her tall, handsome husband, who had gone through torture when she was birthing their son.

A few years after Jane and Jason's son was born, Andy had asked Jane and Jason to stay seated when they had finished their supper. "I want to talk to you two. I'm eighteen now and I have a good start with my horses. Sarah and I want to wed, if it's all right with you two. I love her and she loves me. We are suited to each other and we want a life together."

"That's wonderful, son," Jason told him. "Sarah is a fine young woman and will make you a good partner. Jane is very fond of her too. Whatever you two want, we will help all we can. We want you to be as happy as we are."

"Andy, you're my first son, and I love you dearly; you couldn't have picked a wife I like more or one that suits you so well. Be Happy!" Jane told him with tears in her eyes.

Andy and Sarah were wed at her parent's big house. It wasn't as big an affair as Jason and Jane had experienced—just close friends. They stayed a few days with the Thompsons. Andy was anxious for his own home, and stopped to see Ray and Caroline. He was looking at the section Jason had homesteaded, thinking that he might build there. They told them they wanted to sell out and go to Nebraska, why Andy wasn't quite sure. He and the Hayes' agreed on a price and Andy bought their hundred and sixty acres. They had lived on it for over five years and they could now sell. Andy had been with Jason long enough that he had learned much from him and felt that he had a bargain; with it joining the other two sections, it would be ideal for him and Jason to continue to work together. He looked the cabin over. Some addition would be needed.

Sarah, after seeing the little cabin, said it would do until they could add on to it. They would move in now that the Hayes' were gone. Sarah was wonderfully happy with Andy; they were both so much alike and had so much fun together.

* * *

Jason and Jane sat on the front porch rocking and watching their son trying to catch lightning bugs and put them into a bottle. They laughed with him when he succeeded to catch one and it flashed its light inside the glass.

"Do you feel old, Jason?" Jane asked.

"Old? Sometimes—until I look at you and then I become as frisky as a colt. Why do you ask? Are you feeling old?"

"It seems that time is flying by—everyone settled with children, and now Andy and little Sarah moving into their own home. It seems just yesterday they were little babies. I'll be a grandmother one day soon. That's old!"

"Jane think how lucky we are. We have good health, two fine sons who will be with us through our lifetime, many good friends, money and property, we can do or buy anything we desire.

It's time for us to take life easy and enjoy each other and our children and friends. Time to turn the page on youth and settle down to middle age, and re-live all the happiness the good Lord has granted us. I love you Jane; now that we are at the end of youth's chapter, more than you will ever know, I love you and the memory of the 'Ashes of Roses' of my youth."

THE END